ANNA

ANNA

Part One of
THE KIROV SAGA

CYNTHIA
HARROD~EAGLES

St. Martin's Press
New York

2

Library of Congress Cataloging-in-Publication Data

Harrod-Eagles, Cynthia.
   Anna / Cynthia Harrod-Eagles.
      p.   cm.
   "A Thomas Dunne book."
   ISBN 0-312-06290-7
   1. Soviet Union—History—Alexander I, 1801–1825—Fiction.
   I. Title.
PR6058.A6945A85   1991
823'.914—dc20
                                                    91-4336
                                                    CIP

First published in Great Britain by Sidwick & Jackson Limited.

10 9 8 7 6 5 4 3 2

For Tony – who got me through it – with all my love.

The Kirov Family

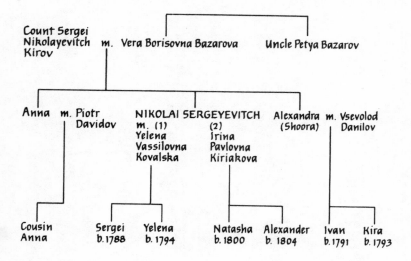

Count Sergei Nikolayevitch Kirov m. Vera Borisovna Bazarova   Uncle Petya Bazarov

Anna m. Piotr Davidov   NIKOLAI SERGEYEVITCH m. (1) Yelena Vassilovna Kovalska   (2) Irina Pavlovna Kiriakova   Alexandra (Shoora) m. Vsevolod Danilov

Cousin Anna   Sergei b.1788   Yelena b.1794   Natasha b.1800   Alexander b.1804   Ivan b.1791   Kira b.1793

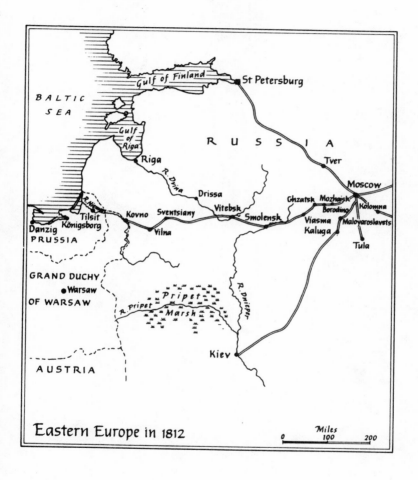

Eastern Europe in 1812

	Miles	
0	100	200

BOOK ONE – 1803

Chapter One

It was a fine spring day in 1803. The sky was a vivid, impermanent blue, and the light – the long sunlight of April – was clear and strong and without heat. Paris had been awake since before sunrise, when the carts from the countryside began to come in, bringing milk and vegetables and meat for the markets; their iron-hooped wheels had battered the milky silence out of the dawn streets, and shaken the birds awake. Now the day was broad, and the city lay, gold-grey and blue-slated in her green frame of fields and woods, humming like a giant bee skep with the intensity of her daily life.

Miss Anne Peters, governess, picked her way along the busy streets with her eyes wide and her senses stretched to the delight of being in this strange, and strangely familiar, place. She had been in Paris since the previous November; by now she could find her way around with gratifying ease, and enjoyed the inward sensation of watching herself do it. But the dual quality of strangeness and familiarity had been with her from the very first: she had always felt as though she had known Paris from some other life.

In London, her employers lived in Margaret Street on the corner of the fashionable Cavendish Square, where all around were broad, handsome thoroughfares and splendid new houses, straight-edged, large-windowed, with the geometrical symmetry made possible by modern skills. From the window of her room at the top of the house, Anne often looked out on the scene with the pleased sense that she was looking at the essence, the very heart of the eighteenth century: clean, orderly, thriving – nature controlled by man.

But here in Paris, the streets were narrow, and the tall, crooked, mediaeval houses reared up in a shoulder-to-shoulder press to cut out the sunlight. Some of them hung perilously over the cobbles as though they might tumble down at any moment. Her employers' present residence, at number 8 rue St Augustine, had no single wall or floor that was quite straight, and the treads of the precipitous staircase sloped alarmingly from the wall towards the stairwell, as if in only temporary alliance with the laws of engineering. Anne's room here overlooked a tumble of roofs and gables and gutters, all at different levels from each other, where slate-blue pigeons cooed and strutted in the sunlight. Anne had been fascinated to see a woman occupying a gable room opposite open the window and put the cat out onto the roof to take its daily exercise – much to the pigeons' consternation. Below roof-level, the houses plunged vertiginously into shadow, and a maze of cold, mossy little yards formed by odd angles of the asymmetrical buildings, jostling each other for space.

Paris, Anne had discovered, was a place of shadows and strange smells, and life of all sorts teemed and thrived without regard to symmetry or propriety. And yet, different though it was in every particular from the surroundings she had grown accustomed to, it appealed to something atavistic in her, perhaps some memory in the blood of times not so long since, before the hand of modern science had drawn in the rein of natural forces. There was something in her that longed for wild places, though a casual observer might not have known it from her plain, neat exterior; but it shone that day in her eyes as she picked her way across the cobbles of the market on the Ile de la Cité, head up, cheeks a little coloured by the brisk breeze running off the river.

Of course, not all of Paris was shabby: there were newer houses, and some of the old sort had acquired modern façades; and now that the destructive turmoil of the Revolution and the stagnation of the corrupt Directory had given way to comparative stability, there were plenty of signs of regeneration. Everywhere there was new work going on: new houses, renovations, and the first public undertakings for more than a decade. The able general, Bonaparte, had turned politician. He had made himself First Consul of the three-man Consulate, and now lived and ruled almost like a king in the splendour of Catherine de Medici's Palace of the Tuileries.

Now England had made peace with the infant nation. It was an uneasy peace, an artificial peace, existing not because the two sides had reconciled their differences, but because ten years of war had led only to a stalemate. The genius of the Corsican general, and the size of the armies he was able to raise, had made France invincible by land; the might of the King's navy had made England invincible by sea. It was internal English politics, and Bonaparte's need for a breathing-space, which had led both sides to the treaty of Amiens, signed a year ago. Then foreign travel had become a possibility for a whole generation who had never set foot outside their native land, and English people flocked in holiday mood to Paris.

The Murrays had come over in November, when England and

4

the Consulate exchanged embassies. Sir Ralph Murray was on the staff of the English Ambassador, Lord Whitworth, and Lady Murray would not for worlds have missed the opportunity of advancing herself and her daughters in society, which she was sure such a trip would mean. Lady Murray had only been a Miss Curtis, daughter of a successful coal merchant, with no recommendations but a pretty face and seven thousand pounds to enable her to get on in the world. She had married very well considering who she was, and she wanted her daughters to do even better. She was shrewd enough to realise that Sir Ralph's, and therefore his daughters', importance would be far greater in the selective diplomatic community of Paris than it was in the wider circles of London society.

She also believed that her girls would stand out much better against a background of French women, whom she was convinced were all flat-chested and ugly. This conviction stemmed from the fact that the only two Frenchwomen she knew well were the elderly emigrée who made her underwear, and the governess of the children of her intimate friend, Mrs Cowley Crawford, both of whom happened to be swarthy and very plain; and she clung to it with the determination of ignorance. Lady Murray had received the fashionable female education of thirty years ago, which meant that she could embroider exquisitely, draw prettily, dance gracefully, and sing three songs in Italian; but if she had ever been able to read and write, she had given it up entirely when she first began to put up her hair.

Anne Peters had been with the Murrays for three years, and at first she had been puzzled as to why a woman like Lady Murray, who had no use for education, had chosen her to take charge of her daughters. Anne's education was extensive. Her father had been a sea-officer, and since Anne was born during one of England's brief periods of peace, he had been at home on half-pay with nothing to do while she was growing up. Her mother had died when she was very small, and her father had not remarried. Anne and her father had lived alone together on terms of unusual intimacy, and he had occupied his time and mental energies by educating her.

He had found her an apt pupil, with a hunger for knowledge which reflected his own restless spirit, the spirit which had driven him in the first place to seek a naval career. He taught her mathematics and geography and astronomy, the academic subjects of his trade; and Latin and Greek and philosophy, the mental furniture of the gentleman. She had inherited his musical ear, and learned French, Italian, and German from him as easily as singing, dancing, and playing the pianoforte. As

5

his close daily companion, she learned to ride a horse and row a boat, to fish and to shoot, and to discuss politics; what she did not learn were the feminine arts.

The revolutionary war began in 1792, when Anne was twelve. Her father received an active commission in the navy, and her world, which, in the way of the child, she had viewed as the permanent and immutable order of things, was shattered without warning. The house in which she was born and raised was given up, and most of the furnishings sold, and Anne was taken in a hired carriage to Miss Oliver's School in Sydney Place, Bath, where her father kissed her, enjoined her to work hard and be a good girl, and left her.

It was a long time before she could obey his injunction. Their very closeness, which always before had been her support and her joy, now brought her her first suffering. She found herself bewildered by the loss of his presence, and for weeks could not settle to her new life, but waited, uncomprehending, like an abandoned animal watching a closed door, for him to come back for her. After a time, the pain of missing him was transmuted into lethargy, and she had no interest in anything, not even eating. She grew very thin at that period, and slept a great deal, slipping away at all times of day, to be found curled up in some obscure corner asleep.

When at last she began to climb out of the darkness into which her uprooting had pitched her, she found Miss Oliver waiting for her. Her father had chosen her new home wisely. Miss Oliver was herself an educated woman, intelligent, novel, and vigorous: the very person to understand Anne's feelings, to enjoy her company, and to stimulate her enquiring mind to reach for something outside her own misery. Miss Oliver continued to educate her new charge along the lines Captain Peters had established, but made sure that the other gaps were filled too, and that Anne learned to sew and sketch and sing the correct songs, and behave herself more conventionally in company. The thin, twig-like twelve-year-old with the burning eyes and the overgrown mind began to fill out into a rounded person.

Anne liked Miss Oliver, and after the first violent reaction to her upheaval, she liked Bath, too, and enjoyed her life there. There was always something doing, something new to think about, someone new to meet. She enjoyed the company of other girls of her own age for the first time, though on the whole she found them so much less well furnished intellectually that she could never achieve any great intimacy with them. It was always she who initiated and guided their conversations and games, and while they looked to her quite naturally for that leadership, they were just a little reserved with her, as they would be with an adult. It was flattering, but it was also lonely, when she saw the others walking in pairs with their arms about each other, or with their heads together in a corner, whispering and giggling over something they would have thought too foolish to include her in.

It was perhaps because of this separateness from her fellow pupils that she never managed to get over the feeling that her residence there was purely temporary, and that at any moment Papa would come back for her, and take her home. In her mind she lived on the verge of departure for the next five years, never quite able to bring herself to unpack and settle in, living from letter to letter, always waiting for the sound of wheels on the cobbles, the knock at the street door, the summons to the principal's room, which would herald her rescue, and the return to real life. Even now, so many years later, in the moment of confusion between sleeping and waking, she would sometimes wonder if today would be the day he would come for her. Then she would wake fully and remember, and the pain was fresh and bitter every time.

In 1797, Captain Peters had attained flag rank, and had been despatched up the Baltic on a diplomatic mission. He had never sailed in Northern waters before, and sent Anne an excited letter describing the marvels of this new territory, the scenery and his trips ashore, the things he had seen, and the people he had met. More precious than that, he spoke of coming ashore again when this mission was over. Since the war began, in common with many other sailors, he had not set foot on English soil; he had not seen his daughter since he left her at the school. But when he had made his report to Their Lordships, he would surely be granted some period of leave, and then he would come straight to Bath.

He also enclosed a pair of pearl earrings for her seventeenth birthday. *My girl is growing up now,* he wrote. *Soon she'll be a woman, and some other man will take my place in her heart. Well, that's as it should be; and though I don't suppose I'll think him good enough for you, my Anne, I know enough of your good sense to be sure that you will not part with your precious self to anyone unworthy. So turn up your hair, my darling, and put these in your pretty ears, and enjoy the things that belong to youth; and think sometimes of one who never ceases to think of you, with blessings.*

Anne put her hair up and wore the earrings at dinner on her birthday, and enjoyed the unaccustomed, luxurious weight, which made her want to move her head slowly and gracefully, like a lady. Miss Oliver, who was very fond of Anne, ordered a special dinner, and allowed Anne and the other senior girls to taste wine for the first time. They drank a toast to her while she sat blushing under the unaccustomed attention, her brown eyes bright, her cheeks pink, and looking, though she had no way of knowing it, as pretty as any young woman could desire to look. There was no gentleman there to notice it, except for the Rector, who had been invited as a special guest, and who, though a bachelor, was above sixty years old. Anne knew no young men; and indeed, her life so far had not taught her to divide humanity by gender, though she had read enough in the Classics to be well acquainted with love in its poetic and dramatic forms. For all her intellectual prowess, she was as innocent as a rose; and, on that day at least, as lovely.

It was on the following day that the letter arrived to say that her father had died of typhus at Riga six weeks before. Contrary winds had delayed his last letter to her; and it seemed somehow a bitter thing, heaping cruel irony needlessly upon pain, that he had already been dead a month, even as she read his happy words to her and unwrapped his birthday gift.

The memory of that time slowed her feet and brought her to a halt. She came to herself to find that she was standing before a stall selling caged birds – chickens, ducks, singing-birds, even swans – and staring at them, though sightlessly, with such intensity that the proprietor had passed through all the stages of anticipation and into apprehension. She met his puzzled eyes, collected herself, and gave him a reassuring smile before walking on.

The mind does not retain a clear recollection of great anguish, only that it occurred. It was as well, Anne thought, or how should we ever survive? She remembered very little of the darkness that overwhelmed her, or of the desperate fear and loneliness that followed when, night after night, she would wake to the knowledge that she was alone in the world, that there was no single soul who bore any responsibility for her, who owed her any affection, care, or protection. For the rest of her life, only her own labours, or cold charity, would keep her from starvation. It was too awesome a thought for a seventeen-year-old – too tremendous to be grasped all at once, except in brief flashes of realisation. That same benign act of nature which obliterates the memory of pain also operates to prevent young minds from anticipating more than they can bear. Understanding came little by little as she grew stronger; and any weight, even that of being responsible for oneself, can become tolerable with familiarity.

Miss Oliver, good friend that she was, kept Anne a year longer at the school, defraying some of the expense of keeping her against Anne's help in instructing the younger pupils. At the end of that time Miss Oliver helped her to find a position as a governess to a private family. Anne was without family or fortune, and it was the only profession open to her, by which she could keep herself respectably.

Her first place was with the Bryants, a newly-wealthy family who had recently bought Marchington Park, an old estate near Bristol. Anne went there with no preconceptions, only glad in a vague way that she should not be too far from Bath and the only point on the earth's surface where she was not a stranger. She was well qualified for her new calling – too well, indeed, for more than half of the subjects in which she was learned would never be required of her – and her salary seemed generous, considering she would have nothing on which to spend it. She travelled by mail, entertaining mild dreams of saving all she earned until she achieved an independence, and of enjoying in the meantime the respect and affection of her pupils, whom she determined to love as well as instruct.

Determination was not enough either for love or instruction. Marchington was as handsome a house and park as anyone could desire, but its elegance and opulence could do nothing to improve the natures of its new inmates. Mrs Bryant was a proud, ignorant bully: a mean-spirited woman whose vulgarity wealth had only exacerbated by giving it the power to expand into new fields; and her three small children had been spoiled and indulged from birth to think well of themselves and to pursue their own gratification at any cost.

Anne had never before known humiliation, and it was a hard lesson. Mrs Bryant treated her like a servant – worse than a servant, indeed, for good servants were hard to come by, whereas impoverished gentlewomen were plentiful, and were expected to be grateful for being fed and housed. Mrs Bryant had money and despised anyone who had not. She spoke to Anne, when she spoke at all, with a coldness and a barely-concealed contempt which made Anne shake with the effort of containing her fury. The mistress's attitude naturally wore off on the servants, and Anne was exposed to their insolence without any hope of redress.

She could have borne these things if there had been refuge in the schoolroom, but the children had none of the restraint of their parents. They tormented, derided, and abused their governess all day long, except when they ignored her. It was impossible either to love or to discipline them. If she attempted to restrain them, they complained of her to their mama, who always sided with them. If Anne abandoned this futile attempt and let them do as they pleased, Mrs

9

Bryant complained to her husband that Miss Peters did not know her business.

For months, Anne went on hoping with the resilience of youth that things would improve. She woke most mornings to a new determination, and the increasingly wistful hope that in time the children would settle down and tire of their wantonness, and come from very boredom to want instruction. All her life she had known no greater joy than learning, and it was hard to believe that other children could be so radically different. But gradually wretchedness replaced optimism, and at last, a little shamefacedly, she wrote to Miss Oliver, as the only friend she had in the world.

She described the difficulties of her life at Marchington – moderating her language a great deal, for she felt that even Miss Oliver would not believe her if she painted the picture in its true colours – and asked for advice. Was this the best she could expect from her new calling? Were all places like this, or was there a possibility that she might be happier elsewhere? Would it be proper for her to seek a new position? And if so, how should she go about it? She apologised for troubling Miss Oliver, and begged her, if she would be so kind, to reply care of the village post office, for she was not entirely confident that a letter addressed to her at the house would reach her unimpeded.

The answer came, prompt and infinitely comforting: that all places were not so uncongenial; that she might quite properly leave at the end of the half-year; and that if she would entrust the matter to Miss Oliver, she would use her contacts to try to find Anne a place where she would be better appreciated. Anne tucked the letter into her bodice, wearing it all day next to her heart like a talisman, and faced her tormentors with a new spirit, in the hope of deliverance.

As a result of Miss Oliver's enquiries and intervention, Anne took up her position with the Murrays in April 1800, to teach Miss Murray and Miss Caroline, who were then fourteen and twelve years old. She was so glad to get away from the Bryants that the Murrays would have had to try very hard to make her feel abused, and for the first few weeks the relief alone made her feel too happy and grateful to notice their faults.

Lady Murray was a very silly, ignorant woman, but there was nothing ill-natured about her, and her placid good humour was only ruffled if she were obliged to do something she didn't like, or if her daughters were not sufficiently admired, or if her son Hartley's extravagances were forced on her notice. Then she would grow vexed and fancy herself ill, and the house would be thrown into a turmoil until she had had enough attention showered on her to soothe her, or the problem had gone away. But she hadn't the force of intellect to be really bad-tempered, and Anne discovered that if caught in time she was easily distracted into a better frame of mind.

The Miss Murrays, though inclined to be uppish, contrary, idle, and conceited, like most girls of their station and upbringing, were good-hearted enough underneath it all, and Anne soon learned the knack of coaxing and jollying them into doing what she wanted. Their abilities were unremarkable, and they had no desire to become scholars, but then neither their parents nor society required them to. Accomplishments fit for the drawing-room were all that was needed, and they worked at acquiring anything Anne could convince them would make them more acceptable in the best circles. For her own pride she extended the frontiers a little, and the Miss Murrays were tricked into learning quite a number of things more than their friends and contemporaries.

There was no conflict of authority in Margaret Street, for Lady Murray's life was dedicated to not being bothered by things, and any attempt on the part of the girls to enlist her support against their governess met with a dismissive wave of the hand. If they persisted, Lady Murray's brows would begin to draw together, and she would say fretfully, 'For heaven's sake, Maria, your father pays Miss Peters a large salary to know best about these things, and what's the point of that if you question what she says?'

Further than that the girls would not go, for they were considerably in awe of their father. But it was rare that they even went thus far, and life in the schoolroom jogged along comfortably for most of the time. The Miss Murrays were as fond of their governess as it was in them to be, and occasionally they even allowed themselves to enjoy her company, when there was no entertainment to compete with it. When they began to turn up their hair and let down their dresses, she became more important to them as holding the key to their future success in the world of matrimony. Though subconsciously, they acknowledged that she was a gentlewoman, and that her taste was superior, and they allowed her to direct and improve theirs, provided she didn't do it too obviously.

Anne had little to do with the male division of the family. Sir Ralph never noticed the servants, amongst whom he classed her, unless they annoyed him; and though Mr Hartley had liked playing practical jokes on her when she first arrived – putting a frog into her bed or a handful of gentles into her reticule for the pleasure of hearing her shriek – he

11

soon tired of it and turned to other sports, after which he noticed her only by a nod of the head if they happened to pass on the stairs.

So she settled in at Margaret Street. Her room was very comfortable, her wages excellent, the servants treated her politely, and she ate with the family unless they had guests. She had nothing to complain of. It irked her at first to be condescended to by a woman who, both in point of breeding and education, was markedly her inferior, but once she came to know Lady Murray, and learned how to keep her in good humour, she even found, unexpectedly, something to admire in her. As the daughter of a man who had made his fortune by the operation of his own wits, Lady Murray had a firm respect for money and hated to see it wasted, which was the principal cause of her dissatisfaction with her son, who liked doing nothing better. She ran her household efficiently and economically, and though she had no natural taste, she was rarely misled by the tawdry or the meretricious. She liked to have everything of the best quality, not only for show, but because her innate shrewdness demanded, and recognised, value for money.

Her manner towards Anne, though offhand, was never insolent, and if she treated her like a servant, it was more by the force of habit than deliberate policy; for she admired, and indeed frequently boasted to her acquaintance of, Miss Peters' intelligence, and was intensely proud that her daughters were taught by a young woman of such good family.

'Indeed, if only the poor thing had had any money, or had been a little more handsome, or had played the harp, or *something*, she might have made a very good match. Well, *quite* a good match, for her mama, you know, was a Miss Strickland, and related to the Talbots of Northallerton,' Lady Murray would say, nodding over the tea-things, and looking, with her round blue eyes and her tiny pink mouth, very much like the porcelain shepherdess on the chimneypiece above her head.

Within a short time of Anne's joining the household, Lady Murray began to call on her for all sorts of services which were not strictly the part of a governess. Lady Murray disliked to write letters, so Anne gradually took on the duties of secretary, sorting and reading her correspondence, accepting and refusing invitations, and replying to personal letters at Lady Murray's dictation. Lady Murray liked novels, but disliked the trouble of reading them, so when there was no company in the evening, Anne was required to sit by her mistress and read to her, or, when even the effort of listening was too great, to play cards with her or play to her upon the pianoforte. Lady Murray discovered that Miss Peters' needlework was most superior, and began to give her those

12

little tasks too delicate to be entrusted to a mantuamaker – repairing the hem of the lace ballgown, embroidering a silk bedgown, trimming Lady Murray's chemises.

All this was quite apart from her normal duties, and the everyday fetching and carrying which would have been the lot of the lady-companion if Lady Murray had not 'detested the very idea of such a person'. Lady Murray never thanked her for these services, or showed her any kind of affection, but Anne carried them out with a good grace, for though she had a great deal of pride, she also craved human warmth. She had no home, no family, no human beings on whom to centre her life, apart from her employers. If she had pondered the matter, the idea that the Murrays might have to become her all-in-all would have depressed her, but she was still too young to think with any kind of continuity about the future.

On the other hand, she had no-one in the world to love, if it were not Lady Murray and the Miss Murrays; and love, where it exists with any determination, will out, and find something to express itself upon. So, though no-one ever acknowledged it, she took pride in being, as she thought to herself, indispensable; and whether ordering the dinner or arranging the flowers in Lady Murray's bedroom, preventing Miss Murray from buying the violently purple silk shawl she saw at the Pantheon Bazaar, or obliging Miss Caroline to practise her piece rather than sit mooning out of a window, she saw to it that the household ran smoothly and that her charges grew up fit to grace a drawing-room.

Everything at Margaret Street was as different as it could be from Marchington Park, and though Anne was grateful and determined to be happy, she discovered that, in a curious way, that very ease worked against her. At Marchington she had been treated so miserably that her immediate unhappiness had swamped the deeper grief for her father and driven it from her consciousness. Here at Margaret Street, there was no counter-irritant to take her mind off her pain. At the end of the evening, when she retired to her room and the swirl of the day's activity died down, she became aware of a plaintive voice inside her whose demands could no longer be ignored. She missed her father, and she was lonely.

Anne reached the open space in front of the cathedral of Notre Dame, and paused to gaze up at the marvellously delicate tracery of the great rose window, set for contrast between the stern Roman arches of the twin towers. Her father had had the mathematician's love of architecture and had taught her how to look at buildings with an informed eye. Like so much in Paris, Notre Dame seemed familiar, and yet subtly alien, and she wished passionately for a moment that Papa were here so that she could discuss it with him. But to be here at all, in a foreign country, was a perpetual source of delight to her, and she remembered how welcome had been the news that the whole family, including her, was to go with Sir Ralph to Paris. Coming as it did at a low point in her spirits, when she had been with the Murrays for a little over two years, the news had brought a grateful diversion to her thoughts and a new interest to her life.

She had been privileged to overhear the first conversation which took place between Sir Ralph and Lady Murray on the subject. It occurred just after breakfast one day when her pupils were upstairs being measured for new pattern gowns, and Anne was writing letters to Lady Murray's dictation. Lady Murray broke off suddenly to address her husband, who was still sitting amongst the bones and shells, reading the newspapers.

'I have been thinking, Sir Ralph, that we had better all go to Paris with you. Mrs Cowley Crawford says Lady Whitworth is to go. She was formerly the Duchess of Dorset, you know,' she added for Anne's benefit. 'She is a charming woman. She has twenty thousand a year of her own, but I hear she is immensely affable.'

'Thirteen thousand,' Sir Ralph corrected her without looking up, 'and she is very proud.' He had met the former Duchess and been treated to a glance from beneath her blue eyelids which had seemed to suggest she regarded him as slightly lower in the order of creation than her pet parrot.

Lady Murray was unperturbed. 'Anyone has the right to be proud, with thirteen thousand a year,' she said easily, 'but I dare say she is very charming after all. Gentlemen never have any idea of these things,' she nodded to Anne, who suppressed a smile. 'And situated as we shall be in Paris, Sir Ralph,' Lady Murray went on, 'there will be no avoiding the intimacy. What a wonderful thing it will be for our girls!'

'How so, ma'am?' Sir Ralph asked absently.

'Why, because the Whitworths will lead society, of course! We shall meet everyone. Our girls will be excessively admired, and Maria will make a great match – a French duke or count with a large estate and several castles.'

'French dukes and counts do not have large estates, since the Revolution,' Sir Ralph replied, turning a page.

'Someone must have them. They can't belong to no-one,' Lady Murray concluded reasonably. 'And though Caroline may be a little young to marry, she may well form an attachment for the future, and she cannot help improving with the society we will keep over there.'

Sir Ralph, who had stopped listening, merely grunted, but as this was as much encouragement as Lady Murray was accustomed to receiving, she continued with her raptures. 'So many of the best families will be there. I hear the Russells and the Mildmays are gone. And we shall all need new gowns, for though I dare say we shall buy a great many when we are there – Paris fashions, you know! – it would not do to arrive with nothing to wear. And then, after all,' she performed an effortless volte-face as her patriotism got the better of her femininity for a moment, 'there is a great deal of nonsense talked about French fashions, as though they must be better than our own. I'm sure my Miss Gilbert makes just as well as any mamzelle in Paris, and I dare say is much cleaner about it too, for everyone knows foreigners are dirty. When we are there, I shall have Simpkins go over the seams of anything I do buy, by hand, just to be sure.'

Sir Ralph turned another page in silence, and Lady Murray, having talked herself into a cul-de-sac, paused a moment before taking a new direction. 'It will not hurt, Sir Ralph, to be taking Hartley away from his present companions.'

At this, her husband did look up, for the conduct of his son and heir was a thing close to his heart. Hartley Murray had come down from an expensive three years at Cambridge only to torment his parents by taking up with the most heedless set of peep-o'-day boys he could find. Since his new friends' allowances were a great deal larger than his own, he had no alternative but to run up bills which, in the manner of curses and young chickens, came home to roost, on the desk in Sir Ralph's business-room.

Remembering, however, what his wife had evidently forgotten, that Anne was present, he said only, 'True, ma'am. Foreign travel and new experiences must do him good; and at least it will break the hold that villainous young Cadmus seems to have over him.'

'Harry Cadmus is the great-grandnephew of the Duke of Bedford,' Lady Murray demurred, shocked; but then she sighed, 'though I must own he does seem very wild, considering his breeding. Well, so it is settled, then, Sir Ralph, that we should all go? I am very glad. Miss Peters, you must pay special attention to the girls' French lessons. It would give them a great advantage over the other young females if they could address these French dukes and counts in their own language. Just a few polite phrases, of course,' she added hastily. 'I should not wish them to be turned into scholars.'

'That is a wish I think you may look forward in confidence to having fulfilled,' Sir Ralph said drily, folding his paper and taking himself out of the room. Since his wife did not understand the force of the comment, she took it for a compliment to her daughters, and smiled complacently.

'You see, Miss Peters,' she said when the door had closed behind him, 'what an excellent opinion Sir Ralph has of my girls? He is not one of your fashionable fathers who pretends to despise his daughters and think them nothing!'

The arrangements for the journey were made by one of the secretaries at the Embassy, while another was sent on ahead to find suitable houses to rent for the Whitworths, Murrays, and other Embassy families. Everything else, from the ordering of a new medicine chest for Lady Murray, to preventing the Miss Murrays from entirely unpacking the only box their maid had succeeded in completing in order to find out whether or not she had put in their blue muslins, was left to Anne. She undertook all the thousand-and-one tasks with her usual quiet efficiency, so that when Mrs Cowley Crawford sympathised with Lady Murray at a card-party the week before their departure over the immense amount of trouble the move must entail, Lady Murray could only raise a mild eyebrow in surprise. She could not conceive what difficulty there could be about it, she said: it was only a matter of ordering the carriage and stepping into it.

The passports were written out, and their passages booked on the packet *Maid of Rye*, which was to leave from Dover on the third of November. Hartley Murray, who had been sulking furiously for weeks over being taken away from his unlawful pursuits, commented tartly that he hoped she wouldn't turn out really to be made of rye, or they would all be done up.

The party left in three separate vehicles: one for the luggage, one for the servants – Sir Ralph's man Betson, Lady Murray's dresser Simpkins, and the Miss Murrays' maid Salton – and bringing up the rear, Lady Murray, her daughters and Anne travelling together in the family berlin. Sir Ralph, his private secretary and Hartley were to go down later by post, so that they might travel fast and not waste their valuable time.

The journey to Dover was not an unmixed delight to Anne, for they travelled very slowly, with frequent stops to change horses and to allow Caroline, who was inclined to be carriage-sick, to get out and walk about. Anne was obliged, of course, to travel backwards. While she did not much mind it, for she felt it gave one a better view of the passing scenery, she did mind having to sit next to Miss Murray and to listen to her endless complaints that, as the eldest daughter, *she* ought to have the other forward seat. It annoyed Anne to have to say again and again, 'But Miss Murray, you know Miss Caroline can't take the backward seat, because it makes her sick.'

'I don't believe she really feels sick,' Miss Murray muttered sulkily. 'She only says it to get the better seat, because she knows it ought to be mine.'

When she had seen the smugness of Caroline's expression on taking the forward seat at the beginning of the journey, the same unworthy thought had crossed Anne's mind; but later when they were jolting heavily over the very bad section of road between Gillingham and Canterbury, and she had glanced at Caroline's green and sweating face, she had revised her opinion. It fell, of course, to Anne to attend Caroline when the lurching of the carriage brought her to the extreme; to calm Lady Murray when she began fussing that all the delays would make them late for their dinner, ordered ahead of them on the road; and to assure Miss Murray that she would find some way of having her gowns pressed before they met anyone important.

In spite of these annoyances, Anne found time to notice and delight in the changing scene outside the carriage windows, until the short November day drew into dusk and the landscape became indistinguishable. Then in charity to her companions, who were much more bored than she, she initiated some word games to keep the young ladies amused. At last, after twelve weary hours on the road, the tedious journey came to an end and the berlin lurched to a halt in the yard of the Angel Inn in Canterbury, where they were to spend the night.

The servants and luggage had arrived long before, so everything was ready for them: fires lit in their rooms, hot water ready, and supper on the table as soon as they wished. They were all very weary, having begun the journey at a very early hour that morning, and stiff and chilled from their long confinement in the carriage. When they had warmed themselves and washed and eaten, there was nothing anyone wanted to do but go to bed. Anne shared a room with Caroline who, once in bed, seemed to revive, and chattered for half an hour about the excitements to come. At last she fell silent, and Anne, relaxing her tired muscles, was in the middle of thinking that it was a pity there would be no opportunity to visit the cathedral where Thomas à Becket had met his end when sleep surprised her; and she knew nothing more until the chambermaid shook her awake at six the next morning.

A short journey of less than three hours the next day brought them to Dover. It was a grey, overcast day, with a chilly wind tearing raggedly at the clouds, and the grey stone houses and cobbled streets made everything seem colourless. As they wound their way down through the town, Caroline let down the window to lean out, and a breath of air penetrated the stuffiness of the carriage. It smelled of horses, as in any town, but along with that familiar scent was a new one: sharper, tangy, thrilling.

Miss Murray, sniffing disdainfully, enquired of no-one in particular, 'What is that strange smell?' while Lady Murray, drawing her cloak closer, protested mildly, 'Caroline, dear! The damp!'

But Caroline, her head stuck out at a perilous angle, cried out, 'Oh Miss Peters, look! Do look!'

Anne, her eyes glowing with sudden foreknowledge, abandoned etiquette for once and craned her head out too. At the foot of the steep hill they were descending, the world dropped away into a wide vista of grey, restlessly heaving water which stretched away into the distance until it joined mistily with the sky. Overhead, white birds wheeled slowly on braced, narrow wings, crying faintly, and stronger with every breath came the exhilarating smell – an unforgettable mixture of salt, weed and tar – which her father must have smelled every day of his professional life.

She met Caroline's excited eyes in a moment of complete sympathy. 'It's the sea!' she breathed.

Chapter Two

It so happened that Anne had never seen the sea before that day in November. It may have been that Captain Peters, exiled from his profession by a peace which, in Anne's childhood, he had no reason to expect would end, could not bear to be near the sea if he could not be on it. However it was, they had lived in a small house near King's Somborne, almost half-way between Salisbury and Winchester, and apart from visits to those two cities to view the cathedrals, Anne had never been further than five miles from her home until she went away to school.

But she had always loved water. Their house had had a stream running along its boundary, a lively tributary of the slow-moving Test, and one of the strongest memories of her childhood was that the chuckle of water over stones was the first sound she heard in the morning and the last one at night. Through her childhood she had paddled and played in the stream, caught guppies in it, dammed it and floated home-made boats on it, slipped over and sat down in it, and so regularly got soaked by it that it became her natural element. When she was older, her father took her boating on the Test and taught her to fish with a line. His mood on those days was always the most genial. Times on the river were happy times, and she came to associate water with happiness.

Here in Paris, the first thing she had done when she had leisure to herself was to find her way to the river, and the walk to the Ile de la Cité remained her favourite, the one which brought her most interest and consolation. To the side of Notre Dame was a newly-laid-out garden, with a stretch of grass and a gravelled walk along the bank of the island, from which, over a low parapet, one could look across the southern arm of the Seine towards the Quai St Michel. Here, Anne liked to stroll or simply to stand and stare at the river moving peacefully by, reflecting the world kindly, the strong, ever-changing pattern of its flow broken now and then by a piece of flotsam, a flotilla of ducks, or a passing boat.

Standing at the parapet now, she remembered the strength of her emotion at her first sight of the sea – her father's element, the strongest love of his heart. It was a tangled rush of feelings: happiness, love, a sense of familiarity, a longing to be near and never to go away again, and a strange, wistful sort of understanding of what her father must have felt. He loved the sea more than he had loved her: she felt now that she had always known it. Through the long years of his unemployment – her childhood – he had never once considered turning to any other profession, any other way of earning a living; and when the war began and he had been offered a commission, he had obeyed the call instantly, abandoning her – yes, that's what it had been – and hastening back to his first love. Oh, he had loved her, she knew that, but he had loved the sea more; and for the first time she wondered about her mother, whether she had known that she could never have better than second place in her husband's heart, and whether she had minded.

Anne had had little leisure to pursue those thoughts on that day in Dover, for as soon as the carriage stopped outside the Ship and Bell in Fore Street, her services were required by all three ladies at once. She established them around the fire in a private parlour in the inn while she made at least some of the enquiries they were urging on her, and was soon able to tell them that the *Maid of Rye* was preparing to sail with the first of the ebb, at half-past twelve; that the luggage was already aboard; that the captain thought the crossing would take about four hours; that he had no apprehension that they would be shipwrecked; and that the gentlemen had not yet arrived.

'I knew it!' Lady Murray said with grim triumph. 'They will arrive too late, and we shall lose our passage. How I wish Sir Ralph had taken my advice and travelled with us!'

Anne imagined with a shudder what her master's temper would have been like after fifteen hours in a carriage with his younger daughter, and said calmly, 'There's still plenty of time, ma'am. It's only eleven o'clock. I'm sure they'll be here in time.'

A tray of hot coffee arrived, which heartened and refreshed them all. Then on Simpkins' advice, Anne persuaded Lady Murray to go aboard. The novelty of being on a boat for the first time was so absorbing that the hour before the gentlemen arrived passed quickly. Anne was kept on the run the whole time, for each of the ladies in turn discovered that some article she could not possibly do without was in one of the boxes in the luggage-hold. The harassed Salton was obliged at last to beg Anne to persuade her charges not to have everything hauled out and unpacked.

The girls exclaimed over the neat way everything was fitted into the cabins and every need catered for in such a small space, although Miss Murray complained about the smell and insisted that Salton scatter lavender water everywhere. The smell certainly was penetrating – a mixture of pitch and bilge, with overtones of cheese – but Anne sniffed it with affection, remembering it was what her father must have been used to.

As well as the sleeping cabins, which of course would not be needed on this crossing, there was a larger day cabin where the Murray ladies soon gathered to exclaim over the cunning hanging-shelves, the silver lamps which were pronounced quite handsome, and the dining-table with the raised edge, which Anne explained cautiously was to stop the plates and knives slipping off. This oblique reference to marine motion passed unnoticed, for each was more interested in drawing Anne's attention to how well she had adjusted already to life afloat, what an experienced traveller she now felt herself to be, and how envious Miss A or Lady B would feel if only she could see her now.

When Sir Ralph arrived, Lady Murray was so excited that she actually met him on deck to tell him that the captain had said they should have a smooth voyage. A handsome collation had been prepared for them below, and Anne had the notion that it was timed to keep the passengers out of the way while the crew went about the business of setting sail and getting out of the harbour. It was thrilling to eat in a real cabin on a real ship. Everyone ate and drank heartily, and a high good humour prevailed, though Caroline jumped up so often to run to the porthole to see what was going on that Sir Ralph was obliged at last to ask Miss Peters coldly if it were not possible to prevent his daughter from behaving like a jack-in-the-box for long enough for him to finish his meal.

Once they were out into the open sea, however, their violent excitement began to dissipate, and one by one the Murrays fell into a more introspective mood. Lady Murray was the first to wilt, saying that all the noise and excitement of the journey had given her a headache and that she was going to lie down. Caroline departed soon afterwards with a moan, calling for Salton. Sir Ralph, who had seemed unaccountably cross for the last ten minutes, said that the Miss Murrays' chatter had given *him* a headache, and stumped off to his cabin, bellowing for Betson with an unexpected edge of anxiety to his voice.

Shortly afterwards, Miss Murray, who had been staring in a fixed manner at the lamp swinging above her head, burst into tears and said that the boat was a horrid, stuffy thing, that she wished she had never come on it, that she was sure they would all die, and that the captain was a wicked man to say they would have a smooth voyage when there was such a storm blowing.

'There ain't a storm, you looby,' her brother Hartley said obligingly. 'The sea's as calm as a pond. You're seasick, that's all.'

'I'm not seasick,' Miss Murray cried indignantly. 'It was the lobster patties. They don't agree with me.' She turned on Anne with the anger born of desperation, and sobbed, 'It was most unkind of you to allow me to eat them! You know I have a delicate constitution!'

Hartley poured himself another glass of wine and remarked that his sister looked damned ugly when she cried, and Anne, seeing that sickness was overcoming even indignation in her charge, hurried her from the cabin. Anne had had some doubts as to the stability of her own stomach, but fortunately she had too much to do to have time to succumb to them. Some time later, when she returned to the dining cabin to fetch Miss Murray's handkerchief, she found Hartley still at the table, hunched over his glass, whose contents had changed by now from wine to brandy.

'Well, seems 'sjust you an' me now, Miss Peters,' he remarked with more affability than usual. 'Even the guv'nor's let me down. Bad sailors, all of 'em. Just you an' me to hold up the side.'

'I think you do me too much justice, Mr Murray,' Anne replied with a slight quaver towards the end of the sentence. Hartley pushed the brandy decanter across the table towards her.

'Have some brandy,' he said simply. 'Best thing for it. Sessles the stomach.'

Anne hardly hesitated. Extreme action was called for. She poured a good quantity into a glass, and though she had never drunk spirits in her life before, she tossed the glassful back in one. Tears sprang at once to her eyes, and for a moment speech was impossible. Then the cauterising draught reached her stomach and spread out into a warm and surprisingly kindly glow, and she felt immediately better and stronger.

Hartley was watching her owlishly. 'Thass the stuff,' he said approvingly. 'Down the hatch!' And he emptied his own glass in courteous imitation. 'D'you know what I think?' he said, reaching out his hand for the decanter which she pushed back towards him. 'I think I'm juss too foxed to get seasick, an' I'm going to stay that way. Have another.'

Anne agreed with his analysis, but a peevish, wavering cry from the sleeping cabin recalled her to her duty. 'I must go to them,' she said, pausing on the way out to add, 'Thank you for the brandy.'

"Squite all right,' said Hartley, slipping a little lower in his seat and closing one eye in a ghostly wink. 'I won't tell a soul.'

The three ladies remained in their bunks all through the crossing, each convinced that her last hour had come, and wishing Divine Intervention might reduce it to a last half-hour in order to get it over with. Anne, a burning glow from her waist to her toes but feeling curiously light and transparent above, ministered to them, along with the sour and glowering Simpkins, who was simply too bad-tempered to get ill. When the administration of a draught from the new medicine chest had got Lady Murray off into an uneasy doze, Simpkins jerked her head to Anne and suggested, not unkindly, that she might go and get a breath of fresh air.

'The air's that close in here, we'll have you going queer next, and who'll look after you then? For I'm sure I won't.'

So Anne climbed cautiously up on deck and found herself in a world transformed. Away from the stuffiness of the cabin, the air was so fresh it was almost intoxicating, while the rolling and pitching of the ship, which below had seemed random and nauseating, suddenly became explicable and even oddly pleasurable now that she could see the waves that caused it swooping in and diving eagerly under the bows and running away jauntily astern. Holding the taffrail, Anne found she could anticipate the movement and go with it, and understood how the sailors ran so nimbly about their work as if the planks beneath them were as unmoving as floorboards.

All around her was the grey-green sea, running on its eternal, purposeful journey, the short waves tipped with white in the distance, striped with shadow close-to, one side glassily transparent, the other bottle-dark. The ship creaked as the sea worked her, the rigging sang in a thousand high-pitched voices, and the waves made a chuckling, gurgling sound as they passed under the hollow hull. Anne felt an enormous, buoyant happiness filling her right down to her toes. I understand, Papa! she thought. Now I know why you couldn't leave it. If only she had been his son rather than his daughter, she could have gone with him to sea and followed in his footsteps; it seemed just then the best, the only life to lead.

It was a brief interlude. Soon Salton came waveringly up on deck to summon her to hold Miss Caroline's head, and she was kept occupied below until the ship passed the harbour bar and sailed into the sheltered waters of Calais. The Murray ladies recovered miraculously as soon as the ship was tied up alongside the dock. First Miss Murray sat up to look out of the porthole for her first glimpse of France; then her exclamations stirred Caroline's curiosity; and finally a loud splintering crash from somewhere outside convinced Lady Murray that it was the box containing her hats which had been dropped, and had her calling for Simpkins and her shoes.

Half an hour later the ladies set foot for the first time upon the shore of a foreign country. Though it was almost dark and there was little to see but shapes and lights, their excited voices rose into the damp sky like the chatter of starlings at dusk as Sir Ralph's secretary conducted them up the slipway towards the Hôtel du Poste, where they were to take dinner and sleep the night.

The rest of the journey was a repeat of what had gone before, only infinitely more protracted. The gentlemen went on ahead, and the ladies, in a hired carriage, spent the next four days discovering that, as Miss Murray had put it in a burst of patriotic pride, 'the French roads were *much* worse than the English.' The journey was tedious and uncomfortable, though for Anne there was the consolation that wherever they stopped, the native people readily understood her French, and frequently praised her accent; and if the compliments were not entirely unstudied, they were sincere enough to please her small vanity. By the time they reached Paris, only Anne had spirits enough to be pleased by the first view of the city – a long misty tumble of roofs from the vine-terraced hill of Montmartre, crowned with its tiny village, down to the shining Seine.

Since then, the Murrays had led a life of continual engagement. Though the haughtiness of the Whitworths was proof against all advances, the Murrays were invited everywhere, and when the ladies were not attending some ball, rout, supper party, picnic, play, or opera performance, they were visiting shops and warehouses, and spending hours closeted with mantuamakers and seamstresses. Once the first shock of the Paris fashions had worn off – never in the history of civilisation had women worn less in public – the Miss Murrays were mad to copy it. French ladies went *décolletée* even in daytime, and the hairstyles – delicious elaborations of Greek curls and Roman ringlets – made Miss Murray mourn deeply her decision last year to crop, and beg Miss Peters to find some way of making her hair grow more quickly.

Hartley Murray had hung about the house for a day or two, annoying his mother and mocking his sisters, and assuming an air of world-weary boredom in place of his former sulks. Then he had discovered that a set of abandoned young rogues, whose sole preoccupations were drink and deep play, haunted the gardens of the Palais Royale. He had hastened to make himself one of their company and was now entirely happy and hardly ever at home, which was more comfortable for everyone.

Anne, of course, had to chaperone the young ladies when they were not accompanied by their mother, but since they had no inclination – and, their mother insisted, no time – for any lessons, she had a great deal more time to herself than ever before. She still had Lady Murray's letters to write, and a great deal of sewing for all three ladies, but on most days she had leisure to go out and look at the shops and explore the city. She discovered a circulating library, newly set up in the rue St Roch for the particular benefit of the English visitors, which contained not only English novels, but books in the French language too. In an access of boldness she had enrolled herself, and since then had been reading steadily through Voltaire, Racine, Diderot, Fontenelle, and even Rousseau, to her own improvement and the evident approval of the Frenchwoman who ran the library.

She had a book in her reticule at this moment – one of the volumes of *Candide* – for it had been her intention to find a sheltered spot under the walls of the cathedral and sit and read for a little; but the sunlight on the river was so pleasant that for the moment she had no desire to do anything but stand and gaze at it. It flowed past her busily, on the way to its appointment with the sea. She tried to visualise the map of Europe and work out exactly where that would be. *All rivers run into the sea; yet the sea is not full.* Her mind idly threw up the quotation, and she spent a moment tracking it to its source, and decided hesitantly that it must be Ecclesiastes. Then she wondered whether a sailor would see the world the other way round from a landsman, and would think of the seas as being bounded by land, and the estuaries as little inlets into the coast, rather than outlets into the sea. The associations of the word 'sailor' inevitably produced a sigh, which she unwittingly uttered aloud.

At once a voice beside her said in French: 'What a sigh! But I think the thoughts were not sad ones, though they were so deep.'

Anne started violently and looked round to find a gentleman standing beside her and looking down at her with interest. He was tall, perhaps about thirty-five, with a long, mobile face – not handsome, but pleasant and intelligent. He was wearing a very fine grey pelisse with black silk frogging and a deep collar of some black fur which looked very soft and expensive, such as she had seen no gentleman in Paris wear before. This and a certain strangeness to his accent made her think he was not French, though certainly not English.

He looked at her quizzically. 'So, mademoiselle? You have been a long way away, I think. Rivers have the same effect on me. I gaze at them and think of them bearing me away to some other place – always to some other place,' he added, laughing suddenly, 'even when I like the one I am in!'

Anne was confused. It was a very odd thing for a young woman to be addressed so familiarly by a stranger; and yet there was no impertinence in his expression, nothing of the slightest impropriety in his voice or his manner. His clothes were expensive, his air distinguished, and he did look faintly familiar to her. Yet she was sure she had never met him: if she had, she could never have forgotten those eyes, large and shining and such an unusual gold-green in colour. They looked at her with interest, as if they really saw her, as no eyes had looked at her since she had left Miss Oliver's school; and the long, flexible lips were curved in a curious, closed smile, as if they liked what they saw.

But what could he mean by speaking to her? Puzzled rather than affronted, she replied in French, 'I beg your pardon, sir. I do not think we have been introduced.'

'I have offended custom by addressing you,' he nodded, 'but I have been watching the expressions flit across your face this quarter-hour, and I feel now as though we are old friends. Pray excuse me, mademoiselle, and allow me to present myself, and then we may continue this delightful conversation with complete propriety.' He swept off his hat, revealing straight, silky, light-brown hair. 'Count Nikolai Sergeyevitch Kirov of the Russian Embassy, entirely at your service! I have had the pleasure of seeing you many times in the company of Lady Murray. The two Miss Murrays I have met – perhaps Lady Murray may be your aunt?'

Anne felt herself blushing. This was dreadful! She must tell him what she was, and then she would see the withdrawal in his eyes. Most people looked at a governess in the same way they would look at a door. He might even be affronted and blame her for the civilities he would find he had wasted on such a menial. She lowered her gaze to her feet and, stammering a little in her embarrassment, said, 'I'm sorry, but I'm afraid you are mistaken, sir. I am Miss Peters, the Miss Murrays' governess.'

A movement caught her attention and made her look up. At the moment of introduction, of course, it was for the lady to offer her hand to the gentleman, and never vice versa; but there was a tiny gesture of intended reciprocation a gentleman sometimes made, to suggest that if the hand were offered he would be more than glad to take it. It was a movement so small it was almost non-existent, and yet to a lady it was quite unmistakable. Anne, brought up as a gentlewoman, responded before she knew it. Her slim, gloved hand came forward, and the Count placed his fingertips under hers, and bowed over it, his lips brushing the air most correctly a fraction of an inch above her glove.

'Enchanted to make your acquaintance, mademoiselle,' he said, and as he straightened, his eyes danced as though he and she were in a delightful conspiracy to mock the forms of polite society.

'*Et le vôtre, monsieur,*' Anne murmured automatically, thinking wildly that perhaps he did not know what a governess was.

But his next words dispelled the doubt. 'The credit must go to you, then, mademoiselle, that the Miss Murrays speak French with such an attractive accent, for I see that you speak the language *à merveille.*'

Anne could not help smiling. 'A pleasing fiction, monsieur!' she said. 'You have heard me speak only two sentences – far too little to judge by.'

'If you will forgive me for so directly contradicting you,' he said, returning her smile, 'it is quite enough when coupled with a face so expressive as yours, mademoiselle.' He frowned suddenly in thought, surveying the face with renewed interest and said, 'Miss Peters! Forgive me, but are you by any chance related to Admiral Peters, Admiral James Peters of His Britannic Majesty's navy?'

It was one astonishing thing too much. Anne passed into a state of euphoria where nothing could surprise her any longer. 'I am his daughter, sir,' she said. 'Why do you ask?'

'I thought so!' the Count exclaimed, evidently gratified. 'You have such a look of him, now I think of it, that it is no wonder I felt I knew you! I had the pleasure of meeting your father in Rugen in '97 when we were both visiting the Prussian ambassador there. We drank schnapps together one memorable night! He is well I hope?'

'He died, sir, at Riga that autumn,' Anne said flatly, and then, feeling she had spoken too brusquely, added in a lighter voice a quotation from *Candide* which she supposed he would know. '*Dans ce pays-ci il est bon de tuer de temps en temps un amiral, pour encourager les autres.*'

The Count did not react, and she felt a little foolish. His expression was grave as he said, 'I am so sorry, mademoiselle. In time of war one becomes reluctant to ask after old friends for just that reason. You have family, perhaps? Brothers and sisters?'

'None, sir.'

He smiled faintly. 'You are all the daughters of your father's house, and all the brothers too,' he said in English.

'*Twelfth Night.* You know Shakespeare,' she said, delighted.

27

He grinned. 'But of course! And you, mademoiselle, know Voltaire! Did you think I did not notice?'

'I have the book in my reticule here,' she said, patting it absurdly. 'I was intending to sit in the sun a little and read.'

'And I have prevented you,' he said with a bow of mock apology. 'But I am sure it is not warm enough to sit, Miss Peters, so I have saved you perhaps from an inconvenient chill. It would be a dreadful thing to miss the grand ball at the Tuileries next week, would it not?'

The words were spoken as part of a continuing friendly jest, but they had the effect of reminding Anne who she was, and of the impropriety of what she was doing. The euphoria dissipated on the instant. She must not stand in this public place talking to a gentleman. Inside her she might be a gentlewoman from the crown of her head to the tips of her toes, but the outside of her was a governess, and so the world would judge her. Disappointment, resentment, and a vicarious shame rose in her and almost brought tears to her eyes, making her speak rather stiffly. 'You need have no apprehension on that score, sir. Governesses have nothing to do with balls. And now, if you will forgive me, I must be going.'

He looked down at her with concern. 'Now I have vexed you! I am so sorry.'

'No, sir, not at all,' she said, turning her face away.

'But I have. You were smiling, and now you are distressed. Please forgive me.'

'Truly, there is nothing to forgive,' Anne said. 'My time is not my own to command. My young ladies will be returning from their drive, and I must be there to meet them. Really, I must go.'

'Your hand, then, to show that you forgive,' he said, holding out his.

Anne looked up and met the kind, faintly-smiling eyes, and felt that here was a man who made anything possible, whom the conventions could not touch, who could conjure happiness out of the air. She had last felt that about her father, and the fact that the Count had known him confused her for a moment, so that as she placed her hand in his, she smiled up at him without reserve, as she would have smiled at her father. It was entirely the wrong sort of smile for a young woman to give to a gentleman of slight acquaintance, but it did not seem to trouble the Count in the least. He pressed her hand firmly and said, 'Au revoir, Miss Peters. We shall meet again, I am sure.'

Then he bowed, replaced his hat, and strolled away, leaving Anne feeling confused, happy, unhappy, puzzled, and exhilarated in more or less equal proportions.

The diplomatic atmosphere in Paris had been electric ever since the middle of March, when the First Consul, Bonaparte, had verbally attacked Lord Whitworth at one of the Sunday Drawing-rooms, pouring out a tirade of accusations and abuse, to which Whitworth had responded by very stiffly walking out. Matters had mended socially since then to the extent that the balls and parties were able to continue, but even Lady Murray had become aware, from her husband's preoccupied frown, that negotiations between England and France were in a delicate state.

Anne, privy to a great deal more information because of her ability to understand French, knew that the governments distrusted each other, and that each was convinced the other was secretly arming for a continuation of the war. There seemed to have been breaches of the treaty on both sides, but of course each was convinced its own breaches were justified, while the other side's were treacherous.

She had not lived in the household of a diplomat for three years, however, without learning that this was a normal state of affairs between countries, and it seemed nothing out of the ordinary to her and caused her no particular apprehension. During the next week she had other more immediate things to think about, principal amongst which was her meeting with the Russian Count.

When she was alone and unoccupied, she went over and over the conversation they had had, analysing everything he had said to her, and interpreting it so many different ways that at last the words seemed to have no meaning at all. Why had he spoken to her at all? It was not until later that he had known her for the daughter of an old acquaintance, so that could not be the excuse. Why had he continued to talk to her when he knew she was a governess? Did he think that because she bore a servant's status, she had only a servant's morals? The notion that he had intended anything dishonourable made her blush with vexation, and then feel ashamed. He was not that sort of man, she was convinced. Perhaps Russians behaved more informally than the English: that was a more pleasant thought. Would she see him again? And if she did, would he greet her as an acquaintance, or be cool with her? And if they met in the presence of her employers, what would their reaction be? She could imagine that they would not be best pleased: they would think her forward.

Any further meeting with him would be fraught with so many difficulties that on the whole she was relieved to think it was very unlikely to happen; and yet she had enjoyed so much the brief human contact, not only with someone who regarded her as a real person rather than a labelled object, but also with someone of wit and intelligence, that she could not help a wistfulness colouring the thought that she would probably never speak to him again.

Meanwhile, there was the grand Embassies Ball to prepare for. It was to be a splendid affair with two suppers and fireworks to follow, and the Murray ladies were reserving their best sartorial efforts for it. The Parisian mantuamaker they had been patronising had made the new gowns in plenty of time, but since they had been delivered, Anne and Simpkins had been called so often to make minute alterations and improvements that it was doubtful whether Madame Beauclerc would have recognised her creations.

Lady Murray's gown had caused particular problems, for her ladyship had been enjoying French cooking with a certain abandon ever since November, and her pattern gown had grown too tight. Simpkins had tentatively suggested making up a new one, and had almost had her ears boxed for presumption, so the new purple satin had been made up to the old dimensions. When it came home, Simpkins had retired upstairs with her mistress and an apprehensive expression for a trial of the gown. About half an hour later, a servant had come to Anne saying she was wanted in my lady's bed chamber.

A few minutes later, Anne scratched at the chamber door and entered to find Simpkins, her face red and her cap over one eye, wrestling with portions of Lady Murray's white dimpled flesh which were refusing to enter the confinement of the shining purple bodice.

'You sent for me, ma'am?' Anne said blandly, biting the insides of her cheeks.

Simpkins rolled a desperate and pleading eye towards her, while keeping a firm grip on the two edges of material she was attempting to bring together.

'Ah yes, Miss Peters,' said Lady Murray evenly, as though the struggle going on behind her were nothing to do with her. Her face rose perfectly calm above her tightly-encased body like a naked woman half-swallowed by a purple whale. 'Perhaps you could help Simpkins. She is being very stupid and clumsy, I fear.'

Simpkins, unable to restrain a growl, gestured to Anne with a jerk of the head to take hold of the dress while she used both hands to cram the unruly portions of her mistress into it. It was a matter, Anne could see, of disposing the bulges where there was room for them, but naturally she could not say such a thing out loud, and could only communicate with the frantic maid by means of eyes and eyebrows. Between them they achieved it at last, and hooked up.

Some of the spare Lady Murray was worked round under the armpits, and the rest went towards giving her a more-than-usually magnificent bosom, which Anne thought would come in very useful for displaying Lady Murray's diamonds.

On the other hand, it was clear from her ladyship's rising colour that breathing and moving in the gown were likely to be restricted, while eating would be quite out of the question. Anne summoned all her reserves of tact and said, 'It is a very handsome gown, ma'am, and the colour suits you to perfection. I think, though, that your notion of having Simpkins go over all the seams by hand was a good one. French makers don't seem to have quite the same way with seams as our English ones.'

Behind Lady Murray's back, Simpkins gaped at Anne with astonishment and incipient fury, and then realised what her plan was. She swallowed. 'Quite right, m'lady,' she said tonelessly. 'It's not the sort of work I like to see in a finished gown.' She gave Anne a grim nod of approval, and probably at that moment almost regarded Anne as an equal.

Miss Murray's gown was of white *mousseline de soie* covered with tiny raised gold spots, cut very low in the front, and with tiny puffed sleeves that left the neck, shoulders, and arms bare. Salton, round-eyed, murmured to Anne that it was little better than a nightdress, and that she knew what her mother would have said if she had dared to go into a public place in such a thing. Anne's help was required in sewing some padding into the bosom, for the deep *décolletage* revealed that Miss Murray had not been generously endowed by nature. She made up for it, however, by having golden hair which, since her crop was now growing out, Salton was able to arrange to great advantage. Caroline's hair was only mouse-fair, but she was the prettier of the two, and plump as a young chicken, and she looked very well in her gown of pale blue silk with an overdress of spider-gauze.

Lady Murray had reached the stage of deciding which of her jewellery she would lend to her daughters for the occasion when, two days before the ball, she was stricken with a heavy cold, and retired to her chamber. Anne was summoned to the bed of pain.

'You see, Miss Peters, how ailing I am,' Lady Murray said tragically. 'I may recover in time for the ball, but in case I do not, you must be prepared to chaperone Miss Murray and Miss Caroline. You must furbish up one of your gowns into something suitable to the occasion. You must do your charges credit, but by no means draw attention to

31

yourself. I'm sure I can trust your judgement. Simpkins will help you, if you need help.'

'Thank you ma'am,' Anne said, 'but I'm sure you will be well again in time.'

Lady Murray waved her away, and Anne left, retaining a grave expression until she was outside the door. Then she could not repress a grin of delight. She was quite sure Lady Murray would not be better in time, and what unmarried female of twenty-three could help feeling an upsurge of joy at the prospect of going to a ball, even if she were only going as a chaperone. She had no intention, she decided there and then, of furbishing up an old gown: two days, even if she had to work all night, was long enough for her to make a new one, and she had not been looking in shop windows for the last six months for nothing. She knew exactly what she wanted, and she had sufficient of her wages saved to buy the material.

Simpkins' recently-acquired approval of her stretched far enough for the dresser to advise against the expense. 'For who knows but what her la'ship will decide to go at the last minute anyway, even if she is still sneezing? And then what chance will you have to wear it? And in any case, no-one will see it. You'll be sitting down in a corner all evening.'

'I know all that,' Anne said, 'but I shall have the pleasure of it myself, don't you see? I must have something pretty, just once, even if no-one but me ever sees it.'

Simpkins sniffed. 'Well, a fool and her money's soon parted, if you ask me. But I'll help you cut out and make up, if you like. Only you'd better not be too fine, or her la'ship'll have it off your back before you can say knife. And you'll have to wear a cap, or she'll think you're being forward.'

'Of course, I understand. Thank you, Simpkins,' Anne said, smiling so rapturously that the dresser felt almost sorry for a moment for the disappointment she felt was inevitably coming Anne's way. Still, she shrugged, each to the devil his own way, and stumped off to answer my lady's bell.

Lady Murray's cold, far from improving, only worsened to the point where even she could not think herself fit to attend the ball, and so on the evening in question, it was Anne who went along to the young ladies' sitting-room to usher them downstairs. Her new gown was of Italian crêpe, light grey, with a dusky-pink silk underdress, which she thought was both sober and becoming. The bodice was shawl-cut, and therefore revealed little of her bosom, but it had very clever Russian sleeves, which had robbed her of a great deal of sleep, for they were extremely difficult to set, and needed a great many tiny stitches. She had draped a shawl of plain grey Albany gauze caught around her elbows, and even with her hair covered by a Mameluke cap, she felt she did not look at all like a dowdy.

Her opinion was soon confirmed. 'Oh, Miss Peters, you do look nice,' said the good-natured Caroline as she entered the room. 'And you have such a way of wearing a shawl! I wish I might wear mine as well.'

Miss Murray only looked sour. 'Do hurry up, Miss Peters. We have been waiting for you this age. Has Mama seen your dress? Does she approve it?'

'Of course,' Anne said quietly. In fact Lady Murray had been half asleep and not inclined to be disturbed and had waved her away without more than glancing at her to see, Anne assumed, that she was not showing too much bosom.

'Have you the sewing-things in your reticule in case anything should tear?' Miss Murray pursued. 'I'm sure it will be a dreadful squeeze.'

'I have; but if you loop up your train as I have shown you, and don't lean towards your partner when you dance, then you won't have your hem trodden on,' Anne said mildly.

'It's only that silly Gregory de l'Aude she leans towards,' Caroline said wittily. 'She's spoony on him, and he has such big feet he can hardly help treading on some part of her if they are in the same room together.'

'Miss Caroline, where did you learn such language?' Anne rebuked her. If Miss Murray were put in a bad mood, it would be she who would suffer.

'His feet are not big,' Miss Murray retorted, reddening with anger. 'They're the right size for his height. Just because you only dance with little, undersized men, Caro – '

'Now that's enough, young ladies,' Anne said hastily. 'If you are quite ready, we had better go down to the drawing-room. You know your father hates to be kept waiting.'

Sir Ralph was alone, pacing up and down the room and occasionally wrestling his watch out of his tight fob in order to suck his teeth at it. Hartley Murray was dining with friends and going on to the ball with them, though Anne privately doubted whether he would arrive much before the end.

'You're late,' Sir Ralph snapped as they entered. 'The carriage has been ready ten minutes. Miss Peters, you understand your duties? I may be called away during the evening to one or other of the embassies. If I am not present at the end of the ball, it will be for you to see the young ladies are brought home safely.'

'Yes, Sir Ralph.'

'And pay particular attention to their partners. To be on the safe side, you had better not give permission for them to dance with anyone who has not actually been received here at this house at some time.'

'I understand, Sir Ralph,' said Anne, seeing out of the corner of her eye the downward curve Miss Murray's mouth had taken.

'And take particular care to remain nearby during supper. It is important that you are *seen* to be present. There is a great deal of informality at the Tuileries, but remember we shall not be in Paris much longer, and it is by our own countrymen that we will be judged when we are back at home.'

'Yes, Sir Ralph,' Anne said, suppressing a desire to blurt out questions. Not be in Paris much longer? What, then, was in the air? It was the first time that any hint had been given of the termination of their visit, and, looking at the frown puckering her employer's brow, Anne felt sure he would not have given away so much now if his mind had not been partly on other things.

Chapter Three

Despite Sir Ralph's complaints, they were still amongst the early arrivals when their carriage turned from the rue de Rivoli into the Carrousel. The First Consul, like the French kings before him, frequently used this enormous open square for parades and military reviews; today it was empty but for the ceremonial guard. The Murrays' carriage drove round the central triumphal arch, surmounted with the great bronze horses of Byzantium which the French had stolen from the San Marco Basilica in Venice seven years before, and joined the tail of coaches working their way towards the main entrance of the palace. It was a splendidly ornate edifice, built in the Renaissance style for Catherine de Medici, and though the interior had suffered badly during the violent days of the Revolution, it had been restored, repainted, and stocked anew with fine furnishings, carpets, pictures, and porcelain, many of which had come from other royal palaces, now in state hands.

'This Bonaparte lives as well as a king,' Lady Murray had complained many times since their arrival last November; but no-one could resist the charm of Madame Josephine, and there was no regal stiffness or ponderous etiquette about the Consul's court. Elegant equality was the watchword, the best of the Ancien Régime mingling with the best of the Republic.

Anne went with the Miss Murrays to an ante-room to ensure that the ten-minute sojourn in the carriage had not impaired their toilette in any way, and then accompanied them into the ballroom, taking up an unobtrusive position amongst the chaperones from which she could watch the arrivals. This must be her pleasure. If she had attended this ball as her father's daughter, she could have looked forward to dancing every dance, for an English admiral was the equal of anyone short of a governor or head of state. As it was, she could only sit by and watch, and her active part would be confined to pinning up a hem or securing a loose curl if her young ladies should dance too vigorously.

And yet the ball was a glittering affair. To be present in any capacity was an honour, something of which she knew she was much more aware than her heedless young charges. Their minds were on their own appearance and the prospect of prestigious partners; that they might be witnessing history in the making was beyond them to appreciate.

Representatives were arriving from all the courts of Europe. The Whitworths were there, of course, casting cold looks upon the First Consul and his closest advisors: the feline Cambacérès, bachelor and gourmet with exquisite but occasionally bizarre tastes; Joseph Fouché, a grey-visaged, cold-eyed man who had already served both the late King Louis and Robespierre, for whom he was rumoured to have carried out hideous atrocities in the provinces during the Terror; and gentle, upright Armand de Caulaincourt, a noble of the old school, fearless, frank, and courteous, whom Beugnot had called the only completely honest man in Europe.

There were the representatives of Prussia and Saxony and Austria, and a little dark man, unmistakeably Italian, whom Anne thought must be from the court of the Two Sicilies. And now here was the Russian Ambassador, Markov, with his party. Anne had not expected to find so much to interest her in the appearance of the Russians, and indeed, they looked very much like anyone else, dressed in French style, though perhaps with rather more colour and jewellery about them, and certainly more appearance of enjoying themselves than the English.

Count Kirov entered at the Ambassador's shoulder, evidently deep in conversation with him. He was the taller man and had to bend his head to reach Markov's ear. The Ambassador turned his head and replied, and both men laughed. Then the Count straightened up and scanned the room, as anyone might who had just arrived at a ball. Why, then, did Anne feel it necessary to shrink back, as though afraid his eye might fall on her, and why again did she feel faintly disappointed when it did not?

The dancing began, and after the first formal minuets, the couples began to form sets for the country dancing. The Miss Murrays were spared any agony of doubt, for their hands had been solicited long before, and having seen her charges walk off with their partners in perfect propriety, Anne was able to resume her seat and allow her eye to wander. It was odd, she thought, how much in evidence Count Kirov seemed to be. Everywhere she looked, it was on him that her eye alighted. Of course, he was a tall man, amongst the tallest present. He had been walking about the margins of the room, and now was leading a splendidly jewelled lady, one of the Prussian Ambassador's party, to the top set. For no reason she could determine, Anne drew a sigh when the music began, and her right foot under the hem of grey crêpe tapped out the rhythm of its own accord.

Nothing at all unexpected happened until the end of second supper interval. Then, in the press towards the door leading out of the supper-room, Anne became separated from the Miss Murrays, who had been making themselves disagreeable to her because she had baulked their plan to eat their supper with their partners, unsupervised. Trying to edge herself out of the main stream of bodies by which she had been caught up, Anne unluckily found herself in the immediate vicinity of Lady Whitworth, whose diamond bracelet caught for a moment in Anne's shawl. The former duchess, who had not noticed that she was attached, moved her arm abruptly and tugged it free. The ripping sound caught her attention, and she looked round briefly to see what had happened. An expression of annoyance crossed her face at having been in such close proximity to a person of inferior status, and Anne shrank back, a flush of anger and distress colouring her cheeks. Lady Whitworth passed on, and Anne managed at last to wedge herself into a corner where she could examine the damage.

There was an ugly three-cornered rent in the delicate gauze, the edges of which were so frayed that it would be impossible to mend it invisibly. Anne was still mourning over her ruined finery when a gentleman coming out of the supper-room bumped her elbow painfully with the hilt of his dress sword, and she was almost vexed enough to cry out.

But the gentleman paused, and a familiar voice said, 'Miss Peters! What a pleasant surprise. But I hope I did not hurt you? A thousand pardons, mademoiselle.'

Anne felt her cheeks grow warm. She had hardly expected the Count to notice her again, particularly at so glittering an occasion, but he was looking at her with such friendly concern that she automatically smiled and answered him lightly.

'For so small an offence, sir, one would suffice,' she said.

'You are too generous, mademoiselle. And this is a famous way to renew my acquaintance with you, to begin by knocking you about! You will think me nothing but a clumsy fool.'

'Anything but that, sir,' Anne said, laughing at his mock-rueful expression. 'Did not Cicero say "The mind of the man is the man himself"?'

The Count raised his eyebrows. 'Now you have really surprised me. Do you understand Latin too, mademoiselle? But no, I mistake. I am not really surprised. It is stupidity which is always so surprising, not intelligence. It is a pleasant ball, is it not? Pleasure shows everyone to advantage. It seems to make the women appear more handsome and the men more distinguished. Are you having an agreeable time?'

'I was sir, until I fell foul of a diamond bracelet,' Anne said, displaying the rent in her shawl. It seemed so natural to talk to him that she found it impossible to be frostily formal, or to check his disastrous tendency to be friendly.

'Oh, what a pity,' the Count said. 'And such a delicate gauze! It is beyond mending, I fear. But perhaps if you cut it down, you might make a fichu of it. It is too pretty to be quite wasted.'

She looked at him with amusement. 'Do you understand such things, sir? It is not the way with English gentlemen.'

'In Russia we take a great interest in clothes. We understand fine materials. And jewels, also. We Russians understand jewels better than anyone in the world.' He surveyed her with a practised eye. 'Your gown is very elegant, mademoiselle, and very becoming, but you should have a necklace. Diamonds would look very well with your colouring, or pearls. No, diamonds, I think, at the neck and in the hair. And not the cap – caps are for old ladies.'

This talk of diamonds embarrassed Anne. 'For old ladies, and for chaperones, sir,' she said lightly. 'I think you have forgotten my station in life.'

The Count looked suddenly serious. 'Forgotten your station? Yes, I understand you very well, mademoiselle, better than you understand me! The English speak of loving their children, but they place them in the care of people they despise. In Russia it is not so. In Russia, a governess is treated with honour, for she is someone whom we regard as most fit to care for and instruct those dearest to our hearts. We love our children, and entrust them only to those we admire and respect.'

Anne was too confused to reply. She lowered her eyes, and managed only to mutter, 'Sir, I beg you will not – '

In a moment the Count spoke again, in a cheerful, matter-of-fact way. 'But tell me, Miss Peters, what do you think of the First Consul? An able man, there is no doubt, but what is your observation?'

Anne recovered herself with an effort. 'He smiles with his mouth, but not with his eyes,' she said. 'I think I would find him rather frightening, if ever I should come close to him.'

The Count nodded. 'You show more discernment than the British Ambassador,' he said, dropping without appearing to notice it into French, which evidently came more naturally to him. 'Lord Whitworth thinks him vulgar, ambitious, and unscrupulous. He hates him, but does not fear him, and that is a man I think it will never do to underestimate.'

'I'm sure you are right. But do you not think the Consul ambitious?' Anne replied in the same language. 'It seems to me he wishes to rule all of Europe.'

'For its own good,' the Count said with a faint smile. 'To free all nations from the tyranny of monarchy.'

'And unite them under the rule of one man, and that man himself,' Anne concluded gravely. 'Pardon me, I am mistaken. Of course he is not ambitious.'

The Count laughed. 'Wise and witty, mademoiselle! And what will be the end of such ambition? You think we shall have war again? Well, I agree with you. This peace was never made of very strong cloth, and now it is beginning to wear thin.'

'And what then, sir?' Anne could not help an edge of anxiety creeping into her voice. 'Who will win? Voltaire says that God is always on the side of the big battalions.'

'Then God will have a hard task in choosing. The battalions will be big on both sides. If war comes, it will be bad, very bad.' The word was unemphatic, but the expression on the Count's face was chilling. 'There are no victors in war. Everyone suffers, and afterwards, no-one can ever remember what it was all about.'

'Do you think it will come soon?' Anne asked quietly.

He met her eyes. 'Yes, soon. The tension grows daily. Myself, I believe that Bonaparte would rather delay matters, but he will make no concessions unless your country evacuates Malta. He has said too often and too publicly that he will have the Treaty, and nothing but the Treaty.'

'I cannot believe the Government will give up Malta,' Anne said. 'From what I have heard my father say, it is as important a naval base as Gibraltar. They will think even war is better than losing Malta.'

'Between ourselves, mademoiselle, Malta is nothing more than an excuse. Your Lord Whitworth is sent new instructions almost daily, to make ever more stringent demands. If it seems that one set will be met, then there comes another. Someone in England wants war, and is determined to have it.'

'Oh no, I can't believe it,' Anne said, shocked, and then, recalling snippets of conversation she had been overhearing for the past year, realised that indeed nothing was more likely. The Peace had never been popular in England, coming as it did, not after a great victory, but as the result of a stalemate; and there were a great many powerful men whose business would benefit by the resumption of war.

The Count, a slight smile on his lips, seemed to be watching these thoughts pass through her head as though she were quite transparent. Provoked, she asked, 'But, pray, how do you know about Lord Whitworth's instructions, sir?'

His eyes shone with amusement. 'We Russians know everything. We have a special arrangement with God for being right. And now, mademoiselle, since we have determined world history between us, and this is, after all, a ballroom, perhaps we should turn to more important things. Will you do me the honour of dancing with me when the ball resumes?'

Again Anne realised how far she had forgotten herself. She looked up at him, profoundly shocked. 'Oh no, sir, you must not ask me! It is quite, quite impossible!'

He smiled easily. 'Indeed. Am I so very repulsive to you, mademoiselle?'

Her cheeks burned with confusion and distress. 'Sir, you don't understand. It is bad enough that I should converse with you, but as to dancing with you – why, even your asking me, if it were known, would bring severe reproof upon me! It would be thought most improper. No, no, you must not! I am a governess. It will not do.'

'You are mistaken, mademoiselle,' the Count said cheerfully. 'I am an old acquaintance of your father, and as such may quite properly ask you to dance with me. But I see Sir Ralph Murray has just come in by the far door. Lest you should be embarrassed, I shall go and explain the matter to him and ask his permission to ask you.'

'Oh no, sir, please do not! He would very much dislike to be troubled with it. And Lady Murray would be so angry.'

'I have observed Lady Murray closely, and if I know anything about humanity, she will only be flattered. How could any *grande dame* object to being reminded that her governess is so well-connected?' His voice was all sweet reason, but Anne was sure that there was a light of mischief in his eyes as he bowed to her and, without allowing her more argument, walked away.

Sick with apprehension, Anne watched him approach Sir Ralph, bow, and speak to him. She saw her employer's expression change from one of polite interest to astonishment, saw the immediate shake of the head as the Count made his request, followed by a growing bewilderment as the explanation expanded. It was, of course, impossible for Sir Ralph to refuse permission, and that alone would have secured his displeasure. He summoned Anne with a crook of the finger, and astonishment and disapproval were equally in evidence as he relayed the substance of the Count's words. It was clear that he was not in the least flattered that this eminent man wished to dance, not with one of his daughters, but with his daughters' chaperone; and only a lifetime in diplomacy prevented him from betraying stark disbelief that the Russian had ever been acquainted with her father.

At the beginning of the ball, Anne had sighed because she could not dance; now, as Count Kirov led her scarlet-faced into the set, and she felt, or thought she felt, the disapproving eyes of every English matron upon her, she would have been grateful to have resumed her former obscurity. In spite of the prospect of half-an-hour's free converse with him, she would have been glad just then to find herself back in her room in Margaret Street, with a cold in the head and a heap of stockings to darn.

The ball ended with fireworks, soup, and pasties, and since Hartley Murray had not arrived at the ball at all, and Sir Ralph had gone off with Lord Whitworth to the embassy to work, it was left to Anne to escort the young ladies home. As they waited in the foyer for the carriage, Anne thought she intercepted some pointed and hostile looks, and felt sure she was being talked about. The atmosphere seemed to her so electric that she was surprised that the Miss Murrays did not notice it; but they chattered happily about the ball, their partners, their flirts and the toilettes of every other woman they could put a name to, with complete unconcern. Astonishing though it seemed, it was evident that they had neither seen Anne dancing, nor had heard of it from anyone else.

On the short journey to the rue St Augustine, Anne sat with her eyes cast down and reflected upon the evening and the probable consequences. How could she have been so foolish as to talk to the Count so freely? It was from that that all her troubles had arisen. True, their meeting at the ball was the purest accident, but he would not have asked her to dance but for their previous conversation on the Ile de la Cité. That was when she should have discouraged him by being properly formal.

Folly! Contemptible, dangerous folly! Of course, she could give plenty of reasons – her loneliness; the longing for intelligent conversation, for human warmth; the flattering nature of his interest in her, and the way he treated her as an equal, not only socially but intellectually; her pique and anger at the accident to her shawl and Lady Whitworth's contemptuous curl of the lip – but reasons were not excuses.

What then if she were gently born, inwardly more than the equal of the Murray women? What if her intellect had gone unexercised for as long as she had been trying to teach these bacon-brained young girls, and fetching and carrying for their even more witless mama? She was what she was, a governess, and as such must keep her place. She was guilty of the sin of pride. She had erred, and would be punished.

But what punishment? She went cold when she contemplated the worst that might happen to her. The Murrays might cast her out without a character, and then, unprotected in a foreign country, she would starve, or worse, fall a prey to some fate too hideous to contemplate. Lady Murray was not a cruel woman, but she was very conscious of her position in the world. Perhaps they would at least take her back to England with them before turning her off. To be destitute in one's native land seemed somehow less terrifying. Without a reference she would not be able to get another place with a respectable family, but in England she might perhaps be able to find a position in a school – an unfashionable one where they were less particular. Miss Oliver might help her to find a place, however mean, where she could earn enough to keep body and soul together without shame.

And then, simply in reaction to these dreadful pictures, she thought that perhaps it would not be so bad. Perhaps Lady Murray would do no more than reprimand her, and her punishment would be to endure rebuke and humiliation and a certain degree of suspicion for a time. That would be bad enough, but if she might escape a worse fate, it would be as well to humble herself before her mistress, admit her sin, and beg forgiveness.

She saw Lady Murray's face in her mind, vacant and foolish, imagined it puckered with anger against her, and mouthing rebuke. For an instant her pride reared up. It went against the grain to abase herself to such a person. She was a gentlewoman: Admiral Peters' daughter! Count Kirov had sought her out, had led her into the set, and had danced opposite her with as warm a smile as he had bestowed upon the wife of the Prussian Ambassador. She hugged the memory of that dance and its conversation to her for a moment. Though she had walked to the set scarlet with embarrassment and apprehension, it had been delightful to take her proper place in the world. If her father had lived, she might have gone to such a ball and danced every dance and never even noticed that the Miss Murrays existed! Was she to be punished for doing what she was born to?

The carriage halted with a jerk outside the house and brought her back to reality, and she busied herself with collecting up reticules and fans and retrieving Caroline's glove, trampled and soiled, from the carriage floor before alighting. She followed the young ladies up the steps into the foyer, and, as they began climbing the stairs, chattering like magpies as they told the story of their triumphs all over again to

Simpkins and Salton, Anne was only too glad to make her way directly to bed. With so much to think about, however, it was long before she managed to drop off to sleep.

She woke early, and since there was no likelihood that her young ladies would stir before noon, she had all the longer in the company of her own thoughts. One of the maids told her that Mr Hartley had not come home last night, and that Sir Ralph was in a terrible taking about it. From the distance of her room, Anne heard some of his fury reverberating about the house, and could not but wonder whether any of it were directed towards her. Silence fell when he left the house to go about his business, and Anne sat quietly and got on with her sewing, wondering whether he had spoken to Lady Murray before he left, and when the summons would come.

It did not come until the early hours of the afternoon, when the young ladies were astir and had sent for trays in their room. Lady Murray was up, but not dressed when Anne entered her room. She had stationed herself on the day bed by the fireplace, and her cold had evidently passed from the feverish into the merely tiresome stage. She greeted Anne with a grave and nasal, 'Come in, Miss Peters. I wish to speak to you.'

Anne closed the door behind her, and stood facing her mistress. Lady Murray surveyed her with cold disapproval, and Anne was surprised to discover that even in her extravagantly flounced and beribboned wrapper, she did not, for once, look ridiculous. Roused from her usual good-natured vacancy, she had attained to a kind of dignity. Anne found that her hands were trembling, and folded them together in front of her to keep them still.

'Miss Peters,' Lady Murray began at last, 'I am at a loss what to say to you. I am profoundly shocked. I never should have thought that a young woman of your education could so forget herself, and forget what was due to her employers, too. We have given you every consideration, Miss Peters, every consideration! Why, I don't suppose there are three governesses in all of England who live so well as you do – and on such terms with the family – and yet this is how you repay us! Presumption, impertinence, and a total want of consideration for our good name! Perhaps it is not well to talk of *ingratitude* between employer and employee, but I should have thought that your sense of duty alone, if not your sense of decency, would have prevented you from making such a spectacle of yourself in a public place. Sir Ralph was shocked beyond measure, and when he told me, I found it hard to believe such a thing could happen! But to dance in that wanton way, you, a governess! and taken to the ball as chaperone to my girls, as one meant to set them an example of genteel behaviour! How could you do it, Miss Peters? How could you bring yourself to do it?'

For all her intentions, Anne was unable to prevent herself from rising to her own defence.

'Indeed, ma'am, I am very sorry it happened, very sorry indeed, and nothing could have been further from my wishes; but I do not know how I could have refused, when the Count had asked permission, and had been given it – '

'*Given* permission?' Lady Murray cried. 'And how, pray, could Sir Ralph do anything else but give it, in front of everyone, when he had been asked? He was placed in an intolerable position.'

'And how, ma'am, could I do anything else but accept?' Anne retorted.

'Do not answer me back, Miss Peters!' Lady Murray said, reddening with anger. 'You know perfectly well that none of this would have happened if you had not encouraged his attentions. Gentlemen do not customarily ask chaperones to dance at embassy balls! A pretty world it would be if they did!'

'He did not ask me, ma'am, because I was a chaperone, but because he was a friend of my father,' Anne said desperately.

'Aye, so you say. And so he said. But as to that, it would be more likely if he had other things on his mind than old friends when he took it into his head to notice you. A count and a governess? I know what everyone at the ball thought about that! What would *you* make of it, Miss Peters, if you heard it of someone else?'

Anne's eyes filled with tears of hurt and anger at the dreadful suggestion. She struggled against them for a moment, and stammered, 'I did not – there was never – there was nothing improper in anything he said or did! Indeed there was not! You must believe me!'

Lady Murray sniffed irritably. 'Well, well, yes, I believe you. Do stop crying, Miss Peters. I only say that that is what everyone will believe. And you did very wrong, you know you did, to speak to him at all, and encourage him in that way.'

'I am very sorry,' Anne began, but was interrupted.

'Sorry? I should think you may! I do not know what will come of this night's work, indeed I do not. I shall have to ask Sir Ralph what is right to do about it. There is no possibility of concealment. Why, already this morning I have had a note from Mrs Anstruther, the cat, asking me in *such* a way whether I was having my girls instructed in the Russian language! It will be all over Paris before the day's out. You have made us look so *particular*, and you know I hate anything of that sort. It is bad enough to have Hartley talked of, though it is only what everyone's sons seem to do, but people will wonder how our girls are being brought up, if their governess acts in such a peculiar fashion. You should have thought before you acted how it would reflect on *them*. It is too much, really it is, to have them brought to shame by such a one as you.'

This was too much to bear. When she thought of her own birth and upbringing, in comparison with that of her charges, Anne was stung into her own defence. 'I do not think I have done anything so very bad, ma'am,' she began.

'It is not for you to judge, Miss Peters,' Lady Murray said crossly. 'Sir Ralph and I are most seriously displeased, and we shall have to decide what is best to be done with you. Naturally there is no question of your continuing to teach my daughters. It would be better perhaps if we were to send you home to England immediately – that would be the quickest way to have this matter forgotten. For the moment you will remain in your room, and I shall ask Sir Ralph when he returns what is to be done about your wages.'

Anne drew herself up stiffly. 'There is no necessity to put yourself to the trouble of consulting Sir Ralph, ma'am,' she said with icy politeness. 'I shall leave at once and find myself other employment.'

'Highty-tighty!' Lady Murray retorted, growing red. 'What, pray, do you think you could do? Other employment, indeed! And don't think I shall give you a reference, for I shan't! Mrs Cowley Crawford was right about you. She warned me from the very beginning that you gave yourself airs because of your education. What use is an education to a female, pray tell me that? Where has it got you? For all that I can see, it adds nothing to refinement or delicacy – '

'Now you have insulted me in every possible way,' Anne said, fighting her rising temper, 'and I must beg you to excuse me. I shall pack my things at once. Goodbye, ma'am.' And she withdrew and closed the door behind her while she was still able to do so quietly.

Upstairs in her room she gave vent to her pent-up feelings by throwing herself down on her bed and bursting into tears. They had more to do with rage than unhappiness, and lasted ten minutes, at the end of which time she sat up feeling much better, blew her nose, and was able in relative calmness to consider her situation.

There was no possibility of her staying here. Even had the Murrays been willing to overlook her first crime of dancing with the Count, and her second crime of refusing to acknowledge the first, her pride would not now allow her to back down from the position she had taken up. Besides, she had become aware of how much servitude had always irked her, although she had always hidden the fact from herself. She felt that any employment, however mean, which would release her from it, would be better than this luxurious enslavement.

Why should she not stay here in Paris and find herself employment? There must be something she could do, and she spoke French now almost as well as English. She could find some cheap but decent lodging, and get herself work as – as – her roving eye fell on the nightgown she had been altering for Miss Murray when the summons had come. Of course! She was a skilled needlewoman and accustomed to making her own gowns, and Paris was the home of fashion: she could get employment with a mantuamaker. Nothing could be easier! And in time, she might start up her own business. She had seen for herself how the leading mantuamakers in Paris were received everywhere, and even made excellent marriages. It was an eminently respectable calling; and best of all, she would be answerable to no-one.

Having thought of the scheme, she could not wait to put it into effect. She jumped up and changed into a plain but well-cut walking-dress of her own making, which she felt would be the best advertisement for her skills, tidied her hair, put on her hat and pelisse, and, going down by the backstairs in case the Miss Murrays were about, left the house and began walking down the rue St Roch towards the main shopping thoroughfare.

As luck would have it, as soon as she turned the corner, she bumped into Mr Hartley Murray, strolling along hatless and looking somewhat the worse for wear. He put his hand automatically to his bare head, stared at it in a rather fuddled way, and then realising who she was gave her a slight bow and a broad grin.

'Miss Peters! Well, here's a famous coincidence. What're you doing out so early?'

'It isn't so early, Mr Murray,' Anne replied cautiously, realising he was probably not entirely sober. 'It is well past noon.'

'That's early for me,' he said, rubbing his hand over his unshaven chin. 'When I dine with Sauvechasse and de l'Aude, anything before five in the afternoon is early. A famous dinner we had last night, I can tell you! We did not even sit down to it before ten o'clock, neither.'

'Your absence from the ball was noted,' she said, amused by his naïve pride in eating so late.

'Who says I wasn't there? No-one can prove it,' he said with a wink. 'For one thing, the guv'nor wasn't there himself a lot of the time; and for another, de l'Aude dropped in on it before he joined us

46

for dinner, and told me all about it, and who my sisters danced with, so I can make a good enough tale of it to satisfy Mama.' He grinned slowly, as one in possession of a good joke. 'And he told about your little adventure, Miss Peters!'

'My adventure, Mr Murray?' Anne said discouragingly.

'Aye, Miss Innocent, dancing with Count Kirov, the Russian Ambassador's aide! It must have been famous! De l'Aude said that all the old dowagers and pussy-cats were almost bursting when he led you into the set. And talking French with him, as if it was the simplest thing in the world! Miss Dalrymple was two down from you, and heard you as plain as anything, and told everyone. Oh, I would give worlds to have been there and seen it! How ever did you keep from laughing, Miss Peters? I know I should have died of laughing, if I'd been there.'

'I wish everyone shared your view of the matter, Mr Murray,' Anne said wryly. 'Your mother, I'm afraid, is not pleased.'

'Why should she mind?' Hartley said easily. 'It was all above-board, for Kirov knew your pa years ago – didn't he, Miss Peters? – and he's old enough to be your father anyway. But he's a capital fellow, all the same! I'm glad it was him that danced with you, of everyone, for he is a trump card, and rides the most capital bay gelding you ever saw! Sauvechasse knows all about him, and says that no-one has ever beaten him at picquet, and he has the most famous hard head for liquor. That should suit you, Miss Peters! I shall never forget the way you downed the brandy that day!' He chuckled. 'It would be a famous thing for you to marry him – only that horse won't go,' he added with a sudden frown, 'for he is married already, now I come to remember. But then,' the frown clearing equally swiftly, 'his wife might die, you know – people do – and you wouldn't care about him being so much older than you, because females often marry men old enough to be their fathers, and no-one thinks anything of it, and I don't say he is as old as *that* exactly, probably not above five-and-thirty, and he rides like a Blood!'

Anne hardly knew whether despair and laughter were the more proper response to such a speech, and at the end of it, she did not manage to say more than, 'It is quite true that the Count knew my father – ' before he had interrupted her again.

'Yes, that's right,' he said happily. 'It would look very well for us if you made such a splendid match. Not that counts aren't two-a-penny in Russia, but he's one of the rich ones, so Sauvechasse says. Only there's this wife to get rid of. But I'm sure someone said she was sickly.' He frowned in unaccustomed thought. 'Yes, I'm sure that was it – he had to leave her somewhere because she wasn't well enough to travel. Well, that's a start, ain't it, Miss Peters?'

Though comforted by his friendliness, Anne felt obliged to disabuse him of his tremendous ideas. 'I am not going to marry anyone, Mr Murray, and I'm quite sure nothing could be further from the Count's mind. Not understanding our customs, he asked me to dance from respect for my father, that was all. I beg you will not run on in that way. Your father, I know, was far from regarding it as a compliment to your family.'

Hartley yawned hugely, and said, 'Oh, the guv'nor has better things to do than worry about balls, I can tell you. There was the devil of a fuss at the embassy last night, lights burning until all hours, and the upshot of it is, we shall all be off home any time now. I wish they would get on with it, and do away with this nonsensical peace. I mean to get Pa to buy me a commission as soon as ever the war starts, and then there'll be some fun at last! It'll be a famous lark, I warrant you! Sauvechasse was in the last one, and he says there's nothing like it, only he says one must get into one of the proper fighting regiments, not one of these fancy Dragoons outfits that do nothing but drill and visit their tailors three times a week.' He yawned again. 'I dare say Mama will kick up a fuss about it, and want me to join a fashionable cavalry regiment. Well, we shall see. Where was you off to, anyway, Miss Peters, when I bumped into you? No, let me guess – the mantuamakers!'

He grinned triumphantly at his own perspicacity, and Anne was glad enough to be able to agree truthfully.

'You guess right, Mr Murray.'

'Those sisters of mine will never rest until they have bought up Paris! If I don't bankrupt the guv'nor, they'll go far to doing it; and however they'll get all their clothes back to England without sinking the ship, I don't know. Well, I'm off home for a clean shirt, and then back to the club. Harrington and Markby and some of the others have some notion of joining the German mercenaries when the war starts. I must say the idea of being out from under the guv'nor's eye, and away from all the old pussy-cats and their wagging tongues, appeals mightily. Good day, Miss Peters. If the Count calls, I'll tell him to wait for you!'

He grinned happily at his own wit, attempted again to raise his missing hat, and ambled away round the corner. Anne watched him go with half a smile, and more fellow-feeling than she had ever thought to have for him, and then resumed her own way towards the first of the dressmaking establishments in the rue St Honoré.

Chapter Four

So preoccupied had Anne been with her own immediate problems, that Hartley's words about the imminence of war had hardly impinged on her. He was, in any case, one of the world's worst rattles, and not to be relied on for accuracy. So when she returned to number eight rue St Augustine at the end of the day, she was not prepared for the scene of confusion which greeted her.

She went in by the service door and ran cheerfully up the backstairs, well satisfied with the result of her endeavours. She had found herself a position with a mantuamaker, which, if it did not promise much immediately, was at least the first step on the ladder, and at the recommendation of her new employer had also secured herself a room in a lodging-house which was clean and conveniently placed. She had thus made herself independent of the Murrays, which alone was enough to put a spring in her step.

Half-way up the stairs, one of the French housemaids pushed past her brusquely with an armful of linen. Then, as she passed the end of the second-floor passage, the maid Salton shot out of the young ladies' room like a peeled grape, impelled by Miss Murray's voice crying shrilly, 'And don't come back until you've found it!'

Anne stopped in surprise. There were boxes standing in the passage, the chair outside the door was heaped with clothes, and from inside the room came the sound of the Miss Murrays chattering excitedly. Anne could not hear what they were saying, but she could tell from the tone of their voices that something tremendous had happened.

'Salton, what is it? Are you packing?' she asked.

The maid, who had been scurrying in the other direction, span round at the sound of her voice, and cried, 'Oh Miss, there you are! Thank heaven! Miss Murray's in such a taking, for I can't find her nightgown with the Marseilles frocking, and there's Miss Caroline's boxes to be done as well, and her taking everything out again as fast as I can put it in, and both of them argufying about whose is what, and I don't know how ever I am to get done if you don't come and help me. Couldn't you p'raps take them away somewhere and read to them, Miss? They'll have everything out again by the time I'm back, even if I can find the nightgown at all, which I'm sure it must have been stolen by that laundress, for I've looked everywhere else I can think of.'

'It's all right, Salton, I have it in my room,' Anne said quickly. 'I was altering it for Miss Murray, don't you remember? Come with me now, and I'll give it to you. But why are you packing? Has something happened?'

'Why, Miss, didn't you know?' Salton said, round-eyed, as she panted up the stairs behind her. 'We're all leaving. Master came home two hours since, and said as how everyone was going as soon as possible, and Mistress gave orders to pack right away. New instructions from home, it seems, Miss. Master was with Lord Whitworth and the Russian Ambassador all day – '

'The Russian Ambassador?' Anne exclaimed.

'Yes, Miss, because nobody knew which way the King of Russia was going to jump, with Malta and all that, and now Betson says Master says he's going to side with the French, so we must go home, Miss, that's what I heard.'

'Yes, Salton, well never mind it now,' Anne said, realising she could not hope for a clearer account of the political situation from a harassed serving-maid. 'Come and fetch the nightgown, and I'll see what I can do to help you.'

But she had no sooner handed over the nightdress, and a heap of silk stockings which had been given her to darn because Lady Murray said they never sat right after Simpkins had been at them, when a housemaid came in to say that Miss Peters was wanted in at once in Lady Murray's room. Anne paused only to take off her hat and pelisse, and went down to face whatever new odium was waiting for her.

Lady Murray's room also bore the signs of imminent departure, but there was no confusion here, for Simpkins was an expert packer, and Lady Murray would never have dreamed of interfering with her. Her ladyship was still on the day bed, and still in her wrapper, but she had her writing-case on her lap and appeared to be in the middle of writing a note. Anne had hardly ever before seen her with a pen in her hand, and it may have been the memory of Anne's services in that department which made her speak more civilly than probably she had intended.

'Ah, Miss Peters, there you are. I have been sending to your room for you half the day.'

'I went out, ma'am,' Anne said briefly. Lady Murray looked as though she meant to challenge this statement, but having regard to the angle of Anne's chin, changed her mind.

'Well, never mind that now. As you see, we are packing everything. Sir Ralph says we must be ready to leave at a moment's notice, though he does not know exactly when the orders will come. When you have packed your own box you had better help Salton with the Miss Murrays' boxes, for I dare say she is behind as usual. Sir Ralph says we shall have to travel post, which I detest above all things, so you will have to travel with Miss Caroline, for there will be no stopping if she is sick, and I cannot have her in the carriage with me.'

'I, ma'am?' Anne said, raising her eyebrows. 'What can you mean?'

Lady Murray frowned crossly. 'Don't pretend to be stupid, Miss Peters. You will travel with us only as far as London, of course, and I hope I can trust you to comport yourself properly during the journey. You will attend Miss Caroline, who I dare say will be dreadfully sick, but we must travel quickly when we go, though I don't think I quite understand why. Then Sir Ralph has said that he will pay you a month's salary in lieu of notice, which I consider very handsome; and – though I don't promise it, mind – if you behave yourself extremely well between now and then, I may bring myself to give you a reference after all, though I shall have to think how to frame it, for I cannot, of course, write any untruths. But I shall say *something*, at all events.'

Anne listened to all this with astonishment giving way slowly before rage. She saw how it was: it had struck Lady Murray forcibly how disagreeable it would be to travel with Caroline in a state of constant upheaval, and with no-one to attend her. Anne's eye flickered towards Simpkins, who avoided the contact and bent unnecessarily low over the box she was packing: Anne could imagine her being appealed to by her mistress and refusing, as flatly as only a dresser of her experience and annual salary could do, to have anything to do with the nursing of the unfortunate girl.

Well then, Anne could imagine Lady Murray thinking, there's nothing for it but to reinstate Miss Peters, just until we get to London, and then turn her off there. They simply wanted to make use of her, she thought; well, they should find she had other ideas.

'I beg your pardon, ma'am, but I shall do no such thing! My arrangements have all been made, and they do not involve travelling with any part of your family. You must get along without me as best you can,' she said.

Lady Murray's eyes seemed to bulge perilously, and Simpkins sucked in a breath at hearing her mistress spoken to in such a manner. 'How dare you speak to me like that?' her ladyship demanded, even more astonished than affronted. 'I have never heard of such impertinence! You will do exactly as you are told, Miss Peters, without answering me back! The insolence! Go and help Salton at once and let us hear no more of this – this – effrontery!'

'I have told you, ma'am, that I have made my arrangements,' Anne replied with a calm she judged rightly would infuriate far more than angry words. 'I shall not be leaving Paris. And I do not take orders from you. I am no longer in your employ. I am a free agent.'

Lady Murray uttered a sound between a gasp and a shriek. 'What? Free agent? How dare you! Nonsense!' she spluttered.

'I know what you are about, ma'am,' Anne said, enjoying her triumph, though there was a layer of sick fear underneath at her own daring. 'You only want me to take care of Caroline because no-one else will. *That* is what has caused this change of heart. You cannot impose on me any longer, Lady Murray.'

'Ungrateful, unnatural girl!' Lady Murray boomed. 'And this is how you repay our kindness, our consideration for you! Don't you know that there is going to be war at any moment? Sir Ralph, all magnanimity that he is, insisted that we could not leave you behind, a stranger in a foreign land, and asked me, *begged* me, to allow you to remain with us, for your own safety. And remain you shall! *I* shall decide when you leave my employ, and on what terms. Free agent, pah! I'll give you free agent!'

'It is pointless to continue this conversation, ma'am,' Anne said. 'I am over twenty-one, and will make my own decisions about my own life. You have no responsibility for me, nor authority over me. I shall go up and pack my belongings now, and go to my new lodgings. I shall send for my box tomorrow – I trust you will not object to its remaining here until the morning?'

Lady Murray had fallen back in her seat, more overcome, Anne guessed, by the mention of new lodgings than anything else that had been said. 'I'll have it thrown out into the street!' she cried vengefully.

'That must be as you choose, ma'am,' Anne said quietly, and turned and left, hearing as she closed the door behind her the words, 'Simpkins! My vinaigrette!' uttered in a despairing shriek.

As she climbed the stairs to her room, Anne found herself trembling. It was not easy all at once to cast off the habits and teachings of a lifetime, and to utter words of such defiance to an elder, and one to whom she had deferred for so long. She felt emptied out, scoured, and yet exhilarated, like a bird which has made the first terrifying plunge into unsupporting air, and found it could fly. Freedom, a new life lay before her. I shall never be afraid to speak my mind again, she thought.

The following morning Anne secured the services of a man with a small handcart, and walked with him from her new lodgings just off the rue Montmartre to the rue St Augustine to collect her box. It was a fine, warm May day, and everywhere the trees were bursting into leaf, and Anne was so deep in the thoughts of how good it was to be here, in Paris, that the man's voice quite startled her when he asked suddenly, 'What number, miss?'

'Number eight,' she said. 'Yes, this is it – oh!' And she stopped in surprise at what had evidently aroused the man's doubts: the knocker was off the door. The shades were drawn down over the windows, too, giving the building the unpleasantly eyeless look of the empty house.

'They've gone,' the man said helpfully. 'Skipped, I dare say. Did they owe you money, miss?'

'No – no, nothing like that,' Anne said. 'There's just my luggage to collect. I suppose their orders must have come after I left and – ' All sorts of speculations were running through her head which were not helpful at the moment. 'I suppose there must be a caretaker somewhere. They may have left my box with him.'

They went round to the service door, and ringing at the bell, soon roused out the elderly hall porter, who had evidently remained as caretaker. Anne was glad it was he, for he had always been friendly towards her, out of appreciation for her unvarying courtesy.

'Oh, there you are, then, mademoiselle. Yes, I've got your box safe here. I'll get it out in a moment, if this fellow will help me.'

'The family has gone, then?' Anne said, stepping into the back hall, and listening to the eerie silence. An occupied house, even if the inmates are not speaking or moving, is never quiet in the same way.

'Last night, mademoiselle. A messenger came round from the Embassy at dusk, carriages were ordered, and they left at eight o'clock. They mean to travel all through the night, so it seems, for this afternoon's packet from Calais. The old lady was very put out. You never heard such a fuss.'

Already, Anne noted, it was 'the old lady', a term of scant respect. 'I was afraid my box would have been thrown out,' she said.

The porter shook his head. 'I'd have made sure it was safe anyway, mademoiselle. But there was so much to-ing and fro-ing, that no-one even thought about it. Your name was mentioned a good bit, though. The young misses were asking for you, and the old lady didn't seem to know whether to curse you or pray for you,' he grinned.

'I can imagine,' Anne said. 'Well, I didn't expect it to be so sudden, but I suppose it doesn't make any difference to me.'

'Will it be war, then, mademoiselle?' the porter said cautiously. 'Is that why they have gone?'

'I don't know,' Anne said. 'I hope not. That would be very uncomfortable.'

'Dangerous, too,' the porter said, looking at her significantly. 'You ought to be careful, on your own as you are.'

'Oh, I shall be all right,' she smiled. 'I am of no interest to anyone. Thank you for looking after my box, anyway.' She reached into her reticule for a coin, which the man took with graceful dexterity and made disappear.

'It was nothing, mademoiselle. I wish you good luck. They should have taken you with them, but you are well away from them in my opinion. I used to serve the Quality – they were one thing. But these – !' He shrugged eloquently. 'You be careful, mademoiselle. There are some funny people about in Paris these days.'

When her box was safely back at her lodgings, and the man with the barrow paid off, Anne felt restless and a little lost. It was one thing to quit the Murrays in a blaze of independence, quite another to find they had quitted her. It came over her how very much alone she was. The last link with England was severed, the last place she had even the slightest right to ask for shelter closed off from her. She felt a little as she had felt when her father died, and she had realised that she must make her way alone through the world.

But after all, she told herself bracingly, that was nothing new. She had had to come to terms with that responsibility years ago, and she was far better able to take care of herself now. There was no point in spending the day sitting here staring at the walls, at any rate. She was not required to start work until tomorrow, so she might as well enjoy her last day of leisure to walk about the city, for she had no illusions about the sort of hours she would have to work from now on. She put on her hat and pelisse, and went out into the sunshine.

It was no difficult decision to choose her usual walk to the Ile de la Cité. Apart from the consolation of the river, there was the market, which had always offered amusement, even in the darkest days of winter. She could imagine how glorious it must appear in the summer, when the great variety of flowers and fruits would spread a carpet of living colour in every direction. Now in May, the first of the spring vegetables were coming in, greens and spinach and infant peas, to supplement the winter store roots, and the polished heaps of pomegranates and oranges from across the mountains in the south, great green and purple cabbages, with leaves deckled at the edge like ladies' skirts, and gleaming bronze onions half as big as melons.

She hurried past the aisles devoted to livestock. Quite apart from the sad-eyed swans, enduring their captivity so patiently, there were monkeys, some with their fur dyed red or green, clutching each other and shivering either with cold or fear; marmosets, parrots, and puppies destined for the drawing-rooms of fine ladies; and white kids with the voices of children, destined for the table.

She had become a familiar sight to some of the tradespeople, who would often call out to her in a friendly way. Sometimes she would stop and talk to them, and they would admire the fluency of her French and the purity of her accent, and ask her what England was really like — whether it was true that everyone lived in a castle, but that the sun never shone, even in high summer. Today, however, no-one greeted her, and as she paused to admire some great sheaves of vivid, scented mimosa, she had the impression that one or two people turned away rather than meet her eye.

Dismissing the idea as nonsensical, she continued across the island to the walk beside the cathedral. She was standing at the parapet gazing at the river when a hand suddenly gripped her upper arm, and at the same instant, she heard a familiar voice saying, 'For God's sake, what are you doing here?'

'Oh, sir, you startled me,' she gasped, looking up into the Count's frowning face.

'Not nearly as much as you have startled me!' he said grimly. 'Why are you still in Paris? Why did you not go with the Murrays? Don't you know you are in danger here?'

'Now, really, Count,' she said with a smile, 'you exaggerate. I am quite capable of looking after myself. And please, would you let go of my arm? You are hurting me.'

He released her automatically, as if he did not know he had done it, saying, 'But something has been going on here. Lady Murray told me yesterday when I called that you were to go with them. She said so specifically, for though I had not asked her directly, I dare say she knew what I wanted to know.'

'You called on Lady Murray?' Anne said in surprise. 'But she didn't mention it to me.'

'I had learned, you see,' he said, drawing her hand through his arm and walking with her in a purposeful way along the gravelled path, 'that by dancing with you I had caused a certain amount of – shall we say, embarrassment?'

'Not quite the word that I would have used, sir,' Anne said wryly.

'It was the furthest thing from my intentions, as I'm sure you must know,' he said apologetically. 'So I paid Lady Murray a formal visit to try to smooth things down, and to make sure your safety was not placed in jeopardy, for it did occur to me just for a moment that she might be vindictive enough to leave you behind last night. It seems I was right.'

'You knew they were leaving? But even Lady Murray did not know when the order would come,' Anne said in surprise.

He made a curious grimace. 'Miss Peters, there is no harm in your knowing now that your country and mine have been involved in some very delicate negotiations with the Consulate over the past week or so, in the hope of avoiding the war. Yesterday it became plain that no agreement was going to be reached, and as we had intercepted a secret message to your Lord Whitworth, ordering him to quit during the night – '

'Intercepted? You mean – you have spies!' she breathed, her eyes wide.

'A disagreeable word, mademoiselle, for a disagreeable necessity. But how does it come about that you did not leave with the Murrays? You must have done something to annoy them, more than simply dancing with me.'

Anne decided this was not the moment to tell the whole story. 'They did want me to go with them, but I refused the offer, and quitted their service. I prefer to stay here.'

He frowned. 'But are you mad, Miss Peters? Don't you know that war will be declared between England and France as soon as the Ambassador is out of the country?'

Anne shrugged. 'I didn't know that Lord Whitworth had left, of course. But in any case – '

'And don't you know that as soon as war is declared, the First Consul will arrest every English person on French soil?'

Anne stared. 'Arrest?'

'Yes, mademoiselle, arrest and imprison for the duration of the war, and who knows how long that will be? Five years, ten – the last war between your countries went on for a decade, did it not? Can you imagine what ten years in a French prison would do to you? Even if you survived it, your health would be impaired for ever.'

Anne thought of the market traders avoiding her eyes, and felt a shiver of fear tighten the back of her neck. 'I didn't know – I didn't understand. I thought I would just live here quietly . . . I found myself a position with a mantuamaker, you see,' she said ridiculously.

'*Borzhe moy!*' the Count exclaimed, turning his eyes up to heaven. He hurried her along so that she had to put in a little hop every few steps to keep up with his long-legged stride. 'Just live here quietly, she says! Thank heaven it is not too late!'

'Where are you taking me?' Anne asked, a little breathlessly, as they crossed the Pont Neuf onto the Quai du Louvre.

'To my house, where you will be safe. After that, we must think what to do with you. It will be best if we speak French from now on, mademoiselle. The order has not yet been issued, but we had better not draw attention to ourselves.'

'Perhaps, then, sir, we should not walk so fast,' Anne ventured, and his frown relaxed into a smile.

'Quite right. You think, as always, very much to the point.'

He set a more moderate pace, and Anne was able to regain her breath and try to stop her head from spinning. War imminent! Herself in danger of arrest! Why had not Lady Murray made those things clear to her? But then, Anne had hardly given her a chance, had very firmly told her to mind her own business, not an experience Lady Murray could have been expected to enjoy. And in any case, Anne thought with a flash of self-knowledge, she would not so readily have believed her former mistress as she did the Count: she would have believed Lady Murray was trying to frighten her for her own purposes.

Anne sighed at the realisation that it was her pride and self-will that had heaped these difficulties on her, and the Count, who had evidently been pursuing a train of thought of his own, said, 'I have been very much to blame in this matter. I have behaved recklessly and selfishly, and brought great trouble to you.'

'No, no, sir, you must not blame yourself. It was by my own decision that I left the Murrays.'

'But if I had not asked you to dance, the situation would never have arisen. There was no other cause of dissent between you and your employers, was there? The breach was caused by my indiscretion.'

'That was the *immediate* cause, sir,' Anne admitted, 'but – '

'No, no, it was all my fault. My wretched high spirits!' he groaned. 'When I was a cadet, I was forever playing practical jokes and finding myself in trouble. My son is the same way – he takes too strongly after me, I'm afraid. And even now, when I am supposed to be a staid and respectable diplomat, I cannot see a lion without wishing to tweak its tail.'

'Then you mean that you danced with me only to annoy the Murrays?' Anne asked.

'What? No, no!' He shook his head in self-reproach. 'That was clumsy of me. I danced with you because I wanted to, and if it is any compliment to be asked by me, then that compliment is all your own.' He smiled down at her. 'I can give reasons in plenty for my bad behaviour. I have been a long time away from home, and away from my wife, whom I love dearly, and I have missed the solace of female companionship. And I so much enjoyed our conversations, brief though they were! You cannot imagine how many stupid people I have to talk to in the course of my work, and how much I long for wit and intelligence.'

'I can imagine that very easily,' Anne said. 'Do you not think I have suffered in the same way?'

'Of course you have! You have a vigorous and original mind, Miss Peters, and contact with it has been a privilege. But you must not distract me from my confession – I was telling you all my selfishness! I enjoyed talking to you, and I wanted very much to dance with you, but I knew – yes certainly, I knew! – that I should not. I allowed myself to be carried away by the moment, but I did not anticipate that it would have such serious consequences for you. If I had, I should certainly have behaved otherwise. I hope you believe that.'

'Of course,' she said, and they walked on in silence for a while. They crossed the place du Théâtre and walked up the rue Richelieu.

'Here is my house, mademoiselle,' the Count said, halting in front of an old, narrow house with new white stone facings. 'Here you will be quite safe. I share it with another member of the Embassy, Poliakov, and his wife and servants, so you need not be afraid to enter,' he added delicately. 'They will be as eager to help you as I am.'

'Thank you, sir,' Anne said, and allowed him to usher her in. An elderly manservant met them, and the Count, having introduced Anne in French, embarked in Russian on what she assumed must be an explanation of her plight. The manservant asked a question, and the Count turned to Anne.

'May I ask where are your belongings?' Anne gave the address of her lodgings. 'Boris will send a man for them, to bring them here. It will be better, I think, if you do not go back for them. Inside this house, no-one can harm you, but if you venture onto the street, I shall have less power to protect you. And now, I am sure you would like some refreshment.'

58

He led Anne into a parlour off the hall, and in a few moments the manservant brought cake and wine for them both.

'Well, now,' the Count said, standing by the fireplace and looking down at her, where she sat on the sofa, 'having brought you so much trouble, I must somehow put things right.' He pulled his chin. 'It should not be too difficult, if we move immediately, to get you back to England, though it might be better to travel by – '

'But I don't want to go back to England,' Anne protested.

'Not want to go home?' he asked in surprise. 'Surely you cannot be serious?'

'That was the greatest part of my reason for not going with the Murrays,' she said. 'It's true that I left them in anger, which affected my decision, but I had also come to realise that I love Paris, and I wanted to stay here. It was a positive choice.'

He looked worried. 'Well, you cannot stay in Paris now.'

'Yes, I understand that,' she said wretchedly. 'But what is there for me in England? I have no family, no home, no friends. All I can do is to try to find myself some work to keep me in food and lodging. The Murrays, I fear, will see to it that I cannot get another place as a governess; at least, not with the sort of family I would prefer. I should probably end up as a seamstress or a serving-woman, and if I must be disgraced, I had sooner be disgraced in a foreign country, where I am not known, than in England.'

'This is too black a picture, surely,' he said tentatively. 'There must be something else you could do.'

She looked up at him with a sort of grim humour. 'There is, but I would not contemplate it.'

He looked embarrassed, and walked across the room and back, twisting his hands behind him, and then paused in front of her gravely. 'I have done you a greater wrong than I feared,' he said. 'I have ruined you, and made it impossible for you to go home. I cannot tell you how much I regret that foolish impulse of mine. If I could only have the time over again, and put things right – '

'Please don't!' she said quickly. 'I am not sorry. If I had the choice, I would dance with you again. It *was* my choice, you know – I could have stopped you, if I had tried hard enough. And,' she added with a small smile, 'I never really liked working for the Murrays.'

His eyes creased up in a smile and he held out his hand to her, and when she offered hers, he took it in both his and pressed it warmly. 'You have all the famous courage of your race, mademoiselle! Well, I promise you you shall not suffer. Tell me, do you like to travel?'

She laughed. 'I cannot say, sir. The only place I have ever been outside my own country is here.'

'Would you like to see Russia?'

She stared at him, stunned. 'Russia?' she managed to say at last. 'Can you mean it?'

'Nothing could be simpler! My tour here is over, and I am to go home in the next day or two. I shall persuade Markov to give you a passport, and you shall come with me. You can travel as my niece. With a Russian passport, you will have no difficulty at the frontiers.'

'The frontiers,' she said, as through it were a magic word. She visualised their route northwards across Europe, through France and the German states, and Poland, and then to Russia! Mighty, mysterious, the most foreign of foreign lands – 'But, sir, what should I do in Russia? How shall I live?'

'Oh, I have thought of that,' he said, smiling broadly. 'Listen!' And he sat down on the sofa beside her, looking, in his eagerness, more her age than his. 'I have two daughters, one nine years old, and one just two. Now Yelena, the elder girl, has a German governess, dear old Fräulein Hoffnung, who taught my sisters when they were young, an excellent woman, though not widely educated as you are, Miss Peters. And Yelena is high-spirited and growing difficult to manage, too much for poor Fräulein Hoffnung, who ought by rights to be sitting by the fire and knitting, at her age. The little one, Natasha, was still with her nurses when I last saw her, but soon she will need the guidance and instruction of a proper governess.'

He jumped up again, and walked back to the fireplace, as if his thoughts were running so rapidly that only physical movement could relieve them. 'Since I first met you, Miss Peters, I have greatly admired your intelligence, your education, your spirit and your character, and in fact it did once cross my mind that I should be very happy to be able to get someone to teach Yelena who had even half your abilities! Of course, the situation was very different then. I should not have thought of asking you to leave your safe employment and travel half across the world to a foreign country, but as matters stand now . . . Would you consider it? Would you come with me to Russia, and be governess to my daughters?'

Anne could not answer. The idea was too sudden and too dazzling. There was too much to think about. The Count watched her face sympathetically, and then said, 'Of course, you cannot decide on an instant. It is a big step to take, and you will need time to consider. There will be questions you want to ask.'

'It would be a great adventure,' Anne said. It was the first thing that came to her tongue, and as she said it, she thought it sounded foolish, but the Count smiled approvingly.

'I believe you have a taste for adventure. I see in you a woman of spirit – am I right? To go back to England would be tame. There is a wide world waiting to be explored.'

'I hardly know, sir,' Anne said hesitantly. 'I think I may have something of my father's nature. He joined the King's service out of restlessness, I believe. I was brought up by him alone, and we were very close, and so I did a great many things that girls are not usually allowed to do. Adventure does not usually fall to the lot of females, but – '

'Yes, you are like him. That is why you wanted to stay in Paris, rather than go back to England. Well, since you must now leave Paris, you must go forward, not back.'

She met his eyes, and hers had begun to shine with excitement. 'You are right. It would be poor-spirited to be afraid. But shall I like it in Russia?'

'Who can say?' he shrugged. 'But there is one thing you may be sure of – you will be treated as you should be, and not as the Murrays treated you. I have already told you on another occasion that we have the greatest respect for those to whom we entrust our children's upbringing. You would not be regarded as a servant in Russia, Miss Peters, by anyone.' He watched her face, waiting for her next question.

'I don't know any Russian. How should your children and I understand each other?'

He laughed. 'In Russia we all speak many languages. Russian is the language of servants, and of the nursery, and for animals, and for the act of love. Adults speak mostly French to each other, although many older people prefer German, because it was the language of the Court while Tsarina Catherine ruled us – she being German by birth. For business we speak English, because all our merchants and bankers are English, and we read English novels, too. And we sing in Italian, of course. My children speak French and German fluently, Russian colloquially, and English sufficiently well – though I should like them to speak it better. So, you see, mademoiselle, I do not think you will have very much difficulty in making yourself understood.'

'You mentioned a son earlier – ?' Anne said.

'Sergei, yes. He is fourteen now, and away at school. I do not see as much of him as I would like. His grandmother likes to have him with

61

her. He, of course, would not be in your charge. He and Lolya – '

'Lolya?'

'Yelena. We Russians are very fond of pet names,' he smiled. 'He and Lolya are the children of my first wife, who died many years ago. Natasha is my present wife's first child.'

Anne was silent again, thinking of the enormity of the step before her. If she went to Russia, probably she would never see England again. If she went, she would be dependent on the Count and his wife for their favour, for if they dismissed her, she would be really destitute, alone in a country incomparably more alien than France. If she were unhappy there, what chance would she have of remedying matters?

Yet what was the alternative? As the Count had said, she must go forward, not back; and what other opportunity would she ever be offered to travel so far and see so many new things? Her father's spirit rose up in her strongly, and only her native English caution made her say, 'Will she like me, your wife? Will the children like me? Do you really want me to teach them?'

He smiled broadly, as if he knew everything that had gone through her mind. 'Yes, yes, and yes. I was never more sure of anything, dear Miss Peters, than that this is the right thing for all of us. Will you come?'

She took a breath. 'Yes, sir, I will come,' she said.

'Then we'll drink a toast to it,' he said triumphantly, filling her glass with such an impetuous hand that it lipped over and wet her fingers. 'We'll do it in Russian, for luck. *Za vasha zdarovia*! Your first lesson in Russian, Miss Peters! To your health!'

'*Za vasha zdarovia*!' she said, and drank.

Later that day Anne met the Poliakovs, a pleasant couple perhaps ten years older than the Count. Poliakov himself was a short-necked, round, bald man, whose unremarkable face was betrayed by a pair of very sharp and humorous eyes. Madame Poliakov had a comfortable face and figure, wispy grey hair, and large, moist eyes, which grew ever more moist as she listened to the Count's exposition of Anne's plight, sympathising all through it in voluble German. The words 'tragic' and 'orphan' were uttered frequently with a wringing of hands, and when the story was told, she at once began offering various items of her wardrobe for Anne's use, despite the fact that any one of her gowns would have fitted Anne twice over.

'My dear Marya,' the Count protested in amusement, 'she is not destitute! She has a whole box of clothes of her own! And it will be high summer when we get back to Russia. There is nothing extra she will need until winter.'

But Madame could not be persuaded, and referred to Anne all evening in melting accents as '*Das armes kleines madchen*', and continued to press gowns, shoes, pelisses, fichus and hairbrushes on her. The two gentlemen went off together to see the Ambassador about a passport, while Anne remained with Madame Poliakov, and when she managed at last to detach the kind lady's mind from visions of destitution, discovered that she had some interesting stories to tell about the court of the great Catherine, where she had been a lady in waiting in her youth.

When the Count returned, he came into the room with a broad smile, and said, 'Everything is settled. We leave tomorrow morning. The horses are ordered and the carriage will be here at eight. I have your passport, Miss Peters, made out in your new name. You are now officially my sister's daughter, Anna. My older sister married a man called Davidov, whose first name was Peter, so with the addition of the patronymic, that makes your new name Anna Petrovna Davidova.'

Anne frowned in thought. 'My surname, Peters, is a contraction of Peterson, you know. If you translated Anne Peters into Russian, presumably you would get – '

'Anna Petrovna, yes,' the count concluded with a satisfied grin. 'A pleasant little coincidence, is it not? I knew you would see it!'

Chapter Five

In years afterwards, when Anne tried to remember that long journey through northern Europe to Russia, she found that the miles and days merged together in her mind, so that she could recall only broad impressions, and not a clear and accurate succession of detail. She began the journey eager to observe and remember everything, and for several hours at the beginning of each of the first few days, she sat well forward on the seat and craned out of the window, eyes wide and mind stretched for new impressions, aware that she might never have another opportunity like this.

But there was just too much of everything for her early enthusiasm to last. In England, even a single day's fast travelling would take one through many different sorts of landscape, with something new to see every mile. But on the continent, everything was so much larger, that the same sort of scenery would go on mile after mile for hours, perhaps even for a whole day. And then the sheer weariness of travelling overcame her. The roads at this time of year, though dusty, were not poached or deeply rutted, and near large towns were often very good. But in the long spaces in between towns they travelled over roads that it was no-one's business to repair, and as they jolted and lurched along, every muscle was kept at the stretch all day to brace the body against the movement.

The Count, for his own reasons as well as for Anne's safety, wanted to travel as fast as possible, so they stayed nowhere for more than a single night, and during the day they stopped only to change horses. They would enter the coach at eight in the morning, and travel until five or six in the evening, when they would descend stiffly at the chosen post-house to bathe, dine, and retire to bed. The unvarying routine soon produced in Anne a feeling of unreality, as though she were trapped in a repeating dream. Day after day they jolted along through flat fields and acres of young crops, through endless stretches of dark coniferous forest, through winding river-valleys where mild-eyed cattle grazed; past rolling green hills or distant mountains, past reedy marshes loud with birds, bare bog-heath, and silent, glassy lakes. The days blurred into one another in her memory, until she felt that this was all she had ever done, and the names of the towns they passed through merged in her mind with every name learned in her geography lessons, so that she no longer knew with any certainty where they had been.

The early part of the journey produced one memorable incident. Having travelled through France, they crossed the Rhine by the bridge at Strasbourg and drove along beside the river to Karlsruhe, the capital of Baden. Here Count Kirov stopped and made a formal visit to the court to pay his respects to the Princess Amelie, who, he explained to Anne, was the mother of the present Empress Elisabeth of Russia.

The Princess received Anne with great kindness, and the Count most eagerly, taking him aside for a rapid conversation in German about the state of international affairs. She had with her a handsome, beak-nosed, auburn-haired man of about the Count's age, who greeted Kirov with a broad smile and an embrace as an old friend. This was Louis-Antoine de Condé-Bourbon, known as the Duc d'Enghien. He was the sole surviving grandson of the Prince de Condé, exiled from France and formerly known as an intriguer on behalf of the Bourbon family against the various Revolutionary governments of France. He now lived a life of bachelor retirement in the nearby palace of Ettenheim, and was a frequent visitor to the court at Karlsruhe.

He and Kirov had met in Italy some years earlier, when the Duc was serving with the army under the Russian general Suvorov, and Kirov was commanding a cavalry troop. As well as being very handsome, the Duc was also high-spirited and charming, and Anne was not surprised to see he was a great favourite with the Princess, who often pinched his cheek or tapped his hand affectionately with her fan while laughing at the evidently entertaining things he was saying.

When Kirov had passed on the news, the Princess pressed him to have dinner with her and the Duc, and to remain at the palace for a few days, courteously including Anne in the invitation. The idea of dining with royalty and staying in a palace was both dazzling and terrifying. Anne immediately began a mental review of her wardrobe, and did not know whether to be pleased or disappointed when the Count made his apologies, and said that he was anxious to press on with the journey. The Duc expressed himself forcibly on this refusal, but the Princess did not press the Count further, saying she knew what it was to be far away from those one loved. She entrusted him with letters for her daughter at St Petersburg, and bid him a kind farewell.

After Karlsruhe they travelled on through Wurzburg, Bayreuth, and Freiberg to Dresden, which they reached ten days after leaving Paris. It was here that they heard the news that England had declared war on France by seizing two French merchant ships on the 18th of May, and had already sent a squadron to blockade Brest. Bonaparte had retaliated by ordering every European port closed to English shipping, and by arresting all English travellers in France – some said as many as ten thousand had been taken up. Part of Anne had never really believed that the Consul would do such a thing, and the reality of it brought home to her forcibly how much she owed the Count. If he had not intervened . . .

'So it all begins again,' the Count said to Anne that evening at the supper table in the posting inn, which stood at the end of the splendid, many-arched bridge which spanned the Elbe. 'The privations and the killing and the suspicion – all the waste and madness of war.'

The innkeeper came in bringing a dish of veal cutlets accompanied by pickled red cabbage, strong-smelling sausage, and the inevitable round of stringy cold beef. He was very voluble on the subject of the war. The talk, he said, was that the First Consul had sworn he would conquer England and utterly destroy the faithless, treacherous islanders. Anne had been very quiet since he had gone out again. 'You must not mind too much what that man says,' the Count went on, eyeing her sympathetically. 'It is a thing that is bound to be said.'

Anne looked up. 'Yes, I know. Probably he exaggerates. And even if Bonaparte does have plans of that sort, he will never succeed while our navy patrols the Channel.'

'You have a very proper faith in your father's service,' the Count said.

She smiled faintly. 'The last war proved the English navy invincible. I am not afraid of any threat of invasion.' But the talk of war had reminded her how far from home she was, and how unlikely it was that she would ever see England again. She had chosen travel and adventure freely and gladly, but she could not repress a pang of sadness at the thought of the small green island that had bred her, of its soft skies and gentle hills and its courteous, independent people – her own people. The Count noted the brightness of her eyes, and took immediate remedial action.

'You will have a glass of wine, Miss Peters – unwatered, I think,' he said bracingly. 'And then early to bed. We begin the harder part of our journey tomorrow.'

Anne obeyed him, grateful for his concern, and hugged that thought to her for comfort as she drifted off to sleep. As so often, she dreamed of travelling, jolting and twitching the miles away in her sleep.

After Dresden, her sense of unreality increased, and she lost all sense of time and distance. The roads grew steadily worse and the towns further apart; the accommodation more primitive, and the food more variable. At one inn she was shown to a room where the bed was jumping with fleas, and at another there were no sheets on the bed, only damp, musty-smelling blankets. But another, though simply furnished, was spotlessly clean, and the hostess, in starched cap and embroidered apron, brought them a delectable venison stew, fragrant with herbs, and a meltingly-delicious cheesecake, freshly baked.

Their rate of travel decreased, and it took a week to reach Warsaw. Shortly after leaving Warsaw, the carriage went off the road into a rut almost deep enough to be called a ditch, and the resultant damage to wheels and axle caused their first serious delay, as they were obliged to stay for two days while repairs were carried out. They were too far from Warsaw to be able to use the time to explore the ancient city, and there was nothing whatever to see or do in the town where they were stranded. Anne took the opportunity to have some washing done while the Count read and slept. Then they took to the road again, passing through towns with increasingly unpronounceable names, some hardly bigger than villages, and through many areas of obvious poverty, where the fields seemed poor and stony, the cattle thin, and the peasant houses mean and dirty.

Four days later, they reached Grodno on the river Nieman, and when they had crossed the wooden bridge to the other side, the Count turned to Anne with a triumphant smile and said, 'Now we are in Russia. Now we are home!'

'And how long will it be before we reach your house?' Anne asked, gazing around her in a rather dazed way, as if she expected to see the roof and chimneys appear on the horizon.

'Another week, perhaps.'

Anne stared. 'A week?'

'A week or ten days,' he said airily, enjoying the effect he was having. Then he grinned. 'Russia is a large country, Miss Peters. We have five hundred miles still to go, to reach Petersburg.'

Anne tried and failed to comprehend the distances involved. 'In England it is impossible to be five hundred miles from home,' she said with a rueful smile. 'It takes a little adjustment of the imagination.'

Once again she looked out of the carriage windows with eager attention; and, whether or not it was her imagination, she seemed immediately to gain an impression of enormous space. The sky was an immense arc, deeply azure, with large clouds dazzlingly white above, bluish on their undersides; the horizon seemed to grow more distant with every mile; and the land stretched away all around as though it were actually uncurling as they moved towards it, like a cat waking from sleep. This part of Russia, she found, was mostly flat, with only gentle undulations, broken here and there by wooded ravines and numerous small streams. There were vast stretches of birch wood and pine forest, and between them lay the cultivated land, the spring seeds ripening fast under the hot summer sun. The roads were unmade, simply tracks of bare earth, and since the cultivated land was unfenced, they were very wide, where, in bad weather, travellers had moved further and further to the side to avoid the churning bog of the centre. The roads were dry and dusty now, but their width added to the impression of great space that was gradually filling Anne's mind.

Space, and emptiness: they saw few other travellers, and mile after mile, few other people of any sort. They might have been alone in the world. It was a strange sensation, rather unnerving at first, but exhilarating too, a heady sense of being unfettered and unobserved, of being free.

'You must have felt so cramped in England,' she said abruptly at one time, turning shining eyes on the Count. 'Such small fields and narrow roads, and so many people!'

And he smiled sympathetically. 'Yes, it's true. I love to visit Europe – there is so much there, such riches! But I miss the *prostor* of Russia – the space. After a while, I feel as though I can't stretch my limbs, as though I were in a cage; and then I know it's time to go home.'

One evening they sat down to supper in the post-house in a town called Mzhinsk. They had been travelling for almost five weeks: French armies had already overrun Italy, captured Hanover, occupied the towns of Hamburg and Bremen, and closed off the Elbe and Weser trade routes, and Bonaparte was reputed to be building a thousand transport ships for the intended invasion of England. But for some time now, Anne had been able to think of nothing in the world so urgently as of getting out of the carriage and never getting back in it again.

They had finished eating when the Count said, 'I have sent off a letter to Schwartzenturm, to warn them that we are coming, and telling them all about you. We will reach there tomorrow.'

Schwartzenturm was the name of the Count's summer house near Kirishi, about twenty-five miles from Petersburg, where, as he had already told Anne, his family had been living while they waited for him to return.

'Tomorrow!' Anne said, and suddenly the thought that this journey was almost over was not as attractive as she had expected it to be.

68

'Yes – one more day's travel will bring us home. We may be rather late, but I intend to sleep in my own bed tomorrow night, whatever happens!' He had been smiling, but now looked at her rather quizzically. 'Is something the matter? You look troubled.'

'No – nothing. I am very excited at the thought of seeing your house and meeting your family.'

'They will make you welcome,' he hazarded. 'You cannot doubt it?'

'Of course not,' she said, managing a rather watery smile. 'I am rather tired,' she added, pushing back her chair, 'and if we have a long day of travel tomorrow, I think perhaps I had better retire early.'

'Of course,' said the Count, rising courteously. 'Good night, mademoiselle.'

'Good night, sir,' Anne said. She paused as she passed him, and looked up into eyes so full of sympathy, that she felt tears rising in hers, and was annoyed at her own weakness. The Count took her hands.

'Don't be afraid. Everyone will love you very much, Anna Petrovna,' he said. 'You must think of us as your family, now.'

Anne thanked him, withdrew her hands, and took flight before she was quite undone. Alone in her bedchamber, she tried to come to terms with the feelings that had been aroused by the news that the journey was almost over, and that her new life was to begin tomorrow. For nearly five weeks, she and the Count had been shut up in a small space together day after day, forced into close proximity, and with nothing to do but either talk to each other, or sit in silent thought. Like a plant in a greenhouse, intimacy was brought on rapidly and flourished in such conditions, and it was inevitable that Anne would emerge from the experience either loving the Count or loathing him, but at all events knowing him very well.

Their early approval of each other had proved to have been based on sound judgement. They both had a similar turn of mind, eager and enquiring, and a ready sense of humour, and were interested in broadly the same things; and while Anne had been well and thoroughly educated, the Count had a great deal more experience of life and the world. He enjoyed telling his adventures to one so quickly appreciative, and she delighted in extending her own experience by all she learnt from him. She had listened with interest as he told her about his childhood and his early loss of his father, his time in cadet school, his army service, his first wife, whose marriage to him was arranged by his widowed mother, and his children; and even more eagerly when he talked of his experiences abroad. He had travelled extensively, both as a part of his Grand Tour, which had taken him to England as well as to France and Italy, and in the course of his services to the Tsar, both military and diplomatic – and, an intelligent and observant man, he had made the most of his opportunities. His expositions often provoked lively discussion between them, and Anne had enjoyed talking to him and being with him more than anyone since her father died.

But now, with the knowledge that tomorrow would bring them to his home, and him to the arms of his wife, Anne was forced to realise that the strong liking she had formed for him was different in a fundamental way from her love for her father. The Count was a vibrantly attractive man, and there had been times in the carriage when she had been intensely aware of his physical closeness. Once, towards the end of a long day, she had woken to the realisation that they had both dozed off, and that their heads were together, hers on his shoulder, his cheek resting against her hair. She remembered now, guiltily and with trepidation, how happy she had felt, and how she had continued to feign sleep so that, even when he woke and lifted his head, she had been able to remain resting against him.

She shook her head in a dazed way at the memory. Tomorrow she would meet the Count's wife, her new mistress. He had told her a little about his second marriage. It had been a love-match: he had met Irina Pavlovna Kiriakova while he was on campaign, fighting the Turks in the wildlands of the Caucasian Mountains, the homeland of her family. They had fallen in love with each other almost at first sight, and he had brought her triumphantly back a bride at the end of the campaign. The Count spoke of his wife with great affection, talking freely of his longing to see her again, but he never offered any description of her. Anne could gain no impression of the Countess, except the inference that if the Count loved her, she must be a very remarkable and delightful woman.

But Anne did not long to meet her. Suddenly, at this late stage, she did not want the journey to end, did not want the Count's attention taken from her and given over to all the other demands of life, and particularly to his wife. She stared out of the window at the black, moonless night, and gripped her hands together, and berated herself bitterly. Is there no end to your folly? Can you have allowed yourself to fall in love with this man, who can never be more to you than employer?

He *is* more, whispered her rebellious, inner self.

He has been kind to you, she replied fiercely. He likes you, yes, but only as he would like any intelligent, educated person. You like him for the same reason. Anything more that you feel is only gratitude for his having rescued you from Paris, and for having appreciated you where the Murrays did not.

Protest, from the inner self.

It *must* be so, she told herself firmly. You cannot live in this man's house and teach his children, and harbour any secret feelings towards him. To do so would be not only wicked, but unspeakably foolish. Admire him, respect him, serve him: there is nothing else. His feelings are all for his wife. Have enough self-respect not to offer, even inwardly and secretly, what is not wanted, would never be wanted.

Suddenly her father's face came clearly before her, looking at her with that expression of affection and pride that she remembered so longingly. I won't let you down, Papa, she thought determinedly. The Count was Papa's friend, and so she would think of him, always, always: her kind employer, and Papa's genial friend. The inner voice retired, vanquished, and Anne prepared herself for bed calmly, almost serenely. You can do anything you want, Anne, if you set your mind to it, her father had said once, and she believed it. She believed firmly in the power of the intellect, even over the atavistic forces of nature.

'Now we are on my land,' the Count said, leaning forward to look out of the window, though since there was no moon, it was almost quite dark, and only the eyes of love could have discerned anything beyond the shapes of the nearest trees. 'We should see the lights of the house soon. If it were daylight, you would get a fine view of it from this road. You must see it tomorrow, Miss Peters. It is quite remarkable – one of a kind,' he added, laughing as if at some private joke.

'Does it have a black tower?' Anne asked, thinking of the name.

'Oh yes. I shall show you everything tomorrow. A complete tour, just as if you were in England and visiting a great house, like Blenheim Palace. Yes, I did those things when I was there on my Grand Tour. I was the compleat traveller, I promise you! Ah, there are the lights at last!'

A few minutes later they turned off the road onto another track, and leaning forward, Anne could see the flaring lights of torches, and the shapes of people moving about near them. She sat back, and in the darkness of the carriage, put a nervous hand to her hair. She had dressed carefully that morning in her blue travelling-dress and her smartest hat, though the sensible part of her mind knew that in the excitement of such a homecoming, no-one was likely to notice what she was wearing. Now there were men running along beside the carriage and voices shouting, and as they lurched to a halt, both doors were opened simultaneously and a babble of voices and laughter surged in. A round-faced man grinned up at Anne, letting down the step on her side of the carriage and holding out a hand like a plank of wood to help her down.

All was confusion for the next few minutes, a jumble of the ragged, yellow light of torches and slashes of shadow, the smell of pitch smoke and horses and sweat, laughter and Russian greetings, and people pressing forward to greet and exclaim. Then there was the Count, his long, cool fingers finding her hand, and drawing it firmly under his arm to guide her through the throng, into a dark doorway, up some chill and echoing stone steps, and into a large, brilliantly-lit hall. Anne glanced around, gained the impression of rococo plasterwork and *trompe l'oeil* Corinthian pillars, crystal chandeliers and enormous dark oil paintings in gilded frames, just like the hall of an English Great House. A large man in livery – the butler, surely? – was wringing the Count's hand and actually weeping with pleasure, while various other domestics and a number of handsome, black and white dogs stood around and grinned their delight. Anne's name was mentioned, and the butler bowed low and said something to her by way of welcome, and she smiled at him in a rather dazed way, and the Count began drawing her towards the door at the far end of the saloon.

And then the door opened, and a small figure came running towards them. Anne thought at first it was a child, for it was so small and thin: little feet in satin slippers flickered below the hem of a white muslin gown; little hands stretched forward from the sleeves of a vivid scarlet and gold silk Chinese jacket; a small face, pinched and eager, was surrounded by curls of soft hair the colour of clear honey. Surely it must be the count's daughter, was Anne's first thought.

But the little creature ran to his arms, the voice cried '*Nikolasha! Eto ti?*' in a tone of such urgent love that Anne knew everything, even before the Count swept his wife off her feet, holding her in his arms well above the ground in a grip that must have hurt her, and saying in a voice made hoarse by emotion, '*Irushka! Milyenkaya! Doushenka!*'

Anne watched with a painful mixture of emotion, pleasure that one must always feel when witnessing real, unselfish love, and a pang of sadness that there was no-one in the world who loved *her* like that. Then at last the Count restored his Countess to the floor, and taking her hand, turned her to face Anne, and said in French, 'Irina Pavlovna, here is Miss Peters whom I told you of in my letter – Admiral Peters' daughter, who has consented to be our little Lolya's new governess. You must make her feel very welcome, for she is all alone in the world and far from home.'

The Countess looked up at Anne with a shy smile, and held out her slender hand. 'Mademoiselle Peters, I am so happy to welcome you to Schwartzenturm. You must look upon it as your home, if you please.' She turned towards a servant who had come in behind her, and took from him a tray, which she proffered to Anne. On it was a silver plate and a small silver dish, the former containing a little round, golden-brown cake, the latter a fine white powder Anne took to be pulverised sugar. Anne looked questioningly towards the Count.

'It is an old Russian custom,' he explained genially, 'to offer bread and salt to a person taking up residence in a new place; but nowadays, we often represent them with cake and sugar instead, as being more palatable. You must taste a little of the cake and a pinch of the sugar – that is your part in the ceremony.'

Anne did so. There was a murmur of approval and welcome, and the Countess smiled as she returned the tray to the servant and said, 'You are completely among friends now, mademoiselle. I hope you will be happy.'

'I'm sure I shall, madame,' Anne replied. The Countess was beautiful, she observed, with that wistful quality of beauty which makes one feel almost sad. The wide Tartar cheekbones, the small, straight nose, and little pointed chin were the delicate setting for her beautiful amber-coloured eyes, fringed with feathery dark lashes, which shone with a soft and lovely light when she looked at her husband. Anne's words were more than a formal politeness. The Countess's expression was truly gentle and benign, shy as a wild animal is shy, but genuinely welcoming. It would be impossible, Anne thought, to do anything but love such a lovely creature, and she felt ashamed at the ambiguity of her thoughts the night before.

'But you must be so tired,' the Countess continued. 'Come into the drawing-room; there is a supper laid out all ready for you, and tea.'

They passed through the end door into the staircase hall, where a great staircase wound ceremoniously round three sides, leading up to a gallery with a wrought-iron balustrade, and vistas through archways to vaulted corridors beyond. Anne caught a glimpse of something white crouched behind the balustrade, and thought it must be another dog, but almost instantly it jumped up and came running down the stairs, to reveal itself as a little girl in a white nightdress, with bare feet and curl papers in her dark hair.

'Papa! You're home! I knew it was you!' she cried in French. 'When it got late, Nyanka said you wouldn't be home until the morning, but I made myself stay awake. I knew you'd come.'

Reaching the foot of the stairs, the child launched herself at her father, and the Count, laughing, caught her up and lodged her firmly on one hip, delivering himself of as least as many hearty kisses as he received, and addressed his daughter with a mixture of French and Russian endearments. Anne was delighted to see how unaffectedly they greeted each other. In England, amongst people of rank, even fond parents preserved formality with their children, and if, unthinkably, such a display of affection had been offered, they would have choked it off with stern rebukes about being out of bed without permission. But the Count put his daughter down only for the purpose of introducing her to Anne.

'Now, Lolya, your best curtsey for mademoiselle, for I want you to make a good impression on her,' he said in French, easing the bare toes down to the ground. 'Miss Peters, may I present to you the Countess Yelena Nikolayevna Kirova?'

'Enchantée, mademoiselle,' the child said, making a deep curtsey with pointed foot and bent arm, in the manner of a ballet-dancer, and fluttering her eyelids like a coquette. Her parents laughed, and she jumped up, pleased, and cried, 'Didn't I do it well? Did you like it, mademoiselle? That is how La Karsevina does it at the ballet, when they throw her roses at the end of the performance. Mama took me last winter when we were in Petersburg, didn't you, Mamochka? Do you like the ballet, mademoiselle?'

'I'm afraid I've never seen it,' Anne replied in French, 'but I think I should like it very much.'

The child looked as though it were very strange for her not to have seen the ballet, and then said, 'I mean to be a dancer when I grow up. And my cousin Kira is going to be an opera singer. We shall travel all over the world together, and have kings for our admirers.'

The Count laughed, and scooped her up onto his hip again. 'So this is what happens when I go away for just a few months! When I last saw you, you said you were going to stay with me for ever and ever, and never get married, because you loved me best.'

'But you were away so long,' she objected, looking seriously into her father's face, which was now on a level with hers. There was little resemblance between them, Anne thought, except for the rather long chin. The child was very dark, with black hair and eyes, and honey-brown skin, and her face had all the charm of irregularity, and of its innocent and animated expression. Over her father's shoulder, she caught sight of Anne again, and with a little, considering frown, she whispered quite audibly into her father's ear, 'Papa, what must I call her? Is it Mademoiselle de Pierre?'

'That is what is comes to, in French,' her father agreed, laughing.

'I think she is prettier than Fräulein Hoffnung,' was the next penetrating comment, to the Countess's evident embarrassment.

'Please, come into the drawing-room, mademoiselle,' she said quickly, and led her through the far door into a large, octagonal room.

'Oh, this is lovely,' Anne exclaimed involuntarily. The unusual shape was determined, she guessed, by the three-sided bay window, now covered by drapes of blue silk damask, directly opposite the door where she was standing. The floor was of polished parquet, the centre of which was covered by a huge Savonnerie rug in shades of blue and rose against a white background. The walls were dark blue, with an elaborate frieze of white and gold around the cornice, and the ceiling was again decorated with delicate rococo designs in plaster. The walls were hung with an enormous number of paintings, mostly portraits, jostling each other for space in a friendly way, and there were several large, comfortable sofas, a handsome pianoforte near the window, and in the centre of the room, a wide, low circular table, on which stood a samovar emitting wisps of steam, and a number of supper dishes. The sight was most welcome to Anne, who was beginning to feel almost faint from hunger.

'It is a pretty room, isn't it?' the Countess said, looking round with a pleased smile. 'You will like it even more by daylight – the colours show up much better. But now, I am sure you must be tired and hungry. Let me take your pelisse and hat – there, now. Come and sit here and be comfortable, and Lolya and I shall wait on you. No, I insist!'

In the most natural, unaffected way, the Countess took off Anne's hat with her own hands, and placed Anne on the most comfortable of the sofas, and went over to the table to make the tea. Russian tea was something that Anne had already come across on her journey from Grodno, and she had gathered that it was something of an institution in Russian society. It was drunk from glasses, instead of cups, which were arranged on the table with a measure of the thick, amber liquid already in them. Boiling water was then added from the samovar, and sugar stirred in, although at some of the inns, instead of powdered sugar being added to the tea, she had been given a piece of sugar snipped off the loaf to chew while she drank, which was the peasant way.

The child Lolya, despite her nightgown, curl papers and bare feet, was behaving in a completely drawing-room manner, and brought tea to Anne and then to her father as though to the manner born. Anne sipped gratefully at the hot liquid, while Lolya placed a little table with a marquetry top just before her, and the Countess brought her a plate of cold chicken, cake, nuts and dried figs. Anne tasted the chicken first. It had been roasted with honey and herbs, and was the most delicious chicken she had ever tasted; and she said so.

'Kerim roasted it specially, when he knew you were coming,' the Countess said, with a laughing glance at her husband. 'He believes that the cooks in London are the best in the world, so whenever we have guests who have been to England, he insists on doing something special for them. You can imagine how excited he was at the thought of a real Englishwoman coming to stay!'

'I won him from Prince Naryshkin in a wager, years ago when we were both young and foolish,' the Count added. 'The next day the Prince offered me fifteen hundred roubles to have him back, but I wouldn't take it. I'd already tasted some of Kerim's cooking, you see. He learned his art from a Frenchman in Moscow, which makes it all the more odd that he believes the culinary art is only understood in London.'

'I believe London society may know all there is to know about *eating* fine food,' Anne offered, and they laughed.

'You must try one of the cakes, Miss Peters,' the Count said later. 'They are curd-cakes, a speciality of the Caucasus, where Irina comes from. She had to teach Kerim how to make them – didn't you, Irushka? I think he begins to make them almost as well as you.'

Anne tried one and found it delicious: a soft brown crust around the outside, and moist, sweet curds and fat Turkish raisins inside. Lolya, who was sitting in the corner of her father's sofa with her legs tucked up under her, was given one and ate it with the passionate slowness of one who knew from experience she would not be offered another. By the time the last crumb had gone, her eyes were heavy, and she made little protest at being sent off to bed again. Looking at her made Anne feel sleepy too, and she was glad when the Countess, with quick sympathy, suggested that Anne must want to go to her room, and offered to show her there at once.

'And tomorrow, I will show you the house,' the Count promised. 'Good night, Miss Peters. Sweet dreams attend you – stationary ones, I hope.'

The Countess conducted Anne up the stairs and showed her into her bedroom. It was a decent-sized, square room dominated by the large bed with a white counterpane and curtains, towards which Anne gazed longingly. The only other thing she noticed immediately was the icon in one corner. It had a small red lamp with a pierced shade burning before it, throwing lacy patterns of shadow onto the ceiling.

'Saint Anne,' the Countess said, noting the direction of Anne's gaze. 'I thought you would like to have your own saint to look after you, but if there is another you'd prefer – ?'

'You are most kind, madame,' Anne said a little blankly. She had been brought up with an English contempt for idolatry and hatred of Popery, but this was obviously meant kindly. It was an example of her new mistress's great thoughtfulness, not an attempt to convert her, and she must respond to it as such. She forced herself to add in a warmer voice, 'It was thoughtful of you. I am content with your choice.'

The Countess indicated the wash-stand. 'There is hot water there, ready for you. I think you should sleep as late as you need to tomorrow. I will tell them not to wake you, but wait until you ring. Good night, Miss Peters. I hope you will be happy here.'

'Good night, madame, and thank you for everything,' Anne said. When the Countess had withdrawn, Anne thought to herself that it would be her own fault entirely if she were not happy in a place where the mistress was at such pains to make her comfortable. She washed and cleaned her teeth, changed into her nightgown, which some unseen hand had unpacked and laid out for her, and then knelt by the bed to offer a prayer of thanks and of mild supplication, that everything would go on being as pleasant as it had begun.

Then she climbed up into the high, white bed. It was a feather bed, and she sank into it deeply and bonelessly, feeling the absolute weariness of five weeks on the road washing over her. Her head whirled rather pleasantly, with mingling images of light and shade, carriages and chandeliers, sofas and trees and samovars. Her limbs were heavy, the bed was soft, so soft . . . as soft as the curds in the curd-cake . . . she was sinking gently into a bed of curds . . . she was asleep.

Anne woke suddenly and completely, and didn't know where she was. White curtains with sunlight streaming through them. White curtains? Oh, she must be at an inn somewhere – but where? Where had they got to last night? Recollection seeped back into her brain. No, of course, they had arrived. She was at Schwartzenturm, the Count's house, in what was to be from now on her own room. That was a pleasant thought: a room of her own again, after so long – a room to unpack in. She sat up and pulled back the bed curtains, and then leaned back against her pillows to examine the room in comfort.

The room was square and the proportions good, but there was no sign of the elaborate elegance of the other rooms she had seen last night. The floor was of wood, painted dark red, with no rug but a sheepskin beside the bed onto which to lower tender morning toes. The walls were of plain plaster, painted white, except for a band at the top where they met the ceiling, which had been painted with a frieze of red poppies, intertwined with green stems and leaves, and yellow ears of corn. It was a scheme of decoration which struck her as simple, novel, and attractive.

The furniture was simple too. There was a handsome, tall chest of drawers made of some light, polished wood – cedar, she guessed – for her clothes, and a heavily-carved, low oak chest, like a church terrier, which she thought would do to hold her shoes and hats. In the corner by the door was the icon with its lamp on a small table before it, and near the window a pretty console table, probably English, with a large mirror above it, in a frame of painted wood. Below the window was a day bed covered in red-and-white-striped silk, which looked French, and on the other side of the room a heavy tapestry chair which looked Dutch.

Add the pleasantness of the sunlight pouring in through the white muslin curtains, the smell of beeswax, and the starch of the white counterpane, and it was a room plain and simple, but eminently comfortable. And on the table beside the bed, alongside the candle, someone – she guessed the Countess – had placed a nicely-bound book of French essays, and a small vase of wild wallflowers, whose faint but sweet scent reached her like a breath of kindness. It was a room in which to be happy, to feel at home, she thought drowsily from the comfort of her pillows.

She must have drifted back to sleep, for she woke abruptly to the feeling that she was being watched, and sat up with a startled gasp to see that the door of her room was open a crack, and an eye was peering at her through the space. It withdrew hastily as she moved, and then reappeared, and, judging by its height from the ground, Anne guessed it must belong to the Count's younger child.

'Hello,' she said. Then, remembering to speak French, she continued, 'It's all right, you can come in if you want. I'm quite awake now.' The door opened a fraction more to allow access to the round soft button of a nose and part of a chin. 'Why don't you come and climb up onto the bed,' she invited, 'and we can introduce ourselves.'

There was a pause while the proposition was evaluated. Then the door opened fully and a small, stocky, nightgowned figure scampered in and scrambled up onto the bed, to kneel before her and contemplate her unsmilingly but with interest from under a tumble of light-brown curls. The solemn eyes were amber, like her mother's, but otherwise it was as yet a chubbily-undefined face.

'Do you know who I am?' Anne asked after a moment. The child nodded, but did not speak. 'How did you know I was here?' she asked next. No answer. 'Did your sister tell you?' A nod. 'So now I know who you are, don't I? You must be' – she paused to get the full name right – 'you must be Natasha Nikolayevna. Am I right?'

Another nod, and then a radiant grin, accompanied by a violent rocking back and forth to indicate approval and good will.

'Well, Natasha Nikolayevna,' Anne went on, 'I am very glad to meet you, and I hope we shall be friends.' Natasha tucked her lower lip under her upper one, and rocked a little harder. 'What lessons do you do? Do you take lessons with your sister?' No answer. 'Do you take lessons with Fräulein Hoffnung?' The bright eyes continued to regard her, but in silence, and Anne was beginning to feel baffled, when there was a small sound at the door of her room and Yelena appeared, dressed, this time, in white muslin frock and blue sash, her black curls tied up with blue ribbon.

'Natasha! There you are!' she cried in aggrieved tones. 'You shouldn't be in here, you wicked thing. Nyanka has been looking everywhere for you. You are to go and be dressed at once!'

Natasha gave Anne one more bright, silent look, and jumped off the bed and pattered out, avoiding with a dextrous swerve the admonitory pinch her sister aimed at her as she passed. Yelena, dropping Anne a curtsey of apology, began to close the door, but Anne called her back.

'Please ask your nurse not to be angry with her, just this once. She was not troubling me,' Anne said. 'I was glad to make her acquaintance; but I could not get her to talk to me. Was I right to assume she understands French?'

Yelena came a step further into the room. 'Oh, she understands French well enough, but she won't speak it,' she said.

'Won't speak it? Why not?'

'She never speaks at all,' Yelena said matter-of-factly. 'Not to anyone. There isn't anything wrong with her – she just won't. Nyanka calls her *Nemetzka* – little dumb thing – but Mama says she'll speak when she has something to say.' She looked around the room, evidently having lost interest in the subject of her younger sister. 'Mama said you weren't to be disturbed, but since you are awake, are you going to get up, mademoiselle?' she asked wistfully. 'Because I want to show you the nursery, and my rocking horse, and Zilka has a litter of puppies in the stable.'

Anne smiled, remembering the urgency of childhood. 'I shall get up this instant,' she promised. 'With the whole of the house to see, I couldn't bear to stay in bed a moment longer.'

Chapter Six

On going downstairs, Anne was directed by the butler into the breakfast room, to the right of the octagon room. It was a smaller, square room, very pretty with its walls hung with green silk damask, its decorated ceiling picked out in pink and green, and its row of long windows reaching down to the ground draped with gently-blowing white muslin. Here, she learned, the family took their informal meals. There was a large, 'state' dining-room on the other side of the octagon room for formal occasions.

The Count and Countess were at breakfast, and both children were sitting and eating with them – another thing Anne had never witnessed in England, where children took all their meals in the nursery. As she entered, the Countess looked up with a smile and said, 'Oh, Miss Peters, you are up so early! This naughty child of mine woke you – I am so sorry.'

'No, indeed, madame, I was already awake,' Anne said hastily. 'Please don't scold her.'

The Count, who had risen to his feet, reached across and ruffled Natasha's curls, and she spared him one golden look from her bowl and spoon. 'Nevertheless, she must understand that she is not to enter your room again without permission – do you hear me, Nasha?'

'You call her Nasha?' Anne enquired as she took the seat a footman was holding out for her.

'It is a little of a joke,' the Countess said, with a smile at her husband. 'In Russian, *nasha* means *ours*.'

'Because I am really only Papa's,' Yelena said unconcernedly. 'My real mother died when I was a baby.' It was said without any malice, but Anne, glancing at the Countess, saw the serenity of her expression falter just for an instant. From what she had so far observed, the Countess treated Yelena like her own child, and indeed she had heard Yelena call the Countess *Mamochka*, which was surely a term of endearment. Yet perhaps there was some element of friction between them. It was something to keep in mind as she got to know her new pupil.

For now, she merely said, 'I see,' and accepted cutlets and coddled eggs from the footman, grateful that breakfast seemed to be much the same wherever one went in Europe: she preferred dietary experiment to come later in the day, when she felt strong enough to cope with it. There was fragrant coffee, too, and crusty bread, a little darker in colour than English bread, with a denser texture and a delicious, nutty flavour. The children were drinking raspberry juice, and eating curds and pieces of honeycomb.

'Well, now that you have been woken early,' the Count said, 'we must see that the day is put to good use. If you will allow me, Miss Peters, I shall give myself the pleasure of showing you the house and grounds, or as much of them as we can see in one day. Tomorrow, I'm afraid, I must go to Petersburg.'

The Countess gave a little involuntary cry, and then put down her fork and said, 'Oh, Nikolai, no! So soon?'

'My dear, I must. But I shall not stay long. I must make my report to the minister and deliver some letters, and then I shall return. After so long away, I think I may be sure of having this summer to myself, at least.'

When they had finished breakfast, the Countess suggested that her husband should show Anne the outside of the house first, and then join her and the children on the terrace later. 'It will not amuse them to talk of architecture, and I must speak to Vasky and Kerim on domestic matters. You will enjoy it much more on your own. Miss Peters is bound to be a better audience than I, who have heard all the history before.'

The Count pretended hurt. 'You are bored with my conversation already! Very well, Miss Peters, you and I will go alone and appreciate the architectural marvels of my house. You will find it a novel experience, I promise you!'

Schwartzenturm was certainly an odd-looking house. Seen from the road, the west front had a solidly Palladian central block, three storeys high. The white stone façade was dominated by a central recessed portico, its four massive Ionic columns thrown into sharp relief by the dark, shadowy space of the loggia behind them. 'Delightful on hot afternoons!' the Count commented. The columns rose to a perfectly normal entablature and pediment, above and behind which the sloping roof and chimneys peeped coyly.

To either side of the central block were one-storey screen walls, linking it to two pavilions. So far, all was perfectly conventional. But the south pavilion, beginning at ground level as a small echo of its parent block, from the first floor upwards degenerated rapidly into a Rhine schloss, complete with round turrets topped with elaborate wrought-iron decorations. It was as if the original architect had been abruptly dismissed, and hastily replaced by someone homesick for the Black Forest.

The north pavilion did not even begin right. From the ground upwards, it was a round, black stone tower, like a castle keep: massive, plain, and mediaeval, as if hewn from the living rock on which it stood. In a remote and gloomy Scottish glen, it would not have looked out of place, but rising from the meek clay of flat grazing-land, it had a most peculiar effect. 'This, of course, is the black tower which gives the house its name,' said the Count.

The curtain walls concealed two courtyards and the necessary jumble of stables, kennels, and outbuildings, as could be seen from the other side of the house. It could also be seen that the back of the central block did not match the front, being faced entirely in soft red brick, with plain Queen Anne windows. The three-sided bay of the octagon room, and the French windows of the breakfast room, gave onto a broad terrace with a stone balustrade and a straight drop down to the park, so that the house appeared to be only two storeys high. If the west front had been designed by an Italian classicist, and the pavilions by nostalgic and romantic Germans, then the east front had evidently flowed from the pencil of a homesick Englishman.

'Palladian palace, Rhineland schloss, Scottish bastion, and English country house – who could have put such things together?' Anne asked, laughing, as she and the Count finished their circuit. 'It is quite, quite mad.'

'The main block was designed by an Italian architect, Gatto, about eighty years ago. It's actually based on one of Palladio's villas, the Villa Emo at Fanzolo,' the Count told her. 'Soloviev had the estate then, and wanted a summer house close to Petersburg, and commissioned Gatto to build him one. But he died before it was finished, and Prince Chernosov bought it for his wife, who was German by birth – one of the Empress's ladies-in-waiting – and added the white tower for her, so that she wouldn't feel homesick.'

'And the black tower?'

'The old Princess, the Prince's mother, added that. She lived here with the Prince and his wife, but after her son died, she grew very strange and gradually retreated from the world. The young Princess only came here in the summer, preferring – despite the white tower! – a modern house in Petersburg, but the old Princess still felt her privacy wasn't complete enough. So she had the black tower built with her own money, and went and lived in the top of it all alone, seeing no-one but the servant who brought her food. She never left her room again until the day she died.'

'Like a prisoner in a fairy-tale,' Anne said, looking quizzically at the Count, hardly knowing whether to believe him or not. He regarded her seriously, divining her thought.

'Oh, but it is perfectly true, I promise you. There are much stranger stories than that in this great land of ours! Well, after that, the young Princess sold it to the Razumovskys, who tore down the east front, which used to house the ballroom, and rebuilt it with the octagon room and the terrace as it is now because they had spent a very happy year in England on their honeymoon tour and wanted to be reminded of it. It's based on a house called Kirby Hall, in your Yorkshire, and they had English bricks brought over specially to make it look as like the real thing as possible.'

Anne burst out laughing. 'Now I know you are teasing me! You must tell me the real story, if you please.'

'I am perfectly serious,' he smiled. 'Why should you doubt it?'

'But surely this is your family home?' Anne said. 'Your father and grandfather must have lived here before you; but by this account, it has had four owners in eighty years.'

The Count shook his head, turning her towards the terrace steps. 'It's not like that in Russia. Until very recently, all the land belonged to the Tsar, and even the richest of the noblemen only held their estates on sufferance. They could be, and were, transferred from one appointment to another, from one part of Russia to another, be deprived of their estate or awarded a new one, all at a moment's notice; so they had no roots in one place, as your old English families have.'

'And might they not refuse?' Anne asked.

'The Tsar had absolute power. Everything in Russia, every stick and stone, every man, woman, child and beast, belonged to him, to do with what he liked.'

'That seems very strange. Did no-one – a rich provincial lord, for instance – ever try to challenge the power?'

The Count smiled rather grimly. 'Emperors have been murdered before now. But all power flows from the imperial throne, reward as well as punishment, and we Russians are born to the system. It's in our blood. And it would be impossible in any case for any provincial lord, as you say, to raise the army necessary for rebellion. There is a very old law which says that a man holding any position of authority over an area may not hold land in that area.'

'I begin to understand,' Anne said. 'A rigid system, but strong.'

'I suppose things may change in the future,' he went on, 'but it's only since the charter of 1785 that we have been allowed to own land as our legal property – a mere eighteen years, far too short a time to change the habit of centuries.'

'So you feel no particular attachment to this house?' Anne reverted to the original point, and sounded so disappointed that the Count laughed.

'To the *pomestie* – the estate – none at all, but only a man devoid of humour could feel nothing for a house as eccentric as this! But I dare say I shall sell it in a few years' time, and buy another *pomestie* somewhere else,' he added cheerfully. 'We Russians have restless feet – we do not like to stay in the same place for very long together.'

'It is very different from the English way,' Anne said thoughtfully as they mounted to the terrace. 'There every man making his fortune longs to buy a piece of land, and to build a house, to plant and improve, and hand them down to his sons and sons' sons. But I suppose if you have never been able to own the land, it would be different.'

'And the land here in the northern territories is so poor it is not worth improving. In the north, it runs in the blood to take a crop or two and then move on.'

'Very poor husbandry, sir,' Anne said sternly. 'What happens when you run out of land?'

'We go out and conquer the next country, of course,' the Count said with a smile. 'Why do you think Russia is so big, Miss Peters?'

The Countess and the children were waiting for them on the terrace. 'Is he talking nonsense, Miss Peters?' she asked with a smile. 'He has a very strange liking for confusing and confounding people. Now you must meet Fräulein Hoffnung, whom Nikolai has told you about, I'm sure.'

Anne stepped forward to shake the hand of a thin, elderly woman, whose face was drawn and pinched with long-endured pain. But the eyes were kind, and the handshake cordial, and she said to Anne in strangely-accented French, 'Ah, mademoiselle, I am very glad to meet you. My little Lolya will be in good hands, I am sure, and I hope she will be a good girl and do my teaching credit.'

'I'm sure she will,' said Anne. The Countess now drew her attention to the stout person who was holding Natasha by the hand.

'And this is Nyanka, the children's nurse, who was my nurse, too, when I was little. Nyanka, this is the Barishnya Peters.'

Nyanka was a fat, comfortable-shaped woman, dressed all in

black with a white apron, and a kerchief tied about her head. It was difficult to tell her age: she might have been forty or sixty. Her face was brown and wide, the weathered skin shiny across the cheekbones like a rock worn smooth by time. She had a strong, eagle's beak of a nose, and bright black eyes under surprisingly delicate eyebrows. Anne thought she must have been very attractive in her youth, perhaps even beautiful, with that mixture of power and delicacy.

Around her neck Nyanka wore a series of crucifixes in graduating sizes – a large wooden one on a leather thong, an elaborately carved one made of mother-of-pearl, and a small, very beautiful one of blue enamel on a silver chain – together with a copper medal of St Nicholas, and a phial made from a small animal's horn, held in a filigree case, which Anne learned later was supposed to contain the blood of one of the obscure Georgian saints she venerated. Anne thought there was something unexpectedly similar about her and little Natasha, standing beside her holding her hand, in the way both of them watched her gravely and silently with bright, almost feral eyes.

'I think, my dear,' said the Countess to her husband, 'that you had better show Miss Peters something of the estate before it grows too hot. The house can wait for another time.'

'Whatever you say, my love,' the Count agreed. 'Shall I order the barouche, and then we can all go together?'

'Oh yes *please*, Papa,' Yelena said passionately. 'And may I ride on the box with Morkin, please? Because he promised he would teach me how to drive, and he keeps forgetting, and if I am there he can't, can he?'

Half an hour later the barouche drew up outside the house, and Yelena urged Anne to come and meet the two large white horses which were harnessed to it. 'They are called Castor and Pollux, after the stars, you know,' she told her importantly. 'They are my great friends, and I always bring them sugar. Nyanka keeps her tea-sugar for me to give to them.'

The horses were pure white, with pink muzzles and ruby eyes, and thick, pale eyelashes, and their topknots had been tied up with blue ribbons which fell forward over their eyes. They bent their heads eagerly to Yelena's hands, and blew and nuzzled exploringly for the fragments of sugar in her small palms. The coachman, Morkin, stood by their heads, watching with a proud smile that revealed a lone yellow tooth like a standing stone in his lower jaw. He wore a tall beaver hat, like an English coachman, decorated with a favour of blue ribbon to match his horses, but below that he was all Russian, in a peasant tunic and trousers, and soft boots which made his ankles turn over. He said something to the Count, evidently about Yelena, who smiled at him happily under the horses' whiskered muzzles.

'Morkin is very proud of Yelena,' the Count translated to Anne. 'She has never had any fear of horses, and he often tells the story of the time when she first learnt to walk, and escaped her nursemaid and wandered into the stables. Morkin found her in one of the stalls, holding herself up by the leg of one of my hunters, quite unafraid. The horse had the reputation of being a kicker, but he never offered the slightest harm to Yelena.'

Yelena now, having had her gloves forcibly put on by Nyanka, climbed with Morkin's help up onto the box, while the Countess, with a foolish little flowered hat and a white lace parasol against the sun, took her place inside the barouche with Natasha on her lap. The Count helped Anne in beside her, and took the pull-down seat for himself.

'By the way, Miss Peters,' he said as they started off, 'it has never happened to come up in conversation, but do you ride?'

'Yes sir – my father taught me,' Anne said. 'I like riding very much.'

'Good,' he said. 'Irina likes to ride, and it makes it more pleasant for her if she has a companion when I am away.'

'Oh yes,' said the Countess. 'I shall be able to show you something of the countryside, too. There are lots of places too far off to walk, where one cannot take a carriage.'

'I have no habit, madame,' Anne mentioned.

'Oh, but you can make yourself one, I'm sure. Nikolai says you are very skilled with the needle.'

'I'll bring back the cloth from Petersburg,' the Count said. 'You shall tell me what colour you like.'

'You are too kind, sir,' Anne began, remembering by contrast how Lady Murray had bid her make over one of her old dresses for the Embassy Ball; but the Count only looked surprised.

'Nonsense. You must have a habit if you are to ride. Ah, look, you can see the church now. I always think it looks prettiest glimpsed through the trees like that.'

The church stood on the main road, which went to the right to Petersburg and left to Kirishi, opposite the beginning of the track leading down to the house, where, in England, there would have been wrought-iron park gates. It was a little white church with a blue cupola, and small, narrow windows. To the left of the door was an arched recess in the wall in which was painted a Byzantine virgin in a dark red robe against a sky-blue background, her head ringed with stars.

'We go to mass here every Sunday and on Feast days,' the Countess said. 'We have no chapel in the house, and I prefer the mass in a small church like this rather than in one of the fashionable churches in Kirishi. It is simpler and more sincere, I think. I suppose, Miss Peters,' she added with a faintly anxious accent, 'that you are a Protestant?'

'Fräulein Hoffnung is a Lutheran,' the Count said briefly, 'which is rather trying for her.'

For whom – the Fräulein or the Countess? Anne wondered. 'I was brought up in the Church of England,' she said as neutrally as possible. It was too early as yet to judge how far the quantity and quality of their alien religion would affect her relationship with the Kirovs. Possibly the Fräulein would be able to enlighten her on that.

The coachman had halted the carriage in the feathery shade of a stand of three false acacias, their trunks white with summer dust, and the Countess now asked in that same, faintly anxious voice, 'Would you like to see the church, Miss Peters? It has some fine icons.'

'Yes, very much,' Anne said firmly, and was rewarded with a relieved smile. They all got down, and stepped out of the bright sunshine and into the cool darkness of the interior. It seemed very empty to Anne, who was used to English churches full of pews or chairs. The floor was of black and white marble, whose chill struck through the thin soles of her sandals, laid in a chequerboard pattern with the points reaching away to the closed altar-screen gates. They were of black wrought-iron, tipped with gold, and elaborately designed, like the gates of a palace. Beyond them, the sanctuary lamp gleamed faintly red.

The air was full of the dry, lilac odour of incense – a strange smell, like dead beauty, Anne thought, like a butterfly or a flower, pressed in a collection, only the sad, dried husk of its living self. After the bright light outside, it seemed dark in the church. Under the cupola, a lustre like an iron cartwheel on a long chain bore a petrified forest of virgin candles, ready for the next service. Around the walls, there was the muted glimmer of small lamps, each flickering flame faintly reflected in the gold of its icon. Near the door, there was an ancient silver font, the engraving worn almost smooth by generations of ardent hands. Against the wall on one side was a narrow wooden chest, and on the other a painted board, almost like an inn sign, depicting the Crucifixion. There was a wide, scarlet wound in the pierced side, and the long dark face was wrenched in a very human agony. The board was supported by a wooden pole on a heavy base, and on the top of the pole was a sinister skull of Adam, glaring sightlessly up into the shadows of the roof.

Anne had been prepared to feel disapproval of the idolatry, or merely an indifferent interest in the architecture, but as she wandered slowly down the church looking at the icons, she found herself unexpectedly moved. The emptiness, the space around her (what was it the Count called it? *Prostor!* Did everything in Russia give that feeling?); the faint smell of incense; the absolute simplicity of the place allied with the passionate beauty of the dark Byzantine madonnas cradling their infants' heads, and the intensity of suffering in the faces of the saints; and the dim, glimmering gold and the dark vivid colours all combined to give her a strange feeling of exaltation, which she did not understand, and was not sure she entirely approved of, yet which she did not want to lose. Stepping out into the sunshine and normality, she experienced a sense of loss.

Behind the church, there was a small churchyard, bounded by a low, white-paling fence, and grouped around it to form a square, there were a number of buildings with which Anne was to become very familiar. To one side of the square were the priest's and deacon's houses – plain, wooden buildings roofed with wooden shingles – the living quarters being reached by an external wooden staircase, for the ground floor of each was used for storage and for keeping animals.

On the opposite side was another similar structure, slightly larger, occupied by the steward of the estate and his wife and children. To the side of it, a road led away, Anne was told, to the peasant village, and to a large house like a sort of barracks, where the estate workers lived. Next to the steward's house was a smaller one, divided into two sets of living quarters, one upstairs and one downstairs. Below, Anne was told, the estate painter lived. She imagined at first that they meant he was the man responsible for painting the fences and barns, but when she ventured on the idea, the Count laughed.

'No, no, I mean painter as in portrait painter! There are plenty of examples of his work around the house. Irina will show them to you. I am lucky in him – he is very good, but he has never been to Petersburg, so he doesn't know it. If anyone ever discovers how good he is, he will be quite spoiled, and I shall lose him, as sure as fate. Naryshkin would like to have him – his painter can't even get the eyes on the same level! Grigorovitch has painted Irina several times, and the children, and all my favourite horses. You must sit for him now you are here, Miss Peters.'

'I, sir?' Anne said, startled. The Count smiled genially.

'Yes – why not? The children will be glad in years to come to have your likeness, and Grigorovitch might as well have something to do to keep him occupied.'

Anne had never had her likeness taken, except by other girls at school, for practice in sketching, and the idea intrigued and rather embarrassed her. She wondered if the Count were saying it to tease her, but then she could not think why he should, and dismissed the idea. If he really wanted the children to have her portrait, she would not object. In her blue dress, perhaps . . .

Upstairs from the painter lived an old woman whom the Countess had brought with her from her home in the Caucasus, and since Yelena clamoured to be allowed to visit her, the Countess took Anne up to meet her too. Yelena ran ahead up the steps calling 'Marya Petrovna! Marya Petrovna! It's me!' and Anne and the Countess followed holding Natasha's hand, while the Count walked off to speak to his steward.

'She is a wonderful needlewoman,' the Countess explained. 'She makes a good many of my clothes and all my underwear, and she embroiders exquisitely. She made Natasha's christening-robe, and she's the dearest creature, and loves the children like her own. Well, you see how Lolya likes her.'

The room into which Anne ducked was spotlessly clean and very bare, with the floorboards painted a lovely amber-yellow, and an icon of the Holy Mother opposite the door, with a pretty silver lamp before it. There was a narrow bed, covered in a white cotton counterpane embroidered with white flowers, a window-seat under the single window, a cupboard against the wall, and a tall-backed, wooden chair in which the occupant sat. She was an old woman, tiny and shrunken, but her skin and eyes were clear, and her fingers were moving nimbly about the work in her lap. The thing that struck Anne as most immediately peculiar about the room was that there was a basket on the floor by the old woman's feet in which a small black pig was lying, curled up like a cat.

When the Countess came in, the old woman's face lit up. She held out her hand, and when the Countess took it, the old woman kissed the Countess's hand and pressed it to her forehead in a gesture of mingled love and homage. There was a rapid exchange in Russian, and then the Countess said to Anne, 'Marya Petrovna greets you and apologises that she cannot get up, but she no longer has much use in her legs. She bids you regard this house as your own.'

The old woman watched closely as the translation was made, and when Anne looked at her and smiled, she bowed her head several times rapidly. Then she reached out hands for the children, who allowed their hair to be stroked and their cheeks patted. Yelena spoke to her in Russian, while Natasha sat on the floor to caress the pig, which woke up and grunted in a genial way and stuck up its wet and quivering snout to sniff at Natasha's face.

'Does the pig live in here all the time?' Anne asked in amazement.

'Oh yes,' the Countess said. 'Marya Petrovna always has a pig. She gets them as piglets and keeps them by her, and feeds them from her own plate. She says it's the only way she can manage, because of her legs. Then, when they get too big, she has them butchered, and lives off the meat for quite a time. She cries dreadfully when they are killed because she gets so fond of them.'

'But don't they – I mean, doesn't it – '

'Oh no, they are very clean. She trains them as you or I would train a dog. She says they are more intelligent than dogs – '

The old woman spoke, chuckling.

'She says they are more intelligent than most people, too,' the Countess translated with a smile.

'Does she speak French, then?' Anne asked.

'She understands it a little, but doesn't speak it very much.'

Yelena had now been despatched to the cupboard in the corner, and returning with a wooden box, hung over the old woman's arm while she opened it. It contained sugar-plums, which the Countess said she prepared herself, and for which she was famous. Natasha and Yelena received one each, and were soon reduced to silence by the sheer size of them. There was some more conversation in Russian between the Countess and her sewing-woman, and though Anne could not understand the words, there was no mistaking the affection and concern which existed between the two. Then the children both kissed the old woman, she kissed the Countess's hand again, bowed to Anne, and they went out into the sunshine.

'She's a remarkable woman,' the Countess said as they descended the stairs. 'She does everything for herself, despite her disabilities, and the children love visiting her, not only for the sugar-plums, but because she is so interested in everything. I'm sure Lolya could talk to her for a day at a time.'

'Mademoiselle, did you know,' Yelena said, turning an urgent face upwards as she preceded them down the steps, 'that Marya Petrovna has tame hens, too? She lets them out in the morning to scratch about in the yard, and they come up into her house at night to be fed and to sleep. They sit along the window-seat, and lay their eggs for her. When we went there once, one of them had a family in the pig's basket – six little chickens. You never saw anything so small! And she let me hold them.'

'I can see the attraction that house must hold for them,' Anne murmured to the Countess.

'It's one of the places they like to go on their morning walk,' the Countess replied. 'Poor Fräulein Hoffnung is allergic to animals, but Lolya managed to persuade her to go there at least three times a week. So you are warned, Miss Peters!'

Beyond the square of houses behind the church was another square made by the range of farm buildings. Here there was the dairy, where the cows were milked and several different kinds of cheese made, and the stables where the working horses were kept. The stable block was a handsome building, with decorative door frames, and a carved frieze around the walls just under the roof. The roof projected a long way out beyond the walls, and between the roof buttresses under the eaves, swallows had nested. The air was filled with their shrill sweeting as they dashed busily in and out, feeding their families. The wooden roof shingles were painted bright red, and for that reason this stable was called the red stable, to distinguish it from the stable up at the house where the riding and driving horses were kept. Yelena was obviously quite at home here. She seemed to know all the horses, and even the long-horned white oxen, who shared the stables, by name, and would have spent all day there petting them and talking to them had not the Count come to find them.

'We had better drive on, or you will see nothing of the estate, Miss Peters. No, no, *galubchik*,' he smiled at Yelena's protest, 'the stables are close enough to walk to. You can bring mademoiselle another time, and introduce her to all the horses.'

Back in the carriage, they drove on down the road in the Kirishi direction, and after a while turned off onto another track to the left, and drove through the parkland belonging to the house. There were cattle grazing, clumps of well-chosen, ornamental trees, gentle undulations of land, pretty streams, and rustic bridges; just like an English park, except that there was a great deal more of it.

'The Razumovskys were responsible for landscaping the park,' the Count told Anne. 'It was all part of their admiration for the English country houses they visited on their honeymoon tour. They had mature trees brought here, some from thousands of miles away, to get the right effect.'

Further on they turned off onto another track, and drove past the estate granary, which stood beside a little stream, and was screened by a stand of larch and pine. Beside it was the Count's distillery where vodka was made. Much of this was sold to the peasants under licence, issued by the government, at the village *kabaks*.

'Not very much like your English village inns, though,' the Count said to Anne. 'They are really just drinking-shops, very bare and functional, no food or accommodation provided. The peasants drink vodka when they have the money. When they don't, they make their own drink called *kvass*.'

'And what is that made of?' Anne asked.

The Count grinned. 'Much better not to ask! It gets them drunk just the same, and I'm afraid that's all they care about. There's no sitting about, sipping and conversing for them. They like to drink a lot very quickly, until they fall into a stupor – they call it *zapoi*, and it's the peasant's idea of heaven on earth.'

'You don't do them justice, Nikolasha,' the Countess reproved gently. 'They make lovely music, too, and sing and dance, and there's a kind of mumming they do at Easter – '

'Yes, *dousha*, I know,' the Count said soothingly. 'I didn't suggest that drinking was all they did – only that when they drink, they do it single-mindedly, and to excess.'

'You will give Miss Peters the wrong idea,' the Countess pursued. 'I'm sure our serfs here are very hard-working, good sort of people. And some of the women do lovely embroidery.'

'Yes, *Irushka maya*, I know. I think there's just time to drive as far as the sawmill,' he said, changing the subject firmly, 'and then we can come back past the paddocks and the orchards and the kitchen garden. When you have time, you must show Miss Peters the greenhouses. We haven't much in the way of ornamental garden, Miss Peters. The change of climate from heat to cold is too rapid here and too extreme to grow many flowering plants out of doors, so we have to rely on greenhouses. There were only two when we first came here. The Razumovskys used them simply to grow potted plants to decorate the house for formal occasions. But I have greatly extended them, added an orangery, and built a whole new range of succession houses, and I mean to do still more in that direction when I have the leisure. I would like to be able to have fruit and vegetables sent in to Petersburg for most of the year. I think you will find them well worth looking at. I got many of my ideas in England. Your gardeners understand such things better than anyone in the world.'

Except the Russians, Anne added inside her head, anticipating his thought. He caught her eye and laughed as if he had heard it.

The Count left early the next morning, and Anne experienced the first day out of his company for a very long time. She felt strangely hollow and listless, which she attributed to the after-effects of the long journey. She was glad that the Countess said there was no question of her beginning her duties at once.

'You must settle in first and find your way about,' she said. 'And besides, I promised Nikolai to show you the rest of the house.'

Over the next few days, sometimes with the Countess as guide, and sometimes alone, Anne explored the vast, rambling house. The main formal rooms were those she had already seen: the hall, staircase hall, and octagon room, which together were intended to form a triumphant progression in the grand manner of the previous century – the 'circuit' – beginning at the main entrance and culminating in the 'state' dining-room. This lay to the left of the octagon, and Anne had only glimpsed it in semi-darkness, for its shutters were kept closed, and its furniture and lustre bagged in Hollands.

To either side of the great hall were four smaller, more intimate rooms, a library, a business-room for the Count, and two sitting-rooms, which the Countess used for privacy, or on dark or cold days when they were more cosy than the octagon room. All the rooms were covered with pictures, struggling for space, frame to frame, and Anne spent many an amusing hour looking at them. They were a motley collection. Some were works by well-known painters – Rubens, Rembrandt, Van Dyck – others by lesser-known Italian artists, endless views of Venice by Pittoni and Tiepolo, and allegorical scenes by Panini and Bonavia; *Alexander and the Gordian Knot*, *Mars and Venus*, *Rebecca at the Well*, the *Death of Lucretia*.

But by far the most numerous were portraits, some of famous people by eminent court painters, others family portraits by artists unknown. Anne found several of the Countess by the same hand, presumably Grigorovitch, and others of her as a younger woman, by a much less skilled hand. The children were represented, and the Count appeared eight times by artists of graduating skill, from quite good to appallingly inept. There were also portraits of dogs, dozens of horses, and various interiors and views of the outside of the house in a variety of styles. It was an amusing mixture of the priceless and the worthless, and Anne contemplated with interest the mind which could have chosen to display them all side by side.

Upstairs in the central block were four 'state' bedrooms, which all led off the gallery in the staircase hall, and a range of smaller bedrooms used by the family. The nursery occupied one whole side of the house, and here the children and Nyanka and her assistant Tanya slept and played. There was a small room designated as the schoolroom, which Anne would use, and Fräulein Hoffnung also had a private sitting-room where she could retire to keep her stern Lutheran Sundays. But unlike an English household, the children were not confined to the nursery. Instead, they had the run of the whole house, and though startled by the idea at first, Anne soon came to feel that it gave the house a more comfortable and genial atmosphere.

The white tower, she discovered, was occupied mostly by the servants, of whom the upper ones had their own rooms there. Other rooms were empty, others again used for storage. There was a great deal to store – furniture, porcelain, carpets, pictures, the expensive, extensive magpie collection of the travelled Russian nobleman. There was a great deal of Italian statuary of various periods, and most of the furniture and carpets seemed to be French – the spoils of the Revolution, Anne supposed. The treasure was heaped, disregarded, in room after room in the narrow circular towers. She wondered if even the Count knew what he had.

The black tower was empty, and unused even for storage. Anne liked to go there alone for there was something intriguing about its stark emptiness. For most of its height it contained no rooms, only a stone staircase which wound round an empty central core, lit by unglazed, arrow-slit windows through which the air blew freshly. At the top of the stairs a solid oak door opened into a large empty chamber, half-moon shaped, occupying half of the tower. Three doors in the straight wall led to a staircase up onto the leads, and into two smaller segments of rooms, in one of which the mad old Princess had immured herself. Oddly, Anne found no atmosphere of gloom up here. The view from the windows at the top of the tower was breathtaking, and she could imagine the self-confined prisoner spending all her days gazing outwards, rather than inwards at her own sadness. On fine days, Anne liked to climb up onto the leads and just sit there in the blessed sunshine, feeling the gentle air brushing her face, and watching the cloud shadows move across the green meadows, the acres of ripening crops, and the distant darkness of the forest.

Yelena was not interested in accompanying Anne and her mother on formal tours of the house, but when it came to the kennels and stables, she could not have been kept away. The stables up at the house were called the 'white' stables, to distinguish them from the red, and here the riding and driving horses were kept. Castor and Pollux, Anne was told, were always at her command for taking out the children in one of the light carriages. There was also a team of bays for the berlin, and a very round dun pony called Limonchik – 'Little Lemon' – who pulled a little park calèche which seated two. The Count's hunters were still out at grass, but there were half a dozen road horses, three of whom were broken to side-saddle, two mouse-grey Tibetan ponies, and the Countess's own chestnut mare, Iskra.

In the kennels were a variety of hunting dogs: English mastiffs, and a flock of elegant, black-and-white borzois, including the Count's favourite, Zilka, who was nursing a litter, of which, Yelena told Anne ecstatically, her father had promised her one of her own.

As well as getting to know the house and the servants and beginning to learn a little Russian – she fully intended to be able to speak it properly within a year – Anne was learning more of those on whom her future happiness depended. Yelena, she soon saw, had got out of hand, perhaps through the growing indisposition of Fräulein Hoffnung, or perhaps simply because the Russians seemed to have a very haphazard way of bringing up their children, and spoiled them dreadfully, allowing them all sorts of liberties that wouldn't have been dreamed of in England.

Yelena was a lively child, intelligent, though Anne thought not at all well taught, and good-natured as long as she had her own way. But she lacked concentration, disliked anything that required prolonged effort or hard work; and though as yet there had been no confrontation between her and Anne – for lessons had not formally begun – Anne had no doubt from the gleam in those dark eyes that there would be something of a battle before she settled down to disciplined ways.

Natasha would not be under her tutelage for another two years yet, but Anne observed her with interest. She had thought Yelena was exaggerating when she said Natasha never spoke, but it was quite true – she not only never spoke, but never made any sound at all. The Countess said that she had cried lustily when she was born, and as a baby had made all the normal gurgling noises until she learned to walk. Then her self-imposed silence began. The Countess, at Fräulein Hoffnung's instigation, had her examined by doctors in Petersburg last winter, but they had said that there was nothing functionally wrong with the child, and she certainly seemed perfectly normal in every other way. Nyanka said that she would speak when she was ready, and the Countess agreed. Anne was surprised at her apparent unconcern, but it seemed to be genuine.

Natasha appeared to be happy and healthy: she played with her toys, listened to stories, pattered about after Nyanka or Yelena, and shared her sister's affinity for animals; but Anne thought her a strange little thing, and sometimes felt disturbed by that bright, watchful gaze of hers. It was too knowing for a little child, almost as though she were laughing inwardly at the adults she cared too little about to wish to communicate.

But if there was something odd about Natasha, there was also something odd about her mother. Anne saw a good deal of the Countess during that first fortnight when the Count was away: she ate all her meals with her, sat with her in the evenings, was shown around the house and taken for drives by her, and yet though they conversed in a far more friendly and informal manner than had been the case with Lady Murray, she could not feel she came any closer to the Countess than on the first day.

There was no apparent reserve: the Countess was uniformly kind and considerate, her manner gentle, her expression kindly. Yet Anne felt that she was dealing with a mask, a shape thrust forward to distract attention, not so much to present a false image, but to prevent an image from being detected. If there were a reality, it was deeply hidden, and sometimes when she spoke to her, and found herself regarded with that golden gaze, like the long, blank stare of a leopard, Anne wondered if there were anything underneath it at all.

She was not alone in finding the Countess strange, Anne discovered. During the two weeks, there were several courtesy calls paid by neighbouring families, and Anne was presented to the visitors, and greeted by them, in an open, warm, friendly manner that was balm to her Murray-bruised self-esteem. The Russian ladies came with their grown-up daughters and small sons and sat in the octagon room, drinking tea and chatting. They asked Anne about England and Paris and her adventures, asked after the Count rather wistfully, listened patiently to Yelena, begged Anne to play for them on the pianoforte, and praised her extravagantly when she obliged.

But she could feel their unease and noted the sidelong way they looked at the Countess, heard the unnatural note in their voices as they chatted to her, and the relief with which they turned to each other or to Anne. They were pleasant, kindly, ordinary matrons, concerned with their houses and husbands and children, with meals and domestics and fashions and marriages; probably they had too little imagination between them to know why, but the Countess Kirova made them feel uneasy.

Anne could see why the Count would have married her, why he loved her. She was beautiful in a remarkable and unique way, and mysterious, the sort of woman to intrigue a man, to make him want to possess her, as he might wish to own a rare and precious work of art. But she was also alien, and Anne wondered how genuine a love could be for something so utterly impenetrable, and how much it was a self-delusion, a fantasy. Anne remembered how he had spoken to her and looked at her, how close their minds had become during the five weeks of their journey to Russia, and she could not believe that he ever spoke to his Countess like that. Surely real love must be for like to like?

Anne remembered the soft glow of the Countess's eyes when she looked at her husband, his passionate greeting of her when he first arrived home, and faltered; but then she remembered also that exchange in the carriage about the serfs, when the Countess had failed to grasp what her husband was saying, and had revealed a shallowness of understanding which a man of his intellect must find daunting. The Count might love his Irina as he would love a beautiful animal, but surely he could not love her mind? In bed at night, alone with her thoughts, Anne felt that he could not, that his singling-out of her in Paris had been in response to a real need in himself; and she looked forward to his return from Petersburg with a guilty eagerness.

Chapter Seven

A rainy day meant there was no going out for a morning walk or drive. The children had already driven Nyanka to slapping-point, and Fräulein Hoffnung had a cold in the head, so in response to Yelena's urgings, Anne took her and Natasha down to the kitchen to make sweets.

The kitchens were on the ground floor under the white tower, a range of rooms connected by stone corridors, around a central chamber ruled over by Kerim. He was a short man, barrel-chested and slightly bow-legged, with a swarthy face, black oiled hair which hung about his neck in love-locks, and protuberant black eyes that shone as though they had been polished, and ran easily over into tears. Despite his Turkish appearance, he spoke French perfectly and with a French accent, and he took an instant liking to Anne the first time she was taken downstairs by the Countess to meet him.

'Ah, how well you speak French, *chère mademoiselle*, like a Frenchwoman! How good it is to hear after the butcherings these Russians make of it! We must converse often – such a pleasure! Come to my kitchen any time.'

Anne knew enough about bad-tempered, autocratic English cooks to accept this as the compliment which was intended. Kerim was remarkably good-humoured, and never seemed to mind having his territory invaded by the children, whom he greeted each time as though he had not seen them for weeks, with hugs, damp kisses, and large sighs.

'The darling little ones,' he would say moistly, 'how I love them! Fair as angels, and so sweet, so gentle! Ah, mademoiselle, if only things had been different!'

'What things, Kerim?' Anne asked, intrigued.

Kerim shook his head lugubriously. 'My life has been full of tragedy! If I were to tell you . . . But then, I would not break your heart, as mine has been broken.'

'But Kerim, what tragedy? What has happened to you?' Anne would ask every time.

And every time, Kerim would only say mysteriously, 'We are

not all made the same, mademoiselle. The good Lord knows why.'

Kerim, though Russian born of Turkish stock, was a Roman Catholic, which scandalised Nyanka, who thought Papists were servants of the Devil, corrupters of the true Faith, and astonishingly, intriguingly evil. It particularly fascinated her that, compared to her practice, Kerim crossed himself backwards, and when she visited with the children, she would try to provoke him into doing it so that she could watch. If that failed, she would use more direct methods, and usually finish by trying to persuade him to convert to the Orthodox faith.

'The faith of your fathers, Kerim!' she would say beguilingly. 'It's in your blood – surely you must feel it! Tradition, reverence, the old ways! Let me get Father Grigori to come to you tomorrow and talk to you.'

Kerim bore it all in silence, until Nyanka was driven through frustration to begin tugging at his sleeve; and then, more often than not, a childish slapping-match would break out, and they would finish by throwing handfuls of flour at each other, Kerim proving himself thereby far more Russian than French.

'Why did you become a Roman Catholic?' Anne asked him once.

'To honour Monsieur Bertin, my teacher,' Kerim said. 'No man could cook like that, unless the Grace of God were in him. What was good enough for my Master was good enough for me.'

With the Count away, and no entertainments in the offing, things were quiet in the kitchen, and Kerim was only too glad to set aside what he was doing and spend the morning making sweets. He enveloped the children in white aprons, tying the tapes with his own hands; set them on stools so that they could see; and made a batch of lemon drops – hard, almost transparent sweets made from boiled sugar-water flavoured with lemon juice. Fräulein Hoffnung was particularly addicted to lemon drops. Anne had discovered that her long-suffered pain was partly bad teeth, and partly severe digestive troubles, the one perhaps being connected with the other.

The sugar-boiling was too dangerous, in Kerim's view, for the children to do more than watch, but he allowed them to help make other things, like 'green roses', a Crimean sweet made of marzipan, and 'mountain', a sticky white confection which he said was a Turkish delicacy. They made sugar-plums, too, and candied almonds, which were set aside in a cool store for the dessert course of dinner. They finished by making a particular Russian favourite called *marmelad*, a sort of fruit jelly, pink or white with a hardish outside and a soft, almost liquid centre, which Anne could see one could easily grow too fond of.

They were happily occupied about these pleasant tasks, and Kerim was telling Anne about his early days in Moscow when he had cooked for the English Club in Arbat Square, and had just embarked on some more eye-rolling and hints about his tragedy when Nyanka came rushing in, greatly excited, to say that the master had arrived home, and began at once tweaking at the children's apron strings and patting at their hair.

Anne's heart gave a violent lurch of excitement and happiness, which shocked her, and she spent an unnecessary minute or two straightening Yelena's dress to give herself time to bring her thoughts back under control, while Yelena, frantic to run upstairs to see Papa, struggled like a bird under her hands. When Anne mounted the steps at last, she did so calmly and with a tranquil smile of welcome already prepared for her lips; but it was of no use. The Count was in the great hall, still in his driving-coat of white drab, while a smiling Vasky held his hat and gloves; the Countess stood beside him, her hands clasping and unclasping before her, and Yelena was bouncing up and down on the spot in order to release some of the intolerable pressure of excitement. As Anne appeared at the door, with Nyanka and Natasha behind her, the Count turned and looked at her with such an open, friendly, glad smile, that all her resolve melted like spring snow in the sun, and she could only smile back at him, with all her heart in her face.

'Miss Peters, there you are! How good it is to see you! Have you taken good care of everything while I was away? And there's my little *Nemetzka*! Come and kiss me, *doushenka*! Yelena Nikolayevna, you've grown two inches! Haven't you a kiss for me?' With Natasha in his arms, Yelena tugging at his elbow, and the Countess standing very close to him as though he gave out warmth like a fire, he moved towards the drawing-room, talking about Petersburg and his journey. Anne, well pleased with her share of the greeting, followed with the footman carrying his cloak bag.

'Petersburg was very hot and amazingly crowded. I don't know what everyone was doing there, when they ought to have been at their *dachas*, but it made it more pleasant for me, when I was not occupied at the court or with the minister,' the Count said, shedding his daughters and his coat and sitting down on the long sofa. 'The Kovalskis were there, and Uncle Petya Basarov, and the Poliakovs, just arrived and on their way to the country. They asked after you, Miss Peters, and I gave them a good report of your health and happiness. I hope I was right?'

Anne could only nod, still a little bemused at her happiness in seeing him again.

'Did you see the Empress?' the Countess asked.

'No, she was indisposed again, poor creature, but the letter from her mother will do her good. The family was at Orianenbaum, of course. I saw the Emperor and the Empress Dowager. They were eager to hear all about my visit to Karlsruhe – not that there was much to tell, but d'Enghien is a great favourite with them both.'

'And what did they say about the war with England?'

'The Tsar didn't say anything much about it. Of course, he is thoroughly disillusioned with Bonaparte, ever since he had himself made Consul-for-life, and he has always had a passionate admiration for everything English.'

Anne was intrigued. 'I didn't know that your Emperor – ' she began.

'Oh yes,' the Count nodded. 'I think in his heart he would rather like to see a parliamentary system like yours in Russia – though with the power balanced a little more in favour of the throne. Certainly there are many senior ministers around him who would like us to move in that direction, and Alexander knows that the administrative apparatus is desperately in need of reshaping. He is not an autocrat by nature. He was brought up by his grandmother, the great Catherine, and she had liberal principles. She even flirted with republicanism at one time, until the revolution in France disenchanted her. She had Alexander educated the same way – he read Rousseau in his youth, you know,' he added with a smile at Anne.

'But Russia could never be a republic, Nikolai,' the Countess said, frowning.

'Of course not, Irushka – no-one suggested it,' the Count said patiently. 'Everything that has happened in France has tended to make the Tsar and his ministers see the dangers involved in too much reform; yet something must be done to revise our governmental system. So they turn more and more away from France and towards England.'

'Then, do you think that Russia will enter the war on England's side?' Anne asked tentatively.

'It depends very much on what Bonaparte does next. The war is not Russia's war, as yet, and God knows we can't afford to get involved. But the Tsar is still young for his age, and idealistic, and if anything should happen to provoke him . . . The decision, you see, would be entirely his. However, for the moment at least, we shall remain neutral. And now, from politics to more important matters! I am home again, and ready to be amused. We must have a dinner, Irushka, and show Miss Peters what Schwartzenturm looks like *en grande tenue*. I should like to ask the Poliakovs, and who else? The Tchaikovskys are in the country, are they not?'

'Yes, and the Tiranovs.'

'And how would it be if we asked Shoora and Vsevka to come and stay?'

'Oh yes, Papa!' Yelena said at once. 'And Kira and Vanya too!'

'Of course, *doushka*,' the Count said, and then, to Anne, 'My younger sister, Alexandra, and her husband, who live in Moscow. They have two children, a son Ivan, and the daughter Kira, who is Lolya's great friend.'

'Yes, she mentioned her the day I arrived,' Anne said. 'The one who is going to be an opera singer.'

'That's right,' the Count laughed. 'Kira always seems to have some unsuitable ambition. We've always taken it in turn to visit each other but I've been away so much lately, I expect we've got out of sequence. Vsevka's family – the Danilovs – are the great family of armament makers. Vsevka inherited a big factory in Tula, about a hundred miles from Moscow, and another in Kiev. He'll be one person who does hope Russia will go to war with France!'

Yelena had been eyeing the cloak-bag all this time, and making a very noble attempt to possess her soul in patience, but now her restraint snapped, and she pressed her father's arm and said, 'Did you bring me a present, Papa? You always bring me something from Petersburg.'

'Yes, I did, little Avarice. I brought presents for everyone, and you shall have yours right away. Oh, by the way, Miss Peters, I brought you some very nice barathea for your riding habit. Vasky will send it up to your room. I hope you like the colour – here is a sample of it.'

He brought out of his bag a small sample square and gave it to her. It was a very dark red, between wine and terracotta, which Anne saw at once would suit her perfectly. She felt warm with gratitude, not only for the kindness, but for the personal quality of it, which made it doubly valuable.

'It's perfect,' she said. 'I don't know how to thank you, sir!'

'Then don't,' he said genially. 'As I said before, you must have something to ride in. It's English cloth, by the way. Isn't that appropriate?'

'I have the pattern upstairs which was used for my habit,' the Countess said in her soft voice. 'I'm sure you will be able to adapt it for yourself. If you do the cutting-out yourself, we can have Marya Petrovna make it up for you.'

'You are most kind, madame,' Anne said, and sat stroking the sample square with thoughtful fingers as she watched Yelena and Natasha attack the presents the Count was bringing out for them from his apparently bottomless bag.

The following day dawned fine, and the whole family went on a picnic. They took the barouche, with Castor and Pollux to draw it, and the calèche with Limonchik between the shafts.

'Bring your sketching-book,' the Count advised Anne cheerfully. 'We are going to the waterfall, our favourite picnic place, and you'll find it well worth the effort of putting pencil to paper.'

It was quite a caravan which set off. The Count drove the barouche himself with Yelena on the box beside him, anxious to take the reins whenever he would relinquish them to her, and Fräulein Hoffnung, Nyanka, and Natasha inside. The Countess drove Anne in the calèche, and promised to teach her to drive by the time they reached the picnic place.

'It is really very easy,' she said, 'and Limonchik knows his business so well, anyone could drive him.'

Third in the procession came a *kibitka* driven by Morkin, containing the food hampers, plates and glasses and knives and forks, rugs to sit on, a table with folding legs from which to serve the food, four servants to attend them, food for them, and all the other things such as parasols, shawls, books, towels, and a balalaika, which anyone was likely to need.

They drove in the direction of the wooded high ground that Anne had seen from the terrace, but which was too far away for her to have visited yet. As they came nearer, she could see that it was an outcrop, sloping and turfed in some places, but with bare, sheer faces like low cliffs in others. Various shrubs and trees grew on the slopes, and at the top, where it became a plateau, the woodland began. It was not very high, not more than about fifty feet at its highest, but in the predominantly level land all around, it stood out.

The waterfall they were aiming for was where a small stream tumbled about twenty feet down one of the sheer faces, making a pool at the bottom before it again became a stream, running down eventually to join the wider stream on which the granary and distillery were built. By the pool itself there was a broad, grassy lawn of close turf, and a scattering of birch, hazel and alder which gradually thickened into denser, darker woods beyond.

'It's a pretty place, isn't it?' said the Countess as Anne, who had taken over the reins, drew the calèche to a halt behind the barouche. 'There are lovely orchids at this time of year, and wild clematis, and in the spring, primroses – you never saw so many – '

'And don't forget the *zemlyanika*,' said the Count, coming to hand his wife down. 'Wild strawberries, Miss Peters. Tiny and scented, and they make the best jam of all. Aren't you glad I made you bring your pencils?'

'Yes, very,' Anne said, accepting his hand in her turn.

Yelena was bursting with energy, and wanted to show Anne everything, and insisted that she must see the waterfall from above as well as from below. There was a rough path leading up the broken slope to the side of the waterfall, and Anne regarded it doubtfully, for it looked as though it would be something of a scramble. Yelena might do it easily on all fours, but that would be rather beyond a grown woman's dignity.

'Oh you must come, you must!' Yelena cried passionately. 'Everyone has to see it from the top. Papa, tell her she must.'

The Count, seeing the problem, said genially, 'I think you might attempt it, Miss Peters, with a little help. There are only two difficult places, and if I were to go first, I could pull you up.'

Anne glanced at the Countess, who said placidly, 'Do go, if you wish. I am quite content just to sit here.'

'We'll wave to you from the top, Mamochka,' Yelena promised generously, taking it as settled. She scampered off, and Anne and the Count followed more soberly.

'It is wonderful to see the freedom of movement children have today,' the Count remarked, watching his daughter with an indulgent smile. 'When my sisters were Lolya's age, they wore stiff brocade gowns, with boned bodices and hoops in the skirts. They couldn't have climbed up that hill, even if they had been allowed to. But now, with just a muslin gown and thin petticoats . . . '

'Yes,' said Anne. 'Even in my own childhood, I remember grown-up ladies wearing panniers and false rumps. It surprises me to think how much they managed to do, with such handicaps. Even getting into a carriage must have been quite an achievement.'

The path was easy enough, with the Count's strong hand to pull her upwards and steady her, and they were soon at the top.

'There, look, you can see the house. It looks very English from here, doesn't it? And over there, in the trees, you can just see a chimney – no there! Do you see it now? That's the distillery.'

'And how far does your estate go?' Anne asked, looking out over the plain.

'As far as the eye can see – that is what one should answer to such a question, isn't it, Anna Petrovna?' the Count teased. 'Do you know,' he added musingly, 'the thing that has always troubled me about the devil tempting Our Lord on the high place, was that he could not have offered Him all the kingdoms of the earth, unless they were his to give.'

'Deep thoughts, sir,' she said, amused, and turned her head to look at him. He was close beside her, and she had to tilt her head upwards to see his face. He was smiling that closed-mouthed, enigmatic smile she had come to know so well. He had left off his hat, and the breeze ruffled the ends of his silken hair which lay across his forehead. A cloud shadow followed the breeze, and the sun, coming after, lay across his smooth tan skin like butter. His green-gold eyes looked directly into hers, as if there were no distance between them. Everything seemed to Anne to pause a moment, and it was as if in that moment she received through all her senses a complete and exact knowledge of him, of everything he was, the essential core of him – perhaps his soul. She was alive to him, dangerously, sensitively, and she felt that he was aware of her in the same way.

It was a perilous instant, lasting only a breath of time, leaving her heart racing too fast, as Yelena broke the bubble by demanding, 'Why did you call her that, Papa? Why did you call her Anna Petrovna?'

The Count turned his head away, and Anne felt as though his gaze had had to be ripped away from her. 'That's what Miss Peters' name is in Russian, *galubchik*. You can work that out for yourself.'

'But she *isn't* Russian,' Yelena objected with the passionate logic of the child. 'So why do you call her a Russian name?'

He moved from Anne's side, and she felt her skin grow cold with his absence. 'If she is going to live in Russia from now on, she will become a Russian, or nearly so. Why, have you some objection?'

'I think it's silly,' Yelena said firmly.

'Do you, indeed?' the Count demanded, reaching out hands to tickle her, and she shrieked and dodged away from him. A lively chase ensued in and out of the bushes which decorated the cliff top. Anne stood where she was, listening to Yelena's shrieks of excited laughter, and looking down thoughtfully at the lawn below, where the Countess, in rose-pink muslin with a white, Chinese silk shawl embroidered with almond-blossom and butterflies, was sitting on a rug with Natasha beside her. Both seemed to be quite immobile, occupied with nothing more than gazing serenely before them, complete in themselves, needing nothing and no-one.

A little later the three climbers went back down the path, the Count going first with Yelena riding him pick-a-back, and turning at each steep place to hold his hand up to Anne. The strong, dry palm and long fingers folded round hers each time with an appalling feeling of familiarity, and their linked hands seemed a channel through which some vital force flowed. Him, and me, and Yelena, her bemused brain murmured to her: man, woman and child. What would it be like to be here with them as of right, to be in reality what she now only appeared to be, the third person of that trinity?

'I hope you're hungry, Anna Petrovna,' the Count said as they regained level ground. 'Kerim's picnics are unsurpassable. I hope that exercise will have whet your appetite sufficiently.'

'That's not her *name*, Papa,' Yelena objected sternly, wriggling to get down. 'It's Mademoiselle Peters.'

'Is it indeed, little piker?' he said in English. 'I'll race you back to Mama. One, two, three!'

How much did he feel? Anne brooded on the question all day, as she watched the children splashing naked in the pool. They all sat around together eating the superb food that Kerim had packed into the baskets: cold roast fowl, and meat pies, and patés, and spiced sausage, and cake, and fruit. Did I imagine the whole thing? she asked herself as she sketched the scene, the pool and the waterfall, and the semi-somnolent people: Fräulein Hoffnung, in a thick, woollen shawl, reading; Nyanka knitting with her eyes shut; the Countess twirling her parasol on her shoulder, very slowly, first this way, then that; Natasha sitting on her supine father's up-bent knees, balancing above him with her hands on his and laughing silently at him.

What must I do about it? she asked herself unhappily as she walked with Yelena in the fringes of the wood, hoping to improve the hour by telling her the English names of flowers and trees, and learning from her, where she knew them, the Russian. The sunny day seemed endless, and the longer it went on, the more bemused she grew, like a sun-dazzled bee on a hot window sill, with no answers for anything, and a growing sense of unreality, so that she began to think she had dreamed everything and was dreaming still.

The servants had got the samovar going at a little distance, and tea was preparing. To eat with it there were little cakes and soft biscuits with raisins in them, and a box of the *marmelad* they had made yesterday.

'We had better be going back soon,' the Countess said eventually, the sun gilding her eyelashes and the soft curls on her forehead. 'The children will be very tired. It's so easy to forget the hour at this time of the year.'

'I was thinking, *doushenka*,' the Count said, sipping his tea, 'that it might be a good opportunity to show Miss Peters the peasant village. She ought to see it once, as part of her education.'

'It's much too far, Nikolasha,' the Countess said unemphatically. 'All the way back to the house, and then another seven or eight versts.'

'I don't mean that one,' he said. 'I mean the one here, on the other side of this wood. If I take her in the calèche, we can drive by the short-cut through the wood, and it's hardly any distance at all. We won't stay long, and if Limonchik puts his feet down smartly, we'll be back almost as soon as you.'

'Just as you please,' the Countess said indifferently. 'But who is to drive the barouche?'

'Morkin, of course, and Stefan can drive the *kibitka*. Would you like to see a peasant village, Miss Peters?'

'Very much, sir,' Anne said, striving to keep her voice even. 'If it will not inconvenience anyone.'

'Of course not. Nyanka and Fräulein Hoffnung can take charge of the children, and we'll be back in time for supper.'

Anne determinedly closed her mind to speculation as she took her place beside the Count in the calèche. It was a tight fit, and he chuckled, 'What a child's plaything of a carriage this is! It's a good job you are so slender. Have you room enough there? Are you able to breathe?'

The sun was much lower, and the air was beginning to cool, and Limonchik, revived after his long sleep in the shade of a tree, trotted briskly with his chocolate-coloured ears pricked, the harness jumping and slapping against his round yellow rump as it bobbed along in front of them. They turned off the track which led home, somewhat to Limonchik's surprise, and onto a narrow path into the wood, and after driving for about ten minutes between the dark trees, they came out at the other side quite suddenly into the slanting afternoon sunshine. The track widened out, leading gently downhill, and at the foot of the slope was the village. The Count halted the calèche half way down, so that Anne could see it all spread out before her.

It was built in linear fashion along either side of the wide earth track, a series of large, stout-looking log houses, with very steep roofs and long, overhanging eaves. Some had dovecotes built into the roof, and pigeons, gilded by the afternoon light, preened and strutted along the roof-tree, cut out against the sky like fantastic decorations. Some of the huts were built with the living quarters raised up and a low beast-shed taking up the ground floor, while others had separate barns and hen-houses attached.

'The huts are called *izby* in Russian,' the Count said. 'They may be a little rough, but they are snug and dry, and when one thinks of the way peasants live in some parts of Europe . . . The two big buildings at the end are the *kabak*, which you know about, and the bath-house – the *bania*. Everyone goes there on a Saturday afternoon to bathe and put on clean linen, so that they are all clean and decent for the Sabbath. For the rest of the week, I'm afraid, they do very little washing.'

Each *izba* had a shade tree or two in front of it, a fuel stack neatly built to shed the rain, and a vegetable patch behind where Anne could see cabbages and what looked like cucumbers growing in neat, well-hoed rows. There were hens scratching about, and small children playing in the dust, a dog or two lying in the sun, and a long-horned, red-and-white cow tethered to a tree outside one house. Half-way down the street was a well with a surrounding wall built of logs, and a wooden crane for raising the water. Most of the activity in the village seemed centred on it, for the women going to and from it with pairs of buckets on long poles across their shoulders were the only adults in view.

'The men will still be out in the fields,' the Count said, flicking a horsefly from Limonchik's flank with his whip-stock. 'They work very long hours at this time of year. The growing season is so short, you see: they have to take two crops off the land between the thaw in May and the frost in October, five or six months at the most. In August, when they have to harvest the oats and plant out the rye, and till their own strips and their landlord's all at the same time, they sometimes work twenty hours a day.'

'I've noticed all the fields are unenclosed,' Anne said. 'We hardly ever see that at home now.'

'We still work the old three-field system – spring seeds, winter seeds, and fallow – which I know you've long abandoned in England,' the Count said ruefully. 'When I visited England on my Grand Tour, I made a particular study of farming methods, and came back full of youthful enthusiasm to improve the land and introduce modern practices. I came into my father's estates when I was a young man, you see, and was eager to make my mark and bring my part of Russia, at least, into the eighteenth century.'

'And didn't you?'

'No. I might have all the enthusiasm in the world, but the peasants can't bear any interference with their ways. They have their routines and traditions, and if anyone tries to change them, they mutter and grumble, and sometimes even take revenge by firing a rick or breaking windows.'

'Even if the changes are for their own good?' Anne said.

'Oh yes. They just don't like to be meddled with. Ask them to plough the soil an inch more deeply, or offer to drain a marshy field for them, and they start to mutter "He is not a good master to us. He torments us. He meddles and oppresses us."'

'How silly – and infuriating for you, too,' Anne said, 'if it prevents you from improving the land.'

'I suppose there's some excuse for them in the shortness of the growing season and the precariousness of their living. One false step, one spell of inclement weather, one mistake, and they face very short commons, perhaps even starvation next winter. It's hardly surprising they aren't tempted to experiment. The margin is too small.'

'But if you explained it to them – '

'They aren't logical thinkers, like us. They are a strange people, you know, stubborn and ignorant and childlike – full of fantasies and visions and magic, and strange beliefs.'

'Strange beliefs?'

'Well, for instance, they believe that all the land in Russia really belongs to them. It seems to date from the time Emperor Peter gave us – the *dvoriane* – our liberties in the charter of 1762, freeing us from compulsory state service. For some reason the peasants believed that the Emperor made another charter at the same time, turning over all the land to them, but that we repressed it and threw him into jail. For years after his death, they went on believing that he was alive and in hiding – some of them believe it still – and that one day he, or his successor on the imperial throne, will get on with dividing up the land amongst them.' He looked at her and smiled. 'They insist on believing that the land belongs to them, and that they belong to us, whereas it is just the other way about: they belong to the land, and the land is ours.'

Anne tried this sentence over once or twice before she could grasp the sense of it, while the Count shook the reins and sent Limonchik on down the slope, turning to the right at the foot of it onto another track. It ran away from the village with oat fields to the left and the

110

pine woods to the right, and, judging by the increased eagerness of the pony's steps, led towards home.

'Would you like to take the reins?' the Count asked. 'Driving is only a matter of practice, you know. There is no mystery to it.'

Anne took over the reins, and the Count took a little trouble with her, correcting the tension and the way she held the whip, and then they went on in silence for a while, with no sound but the muted, rhythmic thud-thud of Limonchik's hooves on the dry track, and the jingling of his harness, and the long, slow whisper of the wind through the ripening oats. Where the woods came to an end, the track joined up with the main road again, and Limonchik turned without help from Anne to the right, trotting on with his ears sharply towards the north, where the blueness of the sky had taken on the mysterious, caressing tone of evening, and one white star shone low and steady above his brow-band.

'It wasn't only to see the village that I wanted you to come with me in the calèche,' the Count said suddenly. Anne said nothing, but waited, half terrified, for what he might be going to say, acutely aware of his physical closeness to her, the small movement of his body as he breathed. She kept her eyes fixed on her hands, and the flat leather ribbons of the reins flowing tautly away from them, and the blurred, jogging yellow rump in front of her; but she could see his face as clearly as if she were looking at it, the long nose and jaw, the curving, cat-smile of the mouth, and the shining hazel eyes.

His hands came into her vision, closed over hers, and took the tension of the reins, drawing back on the eager pony's mouth until the strong thud-thud faltered and broke down into the uneven thud-ub-thud-ub of a walk. The round golden rump ceased to blur, and Anne turned her head slowly, as if it hurt, to look at him.

'When I spoke of the peasants a while ago, and their fantasies and visions and magic . . . it isn't just the peasants, you see. It's in all of us. We all see visions. There's a magic in Russia that we breathe in all the time. We live our lives half drunk with it, with the beauty of it, the *prostor* all around us, drunk with air and sky, drunk with the incense and candlelight of the mass, with the ecstasy of snow in the winter – oh, more different colours and textures of white and blue than you can possibly imagine! And the air so cold and clean it's like vodka, burning and intoxicating! And in the summer, here in the north, there are what we call the White Nights, when the twilight goes on and on until it meets the dawn, and it never gets dark, and the air is so blue and shining you could drink it! That's what I wanted you to see, Anna Petrovna – the twilight, the long northern twilight.'

She looked at him, and felt things in her moved and altered, that could never be put back in place.

'You have been in Russia only a little while, but today I watched you, and I felt sure that you were beginning to feel the magic, and I wanted to make sure of it. I do so want you to love Russia.'

'Yes,' she said, and the Count seemed to accept this as sufficient answer to all he had said. His hands, still over hers on the reins, closed a little, in a pressure affectionate, glad, a little triumphant, and his smile intensified in his eyes and on his lips. How then could she feel so sad? she wondered distantly. The feeling that he had for her was something any woman ought to be glad of, a warm affection based on knowledge, sympathy and respect; it was, moreover, the only kind of feeling she could have allowed herself to receive from him, a married man, and her employer. She ought to delight in his good opinion and personal liking. She *did* delight in it. It was just that it made something inside her want to lie down and howl.

She must speak. 'I do love Russia,' she said. 'And I am so very, very grateful to you for bringing me here, and for taking such care of me. I know I shall be happy in Russia, and with your children, and with – ' Her throat closed up. She tried again. 'I like my Russian name, too,' she said unevenly.

He released her hands. 'Do you?' he said happily. 'I think it is much prettier than Miss Peters. In Russian it is very polite to call someone by name and patronymic like that,' he added quickly. 'Polite, but friendly too. Shall I call you Anna Petrovna all the time?'

'Yes, please do,' she said.

The pony walked steadily on, along the white dust-track, his left side rosy and gilded from the last, low sunlight. To the right the tall oats whispered sleepily, their green-gold heads closing up in the distance into a gently-shifting sea, slicked with mysterious violet shadows, reaching away to where the wooded high ground rose like dark cliffs into the velvet eastern sky. And the evening lengthened all around them, as if, Anne thought, light were a new dimension half way between space and time; as if it were some new element between air and water, blue and pellucid, through which they swam like birds.

They were late back to the house. Yelena had refused to go to bed until her father came home, and when he arrived, demanded to be allowed to stay up to supper. Her father, always indulgent, agreed, but supper was a long time being prepared, and it soon became clear that the child was over-tired and over-excited. She became more noisy and tiresome and rude until Anne could bear it no longer and took matters into her own hands, saying Yelena must go to bed at once. Neither of the adult Kirovs made any objection.

'You're her governess – you know best,' the Count said easily, looking up from the cellar book which he had sent for, to choose some wine appropriate to what he regarded as a special, celebratory evening. 'Go with Anna Petrovna, *galubchik*. You're very tired.'

Anne took the child's hand, but she snatched it back and began running round and round the room. Anne looked towards the Count, but he had evidently turned the situation over to her, so she felt it was up to her to be firm. She caught Yelena on one of her circuits, closed her fingers firmly round the small wrist, and towed her screaming out of the room.

Out in the hall she shook Yelena sharply and said, 'Stop that noise this instant!'

'I won't go to bed, I won't!' Yelena shrieked.

'If you don't walk up the stairs quietly with me now, I shall carry you over my shoulder. Remember who you are, Yelena Nikolayevna,' Anne said quietly, but with all the determination she could muster. Yelena's lip thrust out rebelliously, but she thought of the indignity of such a proceeding, and consented to trail along unwillingly at Anne's side. At the door of the nursery, Anne passed the child over to the care of Nyanka, who summed up the situation in an instant, clucked and tutted and addressed Yelena in soothing Russian phrases, and gave Anne a nod over her head of approval and dismissal.

Supper was finally served. The Countess seemed more than usually silent, and Anne had nothing to say, only sipped the fragrant, flowery white wine the Count had chosen, as if in a reverie. All the conversation was between the Count and Fräulein Hoffnung, who discussed the wines of the Rhineland knowledgeably and, in her case, with nostalgia. When the lamps were lit and the table cleared, the latter three went out onto the terrace while the Countess played pensively on the pianoforte. The air was scented with white summer jasmine, and the notes from the piano dropped into the quietness like small pebbles into a clear pool. The Count lit a cigar, and soft brown moths fluttered out of the dimness and pattered against the drawing-room windows.

Anne stood at the balustrade, her forearms resting against the cold stone. The long twilight seemed to reverberate against the memory like faint music, as if there had been some time immeasurably long ago when she had stood like this, gazing into the luminous eastern darkness, feeling the blue air brush against her skin like warm silk, while the violet shadows of bats flickered shrieking back and forth after insects, half-seen, half-heard.

The Count was near, leaning in the same attitude and smoking his cigar; companionably silent, not touching, and yet connected somehow. Anne felt everything in her, all the thoughts and feelings of the day, and of weeks past, melting and merging together, distilling out inside her towards some single clear drop of perfect experience. All of life, she thought, was a striving towards the place where knowledge was perfectly matched by understanding, where a thing seen or done was felt and known with every particle of the self. That place seemed immeasurably far off, and yet not foreign to her, as if she had known it before, and would recognise it when she came to it, as she would recognise her childhood home.

And he was part of it. She didn't understand how or why; perhaps he was simply another traveller along the same road, someone with whom to share the journey; or perhaps he was more, a guide, or native interpreter. Perhaps, in some strange way, he was part of the journey itself. She didn't know, but she felt just then that he was aware of the connection between them, and was at ease with it.

As if he heard her thoughts, the Count turned his head, and they both smiled, the serene and contented smile of two people at peace with themselves and with each other. Anne was aware even then that such moments of equilibrium come rarely, and that they do not last. Tomorrow, she thought, I shall be as confused and fallible and human and unhappy as everyone else; but as such moments inevitably pass, they always come again. The godlike, untroubled sensation expanded on the warm air, and enclosed the two people in a bubble which seemed both fragile and indestructible.

Chapter Eight

Now the normal routine of life began for Anne. There were lessons with Yelena in the little schoolroom, although at first it was so difficult to make her concentrate, that it was sometimes easier to move her from place to place and construct the lesson around some object or aspect of the house. She had never been obliged to work hard at anything, and, if pressed, grew either sulky or rebellious. She had not yet fully accepted Anne, and, having never been subjected to discipline, was doubly resentful at Anne's attempts to impose it. Anne knew there were fearful battles ahead of them. She was determined to have obedience, but she did not want to crush Yelena's bubbling high spirits, which were one of her most attractive features.

There were lessons on the pianoforte, too, and sketching-lessons, mostly given out of doors when Yelena grew too restless to be kept in the schoolroom any longer, and Fräulein Hoffnung took her for an hour each day to teach German and history, which allowed Anne time to do other things: cutting out her riding habit, doing her own piano practice, and studying Russian, in which she was determined to be proficient as soon as possible, for many of the servants spoke no other language. Nyanka's attitude towards her softened perceptibly every time she acquired a new word, and the more Anne tried to speak Russian, the more kindly Nyanka consented to address her in French.

She did not yet teach Natasha, although sometimes, to accustom her to the idea of education, Nyanka would bring her to sit in the schoolroom during one of Yelena's lessons. Nyanka would sit in the corner, vastly overspilling a little schoolroom chair, and get on with her knitting or sewing, while Natasha sat on the floor at her feet with some doll or toy to keep her occupied. With Natasha there was never any cause to complain about noise: even when pushing a wheeled elephant back and forth across the waxed wooden floor, evidently engaged in some imaginary adventure, she made no sound, though her lips sometimes moved as if in commentary. After the first few visits, Anne noticed, to her amusement, that Natasha would sit her doll up and give it lessons, copying Anne's gestures and making the doll go through Yelena's motions. Every now and then the curly head would lift and the amber eyes would regard her solemnly and carefully for a few moments rather like a portrait painter referring to his subject. Anne did her best not to be unnerved by this minutely noticing gaze, and wondered how she would cope with it when she actually had to teach Natasha.

Every morning, unless it rained, Anne took both children out for a walk, accompanied either by Nyanka or Tanya, or more often by Fräulein Hoffnung. Anne grew to like the elderly governess. Though her education was narrow, she had a native shrewdness, and a great deal of experience of children on which Anne could draw when puzzled. Her conversation was often amusing, full of strange turns of phrase, words of wisdom, quaint adages, and English proverbs imperfectly remembered. She was patient and good, though rather slow, and Anne observed with inner amusement and understanding how Yelena was sometimes driven through frustration to torment her, and then felt guilty afterwards because she was so kind.

The daily walk was usually, by request, to the red stables and the farm buildings. The dairy was a favourite haunt – both children loved to watch the cows being milked, or the cheese being turned out – and they usually finished up at Marya Petrovna's, to stroke the pig and hear a story. The old lady had a fund of Russian folk-tales and fairy-tales, usually involving talking animals and retribution by the world of Nature on human beings who thought too well of themselves. The children could never have enough of these, and would sit at her feet open-mouthed with fascination, while her nimble fingers drew the embroidery silk back and forth, or flashed amongst the lace bobbins as though they were weaving the story right there before their eyes.

With Marya Petrovna's professional touch in the making-up, Anne's riding habit was soon ready, and the Countess donated a smart hat with a veil, hardly used, from her extensive wardrobe. Looking in the mirror the first time she tried them on, Anne saw herself with new eyes. I look almost pretty, she thought. The colour was perfect for her, and together with the smart cut of the habit made her appear striking, where before she had always felt herself to be pleasing enough, but insignificant.

The Count provided her with a bay mare called Grafina, who had pleasant paces and a good mouth, and thus mounted she took out Yelena, riding astride on Tigu, one of the Tibetan ponies, or sometimes accompanied the Countess on the beautiful chestnut Iskra, whose name meant 'Flame'. The Countess adored her mare with a passion she expressed with more than usual emphasis, and the two were in obvious sympathy with each other. The Countess rode well, and with unexpected boldness. She seemed quite a different person out on a horse, and Fräulein Hoffnung said that this was because she was from the Caucasus, where children learned to ride before they could walk.

'They are great horsemen, the hill people,' she said. 'Madame rides like a cyclops, like all her family. They're great horse-breeders, too. Iskra is a Karabakh – their special breed, famed all over Russia for swiftness and beauty. I don't know much about these things, but I do know that Karabakhs can cost anything up to eight hundred roubles.'

On Sunday mornings, when the family went to mass, Anne would sometimes take her work and go and sit with Fräulein Hoffnung in her sitting room, and from the talks they had at those times, Anne learned a good deal about Russia, and about the family's history. The Kirovs were the third family Fräulein Hoffnung had worked for, although she had been with them for most of her life. She had been governess, and then chaperone to the Count's sisters, until he had married and produced children of his own, when she had transferred to his service. Thus she had known the Count since his boyhood, and, a little guiltily, Anne encouraged her to talk about him. Any detail of the Count's life, past or present, was fascinating to her.

'He was the sweetest-tempered child I ever knew,' Fräulein Hoffnung said. 'His own son is the same, my dear little Sergei – not so little now, I suppose, though I can hardly think of him at cadet school when it seems only yesterday that I was watching him take his first steps. But he is the same, sweet-tempered boy his father was. It often works that way, you know – the apple tree grows apples, and the thorn tree thorns.'

'And when Sergei is not at school, does he come here?'

'He visits from time to time, but he lives mostly with his grandmother, the Count's mother. She is very fond of him and likes to have him with her. Grandmother-hunger, we call it. Of course, he has his cousins near-by in Moscow, but I sometimes think it is a pity he should not see more of his sisters – and his new mother, too. But the Dowager Countess is a very determined woman, and it's not to be supposed . . . It was she who chose the Count's first wife for him, Sergei's and Lolya's mother, and she was very fond of her, so it's hardly surprising that she wants to keep Sergei with her, to remind her.'

She sighed and relapsed into a contemplative silence. There seemed to be several intriguing hints here about the family's relationships, but Anne did not yet know her colleague well enough to judge how she would react to probing on such matters. Fräulein Hoffnung was fiercely loyal to the Kirovs, and if there were some question of divided loyalties, she might not like to have to voice them. After a while, to get back onto level ground, Anne asked her if the Kirovs were particularly kind and generous, or whether the kind of treatment she had received were the general rule in Russia.

'Ah, Miss Peters,' Fräulein Hoffnung said, putting down her work to clasp her thin, age-freckled hands at her breast, 'since I first came to Russia forty years ago, I have met with nothing but kindness and respect everywhere I went! Always I ate with the family, not just when they were alone, but on the grandest occasions; taken to the ballet and the opera, to balls; given such presents! *Ach, das is doch ausgezeichnet!* Everywhere, I was welcomed. That is the Russian character, to make one welcome. I cannot begin to tell you!' She reached into her reticule for a handkerchief to dab at the corner of her eye.

'So it isn't just the Count and Countess?' Anne said.

'Ach, no! I could have been married once, you know,' she said, nodding her head significantly. 'A young man of very good family addressed me – this was when I was much younger, of course – and not only did the Count – the present Count's father, you understand – give his complete blessing, but the young man's family set aside all consideration of a dowry. Where else in Europe would you meet with such generosity?'

'Why didn't you marry him?' Anne wanted to know.

Fräulein Hoffnung drew a deep sigh and picked up her work again. 'Ah, my dear, I couldn't leave my young ladies, dear Annushka and dearest Shoora! When a woman becomes a governess, she gives up all thoughts of love and marriage.'

The crisis of discipline with Yelena was not long in coming. One evening the Tchaikovskys came for cards and supper, bringing with them their grown-up son and daughter, Vassili – or Basil, as he preferred to be called – and Olga. The young Tchaikovskys were the leaders of the smart and fashionable younger set, and Anne had heard so many tales of them that she had been quite nervous about meeting them. They were talked of as inseparables going everywhere together, and despite Basil's being nearly thirty, and Olga twenty-seven, they firmly refused to get married, each declaring that no-one they had met even came near to the other's standards of beauty and intelligence. They had large allowances, and divided their time between Moscow and the newly-fashionable Crimea, from which they had just returned after visiting an aunt and uncle of whom they had expectations.

As so often in life, Anne found the reality less daunting than the reputation. The young people were expensively dressed in the 'high

French' style that was fashionable amongst the wealthy, and despite the difference of their ages and sexes, they looked remarkably alike: both tall and slender, with dark, high-nosed faces, thick black hair, and rather bulging, pale-green eyes, like translucent, ripe grapes. They had the air of being handsome, which probably, Anne reflected, served rather better than the reality; and while they spoke with a great deal of self-assurance, neither, to her notice, said anything either very clever or very original.

The Countess was clearly daunted by them, and their parents intensely proud of them. The Count, with his most inscrutable smile, encouraged them to talk, laugh, and give their opinions more and more freely as the evening went on, occasionally catching Anne's eye with a look of unspeakable innocence. It was well for her self-esteem that he did, for in the young Tchaikovskys she met for the first time in Russia something of the attitude she had grown accustomed to in England. Olga looked her over once sharply on being introduced and dismissed her as beneath her notice, and thereafter never spoke to or looked at her again the whole evening, while Basil looked down the neck of her gown as he bowed over her hand, and each time she spoke, used the opportunity to ogle her in a manner Anne thought both lascivious and patronising, as if she ought to be grateful to be thought worth leering at.

Her self-esteem suffered more that evening, however, through Yelena's behaviour. She had hoped that she was beginning to work some good on her pupil, but Yelena grew more and more excited as the evening wore on: she interrupted the conversation, swung on the furniture, knocked things over, and snatched rudely at anything to eat that appeared. Anne's remonstrances served only to provoke her to worse behaviour, and when even old Madame Tchaikovskova's patience was fractured by Yelena's knocking over her glass of wine for the second time, Anne could restrain herself no longer, and swept Yelena out of the room before she had time to resist.

Yelena bellowed, fought, and bit all the way up the stairs, and it took both Anne and Nyanka to detach her from the door-frame of the nursery, where she clung with both hands, howling with rage. Once she was inside, Nyanka gripped her charge round the waist with an arm like a bolster, summoned Tanya's assistance, and dismissed Anne with a jerk of the head. Seeing the red glare that Yelena was directing towards her, Anne thought the child would probably calm down more quickly if she went away and took her leave with haste and relief.

The rest of the evening in the drawing-room passed quietly, and Anne had put the incident from her mind by the time she went up to bed. In her chamber she washed her face, cleaned her teeth, took off her clothes and put on her nightgown, all by the faint but sufficient light of the white night outside. She climbed into bed, and jumped out again much more quickly than she got in: her bed was wet. Lighting her candle, she held it close, and saw that a large patch in the centre was thoroughly soaked, as though water had been poured over it. In a moment of complete bewilderment, she stared up at the ceiling, and then down at the floor; and then noticed a trail of spots of water which, though they had dried out already on this warm night, had left whitish marks on the waxed floor.

Grimly, she put on her wrapper and, candle in hand, followed the trail out of the door and down the passage, already guessing what had happened – knowing it would lead to the nursery and to Yelena's wash-stand pitcher, now standing empty. The nursery rumbled gently to Nyanka's snoring. Anne padded softly over to Yelena's bed and looked at the face against the pillows grimly sleeping, the eyelashes fluttering in their determination not to be tricked into looking.

'Enough,' she said grimly. 'Get up, Yelena Nikolayevna. You are coming with me. Get up, up, up!' And she whipped the covers off with one hand. Yelena, exposed to the night air, jerked together like a hedgehog rolling up, opened her eyes and looked at Anne with a mixture of apprehension and defiance. 'Up,' said Anne again, taking hold of her wrist and tugging her upright.

'What is it? What's the matter?' came Tanya's sleepy voice from the other side of the room. Anne turned, holding the candle near her face so that she could be seen.

'It's nothing,' she said soothingly. 'Go back to sleep.' Tanya sat up, but showed no inclination to interfere, only watched, puzzled, as Anne thrust Yelena's wrapper at her and then urged and prodded her out of the room. 'Go to sleep, Tanya,' Anne said as she passed.

Out in the corridor, Yelena looked up at her darkly. 'I'm supposed to be in bed,' she said. 'I'm supposed to sleep. It's very bad for me to be woken up.'

'Oh, but you weren't asleep,' Anne said pleasantly, 'and you and I have a little job to do.'

'I'll tell Papa,' she offered, rather feebly.

'Good,' Anne said. 'I'll tell him too, in the morning.'

'It was only a joke,' she said now, subdued by Anne's immovability, and Anne took her hand and led her along towards the backstairs, where the housemaids' cupboard was.

'Quite,' said Anne. 'Now you are going to help me make the bed again, and then we'll decide what to do with you. I might have a joke or two I want to play on you.'

Yelena offered no further protest or justification, but went meekly through the process of finding fresh bedclothes, carrying them back to Anne's room, stripping the bed, and making it up anew. The mattress was rather damp in the middle, even when Yelena had sopped it with towels, so they folded several more dry towels over the patch before putting on the sheet.

'Tomorrow it will have to be dried out properly,' Anne said, 'but for tonight it will have to do. I just hope I don't get rheumatism.'

Yelena looked up at her under her brows. 'I'm sorry,' she said abruptly. Anne's heart contracted with relief at the words, the first sign of yielding in her intractable pupil; but she said nothing, only nodded slightly.

Yelena bit her lip. 'I know,' she offered, 'I'll sleep in it, and you can sleep in my bed. And then if I get sick, it will be my punishment.'

It was so genuinely and innocently said, that Anne repressed a smile. 'No, I don't think that's a very good idea. We shall have to think about how you can make it up to me. You can let me know if you have any good ideas. And now you had better go back to bed. Come.'

She held out her hand, and they retraced their steps.

'Will you tell Papa?' Yelena asked after a moment. Anne glanced down, and saw the fan of eyelashes against the rounded cheek as Yelena fixed her eyes on the floor. 'He'd be very angry.'

Anne thought privately that his anger, if it existed at all, would be much more formal than real: his indulgence towards his daughter seemed endless.

'No, I shan't tell him. Not as it was just a joke,' she said. Yelena's hand relaxed in hers. In the nursery, Tanya stirred, watching them, but did not sit up. Anne put down the candle, helped Yelena into bed, and pulled the covers up around her. 'Goodnight, Yelena Nikolayevna,' she said. 'Tomorrow, perhaps, we can think of some more jokes together – really funny ones, this time.'

Yelena regarded her thoughtfully, her eyes black pools with twin candle flames in their centres. 'You can call me Lolya,' she offered. Anne smiled, and the corners of Lolya's mouth moved in response. 'And I'll call you Anna Petrovna, if you like,' she added with enormous generosity.

'Yes, I like,' said Anne.

It was a beginning. Yelena did not become an angel overnight, but now licensed to call her Lolya, Anne found much less difficulty in making contact with her, and began to be able to interest her in her lessons, instead of merely forcing her to endure them. Fräulein Hoffnung noticed the difference at once and congratulated Anne on having broken down the first barrier. It would be a long time, they both knew, before Lolya completely accepted and trusted her new instructress, but it was a start, and as Fräulein Hoffnung said, 'Rome vass not burnt in a day.'

One day, as Anne approached the breakfast room, she heard the Count's voice raised in irritation: 'For God's sake, Irina, don't begin that again! It's stupid, and you know it!'

Anne was shocked, never having heard him raise his voice in anger before; and was even more shocked at the little thread of pleasure she discovered in herself, that he should so berate his wife for stupidity. Rebuking herself inwardly, she made a noise at the breakfast room door before opening it, and when she entered, they were composed: the Count reading his letters, the Countess, eyes down, picking listlessly at a roll of bread.

The under-butler, Yakob, followed Anne in and drew out her chair for her, and a moment later Fräulein Hoffnung brought the children in, and the normal morning routine was re-established. But Anne, watching the Countess from the corner of her eye, thought she looked less at ease than usual. She seemed a little pale, and her lips were tense. Well, I should not like to have him shout at me like that, Anne thought to herself, and tried desperately not to feel pleased about it.

Later, in a lull in the conversation, the Countess spoke up, her voice pleasant and serene as always.

'Really, I must take my poor Iskra out today. She has had so little exercise recently.'

That's right, Anne thought approvingly: the best remedy is to seek the comfort of the great outdoors, and the unfailing love of a favourite animal.

The Countess went on, 'But I do not like to ride alone. Will you ride with me, Anna Petrovna? Fräulein Hoffnung can take Yelena's lessons this morning, can't you, dear Fräulein?'

'Of course, madame –' the Fräulein began, and the Count, without looking up, said, 'I think it will rain. You had better not go far.'

Anne, who was still looking at her mistress, saw her amber eyes shine and her lips tremble, and knew, quite certainly, that the unspoken words hovering there were 'I shall go as far as I please!' For a moment she felt a sympathy with her, liking her better for that flash of temper, repressed though it was.

'I want to come too,' Yelena said, inevitably. 'I want to ride with you. I don't want to do lessons.'

'Not today, Lolya,' the Countess said with unexpected firmness. 'Today I want to ride very fast.' Her husband shot her a brief look at those words, but said nothing, and she stood up and said to Anne, 'Shall we go and get ready?'

Anne got up to follow her mistress, and the Count rose courteously to his feet, watching them both with a quizzical expression. The Countess inclined her head towards him, and Anne, embarrassed at being obliged to stand between them, followed her out without meeting his eyes, hearing behind her Lolya's renewed complaint.

'I want to go too! Why can't I go? It isn't *fair!*'

In the stableyard, Anne looked at the sky while they waited for the horses to be brought out, and wondered if the Count were right about the rain, or if he had simply been trying to spoil his wife's pleasure. It was clear overhead, though there were clouds on the horizon, and there was a small, cool breeze, which served to make the heat more tolerable. She didn't yet know enough about the region to know if rain were likely, but there seemed to her to be no immediate sign of it. And anyway, she thought, if the worst came to the worst, a little wetting wouldn't hurt two healthy young females.

There was a measured clopping of shod hooves on brick, and two grooms led Iskra and Grafina out into the yard, already saddled, their coats gleaming and their eyes bright with pleasure at the prospect of going out. The horses were led to the mounting blocks, and two more grooms came running to check that the girths were tight, and to help the ladies up. Anne freed her habit from under her leg and hooked her knee round the pommel, found her stirrup, arranged her skirts, and gathered up the reins. The Countess turned to her with bright eyes.

'Are you ready? Very well. Stand aside, Yurka!'

Iskra flung her head up and down and jogged even as they walked them out of the yard, and Anne felt a moment's apprehension – she seemed so fresh. But from her own past observation, the Countess really could ride 'like a cyclops' and the present fidgetings did not seem to be troubling her. Anne trotted the sensible Grafina a few steps to catch up, and once they were outside the gates, the Countess said, 'Let's gallop to settle them down.'

Iskra was off before the last word was out; Grafina threw her head up and snorted, and Anne lost a rein, and the bay took off in pursuit. The Countess, Anne saw, struggling to gather her reins, was urging her mare on: she could see her booted foot digging away at the chestnut's side, and she felt rather cross at this unhorsemanlike behaviour. She ought to have waited until I was ready, she thought angrily, and having regained her reins and balance, urged Grafina to catch up. Iskra was much too fast, however, and the flying figure drew further and further ahead. She is showing off, Anne thought, proving she's a better horsewoman than me. It's very silly and thoughtless.

After a while, the distant golden speck slowed and stopped, and Grafina, blowing a little, began to catch up. The Countess turned Iskra and stood waiting as Anne rode up to her. Her cheeks were bright and her eyes moist – though that was nothing, Anne's were too, from the wind – but her expression was almost normal, and she spoke in her usual, unemphatic voice.

'I'm sorry I left you behind. I needed to let go and fly, just a little. We'll go more steadily now, I promise. Are you all right?'

'Yes,' Anne said. 'Poor Grafina is not as fast as your mare. She didn't like being deserted.'

'No, they don't,' the Countess said, turning and walking on as Anne fell in beside her. 'Horses hate to be alone. But then horses are never unkind to each other.'

Surprised, and a little apprehensive, Anne waited for the confidence she thought was to come. But the Countess said nothing more, and they rode in silence for some time. When she did speak again, it was to comment on the scenery and the route they were to take.

They rode in a wide half-circle, coming up through the woods from a different direction to the outcrop where the waterfall was, and halted there to breathe the horses and look at the view.

'It's so flat here,' the Countess said. 'I was brought up in the mountains, you know.' Her eyes moved sideways to glance at Anne. She seemed to want to confide, but not to know how. She couldn't have had much practice at it, Anne thought with some compassion.

'Yes, Fräulein Hoffnung told me so,' she said encouragingly. It seemed to have been the wrong thing to say.

'Ah, the good Fräulein,' the Countess remarked – ironically? 'She was governess to Nikolai's sisters, did you know that?'

'Yes – yes, she told me about that. She often speaks of those days.' The Countess looked straight ahead, her mouth uncompromising. Anne tried again. 'She speaks highly of all the family.'

'She would,' she Countess said shortly. 'The Kirovs make a great impression on everyone.'

Ah, was that it? Anne wondered suddenly. Were there family jealousies, family tensions? Had she quarrelled with the Count's sisters? But she could not imagine this strange, introspective woman quarrelling with anybody. She could think of nothing useful to say, and continued to look out over the plain towards the house. The breeze whipped up a little more sharply, turning a lock of Grafina's thin mane, and Anne noticed that the clouds which had been on the horizon were coming up more rapidly than she had expected. The sky above them was still blue, but there was an unpleasant, steely quality to the blueness that troubled her a little.

She was about to mention it, when the Countess said abruptly, 'Let's get on,' and turned Iskra to the left, picking a way down the slope towards the woods.

'I think it may rain,' Anne ventured, following her.

'We'll be under the trees if it does,' the Countess said indifferently. She seemed to know where she was going, so Anne followed her patiently, wondering if anything more revealing would eventually be said. They entered the trees, and rode deeper into the wood, so that Anne soon lost her sense of direction. It seemed to be growing very dark, and she didn't know if that were because of gathering clouds, or simply because they were under the trees. It was very still and silent in the forest: there was no birdsong, no insects buzzing, and the horses' hooves made little sound on the thick carpet of dead needles. But high above them, the upper branches of the pines were lashing back and forth with a sound like the sea, and once or twice a pine-cone, dislodged, fell with a thud and a bounce on the path before them.

The Countess seemed to be riding automatically, paying no attention to anything around her. Her blank golden eyes stared straight ahead, and her mouth was set more grimly than usual. Anne began to grow both bored and apprehensive. It was definitely darker, and growing quite chilly, and while she did not mind getting a little wet, she did not relish a soaking.

Then suddenly there was a tremendous clap of thunder, like a short, sharp explosion, which startled Iskra almost out of her skin, and made even Grafina flinch. Both horses flicked their ears back and forth nervously, and a moment later a vivid flash of lightning penetrated the gloom of the forest, followed by a long grumble of renewed thunder.

'Madame, the storm –' Anne said, not even sure whether the Countess had noticed. 'I'm afraid it may rain at any moment.'

'Well, we are under the trees,' the Countess said shortly. 'We are sheltered.'

'But madame, I'm not sure if it is a good idea. I was always told not to shelter under a tree if there were lightning.'

'Under a solitary tree, not in the middle of a forest. We are quite safe. Don't fuss so.'

Anne was astonished to hear her speak so shortly and said nothing more, riding on beside and a little behind her, while the wind moaned in the tree tops, and lightning flashes and long rumblings of thunder grew more frequent. Then the trees thinned out, and they were out on the other side of the forest, and Anne could see for herself how plum-coloured clouds had rolled up to cover the whole sky, making a strange and threatening twilight in the middle of the day. It was going to rain, and rain mightily, at any moment!

The Countess, however, rode straight forward, leaving the shelter of the trees behind. Anne shivered, hating to feel so exposed, and paradoxically more afraid of the lightning than she had been when under the trees. Below and to the right she could see the peasant village she had visited with the Count, and she felt a small surge of relief. Now at last she knew where they were in relationship to the house.

'Madame,' she said, 'ought we not at least to ride in the direction of home?'

The Countess opened her mouth to reply, and there was a sudden chill gust of wind which lifted their hair, and the storm broke over them. The rain fell in large drops, the first few warm, and then, as it grew heavier, unpleasantly cold. The horses laid back their ears, and Iskra sidled unhappily, trying to get away from the hard raindrops smacking her rump. The Countess looked about her, almost as if she had woken from a dream, and Anne, raising her voice over the drumming of the rain on the dusty track, said, 'We must take shelter! Shall we head for the trees again?'

Iskra performed several tight circles on the spot, and the Countess, straightening her out with a firm hand, said, 'No, we had better ride to the village. We can shelter in one of the houses. This won't last long — it never does when it's so violent.'

She put the mare into a canter, and Anne followed, bowing her head and turning her face sideways out of the blinding rain, praying that Grafina would be able to keep her feet on the greasy track and pick her own way. They cantered full pelt down the slope, and a moment later skidded to a halt under the sheltering trees outside the first house in the village street. The Countess swung her leg free and jumped down, and at the same moment, an old man with a stick came hobbling out of the house, followed by a young woman in the usual peasant garb of cotton dress, shawl, and handkerchief tied about her head.

Anne heard an exchange going on in Russian as she freed herself and jumped down, and the young woman, who had taken Iskra's reins, held her hand out for Grafina's, and led the horses swiftly away through the teeming rain towards the barn next to the house. The old man bowed several times to the Countess, and then to Anne, and with voluble gestures of his free hand for them to follow, hobbled briskly towards the house.

A moment later, gasping and with water running down her neck, Anne ducked in out of the rain, and had her first view of the inside of a peasant house. It was only a single-storey building, but the ceiling was very high, going right up into the steep pitch of the roof. The atmosphere was warm and close and smoky, for the stove was alight, and there was no chimney. The stove took up about a quarter of the space inside the hut, a huge oblong made of baked clay, with a large opening at one end through which Anne could see the light of the flames inside. It reached half-way up the height of the room, and above it, there was a wooden structure, like two tiers of broad wooden shelves, which Anne could not immediately account for.

The walls of the house were of plain wood, and she could hear the rain drumming against the roof. There was very little in the way of furniture – a large wooden table with wooden benches drawn up to it, and some shelves high up on the walls, on which bowls and jugs and boxes were stacked. Opposite the door, in the corner to the left, was a shelf with a lamp burning on it before an icon of the Mother and Child, and even as Anne entered and looked about her, she saw the Countess bow reverently towards it and cross herself.

The old man now looked at Anne expectantly, and when she stared back, not knowing what was wanted of her, he frowned and growled something in Russian. The Countess turned to Anne.

'Do as I did. Bow to the icon and cross yourself.'

'But I'm not – '

'Do it. They will be horribly offended otherwise,' she said sternly. Anne, with an inward shrug, obeyed, remembering at the last moment to cross herself the Orthodox way. She felt very awkward about it, but appreciated that it would be easier than explaining her to the inmates and persuading them not to mind, and hoped that God would understand.

There were a good many people in the room: the old man, two old women, a middle-aged woman crouching in front of the opening of the stove, and – Anne counted quickly – six children of different sizes, including a baby swinging in a sort of small hammock hung from the cross-beam. As soon as Anne had performed the ritual, they all smiled welcomingly, and a splurge of chatter broke out, and two of the women came forward to help them off with their hats and jackets, tutting and clucking about the rain, and carried them away to prop them on a wooden frame against the wall of the stove to dry.

The young woman came back and said something to the Countess about the horses – Anne knew one or two words now – and then gestured for them to sit down on one of the benches, and went over to feed the stove. Anne sat beside the Countess, with the disagreeable feeling of water in her boots, and began to pull off her gloves, which, being made of soft leather, were clinging to her fingers like a second skin.

'It's customary, you see,' the Countess explained, engaged on the same task, 'for everyone entering the house to make obeisance to the beautiful corner, before they are permitted to speak or sit down. It's a rule they keep very strictly, without exceptions.'

Anne nodded. 'I understand. Is that what they call it – the beautiful corner?'

'Yes – *krasnyi ugolok*, in Russian.'

'But I thought *krasnyi* means "red",' Anne frowned. It was one of the words she knew well, having heard the 'red stables' spoken of every day on her morning walk with the children.

'It's the same word,' the Countess said indifferently. '*Krasnyi* means both red and beautiful.'

'Why?' Anne wanted to know.

'I don't know,' the Countess said without interest. 'We'll shelter here until the rain stops. The young woman will make us some tea, I expect. What do you think of your first peasant house?'

'It's very snug, and bigger than I expected,' Anne said, looking around her. The two old women and the old man were all looking at her, and as she caught their eyes they all beamed and nodded delightedly, and she smiled and nodded in return. This happened every time she looked up, and though rather tiring, was ample evidence of their good will. 'There is one thing that strikes me as odd, though – I can't see any beds. Where do they all sleep?'

'Above the stove, of course, for warmth,' said the Countess. Thus prompted, Anne could see how it was arranged. The lower level of sleepers would lie directly on the clay roof of the stove, and in winter, she imagined would be delightfully snug; those on the upper level, raised above them on the wooden superstructure which had puzzled her, would benefit from the rising warm air.

'What a clever idea,' she exclaimed, and received another round of smiles and nods from the old folk, who didn't understand her words, but were watching her expression carefully. 'I suppose they decide who gets the best place by seniority.'

'I suppose so,' said the Countess indifferently, and Anne thought how much more she would have enjoyed this visit with the Count, who would have told her all manner of fascinating things, and would have delighted in and responded to her interest in everything. It was hard not to think disloyal thoughts about her mistress when in so many small ways she proved herself unworthy of her master.

The samovar was steaming, and soon the tea was brought and handed round with more nods and smiles. Anne essayed a sentence of thanks in Russian, which seemed to go down well. The Countess said something in which Anne distinguished the words *barishnya* and *Angliskaya*, and understood herself to be being explained to the inmates, and there were cries of enlightenment and renewed welcome before everyone settled down again to watch the great ladies drink their tea.

The tea seemed to revive the Countess. After the first few sips, she stopped staring blankly at the wall and looked at Anne a little hesitantly.

'I seem to have behaved rather badly,' she said. 'I'm very sorry you have had a soaking for my foolishness.'

Anne was astonished to receive an apology, and it took a moment for her to assemble the right thing to say. 'Please – I don't mind in the least. I'm always doing things and thinking better of them later.' That didn't sound quite right, and she added hastily, 'I mean, you weren't to know there would be a storm.'

The Countess actually smiled, the first frank and natural smile Anne had ever received from her. 'Oh, but I knew perfectly well there would be a storm. I *wanted* to get wet. But I shouldn't have made you suffer too.'

'I'm not suffering,' Anne said. 'I'm seeing the inside of an *izba* – is that right? – which is very interesting. And I enjoyed the ride. But I wonder why you didn't go out alone, if you felt like that?'

'I thought . . . ' The Countess hesitated, and then shrugged. 'I have been very much alone this last year, while Nikolai has been away. At home I always had my sisters to talk with, although I never missed them while he was at home. And now I thought – I hoped – that perhaps I could talk to you.'

Anne felt a rush of renewed shame at the unkind private thoughts she had been harbouring. Her cheeks grew warm, and she was glad that the Countess was not one for looking at the person she was speaking to. 'Of course, if you wish,' she said, and then, thinking it sounded churlish, she added, 'I should be honoured by your confidence.'

There was a silence, as the Countess arranged her thoughts, and then she said hesitantly, 'I was upset, this morning, you see. I suppose you guessed that. That was why I wanted to ride out. I had to get away. It's foolish, but . . . when I am troubled, the only thing I want to do is to saddle Iskra and gallop and gallop.'

Anne thought of the Count's sharp words she had overheard, and felt embarrassed. It would not do for the Countess to confide anything of too intimate a nature to her. 'I can understand that. And I guessed you were a little – unhappy,' she said cautiously.

It seemed to breach the dam. 'Unhappy? Yes, yes, that's the word! Unhappy, and afraid. Unhappy because I'm afraid. Nikolasha says it's stupid, and I can see that to him it must seem so, but he does not know – he cannot know – he thinks her the model of womanhood.'

Her? Anne thought. Oh God, am I to hear of some *affaire* she has discovered? No, no, it couldn't be. He would never do such a thing. 'Who, madame?' she asked bravely.

'His mother,' the Countess said, and gave a groan as if speaking the word had been a relief. 'Vera Borisovna, the Dowager Countess Kirova! How she hates me!'

Anne glanced anxiously at the peasants, for the Countess's voice was vehement, but she intercepted the glance and said, 'Oh it's all right, they don't understand French. Nikolai had a letter from her this morning to say she is coming to stay, and that was what began it all.' She stared at her hands. 'You can't imagine,' she went on in a lower voice, 'how she terrifies me. She criticises everything I do, and finds fault, and asks me questions only to catch me out. She did not want Nikolasha to marry me. She thought I was unworthy to take the place of the woman *she* chose for him, and she makes me know it all the time. That was why she took Sergei away, to show me I was not fit to bring up her grandson. But of course,' she added despairingly, 'Nikolai never realises any of that. To him she speaks politely about me, even praises me. He never hears that she is being ironic.'

'I'm surprised,' Anne said. 'I thought him a sensitive man.'

The Countess looked up. 'All men are blind when it comes to

130

their mother. You will learn that one day.' She sighed. 'Besides, she brought him up alone from an early age, after his father died, so her influence with him is very great. He thinks her a saint. He can't see – ' She stopped abruptly and relapsed into silence.

Anne looked at her averted profile with perplexity, half wishing the Countess had not confided in her, for it gave her something else to complicate her feelings. One part of her sympathised, as woman to woman, able easily to imagine how difficult a predicament it must be, and how impossible it would be to persuade any man that his mother was not as he thought her; another part felt that *she* would have managed somehow to get on with Vera Borisovna, or at least have explained matters to the Count so as to win his support. It seemed to her feeble and poor-spirited to be so upset over the attitude of someone who at most would be inflicted on one for a few weeks of the year; and then she looked at the unhappy droop of the Countess's mouth and remembered the Count's harsh words, and was angry with him for being so unfeeling towards one whom it was his duty to protect and support.

'Have you tried to explain to him how you feel?' Anne said at last.

'Oh yes. But it makes him angry. He wants me to welcome his mother when she visits, and I try to, but it isn't enough because he knows it isn't from the heart. He should never have married me,' she added in a small, sad voice. 'There was no need. He already had a son, and my dowry was nothing, nothing.'

Anne forced herself to speak. 'You mustn't say that. He married you because he wanted to. He loves you, madame, surely you know that?'

She glanced up. 'Do you think so? I wonder sometimes. I am not clever like you, and he has always admired intellectual women.'

Oh this was bitter! It was so innocently spoken. 'He loves you, I'm sure of it. I've – I've seen the way he looks at you. Truly, I could not be mistaken.'

The Countess drew a small sigh. 'Thank you,' she said, and then, 'Thank you for letting me talk to you like this. You cannot know what a comfort it is to have a female companion again. Oh, Fräulein Hoffnung is a kind woman, but she is not a companion, and besides, she is Nikolasha's, to the bottom of her heart, not impartial, like you.' Anne said nothing. 'I am so glad you have come to us, Anna Petrovna. Glad for Lolya, but glad mostly for me.'

Anne tried to crush the feelings down and speak evenly. Perhaps this was to be her punishment for the sins of thought she had already committed, to be the friend and confidante of the woman she had wronged in her mind. 'I have everything to thank you for, madame, You have been kind and generous to me,' she said with an effort.

'Please, call me Irina Pavlovna. But not when my mother-in-law is within hearing,' she added with a faint smile. 'Will you help me prepare for her visit? There will be a great deal to do. Vera Borisovna always expects everything to be up to Petersburg standards, even in the country. I suppose we will have to have a formal dinner and a ball.'

'Will you not enjoy them? Dinners and balls are thought to be pleasant things,' Anne said.

'I hope only to survive. But you will enjoy them, I hope.'

'When is she coming?' Anne asked.

'Next week, she and Sergei – and the Danilovs the day after, to stay until we leave for Petersburg. No more quiet rides alone,' said the Countess sadly. 'We shall have the house full for the rest of the summer. Oh, how I dislike to have lots of people around me. I hate company and crowds.'

How differently we feel, Anne thought. And how could the Count, that conversible, sociable man, have chosen such a weak and retiring woman for his mate? Despite the kindness and the confidences, she still could not feel she *liked* the Countess, although she could not refuse the intimacy offered, nor the responsibilities it thrust upon her.

'The rain seems to have stopped,' she said, cocking a head to listen. 'I think perhaps we might be on our way.' She stood up, feeling the now lukewarm water rushing down to the toes of her boots, and her heavy skirts clutching damply at her legs. But at least their jackets were almost dry. They put them on, and thanked the peasant family for their hospitality, and received shy smiles from the woman, though the old man looked to Anne as though he would have liked a more tangible sort of gratitude.

'When we get home,' Anne added, following her mistress to the door, 'perhaps we can make a list of the things that have to be done. I shall be very glad to help you in any way I can.'

The Countess gave her a glance of burning gratitude. If I cannot love her, Anne thought, I can at least be kind to her: I must do no less. But how much I would have preferred it if she had never existed, poor creature.

Chapter Nine

If Anne thought the Countess was exaggerating about the amount of work involved in preparing for a visit by the Countess Dowager, she soon learned her mistake. Her experience so far of Russian servants was that they were an easy-going tribe, who liked to move about their tasks in a leisurely fashion, and were more often than not to be found lounging against something and chatting, much preferring to discuss the jobs that needed doing than actually to do them.

The very mention of Vera Borisovna changed all that, and sent them scurrying in all directions, bumping into each other, dropping things, and exploding into vehement arguments about who was impeding whom, and whose fault it would be if things weren't ready. It seemed that the whole house had to be scoured and polished from top to bottom before the Dowager stepped over the threshold. Carpets were beaten, floors waxed, windows cleaned inside and out, every piece of china and porcelain washed and dried by two senior servants who set Anne's teeth on edge by their inability to converse while they worked without waving their hands.

Every lustre in the great rooms had to be taken down and dismantled, and the individual crystal drops washed in vinegar and polished with soft cloths before being put together again and supplied with fresh candles. Silver, which had languished unnoticed and dull since the last formal dinner, was polished to midday brightness, and Grigorovitch justified Anne's first assumption about his job by appearing with ladder and pots to touch up the paintwork inside the house wherever it was damaged, finger-marked or dingy.

The great dining-room was opened up, and the largest of the state bedchambers, which Vera Borisovna would expect to use, and more modest bedrooms were prepared for the other guests. Gardeners came and went, followed by cursing housemaids with brooms, bringing pots of flowering plants and shrubs to decorate the formal rooms, orange trees in lead troughs to place along the terrace, and cut flowers for the Dowager's chamber. The estate musicians were brought together and given their instructions, and the sound of their rehearsal issued at all hours from one of the rooms in the white tower; while down in the kitchens, such pandemonium reigned that the ants' hill activity upstairs paled into insignificance beside it.

The Countess went about with her face creased in a worried frown, the list she and Anne had made between them clutched like a talisman in her fingers and growing more and more dog-eared and difficult to read. Fräulein Hoffnung took charge of the children, to release Anne to help the Countess, and Nyanka to oversee the linen-cupboard, which was her special province; but Lolya grew more ungovernable by the hour, and with Natasha at her heels, continually escaped Fräulein Hoffnung's restraint to tear up and down corridors, toboggan down the newly polished stairs, and play hide-and-seek among the dust sheets.

The Count stepped serenely over and around the commotion with a smile of inward amusement, and, sitting down to the picnic meals which appeared at irregular intervals, told his wife that he couldn't understand why everyone was making such a fuss. 'The servants ought to know their jobs by now. It's only a matter of cleaning everything and setting it all to rights. Let them get on with it, Irina – don't trouble yourself with it. Go out for a walk, or go and read a book somewhere.'

Irina forbore to point out that there was nowhere in the house where one could sit down with a book without being dusted, and ate her cold meat and stale bread with a meekness Anne would not have emulated. The Count's attitude certainly made her want to wring his neck – it was not *he* who would be blamed if everything were not perfect – but on the other hand, the Countess was ineffectual and inefficient, often increasing muddles by her attempts to direct the servants' labours and by her inability to make decisions and stick to them. Anne tried as far as possible to direct matters herself and to persuade the servants, without appearing disloyal, to come to her for instructions. Her Russian improved by bounds during the week before Vera Borisovna's visit.

Then the dreaded day arrived, and all the servants were assembled in the great hall in clean dresses and aprons, best livery and white gloves, because the Dowager liked to be received in formal manner by the whole household. It was difficult to keep them all together, for individuals kept remembering something they hadn't done, and slipping off to turn off a tap or retrieve a duster left in a prominent place. Vasky went along the line inspecting everyone's fingernails, while Yakob, in a last-minute fit of panic, suddenly took it into his head to climb onto one of the hall chairs and check that the tops of all the doors had been dusted.

The children, washed to smarting-point and dressed in their best, were confined with Fräulein Hoffnung in one of the parlours off the great hall, ready to be brought out when the moment arrived. Anne and Nyanka were checking for a last time that everything was ready in the bed chambers, and that Lolya hadn't done anything in her excitement like putting a frog in Vera Borisovna's bed. Outside in the entrance courtyard the orchestra was tuning up for the moment when the carriages would come into sight, and the grooms were lined up round the walls to run to the horses' heads. Anne thought that if the Prince of Wales had taken it into his head to go and stay with the Murrays for a week or two, there would not have been more fuss and work and worry than had been expended over the impending visit of the Dowager Countess Kirova.

When she arrived, however, she did it in grand style, in a large and gleaming black coach picked out with crimson and gilding, drawn by four milk-white horses. Behind it came two more carriages and a cart, bringing her servants and luggage, for where Vera Borisovna went, a nucleus household went too. She brought with her her waiting woman and her dresser, a chambermaid to take care of her linen, and a chamberlain who took charge of her china and silver, and who also looked after her jewels; a secretary-courier, for she could neither read nor write; her own coachman and footman, two grooms, a cook, two housemaids, and a lamp boy. In her youth, she had been lady-in-waiting to the great Empress Catherine, and she had never forgotten what that lady had taught her about the importance of ceremony. She also had her generation's fear of the hazards of travelling, and was convinced that anywhere outside Moscow and Petersburg she would meet with nothing but insolent servants, damp sheets, bad food, and cracked china.

Anne's first view of her was not a disappointment. She had been prepared to be impressed, even if only because a woman who believes herself to be impressive will usually manage to be so, but Vera Borisovna was the mistress of the grand entrance. She halted in the doorway, with the sound of the orchestra drifting in behind her, and her crowd of retainers just visible beyond her, and stood, head up, to be viewed.

She was not a tall woman, but she was large – not fat, precisely, more bulky and hard-looking – and she looked larger by virtue of her clothes. She wore a voluminous pelisse of royal-blue velvet, trimmed with dangling squirrel-tails, and, despite the summer heat, an enormous round hat of dark fur decorated with a diamond spray. Her arms were encased to the elbow in soft suede gloves of sky blue, the wrists clasped by diamond bracelets, and she held in one arm a goggle-eyed Chinese dragon-dog, pure white and sporting a diamond collar. In her other hand she carried a large, jewel-encrusted lorgnon, which she opened with a practised flick and used to subdue anyone not completely undone by her entrance.

Her face was long, like the Count's, but the jaw was more pronounced and the nose less shapely. She had grey-green eyes, rather protuberant, even without the magnifying effect of the lorgnon, and a sharply down-turned mouth. Her whole expression was one of haughtiness and readiness to be displeased. A woman of no particular talent or mental attainment, she had early learnt that one sure way to avoid the charge of mediocrity was to become famous for ill-humour; Anne could well understand the Countess's apprehension. For the moment, however, having surveyed the room, the Dowager put down the dog, stitched a terrifying smile into place, flung out her arms, and cried 'Koko!' in a voice so vibrant that she managed to infuse five inflections into the one short word.

The Count, so designated, stepped forward to put his arms around her and kissed both cheeks. 'Mother dear,' he said. 'You're looking well.'

'Koko, *mon cher fils*!' The Dowager advanced her head without moving her body, like a tortoise, to receive the greeting. 'It has been such a time – such a disagreeable time – since we met! You have been away far too long, you wicked boy. What can there be in Europe to keep you from home?'

'The Emperor's business, Mama,' the Count said mildly, and looked towards his wife. Thus prompted, she stepped forward dutifully, looking as blank and beautiful as if she had no fear in the world, and curtseyed to the dragon.

'Ah, Irina Pavlovna,' the Dowager said, as if she had only just managed to remember the name at the last moment. As the young Countess rose, the old one placed her hands on her arms and kissed the air over each shoulder, with a smile that made Anne want to scratch and spit. 'How very – exotic you look, *ma chère*! And what an unusual gown! But you always do manage to wear something surprising. How lucky you are, Koko,' she went on, her voice creaking with acerbity, 'to have a wife with such *imagination*.' Imagination, it was clear from her expression, was an attribute more usually to be found in criminals, beggars, and lunatics.

'Fräulein Hoffnung, you know of course,' the Count went on, apparently unaware of these undercurrents.

'Of course. How are you *dear* Fräulein Hoffnung?' Vera Borisovna cried with so marked a warmth in comparison with her greeting of her daughter-in-law, that Anne thought the Count must surely notice it. She smiled sweetly, and the Fräulein's cheeks grew pink.

'Very well, thank you, madame,' she said, her eyes bright with gratitude at the attention.

'How is your old trouble? Better? Ah, but not worse I hope? We must have a long talk together, as soon as I have settled myself.'

'And here,' the Count went on, 'is a new addition to our household, Mama: Miss Anne Peters, who has kindly consented to teach our little Yelena.'

The smile snapped off, and Vera Borisovna raised her lorgnon to look at Anne, and did not, it seemed, much care for what she saw. Anne curtseyed as slightly as she thought she could get away with. The Dowager made no sign of acknowledgement, and said rudely to her son, as if Anne were not present, 'What sort of a name is that? Is she English? An English governess?'

'Yes, Mama. Anne Peters is an English name,' the Count said with patient humour. 'But we call her Anna Petrovna.'

Vera Borisovna stared at Anne offensively through the lorgnon.

'Why?' she demanded coldly.

Anne caught the Count's eye over her shoulder, and had to bite her lip to prevent herself from laughing.

'Never mind, Mama,' the Count said hastily, laying a hand on her arm and turning her away. 'Come, let Vasky take your coat. The children are waiting to be presented to you. And where is Sergei? Don't tell me you left him behind in Moscow?'

'I was obliged to,' the Dowager said, successfully diverted. 'It is impossible to travel in the same carriage with him. The child cannot sit still for a moment. I don't know what they teach them at school nowadays, Koko. I'm sure when you were his age, you were not so wild. But Alexandra's children are just the same. She hasn't the way of managing them. I left him with her to travel in her carriage.'

Vasky came forward with the bread and salt. The Dowager nodded it away, and then waved a hand for her own people to come forward and help her off with her hat, pelisse, and gloves. Thus divested, she stood forth in a gown of puce silk, an elaborately arranged head of grey curls, complete with false-front in the style of twenty years before, a surprising quantity of pink powder and rouge, and a great many glittering jewels, including the diamond bracelets, several rings on each hand, and a massive necklace of rubies and diamonds with matching earrings.

The Count escorted her into the octagon room and placed her on a sofa with the little dog beside her, where she sat looking about her with sharply critical eyes. 'Well, Irina Pavlovna, you have not seen fit to move that table, as I suggested to you the last time I was here,' she began. 'No doubt you had your reasons for leaving it in the very spot where the sunlight will strike it and take all the colour out of it. And the pictures are crooked. When the servants dust them, they must make sure they are hanging straight afterwards. It is precisely attention to such details that mark out the mistress of the house who is worthy of the name, from one who merely enjoys the privileges of the position.'

Irina bore all this with a pallid, 'Yes, *Belle-mère*,' while Anne longed for the distraction of the arrival of the children, whom Fräulein Hoffnung had gone to fetch. When at last they came into the drawing-room, Yelena pulled free at once, and ran eagerly forward crying, '*Gran'mère, Gran'mère*, here I am! Oh, you've got your rubies on! I like them best of all. Did you put them on for me?'

To Anne's astonishment, the Dowager did not in the least object to the familiarity. A smile, which seemed in danger of cracking something, it was so sincere and natural, transformed the enamelled visage, and she held out both hands and said, '*Ma Belle Hélène*! Come here, my love, and let me see how you've grown! Oh, you have such a look of your dear mother about you! I'm sure you are lovelier every time I see you. Kiss your grandmother, my precious.'

Yelena did so noisily but briefly, and then repeated the salute on the dog. 'And there's my darling Nu-nu! I like his pretty collar, Gran'mère. It's just like the one you wore with your grey dress at New Year. Where's Seryosha? Did you bring me a present?'

'Your French accent has improved a great deal, Hélène. Is that dear Fräulein Hoffnung's work?' the Dowager cooed, reaching for her reticule. Yelena, who had taken up a position leaning on the arm of the sofa with her elbows, rocked her feet off the floor and down again rhythmically as she watched the hand in the reticule with avaricious eyes.

'No, Anna Petrovna teaches me French now,' she said. 'Is my present in there? What did you bring me?' The Dowager had brought out a pretty gold cachoux-box with an enamelled lid and tiny diamonds round the edge, doubtless intending to take a cachou for herself, but Yelena said, 'Oh, it's so pretty, Gran'mère! Is it really for me?'

To Anne's surprise the Dowager, with hardly a hesitation, said, 'Do you like it? Yes, Hélène dear, it's for you. Here – ' Her hands lingered only a little regretfully on it as she relinquished it into Yelena's eager fingers. 'Take good care of it, won't you, *ma chère p'tite*, because it belonged to the poor dear martyred Queen of France.' Yelena bent her head over it with close interest, and the Dowager turned a less hostile eye on Anne, and lifted her lorgnon only half way as she said, 'So, you teach my granddaughter French, mademoiselle?'

'Yes, madame. That is, I improve her French, for she speaks it very fluently already,' Anne said diplomatically.

The Dowager lowered the glass a little more. 'Hmm,' she said grudgingly. 'You have a good accent, mademoiselle. English? I would not have thought it.' She pulled herself together, and turned to frown at Irina. 'There is no call to learn English as far as I can see. It was never required in my day, and what use will it be to Hélène? French is the language for a gentlewoman, French and only French. I'm surprised at you, my dear.'

Fräulein Hoffnung, anxious to protect her young mistress, now made a mistake. She had been holding Natasha by the hand all this time, and now, to draw attention away from the Countess, said, 'Dear madame, here is your other granddaughter, come to greet you. Natasha Nikolayevna, curtsey to your grandmother.'

Vera Borisovna's head swung round and her eyes narrowed, and she looked so coldly at the elderly governess that the poor Fräulein turned quite pale, dropped Natasha's hand, and fumbled in her sleeve for a handkerchief which she pressed to her face as though hoping to hide in it. Natasha curtseyed quite prettily, but the Dowager stared, unmoved. 'Yes, so I see.' Then she looked at Irina Pavlovna and said frostily, 'She looks like her mother.'

The words themselves were unexceptionable, but the tone of voice suggested that it was a grave misfortune for the child, and Irina Pavlovna's lips quivered with distress. She held out her hand to her daughter, who ran to her, unconcerned, and climbed onto her lap. Anne could see how hurt she was, and also how the Count had – at least apparently – noticed nothing untoward in the exchange. Fortunately Yelena broke the tension by asking again after her brother, and the moment passed.

The Dowager, to mark her disapproval of Fräulein Hoffnung's blunder in asking her to notice Natasha, decided to be gracious to Anne, invited her to take a seat near her and engaged her in conversation about Yelena's education, beauty, and amazing talents. She referred to her granddaughter always in the French form, Hélène, and lavished praise on her in her hearing in a way Anne thought calculated to make her own life more difficult in future. A conversation with the Dowager was in any case like a cross between a surgical probing and a stroll in the open under shell-fire, and Anne would have been happy to dispense with the honour. But it was obviously better to be one of Vera Borisovna's favourites than one of her anathemas, so she picked her way carefully, answered patiently, and closed her mind to the Dowager's offensive manner and her insulting opinions. It astonished her, then and on reflection, how the Count could have grown up so intelligent, liberal and kind, and even more how he could now be so blind to his mother's multiple faults.

The following day, the Danilovs arrived, bringing Sergei with them. The Count's sister, Alexandra, whom everyone but her mother called Shoora, was a round-faced, sweet-tempered, merry romp of a woman, seeming much younger than her age and certainly too young to be the mother of her two children. She didn't look in the least like the Count, so Anne assumed she must favour her father. She had a frank, open face and round blue eyes, and when Anne was introduced, she took hold of both her hands and said, 'Ah, you poor dear! How dreadful it must be to have no family and to be so far from home. Well, we shall be your family now. You must look on me as a sister, and you shall call me Shoora – none of this "madame" business. And how sensible of Nikolasha to give you a Russian name! It makes you seem immediately like one of the family. You must come and stay with us in Moscow as soon as Irina can spare you, mustn't she, Vsevka?'

Her husband, Vsevolod, was less voluble, but equally kind. He shook Anne's hand heartily, gave her a steady, friendly look, and said, 'Yes, of course you must, Miss Anna. You mustn't miss seeing Moscow. It knocks Petersburg into a cocked hat!'

Their children, Ivan – Vanya – who was twelve, and Kira, who was ten, were remarkably attractive children, with the free, open manners of their parents, and a good deal of fun about them. Kira, indeed, was so pretty, with neat, regular features and a mischievous smile, that if she hadn't been one of Vera Borisovna's grandchildren, the Dowager would have given her a very uncomfortable time. Shoora and Vsevka treated the Dowager just as they treated everyone else and were impervious to her criticisms, shrugging them off with a laugh; and she was a good deal less formal and frosty with them. It went to prove, Anne thought, that the one thing one should never do with a bully is to lie down under their feet. But it was impossible, of course, to tell the Countess that.

The Count's son, Sergei, was very like his father in looks, quite startlingly so, in fact. He was almost fifteen, and in the borderland between boyhood and manhood, capable of romping unselfconsciously with his sisters and cousins, but with the occasional painful access of dignity. He liked to talk seriously with his father and Uncle Vsevka about politics and military matters, standing with his hands clasped behind him, nodding like a sage in a way that made Anne and the Count catch each other's eye and repress a smile; and yet the next moment he would be in the throes of a very childish bout of horseplay with Vanya and Lolya, involving battering each other with cushions until they fell to the ground breathless.

His grandmother obviously adored him even more extravagantly than Yelena, and he bore her attentions patiently. The only time he rebelled was when she called him 'Serge' instead of Sergei or Seryosha. Then the high colour of youth in his cheeks would deepen with embarrassment and annoyance, and he would say 'Don't, Grandmère. That's not my name.' All the children called her Grandmère. She spoke nothing but French, and would understand no other language, and they would not have dared address her as Baboushka, even had anything in her resembled that comfortable word.

Sergei treated Anne with friendly deference, as an unobjectionable adult outside his immediate circle of concern, which was all she would have expected of him. His attitude to his step-mother was harder to define. He was perfectly polite to her, and Anne, though she watched him closely, could not detect any hostility in his attitude; yet he was not at ease. He seemed to want to get away from her, answering her briefly when she spoke to him and never meeting her eye. He seemed to become subdued in her presence, as if all the outflowing of his personality and young spirits were suddenly damped down. He seemed almost to become smaller when he was near her.

The visitors settled in, and the house was filled with sound and movement, talk and laughter, which Anne found perfectly delightful. Shoora was a great asset to the company. She was full of fun and chatter, keeping the conversation going through every awkwardness and deflecting the worst of the Dowager's malice from the Countess. With her brother's help, she organised all sorts of games and frolics in the evenings that kept everyone amused until the children fell asleep, despite themselves, from sheer exhaustion.

Anne liked her enormously and was glad that Shoora seemed equally disposed to approve of her. They had a long talk one morning in the linen cupboard, where they had gone to find some particular embroidered sheets which Vera Borisovna remembered having used on her bed on some previous visit.

'Of course, Mama is very down on poor Irusha,' Shoora said, leaning an elbow on a convenient shelf. 'She didn't think Nikolasha ought to have married again, and then when they had another child – well, that was the end of it! Nikolasha's estate has to be divided up between his children, you see – when he dies, I mean of course – and the more children he has, the less there will be for Seryosha. Lolya has money in trust from her mother, so Mama isn't worried about her. And Irusha's young, and there's no knowing how many more children they'll have, so of course Mama takes it out on her.'

'That's very unfortunate,' Anne said.

'Very unfair, you mean,' Shoora said with an impish grin. 'It's all right, you needn't mind saying it to me. Well, Mama did read Nikolasha a terrible sermon when he married, saying he was selfish and irresponsible and all that sort of thing; so she blamed him as well as Irusha, but he doesn't mind, while it really upsets her. If only she'd stand up to Mama, it wouldn't be so bad. The worst thing you can do with Mama is to let her see you're afraid of her.'

Anne could hardly say that was just what she had thought, so she simply nodded sympathetically.

'And Nikolasha made it as bad as he could by telling Mama he was in love. Mama chose his first wife for him, and as far as she was concerned Yelena Vassilovna was absolutely perfect. To her mind, Nikolasha should have buried his heart along with his wife, especially as he already had a son to follow him. She thought it was in bad taste to marry again, and then to marry for *love*, and to a woman of no family, and with no dowry – or next to none. And then Irusha's from the Caucasus, which Mama regards as practically *Turkey*.'

'I see. She couldn't ever have had much hope of winning approval, then,' Anne said.

'She might have been all right, if she'd been richer, or much plainer than Yelena Vassilovna, or if she'd even managed to be a *Frenchwoman*,' Shoora sighed. 'But as it is, she's done everything wrong, poor creature. Ah, wait, are those the ones? Oh no, they're the lace-edged sheets Vsevka and I gave for the wedding. Well, I don't know where these embroidered ones are. I think Mama must have dreamt them.' She looked at Anne with a frank smile. 'I like you, Anna. I think you will be very good for Irina, bring her out of herself a little. And good for Nikolasha, too.'

'What do you mean?' Anne asked with difficulty.

Shoora's round blue eyes were fixed on her face. 'Oh, give him someone to talk to, I mean. You're of his kind, a real intellectual. I'm not, and poor Vsevka knows about nothing but bang-bangs, and Irusha, poor child, is as cloudy as pond-water. But you can really talk to him. He needs that. His poor mind gets like a hunter shut up in a stable and fed too much corn. We should all count it a great service, Anna dear, if you'd give him a little exercise from time to time. What a pity,' she added with a sigh, 'that he couldn't have married someone like you. I'm sure you could have made him happy, and made Mama like you.'

Anne fought to keep her countenance and hoped that the colour of her cheeks might be attributed to the warmth in the closet. 'I think we ought to give up the search for those sheets,' she said desperately. 'I don't think we're going to find them.'

'I'm sure we won't,' Shoora said equably. 'I'd have taken Nyanka's word for it – she ought to know, after all – but Mama never trusts servants, and especially not Georgians. She thinks they all live in caves and eat little children.'

All meals were now formal occasions, taken in the great dining-room, and with the best crystal, silver, and china. The breakfast-set was Meissen, patterned with brightly-coloured insects, butterflies, and dragonflies; the dinner service was newer, Sèvres *famille vert* with a deep gold border. All the children sat down with the adults, and Anne was impressed with the way they handled the priceless articles – the exquisite porcelain, the delicate crystal, the heavy silver cutlery – and never spilled or dropped anything. There was a liveried footman to each chair – Vera Borisovna's own footman waited on her, his scarlet livery clashing horribly with the Kirov strawberry red – and Vasky attended to the wines, while Yakob, quivering with nervousness, presided over the side-board and dressed the joints. There were two full courses every evening, and dinner often went on until half past eight or nine o'clock.

The neighbouring families all made formal calls to pay their respects to the Dowager, and on most days there were guests to dinner, or to cards and supper. Vera Borisovna was a great card-player, and in the style of her youth, played for high stakes and was usually a winner. These occasions were a refined torture for the Countess, who, though understanding the rules of play, had no more grasp of strategy than a bullfinch. She lost every hand, and though the Count paid her losses cheerfully, even jokingly, she could not but be aware of her mother-in-law's contempt. Even worse was when the draw partnered them: either they lost, and the Dowager abused her stupidity, or they won, and she was placed in the Dowager's moral debt.

The Countess's only moments of happiness were when she rode out, usually now in the company of Shoora and the children, and sometimes the young people from the neighbouring families. Vera Borisovna did not ride and so for a few hours the Countess could legitimately avoid her company. The weeks passed, and though there had been informal dinners and various evening entertainments, nothing had yet been said about a formal dinner or ball. Anne was aware that the Countess was evading the issue; and was aware, too, from covert glances and pointed remarks, that a subtle pressure was being exerted by the Dowager for a date to be set. It was plain that for the Countess, to give a formal reception would be worse torture than not to. Anne was only surprised that she managed, with that stubbornness weak people sometimes display, to continue to resist.

One morning while they were at breakfast, Vasky brought in a pile of stiff white cards together with a letter for the Countess.

'Invitations!' Shoora exclaimed at once. 'Don't tell me – nothing else looks like an invitation card. How exciting! Who is it, Irusha? Dinner or ball?'

'It's from Princess Kovanina,' Irina said, reading her letter. 'They have just arrived from Petersburg, and ask us to a formal dinner and ball at Grubetskaya next week, especially in your honour, *Belle-mère*.'

Anne saw Vera Borisovna cast a sharp glance at the Countess. This might well be used as an excuse for Irina not to give a ball of her own, especially as the summer was now well advanced. Yet from her expression, she might as well have been invited for a short spell of imprisonment followed by execution by guillotine, and Anne felt a faint irritation with her mistress that she seemed so incapable of enjoying life.

She was thrilled, however, to find that there was an invitation for her in the pile of thick, gold-edged cards, and after breakfast Shoora hastened to tell her how much she would enjoy it.

'Grubetskaya's a beautiful house, not like this dreadful old pile – just like Versailles, only not so big, of course, but with a beautiful ballroom, all mirrors, and a terrace overlooking the river. The Kovanins are wonderful hosts, quite young, and not a bit stuffy. Nikolasha says the Poliakovs probably told them about you. Have you something to wear, by the way?' she added.

'The grey crêpe is my best dress,' Anne said. 'The one I wore at dinner last night.'

'Oh, no, it's too severe, and cut too high,' Shoora protested. 'Besides, it's not really a ball-gown. She should have something much younger and prettier to dance in, shouldn't she, Irusha?' she added as her sister-in-law came in. 'You aren't required to dress like Fräulein Hoffnung, you know! You could have one of my gowns to make over, if you like, only they would all go round you twice over, you're so slender.'

'No, no,' Irina said calmly, 'she must have something new. I have some very pretty figured muslin upstairs which I bought in Petersburg but never had made up. You shall have it to make yourself a new gown – something fashionable and pretty.'

'Excellent! And I have some ladies' journals you can look through. This gets better every moment,' cried the irrepressible Shoora. 'Just like dressing up a doll!'

Anne felt ridiculously excited. She was to go to a ball, the first she had ever attended as a guest, a ball and a grand dinner, the guest of a Prince and Princess! She tried to tell herself that she should not care so much for such worldly pleasures, but she was only twenty-three, and her natural spirits bubbled up in her like champagne. To attend a ball in a new gown, to dance! But would anyone ask her? Would – tremulous thought! – the Count ask her? Well, someone would surely ask her at some point in the evening, even if it were only kind Vsevka Danilov. She would have at least one dance – and what heaven to be at a ball, properly, in a new gown!

In her spare time during the next week, she laboured long and carefully over the new gown, and took it to Marya Petrovna to put in the rather ambitious finely-stroked gathers she wanted for the sleeves. The material the Countess had so kindly given her was a fine Indian muslin, figured with raised, glossy white spots, and Anne had cut out a very simple but elegant gown, with a low neck, and short sleeves with the cuffs bound with white satin ribbon. She had unpicked the silk underskirt of her crêpe gown to go under the muslin, which was so fine that the dusky pink colour showed through rather prettily.

On the day of the ball, everyone went upstairs very early to dress, the timing being adjusted to Vera Borisovna's lengthy requirements. Anne had little to do to prepare herself, and was dressed and ready within half an hour. She was sitting in her room reading, to pass the time, when there was a knock on the door, and the Countess's maid Marie came in to say that her mistress had sent her to dress Anne's hair. It was another example of her great kindness, and Anne sat before her looking-glass feeling a now-familiar mixture of guilt and irritation over Irina Pavlovna's character, as she watched the maid's skilful fingers rearranging her hair. Marie brushed it until it shone, then curled it into ringlets and drew them up to the top of Anne's head, bound them there in a bunch with pink ribbon and some white rosebuds, and then cut and curled her front hair.

'*C'est ainsi que Madame Josephine les porte, mademoiselle*,' Marie assured Anne when she had finished, and then stood back to regard the reflection critically. '*Mais vous avez besoin de quelque chose – un collier, certainement, et des boucles d'oreille pour completer la toilette.*'

Anne produced the pearl earrings that her father had given her, and Marie looked at them rather doubtfully, and handled them with the tips of her fingers.

'They were my dear father's last present to me,' Anne said firmly.

Marie sighed and put them on for her and said bravely, '*On voit qu'elles sont assez jolies, enfin, pour une demoiselle.*' However, when it appeared that the only thing Anne could offer by way of necklace was a simple gold chain, she rebelled firmly and finally, and scurried off to consult with her mistress.

A little while later, in spite of all her protests, Anne was obliged to accept from the Countess the loan of a handsome necklace of three strands of pearls clasped at the front with a ruby, and a pair of coral and pearl bracelets. Anne was reluctant to wear borrowed jewels, and insisted that she was perfectly happy with her own modest things. The Countess, seated before her mirror with a worried frown, was obliged at last to turn round to impress Anne with the urgency of the matter.

'Please, for my sake, do wear them! You will not be formal enough without something by way of jewellery, and Vera Borisovna will take exception if everything is not just so. You really ought to have something better than those, but I chose them because they will go with your father's earrings, which you were so anxious to wear.'

Anne had no wish to increase her mistress's burdens, and with this veiled threat of more costly jewels, accepted with as much grace as she could and made her way down to the octagon room to wait for the hour of the carriages. Vsevka and the Count were there, chatting. Both stood as she entered, but Anne's eyes were for the Count alone. In evening dress, powdered, with a glittering ribbon and star across his chest, he looked so handsome and noble that her heart skipped like a roe, and she would have found it impossible, if challenged, to say anything about Vsevka's appearance, or even what colour his coat was.

She walked a few steps into the room and stopped, looking at him almost shyly, like a child in her first grown-up dress waiting for approval. His eyes shone warmly as he looked at her, and with a whimsical gesture of one hand, he bid her turn around to be viewed.

'So that's the new gown,' he said at last. 'Yes, it will do very well. I thought at first it was too plain, but after all there is a kind of simplicity, which beside some – ' He paused. 'Which is very agreeable. I still think,' he added with a smile to remind her of the other ball, 'that you should have diamonds, Anna Petrovna. But at least I shan't have to ask anyone's permission to dance with you.'

'No-one's but hers,' Vsevka commented drily. 'You have no manners, Nicky! I'll show you how it's done. Anna Petrovna, will you do me the inestimable honour of reserving a dance for me tonight?'

Anne tore her eyes from the Count for long enough to smile at Vsevka's low bow, and say, 'Yes – thank you – with pleasure. You are very kind, sir.'

'No, you are kind, mademoiselle. And now, since Nikolasha seems to have been struck dumb, come and sit here by me, and let me pour you a glass of wine. The others will be hours yet. I don't know what women take so long about up there! I mean, look at you: you have done everything a woman needs to appear ravishing, and you're still ready at a reasonable hour.'

Anne could have wished Vsevka anywhere but here, as he obliged her to sit down and chatted pleasantly, destroying what she had seen as a tender moment between her and the Count with his commonplace kindness. But perhaps, she reflected a while later, he had been doing it for her sake: perhaps she had been wearing rather too much of her feelings on her face. When the other ladies finally arrived, she was able to greet them with complete composure, and even endured, unmoved, a long and searching examination through the lorgnon by Vera Borisovna, who, in a parure of pink diamonds and amethysts the size of plover's eggs, was as splendid and glittering and gem-encrusted as an Indian potentate – which, with her sallow complexion and jewel-clasped turban, she even rather resembled.

In the long, pillared and gilded drawing-room at Grubetskaya, the dinner guests assembled: the women deeply *décolletées*, all bare arms and bosoms, and more jewels than an English lady would have thought quite the thing; the men in silk breeches and stockings, velvet or satin coats, ribbons and stars and orders, dress swords, powdered hair. There was something rather engaging about the evident delight everyone had in dressing-up, even for what Anne had been assured was not the most formal of occasions, and the overt pleasure with which they wore their princes' ransoms of jewels.

Anne was introduced to the Kovanins: the Princess plump and golden-haired, with a short upper lip and a merry smile that reminded Anne of Kira's, and the Prince very small and dark and slightly bow-legged, rather frog-like, and very knowledgeable about horses. Both welcomed her very kindly.

The Tiranovs were there, and the Fralovskys, and all four Tchaikov-skys arrived shortly afterwards. Olga, her black curls piled high, was the only other woman all in white, like Anne; but unlike Anne was sparkling with crystal spars and diamonds, like an ice-queen. Her brother Basil, his dark face seeming darker against his powdered hair, claimed Anne, surprisingly, as an old acquaintance. He bowed lower than ever over her *décolletage* and spoke quite pleasantly about Paris and London and the difference between public and private balls, with the pleasant assumption that Anne would have attended enough of them to have an opinion.

When everyone had been assembled for some time, chatting, the doors were flung open, and footmen wheeled in several long tables covered in white cloths, on which a large number of silver dishes were arranged. Vsevka, who was standing beside Anne at that moment, intercepted her look of enquiry and explained, 'It's called *zakuska* – different sorts of small things to eat, which we have before dinner begins, to whet the appetite.'

The tables had been set up at one end of the room like buffets, with the footmen standing behind them ready to serve, and people were beginning to move towards them. Prince Kovanin offered Vera Borisovna his arm, and the Count escorted Princess Kovanina. Anne had the impression that Basil Tchaikovsky was about to offer her his arm when his sister thrust her hand under his elbow and pulled him away, saying, 'I must go with you, *mon cher*. It is bad enough that we shall be separated at dinner, for there is no-one else here fit to talk to.'

Vsevka smiled kindly down at Anne. 'Will you do me the honour of taking my arm, Miss Anna? I'll tell you what everything is, and make sure you taste everything you ought.'

'Yes, gladly,' Anne said. Later, learning to balance a plate and glass and still to manipulate a fork, she reflected that it was a strange way of eating, though novel and enjoyable. The footmen helped each person to a selection from the dishes, some of which were hot and set over chafing-dishes, and others cold, and the guests stood about in groups, plate in hand, talking and laughing as they ate, and returning to the buffet to replenish.

With Vsevka, genial and amused, to help her, Anne went a fair way to trying everything. There was caviar, grey and unappetising to look at, but quite delicious; various kinds of salt fish; strips of smoked duck and of smoked chicken rolled about olives; and slices of spicy sausage like little marbled coat buttons. There were tiny tartlets, filled with creamed chicken, with buttered egg, with fillets of anchovy in a savoury paste; there were hot dishes of stewed prawns and stuffed eggs and pickled mushrooms; there were hearts of artichokes, radishes, and a dozen different kinds of cheese.

Every time Anne was about to discover what the pattern was on her exquisite porcelain plate, it was taken out of her hand and a new selection of delicacies appeared, while her glass never seemed to have a chance of becoming empty. There was vodka to drink, from the Count's own distillery, but of a finer brew than what was sold in the peasant *kabaks*, she was assured by Vsevka; and champagne, both kept chilled in great wooden coolers full of ice. It was well, Anne thought, looking around the room at the munching, laughing company, that she had not eaten that day since breakfast, or this extensive preliminary feast would have spoiled, rather than whet, the appetite for what was to come.

It was well after six o'clock when the Prince and Princess led the way into the huge dining-room for dinner, and ten o'clock before any of them set foot in the ballroom, where the orchestra, on a raised dais at one end, was playing quietly to itself as if to pass the time. Anne had never been at Versailles nor seen a picture of it, so she did not know whether the comparison were just, but the ballroom at Grubetskaya was the most beautiful and magnificent room she had ever seen. It was about a hundred feet long and thirty feet high, with three of the walls entirely covered with gilt-framed mirrors, interspersed with gilded, three-branched sconces. From these and from the huge crystal lustres, the light of hundreds of candles was reflected in the mirrors to dazzling effect.

The fourth wall was pierced all along with pairs of glass doors leading out onto the terrace, a broad, marble-paved walk, set here and there with flowering shrubs and ornamental trees in pots, and a stone balustrade, beyond which was a sheer drop of thirty feet to the river, from whose far bank rose up beautiful hanging woods. The whole scene was reflected in the mirrored walls, so that, as the ballroom filled with guests, it seemed to hang suspended in a vast space like a gold and crystal box filled with jewels and flowers.

Anne found she did not need the kindness of Vsevka to ensure that she danced. He claimed the first dance with her, but when it was over, young Boris Tiranov came up to ask her, and after that she never lacked a partner. Russians, she discovered, from the youngest to the oldest, loved to dance, so there was no fear that anyone young and personable would languish against the wall. She danced the third with Borya's grandfather, old Admiral Tiranov, who, like the Count, claimed to have met her father, but could give no clear account of when or where; and when pressed, admitted with a twinkling eye that it might have been Admiral Parker, not Admiral Peters, but that it was a good enough excuse to talk to her.

Half a dozen partners later, Borya's brother Pavel came and bowed to her, only to be gently but firmly brushed aside by Basil Tchaikovsky, who said, 'You Tiranovs can't expect to monopolise mademoiselle all night. Wait your turn, young Pavelasha! She is promised to me since before dinner – you may have her next, perhaps.' And before Anne could have any say in the matter herself, she was swept away into the set.

Facing her partner a little stiffly, she said, 'Do you always dispense with the ceremony of asking, before claiming a partner, sir?'

'Now, mademoiselle, don't poker up with me!' he returned, completely unabashed. 'You know quite well I meant to ask you at *zakuska*, only I couldn't get near you.' He smiled vividly at her, displaying his white teeth, a feature for which he was famed. It was to emphasise their whiteness that he had grown a narrow black moustache like a Frenchman, which Anne regarded with particular dislike.

'How should I know it,' she replied coolly, 'when you made no attempt to ask me, or even to speak to me until this moment? Why should I suppose you had the least desire to dance with me?'

'Every man in the room desires to dance with a pretty woman,' he replied, leaning towards her, his eyes bulging softly. His upper eyelids, she noticed, were abnormally short, and for an instant she was absurdly afraid that they might fall out, and had an image of herself leaping forward nimbly to catch them. 'Ah, that's better,' he said, watching her closely. 'You almost smiled. You look so very pretty when you smile, mademoiselle.'

'Absurd,' she said. 'I, pretty?'

'Well, not just in the common style, perhaps,' he said appraisingly, 'but you have something, mademoiselle, I assure you; and my opinion is worth having. I am acknowledged as an expert on women. It was I, for instance, who brought La Karsevina to Moscow – and kept her there for a twelvemonth! Now there's something about you, mademoiselle, something very fine and original, that shows in your face. Intelligence, too – '

'Too much intelligence to take your nonsense seriously, I promise you,' Anne said firmly.

He lifted his hands in a gesture of innocence. 'Mademoiselle, I protest! I could make you the toast of Petersburg, if I took you up, you know. My opinion is much sought. You could have anyone you wanted.' Anne was not really paying attention to him, and her eyes had involuntarily strayed to the next set, where the Count was dancing with the Princess. Basil followed the direction of her gaze and gave a shrug. 'Kirov? No, no, I assure you, you are wrong.' Anne looked at him, startled, and he showed his teeth again. 'Kirov may have a very pretty woman for a wife, but he has not the power to make you fashionable, as I have. No-one asks his opinion about women. About horses, yes; but everyone knows dear Vera Borisovna chooses his wives for him, and does it very well indeed.'

Anne could not prevent herself from laughing at the absurdity of his opinions. Was this the man Shoora had said was toasted as both handsome and clever? He had not even the penetration to see what Vera Borisovna really thought of her daughter-in-law. She laughed, and Basil took the compliment to himself.

'You see how I amuse you? Dear mademoiselle, you and I go very well together. I think we shall see a great deal of each other in Petersburg.'

'And what will your sister think of that?' Anne asked unkindly.

'My sister? What can you mean?' he asked, his cheeks growing a little pink under their sallowness.

'I mean, dear sir, that she is looking at us this moment, and to judge by her expression you will not be seeing anything of me in Petersburg.'

He looked hastily round, and then turned back to lean perilously over Anne, so that she began to think the eyes, if they did drop out, would fall down inside her bodice. 'Dear mademoiselle, have no fear! I have not yet told her that your father was an *admiral*. All will be well, I assure you!'

And as Anne continued to laugh merrily at almost everything he said, he was well pleased with the beginning of his campaign, and was ever more impressed by her intelligence, which was demonstrated by her ready appreciation of his wit.

At the end of their dance, she curtseyed and escaped, and managed to slip through the crush to one of the doors to draw a breath of fresh air and let the last of her laughter shake itself free.

'You seemed to be getting on very well with your last partner,' murmured the Count into her ear. She looked round and found him standing at her shoulder, resting his hand on the door-frame above her head; and, looking up into his smiling face, felt a sense of peace and contentment stealing over her. His presence was all she had needed to make the evening perfect.

'I found him vastly entertaining,' she said.

'Oh? Well, he is said to be a very charming young man,' the Count said, observing the glint in her eye.

' "Charming young man" isn't quite the description I would use.'

'Really? What then?'

'I think – ' she pretended to ponder. 'Yes, I think "egregious ass" fits him rather better.' The Count snorted with laughter. 'Really, how can he have won such a reputation for wit? And his sister for beauty? Is she as like him in intellect as she is in looks?'

'Another moment, Anna Petrovna, and I shall suspect you of being jealous. It doesn't do to tilt at reputations, you know.' He glanced over his shoulder. 'Damn, here's that young Tiranov boy, looking for you to dance with him, I don't doubt. I've been waiting all evening to talk to you – he shan't have you. Come, step outside with me for a moment. He hasn't seen you yet.'

He stepped behind her to shield her from view and propelled her gently out onto the terrace, and then tucked her hand under his arm and strolled with her along the walk. Anne matched her steps to his, blissfully happy. He had sought her out – said he had been waiting all evening for her. She had nothing more to wish for.

'So what was Basil Andreyevitch telling you that was so very amusing?' he asked.

'He said that if he took me up, he could make me the toast of Petersburg.'

'Did he? Curse his impudence! What else?'

'That you could not do it for me,' Anne said, glancing up at him, 'because your taste in horses was famous, but not in women.'

'Ha!' The Count's mouth curled into its closed, cat-smile. 'What else?'

'That I was not handsome in the common style,' she said, smiling now. They reached the end wall and stopped, and the Count felt in his pocket and took out a cigar.

'Do you object to the smell?' he asked.

'No, I like it,' she said. 'I used to light Papa's for him.'

He took a moment to cut his cigar, light it, and get it drawing. Then, blowing a plume of fragrant smoke high in the air, he turned to look at her, leaning on the balustrade and studying her with a humorous but intent look. 'Well,' he said at last, 'egregious ass or not, he was not entirely mistaken.'

'About what?' Anne asked. She rested her forearm on the stone sill, and tilted her head back to look at him, and felt her throat tighten as she met his shining, laughing eyes.

'He could make you the toast of Petersburg, for one thing. He has great influence amongst the young people of fashion. God knows why!' He gave a bark of laughter. 'But you should not dismiss him too lightly,' he added seriously. 'It would be a good thing for you – a great thing, perhaps.'

'Why should I want to be a toast?' Anne said dismissively.

'Because, little sceptic, you might make a good marriage through his recommendation. You might marry someone of position and wealth, and be fixed for ever.'

'I don't want to marry,' she said.

'You say that now,' he said, 'but you may think differently one day.'

She shrugged. 'And what else was he right about? That you couldn't do as much for me?'

'I *would* not,' he said, and she flinched inwardly at the changed emphasis. 'It wouldn't be in my best interests,' he added quietly, 'to help you leave my household, now would it?'

'And what else?' she asked unsteadily.

'That you are not handsome in the common style,' he said, looking at her searchingly now. 'In fact, you are quite uncommonly beautiful, Annushka, only he is too much of an ass to see it.' And he put out his hand, and brushed her cheek with the backs of his fingers. Anne felt as though the whole night were holding its breath in the fluttering silence that followed. 'Don't leave us too soon,' he said at last. 'I am selfish to ask it, but I should miss you very much if you left, even to marry someone as good and great as Basil Tchaikovsky.'

'I don't want to marry,' she said again, but this time the words did not, perhaps fortunately, reach the air. After a moment, the Count turned to lean on the balustrade and look out across the river, drawing again on his cigar and blowing the haze-blue smoke into the luminous sky. Anne turned too, and leaned beside him, close enough to feel the warmth of his body against her bare arms, and they stood in companionable silence staring at the dark line where the trees curled against the sky. Presently the moon rose, and lifted itself above the trees to sail clear: a full moon, white and transparent as a lemon-drop.

Chapter Ten

In October, when the frosts came, riming the drifts of fallen leaves and blackening the late buds on the roses, the Kirovs left Schwartzenturm and went back to St Petersburg. The Danilovs took their departure too, for Moscow, taking Sergei with them, but the Dowager Countess decided to stay with her son and daughter-in-law for a while longer in order to visit old friends in Petersburg.

'I might stay with you until Christmas, perhaps,' she said, as though conferring a great favour. 'I still have a large acquaintance at Court; and I ought to pay my respects to the dear Empress-Mother.'

At Schwartzenturm the double windows were fitted, the shutters put up, the furniture and lustres bagged in Hollands, the carpets rolled, the plate and china packed carefully away. Only a skeleton staff would remain, living in the white tower, until the house was needed again. The rest of the indoor servants, along with the family and their luggage, made part of the huge cavalcade that set off for the short journey up the wide, bone-hard road to Petersburg.

Anne had heard so much about it already, this great city which Emperor Peter had raised by an act of will and at the cost of thousands of peasant lives, from the swamps and salt-marshes and reed-covered islands of the Neva estuary. Not quite a hundred years later, Peter the Great's 'Window on the West', begun in such unpromising conditions in one of the worst climates imaginable at the northern end of the Bay of Finland, had become 'the Venice of the North', and the most beautiful city in the world.

It was a city of broad avenues, gigantic squares, waterside promenades and massive granite quays lining both sides of the wide, genial river. With its interlinking network of canals, it was a city of light and movement and rippling reflections, bright-coloured boats and the chuckle of water against hull. It was a city of buildings designed on a magnificent scale: grand, elegant, symmetrical, pillared and porticoed, and – what was most delightful to Anne's first sight – stuccoed and painted in bright, cheerful, harmonious colours. Every other city was dull and shabby in comparison. Where in the world, for instance, was there anything to equal the seemingly endless, blood-red façade of the rococo Winter Palace, or the chrome-yellow Admiralty building, almost a quarter of a mile long, with its gilded spire, its white columns and projecting porches flanked with marble statues?

The Kirov palace on the *Angliskaya Naberezhna* – the English Quay – was painted a pale, bright blue, classical in style, with the windows, frieze, and pediment picked out in contrasting white. Anne was struck speechless with the sheer size of it. And when the Count told her it was one of the smaller palaces, she gave him a reproachful look.

'But it's true,' he said, divining her trouble. 'Everything in Petersburg is big, compared with European cities,' he added almost apologetically. 'You must remember that here in Russia, space is what we have plenty of. And particularly here at the mouth of the Neva, where the land was not useful for anything else.'

Anne's new room was so large that at first she thought regretfully of her snug chamber at Schwartzenturm, particularly when she began at last to appreciate how cold it was going to be. There was no doubt though, that it was handsome. Her massive bed bore a canopy and curtains of ochre silk-damask; the drapes were of sea-green velvet, the carpet green-and-gold Savonnerie; the walls were panelled in a pale, honey-coloured wood, and the furniture was light and modern, with chairs upholstered in sea-green to match the drapes.

The fire in the massive marble fireplace, supported by rather snub-nosed caryatids, was kept alight all the time. It was flanked with two sofas, while nearby was a neat little satinwood writing-desk, positioned to catch the light. It was a room not only to sleep in, but to retire to at any time of the day, to be comfortable and private. As soon as Anne's eye had adjusted to the difference of proportion of everything in Petersburg, she began to think of it as being just as snug as her room in Schwartzenturm.

The first few days were very pleasant, as the Kirovs devoted themselves to showing Anne the sights of Petersburg. The Dowager was engaged elsewhere, renewing old acquaintance, so it was a relaxed and happy Countess who introduced Anne to this magical city. Sometimes alone, and sometimes *en famille*, she took Anne to watch parades in front of the Winter Palace, reviews on the Champs de Mars, and impromptu carriage-races along the quaysides, and again and again to visit the shops along the Nevsky Prospekt, each like a little palace in its own right, where French fashions and furniture and the most fabulous jewels and furs in the world were on glittering display. The weather was cold but bright, and Petersburg looked at its best under a dark-blue autumn sky, the heatless sunshine flashing off the gold of spires and cupolas and refracting into dazzling rainbows in the spray from a hundred ornamental fountains.

Even when lessons began again, Anne found herself with more time to herself, for while in Petersburg, Lolya went to fashionable tutors for her music, dancing, and drawing lessons. After a week or so, there was also another interruption: Vera Borisovna took to coming into the schoolroom at various times and taking Yelena away to accompany her on shopping expeditions or to visit friends. Anne guessed that the Dowager enjoyed the child's uncritical company, and also that she liked to show her off to her contemporaries, for Yelena was certainly both pretty and attractively vivacious. But it was very bad for Lolya to be displayed like a pet monkey, praised and admired extravagantly, and generally allowed to go her length unchecked; and the more Gran'mère called her Belle Hélène and promised her a career of social adulation and heart-breaking, the more idle and inattentive she became in the schoolroom.

Finally, Anne felt driven to remonstrate. It was difficult to find an opportunity to do so, for she would not argue with the grandmother in front of the child, and Vera Borisovna was largely engaged elsewhere in the evenings. The occasion arose, however, one day when Tanya had taken Lolya early to her dancing lesson, while the rest of the family was lingering over breakfast.

'My sweet Hélène,' Vera Borisovna was saying, gazing affectionately at the door through which Lolya had just left. 'I've seen the most delightful ermine hat in the Pantheon bazaar which would look charmingly on her! I have half a mind to buy it for her this afternoon before I take her to the Shuvalovs. Princess Shuvalova's granddaughter is coming to visit her, and she's as plain as a staff beside dearest Hélène! And as for her playing on the pianoforte, well, I hardly know where to – '

'I beg your pardon, madame,' Anne interrupted, feeling her blood mount, 'but do I understand that you are intending to take Yelena out of her lesson *again?*'

The Dowager's brows contracted sharply across her nose, and the Countess choked a little over her coffee, and retired into her napkin.

'What is it to you, mademoiselle, if I do?' the Dowager snapped. 'Pray do not interrupt me when I am speaking.'

'I must interrupt, madame, when it is a matter of Yelena's welfare,' Anne began bravely, hearing her own voice with a kind of detached amazement, for she was almost as frightened of the Dowager as the Countess was. 'It is not good for her continually to miss her lessons – '

'How dare you speak, mademoiselle, when I have bid you be

silent?' the Dowager said, her cheeks mottling ominously. 'Remember your place!'

'My place, madame, is to teach Yelena, and I cannot do so if you interfere with my – '

'*Interfere!*' the Dowager boomed in horrified astonishment. The Countess moaned quietly behind her napkin. 'How dare you use such a word to me? Do you think I do not know better what is good for my own granddaughter, my own flesh and blood, than a foreigner, a *hireling*, engaged merely to teach her English, though what good that will do her I still have not been brought to understand? You see, Irina Pavlovna,' she went on, rounding on the Countess with a sort of savage glee, 'what comes of going against tradition? No gentlewoman would speak any language but French, as I've told you many times, and now this – this *person* – '

'I was engaged, madame, as Yelena's governess, to educate her in all subjects, not just English, and I will not remain silent when I see her being made vain and idle and thoughtless by a diet of flattery and spoiling,' Anne cried, her face growing as red as the Dowager's.

Vera Borisovna let out a shriek. 'Insolence! You impudent hussy! Koko, I insist, I absolutely insist, that you dismiss this – this creature at once! Do you hear me, Koko? I want her out of the house within the hour! I will not have – '

'Sir, I appeal to you,' Anne said desperately over the top of the tirade. 'You engaged me to make an educated woman of your daughter, and I cannot do so if – '

The Count stood up, and held up his hands. Both protagonists lapsed into silence, their eyes fixed on him in mute and burning appeal, and he surveyed them a moment with his most infuriating faint smile. The Countess looked from one face to another apprehensively, knowing that that particular smile boded no good.

'Mother dear, consider! I can't turn Anna off in a strange land, when it was I who brought her here. I have a responsibility towards her. I owe it to her father, my friend, to take care of her.'

'But Koko, you don't mean – !'

'Sir, you must know – '

'Anna dear,' the Count said soothingly, turning to her as he left the table, 'don't make such a fuss. There's plenty of time to teach Lolya everything she needs to know, and to let her enjoy herself. She's only nine years old, you know.'

With that he strolled out of the room, having resolved nothing, leaving the Dowager baffled and Anne annoyed but resigned. Irina got up hastily and made her escape too, catching Anne's eye a moment as she passed, and for an instant Anne felt a close sympathy with her mistress. The Count was many delightful things, but he was not perfect, and his enjoyment of teasing people could be very tiresome. But just as Lolya's imperfections of face made her the more truly beautiful, Anne's very feeling of resignation was evidence, had she needed it, that his imperfections of character only made him more attractive to her.

One day when she was accompanying the Countess and the children in the carriage, Anne saw the Emperor Alexander from only a short distance away. He was tall, well made, and handsome, with high-coloured cheeks, blue eyes, and dark auburn hair, looking very elegant on horseback in one of his many brightly-coloured uniforms. She thought he looked pleasant, kindly, romantic, and good, but very young, younger even than his twenty-six years, and it was hard to reconcile his appearance with the fact that not only was he ruler over the largest territory and population in the world, but that he was absolute ruler, answerable to no-one in the world. He was not just the sovereign, he was the *owner* of every man, woman, and child, every acre of land, every cow, sheep, tree, and ear of wheat in all of Russia, and he could do with them exactly as he wished.

Of course, Anne realised that it was only outsiders like her who thought of it in that way. To the native Russians it required no thought or comment, being to them as natural and inevitable a state of affairs as that it should be cold in winter. And how cold! Anne had been told about the cold, and expected it, but no exercise of the intellect could prepare her for the actual experience of temperatures that passed freezing point and went on falling to the stark and astonishing regions of -21°C.

It was a cold past comprehension, a cold like death, and yet there was a curious liberation in it, a strangely exhilarating sense of freedom. There was a feeling of the city gradually waking up, as if it were only waiting for certain landmarks of cold to be passed to come alive. First the river skimmed over with ice, frost fingers making long patterns like ferns on the surface; and boys idling along the quays threw stones at it, breaking the thin sheets with a sharp noise like window panes. The temperature fell, and the ice thickened and hardened, and then the day came when the flung stones skittered across the surface without breaking it; and the first daring soul took a tentative step onto it and found it bore his weight. The next instant, it seemed, there were skaters in coats of sheepskin dyed scarlet and deep blue and green, whirling and darting like bizarre winter dragonflies; and high, narrow horse-drawn sleighs, laden with goods or with fur-swathed passengers, flying along the river as on a road, the drivers ringing their bells and cracking their whips for clear passage.

The snow came, falling feathery and soft, melted at first by the wheels of the carriages, and piled into ridges down the broad thoroughfares. And it grew colder, and the snow settled, and fell all night in a silent wilderness out of the black sky, and the next day the carriages were put away and the sledges and troikas were brought out, and travel in the city became like something in a dream: unbelievably swift and almost soundless over a glittering carpet of crushed diamond. It grew colder still, and the surface of the snow froze, and more snow fell on the roads and on the river and the canals, obliterating them, so that the city seemed to grow larger as the boundaries disappeared, and movement seemed freer – no difference now between the elements of earth and water, bound together in a single plane beneath the enveloping icy air.

The days grew shorter and the nights longer. Anne saw the other side of the coin from the white nights now, in those long nights beginning in mid-afternoon and lasting until mid-morning. Yet the nights didn't seem so dark after all, filled as they were with movement and laughter and torchlight and the hissing of the snow under the runners of a thousand sleighs, their swinging coach-lamps spilling yellow light like honey into the shadows as they hurtled round corners on their way to some urgent pleasure.

All the families were back from their summer retreats, ready for the almost frantic sociability of the Petersburg winter Season. The circle in which the Kirovs moved included the families Anne already knew – the Fralovskys, Tiranovs, Tchaikovskys, and Kovanins – together with dozens more she had never met. Uncle Petya Bazarov, Vera Borisovna's brother, was an early caller – a huge man with a beard, dressed in Cossack tunic and trousers – who lived a strange and eremitical life in a house on the Vassilevsky Island. He drank hugely, though he never appeared to be drunk, and spoke Russian instead of French, but he was a great favourite with everyone, even the fashionable set, and Anne was once again impressed with the generosity of the Russian mind, which enjoyed people as they were, without applying restrictive social rules to them.

Every day now had its engagements. There were dinners and balls and routs and card-parties and supper-parties; there was the theatre and the ballet, Court receptions, military reviews, and parades; there were troika races and skating-parties and masquerades. Anne was included in almost everything, and her wardrobe could not have stood the strain had not a great deal of her newly-free time been devoted to buying materials and making up new gowns.

As for her outdoor clothes, as soon as the first frost came, Irina had given Anne a *shooba*: a heavy coat of felted wool, with a thick, quilted lining stuffed with kapok. When the snows began, the Count made her a present of a fur-lined cloak and a fur hat with long lappets, and the Countess gave her a fur muff. Anne was overwhelmed by the magnitude of the gifts, but her employers made nothing of it. It was obvious, they said, that she must have the right clothes for the Russian winter, and who should provide them but themselves? Anne bought herself a pair of sheepskin gauntlets and a pair of the white felt boots called *valenki* she had so admired in the shops. With the memory of English snow and slush, Anne had some doubts as to the wisdom of the colour; but she soon learned that the Russian snow was so cold that it remained powdery and quite dry, so the boots never got dirty or discoloured.

Wrapped in all these, and further protected by a huge bearskin rug, Anne would sit beside her master and mistress in the large, three-horse sleigh, its eight bells ringing in harmony like a strange kind of frozen music, and be sped along through the torch-lit streets to yet another party. Parties often began late and went on until the early hours of the morning, and Petersburg never seemed to go to sleep.

Anne met Basil Tchaikovsky at Princess Kovanina's soirée, and despite her poor opinion of his intellect, could not help feeling a little flattered at the haste with which he came to bow over her hand.

'Anna Petrovna! How delightful to see you again so soon!'

'Basil Andreyevitch!' she replied in kind. 'What a surprise! I thought you lived in Moscow and found Petersburg strangely insipid?'

'Why, who told you so?' he said indignantly.

'You did yourself, at the ball at Grubetskaya.'

'Oh, one cannot be bound by what one says at balls,' he said airily, waving one of the white hands of which he was so proud. An emerald ring caught the light so attractively that he was pleased with the gesture, and repeated it. 'The conversation at balls obeys different rules from conversation anywhere else.'

Anne smiled. 'Yes, you're right. That's very witty,' she said kindly.

'My dear Anna Petrovna, must you sound so surprised about it? I am famous for my wit in three capitals.'

'Yes, so I've heard, and from a good authority.'

'Which is – ? No, don't answer. You will say I told you so myself.' He surveyed her critically. 'There is a new confidence

161

about you, Anna Petrovna. It suits you. But where does it come from?'

'Why sir, you must know better than anyone,' she said, enjoying herself. 'Did you not cross this room to claim me as an acquaintance? What could give a woman more confidence than the approval of Basil Tchaikovsky? Did you not say that if you took me up, I should be made?'

'Well, it's true,' he said, narrowing his eyes, 'but I cannot help feeling that when you say it, you are funning me.'

Anne tried for a more sober look. 'Are we not to have the pleasure of your sister's company tonight?'

'No, Olga is engaged at Court. I have been working for an appointment for her, as lady-in-waiting to the Empress. I have some influence with dear Maria Feodorovna, you know. She quite dotes on me, the dear creature.'

'Yes, I've noticed that you have a way with the older ladies, as well as with the young ones,' Anne said. 'I was observing you just now engaged in a tête-à-tête with Princess Shuvalova. She seemed enthralled by what you were saying.'

'Oh, I was talking scandalously to her,' Basil said lightly. 'The older they are, you know, the bolder they like you to be. But I must tell you,' he went on, leaning closer, 'how much good I have done you already. Dear Princess Kovanina told me yesterday that she is to get an English governess for her own little Anastasia! By the end of the season, it will be the height of fashion, I promise you! There will be a whole community of English women in Petersburg, but with you at the head, of course. So now, dear Anna Petrovna, will you be kind to me?'

'But I am kind to you, sir. You see how I smile and talk to you, thus confirming your own good taste in choosing to converse with one upon whom you yourself have bestowed the accolade of approval?'

She gave him her most innocent look as he attempted to unravel the sense of what she had said, and, failing completely, could only give a sickly smile and say, 'Quite so. You are right, of course. Pray, mademoiselle, as there is to be no dancing tonight, may I prevail upon you to play for us on the pianoforte later?'

'Provided I play only to accompany a song from you, sir,' Anne replied, and he smirked and bowed his pleasure at the compliment.

However much it piqued her, Anne had to acknowledge that Basil's attentions did make her sought-after. Hostesses asked her to play and sing for them; young men asked her to dance; and young ladies chatted to her politely and begged her to sit beside them or

162

take a turn about the room with them. However little she understood society's propensity to think him intellectual and witty, she found that his good opinion secured everyone else's – with the exception of his sister. She plainly disliked Anne, though even that conferred a sort of distinction, since she treated most people with lofty indifference. Olga, Anne decided, was courted more for her brother's sake than her own, though her very frigidity made her attractive to those who preferred the excitement of a challenge to the insipidity of easy friendship.

It amused the Count as much as it annoyed her that her popularity and rapidly-acquired reputation for intelligence came from Basil's recommendation, and he frequently teased her about it.

'You should be grateful to him,' he said once. 'There are few young men in Petersburg with sufficient wit to recognise yours. If Basil Andreyevitch had not told them how clever you are, they would never notice it for themselves.'

'You are too kind to him, sir,' Anne retorted. 'He has no opinion of your intelligence at all.'

The Count only laughed. 'I should be unhappy to think he was able to understand me! Make the most of the situation, Anna. Enjoy it – that's my advice.'

Anne soon met the Kovanins' new English governess, a Miss Emma Hatton who originally came from Hampshire. She was some years older than Anne, and of a limited education, but Anne found it delightful to have an Englishwoman to talk to again, someone who had grown up under the same skies and the same social conventions, who spoke English without translation and remembered the same history. Miss Hatton's duties were only to teach Princess Anastasia, who was eleven years old, to speak and read English, so she had even more free time than Anne. They met frequently and went shopping or for walks together. Miss Hatton had been several years in Petersburg and knew most of the great families at least by repute, and she proved a useful source of gossip and news.

Despite the below-zero temperatures, Anne still took the children out for their daily airing. Sometimes they would go for a walk – Nyanka thought this a peculiarly English insanity and would have nothing to do with it, so when they walked, it would be Tanya who came with them to hold Natasha's other hand. A small one-horse sleigh had been put at Anne's disposal, and sometimes she and the children would cram into it together, and go for a drive along the frozen river or over the glittering fields. The children also introduced her to the delights of tobogganing. An artificial slope was built in the garden of the Kirov Palace for their private delight, and Nyanka's services were frequently called upon to weight the roller with which the level at the end of the slope was kept smooth and flat. Miss Hatton sometimes brought her Anastasia to join the party, and a cautious friendship grew up between her and Yelena. It would have flourished more freely had not Vera Borisovna encouraged it so blatantly. She approved of the Kovanins and pushed so hard for Yelena and Anastasia to become bosom-bows that a certain amount of hostility between them was inevitable.

Having Yelena taken off her hands for so much of the day, Anne interested herself more in Natasha, and began to teach her to write and draw. She displayed a considerable talent for sketching, especially people and animals, which, though childishly inaccurate, displayed a life and vigour all their own. Despite the fact that she still would not speak, she extended her mastery of the pencil to her pot-hooks and was soon able to write 'Nasha' and 'Mama' and 'Anna' underneath her portraits in large, wobbly letters. In a short time she had grown much attached to Anne and listened with keen if silent attention as Anne told her the names of the stars or the Kings and Queens of England. She had her third birthday, and the Count bought her a toboggan of her own, painted in blue and white, with a swan's head with a gilded beak. She loved it so much, she insisted on taking it to bed with her every night, and only a great deal of firmness on Nyanka's part persuaded her to keep it beside rather than in her bed.

In February, the winter fun reached its peak in the carnival season, which would culminate in the *masslenitsa* – Shrovetide – festivities, a sort of last grasp at gaiety before Lent began. A great fair was held on the river, with all sorts of displays and stalls.

'This is something you mustn't miss, Anna,' the Count said. 'Shall we take her, Irushka? And the children, of course.'

The Dowager was visiting a friend at Court and would be away all day, and probably all night too, and Anne expected the Countess to leap at the opportunity of an outing with her husband and children without interference. But she only shook her head without lifting her eyes from her work. 'Oh, no, forgive me, Nikolasha, but I don't think I could bear the crowds and the pushing and the noise.' She did not see the expression of disappointment which passed across his face, and was quickly suppressed. 'But you should go, Anna. It will be very good fun for you. Perhaps you could make up a party with the young Tiranovs and the Tchaikovskys.'

The Count demurred. 'Oh no, I don't mean to go in a regular

party, and particularly not a party in which I am regarded as an elderly nuisance!' He fixed Anne with a sardonic eye. 'To have Basil Tchaikovsky make me feel *de trop* would be too much for my frail self-confidence. Just a family outing was all I had in mind. Wait, I have it! Uncle Petya shall come with us. He's the very person to make the most of the fair. You and I, Anna, and Uncle Petya and the children – what do you say?'

Uncle Petya's size and bulk, Anne discovered, were certainly useful for thrusting a way through the crowds; and after a few minutes he swept Natasha up onto his shoulders, where she rode like a monkey clinging onto his huge fur collar and getting the best view of everything. There was plenty to see. There were boxing-booths, musicians, sword-swallowers, fire-eaters, dancing bears and dogs, acrobats, and jugglers. There was a troop of Cossacks who did tricks on horseback, jumping on and off at full gallop, standing on the saddle, and jumping from one horse to another. They also gave a display of Cossack dancing, full of curious leaps and leg-kicks; and there was a troupe of gypsy dancers, too, all in red and gold, the women's dresses sewn all over with shining metal discs, who twirled and clapped to a sawing tune on the fiddle.

There were wandering peddlers selling ribbons and trinkets and sweetmeats, and stalls where you could buy anything the heart desired, from a pewter plate to a handful of treacle cakes – *pryaniki*. Anne now discovered what the peasants did during the long frozen winter when they could not work the land. The fruit of the dark days was on sale all around: wooden shoes and *valenki*, gloves, stockings, furniture, pots and pans, blankets, toys, icons, preserved fruit, bead necklaces, decorated trinket-boxes, saddlery, dog collars, whips, painted baskets, and bird cages.

Anne was enjoying it all enormously, and was guiltily glad that the Countess had not come with them. Everything was so much more informal and relaxed as they were: Uncle Petya forced a way through for them, and the Count and Anne, with Yelena between them, slipped in after him like gulls riding a wake. Once when they were in a particularly dense part of the crowd, the Count took hold of Anne's hand to stop her getting separated from them, and he forgot to release it for quite a time. There was no reserve or tension between them. She felt, as she had felt that time at the waterfall, that it was they who were the family, they and the children.

They wandered amongst the stalls and watched the displays, marvelled at the acrobats, laughed at the puppet-play, clapped in time to the stamping of the dancers, ate hot pasties and roasted apples and *pryaniki*, and drank hot tea sweetened with raspberry jam. Uncle Petya bought Natasha a wooden doll, and Lolya a coral necklace; and the Count bought Anne a cross of blue enamel from Kiev set in delicate gold filigree. Uncle Petya bought a flask of vodka from a drinking booth, and the Count tasted it and pronounced it vile stuff, and then, laughing, produced a small flask of his own from under his coat.

The short day darkened, and flares and torches were lit. On the frozen river, skaters danced to the music of a band playing in a wooden shelter with charcoal braziers all around to keep their instruments from freezing. Dominating the scene was the great artificial ice-hill, a stout wooden frame covered with packed snow, down which the fur-hatted citizens were tobogganing with wild shrieks of glee onto the three-feet-thick ice of the river.

'Oh Papa!' Yelena cried, turning a passionate face up to him.

'What, risk your beauty, my little rose petal?' the Count smiled, cupping her pink cheek with one hand. 'Suppose you overset? What would Grandmère say if I brought you back all black and blue?'

'Oh, I don't care about that. And anyway, we won't overset. Oh Papa, please let's! Uncle Petya, please!'

The Count smiled at Anne. 'What about you, Anna Petrovna? Are you pining to try it?'

'It does look very exciting,' Anne said, 'but I don't know if it's quite proper. Do ladies toboggan in public?'

'Now you have said the one thing that would persuade me,' he grinned. 'Proper? Is that my English Anna, two thousand miles from home, wondering about propriety?'

'I have a reputation to preserve, sir,' Anne laughed. 'What would Basil Tchaikovsky say?'

'After I danced with you at the Embassy Ball at the Tuileries, you had no reputation left to lose,' he said firmly. 'Come on then, let's to it! We'll scale the mountain! Uncle Petya, hold tight to Nasha. Lolya, give me your hand.'

There were toboggans to hire at the foot of the slope for those who had not brought their own. Anne, still wondering if it were quite the thing, and perfectly sure that Lady Murray would have had ten fits if she had been here to see it, took charge of a battered red one and climbed, not without apprehension, to the taking-off stage at the top of the hill. The Count showed her how to sit on the sled and how to hold the rope, set her straight, and pushed her off.

There was a moment of sinking terror as she lurched over the rim of the slope; and then a mixture of wild exhilaration and fear as she gathered speed and the little wooden frame rocked and rattled over the streaked and glassy surface of the hill. The icy air streamed past her cheeks and tears broke from her eye-corners, and she had a brief watery impression of the lights and colours and pink faces of the crowds below on the river rushing up towards her; and then it was all over. She was jolting over level ground, and two huge men in peasant *tulups* and sheepskin gloves had caught and halted her, and were helping her to her feet.

She staggered a little, feeling dazed and dizzy. Her lungs seemed to be full of ice-cold space; there were tears on her blood-burning cheeks; and she felt horribly disappointed that it was over.

The Count and Lolya appeared beside her, having come down together. He grinned at Anne, and she knew by the cold air on her teeth that she was grinning too, in a ridiculous, exhilarated fashion.

'You were shrieking all the way down,' he said.

'Was I? I didn't know I was.'

'Again! Papa, again!' Lolya cried urgently, tugging her father's sleeve. Uncle Petya appeared with Natasha.

'Just once more, then,' the Count said. 'Coming, Anna?'

'Certainly,' she said. 'And I won't scream this time.'

The same fear and excitement as before; and as she hurtled down, Anne could feel herself shrieking, though she could not hear it, and could not have stopped herself. 'It's better than galloping on a fast horse,' she said afterwards.

'Not better – different,' the Count said.

'Again, Papa! I want to go again!' Lolya shrieked.

Anne shook her head involuntarily – the child seemed too excited – and the Count hesitated too, but Natasha was tugging at Uncle Petya's sleeve, her face turned up urgently like a pink flower, and he said, 'Oh, once more won't hurt them, Nikolasha.' He touched Natasha's head. 'You'd like to go just once more, wouldn't you, Nashka maya?'

'Very well, but this is the last,' the Count said.

'Enough for me,' Anne said. 'I'll wait here.' Her legs were trembling. She caught the Count's eye, pleading caution. It was too exciting to be entirely safe.

She stood at the bottom of the slope, waiting for them to appear up above. It looked very far away, and it was hard to tell one black shape from another in the crowd at the top by the wavering light of the torches. Each sled as it came down made a thud and a hard swishing sound; a hurtling, rigid bundle of colour with a pink circle at the top of it, and a black circle within the pink circle of the open, shrieking mouth. All around her there were people talking, laughing, shouting to one another; stall holders crying their wares; music from three different bands crashing together like waves hitting a rock; and suddenly all the sounds merged into something solid, so that she could no longer pick out individual sounds, and the noise became a single seamless thing, like a wall of silence.

And in that silence, she saw the Count and Uncle Petya with the children starting down. They were too small and bundled up for her to be able to recognise their features, but she knew it was them; and with another part of her attention she saw also the two young men, laughing and probably drunk, run onto the slope from the bottom, towing their toboggans, and trying to climb upwards, slipping back helplessly and falling over on the glassy surface. It all happened so quickly, that she could not understand afterwards how there seemed to be time to notice everything: the thin, fair beard of one young man, and the slate-blue colour of the other's greatcoat, and his gloved hand dark like a starfish against the ice as he fell sprawling, and the bottle he had been holding slithering and spinning like a live thing down the slope away from him.

She saw people's mouths opening and shutting in shouted warnings, but she could hear nothing in that wall of silence. Her own mouth was stretched open too – she felt a pain under her jaws. People were moving forward like a surging wave. The toboggans, one behind the other, sped like bullets, and the young men, still laughing, tried to scramble out of the way. The Count, with Yelena between his knees, missed them by inches. Uncle Petya's sled did not. He and the young men, in a sprawl of arms and legs, went sliding down the rest of the slope together like an untidy mat. Natasha, jerked out of his grasp like a projectile, went flying in an arc over the side of the hill and fell into the snow with a heavy thud.

Anne had no memory of moving, but she must have been running already, for she reached Natasha before anyone had had time to touch her.

'Nasha! Nasha!' she cried as she flung herself down, reaching out hands for the little bundle of red coat and rabbit-furred hood. The cold wetness of the packed snow struck through her knees, and the sounds were suddenly back, a blurred babble of cries and expostulations. Natasha opened her eyes and stared upwards unrecognisingly. 'Nasha, are you all right?' Anne said foolishly, touching, brushing away snow, trying to find out what damage had been done. She felt the Count arrive at her shoulder, saw Natasha's eyes uncloud and recognise first her and then her father.

'Yes,' Natasha said. 'Not hurt. Want to go again.'

The Count made a sound between a sob and a laugh, and his hands came past Anne to seize his child and lifted her into his arms. 'What?' he said unsteadily. 'What did you say? Nasha, Nashka, what did you say?'

'Want to go again,' she repeated, putting her arms round his neck as if nothing out of the ordinary had happened. The Count, holding her tightly, looked across her at Anne, his mouth laughing, while his eyes quite independently went on crying.

'Did you hear that, Annushka?' he said. 'She wants to go again. Did you hear?'

Anne nodded, knowing that if she spoke she would sound as drunk and foolish as he. She patted Natasha's back with a helpless gesture, and the Count encircled her with his free arm and drew her against him too, holding them both tightly against him until he could stop trembling.

Natasha didn't say anything else, but she was plainly unhurt: she moved freely and smiled normally, and the minutest search on Anne's part could find no injury beyond a slight bruise on one cheek. Her infant limpness and the bundling of her clothes must have protected her and cushioned the fall. Once they were in the troika going home, she fell asleep on her father's lap. Anne wondered anxiously if she might be concussed, but it seemed a perfectly natural sleep, and even Lolya was heavy-eyed after all the exertion and excitement.

'I shan't feel easy until she has been seen by a physician,' Uncle Petya said. 'Oh God, if only I hadn't taken her down the third time! I'll never forgive myself if she's been hurt!'

'Don't,' the Count said shortly. He looked bone weary, and Anne, beside him, longed to touch him, to comfort him in some way. 'It wasn't your fault. She'll be perfectly all right after a good night's sleep.'

'Yesilev's a good physician,' Uncle Petya went on, twisting the end of his beard between his fingers. 'He took care of the young Fralovskys when they had the measles. Shall I send for him?'

'Tomorrow,' the Count said. 'Tomorrow will be soon enough. Look, you see there's nothing wrong with her. She's sleeping naturally.'

'Oh God, pray it's so,' Petya said, uncomforted.

Vasky opened the door to them, and the Count, carrying Natasha, headed straight for the stairs. 'Where's her ladyship?' he asked.

'Her ladyship retired early to bed, sir. She felt rather tired. Has something happened, sir?'

'A slight mishap, nothing serious,' the Count said, already half-way up the first flight. Anne, hurrying behind him with Yelena, heard Uncle Petya begin a voluble explanation.

In the nursery, Nyanka, tutting but blessedly calm, took over her charge and undressed her and put her to bed without waking her, and then took Lolya off, promising her a hot bath, a bowl of bread-and-milk, and a story too, if she was good. Left alone, the Count and Anne stood for a while watching the sleeping child. Her fair eyelashes lay in a thick fan on her pink cheek, and her curled fingers rested beside her lightly-parted lips. She looked healthy and peaceful.

'I think she'll be all right,' the Count said, and then looked up at Anne. 'It did happen, didn't it? I didn't dream it? Nasha did speak?'

'Yes,' Anne said with a faint smile. 'Her first words.'

'Not particularly special ones, considering how long we've waited for them,' he said, 'but thank God for them, all the same. No matter how often one reassures oneself – '

'Yes, I know,' Anne said. 'But she's perfectly normal. A perfectly normal little girl.'

He looked down at the sleeping child. 'Little Nemetzka,' he said with a rough tenderness. 'Her first words, Anna!' He looked up. 'I'm glad you were there to hear them.'

She met his eyes, shining with tiredness and emotion, and felt too much, and tried to cover it up. 'Before long, she'll be chattering so much, you'll long for her to be silent again,' she said with an attempt at lightness.

The Count took her hand and lifted the fingers to his lips for an instant before turning away. 'And now,' he said, 'I had better go and see if my wife is still awake and break the news to her before some servant scares her out of her wits with tales of horror. Will you go and keep poor Petya company, Anna? I'll be down soon. Try to stop him beating his breast, will you?'

The next morning Anne hurried to the nursery as soon as she was dressed. Natasha was up and in the process of being dressed by Nyanka, and she ran to Anne as soon as she saw her and gave her a silent hug around the knees, turning her eyes up to her with her usual golden smile.

'She's all right,' Nyanka said gruffly. 'No bones broken. What's this Lolya is telling me, that my baby spoke last night?'

'Yes, it's true,' Anne said. 'Isn't it, Nasha?' She ruffled the tumble of mouse-fair curls, and Natasha nudged against her hand like a cat before running back to Nyanka to offer a foot for a stocking.

'Well, if you say so, Barishnya, it must be so,' Nyanka said grudgingly, 'but she hasn't spoken to me.'

She didn't speak to the physician who came later that morning, either, or to anyone else. The words of the night before, jarred out of her, perhaps, by the shock of the accident, remained her sole venture into the world of speech, and once again Nyanka was driven to fall back on her old comfort of 'she'll speak when she's ready'.

The physician pronounced Natasha unharmed, but recommended that she be kept quiet for a day or two, with no undue exertion or excitement. 'There may be some nervous reaction,' he said. 'Watch her carefully. I'll send round a tonic I recommend in these cases, and I'll call again tomorrow.'

Later, Anne went down to the morning room, and found the Count and Countess alone there, standing by the window and looking out into the street. They had the appearance of having been interrupted in a private conversation, and Anne hesitated at the threshold.

The Countess turned and held out a welcoming hand to Anne. 'Yes, come in! I have something to tell you. Is the doctor still upstairs?'

'No, madame, he left a few minutes ago. Did you want to see him?' Anne said.

'It doesn't matter. I can send word after him,' the Countess said. 'I wish to consult him, although it is only to confirm what I already know.' She smiled, and her face seemed alight and alive in a way Anne had not seen before. 'Dear Anna, have you not guessed? You are to have a new pupil! There is to be a new addition to the nursery! I am with child again!'

Anne's mind worked with feverish rapidity, assembling all the tiny pieces of evidence which she had noted and failed to put together over the past weeek or so. She was desperately aware of the Count's presence and kept her eyes forcibly from him, lest she betray herself. She remembered in a painful jumble of images the evening they had just shared, and the moments of intimacy which had seemed, then, so important to her.

Intimacy! She felt a withering sensation inside her, as she tried not to think of exactly what this news meant. It was a knowledge she had refused all along, shutting it away in some inaccessible part of her mind, even – inexcusable folly! – allowing herself to believe it was not so. Now the truth was being forced upon her. This

171

woman was his wife. She was with child. He had shared a bed with her.

Anne heard her voice saying the right things, congratulating them both with amazing calmness, even with the appearance of pleasure. And now her treacherous eyes, despite all her efforts, escaped her control. The Count stood beside his wife, not quite touching her, and met Anne's regard like a stranger, receiving her congratulations with a smile of perfect politeness. His face was a meaningless blank, his eyes opaque to her. For the first time since she had met him that day on the Ile de la Cité almost a year ago, she looked at him and had no idea what he was thinking or feeling.

BOOK TWO – 1807

Chapter Eleven

It snowed again that morning, the flakes falling with cat's-paw softness onto the glittering, frozen city. Anne stood at her window and watched the endless, silent whirling from a sky the colour of a gull's back, blotting out the view and making instead for her a magical, miniature landscape of drifts and hollows along the glazing bars of the window. It was March, still a month away from the thaw.

Ottepel – the thaw: an event so dramatic, so overwhelming, that Russian poets without number had used it as a simile for every kind of violent change from the emotional to the political. Anne had seen three of them since she came to Russia, as each year the revolving world turned back towards the sun, and the lengthening daylight hours began at last to warm the frozen northlands.

The first intimation would be the pink-tinged mist at dawn, and the long-absent sound of water dripping from the eaves and gutters. Then the ice on the Neva would suddenly split with a violent report like a cannon shot, and begin to break up. For a week, huge ice floes would move slowly downstream towards the Gulf, more and more of them, fed in from the ice-bound Lake Lagoda. They passed in endless procession like a migration of primordial beasts, magnificent in their heedlessness, grinding their shoulders against each other like rocks, jostling against the quays with a booming thud. The river, which all winter had been a road, and all summer would be a waterway, for a time was unusable. The banks were cut off from each other, except when some daring soul ventured out onto the ice and risked the crossing by jumping from one floe to the next, like stepping stones.

And as the ice melted, so would the snow in the streets. Underfoot it turned to slippery, treacherous slush, and galoshed boots replaced the felt *valenki* for those determined to walk. Sledges were put away, and the first wheeled vehicles churned the streets into grey-brown mires, flinging icy water over unlucky pedestrians. The dripping sound hastened into gurgling as the world threw off its winter-long accumulation of water: butts filled, gutters overflowed, and masses of softened snow slid suddenly and perilously from roofs. Everything was wet, cold and wet, and the air became a damp, grey blanket of fog through which the sun shone dimly, tracking across the sky a little higher each day.

And yet in the space of only two or three weeks, the whole thing was accomplished, and the blue-white, smooth and glittering world of winter would be gone, dislimning as rapidly and completely as a dream. Suddenly there was colour again, the greens and browns of nature, the blue of cupola and the gold of spire. And the sun shone, pallid but daily strengthening, from a vivid, spring-blue sky.

Then would come the day when the Peter and Paul Fortress at the mouth of the river fired its cannon as a signal that the river was open for navigation. As if conjured from nothing by the sound, hundreds of little boats, like gaily-coloured insects, would instantly appear, filling the miracle of reflection between the banks. That first day, the tall, lovely buildings would echo with voices and laughter and music, as if the pent-up mirth of the city had been set loose to flow again, as the clear water bubbled up out of the unlocked earth like joy. Then the Governor of the Fortress would be rowed in a ceremonial barge, ornate and canopied as a Venetian gondola, to the quay in front of the Winter Palace, where he would present to the Tsar a glass of cold water as a symbol that the winter was truly over.

But that was all a month away at least, and, looking out on the smooth, unbroken integrity of the frozen world outside her window, Anne had her usual spasm of disbelief that this could be anything but the permanent order of things. While she had been standing there, deep in her reverie, the snow had eased and stopped, and now the thermometer on the window-frame outside told her that it was freezing hard again. The sky was like stone, heavy with the threat of more snow to come, and her heart was numb, too, with apprehensions of disaster and the weariness of waiting for news. A month ago there had been a battle in snow-bound Lithuania between the French and the Russians. The Russians had claimed it as a victory; but the Count was missing.

It was odd to think, Anne reflected, that it had all started with the Duc d'Enghien, that handsome, auburn-haired Bourbon prince whom she had met briefly at the court at Karlsruhe. She remembered his gaiety, his lightness, the way the Princess had tapped his cheek affectionately with her fan, and could hardly believe that he had ever had anything more weighty on his mind than hunting, dancing, and flirtations. But in February 1804, the French police had uncovered a plot to assassinate Bonaparte, one of many such since the Corsican had taken supreme power. It was secretly financed by the British government, and a leading figure in the conspiracy was said to be this same Duc d'Enghien.

It seemed that his role was to liaise between the emigrants in England and the Breton royalists who were fomenting the plot, and in particular to ride post-haste to Paris as soon as the Consul was dead, and proclaim the restoration of the Bourbon monarchy. Such plots, of course, were a serious threat to Bonaparte, and he evidently decided to make an example of the young Prince. In March 1804 he dispatched a force of three hundred dragoons secretly to Strasbourg. They crossed the Rhine in the dead of night, surrounded the castle of Ettenheim, dragged the Duc from his bed, and bundled him, protesting, into a coach, in which he was galloped under strict guard to Paris. There he was brought before a military tribunal, and summarily condemned for fomenting civil war. At two-thirty in the morning of the 21st of March, he was executed by firing-squad in the waterless moat of the fortress of Vincennes.

The news of this abduction and judicial murder caused a violent wave of reaction in all the courts of Europe, and nowhere more than in St Petersburg. By his act, Bonaparte had violated the territorial integrity of Baden, which was the principality of the Empress's mother; and to this political indignation was added personal grief for the handsome, high-spirited young Prince, whom the imperial family had known and loved. The Empress Elisabeth broke down and wept at the news of his execution, and a full week of formal mourning was ordered for the Court.

The Emperor was incensed, regarding the incident as a personal affront; and his antipathy towards Bonaparte was further strengthened when, only two months later, the Corsican had himself declared Emperor of the French. When that piece of news had arrived, Anne had reminded the Count of their discussion at the ball in Paris about ambition.

'Emperor of France today; ruler of the world tomorrow. Can anyone now doubt that that is his desire?'

'It was inevitable he should take this step,' the Count replied with a shrug. 'Ambition of his sort has only one, well-marked path it can tread. As First Consul, he had the power, but not the mystery: he was too vulnerable. You remember that line from Hamlet – "There is a divinity which hedgeth round a king"?'

'But can he think it will protect him?' Anne said. 'Kings are made of flesh and blood: they can be murdered.'

'It isn't simply a matter of that. He has a large country to rule, and hopes to make it larger. An elected consul is only one government official ruling over others, and in every province there would be other ambitious men eager for promotion to his eminence. But a king – or an emperor – occupies a realm far removed from government office. He can be adulated by the people – almost worshipped – and he cannot be demoted.'

'Yes, I see that,' Anne said. 'And I suppose in time people would forget how he came by his royal state.'

'Don't forget, either, that kings can also leave sons to carry on after them,' the Count said. He sighed and rubbed a hand over his face. 'It is all inevitable, you know – everything that has happened, and that will happen, in France. Men do not change. Once the Revolution began, it was inevitable that one man would emerge to take power, and that having power, he would seek to establish his own new dynasty. Now every man's hand will be against him. Europe will be convulsed with war, and men will die, and eventually Bonaparte will be defeated, at great cost to everyone; and all of that is inevitable too. We learn nothing from history; it is in our nature that we never will.'

'And will Russia go to war?' Anne asked.

'I think so,' the Count said. 'I told you once that whether or not we joined the war would be the personal decision of the Tsar; and this business with d'Enghien has afforded just the personal reason he needs.'

The Count had proved right. By April 1805, Russia had signed treaties of alliance with Austria, Sweden and England, and in August, Kirov, resplendent in the white and gold uniform of a colonel of cavalry, rode off to take up his command in Poland.

That had been an anxious year for Anne, waiting day by day for news of the planned invasion of England by Bonaparte – now calling himself the Emperor Napoleon – with the army he had assembled along the Channel coast. Deprived of the support of the Count's presence and worrying for his safety, she yet had to try to comfort the Countess for the same pains she was suffering herself. The news of the great sea battle off Cape Trafalgar in October 1805, in which the English fleet under Admiral Nelson had utterly destroyed the combined French and Spanish force, relieved Anne's mind of one anxiety. It was impossible that the French would be able again to raise a sufficient force to support the invasion of England. Blockaded as they were, they would simply never be able to assemble sufficient materials to build a new fleet: any naval warfare on their part from now on must be confined to single-ship activity. As long as the English navy sailed the seas, England herself was safe.

But bad news followed good: in December a terrible and bloody battle was fought at Austerlitz, seventy miles from Vienna, and the combined Russian and Austrian army was utterly routed by the French. In an incredibly short time, Napoleon himself had marched the army which had been assembled at Boulogne for the invasion of England over 700 miles across France and Bavaria into Austria, there to defeat a force twice as large. Of the allied army, twenty-seven thousand men were killed or captured; after the battle, the Emperor Alexander, who had insisted on directing the campaign in person, sat down among the Russian dead and wept.

With Vienna occupied by French troops, the Austrian Emperor was forced to submit to Napoleon. The Holy Roman Empire was no more: Austria was stripped of half its territories in the Treaty of Pressburg, and Napoleon was recognised in his newly-assumed title of King of Italy. With Tsar Alexander back in Petersburg and his army licking its wounds in winter camp, the war might have ended there; for with the death of Pitt there was a change of government in England, and the new government under Fox was anxious for peace.

Through spring and summer of 1806, tentative talks went on between the emissaries of England and France, with Hanover – principality of the King of England, but at present occupied by French troops – as the bait and the prize. But even as they talked, Napoleon formed sixteen small German states into a single entity, called the Confederation of the Rhine, making it a state within the French Empire with himself as Protector, and it seemed increasingly unlikely that he meant to let Hanover go. When he prepared to invade the previously neutral Portugal, the English sent a fleet to Lisbon to protect it, and the prospect of peace receded.

The Count spent a month at home in August 1806, and Vera Borisovna brought Sergei to visit his father. The talk was inevitably of war, with Sergei fretting that he was not old enough to serve alongside his father.

'Don't worry, Seryosha,' the Count said with a grim smile. 'There will be plenty more fighting to come. You will have your share.'

'But isn't it all over?' Sergei asked. 'I thought, after Austerlitz – '

'No, no, my dear. Napoleon has Austria; now he will have Prussia. The Confederation of the Rhine is the first step towards extending his empire northwards, right to the banks of the Nieman. He has a great belief in what he calls 'natural territory' – a sort of geographical logic, you know.'

'You don't think – he won't try to take Russia too?' the Countess asked faintly.

The Count frowned. 'I think not – '

'He could not do it,' Sergei broke in boisterously. 'No-one could

179

conquer Russia – it's too big! He would not be so mad as to try!'

'Apart from that,' the Count went on calmly, 'I don't believe Napoleon would attempt it for another reason. He has a strange admiration for our Emperor – looks upon him as a sort of spiritual brother. It is not widely known that before Austerlitz he sent twice to our camp asking for a personal meeting with the Tsar to talk peace; and that after the battle, he sent another message along the same lines. It's my belief that he thinks it would be a fulfilment of the natural order of things, if Europe were divided into two great empires, France and Russia, ruled by himself and Alexander, bound together in brotherly love.'

'He is mad, then?' Anne said quietly.

The Count looked at her for a moment. 'Yes, I think so,' he said at last. 'And yet – there is something appealing about such magnitude of vision. It is the faint scent on the breeze, the hint that man could be greater than he is.'

'At the price of so many thousands dead,' Anne reminded him.

'Yes,' the Count said. 'An unacceptable price, of course. We do not yet seem to have found another way to greatness.'

'But what about music, painting, architecture?' Anne protested. 'Look at Petersburg, for instance. Is that not greater than the sum of the men who built it?'

The Count smiled at her in perfect sympathy. 'You chose your example badly – thousands of serfs died to raise Petersburg from the swamps. But I grant you the point. Perhaps a great cathedral is almost as grand a vision as a mighty empire.'

Sergei looked bored with the turn the conversation had taken. 'But Father, will Napoleon really fight Prussia? We heard that he had offered them Hanover in exchange for their neutrality.'

'He won't give Hanover to Prussia any more than he will give it to England. Why should he? He has little to fear from Frederick William.'

'Who are you talking of, Koko?' said Vera Borisovna, walking into the room at that moment. 'The King of Prussia? Oh, he's a poor creature, nothing like his great-uncle, Frederick the Great. Now there was a ruler! He was on the best of terms with our dear Empress Catherine, you know. In those days, Europe was ruled by great monarchs, a giant breed who seem, alas, to be extinct in these poor modern times! Now there is nothing but an unprincipled Corsican bandit, and spineless creatures like the Austrian Emperor, signing away his patrimony, and that half-witted, vacillating oaf in Berlin. His wife is more of a man than he is. Why doesn't he drive Bonaparte out?'

'He will probably try, Mama,' the Count said mildly, 'but I doubt whether he will succeed. Napoleon's star is still rising. The time has not yet come when he can be defeated.'

The Countess was looking at him with wide, surprised eyes, but Vera Borisovna had merely snorted contemptuously. 'Mystical rubbish! He is a common little man who rose through the ranks, and he can be sent back the same way. He has armies – send armies against him! He lives by the sword – let him die by the sword!'

There was never any point in arguing with Vera Borisovna, so the Count changed the subject at that point; but after dinner, while strolling on the terrace, he told Anne that Frederick William was even then in negotiation with the Tsar, for his support if he declared war on France.

'I don't think the Tsar will refuse to help,' the Count said. 'As soon as they reach an agreement, war will be declared, and I will have to leave you all again.' He lapsed into silence, leaning on the parapet and staring sightlessly at the blue wreaths of smoke rising from his neglected cigar.

'Will it be for long?' Anne asked quietly.

'Yes, I think so. It will not take long for Napoleon to defeat Prussia; but my fear is that he will interfere in Poland, and that will mean that we will enter the war on our own behalf, not just to help Frederick William.'

'I don't understand,' Anne said.

He smiled. 'No, how should you? I will explain, if you are ready for a little history lesson.'

'You know that I am always eager to learn,' Anne said.

'Yes, I know. That was one of the things I always liked about you, Anna Petrovna: your mind is not closed and shuttered like most women's – like most people's indeed! Well, then, we must go back to the last century, when, as my mother told us so eloquently, the world was ruled by those giant figures, Catherine of Russia and Frederick of Prussia. Catherine the Great and Frederick the Great.'

'Were they so great?' Anne asked.

'You doubt it? Little cynic! They were, at least, ruthless, which often does just as well in a ruler. At any rate, they, with the help of the Emperor of Austria, carved up the Kingdom of Poland into three portions, and swallowed them. Austria took the southern Polish province of Galicia; Russia took the provinces bordering the Ukraine, along with Lithuania and the northern seaboard territories; and that left

181

Prussia with the ancient Polish Crown lands, the capital of Warsaw, and the seaport of Danzig – which up until then had been a sort of free state with its own autonomous government.'

'Rather hard on the Polish people,' Anne suggested.

'Straight to the heart of it, as usual,' the Count nodded approvingly. 'Yes, it was; and the Poles are a fiercely patriotic people. Well, we Russians haven't had much trouble with our share of the partition, because our way of life isn't much different from theirs, and we leave them alone a good deal; and of course Lithuania had only been a territory attached to Poland. But the Crown Lands were the heart of Poland, and they have always hated Prussian rule. That's where the trouble is likely to begin. Last year Czartoryski, our Foreign Minister, who happens to be a Pole himself, begged the Tsar to help the Polish cause; but he wouldn't interfere, and that, of course, leaves the way clear for Napoleon to become their national hero instead.'

'But how?'

'By helping to recreate the Kingdom of Poland – with himself as overlord, of course, in some capacity or other. I imagine he will offer to help them free themselves from Prussia, in return for their becoming a satellite kingdom within the French Empire. The Poles are proud, and Napoleon is not without tact, so he will probably not ask to be called King, or Emperor, or Protector, or whatever is this year's title, but that's what it will amount to. And then, naturally, the Poles will want their lands back, which now belong to Russia.'

'And the Tsar, of course, will not agree,' Anne said thoughtfully.

'Of course not. It will mean real war between us and France, not this half-hearted business of helping Austria and helping Prussia.'

Anne sought for something comforting to say. 'Perhaps if it is real war, it will be over the sooner,' she said.

He looked at her for a moment, and then laughed. 'Well tried! But it would be more to the purpose if you offered to play to me on the pianoforte. Music has charms, you know, to soothe a savage breast.'

'Likewise, "music oft hath such a charm to make bad good, and good provoke to harm," ' Anne returned.

The count considered. 'Shakespeare,' he said at last.

'That,' she said severely, 'was purely guesswork.'

'It's a long time since we played that game,' he smiled, and offered her his arm. 'Come and play to me, and we'll see who was right.'

Prussia declared war on France in September 1806, and the Count rode away again to join his regiment, this time in Lithuania. Napoleon defeated the Prussians in a devastatingly short campaign, crushing their armies at Jena and Auerstadt on October the 14th in a single day. Thereafter, the Prussian Empire collapsed in a series of retreats and surrenders; and by December, French troops were trotting into Warsaw to be greeted as deliverers by the delirious inhabitants. From every side, Polish nobles and their followers streamed into Warsaw, eager to offer their services. Napoleon had made the offer the Count had foreseen, and as the bitter Polish winter closed in on the armies of France and Russia, a new Polish state was being created under the leadership of Prince Joseph Poniatowski, the nephew of the country's last king.

The Count had written what he knew of these events from a camp somewhere near Königsberg, where he was with his regiment under the overall command of the Tsar's brother, Grand Duke Constantine, as short, pug-nosed, and hot-tempered as Alexander was tall, handsome, and serene. News came infrequently, much delayed and frequently garbled or contradictory. There had been a short, fierce but inconclusive battle in December between the Russians and the French at Pultusk, after which the French had retired into winter quarters, and nothing more was expected to be heard until the thaw.

But three weeks ago news had filtered through of a further engagement. The Russians, it seemed, had attacked the French in winter quarters at Preuss-Eylau. A running battle had been fought through the town, with heavy losses on both sides, but the French, it was claimed, had had the worst of it. It was the nearest thing the Russians had had yet to a victory, and there was rejoicing in Petersburg, which in the Kirov Palace rang rather hollow. The Count's regiment had been one of those engaged, and as yet there had been no news of him.

A scratching on the door of her chamber roused Anne from her reverie, and a maid came in to say that Fräulein Hoffnung had finished giving the girls their German lesson and wondered, as it had stopped snowing, whether they ought to take their walk now, in case it should begin again.

'I'll come,' Anne said, having little difficulty in translating this as a cry for help. Bad weather lately had confined Lolya and Nasha to the house a great deal, making them even more boisterous and high-spirited than usual; and Fräulein Hoffnung had a head cold.

'Run along to Nyanka, girls, and put on your outdoor things,' Anne said as she lifted the siege. The Fräulein rolled grateful eyes in her direction, and drew out her third handkerchief of the day. 'And you had much better go to bed,' Anne added to the sufferer as the children ran away. 'You don't look at all the thing.'

As soon as they were outside, Lolya and Nasha rushed off like dogs frisking, and were soon snowballing each other and shrieking with all the force of their pent-up energy. Lolya, now almost thirteen, had reached the age when her normal propensity was to rush about and behave like a hoyden. She bubbled over all day long with energy, and her high spirits were sometimes violent, especially when bad weather confined her indoors for any length of time; but she was gradually learning the accomplishments of a woman and beginning to take an interest in her future marriage prospects; and had fits of worrying that she was little taller at thirteen than she had been at nine.

'When will I grow, Anna Petrovna?' she would ask anxiously. 'How tall were you when you were my age? What if I never grow any more, ever?'

Anne's attempts to reassure her were defeated by the fact that her cousin Kira was six inches taller than her, and even more so by the fact that Nasha had suddenly shot up like a weed in a greenhouse and, at six and a half, could easily keep up with her sister. Anne had been very glad to see the friendship growing between her young charges. Natasha was mature in advance of her years, and Lolya now found in her an acceptable companion for her games and a sympathetic listener to her troubles.

Nasha was a good listener. After the incident at the ice-fair, she had not spoken again for some time, but it was clear that it was from disinclination, not inability, and her reading and writing skills grew rapidly from that point. Anne took great pleasure in teaching her, because she was so eager to learn. Lolya only learned to please Anne, or because she thought it would be useful to her in later life; but Nasha had a real love of, and hunger for, knowledge for its own sake. She still spoke very little, rarely volunteering a remark, and answering more often than not with gestures and nods of the head; but she wrote reams, stories and poems and strange internal monologues, and made pencil sketches and tiny coloured paintings which she showed to Anne with the confidence of love.

Anne received them with intense pleasure and a certain tingling of unease. Both the writing and the drawing presented a view of the world which was strangely familiar, and yet which gave the impression of being slightly distorted in a way Anne could not quite pin down. It was as if she were looking through one of the crystals of the lustre in the great hall: everything appeared

184

tiny and radiantly clear, rainbow-edged, and infinitesimally out of shape.

As well as her silence, Nasha had retained her self-absorption. Left alone, she would amuse herself quite happily all day long, writing or drawing, or simply staring into the fire or out of the window for hours at a time, her golden eyes blank and shining, her face serene as she travelled through some landscape of thought which was entirely satisfying to her. While Lolya had the normal child's love of novelty, playing with a thing briefly and discarding it easily when her attention was diverted by something else, Nasha had an intensity of focus which could shut out interruptions, like an anchoress, and she would carry one thing around with her all day, to feel it and touch it and look at it until she knew it absolutely.

But with all that, there were enough times when, as now, she rushed about, shrieking and romping with Lolya, for Anne to feel there was no need to worry about her. Nasha had unusual talents, but she was a normal, healthy child as well. Anne was not entirely sure that it was always Lolya who initiated their naughty pranks, though it was usually she who took the blame. Yesterday, for instance, when they had tried to make an indoor skating rink in one of the unused rooms of the palace, by opening the top windows and pouring water on the floor ... There had been something about Nasha's face that had made Anne suspect it was she who first thought of it; but Lolya was the one who had argued, justified, defended, and finally sighed and admitted guilt.

They needed a firm hand, Anne thought with a sigh, and though they minded her pretty well, there were times when her life would have been made easier if there had been a higher authority to whom to appeal for confirmation of her decrees. But the Count was away, and the Countess, though physically present, was growing more absent, it seemed, day by day.

Walking along the quay behind the children, Anne thought about her with a mixture of anxiety, pain, and exasperation. Irina had never been the same since Sasha was born. In fact, she had begun to change even during that pregnancy. Anne remembered how for the first few happy days, she had basked in the joy of accomplished love, and the Count had treated her like something fragile and precious, and Anne had been driven nearly mad with suppressed and fiercely-resisted jealousy. But then Vera Borisovna had returned to the palace from her visit and had been told the news that the hated interloper was pregnant again. Anne had watched the Dowager's lips whiten with fury, and for a moment

185

had thought that she would actually forget herself and let out all her rage and spite.

But the moment passed. Vera Borisovna controlled herself, and uttered a few words of congratulation, though in such a cold and loathing voice that even the Count could not have believed she meant them. Irina seemed to shrink together under the icy glare like something blighted by frost, and the joy of the pregnancy had gone out of her in that moment. From then on it brought her only misery. Physically she was unwell, troubled with continuous nausea, cramps, headaches, insomnia, and later backache and painfully swollen legs. Yet those were the least of her problems: it was the Dowager's persecution which really made the pregnancy a torment. Vera Borisovna was furious that another half-caste was to be brought into the world to steal her precious grandchildren's inheritance from them, and in every way she could, she vented her spite on Irina.

It was a subtle and unrelenting campaign. The Dowager could not attack openly, or do anything that might provoke-her son to remonstrate; but she was a past master in the art of the veiled insult, the criticism disguised as kindly advice, the reminiscence designed to undermine confidence. The Count, seeing his wife grow pale and thin, expressed his concern about her and unwittingly gave his mother a new opening; for now, under the guise of concern for Irina's health, the Dowager could describe in lingering detail all the miscarriages, birth agonies, and childbed deaths she had ever witnessed or heard about.

There came a day when Irina, while talking to Nyanka about the state of the linen-cupboard, collapsed in tears on that broad, familiar breast and sobbed out her fears that the Dowager was ill-wishing her, that she would give birth to a deformed child or die in childbed. Nyanka, fierce in her motherliness like a mountain bear, offered to go at once and turn the Dowager bodily out of the house. But Irina, her sobs subsiding, begged her to say and do nothing, afraid that any intervention would only make things worse. Nyanka insisted on giving her the phial of St Nino's blood to wear around her neck as protection against the Evil Eye and stamped about the house muttering imprecations, ostentatiously crossing herself whenever she passed the Dowager. At the end of the day, when the Count returned home, Nyanka cornered him and told him bluntly that if the Dowager did not leave, she could not answer for the consequences.

'My mistress's nerves are all to pieces,' Nyanka said, fixing him with a steely eye, 'and if you want your son to be born alive, you must do something about it.'

Anne was not privy to the interview which took place between the Count and the Dowager. The Dowager did not leave for Moscow for another month, but during that time, she kept herself distant from the Countess, and persecuted her only by treating her to a cold politeness whenever they met. After she had departed, the Countess revived a little, but like a flower left too long out of water, she did not regain her spring. The Dowager seemed a continuing presence, and even from the remoteness of Moscow managed to continue the campaign by writing weekly letters describing the excellent qualities of Yelena Vassilovna's son and doubting that anyone else's child could begin to match him, wondering if Irina Pavlovna's delicate health had improved at all, and uttering vague threats about the future disposition of her personal fortune. Anne, urged on by Nyanka, would have kept these letters from the Countess, even going so far as to beg her not to open them, but they seemed to exercise a black fascination over her. The Countess read them because not knowing what they said was worse than the reality.

The baby was finally born at Schwartzenturm in August, a perfectly-formed, if rather small, baby boy; but the labour went hard with Irina, and she was unwell for a long time afterwards. Even when she did rise from her bed, she did not regain her former strength and spirits, but remained listless, depressed, and more silent than ever. She seemed unable to take any interest in the child, whom they named Alexander; and as soon as he was done with his wet-nurse, he seemed to turn quite naturally to Anne for mothering.

From his small beginnings, Sasha had thrived and grown, filling Anne with a different kind of love from anything she had ever known before. It was the first time she had ever known a human creature from birth upwards, and as Irina turned away from the boy, Anne began to feel almost as if Sasha were her own son. Everything to do with him gave her great joy: to feed and bathe him, rock him and play with him, even to stand by his crib and watch him sleep. She was fascinated by his growing intelligence, and at times she felt she could almost see the unmarked, malleable clay of his infant mind taking shape as each new experience was impressed upon it. From the first moment he reached out a hand and encountered the bars of his crib, he was discovering where his own self ended and the rest of the universe began. It was a process Anne loved to watch, and with only a light hand she guided his exploration of the world, and his learning, day by day, the nature of things and how to respond to them.

It was for Anne that Sasha first smiled; it was she who placed objects in his fat little hands to examine and, inevitably, suck; towards her he made his first crawling movements, and with her aid first stood upright and took a bowlegged, wavering step; and when he spoke his first word, it was *Annan*, uttered with a beaming smile and outflung arms towards his adoptive mother.

Now, as she walked along the quay watching Lolya and Nasha race ahead and snowball each other, Sasha was stumping along manfully beside her, and his hand locked fast in hers seemed as natural a concomitant to walking as her own legs. He was the more absolutely hers because his father had been absent from home, with only two brief visits, since he was a year old. The Count barely knew his son; Irina had no interest in him; Vera Borisovna refused to acknowledge he existed. Sasha was hers, her own; and while with her conscious mind she might rationalise her feelings, might tell herself that as governess to the Kirov household it was her business to take an interest in Alexander and to direct his upbringing, there was a dark, atavistic place inside her that loved the child with a fierce, maternal passion. She would not acknowledge it, even to herself, but it was to do with her feelings for the Count: Sasha was the child of his that she should have borne.

Tanya, who was walking beside her pushing the baby-sledge, a sort of baby-carriage on runners, for when Sasha's legs grew tired, said, 'There's a gentleman over there waving, mademoiselle. I think it might be Count Tchaikovsky.'

Anne turned her head. 'Yes, you are right. We'll wait for him. Call the children back, Tanya.'

The figure in fur hat and long sable coat would not have been recognisable at that distance as Basil Tchaikovsky, except for the white boots he affected, which he claimed were made from polar bear fur, and his gold-headed ebony walking-stick. Anne waited for him to close on her with a degree of pleasure she would not have imagined possible three years ago; but he had changed in the time she had known him, becoming a great deal more sensible and a little less conceited. The Count had been struck by it the last time he had been home and had teased Anne on the effect she had had on her lover.

'He is trying to win your approval, Anna, that's what it is. You will make a man of him yet.'

Anne had denied it hotly, protesting that she was not so vain and foolish as to suppose that she could have wrought any change in him; yet it was hard not to conclude that his idle plan of making her popular had resulted in his coming genuinely to admire her. She could not say he precisely *courted* her; but he sought her company, listened to her opinions, and was at pains to please her; and this winter, for the first time in his life, he had come to Petersburg without his sister.

It was he who had brought the first news of the battle at Preuss-Eylau to the Kirov household, and since then had oscillated between the Court and the Angliskaya Naberezhna, using his influence at the former to beg intelligence for the latter. His attentions had been kind, and though he was still very much a man of fashion, he seemed to Anne much less of a coxcomb, and she liked him the better for it.

He reached her now, his breath smoking with his haste, the tip of his thin nose crimson with the cold, and held out hands encased in huge sable gauntlets, like a bear's paws.

'Anna Petrovna! I'm glad I spotted you walking along. I was just on my way to call on you at the Palace.' His bulging eyes were alight with some excitement, and he closed both paws over the hand she offered.

'What is it? Is it news?' she asked, suddenly breathless.

'Yes,' he said, looking down at her with some unfathomable emotion. 'It is news of Kirov. He is found. He is alive.'

Anne's apprehensions seized on the words. 'Alive! But what do you mean? Is he hurt?'

Before Tchaikovsky could answer, the children came running up.

'Basil Andreyevitch!' Lolya called. 'Why are you walking? Where's your troika? Are your greys lame? Are you going to walk with us? If you come with us, we could go as far as the winter garden, and see the aviary.'

'Basil Andreyevitch does not want to see the aviary, you foolish child,' Anne said with a nervous smile. 'We are going to turn back now, so that he can pay his respects to your mama.'

Lolya pouted. 'Oh, pooh! He doesn't need us to come, to do that. I don't want to turn back – we've only been out a minute. Anna, *do* let's go on! There's a new scarlet parrot at the aviary and you can see Basil Andreyevitch any time.'

But Nasha, watching Anne's face carefully, tugged briefly at her sleeve and mouthed the word 'Papa?' Anne nodded, tears jumping to her eyes. Lolya had not noticed this exchange, and Basil, trying to be helpful, solemnly offered her his arm, and said, 'I think it is going to snow again very soon. Your walk had better be postponed until a finer day. Won't you do me the honour of allowing me to escort you, Yelena Nikolayevna?'

Lolya hesitated, torn between the pleasure of such grown-up

attentions and her disapproval of this particular gentleman. 'Well,' she said, placing her hand doubtfully on his arm, 'I suppose I might. But I still think it's very poor-spirited of you not to go and fight the French. If I were a man, I'd have gone.'

'I'm sure you would – and heaven help the French if you had! But someone had to stay, you know, to look after you ladies,' Basil said gravely.

'We'd have looked after ourselves,' Lolya said stoutly. 'I don't see that *that* was very important.'

Anne could not listen to any more of this. 'Children, why don't you run on ahead of us? You needn't go indoors yet. Ask Stefan to take you tobogganing in the garden. Tanya, go with them – and take Sasha in the sledge. I think he's walked far enough.' Lolya was happy enough to comply, but Nasha flung Anne a burning look of appeal. 'Yes, I'll come and see you later,' Anne replied to it.

The children ran off, with Tanya following them pushing the sledge, and Anne was at liberty at last to turn to Basil and say, 'For God's sake, tell me! What do you know? Where is he? Is he hurt?'

'He is safe. I'll tell you everything I know, but take my arm, at least. You're trembling. That's better. Well, you know that there was a battle in Preuss-Eylau?'

'Yes, yes, go on!'

'It seems it was a pretty fierce affair, right in the town itself, a sort of running fight from house to house. Barclay de Tolly was commanding our men, but Soult's soldiers gave them plenty of trouble at first, driving them back to the gardens at the edge of the town. It came on to snow, and our men were tired and half-starved, but Barclay rallied them and they fought their way back into the town square in the centre. Hundreds of French fell and even more were taken prisoner.'

'But what of the Count?' Anne asked desperately.

'Hush, I'm coming to it,' he said. 'Well, the snow was blowing, making it hard to see anything, and dusk was falling, too, and the last of Soult's men were holed up in the church and the graveyard, and making a sort of last stand there behind the snow mounds which had formed over the gravestones. Barclay sent in the cavalry to clear them out. Kirov was leading his own men in the charge when it seems he was hit by a round of grapeshot – '

'Oh, dear God!' Anne cried, her hands going up to her mouth.

'Wait! Let me finish. He came off his horse and was probably knocked unconscious by the fall, or the shot, or something. His sergeant saw him go, but couldn't stop, being carried forward by the charge.

All was confusion. You can imagine how it was – darkness, driving snow, galloping horses. Kirov disappeared under the horses' hooves – God knows why he wasn't killed! He must have been rolled around like a stone in a whirlpool. Anyway, the charge was successful, and the French were completely knocked out, but when Kirov's sergeant, who'd seen him fall, went back to help him, he couldn't find him. He searched everywhere, and then reported him missing.'

'And where was he?'

'It seems some other soldier from another troop, who didn't know who he was, had found him and took him to a dressing station. The Count was unconscious at the time, of course, and when he came to himself, they discovered he'd lost his memory – couldn't remember his own name, or anything. So that's why no report came through to us that he'd been found.'

'What are his injuries?' Anne managed to ask.

'Well, he'd taken a lot of bruising from being under the horses, and one of them must have given him a kick in the head, for he had a head wound which was obviously what caused him to lose his memory. And his left arm was pretty badly knocked about.'

'Have they – did they – '

'Cut it off?' He anticipated her with devastating ease. 'I don't know. I don't think so. The message says it's pretty bad, that's all.'

'And does he still remember nothing?'

'Oh, as to that, he's quite himself now. What happened was that they moved him from the dressing station almost at once to a hospital camp at Koñigsberg, which is why no-one from his own troop could find him. And from there, they took him by sledge to military headquarters at Olita. That's where he was when his mind cleared, and he remembered who he was and what had happened. So they sent off a message, and it came through in the despatch bag to Czartoryski's office today. And that's all I know.'

There was a brief silence while Anne digested the story, and then she said, 'Thank you for telling me. I could not have endured to wait until we reached the Palace. But you will have to tell it all over again to the Countess.'

'Of course,' Basil said simply. 'I wonder how she will receive it. It will be as well for you to be on hand, in case she faints away, or something.' His eyes shone with approval as he looked down at her. 'All women have not your spirit, Anna Petrovna.'

Anne bit her lip, hardly hearing him. 'It is intolerable to know so little! There must be a way to find out more.'

191

'Well, of course, now we know where he is, we can send for news. But whether it will arrive before the thaw, there's no knowing.'

'But you will do everything you can to hasten any news to us – to the Countess?' she amended hastily.

'I will come to you daily,' he promised, 'even if it is only to tell you that there is no news. But try not to worry. If there were apprehensions about his life, they would surely have said so.'

'You think so?' Anne mused. 'Yes, perhaps you're right. And perhaps, now he has been wounded, they will send him home after the thaw.' She imagined the summer at Schwartzenturm with him, with a wound only just bad enough to stop him going off on business all the time. She imagined driving him about the estate in the calèche, helping him to get to know Sasha, walking with him on the terrace after dinner . . . She sighed. 'We must go and tell Irina Pavlovna,' she said, and they resumed walking towards the Palace.

Chapter Twelve

It was a beautiful, clear May day. Lolya had gone riding with her mother, and Anne was walking back from a visit to Marya Petrovna with the two younger children. Sasha had fed the chickens from his hand, and smiled in delight as the old red hen's single chick came running with a shrill *tseep-tseep* and thrust its little clown bill between his fingers for the grains of meal. Nasha was trying to teach tricks to the latest pig, whom she had named 'Pushka' – cannon – because he was black and barrel-bodied. She said he had learned his name already, and certainly he came to her when she called, but Anne thought secretly that it was rather because all animals loved Nasha and came to her whether she called or not.

After a while, when the children had run off to the red stables to feed the white oxen with sugar, Marya Petrovna, her fingers flashing back and forth in her lap amongst the lace-bobbins as if they had a separate life from hers, had told Anne the village news: of marriages arranged and deaths anticipated; of new friendships and old jealousies; of a lame horse and a twin calving; how Zina Andreyevna had prayed to St Anthony, and the very next day had found the ring she had lost; how wicked old Nikita, who had barely drawn a sober breath since last harvest, had sworn to the *Pop* – the parish priest – that the reason he had not come to Mass last Sunday was that he had seen Our Lady in a vision and had been too overcome to stir out of his bed.

Anne listened with interest and a sense of peace, which always came to her in the presence of this old lady. The little village concerns – small, unimportant, universal – stroked her mind into the same kind of blissful calm that Nasha induced in Pushka by scratching his back with the rounded end of a bodkin. Beyond the borders of Russia, armies marched and counter-marched, battles were fought, men cried out and suffered and died; but here in the heart of this great country, the fields bore no treading foot but the farmer's and the oxen's, and the hills echoed only to the whistle of a man to his dog, and the clamour of rooks going home at dusk.

She had tried to explain this to Marya Petrovna, but her Russian was not yet good enough to express so nebulous and complex a thought. But old Marya had nodded as though she understood, and her snake-dark eyes had looked long into Anne's.

'Ah, Barishnya, you have an old head on your young shoulders! Some people can look at a field and see only earth and stones, and maybe next winter's hay. But you can look at a field and see Russia. Yes, it is there, and whatever comes, it will always be there for those who can see. Men bring evil into the world and breed it up for their sport the way they breed their hunting dogs. They change and spoil and destroy what is within their reach; but women go on, unchanging as the wind. Women go on, and Holy Russia goes on. God made it so.'

Her fingers stopped and were still. She was silent a moment, and then continued, holding Anne's gaze intently. 'The little one, Barishnya, she is another who sees more than is there.'

'Natasha?'

Marya nodded. 'Since she was born, I've watched her and wondered. She is not of us, Barishnya. She moves to a music we can't hear. Sometimes I think – ' She paused to pursue a thought. 'I lived in a house in Moscow once, where the beams and floorboards were made from an old ship's timbers. When there was a storm at sea, the timbers used to creak and groan, even though the air around the house was quite still. The house was very old, and those timbers hadn't been near the sea for a hundred years or more, but still they remembered. In their dreams they heard it sing, and they wanted to get back to it.' The black old eyes were unfathomable. 'The little one may walk away, one day. You should keep an eye on her, Barishnya. Don't let her stray too far.'

The sun was westering as Anne walked back along the dusty track towards the house, with Nasha skipping ahead, and Sasha walking beside her, holding her hand and chattering in his happy way about the chickens and the oxen. Both children looked so normal and healthy and happy, it was hard to take old Marya's warning seriously, or to believe that anything other than good could come to them. How rich I've become, she thought, with a home and a family, a future to look forward to, and this feeling of belonging. England seemed as far away as a dream; but her father was always near, his memory drawing substance from the unchanging earth, and all the things which, added together, meant *home*.

The house came into sight, and her steps quickened automatically. The family would have gathered on the terrace, she thought, for once the sun had gone round, it was shady and cool for most of its length; and the Count would be there, reclining on the day bed Vasky brought out for him from the small parlour. She walked round the side of the house with the children so as to approach by the terrace steps from the garden. Her eyes flew to him first in hope, and then her heart sank at the realisation that he was looking no better: in fact, his face was more drawn and pinched today than ever, and he lay back on the day bed in the flattened manner of one exhausted. He smiled as she appeared, but he did not speak or move, and his immobility was too complete to be natural.

Irina and Lolya were there too, still in their habits and talking about their ride. Lolya was sitting on the top step, and with her long hair in a plait hanging over one shoulder, was twiddling the end of it for the white stable cat, who was watching it with a lofty indifference belied by a certain tension in his posture.

'And then when we came to the stream, I had to go round by the ford,' Lolya was saying. 'I do think I ought to have a proper lady's horse of my own now, Papa. Poor Tigu simply can't keep up with Iskra. Oh, here they are! Anna Petrovna, don't you agree I ought to have a horse of my own? I mean, thirteen is nearly grown up, isn't it?'

As she looked away, the white cat struck at last with a massive white paw and needle-claws half extended, and having speared the thick tuft of hair, curled his paw over sideways, revealing pads as pink as *marmelad*, and tried to draw it to his mouth.

'I thought you loved Tigu,' Anne temporised, her eyes on Nasha, who had run to her father and knelt beside the day bed to look passionately up into his face. With what seemed a disproportionate effort, he reached out his hand and stroked her hair briefly, and said, 'Hello, my Mouse. What have you been doing?' Nasha didn't speak, but for answer pushed her head against his hand as a cat does, and settled herself with her elbows resting on the edge of the sofa so that she could continue to look at him.

'Well, I do,' Lolya said, 'but now I'm thirteen I oughtn't still to be riding a pony. Kira's having a proper horse for her birthday. When I go to stay with Aunt Shoora next time, it will be hateful to have to ride a pony, when Kira has a horse.'

Vasky, alerted in some mysterious way to Anne's arrival, appeared at the door of the parlour with the tea-tray, and Stefan came behind him carrying the samovar. Behind him, looking suspiciously from side to side as he emerged into the open air, as if he expected to be ambushed, came Adonis, the latest addition to the household. He was a soldier of fortune who had befriended the Count at the dressing station after the battle and had insisted on going with him whenever he was moved.

When the Count had come home from Olita, Adonis had come with him, like a fierce and ill-favoured but unshakably loyal watch-dog.

'But what is he to do, sir? What is his position to be?' the despairing Vasky had asked his master on their arrival, while Adonis glowered from the corner of the hall, just out of earshot.

'He will decide that for himself, I daresay,' the Count had said with weary humour. 'He seems to believe that I need him, and he will find some way to serve me. Make sure the other servants are polite to him, Vasky, and try to make him welcome. I owe him a great deal.'

Adonis' appearance was not reassuring to a highly-trained house servant. He was short and stocky, massively muscled about the shoulders and thighs, and with strong but surprisingly delicate hands with which he could do fine needlework as well as control a team of horses. His face was disfigured by a scar which ran slantwise across the left cheek and crossed the eye, which was white and blind. The eyebrow, too, had been cut almost in the middle, and the outer half grew wild and shaggy, while the inner part matched the smooth arch of the right brow. As Anne came to know him, she felt that his appearance in some strange way mirrored his nature. It was as if his inner self had been bisected by the wound, leaving him half-savage, half-civilised.

His name, she had assumed, was a joke.

'It was like this,' he told her later. 'I come from Hungary, from a town called Puspokladonysz. When I first went a-soldiering, no-one could pronounce my real name, so they called me by the name of my home town — just the end part, of course. In those days, I wasn't so bad looking. Before I got this.' And he touched his seamed cheek.

He had left home at a very early age to fight for anyone who would hire him. 'There was nothing to do at home but work in the fields. I wanted to see the world and make my fortune. I've fought for the Turks and the Austrians and the French and the Prussians and the English. The Austrians paid best, and the Turks ate best, and the French had the most women, but the English were the best soldiers. I nearly went to England once, because they have such fine horses, but I didn't want to be a servant. The English treat their horses like people, and their servants like animals.'

For one so alien-looking, Adonis had settled into the household very quickly, serving his master like a military body-servant, with a curious, touchy pride, which made him seem almost more like the Count's friend than a domestic. He took an immediate liking to Anne and, with the slightest encouragement, would settle down beside her in the evenings with his piece of work and tell her his adventures. He was a natural story teller, and many an evening she had sat spellbound, watching his hard, pointed fingers stitching delicate embroidery on a nightshirt for the Count, while he described desperate sorties, bloody battles, boar hunts, and wild affairs with half-savage gypsy women. The latter stories, of course, were quite improper, but Anne, quite rightly, took it as a compliment to her intelligence that Adonis did not feel inhibited from telling her them.

Vasky and Stefan had set the tea-things down in front of Anne. It was always she, now, who presided over the samovar, and she had grown skilled in the ritual, learning just when to add more boiling water to the pot of very strong liquor which stood keeping warm on the top, so that the tea was always at the right strength. Lately Vasky no longer even troubled to ask the Countess whether she wished to preside, acknowledging her by a bow of the head as he placed the tray on the table by Anne. The Countess nodded in reply. She was sitting on one of the stone benches, flicking the tip of her boot idly with her crop and watching Lolya play with the cat; but Anne, at least, knew that her attention was really fixed on her husband.

Lolya, receiving no satisfaction on the subject of horses, allowed her train of thought to follow another connection.

'When *are* we going to Moscow, Papa? It must be soon, surely? Shall we visit Aunt Shoora's, too?'

Irina, her voice as mild and languid as the little breeze which stirred the air beyond the terrace, expressed her surprise to her husband.

'Is there a plan to go to Moscow, Nikolasha? I didn't know. What for?'

The Count looked a little conscious. 'For Sergei's passing-out ceremony, to be sure,' he said. 'Didn't I mention it to you?'

Adonis appeared at Anne's elbow to take the Count's cup. Since he had arrived, no-one but him was allowed to hand the Count anything to eat or drink. She wondered if he had once served a master who had feared to be poisoned – a Turk, perhaps? What little she knew of Turks suggested they lived darkly volatile lives.

'But Mamochka, you *knew* Seryosha was to graduate in June,' Lolya interrupted with wide-eyed surprise. She straightened abruptly, snatching the plait end from the white cat's grasp. The cat stood up, offended, and walked away down the terrace steps with a flounce of his furry Scythian trousers. 'Of *course* we must be there to see it. There will be a parade, and manoeuvres, and a musical ride, and a ball in the evening – though I don't suppose,' she added in a voice which did not quite exclude hope, 'that I shall be allowed to go to that.'

'I do not recollect being told about it,' Irina said in that same unemphatic tone. 'Perhaps I did not attend.'

'But they always have them, every year,' Lolya insisted. 'You must have known *that*.'

The Count moved to take his cup from Adonis and winced, and Anne met his eyes with a look half afraid, half accusing. He evaded it and said to his wife, 'Perhaps I should have raised the subject with you sooner. Mother wants to give a party for Sergei's graduation. The passing-out ceremony is on the 21st of June and there will be celebrations of all sorts during the week following. After that we might all go and stay with Shoora and Vsevka, if you like. Anyway, there is no need to decide all at once. There's plenty of time.'

He exchanged a look of mingled apology and entreaty with Irina, for they both knew it was Vera Borisovna's plans which mattered, and which were the reason that, man-like, he had put off discussing the business with his wife.

Irina sighed a little, emptied her cup, and stood up. 'Just as you wish,' she said. 'I must go and change – and Lolya, so must you.'

'Now, Mamochka? *Must* I?'

'Of course. Besides, you must be so hot in that heavy skirt. Ah, here is Nyanka for the little ones.' Nasha jumped up and ran to Nyanka, while Anne rose automatically and bent to pick up Sasha; but Irina forestalled her, holding out her hand. 'No, do not disturb yourself, Anna. Nyanka and I will manage. Come, Sasha, will you come with me?'

Sasha flung a brief look of enquiry towards Anne which she reflected could not but be hurtful to the Countess. She gave him a little helpful push, and he went, placing his hand in his mother's, not precisely hesitantly, but without enthusiasm, and allowed her to lead him away, turning his head again at the door to bestow a look of entreaty on Anne.

When the children had gone, Anne turned to the Count and saw that Irina's manoeuvres had not been lost on him. He waited for her question with as much humour in his eyes as he was capable of in his present state.

'The wound is still troubling you, isn't it?' she said, obedient to his silent prompting.

'She thought I would tell you sooner than her,' he observed with some irony.

Anne frowned a little, wondering whether, or how much, he minded. 'She knows you try to protect her from things,' she said. 'Besides, she has had no training or experience in nursing the sick. When the children are ill, Nyanka won't let her near them.'

'You, of course, have a lifetime's experience of caring for wounded soldiers,' he said. 'I should have remembered.'

Anne ignored this. 'Will you let me look at it, at least?' she said. Refusal was instantly in his face. Then Adonis, whose presence they had both forgotten, made a small, admonitory sound. The Count looked towards him enquiringly, and then gave Anne a resigned nod. 'Very well.'

She drew a chair up beside the couch, and Adonis came to help her ease off the sling and unwind the bandages from the wounded limb. Even through the gauze, she could feel the heat of it, and when her cool fingers touched his skin, she felt it flinch. The scars which seamed the upper arm had healed together, but they were red and sore-looking.

'This isn't right,' she said, frowning.

Adonis growled. 'Army surgeons! Know nothing and care less, and drunk by noon every day, most of 'em! You see how it is. I'll give you odds there are bone splinters left in there. That wound ought to be searched again.'

Anne looked up at the Count's face and was shocked to see the apprehension which he was struggling to control. He tried to smile, but his mouth-corners wouldn't obey him. She bit her lip. 'Something must be done,' she said. 'Will you let me send for another surgeon?'

Adonis snorted. 'Don't ask him – tell him! He'd suffer and say nothing; but every man takes orders from someone. *She* knew that – ' he jerked his thumb in the direction of the door through which Irina had left. 'That's why she went away. Knew he'd show it to you sooner than her. You tell him he's got to see a surgeon – a smart one from the city. I don't know who is the best in Petersburg, but I can soon find out. You tell him and I'll fetch one here snick-snack.'

'You are insolent,' the Count said, with a feeble attempt to regain the initiative. 'You had better mind your tongue, or – '

'Or what? I'm not a serf, thank God! I'm a free man, Colonel, and I talk as free man to free man. If you don't like it, you may do otherwise!'

Despite her anxiety, Anne could not help being amused at the baffled expression on the Count's face, and the defiance in Adonis' one fierce eye. 'This is not the moment to quarrel,' she said hastily. 'Sir, will you let me send for a surgeon?'

The Count met her eyes and nodded once briefly, and then looked away. His face seemed grey and exhausted.

She stood up and gestured to Adonis to accompany her into the small parlour. There she rang the bell and sat down at the desk to write a note for the surgeon, while he stood behind her and looked over her shoulder.

Vasky came in, and Anne said, 'Adonis is going into Petersburg to fetch a surgeon to the master. Will you give orders for a good horse to be saddled for him? And he will need a little money for his expenses.'

Vasky gave them both a comprehensive inspection, and then said, 'Very good, mademoiselle. I will see to it.'

When he had left the room, Adonis said, 'Read me what the note says.' Anne glanced at him in surprise, and he said, 'No, I can't read. What use would that be to me?'

'It's useful to everyone,' Anne reproved automatically. 'It opens up a whole world of experience, such as you can hardly imagine.'

'Maybe you shall teach me one day,' he said generously. 'But now read.' Anne complied, and at the end, he nodded. 'That will do. Give it to me. I'll go at once, Little Mistress, and I'll find which is the best man in Petersburg, and bring him back as soon as possible.'

'What if he won't come?' Anne asked.

'I'll offer him gold,' Adonis said with a quick nod. 'And if that doesn't move him,' he added with a grin, drawing out the knife he always carried, a long, slender blade with a well-worn ivory handle carved at the end into the shape of a snarling tiger's head, 'I'll think of some other way to persuade him.'

When Adonis had gone, Anne went out onto the terrace again. The Count's eyes were closed, but when she drew near him he opened them and looked up at her unsmilingly. He looked worn with pain.

'He is leaving at once,' Anne said. 'Does it hurt you?'

'It aches all the time; and when I move, the pain is like a knife,' he said shortly.

'You should have said something before now,' she said.

His mouth was wry. 'I hoped it would heal on its own. You know what this means? If the surgeon decides there are bone splinters, he will want to probe the wound again to extract them. There,' he added, meeting her flinching eyes, 'I am a coward. You know about me now.'

'No,' she said. 'No. It is not cowardice to be afraid of pain. God knows – ' Her mouth was dry, and she could not go on. His sound hand reached blindly for hers, and she did not think it improper, in the circumstances, to give it. They sat in silence for a while. 'Adonis was right,' he said at last, obscurely.

'He's a good man,' Anne said. 'I'm glad you have him.'

He gave a rueful smile. 'I rather think he has me. Anna – '

'Yes?'

'If – if it has to be done, will you – could you – ?'

She met the fear in his eyes and strove to thrust her own down out of sight, out of knowing. The thought of being obliged to witness such an operation – to witness his suffering – filled her with horror. But she answered almost without pause, 'Of course I will stay with you. I wish to God,' she added in a low voice, 'that it could be me instead.'

He shook his head at that, but he looked comforted.

The operation was performed two days later, in the early hours of the morning, as soon as it was fully light. The surgeon Adonis had chosen was a firm-faced, soldierly man of middle years, with a quiet bearing and expensive, but not elaborate, clothes. He was evidently quick-witted and had gathered enough on the journey from Petersburg in Adonis' company to understand that nothing short of death would have prevented the ex-soldier from assisting at the operation; but he looked askance at Anne's presence and only agreed to allow her to help if someone else were there as well.

'If you faint away, mademoiselle,' he said abruptly, 'I shall not be at leisure to attend to you.'

'I shan't faint,' Anne said, with more defiance than conviction. But Nyanka offered her services and privately to Anne gave her opinion that it was Adonis who was more likely to faint away. In her home village in Georgia, she said, most of the doctoring was done by the women, because the men were too squeamish and could not bear the sight of blood.

Anne was glad of her presence, solid and boulder-like, holding basins and handing towels as if she were presiding over the bathing of a baby, rather than the bloody and disgusting spectacle it really was. Anne did not faint, but again and again she had to think hard about something else to prevent herself from retching.

When it was all over, and the surgeon was sitting quietly beside his patient with a hand over his heart, and Nyanka and Adonis were clearing up the mess, Anne slipped away and climbed to the top of the black tower. Out on the leads, the air was clear and cool. It had not taken so very long, all in all: the day was still new and unused, and below, where the shadow of the tower had only just withdrawn, the dew was still thick on the grass like grey gossamer. Anne rested her hands on the cold stone of the parapet, and tried to clear her mind of the images which were as sharp and jagged as the bone fragments the surgeon had drawn out from the wound.

The liquid thrilling of wren's song rose from the wild pear tree which grew at the foot of the tower. 'It will heal soundly now,' the surgeon had said. 'The arm may always be a little weak, but he will have the use of it, at least.'

I wish it could be me, Anne had said. But that was before. Could one really, *really* wish to suffer another person's pain? Easy to say; not so easy to mean. She felt troubled, ill at ease with herself. It is not cowardice to be afraid of pain, she had said. Surely that was true? Then the image of what she had just witnessed jumped again into her mind. Perhaps it would almost have been easier to suffer than to witness: the Count had lost consciousness quite soon after it began.

There was a sound behind her, and she turned to see Adonis standing near. 'He said you would be up here. He is awake and wants you.'

'Have you told the mistress that it is all over?' Anne asked quickly.

'The old nurse told her. She has been to him. Now he wants you.'

'Very well, I'll come,' Anne said, starting for the hatchway.

Adonis took her arm as she reached him. 'It is good that he has you,' he said, unconsciously echoing her words. 'The outsider sees most of the battle. I know who is really mistress of the house.'

'You mustn't say such things,' she said uncomfortably, pulling her arm free.

Adonis nodded. 'Aye, I know. It is bad for you, Little Mistress. He doesn't yet understand himself. It's her he loves, with his head, at least – but it's you he turns to.'

'You're wrong,' she said, gripping her hands together. 'He loves her truly. Please don't talk like that. It's improper and – and untrue.'

Adonis gave a sardonic smile and stepped out of her way. 'Have it your own way. But it was not her he called for in Königsberg, when he was delirious.'

Anne shook her head, frowning, and hurried away.

The difference was astonishing. For a day or two, the Count was groggy and in pain from the new wounds; but within a week he had begun to mend, and his spirits were returning to normal. Though he felt so much better, the surgeon insisted on his resting as much as possible and spending his days upon a couch. Like a child, he grew restless with boredom and needed to be distracted. Irina and Anne read to him, played chess or picquet with him, conversed with him, begged the neighbours to come and visit him, and even had the children play spillikins with him, but still he sighed and fidgeted.

Then, to amuse himself, he resurrected a scheme of which nothing had been heard since Anne first arrived at Schwartzenturm, and had Grigorovitch in to paint Anne's portrait. The sittings took place in the small drawing-room so that the Count could watch. He decided everything, from the gown Anne was to wear, to exactly how she should place her hands, and what was to be painted in the background. He observed and criticised every brush stroke, and thus distracted, the Grigorovitch took a week to finish the job; and when it was done, the Count was far from satisfied.

'It doesn't do, somehow. It doesn't capture you,' he said critically, moving his head restlessly to get the best light on it. 'We will have to have it done again – outside perhaps. Yes, that is a better idea. Grigorovitch is excellent at horses. We shall have you taken on horseback, in front of the house – in a blue habit, I think. Oh, if only I were allowed off this wretched sofa!'

By the end of May, he was up and about again. The arm no longer pained him, and he was beginning cautiously to use it again, taking it out of the sling for a few minutes each day to exercise the muscles. This was more like the convalescence of which Anne had dreamed: when her duties allowed, she sat with him on the terrace, or strolled with him about the garden; but she was never alone with him. On the rare occasions when Adonis was absent from his side, the Countess was there, bathing in the glow of his restored health; and it was she who took him out for drives about the estate in the calèche, guiding Limonchik carefully over the smoothest parts of the tracks.

The Count began to spend a good deal of time in the stables talking to his head groom, and the Countess suspected that he was longing to begin riding again and feared they would have difficulty in restraining him. But it soon became plain that he had had other plans.

One day when they had no visitors, they were sitting on the terrace in the drowsy part of the afternoon which Anne, because of her father, still thought of as the dog-watches. Sasha was sleeping on a rug in the deepest shade; Anne was instructing the girls in a desultory way in geography; and the Countess and Fräulein Hoffnung were engaged in needlework and chatting in low voices – a sound as small and soothing as distant running water. Even the white cat was stretched out on its side, immobile except for the very tip of its tail.

Then Silka, the borzoi bitch, was amongst them, dabbing them each in turn with her wet nose, and the white cat was gone in an instant. The Count appeared, coming up the terrace steps, and said, 'Lolya, I have been thinking about what you said – about wanting a horse instead of a pony.' Lolya's head came up: Anne could almost see her prick her ears. 'I think you are right, and I have decided to give you Grafina for your own. She's a good mare and will carry you safely; and when you are fifteen, you shall choose your own horse – a youngster if you like, to break in for yourself.'

'But Papa,' Lolya found the only thing to object to in the proposal, 'Anna Petrovna always rides Grafina. What is she to ride? You don't mean we must share her?'

'No, that would not do at all. I have something else in mind for your Mademoiselle de Pierre.' He smiled at Anne and then beckoned her over to the edge of the terrace. 'Come and look, Anna Petrovna.'

Puzzled, Anne got up and went to stand beside him at the parapet. Below, she saw a groom come into sight around the corner of the house, leading a horse. It was a beautiful mare, glossy and black, breeding in every fine line from her delicate head to her small, hard hooves.

Anne's astonished eyes met the Count's, and he smiled and nodded. 'Yes, she's for you,' he said.

Lolya had joined them and was frankly gaping. 'Papa!' she cried. 'Where did she come from? Isn't she fine! Have you just bought her?'

'She's a Karabakh,' the Count said imperturbably. 'I bought her from Volkonsky – he'd bought her for his wife, but she isn't a great horsewoman, and the mare was wasted, standing in the stables eating her head off most of the time. I hope you like her, Anna. She's called Quassy.'

Anne could find no words. She knew enough to know that Karabakhs were extremely expensive, the best horses money could buy, and such extravagance, such generosity towards her, seemed out of proportion to anything she had ever done – almost unseemly, given her situation. Everyone was now standing at the parapet looking down at the glorious black mare below, calmly swishing her tail against the flies and mouthing her bit as the groom held her for their inspection. Anne was acutely conscious of the Countess's silent presence. Irina's small hands were resting on the parapet wall within her vision, and it seemed to Anne that they were gripping the stone rail rather harder than was necessary.

It was Lolya who spoke, her voice innocent of anything but frank admiration. 'She's *beautiful*, Papa! She must have cost the earth!'

The Count looked at his daughter with a self-conscious grin. 'Oh, not more than she was worth. I can see *you* are aching to try her, at any rate, but remember she's Anna Petrovna's horse, and if you dare to touch her without permission, you'll have me to reckon with. Come and look at her, Anna! She has a mouth like silk.'

'Papa, you've been on her!' Lolya said accusingly. 'And the surgeon said!'

'Oh, round the paddock, that's all, just to try her paces,' he said, and he looked absurdly guilty, like Sasha caught eating jam in bed.

They were half-way down the terrace steps when Anne realised the Countess had not moved to follow them. She looked back hesitantly and met Irina's eyes, and saw the puzzled, questioning look in them change to despondency. Natasha, standing beside her mother, looked from one to the other, and when a moment later the Countess turned and walked away towards the house, Nasha hesitated only a moment before following her.

There were several reasons why Anne would have preferred to remain at Schwartzenturm instead of going to Moscow for Sergei's graduation. Quassy was one of them: riding the mare was an experience so delightful that she was reluctant to give it up even for a day, and the Count must have paid so much for her that it seemed absurd to be going away so soon after receiving her.

Then there was the slight coolness she had detected in the Countess since the mare's arrival. It was so little that it was barely quantifiable, but Anne could not help feeling that the Countess was hurt by the Count's gift. It was not that she objected to his generosity, for he was generous to everyone, and the Countess was not so small-minded as to wish him to buy no-one presents but her; but it was a more tangible evidence of the many small ways in which he showed his preference for Anne. Almost any other expensive gift would have aroused no emotion in the Countess; but a horse was such a personal thing, and he had obviously expended a great deal of time and trouble on choosing the perfect one for Anne – just as, years ago before Nasha was born, he had chosen Iskra for Irina.

Anne had done her best, since that day, to avoid the Count's presence, to leave him alone with the Countess whenever she could do so without drawing attention to her design; and she felt that if the Count and Countess went to Moscow without her, things would mend and the matter would assume its proper proportion in Irina's mind. When the plans for going to Moscow were discussed, Anne begged to be allowed to stay home to look after the baby and ride Quassy, while Fräulein Hoffnung accompanied Lolya and Nasha. But Fräulein

Hoffnung pleaded off, saying that the journey would be too much for her, and indeed, she looked so frail, that no-one could suspect her of exaggerating.

'It will not do,' the Count said at last, cutting across the argument. 'You must come to Moscow, Anna. You need not worry about Sasha – Nyanka can stay and help Fräulein Hoffnung with him, and Tanya shall come to take care of the girls. I'm sorry you will have to leave off riding your horse for a while,' he added ironically, 'but life is full of these little disappointments.'

Anne saw there was no help for it. 'Of course I'll come, sir,' she said hastily. 'I have no wish to seem disobliging. Whatever Irina Pavlovna decides, I shall abide by.'

'Besides,' the Count went on, 'you must not disappoint Basil Tchaikovsky. He will be at the Graduation Ball and will expect to dance with you. Fräulein Hoffnung could not take your place there!'

'Oh Papa, mayn't I go to the Ball?' Lolya broke in passionately. 'I'm sure thirteen is old enough, and if Anna is to be there anyway . . . '

His denial led to the usual argument, and the moment passed without further awkwardness.

The day of the passing-out ceremony was humid and overcast, but the weather was kind enough to stay dry, and all the fine ladies who went to watch in open carriages were saved from having their elegant toilettes and elaborate hats spoiled by a soaking. It was one of the main social events of the year in Moscow, for every noble family had at least one sprig in the Academy, which was the fashionable, as well as the best, institution for educating boys.

'In my grandfather's day,' Vera Borisovna explained more than once during the day, 'boys were taken from home when they were ten, for five years' compulsory education, and then enrolled in the Guards at fifteen. Of course, state service was for life in those days. Even my father was obliged to perform twenty-five years' compulsory state service, though to be sure, they had raised the age of enrolment to twenty by then. You don't know how lucky you are, Koko,' she concluded severely.

'Yes I do, Mama,' the Count said patiently.

'Things are very different in modern Russia,' she went on unregarding, 'and I don't know that we are better off for it. Young people are sadly heedless. You had your freedom from the very beginning, Koko, to do what you chose, and go where you pleased. No state service for you! Not that you haven't served our dear Emperor very well, travelling all over Europe. living in foreign countries, and I'm sure he is very grateful. And it will be just the same for my dearest Serge: he will be able to travel wherever he likes. In my grandfather's day no-one was allowed to leave Russia without a special permit from the Tsar, and precious few of those were ever issued, you may believe me! What a wonderful thing it is, this progress!'

'Very true, Mama!'

She sighed and frowned. 'But I don't suppose he is grateful for it. People are never grateful for liberty or indulgence. It is a great mistake, to allow young people to do as they please. The folly and nonsense of young people's setting up their opinions in opposition to their elders and betters, is not to be believed! Discipline, firm discipline, that's what people need – and a good whipping, if they disobey. I never spared my children, though your father, Koko, was foolishly soft-hearted! Many a time I had to beg him to beat you when you had done wrong, for he would have let you off, if left to himself.'

'Yes, Mother, I remember,' the Count replied with admirable self-possession. 'My gratitude to you is beyond expression.'

They attended the open-air ceremonies in two carriages: a new, smart barouche, in which Vera Borisovna rode with her son, and a larger, four-seat vis-à-vis, which was provided for Irina, Anne, and the children. As the barouche only held two, the division seemed a natural one, and Anne thought nothing of it at first. The carriages were drawn up side by side at the edge of the parade ground where they were joined by another containing Shoora, Vsevka and their children, who had come up from Tula for the occasion.

There was soon a throng of carriages drawn up close enough to each other for conversation, each one filled with the first in rank and fashion of Moscow Society. Older ladies remained seated, nodding to each other from a distance, but gentlemen and younger ladies visited between carriages rather as they visited between boxes at the theatre or the ballet. Many were the polite calls of congratulation paid to the barouche on Sergei's account, for he was not only popular amongst his fellow cadets, but well liked in Moscow Society generally, and particularly by those families who had unmarried daughters upon the market.

The visits, Anne noticed with the beginnings of unease, were all to the barouche, and the congratulations were directed towards Vera Borisovna, with the Count receiving the overspill. Even when the ceremonies began, there was still a constant coming and going of gentlemen to pay their respects to the Dowager and chat about the war to the Count. Vera Borisovna was clearly revelling in the attention, and made as much use of her fan and parasol as a debutante.

The Count made one or two attempts to include his wife in the visits and the congratulations, but geography and his mother made it impossible; so after a while, he gave her a bow and stepped down to go around to Irina's side of the vis-à-vis and ask if she was sufficiently amused.

'I'm sure it will be a spectacle worth watching,' he said apologetically.

'Yes, I'm sure it will,' she replied calmly.

'But there is a disappointment for you, Anna,' he went on, giving her a mock-sympathetic smile. 'Your admirer is not here! I cannot think what he is about, but perhaps he is saving himself for the ball. I believe it takes him fully three hours to dress for a formal occasion.'

'If you mean Basil Tchaikovsky, Nikolai, he and Olga are in the Crimea. Their uncle is sick.'

The Count raised his eyebrows. 'Is it so? Then, Anna, your disappointment will know no bounds. But I shall try to make it up to you. I shall dance with you, at all events.'

Anne felt uncomfortable. 'I shall not be going to the ball, sir. My place is with the children.'

'Nonsense!' he retorted at once. 'Your place, like that of any handsome young woman, is to enjoy yourself! The servants can watch the children sleeping.'

'Really, sir,' Anne said in a low voice, 'I am quite decided. I do not wish to go.'

'Nonsense,' the Count began again, but Irina interrupted.

'Let her be, Nikolasha. Anna knows her own mind. If she does not wish to go, do not press her.'

'Oh, I do not press her,' he said with a wicked grin. 'I can see I am no substitute for Tchaikovsky. The young men carry all before them – especially those with two sound arms!'

He gave them a laughing bow and went back to his mother's carriage, leaving Anne to think that never before had his sense of humour been so displeasing to her.

The cadets paraded and were given their scrolls. From a distance Anne could not pick out one from another, but Lolya was perfectly sure she knew which was her brother, and pointed him out in a shriek at every opportunity; and when the review began, and the cadets' manoeuvres brought them closer from time to time, she proved to have been right.

While the cannonades were going on, and before the musical ride, in which he was to take part, Sergei rode over to the carriages, a little red in the face from his exertions, to speak to his family. He seemed very pleased with himself and greeted everyone exuberantly, promising them good entertainment from the displays to come.

'And the ball tonight is going to be first-rate!' he exclaimed. 'There are to be fireworks at the end, and the set-piece – well, I won't spoil it for you, but if you ever saw anything half so fine, I shall be astonished! I must go now, however. I see I am wanted.'

And he rode away to the sound of Lolya's renewed demands to be allowed to go to the ball. 'Fireworks too! Oh Mamochka, Papa can't be so cruel!'

After the open-air spectacles, they returned to Vera Borisovna's house to change for dinner.

'Just a small dinner,' the Dowager had promised. 'Just family and a few intimate friends.' She was giving her grand party for Sergei on the following day; this, she had taken pains to point out, was just an intimate affair. When Anne learned, however, that Sergei was to ride over to eat with them before accompanying them to the ball, she was not entirely surprised to discover that the long table was set for forty, and that the Dowager intended to receive at the head of the stairs in the formal manner, rather than in the drawing-room.

Lolya was still grumbling about not being allowed to go to the ball when Anne accompanied her and Nasha down to the drawing-room, well before the first carriage was announced.

'Do stop, Lolya,' Anne said as they reached the drawing-room door. 'You'll have plenty of balls when your turn comes, all just as exciting as this one, I promise you.'

'But *everyone's* going!' she cried tragically. 'And there will be *fireworks*!'

'I'm not going,' Anne pointed out. 'And as to the fireworks, we'll be able to see most of them from the upstairs windows. If you're a good girl and don't make any more fuss, I'll come and wake you up when they begin, and watch them with you.'

Lolya accepted the compromise reluctantly, and they entered the drawing-room to find that Sergei had already arrived, and was standing in the centre of the room with his father beside him, the centre of attention. He had grown handsome since she last saw him, Anne thought, though his face still had that unfinished look of a very young man. His pale blue uniform suited his golden looks to perfection, but most of all, she thought with an inner pang, he looked very, absurdly like his father. He was a little the taller, slightly larger-boned, and his hair was a shade lighter; but as they stood side by side with that same long, curving face, shining gold-green eyes, and mobile, quirky mouth, it was as if some kind of magic had brought the Count as a young man from the past to stand beside his adult self for comparison.

Both pairs of eyes came round to her as she entered. The Count smiled warmly, Sergei shyly, and then Lolya ran forward to claim their attention and her brother's hugs, and to display her new best dress, put on for the dinner and perfectly fit, she assured them eagerly, for dancing. Anne took Nasha to sit on a sofa to one side. Shoora engaged her in conversation across the Countess, who was sitting between them, silent but faintly smiling as she gazed at her husband and her stepson with what appeared to be both pleasure and pride.

Then the door opened and Vera Borisovna sailed in, magnificent in puce satin decorated all over with glinting crystal spars and beaded fringe, and with her famous pink diamonds glittering on her bosom and in her hair.

'The first carriage is approaching. Come Serge, Koko, we must take up our positions at the head of the stairs to greet our guests.' The Count looked towards his wife, who made a move as if to rise, but the Dowager crushed her back with a kindly smile. 'No, no, my dear Irina Pavlovna, we need not trouble you. There is no need for you to receive – not the least in the world! My son and grandson and I will do all that is necessary. Pray do not disturb yourself.'

The Countess sat very still, her face seeming very pale, her eyes carefully blank. The Count and his son exchanged a quick glance, and Anne thought how, in the Dowager's presence, they were like two guilty children. Her influence over both of them was absurdly strong; but the Count could not refrain from at least beginning an objection.

'Surely, Mother, Irina, as my wife, ought to be with us.'

The Dowager's smile was wider and whiter than ever. 'No, no, my dear, there is not the least occasion to trouble the dear Countess. People will not expect it. Serge is merely a relation by marriage to her, and it is I, after all, who have been a second mother to the dear boy – have I not, mon cher?'

'Yes, Gran'mère,' Sergei said automatically, but he was watching his father enquiringly.

'Mother, I must insist –' the Count began.

'No, my dear, this is a Kirov affair, you know. There is no need for this debate – and no time! I hear people below. Come now, we must take our places at once!'

She swept them out without allowing any further argument. It was done so cleverly that there was nothing on which anyone could have hung offence; and yet Anne knew it was meant to offend, and that it had offended. Lolya was chatting to her aunt and uncle, who had not observed the piece of business at all, and Irina remained motionless, displaying no distress, but Anne could feel her pain like a separate person standing between them. She went across and sat beside the Countess and began talking about the first thing that came into her head.

'I wonder if we shall hear more, ma'am, of this shocking new dance they have invented in Germany? I cannot believe we shall ever see men and women holding each other in public in that way; but perhaps the reports have been exaggerated. What do you think? Would you countenance the Waltz in your drawing-room?'

The Countess could not answer at once; but after a moment made some kind of reply, and Anne continued to talk, hardly aware of what she was saying, only using her voice as she would to soothe a frightened animal. In a little while, Irina looked up and met Anne's gaze with eyes that were too bright and gave her a small, tight smile of gratitude.

The dinner was magnificent, but Anne, whose appetite was usually healthy, ate unexpectedly little of the procession of delicacies which passed her way. As the Countess was seated on the same side of the table, Anne could not see her, or judge how she was feeling; and Lolya, beside her, demanded a great deal of attention. But it was still unhappily plain to Anne that Vera Borisovna, at the end of the table with Sergei on her left hand, was taking all the congratulations of the occasion to herself, not only as hostess, but as patroness and surrogate-mother of the newly-graduated cadet.

The Count was at the other end of the table, and Irina, seated insignificantly half-way down one side, was being pointedly ignored. Anne began to wonder apprehensively what would happen at the party tomorrow. If Vera Borisovna stage-managed another slight to Irina, would the Count protest? Anne hoped so fervently, though her imagination shrank from the prospect of a quarrel between mother and son: so distressing, so improper. The situation would be unpleasant, whether he intervened or not; and she wondered whether she might somehow speak to him, persuade him to confront his mother privately during the course of the next day, before the party, and somehow force her to be properly civil to her daughter-in-law. Yet that would be an unwarrantable intrusion on her part. It was not her business to intervene, however much she longed to.

She was so preoccupied with her thoughts that she hardly noticed the Dowager's butler approach his mistress with an unusually agitated expression to murmur something into her ear. The Dowager's expression altered. She spoke a few rapid words, and the butler hastened towards the door; but before he reached it, a new figure appeared in the doorway. It was a young Guards cadet in uniform, booted and caped and a little tousled, as if he had ridden fast. His face was pale, his eyes, as they swept the room, almost unseeing from some kind of emotion, and as he strode up the room towards the Dowager, all eyes turned to him, and the clamour of conversation died rapidly away.

He stood before Vera Borisovna, but seemed unable to speak in his agitation. His mouth opened and closed a few times without words, and he looked around him again, as if seeking help.

The Count stood up. 'What is it?' he said into the chill silence. 'You have a message for someone? Pull yourself together and spit it out, man! Remember you're an officer.'

The young man straightened up, gratefully, and turned towards the Count, composing himself, almost visibly separating himself from his emotions.

'News, sir,' he said at last. 'A despatch has just arrived from Olita. I have been sent from military headquarters to request you to come at once – and you, sir,' he added, his eyes flickering round towards Sergei. Sergei made a movement as if to rise; his hand, with his napkin crumpled in it, going down onto the table to push himself up, knocked a knife lying on the nap, so that it swivelled and struck the stem of his wine glass, which rang with a tiny, clear sound. Anne always remembered it afterwards: it was as if someone had rung a bell, as they do during the Mass, to draw attention to the moment of transubstantiation. What came next would change everything.

The Count recalled and held the messenger's gaze. 'A despatch from the front?' It must be serious, if they were summoned immediately. 'Is it news? For God's sake, what is it?'

The boy's precarious self-possession crumpled, and he looked at once very young and very scared.

'There's been a battle, sir, against the French, at Friedland. A terrible defeat! Our men are in retreat to Danzig. They are evacuating Königsberg, and taking the wounded to – the wounded – ' His voice trembled and failed, and nothing followed it in the palpitating silence. His eyes filled with tears. 'Oh sir, it's horrible! They say our dead number more than twenty thousand!'

Chapter Thirteen

In May 1808, the Countess Irina set out with her two children and their governess on the long journey south to her family home, the Kiriakov estate on the warm, dry, sunny northern slopes of the Caucasian mountains. It had been a sickly winter. Everyone had had colds and aches and pains, and Irina had suffered a particularly bad attack of influenza, which had left her thin and pale and with a troublesome cough; and when a letter came from her sister Ekaterina, recently widowed and returned to the family home, Nyanka suggested that it would do her mistress good to do the same. The climate would benefit her health, and the companionship of her brothers and sisters would raise her spirits, which had been very low since the news of the defeat at Friedland had taken the Count away from home again.

The day of the Graduation Ball was burned on their memories. The ball had been cancelled, of course: no-one could have danced with the cadet's words still ringing in their ears. The Count and Sergei had gone straight to headquarters and had remained there all night, returning the following morning only to pack for their immediate departure to Olita to join the Tsar's retinue – the Count as diplomatic advisor, Sergei as a subaltern in the prestigious Preobrazhensky Guard. The latter appointment was made as a favour to the Count, and it was a sign of his high standing with the senior military officials that they could think of it at a time like that.

Shoora and Vsevka had invited Irina and the children to return with them to Tula, but she had wanted only to go back to Schwartzenturm, in which Anne had whole-heartedly agreed with her. To be away from home at such a time was unbearable. If *he* were to be gone, the only comfort could come from familiar surroundings. Lolya had begged to be allowed to go with Aunt Shoora, however, and Irina had admitted her plea. There she had remained ever since, while Anne and the Countess had taken Natasha back to Schwartzenturm. Since then, Anne had been able to distract herself for much of the time with her duties to the children; but Irina had nothing to do to stop her thinking about her husband and missing him, and her spirits had never been lower or more in need of a visit to her loved and distant home.

The thousand-mile journey was not undertaken lightly, and it was almost a caravan which eventually started out from Schwartzenturm. The Countess took along her maid Marie; Nyanka and Tanya to take care of the children; Kerim the cook, and one of his assistants; two footmen; Morkin the coachman; six grooms; and eight other servants. There was also one of the estate carpenters, who was also a skilled wheelwright, and Marlinski, the farrier-blacksmith, who, besides being able to shoe horses and repair broken carriage-frames, could doctor almost any living creature who did not object to it.

There was a mountain of luggage, too, which included bed linen, cooking pots, spare harness, tools, medical supplies, soap, a large number of firearms, and emergency rations in the form of dried meat, dried peas, and a kind of hard bread like ship's biscuits, which though as unappetising as wood had the virtue of remaining edible for long periods.

Anne, used to travelling in England, and even with the experience of her journey from Paris behind her, rather stared at all these preparations; and wondered, too, that the Countess should choose to travel in a peasant *kibitka* rather than her own comfortable berlin. She also wondered at the small chest of gold, which was stowed under the driving-seat of the first cart, to be guarded by a groom with a horse pistol. Anne, the Countess, and the two children travelled in the first cart, and behind it came four others. At the rear of the procession rode Stefan, leading Iskra and Quassy.

The journey was a slow one. As soon as they were away from the immediate environs of Petersburg, the roads worsened rapidly, for in the winter ice and snow, driven by the wind across the tracks, formed deep waves, like the sea, which, after the spring thaw, turned the roads into broad morasses of mud, over whose vast ruts and troughs the horses dragged the carts with great difficulty. This kind of going was hard on both horses and vehicles, and wheelwright and blacksmith between them had repairs to do at the end of most days. The sturdy peasant *kibitkas* and *telegas* were best suited to the job: a smart European berlin or barouche would have been jolted to pieces within days.

The lurching of the vehicles was sometimes hardly to be born by the passengers. The children retched with travel-sickness while the adults were flung violently against the sides of the *kibitka* and cracked their heads on the roof. At the end of the day, Anne would undress cautiously to find herself black and blue, despite the bulky clothing Irina had advised her to wear. They dressed each other's bruises with arnica each evening in the most friendly way: the shadow of coolness that had come between them over Quassy had been driven away by subsequent events.

The necessity for the box of gold was explained by what Nyanka described as 'galloping consumption' in the pockets of postmasters, inn-keepers, and local constables, all of whom had to be sweetened by large sums of money in order for the travellers to proceed, and to obtain passes or beds for the night and fodder for the horses. Iskra and Quassy had to be guarded at night by a groom, who sat up with them in whatever shelter had been obtained for them, watching over them with a lamp and a shotgun. Imperial couriers and other officials of the Empire took precedence on the roads in all matters, and sometimes, despite the bribes, the party was turned out of a posting-inn to make room for them, and had to make do with some rough peasant hut, or even sleep in the carts. But the servants showed the proverbial adaptability of the Russian peasant, and managed to make everyone reasonably comfortable.

Things were better when they reached the Steppes, for here the tracks were wide and level, and the horses were able to make good speed. The children's spirits improved: they began to take notice of things, and enjoyed riding sometimes in one cart and sometimes in another, while Anne and Irina took the opportunity to refresh themselves by riding for a spell, galloping over broad grasslands as smooth as bowling-greens, sewn with an incredible carpet of wild flowers. The vast grasslands rolled away, level and featureless to the horizon in every direction. In the distance they saw herds of horses and cattle, being driven by mounted herdsmen on small, swift ponies, which they rode bareback, and turned with a dig of the knees, leaving their hands free for their whips and weapons. It was all as new to Anne as to the children, but Irina answered their endless questions patiently.

Beyond the Steppes the country changed again. It was as if the flat grasslands had been crumpled up like bedclothes into a series of gentle rolling foothills. The tracks were dusty, the blue sky windless, and the heat at noon was oppressive, and made the horses sweat, so that at the end of the day their coats were matted and pale with dust. There began to be trees again, oaks and maples, and the strange feathery grasses of the drylands, giant thistles and poppies, bellflowers and yellow mullein, and sometimes patches of marsh sewn with reeds. The cicadas sang all day long; there were vultures with hideous bare necks perched unnervingly near the track; and sometimes a pelican flew over from the Sea of Azov. Anne never quite got used to the sight of these extraordinary birds, but Nyanka said even the sight of them was lucky, and crossed herself fervently every time one flapped slowly by.

One day, when they were a short way from Stavropol, and Irina was telling Anne and the children an anecdote about her childhood at Chastnaya – the name of the family estate – Morkin suddenly reached for his shotgun, and said tersely, 'Horsemen, Barina.'

The effect on Irina surprised Anne: she broke off in mid-sentence, her whole body grew rigid, and her hands gripped together in her lap. 'Tcherkess?' she asked abruptly.

Morkin did not immediately answer, straining his eyes towards the group on the track, far ahead where it met the horizon. He transferred the reins of the horses to one hand and held the shotgun ready in the other, and his and the groom's bodies were tense in every line. Then at last he seemed to relax. 'Cossacks,' he pronounced.

At the single word, Irina's breath sighed out of her, and she looked towards Anne. 'We are almost at the Line,' she said. 'This is the dangerous part of our journey.'

'The Line?' Anne asked.

'It's a line of fortresses, guarded by Cossacks. Travellers like us pass along it, and the Cossacks protect us from the Tcherkess – the Circassians,' Irina said. 'They are mountain people, and they live by war and plunder. They like to attack and rob travellers, but the Cossacks prevent them.'

Her eyes flickered towards the children to indicate to Anne that she did not want to make more of the subject in their presence; but Morkin, the shotgun across his knees now, said, 'Sometimes they prevent them, Barishnya. When there's enough of them, and they haven't gone to the bad themselves. I've heard stories that would curdle your blood, about Cossack troops deserting to the hills and – '

'Enough, Morkin,' Irina said sharply, cutting his voice off instantly. But the damage had been done, and everyone was silent with apprehension for the next few minutes, until the horsemen waiting ahead were close enough to be identified as friendly. There were eight of them, in sheepskin coats, bearing red lances, and with muskets slung over their shoulders, mounted on small, swift horses. They were the first true Cossacks Anne had seen, though she had heard a great deal about them, mostly from Nyanka and Adonis, who held them in some respect. They saluted the travellers cheerfully, and whirled their horses around the carriage, inspecting the women frankly and joking with the children. They had high Tartar cheekbones and hawk noses, and fierce smiles under their long moustaches. Their Russian sounded very strange to Anne: she could only understand half of what was said.

216

Though a mood of apprehension kept the party rather subdued, under the escort of successive bands of Cossacks, they continued their journey without incident. They passed down the line of look-out posts, where a single guard watched the horizon, ready to light a signal beacon if a raiding band were sighted, and the fortresses themselves, which were little more than an enclosure of earthworks and ditches, but which provided necessary shelter, a barracks, a church, and the protection of a two-pounder gun.

A little before Georgievsk, Irina suddenly sat up straight, straining her eyes ahead, and cried out in a joyful voice, 'Oh look, there's Mount Kazbek! Isn't it lovely? Look, children, the Caucasus at last!'

Mile by mile it grew more distinct on their horizon, the triangular white peak of Mount Kazbek cutting into the blue sky, and beyond it, the three-hundred-mile sweep of snow-capped mountains refracting a thousand colours from the sunlight, the spires and pillars and minarets of the countless peaks like some magical city of the clouds: awesome, beautiful, longed-for, and unattainable. It was a magnificent spectacle, and Anne and the children exclaimed over it again and again. But the Countess only gazed in silence, with her eyes shining with a joy that Anne had never witnessed before.

At Georgievsk they had to wait two days for the formation of the weekly imperial convoy. From here onwards, the risk of attack by the Tcherkess was too great for the protection of a single troop of Cossacks to be adequate. The convoy was guarded by seventy or eighty Cossacks armed with guns and some small artillery, and its purpose was to escort the Tsar's mail and treasury through the mountain passes along the Georgian military highway to the Governor General of Georgia at Tiflis, on the other side of the Caucasus. So dangerous were the lands beyond Georgievsk that anyone who wanted to travel that way waited for the convoy and took advantage of the heavy guard, and the procession that the Countess and her party eventually joined was formed of more than a hundred vehicles, a very mixed party of travellers ranging from peasants to high-ranking government officials, and herds of cattle and roped teams of horses to add to the confusion.

Marshalling this unwieldy convoy into two columns for marching took a very long time, with officers shouting orders and Cossacks shouting abuses, cracking their whips, and riding up and down the lines on their sweating horses to prod stragglers into place. When they eventually got on the move, progress was as slow as it had been at the beginning of their long journey. They were reduced to the walking pace of the slowest ox: twenty miles took sometimes as long as twelve hours.

There was always something interesting to be observed, and the children were full of chatter, and thoroughly enjoyed the altercations between the Cossack guards and the travellers who strayed out of line or held up progress or allowed their cattle to graze. Anne noted one or two incidents to include in the long letter she was writing to her friend Emma Hatton in Petersburg: the description of the convoy and the colourful characters in it alone was likely to take up two pages.

One particularly noticeable figure was a man to whom Irina had first drawn Anne's attention in Georgievsk, when he had arrived to join the convoy accompanied by an impressive number of servants and a quantity of luggage. She said he was a Tartar prince. He was tall, and blackly handsome and moustachioed, and he wore pearls in his ears. His clothes were magnificent: a dark green and purple striped surcoat over silver-gilt chain mail that flashed in the sun; pantaloons of sky blue embroidered with silver, bound at the knee with scarlet leather garters; a leather cap shaped like a cupola, trimmed with a band of black sheepskin; and long boots of red and yellow leather with long pointed toes, fastened close all the way up to his knees by laces.

He carried a whip of crimson leather with which he made a great deal of noise, slapping the stem of it against his saddle flaps to make a path for himself through the crowds. He wore a sabre of Damascus steel with an ivory handle, and a short Circassian bow slung over his shoulder, together with a quiver full of arrows, ready for use. He rode a magnificent, curvetting bay horse, whose harness was decorated with crimson tassels and gold discs, and he was accompanied everywhere by his mullah, also on horseback, in a white turban, flowing scarlet robe, and yellow boots.

Anne had enjoyed looking at him, and memorising his appearance for her letter to Emma. Once or twice she had caught his eye and hastily removed her gaze, not to appear rude, but had thought no more about it; until one day while they were on the road, and Anne was wishing longingly that she could rest her bones by riding Quassy, the Prince appeared beside her, forcing his way up to the *kibitka* and pacing his horse to the cart's speed.

He bowed towards the Countess, who had made an instinctive shrinking movement at his appearance, but ignored the children, who were frankly goggling at him; and, fixing his glittering eyes on Anne, he said in a strange and barbaric Russian, 'The mare – the black Karabakh – is she yours?'

Anne was too surprised at the question to feel much afraid. The bay horse close beside her fretted against the curb bit, making its harness discs ring, and spattering a little foam on the side of the *kibitka*, and the Prince checked it minutely with hand and foot. It was so close to her that she could feel its heat, and the barely-restrained power of it; its bright eye and foam-whitened lips were on a level with her face.

'Yes,' she said. 'The black mare is mine.'

'So *he* said,' the Prince replied with a jerk of his head, evidently meant to identify Stefan. He examined her fiercely and without apparent approval. With his hard eyes and hooked nose, he reminded Anne of an eagle. 'You are not Russian,' he said finally.

'I am English,' Anne replied. Despite his abruptness, she saw no particular threat in his presence – indeed, she was rather enjoying the exchange with so exotic a character. This, surely, was why one travelled in foreign parts!

'Ah, English!' said the Prince, baring his teeth in what Anne took to be a smile. 'English love horses, this I hear! How you like your Russian horse?'

'She is very beautiful and very swift,' Anne said. 'I like her very well.'

He nodded in approval. 'Russian horse,' he affirmed.

Anne felt her native honour at stake. 'Our English horses are also very fine,' she said. 'They have Eastern blood too, you know.'

The Prince ignored this puny attack. 'The black mare, I buy her from you,' he said, throwing back his head and looking down at her fiercely, in a way, she thought, that was calculated to suppress any desire to refuse. 'I give you much gold – one hundred gold pieces for this horse.'

'But I do not wish to sell her,' Anne said calmly, and felt Irina touch her hand warningly.

The Prince glared at her a moment, and then turned away to stare thoughtfully at the sky. 'Two hundred,' he said at last, looking down at her again. 'This is enough, even for a mare.'

Anne met his eyes steadily. 'I will not sell her,' she said. 'Not for two hundred, or four hundred – not even for a thousand.'

'You sell!' he growled threateningly.

'I will not,' she said firmly.

The Prince's brows drew down in a ferocious frown, and he leaned down from the saddle to put his face on a level with Anne's, so that she could get the full benefit of it. At close quarters he was quite frightening, but there was that in her which could not endure to be bullied, and she forced herself to meet his gaze without flinching; and in a moment

219

he straightened up, and without another word whirled his horse away, and galloped off down the line. Anne let out her breath in a long sigh and then smiled reassuringly at her round-eyed charges.

'He meant no harm,' she said. 'I expect that's just his way of striking bargains.'

'It was very incautious of you, Anna Petrovna,' Irina said, shaking her head. 'You should not have provoked him. You don't know what he's capable of.'

'Would you have let him have Iskra?' she countered reasonably.

Irina smiled a little. 'No, I wouldn't,' she admitted. 'But these people can be dangerous. You should not take them lightly.'

'I assure you,' Anne said, lifting her hand from her lap and shewing the Countess how it trembled, 'I did not take him lightly.'

The second act in the drama took place that evening when they reached the fortress at Prokhladnoye. The Kirovs were just settling down around the fire in one of the huts when the Prince appeared in the doorway, hand on the hilt of his sabre, and strode towards them, followed by several servants carrying baskets.

'I have come,' he announced firmly, bowed, and gestured forward the baskets. 'You will take dinner with me, Engllish lady – and your people,' he added, waving a hand towards Irina and the children, as if they were very much a secondary consideration. 'Never before was I beaten in bargaining – and by an English lady. So, dinner – eat!'

The baskets proved to contain caviar, cold pheasant, meat patties, fruit, including a magnificent bunch of muscat grapes, and several bottles of real French champagne from the Widow Clicquot's estate. This was better fare than they had expected to enjoy that evening. The Prince was in great good humour, filled their glasses, and raised his towards Anne with a flamboyant gesture that baptised everyone. 'To your horse!' he cried.

They drank the toast and then fell with a will on the delicious food. The Prince drained his glass, refilled it, and examined Anne closely and at length. Then at last he reached across and tapped her arm with his whip to gain her attention, and said with decision, 'I marry you.'

'What!' Anne could not help exclaiming, while the children giggled, and Irina looked nervously from one to the other.

'Yes,' he said, nodding firmly. 'English lady with horse, you make a very good wife. And,' he added, looking at her sidelong, 'if I marry you, I get the horse too.'

There was a moment's silence, and then Anne burst out laughing, realising that he was teasing her. He laughed too, very loudly, showing

220

all his teeth and turning his face from one to another to make sure they were appreciating the joke. After that, the evening went very fast. Despite the language difficulties and the radical differences in their culture, Anne and the Prince managed to get along very well. His harsh laughter and abrupt manner no longer worried her, and he asked her many interested questions about her country and told her stories of some of his more dangerous exploits against the Tcherkess.

When at last he rose to leave, he said with sincerity, 'English lady, I like you very well. Send to me, Akim Shan Kalmuck, if you change your mind. I think you make a very good wife!'

It would make a good story, Anne thought, to tell the grandchildren one day — if only she were ever likely to have any! It would certainly amuse Emma Hatton. She only wished the Count could have been there to enjoy it, for it was the kind of absurdity that he would like.

At Vladikavkaz, they left the convoy, for here they were met by a smiling, exuberant party of Cossacks from the Kiriakov estate, come to escort them over the last stage of the journey to the safe haven of Chastnaya. It was a large plantation of more than five hundred serfs, containing vineyards, groves of fruit trees, and acres of mulberry trees, on which lived the silkworms whose industry supported the Kiriakov fortune. It was set in the pleasant country where the Caucasian foothills ran out into the plain of the Caspian, a green and smiling landscape of gentle rises and hollows, a sprinkling of deciduous woodland, and numerous little streams making their way downhill to join the great River Terek.

The house itself was different from any that Anne had yet seen, being long and low and rambling, made almost entirely of wood, and surrounded by a deep verandah where a great deal of the family's life took place. It was sheltered by clumps of dusty false-acacia and tall elms loud with rooks. White jasmine clambered exuberantly over the verandah roof, filling the evening air with its rich scent, and to one side an attempt had been made at planting a pleasure-garden: roses, lavender and rosemary bushes, separated by gravel paths.

The Kirov party was greeted rapturously, and Irina was clasped to bosom after bosom, embraced, petted, and called any number of pet-names by her numerous and affectionate family. Anne, watching her smile and bloom under this treatment, began a little to understand the Countess's intense reserve when away from them. To have been brought up amongst such an exuberant and demonstrative family, and then to be taken away from them to the formality and reserve of Petersburg life, must have its effect.

The children were next seized, hugged, exclaimed over, and borne away to be regaled with honey cakes and kissell; and Nyanka was openly blubbering in her joy at being home again, and was sprinkling one of her former charges after another with her happy tears. The whole of Irina's large retinue was absorbed into the Chastnaya household with the ease of a minnow embraced by an octopus; in their warm hearts, and in the rambling honeycomb of rooms which was the house, there was space for everyone.

There seemed so many of the Kiriakovs that Anne had difficulty for a few days in separating them out in her mind. They all had Irina's fair, Tartar looks, and a friendly, forthright way of speaking that she found very attractive. Irina's parents were dead, so the head of the family was now her eldest brother, Feodor, who had a wife and four grown-up children. Next came Zina, who was unmarried, and more or less ran the household, though Feodor's wife was official mistress of the house.

Then came Dmitri and Danil, separated by a year, but looking and behaving like twins, the more so because they had married twin sisters, which added enormously to Anne's confusion. They had seven children between them. Ekaterina came next in age, widowed and returned for a long visit with her two children. She was the closest to Irina in age, being just eighteen months older.

After Irina came the unmarried brothers, Mishka and Grishka, and the unmarried daughters, Nadezhda and Zinaidia. Nadezhda had recently been betrothed by their eldest brother to a steady young man who would be allowed to marry her in nine or ten years' time, when he had proved himself worthy. Anne saw that Irina's whirlwind courtship and marriage to Count Kirov was not the way things were usually done, and that they had worried a great deal about her and were upset but not too surprised to find poor 'Rushka' looking so pale and thin.

'Now you're here,' Zina said, putting an arm round her little sister, 'we'll soon make you rosy and plump. You must stay a good, long time. No need to hurry away, since that husband of yours is not at home. In fact, since you've brought the children with you, there's no need to go back at all,' she said, and at Irina's startled look added hastily, 'until Kirov comes home again, I mean.' But it was plain that it was not what she meant, and that she could see no good and sufficient reason why any Kiriakov should ever live anywhere but at Chastnaya.

Life at Chastnaya was very much less formal than at Schwartzenturm.

Anne was surprised but pleased to see her mistress put off her fashionable French clothes and adopt a plain and serviceable mode of dress; and was amused at Marie's outrage when Irina stopped having her hair curled, and wore it instead in a single plait down her back, like a child. One day she even put on Scythian trousers, and went out on Iskra riding astride, the way she had when she was a little girl. The change in her was astonishing: she blossomed under the kindly warmth of her family's love, and became smiling, talkative, even mischievous, enjoying romps and old family jokes as much as any of the children.

It was a happy, haphazard house. Everyone had their tasks to perform, and their own interests to pursue, and though the greeting they gave Anne was warm and sincere, she was a little startled, but not displeased, to find that they expected her to look after herself. Whatever she wanted she could have for the asking, or better still, help herself to. She might please herself how she dressed and what she did; and until everyone gathered on the verandah at the end of the day for the long, social evening of eating and drinking and talking and laughing, no-one felt it was their business to entertain her, or advise her what to do.

Riding took up a great deal of everyone's day. Chastnaya was a large estate, and just to get around it all the brothers spent many hours each day on horseback. The children were taught to ride almost before they could walk, and scrambled about on ponies, bareback like the hill children, as easily as on their own legs. Because of the threat from the Tcherkess, it was not possible to go outside the estate, and even within its bounds there was some danger, though all the Kiriakovs affected at least to ignore it. Their father had been killed by a Circassian raider, who picked him off while he was riding about his business in one of the outlying parts, and his sons felt that to show any fear of the same fate would be to dishonour his memory; but the women never went near the boundaries unescorted, and the children kept strictly to the fields nearer the house. The estate was so large, however, that this was not a hardship.

Anne rode for a good part of every day, and could hardly have desired a more agreeable occupation. Quassy had quite recovered from the journey, and Anne was discovering all over again the particular joy of riding her perfect horse. Her paces were smooth, her mouth like silk; but best of all, as Anne had found the first time she mounted her at Schwartzenturm, Quassy had a great natural exuberance which made riding her a particular delight. The mare loved to go out; and as they explored Chastnaya together, Quassy's ears were pricked, her nostrils quivering, and she looked about her, bright-eyed with the intensity of her interest in everything around her.

The good-natured Grishka had built a series of small obstacles in one of the paddocks and was teaching Anne to jump.

'I'll teach you to ride astride, too, if you like,' he offered one day. Anne was reluctant at first to try it. It looked comfortable, but somehow immodest, she said. Grishka laughed, and pointed out that he had taught his two younger sisters to ride astride, and he would hardly have done that if there were anything improper about it; so she consented. The lessons were so successful that Danil offered next to teach her to shoot, and promised she would be a very fair shot by the time he had finished with her.

As to her pupils, she hardly saw them. There were so many people at Chastnaya eager to take care of them that she was never called upon to accompany them; and as to lessons, it was not thought of. They ran and played and rode with their cousins from dawn to dusk, growing brown and strong in the delightful Caucasian sunshine; and Anne comforted herself with the thought that the things they were learning then might be just as useful to them as the ability to put the map of Europe together, or recite the Tsars in order, with their dates.

One day in June, Anne was coming in with a basket of roses she had picked for the house, and to her astonishment found Sergei standing on the verandah talking to Zina, who had been called away from overseeing an important culinary event by his unexpected arrival. He turned as Anne approached, and his face lit up with a very flattering smile.

'Anna Petrovna!' he said. 'There you are! I was told you were all here, so I thought I'd call and see you. I've been seconded to the Independents – the Independent Caucasian Corps, you know – and we're stationed at Grozny, which is only twenty versts away. How are you? You are looking so well! And how is my mother?'

The second question sounded rather more perfunctory than the first, but Anne answered it as if it were not merely polite. 'She is so much better, you would hardly know her. She grows quite plump – doesn't she, Zina?'

'She does; but none of us will have anything to eat today unless I get back to the kitchen and stop my cook and Kerim from killing each other. So I bid you welcome and farewell for the present, Sergei Nikolayevitch. Anna will take care of you, I know, and the men will be back soon. Forgive me – I shall see you at dinner.' She hurried away, and though she had spoken in a friendly way, Anne wondered if she rather disapproved of Kirov's son, and whether some other visitor might not have been deemed worth the risk of a domestic disaster.

Sergei seemed to notice nothing, however. He was looking at Anne, and as she put down the basket of roses he reached out and took both her hands, and said, 'You look so well, Anna Petrovna! And different, somehow, I wonder what it is?'

'Nothing in the world, except that I dare say I am rather brown, from riding all day,' Anne said with a smile.

'No, no, it is something. You look happy and – I don't know.' He was staring at her with such intensity, that she began to feel a little uncomfortable. She drew her hands back and gestured to him to sit down on one of the large sofas in the deep shade of the verandah.

'Now, tell me all your news,' she said. 'I haven't seen you since you left Moscow with your father last year. You must have so much to tell! You were with him for some time, weren't you?'

She managed to keep the wistful note out of her voice, though she longed for news of the Count. Sergei leaned back in the sofa's embrace, and stretched out his elegant legs, crossing them at the ankle, and she studied his face unobserved for a moment. He had changed, too, she thought: his face had gained authority, his neck was thicker, his shoulders heavier. He no longer had that unfinished look: he was almost twenty, and had come into his young manhood, which suited him very well. He had grown very handsome, she noticed; and also, with a pang, that he looked more than ever like his father.

'Yes, until December,' he was saying. 'Then he went to Paris, and I went to Lvov. Provincials! How I hated that! And then to Kiev, which I liked very well; and now here. Have you heard from Papa? He is lucky, to be sent to Paris again. How I long to see Paris!'

'I think he would sooner be here,' Anne said, 'and let you go to Paris in his stead.'

'Do you think so, indeed?' Sergei said seriously. 'I wonder. He loves his work, you know. He told me when we were together at Tilsit that diplomacy is in his blood. I think he soon grows bored with sitting at home and riding about his estate, and nothing to do in the evening but talk to his – ' He broke off, and blushed a little, and Anne affected not to notice what she imagined was to be a disparaging remark about Irina.

'Was he in good health when you saw him last? His letters never mention such things. Does his arm trouble him?'

'He says it aches a little in cold weather, but otherwise it seems to hold up very well. He told me,' he added in a burst of confidentiality, 'about your standing by him, when the surgeon searched the wound. I must say, Anna Petrovna, you are very brave, and a good friend to Papa. I know he thinks very highly of you – and I do too. And,' he added, looking closely at her, 'if you won't think me impertinent, I'll say you are looking very handsome today.'

Anne laughed. 'I shall think you not only impertinent, but very foolish! Handsome, indeed, in this gown, and with my hair undressed!'

'Well, I'm sorry, but it seems so to me,' he said, seeming more puzzled than rebuked. 'Perhaps – '

'Ah, here is Yurka with some tea for us,' Anne said with relief. 'Or would you rather have something else?'

'Tea will do very well. Papa told me how you preside over the samovar at home, in my mother's place. I shall like to see how you do it.'

'You are determined to put me out of countenance, but I shall not give you the satisfaction,' Anne said, laughing. 'Now do tell me what has been happening to you. What did you do in Kiev? I know very little about it, except that there is a fine cathedral there. Did you see it? Tell me all about it.'

By skilful questioning, she persuaded Sergei to drop the subject of her looks and character, and to talk instead of his own experiences. If he had been anyone other than her employer's son, she would have thought him trying to flirt with her, or at least finding her attractive; but she was eight years his senior, no small difference at their respective ages, and her position within the family alone should have made her invisible to him as a woman. Yet she was a little put out to find how attractive he had grown, and even more so to find herself noticing it when she was with him.

Zina's slight coolness towards Sergei was not echoed in the greeting of any of the rest of the family, and soon wore off in the face of his personal charm and the family's tradition of hospitality. Even Irina seemed less reserved with him than on former occasions, and she questioned him eagerly about his father, without seeming shy of him. Anne thought he still was not at ease with her, but he greeted his half-brother and half-sister affectionately. Nasha, in particular, seemed pleased to see him, and wound herself briefly but fervently round his waist.

He came evidently prepared to stay, and after dinner revealed that he had been given a month's leave, which he thought not long enough to go even as far as the Black Sea. Feodor said at once, 'Then you must stay here; of course you must stay with us!' and so it was settled. As the family accepted him so easily into their number, so also they treated him as one of them, without troubling themselves to entertain him. Before long, Anne found he was attaching himself to her as being the one person who would interest herself in his feelings and enterprises. If she sat down on the verandah with a book or a piece of work, he would drift up and sit beside her; if she changed into her riding-skirt to take Quassy out, he was sure to appear at her elbow and offer her his escort; and after a day or two, she stopped struggling against the inevitable, and accepted that whatever she did, he would be her shadow.

She found herself enjoying his company much more than she had expected. She tended always to think of him as the child he had been when she first came to Russia, but he had grown up so much in the last year or so that the difference in their ages was less obtrusive than before, and his experiences since he had graduated from the academy and left the stifling folds of his grandmother's care had made him enormously better worth conversing with.

On the first day that they took a long ride together, he told her the extraordinary story of what had happened at Tilsit. After the defeat of Friedland, the Tsar's brother Constantine, along with other senior generals, argued that to continue the war was like holding a loaded pistol to the head of each Russian soldier. The war was in any case being fought for no vital Russian interest, and to drag the weakened and demoralised army into another confrontation with the highly-trained French would simply be to court another defeat, which might bring Napoleon to the very gates of Russia itself.

Besides that, the war was unpopular at home; and the peasants, on whom it fell to provide the manpower, detested the compulsory military service, and there had been outbreaks of violence and arson in protest against it. Galling though it was to deal with an upstart general whom the Synod of the Russian church had stigmatised as 'the raving foe of mankind', common sense dictated that it was necessary to make peace.

'Papa said that Napoleon had never wanted to fight us; that he had always looked on France and Russia as natural allies,' Sergei said as he rode his horse casually one-handed alongside Quassy. 'He said that Napoleon had made overtures to our Emperor before, but that the Tsar would have nothing to do with it; and it was very hard, even though the Tsar agreed we must make peace, to get him to meet Napoleon at all. Especially, it was hard to find a place to hold

227

the meeting. Napoleon has his pride, too, so it had to be on neutral ground.'

'And hence the raft on the river?' Anne prompted.

Sergei laughed. 'Oh, you heard about that? Well, of course you would have! It was so fantastic, we all thought from time to time that we must be dreaming! Only it wasn't a raft, you know, but a barge.'

'But how did it come about?' Anne asked.

'It was Papa's idea,' Sergei said with evident pride. 'Every place we suggested, the French objected to, and vice versa, and in the end Papa said, why not meet in the middle of the river? Because the Nieman is the boundary you know, Russia on one side and Prussia on the other. He swore afterwards that he said it as a joke, but you know Papa — he always means more than you think when he says things.'

'Yes, I've noticed that,' Anne said.

Sergei nodded. 'Well, whether he meant it or not, the idea seemed to take, so we had a barge built, and towed it out into the middle of the river and moored it with ropes to the central piles of what had been the bridge, before it was destroyed, you know. Then we had a tent made, with N for Napoleon on one side and A for Alexander on the other — oh, you'd have laughed, Anna! — and the two Emperors were rowed out there, and sat in the tent on either side of a table and talked.'

A quail got up from the grass beside the path, and his horse startled, and he took a moment to quiet it. 'But after the first two days,' he went on, 'everyone said it was too cramped on the barge, so it was decided that Tilsit itself should be declared neutral territory, and the rest of the talks took place there. But the barge was a good idea. I don't see how we'd ever have got the Emperor to sit down in the same room with Napoleon if it hadn't been for that.'

'Did you see Napoleon? What did you think of him?' Anne asked, checking Quassy from snatching at some tender leaves on a low branch over the path.

'Well, I was lucky, because naturally everyone wanted to be appointed to the duty, but Papa being who he was, he was able to get me on the roster to attend the Emperor himself. So I was actually in the room some of the time. I must say, our Emperor beat the Frenchman to flinders!' Sergei exclaimed with evident satisfaction. 'He's taller and handsomer and much more like a ruler in every way. But there's something impressive about Napoleon all the same,' he added thoughtfully. 'I don't know what it is.'

'You sound surprised,' Anne said.

'Well, he's so short, to begin with – our Emperor towers over him – and he's got a short neck, and a pasty face, and thin, dark hair – and not too much of it, either! But his eyes are extraordinary – blue, though not such a bright blue as our Emperor's, more a sort of grey-blue – but so bright and piercing, you have to look away from them. They make you feel very strange when they fix on you. He looked at me once, when he was asking for some more paper to be brought, and it made my head swim. I didn't like him,' he confessed, 'but there's something about him you can't ignore.'

'What was his manner like, to the Emperor?'

'Oh, he was very polite – conciliatory, even. He called him "brother" – I don't think the Tsar liked that at first, but after a while, he seemed to take to Napoleon more and more, as though he were casting a spell on him. They sat down after dinner and talked into the early hours, night after night, and from what I could hear, they seemed to be carving up the world between them – as if no-one else had any say in it! Papa said they both got carried away. He says that Napoleon is quite mad, and that he fascinated our Emperor, but that their plans were grandiose, like children with no idea of how things really are. He says that it will destroy Napoleon in the end – but not until thousands have paid the price of his madness.'

Anne could hear the Count saying the words, and for a moment, Sergei was him, riding beside her and explaining the world to her, as he had done so often before.

'I've heard some of the terms of the treaty, of course,' Anne said thoughtfully. 'France to help Russia against the Turks, for instance, in return for recognising the French in the Adriatic. But it doesn't seem as though we came out of it very well. There's Poland, for instance.'

'Yes, the new Grand Duchy of Warsaw ratified,' Sergei said, without apparently noticing that Anne had referred to Russia as her country, 'and Moldavia and Wallachia handed back. And though Napoleon encouraged the Emperor to take Finland from the Swedes, he didn't offer any help, and he's claimed the right to keep garrisons in the Baltic ports. I can't help feeling,' he concluded uneasily, 'that all the treaty has done is to make Napoleon stronger. Perhaps we ought to have gone on fighting after all. And yet, there seems no chance we would have beaten him.'

'The time hasn't yet come when he can be beaten,' Anne said, remembering the Count's words.

Sergei looked at her strangely. 'Sometimes you sound so like

229

Papa,' he said. 'I must say, it's wonderful talking to you, Anna Petrovna. You have such a quick grasp of things. The girls I am used to talking to can think of nothing but French gowns and dancing! In Kiev we had two balls a week during the season, and how bored I got with the giggling, feather-headed creatures I had to dance with! But of course, they are just girls – you are a woman, and an educated woman at that. No wonder Papa – ' He broke off abruptly.

'No wonder what?' Anne asked, intrigued.

'Nothing,' Sergei said, blushing a little. 'Only Papa thinks a great deal of you, I know. He often talks about you – and I begin to see why.'

This was growing too close for comfort. Anne changed the subject. 'So how did you occupy your time at Tilsit, when you weren't on duty with the Emperor? Was there lots to do?'

He was successfully distracted. 'Lord, no!' he said with a disdainful curl of the lip. 'Tilsit is the most beastly little town, shabby and down-trodden, and nothing decent to be had, not so much as a pair of gloves! There were a couple of banquets, but the food was dismal – everything tasted of river water, you know how it is in these provincial holes! And of course, the place was crawling with French.'

'You didn't like them?' Anne hazarded.

'Sneaking, air-blowing braggarts,' Sergei said with unexpected passion. 'Strutting about the town as if they owned the world, and not one of them from what we would call a decent family. But in the French army, anyone can become an officer, so what can you expect? We of the Guard refused to mix with them; and we didn't like it above half when Grand Duke Constantine got friendly with their General Murat, and gave him a pair of Cossack breeches. Seeing that frog-eating blowhard swaggering about in them was enough to make one sick! He looked ridiculous, but he didn't seem to know it.'

'Perhaps the Grand Duke knew he would. Perhaps he did it as a joke,' Anne said.

The notion seemed to appeal to Sergei, and he smiled. 'Perhaps. Well, the French at least had the decency to send us their one remaining gentleman as Ambassador to the Court of St Petersburg. Have you seen anything of him?'

'Armand de Caulaincourt? Yes, in Petersburg last winter. The Emperor has given him the Volkonsky Palace, practically next door to us, and we were invited to several balls and receptions there. Your father knew him in Paris, of course, and I saw him there once, at an embassy ball. He seems a very agreeable, intelligent man, and gets on well with everyone at Court, from what one hears.'

'And lives like a prince, with fifty indoor servants,' Sergei said with a grin. 'They say his cook, Tardif, is the best in the world. Have you experienced his skills yet?'

'Oh yes, at the banquet before his first ball. The food was certainly delicious, though Kerim tells me that there is nothing that comes out of the Volkonsky kitchen that he could not do just as well, or better! But de Caulaincourt certainly likes to entertain, and he will be a great asset to Petersburg society. I wish the French may do as well in Paris, with our Ambassador.'

'What, Rumiantsev? Oh, he's a gentleman of the old school, but no great gourmet,' Sergei said carelessly. 'You know that the Emperor wanted Papa to go?'

'What, as Ambassador?' Anne said in astonishment. 'I did not realise – I had not thought he stood so very high, though to be sure – '

'Oh yes, the Emperor thinks the world of him, and he said that as Papa had spent so much time in Paris, and knew everyone, he was perfectly suited for the position. But Papa refused it. He suggested Rumiantsev instead, and offered his services in an advisory capacity.' He shook his head in wonder. 'I should not, myself, like to refuse the Emperor anything, but Papa is as brave as a lion.'

'Why did he refuse? Did he happen to mention to you?'

Sergei frowned. 'I'm not absolutely sure. Papa jokes, you know, and sometimes one cannot precisely pin down what he *does* mean. But he told me that Rumiantsev was the best man for the job, because he really believes in the alliance with the French. He thinks that the French are sure to help us secure the Turkish lands we need to complete the old Byzantine Empire; and that what happens in the rest of Europe doesn't matter, as long as Napoleon leaves our western border alone.'

'By which we must infer that your father does not think so.'

'Papa thinks Napoleon is the enemy of civilisation, and that he must be defeated sooner or later. He thinks what happens in Europe *does* matter, and that we should resist it; and that the treaty solves nothing, only pushes the problem under the carpet.'

They reached the top of a rise, and he halted his horse and turned it a little so that he could look at Anne. She reached forward to stroke Quassy's neck and turn over a lock of her mane, and then straightened up to meet Sergei's searching gaze.

'The worst thing about the treaty,' he said, 'is that our Emperor was obliged to side with the French against England. It makes me feel very bad to think that Russia is now England's enemy; though I'm sure,' he added hastily, 'that the Emperor doesn't mean to do anything about it, beyond the boycott of British shipping. This talk about a secret treaty to declare war on England is all nonsense, I'm sure.'

Anne was touched by his concern; and a little puzzled to know what her own feelings were. 'My dear,' she said, trying to make light of it, 'there's no need to apologise for the actions of the Emperor of All the Russias. I'm sure if he had consulted you, things would have been different.'

Sergei bit his lip. 'You are all generosity to joke about it, but I hate to think that we are now on opposite sides.'

'You mean that officially I am now your enemy?' she teased gently. 'No, it's all right – I am joking you. And, indeed, I hardly know what I feel. I have been five years in Russia, but it seems like half a lifetime. I think I am becoming more Russian every day, and England seems so far away – far away, and lost to me.'

He observed her intently. 'You miss your home?' he asked gently. 'You must often wish to return. I'm sorry if I have spoken clumsily, and made you remember it.'

She gathered herself together. 'Don't look so tragic, Seryosha! England is still there, and still safe, whatever Alexander and Bonaparte may decide between them. While the British navy rules the wave, no harm can come to my country. And the war won't last for ever. One day I shall be able to go back.'

'Go back to visit – or to live?' he asked hesitantly.

She stared unseeingly at Quassy's ears. 'I don't know,' she said at last. 'At this moment, I really don't know.'

There was a silence; and then Quassy tugged impatiently at the bit, and Anne shook herself and smiled at her young companion's grave expression. 'Come on, let's gallop,' she said cheerfully. 'I haven't felt the wind in my face all day. I'll race you down to the brook and see if that bay of yours is as great a sluggard as it looks.'

Sergei rose to the challenge. 'He'd beat your mare over any ground! Name your stakes!'

'The winner shall name them! Are you ready? Go!'

Chapter Fourteen

Anne was sitting on the verandah enjoying a late breakfast of yoghurt, honey, figs, grapes, and the strong, cloudy coffee which had taken so much getting used to, but which she now relished almost more than the usual kind. Sashka was lolling against her knees, picking idly at the grapes on her plate as he took a short respite from the energetic games he had been playing with his cousins since dawn. He had grown visibly that summer, since arriving at Chastnaya, and Zina said proudly that it was the Caucasian air and food, which, she firmly believed, could have made a dead man get up and dance.

His father, Anne thought, half-fondly and half-sadly, would hardly recognise the boy when he saw him again. When that would be there was no knowing. The Corsican general who had made himself Emperor now ruled half the world: with Portugal overrun and Spain become a subject kingdom, the French empire now stretched from Gibraltar to the Russian frontier; from the chilly Baltic to the blue Ionian Sea; and with Russia complaisant and Sweden helplessly neutral, England alone resisted, maintaining the war against the most successful soldier the world had ever known, not in hope of success, but because there was no choice. Already the European embargo on British goods, or goods carried in British ships, had bitten hard: Napoleon hoped to starve his enemy into submission, since he could not invade England's shores without control of the sea – and that, Anne still firmly believed, he would never have.

Meanwhile, life for her at Chastnaya was very pleasant, and she missed the stiff formality of Petersburg not at all. Like her mistress, she had taken to wearing her hair in a plait, and dressing with simplicity in a cotton skirt, peasant blouse, and sandals, or soft boots for riding. Occasionally a feeling of guilt would drive her to gather the children together for a lesson, or to take them out on an escorted ride to teach them the names of the trees and flowers; but otherwise she spent her days in idleness and pleasure, and enjoyed every moment.

Sergei came out of the house, smiled a greeting at her, and flung himself down in a hammock, one leg trailing idly over the edge, one arm hooked under his head so that he could look at her.

'What are you going to do today, Anna Petrovna?' he asked. Sashka left Anne's knee to climb onto the hammock and sit astride his half-brother, who held him off gently with one strong hand. 'Don't kneel there, Sashka! I've breakfasted on quails and champagne and I should hate to lose them!'

'Quails and champagne?' Anne said with a quizzical smile. 'Is that the way you Guards officers live? What luxury! I suppose that's what you learned in Kiev?'

'That, and how to dance and make love to the Ukranian girls,' he smiled from under his eyelids. 'I am an excellent dancer, you know, Anna. They all said I was a pleasure to dance with.'

'I'm sure you are,' Anne said, sipping her coffee.

'So, will you entrust yourself to me tomorrow, at the dance after the muster? I think we should make a very pretty couple.'

Anne raised an eyebrow. 'You want to dance with *me*?'

'Why not?'

'I should have thought you would want to dance with Zinaidia and her friends. They are closer to your age, and Zinaidia is very pretty. That's what *I'd* call a pretty couple.'

A pink spot of vexation showed on his cheek, but he kept his eyes on Sashka, who was pretending he was a horse, and slapping his thigh to drive him on faster. 'What nonsense you talk! Anyone would think you were a matron in a cap, to hear you. The difference in our ages is nothing. I regard *you* as my contemporary; Zinochka and her friends are giggling schoolgirls as far as I'm concerned, and I have no interest in them.'

She saw his dignity had been touched, and did not want to upset him further. 'I am rebuked,' she said calmly. 'I shall dance with you, with pleasure, if that's what you want.'

He sat up abruptly, swinging Sashka down in one movement, and regarded her with bright eyes. 'Do you mean it? Any dance?'

'Any dance,' she smiled. 'You choose. Now I think I'll go and put on my riding boots, and take Quassy out to look at the view from Picnic Point.'

'Good idea! May I come with you?' Sergei said at once. 'Here's a thought: why don't we take a picnic with us, and go the long way round, by Valley of the Horses? After tomorrow, you know, you won't see the great herds grazing there, so you ought to go and look at them once more. Then we can take a nuncheon under the trees, and ride back through the woods, which will be nice and cool in the hot part of the day.'

The plan was very appealing, but there was something in the eagerness in Sergei's eyes that made Anne hesitate. He did not look at her as she would expect a boy to look at the governess, his father's employee; but then, she reminded herself, he was not a boy any longer, and it would be as well not to forget that again. She met his eyes, and felt a strange flutter inside herself, which she immediately and sternly crushed down.

'What a good idea,' she made herself say lightly. 'We could take Nasha and Sashka, too. Would you like that, Sashka? How kind your brother is, to think of it! Run and find your sister, and we'll send for the horses, and get Kerim to make us up something to eat. We could carry it in saddle-bags, so as not to have to take a groom with us.'

Sergei took it very well, but seeing, out of the corner of her eyes, the disappointment in his, Anne felt she had been right to include the children in his plan.

Three hours later, they were riding in single file along the path which ran along the side of the hill for the whole length of the Valley of the Horses. As they wound in and out of bushes and rocky outcrops, they could see down below them the silver thread of the little river which tacked back and forth across the valley floor. In some places it ran brown and deep between green banks, and there were fish to be caught, flickering suddenly out of the overhang, or rising to snatch a fly with a faint popping sound; in other places it became shallow, and tumbled noisily over natural dams of grey rock, refracting the light into dazzle; clattered hollowly over smooth bare stones; and spread silver ripples over wide gravel beaches.

And scattered over the whole valley floor, everywhere they looked, there were horses, grazing on the good, rich grass, peacefully unaware of the muster to come on the morrow. They were mostly bays and greys and a few blacks, Karabakhs and Kabardas, highly-prized throughout Russia and the Levant: intelligent, fast, and hardy. As they rode along, Quassy turned her head continually from the business of picking her path, to gaze intently at the grazing herds below, as if she recognised her kin; and now and then she would stretch her nostrils wide for the smell of them and make a little whickering sound of excitement. She had been born in just such a herd in such a valley, and her eyes were bright with the memory. Sergei's horse, and the children's ponies, being geldings, paced along unemotionally, their ears at the usual half-mast of indifference.

At the head of the valley, the flanking hills closed together, and met in a flattish headland, with a broad grey patch where the underlying granite broke through the thin turf. Behind it rose a rough cliff, topped with wind-bent thorn trees; but around the natural rock table was a pretty clump of birch which afforded shade from the noon sun, and relief to the eye. This place was called Picnic Point, for it was a natural place to stop and enjoy an alfresco meal, and admire the view.

Kerim had exercised his imagination in the matter of the nuncheon; perhaps enjoying the challenge, for much of his time hung heavy on his hands. He was under-occupied at Chastnaya, for the Kiriakov cook was even more fiercely autocratic than Kerim, and only grudgingly allowed him to help in the kitchen, except for the one day a month when he took a holiday on vodka and became incapable for twenty-four hours of anything but snoring. Then Kerim came into his own, not only cooking, but passing through the kitchens like a whirlwind, cleaning and reorganising everything along the lines he approved and had learnt from his Moscow master; only to see the new order overturned the following day when Bablash returned to duty with his temper soured by a thick mouth and pounding head.

A nuncheon to be packed in saddle-bags was beneath Bablash's notice, however, and he had made no objection to Kerim's being asked to prepare it personally. Had he been given sufficient notice – say, a day or two – Kerim would have put up a feast fit at least for a count; as it was he had done his noble best by assembling all the good things he could find that didn't need cooking.

While Sergei unsaddled the horses and tied them up, Anne spread a cloth and the children trotted back and forth bringing the quail's eggs, pickled mushrooms, cold roast duck, smoked eel, salads, strawberries, raisins and honey cakes with which Kerim had solaced his thwarted creativity.

'Quassy's very restless,' Sergei reported as he came to join them, bringing the bottles which had been packed in his saddle-bags. 'We shall have to keep an eye on her, in case she breaks her rope.'

'I expect it's the herds down below upsetting her,' Anne said, making room for him.

'The other horses aren't excited,' Sashka pointed out.

'Perhaps she can smell the stallion,' Nasha said unexpectedly, and Anne and Sergei met each other's eyes, and suppressed a smile.

'Maybe so,' Anne said hastily. 'Sit down, Nasha, and have something to eat. What has Kerim given us to drink, I wonder?'

'Buttermilk,' Sergei said, making a face. 'That must be for the children. And Rhenish for us, Anna.' He smiled into her eyes. 'It should have been champagne.'

'Not in the heat of the day,' Anne said off-puttingly.

Sergei seemed suitably chastened, and laid himself out instead to be pleasant and amuse the children. He told them tales of his adventures; described their father 'being the arch diplomat, all lowered eyelids and inscrutable smiles'; even played guessing games with them while they ate Kerim's delicious food. Now and then, to Anne's amusement, he glanced at her for approval, but she kept her eyes on her plate and feigned not to see. When they had finished, the children, energy restored, jumped up to wander off to explore while Anne and Sergei made themselves more comfortable, gazed at the view and chatted.

'I must say,' Anne said, 'I'm really looking forward to the muster tomorrow. It promises to be quite a day! And Grishka says there will be riding displays, and mock battles, and gypsy dancing, as well as the feast and the dance afterwards.'

'Yes, they always make a festival of it, at Chastnaya,' Sergei said. 'People come from miles around to buy horses and sell other goods in exchange. It's like a regular country fair. Not that I've ever been here before, but Papa has told me of it often. It was at the muster that he first met Irina Pavlovna.'

'I didn't know that. How did it come about?'

'Well, he was serving with the Caucasus Highland Guard at Pyatigorsk, and they had an anonymous warning that the Tcherkess were going to attack Chastnaya in force during the muster, and steal the horses to sell to the Turks. So he was ordered to bring a troop down to guard the plantation; but the Tcherkess never came, and instead he fell in love with Irina Pavlovna, and married her and took her away within the month.'

'So quickly!' Anne said. 'Was it love at first sight?'

Sergei shrugged. 'I only know what Papa's told me. The story is that he saw her coming in from riding with her hair in a plait and a scarf round her head, and took her for a peasant girl, and asked her to bring him some lemonade. Later when he was introduced to her as the daughter of the house, he didn't realise it was the same girl, until she asked him if he wanted anything more to drink. It made a sort of joke between them, I suppose.'

Anne didn't think this sounded like a sufficient reason for marrying anyone, but could hardly say so. Instead she said lightly, 'So the Kiriakovs kept their horses, but lost a daughter.'

Sergei gave a quirky smile. 'I wonder if that's why Zina doesn't take to me – maybe she's afraid history is about to repeat itself, and that I'll run off with Zinochka! Perhaps I should set her mind at rest.' And he sang in his small but tuneful voice a verse of a popular local song:

> *The mountain girls are honey-sweet,*
> *With midnight in their eyes,*
> *But wind and sky and freedom*
> *Are still the better prize.*
> *So I'll not wed, and die in bed:*
> *I'll save my cash*
> *And buy a horse instead!*

Anne laughed and said, 'That's a thoroughly reprehensible song, but I don't know that I can find fault with the philosophy, feeling as I do about Quassy! Did I tell you about the offer of marriage I had from a Tartar Prince? If I had been willing to part with my horse, I could have been a princess by now!'

'In Papa's case, he'd have done better to take the horse,' Sergei said unguardedly.

'Sergei, you mustn't say things like that,' Anne said quickly.

'I can't help it, Anna – I don't like her. Oh, I do my bit and behave pretty, and call her Mother, but I've never liked her.'

'I've seen you try and applauded it, but I wish you need not find it such an effort. What is it you dislike?'

He shrugged. 'There's something about her and all her people that's – I don't know – different. Not civilised. They aren't really Russians at all, you know. They're like half-tamed dogs – they might turn at any moment and bite you.'

'But you must believe that Irina Pavlovna loves your father very dearly, and he her.'

'Why must I? I don't believe it,' Sergei said, frowning. 'I don't know what they may have once felt for each other, but I don't believe he loves her now, and as for her – well, look where she is! If you loved my father, wouldn't you go with him to Paris? Would you stay behind?'

'Seryosha, it's most improper for us to talk like this. Please, don't say any more. You forget my position.'

He flung himself back on the grass on one elbow. 'Your position! How could I forget? You're always reminding me of it!'

Anne looked at him in distress, wondering how to cope with the jumble of emotions being presented her. But before she could draw breath to tackle the situation, there was a sound behind them, a little rushing rattle of small loose stones, and she turned her head to see that Nasha had climbed half-way up the cliff face and was sitting on a ledge, watching them.

Anne called out an automatic warning. 'Nasha, be careful! You shouldn't have climbed up there! It's dangerous.'

Nasha looked down at her unperturbed. 'I'm all right,' she said calmly. 'I shan't fall.' She regarded them steadily, her eyes impassive and bright, and Anne wondered uncomfortably if it were possible that she had heard what they were saying. But surely she was too far away?

'Nasha, come down now,' Anne called, but Natasha did not move to obey. Instead she looked away, and fixing her eyes dreamily on the middle distance, she said unexpectedly,

'Anna, are all the people who hear voices mad?'

'What do you mean? What voices?' Anne asked, some undefined apprehension sharpening her voice.

Nasha's gaze slid from the infinite to focus on Anne's face. 'Marie was telling me about Jeanne d'Arc hearing a voice that told her to dress as a man and go to war. But when I asked Kerim, he said that it was a sign of madness to hear voices.'

Anne regarded her cautiously, wondering what new mischief this heralded. Was Nasha hoping to be allowed to dress in trousers and ride at the muster tomorrow? And did she hope to enlist Divine aid for the purpose? 'In the case of Jeanne d'Arc, we believe that the voice she heard was a command from God,' she said, aware that Sergei was watching her with amusement at her predicament.

'And what if someone else heard voices?'

'I suppose it might be a Divine command,' Anne began cautiously.

'In the case of Bablash,' Sergei interrupted, 'it's the voice of the genie in the bottle. Commands of a very different sort.'

Nasha considered. 'How would anyone know which it was?'

Sergei was grinning at her discomfiture, and Anne firmly avoided his eyes. 'I think if the voice were from God, the command would probably be to do something difficult that you didn't particularly want to do.'

'Because if it was something you liked doing, God wouldn't have to tell you – you'd do it anyway?' Nasha hazarded.

'Something like that,' Anne said, wondering how she could change the subject.

Nasha appeared to be pondering the matter, staring away into the distance. Suddenly she straightened and said in a very different voice, 'Oh look, there's the stallion!'

At the same moment Quassy let out a piercing whinny, and they turned to see the herd stallion standing on a rocky outcrop only a little way off, separated from them by a shallow gully. Anne drew a breath. She had never seen anything so magnificent: he was no mere horse, but a creature of raw power and commanding presence. He stood watching them, his head turned, his bright eye showing a little white, his whole body gathered and tense like a coiled spring. He was pure white, not tall for a horse, almost too stocky for beauty; his chest was deep, his ribs widely sprung, his quarters broad, muscle packed over shoulder and loin, and arching his massive neck into a crest; but his head was fine-cut and intelligent. Power and delicacy were perfectly combined in him as he stood there outlined against the sky, his ears pricked, his nostrils flaring as they sought to trap and identify the scents coming to him on the light air.

'He's beautiful,' Anne breathed, enraptured. The stallion arched his neck and raised his tail into a banner, and stamped his hoof threateningly against the rock as he looked warily from one to another of the group before him. Then he fixed his eyes on the horses, and made a deep knuckering sound. Instantly Quassy answered, whickering and fidgeting in excitement, and even the geldings began shifting nervously at their tethers as the tension in the air reached them.

Sergei was half-way to his feet. 'We'd better get to them,' he said. 'There's no knowing what – '

But the stallion had caught Quassy's scent, and he made another sound, quite different this time, a deep and powerful whinny, to which Quassy replied with an excited squeal. She flung herself abruptly back on her haunches and jerked at her head-rope, and as the stallion called again, she reared up and struck out at her tether, and came down with a leg over the rope.

Now all was confusion. The horses were milling, the stallion stamping and calling, and Quassy was trapped, unable to free her leg from the rope which she was pulling taut in her efforts to escape. She was whinnying and struggling in a mixture of excitement and panic, and Anne and Sergei were both up and running.

'Oh God, she'll break her leg!' Anne cried. The slender foreleg looked so fragile, as though it might snap at any instant.

'Get to her! Hold her!' Sergei called. 'I'll try to drive him off!' He ran past the horses, waving his arms and shouting to try to frighten the stallion away. Anne reached Quassy, grabbed her rope close to the head, and tried to pull her head down so as to slacken the rope enough to free her leg. But Quassy was too frightened now, strong in her panic, and strained back with all her strength, pulling the rope ever tighter under her knee.

In terror that the leg might break, Anne saw there was nothing to do but untie the rope. Sergei had hitched all the horses with safety knots, and she had only to reach for the loose end and tug. Her fingers closed on the rough hemp, just as Sergei, turning his head, saw what she was about to do, and shouted, 'No! For God's sake, don't untie her!'

He was to late. The rope came free, and for a blessed moment all seemed well, as Anne dropped the slack of it and Quassy was able to put her foreleg down; but in the same instant the stallion called again, and the mare, her whole body quivering, flung up her head, her ears pricked towards him, and obeyed the imperative summons. The rope was jerked free, running through Anne's hand, and burning her palm as she tried to hold on. She cried out; Quassy gave a violent breenge, shook her head, and leapt away, almost knocking Sergei over as he tried to grab her. She was over the dry gully in one bound; the stallion whirled and snorted excitedly, circled her, and then closed his teeth on her crest, driving her towards the herd. Quassy squealed and obeyed, and the two of them disappeared over the edge and down the hillside.

Anne ran forward automatically, but Sergei caught her, almost pulling her over.

'Anna, for God's sake!'

'We must catch her! He'll hurt her! Let me go!' Anne cried out, struggling.

Sergei tightened his hold, turning her to face him, shaking her a little to get her attention. 'Don't be a fool, you can't go after her on foot! He wouldn't let you get near her anyway. Be still, Anna! There's nothing we can do now. Oh Lord, we'll lose the other horses if we don't calm them!'

And he let go of her to run to the head of his gelding, who was snorting and tugging at his rope. Nasha was there, too, soothing the ponies, and Sashka looking frightened. Anne suddenly became aware of the pain in her hand, looked down at the red rope-burn across her palm, and burst unexpectedly into tears.

In a moment, Sergei, abandoning the horses to Nasha, had crossed to her again, and taken her in his arms, holding her close against him and murmuring, 'Anna! Annushka! It's all right. Don't cry.' Anne wanted to obey him, but the excitement and shock of it all had for once overset her usual self-control, and she was unable to stop herself. 'Oh don't cry, *doushka*! She'll be all right. He won't hurt

241

her, you know – he just wants her for his herd. It's a compliment really.'

Anne tried to respond, but only cried harder. His arms were unexpectedly strong and comforting, and she leaned against him gratefully, and tried to say something, which came out as a gulp and a sob.

'What is it, Annushka? Oh, there, don't cry! We'll get Quassy back, don't worry.'

Over Sergei's shoulder, Anne caught sight of the children watching her gravely, and it was enough to make her recover her senses. She must not take comfort from Sergei like this. She pulled away from him, and he allowed her to go reluctantly, transferring his hold to her wrist, and uncurling her wounded hand gently.

'Oh, your poor hand! Poor darling, does it hurt very much? Wait, I have a clean handkerchief here. Let me bind it up for you.'

'No, no, I'll do it,' Anne said hastily.

'Nonsense,' Sergei said with an engaging smile. 'How would you tie it, one-handed?'

She submitted, allowing him to fold the clean linen and bind it around her palm. 'We'd better get back to the house, so that we can dress it properly with something,' Sergei said. 'And then perhaps you ought to go to bed and rest. It's been quite a shock for you.'

Anne almost smiled at this picture of her fragile sensibility. 'Thank you. I'm quite all right now,' she said, fumbling for her own handkerchief. She dried her face, and thought as Sergei watched her solicitously how absurdly young he looked when he was being protective. 'As for going to bed, there's no question of it. We'll have to ask Mishka to get a party together at once, to go after Quassy. She still has that rope on her headstall. I'm so afraid she'll catch it in something and hurt herself.'

Sergei shook his head. 'Don't be silly. The stallion would never let us get near her, even with a dozen men. The only way to separate her now is to drive the whole herd in and corral them, which is what will happen at the muster tomorrow. We'll get her back then. Don't worry, she'll be all right.'

'But supposing – '

'Don't suppose! There's nothing else to be done. Come, we had better pack the things and get back. We've got Quassy's saddle to carry, too. Look, do you think you could ride Nabat astride? He's not broken to side-saddle. Then if you could take Nasha up behind you, I can ride her pony and carry the saddle. That will be the best way. Can you manage the reins, with your hand, or should I lead you?'

'No, I'm sure I can manage,' Anne said, and meekly allowed Sergei to go on organising everything since he seemed to be enjoying it. He helped her mount his gelding, and Anne was very glad now that she had had those lessons from Grishka. Nabat felt horribly broad after Quassy. Her thigh muscles ached from the unaccustomed position, and her hand hurt her, but there was nothing to be gained by complaining, so she bit her lip and held her silence. Sergei threw Nasha up behind her, helped Sashka to mount his pony, and almost stepped onto Nasha's pony with the spare saddle over his arm.

It seemed a very long ride back, and by the time they reached the house, Anne felt exhausted by the emotions of the day. Zina exclaimed and tutted over her hand, and dressed it with sweet oil, and even while Sergei and the children were describing the excitements of the day, she noted the heaviness of Anne's eyes, and insisted that she have a warm herbal bath and retire to her room for a rest. 'You will need to be fresh for tomorrow,' she said reasonably. 'It will be a very long day.'

Anne allowed herself to be persuaded.

Naturally, neither Anne nor the children were allowed to take part in the muster itself, but mounted on quiet ponies, they were able to watch the beginning of it from the hillside above the valley. Irina was there too, but not on Iskra. She had been very much upset by the narration of what happened to Quassy, and had taken the precaution of shutting her own mare in the stable for the day, and coming out on a safe pony.

Down below the herd grazed. Anne strained her eyes, but could not pick out Quassy from that distance, even allowing for the rope and headcollar. The stallion was on a little rise to one side, scenting the wind, seeming already uneasy, though he could not yet have caught the smell of the men who were approaching from downwind, thirty of them on horseback, and another twenty on foot, with whips and sticks with which to make a noise to head off the horses if necessary. The watchers on the hillside could see the cordon of riders approaching, stretched out across the open end of the valley. The plan was to drive the horses up the headland and through the gulley, and down the woodland track to the bottle-necked corral which had been built about half a mile from the house.

A horse whinnied, and the mares stopped grazing and looked about them uneasily, and called their foals to their side. The stallion's head was up high, turning this way and that, and then he saw the movement out beyond his herd, and stamped his foot warningly. He left his eminence and trotted down the side of the herd, and his gait was long and smooth and floating; despite his solidity he moved with effortless grace, barely seeming to brush the grass.

The mares were beginning to draw together and move away from the approaching cordon, but the stallion was suspicious. He reached the far side of the herd and halted, head up, staring at the riders, trotting a few steps one way, then whirling on his haunches and trotting the other way, keeping between his mares and the threat, yet not knowing quite what the threat might be. He could smell the men, but the ridden horses confused him; and all the while his herd was drifting away from him up the valley, bunching in closer as the valley narrowed.

Finally he whirled away and raced the length of the herd, turning at the front to halt the mares, who looked uneasily over their shoulders, and then at him, uncertain which imperative to obey. One or two tried to break back, their foals running and turning with them as if attached to their flanks by invisible cords, and the stallion whinnied to them anxiously. Then Anne saw a glint as one of the leading riders – probably Mishka or Grishka – raised his shotgun in the air, and a moment later there came the flat slamming sound of an explosion, which echoed back and forth across the narrow valley.

It was all that was needed. The mares who had tried to break turned away from the sound in panic, and the whole herd began to move up the valley at a trot. The stallion went with them, circling at that same, effortless, flying gait, bunching the mares closer together, unwittingly doing exactly what his pursuers wanted.

'We'd better go now, if we're to get to the corral before they arrive,' Irina said. 'You mustn't miss that part, Anna – it's so exciting! One year they managed to break out, and it took two days to drive them back again once they had scattered. That was in the days of the old stallion, of course. He was very clever, and very fierce, and he knew all about the muster. This is the new, young one – there's no knowing what he may do.'

'I don't understand what's to keep them on the path through the wood,' Anne said as they turned their ponies away from the valley. Across country, they should easily reach the corral first. 'They could scatter amongst the trees, and you'd never catch them.'

'Instinct,' Irina said with a smile. 'They always try to keep together, and run for open country. It isn't in their nature to go in amongst the trees, and the stallion wouldn't let them, either. Horses don't hide for safety – they run. They obey their nature – and it will be their undoing,' she added thoughtfully.

On the other side of the headland, at the end of the wood, there was another gully, and beyond it the corral had been built, a wide-open funnel at the end from which the horses would approach, narrowing into a bottleneck with a double gate. Up on the top of the gully another group of men waited with brushwood hurdles to jump down behind the herd and close the gap to stop them breaking back; and here, too, Anne and Irina and the children joined the other women and children to watch from the safe eminence.

It was hot, even so early in the day, and airless, and clouds of tiny black flies rose from the bracken to torment the ponies; but the ring of their bits as they shook their heads, and the occasional stamp of a hoof, were the only sounds. Everyone was silent, waiting in almost unbearable tension for the arrival of the herd.

They heard them before they saw them, a soft drumming sound that was so low and heavy it was almost felt rather than heard, like the beating of one's own heart. Its vibration increased as it drew nearer, and became audible as a thunder of hooves on the hard-baked track; and then the distant sound of pursuit reached their ears, the men yipping and cracking their whips to drive them on.

Then suddenly out of the wood the stallion appeared, leading his mares now that the track was too narrow for him to circle them. He cantered, head up, bright eyes everywhere, his mane and tail streaming out with the wind of his passage. Then, as he reached the point where the gully sides rose short but sheer like cliffs, he stopped dead. Behind him the mares crowded up but did not pass, while he stood staring suspiciously about him.

Anne thought how beautiful he looked: wild and proud, the master of his mares, but their protector, too, going first into danger on their behalf, offering his life for them, and for the right to mate them; and somehow the beauty and the pride made her feel sad. She wanted to cry, because they, the human beings, were deceiving him, trapping him; and though she knew it was foolish, because no harm would come to him, she felt they were small, mean creatures, beside his greatness, his noble strength.

He looked at the people lining the gully top, and at the inviting open space before him at the gully mouth, and he seemed to sense that something was wrong. His mares pressed against him, and one tried to pass, but he snapped at her to hold her back. His ears went forward and back, and he snorted, misliking the situation, and held the great

245

press of bodies behind him by the sheer force of his presence.

Then Natasha tugged urgently at Anne's arm, and whispered, 'Oh look, there's Quassy!'

Anne had seen her at the same instant, as she flung up her head and the headcollar and rope became visible. She was near the front, and apart from the headcollar she looked no different from any of those other black and brown and grey bodies; with her dusty coat, tangled mane and wary eyes, she was just another wild mare trying to escape from the hated smell of men. Anne's heart ached for her, too.

Behind them the men redoubled their shouts and whip-cracking, and the mares surged forward more urgently. The stallion looked again suspiciously at that inviting gap; and then, there being nothing else for it, trotted forward. Anne was conscious of everyone's letting out their breath in relief. The herd surged by, a sea of long bodies, wild manes, upflung heads; the foals pressed to their mothers' sides, only their tiny faces visible in the mass of warm bodies, as they did what was born in them for survival. In a brown and black and white stream, the horses poured through the narrow gap and spread out into the space beyond. Anne turned her pony and rode to the other edge of the gully to see the finale.

The paddock rails were visible to the stallion now; and all around the circumference were people, lining the rails, making escape impossible. Now the lie was exposed to him. The open space was not what it seemed: the paddock rails curved in again, narrowing ahead into a trap. He snorted and began to run back and forth across the width of the paddock, whirling, ears back, just out of reach of the hated men who hemmed him in. The mares pressed in behind him, driving him towards the bottleneck; he ran back and forth, more and more urgently, kicking out as he span around at the end of each shortening run, angry, afraid.

'What will they do with him?' Anne asked breathlessly, of no-one in particular. Surely no-one could hold that white storm? Then there was a confusion of shouting and a flurry of movement, as at the last moment when it would be possible, the stallion charged the rails, and with a power born of desperation sprang into the air, clearing both the rails and the instinctively ducking heads of the men beyond them. It was a soaring, stunning jump, at least five and a half feet upwards, perhaps fifteen feet outwards, hard to believe even though they witnessed it with their own eyes. He landed in a spurt of dust, and swerving violently, galloped at an astonishing speed for the open country.

Everyone was shouting and exclaiming with excitement. 'Did you see?' Irina cried needlessly, her eyes shining. 'What a jump! He must have cleared six feet!'

'I'm glad he got away. They'll never catch him now,' Anne said, her eyes unaccountably moist.

'They don't want to. Once he was through the bottleneck he'd have been let go anyway,' Irina said. 'His job is to look after the mares out in the wild – he is never brought in or tamed.'

'Where will he go now?'

'Not far,' Irina said. 'He'll hang around just out of reach, waiting to see what becomes of his wives, and when they are released, he'll come and gather them up, and take them back to the valley. But I'm glad I saw that jump! I don't suppose anyone's ever seen a horse jump higher.'

The corral was filling up now, and Sergei came riding up to the gully-top to say to Anne, 'Quassy's up there, and she looks all right, as far as one can see.'

'Yes, I saw her go past. What happens now?'

'Since the stallion's gone, Feodor's going to go in and try to get hold of her. She may be a little wild. Do you want to come down and watch?'

'Of course,' Anne said. 'But wouldn't it be better if I went in to her? She knows me.'

Sergei grinned. 'Foolish! You don't really think anyone will let you climb into a corral full of wild horses, do you?'

With no-one driving them, and no stallion to lead them, the mares were growing quieter, no longer milling about, but standing still, watchful, yet not panicking; one or two even suckled their young foals. When Anne and Sergei reached the paddock rails, Feodor with a rope in his hand was preparing to climb in.

'Going to see if I can get up to that mare of yours, Anna,' he said as they came up. 'See if she'll let me near her.'

'She ought to,' Anne said. 'She's as gentle as a kitten to handle.'

'That was before she had a whole day of freedom on the range, and with the stallion for company,' Feodor said with a grin. 'It changes priorities, you know. But we'll see.'

Anne watched with amazement and distress as her previous docile, gentle mare proved impossible to catch. In a while, Feodor was back.

'She's not having it,' he said, climbing back over to safety. 'Unfortunately, there's just enough room in there for them to move about. If they were packed tighter, I'd be able to take her, but I don't want to upset them any more. We'll get her when she goes through the bottleneck. One thing, though – she's not lame. Seems to be perfectly sound, from the way she was dodging me and kicking out.' He turned to his head man, hovering at his side. 'All right, let's get on with it.'

Half an hour later Quassy was driven by the press of bodies into the bottleneck, and trapped between the two sets of gates. Leaning over, Feodor caught the rope hanging from her headcollar, while Mishka reached over from the other side and attached a second rope; then the further gate was opened, and she exploded out of the trap, towing the two men with her. Anne watched in amazement as for the next few minutes, Quassy bucked and struggled like a mad thing to get away; then she seemed quite suddenly to resign herself to her fate, and stood quietly, though trembling all over from her head to her feet.

The two men examined her, ran their hands down her limbs, and pronounced her sound.

'She's very upset, though,' Mishka said. 'We'd best shut her in the stable for the rest of the day, let her get over it.'

Anne came towards her to try to stroke her, but she flinched away, staring over their heads with wild eyes, and when they led her forward, she went with them reluctantly, turning her head back and whinnying shrilly, as though calling to her recently-acquired sisters for help. The men took her into a loosebox and released her, and she ran at once to the half-door and put her head out, staring into the distance and ignoring Anne's attempts to stroke or pet her or give her sugar.

'She'll settle better if we shut the top door, too,' Feodor said. When he had bolted the door at the top, he looked sympathetically at Anne and said, 'Don't worry, she's not hurt.'

'But she sounds so unhappy,' Anne said miserably. From within the loose-box came the rustling sound as she moved restlessly around in the straw, and the occasional angry thud as she tried kicking the door. Then, even harder to bear, a series of piercing neighs, as, shut up in the semi-darkness, deprived of her freedom and the excitement and the companionship she had tasted, Quassy called and called to the herd she could no longer see or smell.

Sergei hovered near, looking at Anne sympathetically. 'She'll forget all about it in a day or two,' he said.

'Yes,' Anne said, 'but I wish she didn't mind so much.'

'You'll have to be careful with her while the stallion's nearby, or he'll come and steal her back,' Feodor said. 'Best keep her shut in, until the herd's back in the valley.'

Gently, and with Sergei's help, he urged Anne away from the box and out of earshot of Quassy's piercing, plaintive cries, back towards the corral.

'By the way,' he said suddenly, cocking his head at her quizzically, 'have you thought what the result of this little adventure might be?'

Anne looked puzzled. 'What do you mean?'

Feodor grinned. 'Well, she was out with the herd for a whole day, and that's a very eager young stallion. Ten to one he covered her in that time. Your Quassy may present you with a foal next spring!'

Chapter Fifteen

It was a day of hard work, filled with the sound and smell of horses, with dust, sweat, shouts, whinnies, and the soft drumming of unshod hooves. Anne's mind was filled with a tessellation of images: a horse's head flung up against the sky, nostrils wide; a foal determinedly suckling in the midst of turmoil; a man laughing, wiping a bloodied nose on the elbow of his coat; Zinochka in a red kerchief bringing out a jug of ale on her shoulder, the gold rings in her ears flashing in the sun; Mishka whirling a rope into blurring patterns around his head; Sergei astride the dozing Nabat, leaning back with a hand on the sun-warmed bay rump.

One by one the horses were driven through the bottleneck, and the ones that were to be sold at the fair were herded into a second paddock, while the others were released. None of those set free had any doubt as to where to go: they galloped as fast as they could lay foot to ground back towards the valley, where the stallion waited anxiously for them, keeping sentry on a prominent rock above the path that led to the pass.

The house-serfs meanwhile were making preparations for the evening's amusements, digging a cookpit for the whole ox which was to be roasted, setting up lanterns and benches around the area marked out for dancing, labouring under Bablash's caustic direction to prepare the feast which would accompany the ball. Other preparations were a grim reminder that here at Chastnaya they were on the very edge of the civilised world. Bars were fitted over all the windows of the house; the two elderly two-pounder guns mounted in front of the house, which Anne had thought merely for decoration, were loaded and primed and kept manned; and a guard of armed serfs was told off to patrol the house and the paddock, in case of raids in the night.

But the Kiriakovs did not allow the threat of danger to damp their enthusiasm for the pleasures of the evening which were to follow the labours of the day. As the sun began to go down, the men came back to the house, and there came sounds of tremendous washings and scrubbings as they plunged their sun-reddened faces and dust-whitened hair into tubs of water, or submitted themselves to the chilly gush of the back-yard pump, with a grinning serf at the handle.

The sun sank, swollen and dark orange, and the spectacular display of gold and pink and purple that flushed the western sky went unobserved as the Kiriakovs sought out their finery, the billowing fragrance of clean linen, the tender whisper of silk, the gratifying weight of gold-thread embroidery. Perfume expanded upon warm skin; ears and wrists and necks were hung with gold and jewellery; heartbreaking little kid slippers, or soft boots of mellowed leather, were drawn on to eager feet; hair was brushed and curled and pomaded with as much care as if each head were a thoroughbred horse being groomed for exhibition.

The last rim of molten gold sank below the hills, and the mysterious twilight drifted silently in from the eastern sky. The servants lit the lamps on the verandah, and the vibrant blue air beyond the rails was alive with the flicker of bats and the soft madness of downy-winged moths; and the Kiriakovs began to assemble, drifting out one by one to sit or lounge, to gaze out into the dusk, to light the first cigar, to converse softly, in tentative phrases, as though their thoughts were assembling as imperceptibly as the twilight was stealing into darkness.

Mishka lay upon a hammock, one leg spilled carelessly over the side, and picked out a tune on the balalaika, in tenuous, almost disconnected notes; while Zinochka, her hair turned up and piled on top of her head for the first time, so that her slender neck was like a stem bearing some great top-heavy flower, sat on the verandah rail beside him and sang the words in a sweet, husky undertone. Feodor came out, lighting a cigar from a taper, his head bent over the glowing cave of his cupped hands, his profile and his fine Tartar nose illuminated suddenly like a religious painting. As he passed Zinochka he reached out a hand to touch her cheek fondly, and she turned her head and smiled – a wistful, almost a sad smile. She was in love for the first time, and could hardly bear herself, or the beauty of it.

Anne came out and walked to the end of the verandah, and stared out into the twilight. The air was as warm as milk on her skin, and filled with the intense fragrance of white jasmine and night-scented stock. Behind her were the sounds of softly clad feet moving on bare wooden boards, and the lilt of voices conversing quietly in Tartar Russian. A night-flying beetle, as big as a mouse, flew buzzing in like a clockwork toy to land on the verandah rail, folding its iridescent wing-cases with an audible click; and suddenly she became aware of how different it all was, how foreign to her. She thought of England, and for an instant it was close and dear, lying cool and green across her memory: her home, now utterly lost to her. Her eyes filled with tears; foolishly she had not brought her handkerchief out with her; she turned blindly to go into the house, and found Sergei beside her.

'Here, have mine,' he said, thrusting the clean linen into her fingers, and positioning himself so as to shield her from the others while she dried her eyes. 'What was it?' he asked, when he judged she had recovered herself.

'I thought of home – I was homesick,' she said. She managed to smile, touched by his ready – and practical – sympathy. 'It's all right – it's passed now.'

'Poor Anna,' Sergei said tenderly. 'I'm so used to your being here, that I forget Russia isn't your home too.'

'I forget it, most of the time,' she said. 'It's just occasionally . . . Things are so very different here. And there's so much of everything, that sometimes I feel overwhelmed.'

She saw that he didn't understand her – and indeed, how could he? He had never been to England; and if he had, he would have felt, like the Count, confined by the smallness. Only someone born there could understand that a place might be larger on the inside than on the outside; that to be encircled by a closed horizon could give one more freedom than to stand in the middle of a vast and featureless plain.

It was a little, she thought, like the freedom of religion, the power and scope that was granted to one by virtue of belonging to God: the atheist might think he was free, but the very emptiness of his life was a prison. She thought of the Second Collect for Peace: ' . . . whose service is perfect freedom'.

She could have explained those things to the Count, perhaps, but not, she felt, to Sergei. He was watching her now with his head a little cocked, alert but puzzled.

'You were a long way away, then, thinking deep thoughts,' he said. 'What were they?'

'Paradoxes,' she said in English, not knowing the Russian word for it. He waited. 'A thing which has two opposite qualities both at the same time.'

She hadn't expected him to understand, but he said, 'Yes, I know – like the White Nights, or like snow being so cold it burns, or being so comfortable in bed you ache with it!'

'Yes!' she laughed. 'Just like that.'

Natasha came out from the house and headed straight for Sergei, pushing her small but solid body determinedly between him and Anne, looking up at him with gold eyes that seemed to shine preternaturally

252

in the twilight. Her soft, pale brown hair was drawn into one long plait behind, as Irina wore it. She looked very like her mother just then. Sergei caressed her head with an absent hand, and she sighed and nudged against his arm with pleasure.

He was still pursuing a thought. 'Or like being in a church, and staring so hard at the candles on the high altar that after a while they seem to turn black. Have you ever done that? I sometimes think God must be like that,' he added, with youthful apology. 'Darkness which is light.'

Anne was startled that his thoughts should have taken a similar turn to hers. 'Henry Vaughan,' she murmured. He made an interrogative sound. 'An English poet,' she explained. 'He lived about a hundred years ago. He wrote: "There is in God – some say – a deep, but dazzling darkness". I never fully understood it – our churches are not like yours. But now I can see how it would be . . . ' she mused. 'Like staring at the sun.'

'And then would you see God?' Natasha asked, surprising them both, for they had almost forgotten she was there.'

'No Nashka, of course not. If you stared at the sun you would go blind. No-one can see God,' her brother explained kindly.

'Some people do,' she insisted; and sighed. 'I suppose they must know where to look.'

'We'll all see God after we're dead, Nashenka-maya,' Sergei said cheerfully, 'and that's soon enough for me, I think. Look, here's Zina coming out at last – that must mean the feast is ready. Let's go and find out – I'm starved! Coming, Anna?'

'Go on – I'll follow,' Anne said, amused at his abrupt descent from the supernatural to the physical plane, and watched him grab Nasha's hand and dash off exuberantly.

Outside the ring of torchlight and firelight, it was quite dark now. A band of serfs was assembled at one end of the marked-out floor, with a fine collection of musical instruments – fiddles, balalaikas, bagpipes, fifes, a tambour, a set of bells, and a kind of primitive hurdy-gurdy, which creaked and wheezed in the background, to the evident satisfaction of the sublimely deaf old greybeard who wound it.

Beef-scented smoke drifted over from time to time from the cookpit as the gentle night air changed direction. A second circle of torchlight illuminated the trestles on which the feast was assembled, where Bablash, growing ever more red-faced from a mixture of heat and alcohol, presided over the mountains of cold meats, pies, pasties, salads, cheeses, breads, cakes, creams, syllabubs, fruit, and sweetmeats he had created for the delight of the Kiriakovs and their guests. Besides the whole roast ox, and one or two sucking-pigs charring in the embers, there was a huge cauldron of a local delicacy called *pilaff*, a mixture of rice, prawns and chicken, flavoured with a peppery sauce which could never be too spicy for the true aficionado. Urged on by Bablash, Anne tasted some cautiously, and tasted nothing else for over an hour.

To drink there was wine, of course, and home-brewed ale and cider, lemonade and raspberry juice to quench the thirst of the dancers, and a potable equivalent of the pilaff in the form of *jonka*, a rum punch in which it was the custom to float burning sugar lumps. Grishka could do a trick with it: tilting his cup gently and allowing the sugar to float into his mouth while still burning, he then exhaled gently, igniting the vapours and blowing out flames like a dragon in a fairy-story, to the hysterical delight of the children, who hung on his sleeve shrieking, 'Do it *again*, Uncle Grishka! *Again!*'

Eating, drinking, dancing, conversing. The torches burned red and smoky, the cookpit spat golden sparks, the lamps on their poles were fat yellow buds on bare trees. The music sawed and thumped, the dancers whirled and sweated, and the watchers clapped their hands and cheered them on, and sang the words of favourite tunes. The children ran back and forth like maddened dogs, their shadows jumping up blackly as they crossed the light, their hands always full, their mouths stretched to accommodate cakes and laughter. And the gibbous moon rose at last, clear and lemon-pale, sailing free of the shadowy trees and casting a new and different light, silver-blue, on the dark places outside the lamp light.

Half-way through the evening, Sergei stood before Anne, looking eighteen again with his hair ruffled from his exertions.

'We must have our dance!' he shouted over the noise of the band. 'I claim my dance, Anna Petrovna!'

She looked past him at the violent Cossack contortions being practised on the dancing-lawn. 'What!' she cried.

He laughed aloud. 'No, no, not this! The next dance will be a country dance. When this one is ended, you will stand up with me?'

She shook her head deprecatingly. 'You don't want to dance with me.'

He looked surprised. 'But it was a promise. Don't you remember?'

'Yes, I remember. But there's no need, Seryosha. I don't hold you to it.'

'But I *want* to dance with you!' he cried, looking hurt. 'And you promised! You cannot go back on a debt of honour, you know.'

She looked past him again, and saw Zinaidia standing watching the dancers, her faint, sad smile still intact, though her lovely hair was tumbled. The neighbour's son with whom she was in love was one of the dancers: aware of her eyes on him, he made spectacular leaps, slapping his feet behind him in midair. Her love for him just then needed no reciprocation; it was sufficient unto itself. She stood, patient under the burden of her beauty, absorbed in love, and the exquisiteness merely of breathing the same air as the beloved.

Sergei followed the direction of Anne's eyes, and then stepped sideways, placing himself in line of her eyes and blocking out any other view. 'Anna Petrovna, I want to dance with you,' he said seriously, 'and no-one else will do. Don't you want to dance with me?'

She could not hurt his feelings. 'Of course, my dear,' she said.

His eyes seemed to glow. He took hold of her hand and raised it to his lips. 'Am I your dear?' She looked up at him, startled, but at that moment the music ended, and he whirled round, keeping hold of her hand, but only, it seemed, to draw her towards the dance floor. 'Now it is time! Our dance – come, Anna. Don't worry, I'll teach you the steps if you don't know them.'

The set formed beyond them. There was Irina, laughing, her face wearing the Chastnaya animation that made it so much more beautiful than it appeared in Petersburg, taking her place with Dmitri. His beard – so shocking at first to Anne, who was used to clean-shaven men – fanned out over his chest, and there was a long, dark wine stain on his white Cossack tunic which looked like a continuation of it. As the music began, his youngest child, little Olga, her cheeks rosy as Crimean apples, came running to him with arms upheld, and he lifted her up onto his shoulder and danced with her clinging madly to his hair.

Sergei called the steps as he danced, and Anne suddenly cast restraint, reflection, sadness to the winds, and danced with Russian exuberance, clapping her hands above her head, whirling in the turns so energetically that her hair began to loosen. Sergei laughed, calling encouragement to her. 'That's the way, Anna! Again! And turn – and leap!'

He caught her crossed hands to spin her, and she leaned back to give them more momentum, feeling herself laughing, as, long ago now, she had felt herself screaming coming down the toboggan run in Petersburg. I must be a little drunk, she thought happily. Sergei looked so like his father, that for a confusing moment she forgot where she was, and imagined it was with him she was dancing.

'Set across – and turn – clap!'

Zinochka, her melancholy love forgotten for a moment, dancing with Dmitri's twelve-year-old son Pavel, her hair now entirely loose and flying like an animated cloud about her head. Natasha amongst the musicians, being allowed to turn the hurdy-gurdy's handle, while the greybeard gazed at her admiringly and wagged his fingers in encouragement. Zina amongst the onlookers, sleepy Sashka in her arms, watching Sergei with a thoughtful frown.

The dance came to an end, leaving Anne feeling breathless and happy and little more than fifteen years old. Sergei, smiling broadly, led her off the dance floor towards the trestles where the feast was spread.

'Something to drink,' he suggested. 'Are you hot? Some lemonade, perhaps. That was well done, Anna Petrovna! You danced like a Russian!'

'I felt like a Russian,' she laughed, glancing back at the next set gathering. 'It would not have been possible in England,' she said. 'I should have been shamed forever, if I had danced like that.'

There was no-one at the tables at that moment. Bablash had long since abandoned his place, and with a flask of vodka had sought the comfort of a secluded tree trunk; the remains of the feast were there for anyone to help himself, and Sergei searched and found a jug of lemonade, but could not find any clean drinking vessels.

'If I hold it for you, could you drink from the jug?'

'Tonight, anything is possible,' Anne said solemnly.

The attempt caused a certain amount of hilarity, and one part of Anne, standing back, was amazed at her continued freedom from restraint. When she had succeeded in drinking enough, Sergei dried her face and hair with his handkerchief.

'There! You're just like an obedient kitten, being licked by your mother cat,' he said. 'I should – ' He broke off, looking at her abstracted expression. 'What is it?'

'Listen!'

'What? The music?'

'No, listen – from the stables! That's Quassy.' She looked distressed. 'I wish she would settle down. I can't bear her to be so upset.'

'Would you like to go and see her? Maybe she's just lonely.'

'Oh yes! Wait – I'll take her an apple. It's all right, you needn't come. I don't want to drag you away from the dancing.'

'Nonsense. You can't go alone – you never know who might be wandering about in the dark. Come, take my arm – you might stumble.'

They almost stumbled on one of the guards, who had fallen into a profound slumber, his cheek cradled peacefully on his musket stock. Sergei stepped instantly into his military persona, and was every inch the Guards officer as he berated the unfortunate serf, who claimed feebly that he had just crouched down for an instant to examine a suspicious footmark, and must have accidentally fallen into the recumbent posture in which they had found him.

Quassy whinnied again, and Anne tugged at Sergei's sleeve anxiously. He delivered a final threat, and led the way to the tack room to collect a lantern, and then opened the door of Quassy's box and ushered Anne in.

The black mare came forward instantly, her dark eyes glowing in the lamplight, and she knuckered welcomingly and nudged at Anne's hands.

'There, you see, she was lonely,' Sergei said. 'She'll be all right now.'

'Poor Quassy,' Anne crooned, rubbing the mare's crest and fondling her ears. 'It must be so hard for you, to taste a little freedom, and then to have it snatched away.' Quassy nudged her briefly in the chest, and then pushed past her to thrust her head out over the half-door and stare into the darkness, her nostrils stretched to catch the scent of her lost sisters. She gave a piercing whinny, and one of the corralled herd answered her. Anne looked despairingly at Sergei, and tried offering the mare the apple. Quassy took it and crunched it up, but her attention plainly was not on the treat. 'You see, she's still upset. I wish I could make her forget.'

Anne stood close to her and stroked her neck soothingly, and after a while Sergei said, 'It's hard for women, isn't it – made to go here and there, as men decide for them.' Anne glanced at him enquiringly. 'I was thinking of cousin Nadya – when she marries Yurka, she'll have to go and live with him at Slovolovsk, which is a horrible place compared with Chastnaya, and I don't believe she really wants to leave home at all. And then it's the other way round for Zinochka – she's in love with Mishenka Uvarov, but she won't be allowed to marry him, because he isn't suitable. Like poor Quassy being dragged away from the stallion,' he added with a small smile.

Anne thought, painfully, of Irina. 'It isn't always like that,' she said.

He looked at her cannily. 'You know, it would have made me very unpopular if I had asked Zinochka to dance. They've never forgiven my father for taking their sister away, and if I were to show any signs of wanting to steal Zinochka, they'd send me about my business so fast my head would spin. In fact, I think you are the only person they'd feel happy seeing me dance with – which happens to be the way I feel, too.'

Anne, following her own thoughts, didn't notice the last remark. 'She went of her own free will. It was her own choice,' she said.

'Was it?' he said coolly. 'She's never been happy away from here. If she could have had the choice, she'd have made Papa live with her here.'

'Oh, of course – but one never has everything one wants. There must always be compromise.'

'Unless –' he hesitated. 'Unless you choose someone who has nothing to begin with.'

She looked at him, puzzled. 'What do you mean?'

'Nothing. Anna Petrovna, will you really go back to England?'

She leaned her cheek against Quassy's neck. 'No, I don't suppose so,' she said. 'What would I go back to? Everything I have, now, is here.'

He was silent a moment, contemplating her profile. Then he drew breath to speak; but at that instant a flicker of movement outside the box simultaneously drew his attention, and made Quassy prick her ears and snort.

'Who's that?' he said sharply, drawing back the bolt of the door. Anne looked round, startled. 'Whoever it is, show yourself!'

Quassy knuckered softly, and the moving shadow paused and returned slowly, coming into the edge of the light.

'Nasha! What are you doing here?' Anne said.

The child stood quite still, looking from one to the other calculatingly, like a cat judging a distance before a spring.

'Don't you know it's dangerous to wander about tonight?' Sergei said angrily. 'There's an armed guard, and if you startled one of them, they might shoot you by accident.'

'They won't shoot me,' she said unemphatically.

'Never mind – Sergei's right, you shouldn't be here,' Anne said. 'What were you doing?'

'I heard Quassy calling. I came to see if she was all right,' Natasha said. She stood facing them, hands down by her side, like a soldier on parade, her face expressionless, waiting to see what they would say or do. Such self-possession, it seemed to Anne, was unnatural in a child so young, and she shivered, suddenly convinced that Nasha was lying, or at least, not telling the whole of the truth. But what was the purpose of the prevarication? She couldn't imagine.

'Well, you'd better come back with us now,' Sergei said. 'I expect it's time you were in bed, anyway.'

Nasha waited patiently while they shut Quassy in again, and

258

then walked obediently beside them back towards the lamp light.

'What *were* you doing, Nasha?' Anne asked after a moment.

'I came to see Quassy,' she said again. She flickered a glance upwards under her eyelids.

'And what else?' Anne persisted.

'And the other horses,' she said with the air of one admitting the truth. 'They're restless, because of the herd.'

'How do you know? They aren't making any noise,' Sergei said suspiciously.

Natasha looked up, and now her gaze was limpid. '*I* hear them,' she said.

At first light, while the revellers were still sleeping the first profound slumber of exhaustion, the groups of tribesmen began to arrive at Chastnaya for the horse fair. By the time the family was up, considerable numbers had already assembled, had tethered or hobbled their horses, and were sitting on the ground eating, or setting out the wares they had brought with them to sell. This makeshift bazaar was always a secondary feature of the horse fair.

After breakfast, Sergei constituted himself Anne's bodyguard in order to allow her to take a closer look. She viewed with amazement the diversity of different physical types amongst the tribesmen, which was to her far more extraordinary than their strange dress or customs. It was as if she had suddenly discovered herself to be living at the edge of a place where the Creation was still going on, where God was experimenting with the very stuff of mankind.

'Those are the Eastern tribesmen – the Lesghians and the Avars,' Sergei murmured to Anne, pointing them out. 'They're from Daghestan, and they're the least civilised of the tribes – except for the Chechen, but I don't suppose they would come to a fair like this. I don't suppose they'd be welcome, either. Even the other Tcherkess don't trust them.'

Anne thought they seemed closer to animals than men. They were short, stockily built, swarthy-skinned and black-haired, as if they had been hewn out of the black rock of the region they inhabited. Their dark, bright eyes were quick and cunning, and they kept close together and eyed the strangers amongst whom they found themselves with suspicion, snuffing the air for danger with their broad nostrils. The horses they rode in on were slender and fleet and beautiful, strange contrast to their atavistic ugliness.

'When I first joined the Independents, we were warned never to underestimate them,' Sergei said. 'And never to be captured alive. They torture prisoners, especially Christians, in the most hideous way – or bury them alive.' Anne shuddered, and he glanced at her, gratified at the response. 'But they love their horses,' he added. 'Odd, isn't it, that they have so little regard for human life, but so much reverence for a dumb beast?'

'Why does Feodor allow them to come at all,' Anne asked, 'if they are so savage?'

'For trade, of course. Who else would he sell his horses to? Of course, he sells some to Russians, but the bulk of his trade must be with the tribesmen. The Eastern clans in particular are great horsemen, and prize karabakhs beyond anything. And they pay good gold for them, which is more than the Russians always do. Of course, they'd sooner steal them than buy them, and sell them to the Persians and the Kurds,' he added with a chuckle, 'so it's best to keep a sharp eye on them.'

'Are all of them so dangerous?' she asked, glancing round warily at the nearest groups.

Sergei shrugged. 'On the whole, the Western tribes aren't so bad, from living shoulder to shoulder with civilised Russians for so long. Some of them – the Kabardins and the Nogays of the plains, for instance, we talk of as "tamed tribes", because we've held them in subjection for generations, and we trade with them as with civilised people. But even they are not entirely to be trusted. They may come openly by day to buy salt and gunpowder from you, and then slip back at night and steal your horses, and like as not put a knife between your ribs. The best plan with any of the Tcherkess is to keep your eyes open and your hand on your gun.'

He pointed out the Ossetins, red-haired, blue-eyed mountain people from the region of Mount Kabak. They wore a great many gold chains and discs which caught the light dazzlingly, and their surcoats of dressed leather were patterned in red and blue. They looked very handsome, but Anne soon discovered it was advisable to keep upwind of them, for they had a custom of rubbing their bodies with rancid mare's milk to protect themselves from the cold and the bitter wind, and the warmth of Chastnaya's summer sunshine, even so early in the day, had ripened it to a kind of cheese inside their leather garments.

The Nogays, she discovered, were small men, made shorter by the fact that they were mostly bow-legged, from having been upon horseback since infancy; and their yellow skin and high, protruding cheekbones betrayed their origins. 'Their ancestors came to Russia with the Golden Horde,' Sergei told her. The mountain Nogays were distinguished from the plainsmen by their shaven heads, and their heavy felted cloaks, which protected them equally from the burning sun, the bitter cold, and the torrential rain of the Caucasian heights.

'And at night, they fling it over a heap of straw or brushwood, and it makes a very respectable mattress.'

One or two of them had spread their cloaks on the ground to display the goods they had brought to sell – objects carved from wood and animal horn, dressed and painted leather, harness, necklaces of polished stones. The plainsmen had brought flasks of oil, bags of sunflower seeds, salt, dried meat, lengths of cloth, and – to Anne's surprise – a great many sweetmeats: gingerbread and curd cakes and candied fruits. The wilder the tribesman, she discovered, the sweeter the tooth: the black-browed, grim-looking Lesghians from the bleakest mountain heights on the borders of Kakhetia crowded around the heaps of glistening sugar plums like eager children.

The Kabardins were the largest group, and Anne admired their proud bearing, and their slender, graceful bodies, which looked so well astride a horse. They were an aquiline-nosed, dark-eyed people, proud and cruel, living by war and plunder, reverencing above all the attributes of the warrior – steadfastness, physical courage, skill in arms. Their clothes were colourful and splendid, and their horses were as elaborately caparisoned as the riders.

They reminded her, in their physiognomy and their dress, of the Prince who had tried to buy Quassy from her. She was not entirely surprised, therefore, when during the course of the morning, he rode in to Chastnaya with a small retinue of followers, and claimed her exuberantly as an old acquaintance.

'English Lady, I have come! I greet you, in the name of the Most High,' he said, with a graceful bow from the saddle of his handsome horse. Anne had forgotten how overpowering he was, and was glad of the presence of Sergei close behind her shoulder. The Prince turned his eagle's beak of a nose in Sergei's direction and surveyed him with bright, feral eyes, taking in his youthful courage, good looks, and military bearing. 'It is your husband, the light-eyed one?' he asked, not without a hint of approval.

'It is not,' Anne said firmly. 'But, sir, you spoke as if you knew I would be here.'

The Prince raised his eyebrows. 'Assuredly I knew it.'

'But how? How could you?'

The Prince looked loftily amused. 'Akim Shan Kalmuck knows everything. It is his business to know everything. I wish to see the

English lady again, but also,' he added sternly, 'I come to buy horses. At Chastnaya are the best horses in the Caucasus – yes, better even than the horses of the Five Hills of Pyatigorsk. So I have said – and it is true.'

He pronounced the words as one speaking Holy Writ, and then glowered around him, as though anyone were likely to argue the point. Sergei, at Anne's shoulder, whistled the tune of the song he had sung her on the day of the picnic, and she suppressed a smile. Evidently the Prince knew it too, for he bared his white teeth in his savage smile, and said, 'I come to buy horses – women I never buy. Always, since I am young man – younger than you – I have any woman I want. Except English Lady. Still my offer is good – I will marry you,' he offered generously, 'with no dowry but the black mare.'

'That's very kind of you,' Anne said gravely, 'but I do not wish to marry.'

The Prince looked from her to Sergei speculatively, and then shrugged. 'And how is she, my horse, my black karabakh mare with the north wind in her blood?' he went on.

'She is perfectly well, but her spirits are oppressed,' Anne told him, and explained the circumstances. The Prince listened attentively, frowned a moment in thought, and then to Anne's surprise and slight alarm, prepared to dismount.

'I will see her,' he announced.

'Really, sir, she is not for sale,' Anne began, and he frowned at her.

'I will see her. Akim Shan Kalmuck knows everything about horses. I will cure her of her melancholy – yes, for you I will do this, though I am begged in vain by men from Batoum to Kizlyar to give of my great wisdom. Bring me to the karabakh!' He raised a hand in an imperious and theatrical gesture, which so delighted Anne, reminding her of the Demon Prince in a farce she had once seen at Drury Lane, that she had no more thought of resisting him.

The Prince handed his horse to his nearest attendant, waved them back and spoke a few words to them in the language Anne didn't understand, and then drew his robe about him in a lordly way and looked to her to lead the way.

Sergei didn't like it at all, but since the Prince, most courteously, was leaving all his bodyguard behind, it would have been churlish to object. Besides, he comforted himself, whatever else he was, the Prince was a horse lover, and would not harm Quassy; and as long as he, Sergei, was present, he could do nothing to harm Anne.

As the strange trio crossed in front of the house on the way to the stables, Nasha and Sashka came running down from the verandah. Nasha thrust her hand into Sergei's, while Sashka too flung himself passionately around Anne's knees, so that she was obliged to pick him up to release herself.

'Where are you going?' Nasha cried.

'Take me!' Sashka pleaded.

The Prince looked at the scene with interest.

'Your children! Ah, so you are married! That is why you refuse me! Of course, I am a Christian too – I may have only one wife. A pity – that is a healthy boy! I said you would make a good wife. Akim Shan Kalmuck is never wrong. About horses and women, never wrong.'

Though she was blushing, Anne had no great wish to disabuse the Prince, especially as the truth would have been too complex to explain, so she merely averted her eyes, hitched Sashka up against her shoulder, and continued towards the stable.

The grooms were made very nervous by the sight of the Prince, even in the company of Anne and Sergei, and they backed away and glanced this way and that, like horses who have smelt a mountain lion. Anne set down Sashka and unbolted the stable door, and stepped aside for the Prince to enter, wondering how Quassy would react to him.

She needn't have worried. He stood in the doorway and slowly held out his hands, speaking in a continuous low murmur words which she didn't understand, and which she guessed from Sergei's expression he didn't either. But Quassy understood them. Her ears shot forward, and she looked at the Prince intently. Still talking, he began to smile, his eyes taking on a soft shine, his voice caressive. Quassy's eyes began to glow too, her body relaxed, and her head lowered, and after only a few moments she stepped forward confidently and dropped her muzzle into the Prince's outstretched hands.

'God! How did he do that?' Sergei muttered. Anne watched, enthralled, as the Prince examined the mare, running his hands over every part of her, resting his ear to her neck and breast and flank to listen, smelling her breath and her skin, looking into her eyes. Finally he stepped up close to her, put his arms round her neck, and resting his cheek against hers, closed his eyes and remained quite still for several minutes. During the examination, Quassy stood as still and docile as though she had been mesmerised – which, Anne thought, she probably had.

The Prince sighed, released the mare, and stepped back, turning to Anne to say firmly, 'She has a broken heart, but I can cure her.'

'You can make her forget?' Anne said.

He looked approving. 'Ah, you understand! Yes, I can make her forget. I need herbs – quite common herbs, easily found. Your serfs will fetch them for me. While they are gone, you will serve me with refreshments – ' he looked around ' – there, under that tree.'

It was a strange, dreamlike interlude. Two astonished, and very nervous, serfs were told off to collect the herbs, and sped on their way by the addition of what was evidently a blood-chilling threat from the Prince, though fortunately for Anne she did not fully understand it; she herself ordered another serf to bring suitable refreshments at once. Then they all sat down on the ground under the tree, the Prince with his back to the trunk, and Anne, Sergei and the children in a semicircle in front of him, and he began to talk.

The children were enraptured, and even Anne was soon drawn out of herself, away from the sensible, practical world she had always tried to inhabit, into a realm where the most exotic fantasy seemed to be able to come true. He told them of battles and feats of daring, of single combat with the champions of oriental kings, of chests of treasure discovered and princesses' hands won, of elephants and dragons and monsters and talking beasts. When the refreshments came, he consumed them without once pausing in his narrative flow, and no-one would have dreamed of hoping to share the contents of the tray with him.

When the serfs came back with the plants, Anne saw that they were indeed unremarkable – yellow mullein, common cinquefoil, leaves from the horse chestnut tree, catnip, camomile, and feathery blue-green sprays of rue.

'Fetch me a bowl, boiling water, and thread,' he commanded. A serf went for the water, while the children scurried off after the bowl and the thread; and then they watched in breathless silence, Nasha's golden eyes utterly unwavering, as the Prince went to work. The chestnut leaves and the rue he bound with thread and quickly and skilfully fashioned into a garland, and tied the ends together. The other plants he tore up and threw into the bowl, and then poured on the hot water and waited for the mess to draw, much in the way one would make camomile tea.

'Now, a bottle. And you, English Lady, will come and help me, for she will not like to take the medicine.'

'I had better help you, sir,' Sergei said firmly. 'If the mare struggles – '

The Prince held up his hand. 'We will not force her – we will persuade her. Come, all of you – you may watch.'

A number of grooms gathered at a safe distance beyond the stable door, too, so that it was quite a throng which eventually witnessed the

Prince gently lift the garland over Quassy's head and hang it round her neck.

'For forgetfulness,' he murmured to Anne. 'The smell of these plants drives memories out of the head. And the medicine for calming, for easing of the heart's pain, and for forgetting. Hold her head up – so – and I will do the rest.'

Quassy rolled her eyes as the Prince pushed her head up so that her muzzle was pointing at the roof, but she did not struggle, and Anne had no difficulty in holding her in that position. The brownish liquid had been poured off the mashed leaves into the bottle that was kept in the tack room for adminstering drenches, and now the Prince, crooning to Quassy, slipped the neck of the bottle into the corner of her mouth, upended it, and stroked her throat firmly so that she was obliged to gulp it down. When the bottle was empty he nodded to Anne to let her go, and the mare lowered her head, sneezed a few times, smacked her lips, and then shook herself violently from head to foot and looked about her like one just waking up from a deep sleep.

Nasha clapped her hands and cried out. 'Oh, she's better already! You can see! Anna, see, she's better!'

Anne smiled at her. 'Yes, I see.' She turned to the Prince. 'Thank you sir,' she said. 'I am most grateful to you. And what must I do now?'

'Do? Nothing! Let her wear the garland until tomorrow. After that, you are quite safe. You may ride her as usual – yes, even to the valley of the horses itself. She will ignore the herd as if they were not there. Even the stallion she will treat with indifference.'

Anne thanked him again, and he turned to the children. 'You have seen a wonder here today, and heard many more. You will not forget the name of Akim Shan Kalmuck.'

They nodded acquiescence to the proposition, and Anne was inwardly amused at his desire to impress the children, which seemed to her akin to the Lesghians' craving for sweetmeats.

'And one day,' he went on magnificently, 'you may come to my village, and I will show you the tiger, which was given to me in tribute by the Pasha of Kavzan, and which lives in a cage and eats from my hand, and wears a collar of magnificent emeralds from Marakata.'

The children's eyes were as round as saucers, and Anne privately thought it was an exit line better than anything Drury Lane had ever offered. Sergei was evidently less impressed. They escorted the Prince back to his people, and returned the children to the care of Nyanka, and when they were alone again he said, 'It's as well there was nothing more than common herbs in that potion, or I should have been forced to prevent him administering it.'

Anne looked at him with amusement, wondering how he would have hoped to achieve that. 'Just as well,' she agreed, 'for I don't think he'd have relished being prevented.'

Sergei looked a little angry. 'You think I'm afraid of that — that posturing barbarian?'

'Not at all, Seryosha. I'm sure you aren't, which is what worries me. But he hasn't hurt Quassy, and perhaps he may have helped. She certainly responded to him.' He only grunted, and Anne went on, 'If she seems calm tomorrow, I shall be very glad to be able to ride her again.'

He brightened. 'There are other horses you can take. Why don't we go out for a long ride tomorrow? There are lots of places you haven't seen yet. I'd like to show you the beechwoods and the deer and the place where the eagles nest. Just you and I,' he added hastily, perhaps reading her mind. 'I don't want to take the children, because they'll slow us down, and there is such a lot to see. Do say yes, Anna!'

'I shall have to see if I'm wanted for anything,' Anne said. 'You forget, Seryosha, I am supposed to be Natasha's governess.'

'Pho!' he protested. 'As if any of that matters here!'

By the evening, the horse sale was over, and the tribesmen were dispersing, packing up their wares, and the goods they had acquired from each other, hitching the new horses they had bought together for the long ride back to their territories. The corrals were dismantled, the hurdles stacked away in the barn, the manure raked aside and carted to the dung heap, the bars dismounted from the house windows. Soon there would be nothing left to show there had been a horse fair, except for the beaten patch of earth, the fire-scarred cookpit, and the smell of horses lingering in the air.

The Kiraikovs began to think of returning to their normal routines, though it was hard that evening to shake the images of the last two days out of their minds. A simple meal was served, and the gathering on the verandah afterwards was more than usually thoughtful.

Urged by Sergei, Anne asked Irina rather diffidently whether she might go out for a ride the next day.

'Is Quassy safe?' Irina asked. 'I heard about your friend the Prince and his magic cure.'

'I'll go and check on her in a little while. But if she's still restless tomorrow, perhaps I could take one of the stock horses. Sergei wants to show me some of the places I haven't seen yet.'

'Of course you can,' Feodor said promptly, 'but I advise you most strongly not to go too far afield. Seryosha, you know where the safe places are. Don't forget that the local tribes are often attracted further down from their usual hunting runs by all the coming and going of the horse fair. You may come across them in unexpected places. Stay to the well-marked paths, and keep your gun ready to hand.'

Sergei nodded gravely. 'Of course.'

'The children mustn't go,' Irina said. 'It's too dangerous.'

'We weren't thinking of taking the children, Mama,' Sergei said, repressing his gratification, even as Nasha's mouth turned down in disappointment.

'If it's really dangerous . . . ' Anne began doubtfully, thinking of the savage aspect of some of the tribesmen she had seen; but Sergei interrupted.

'Of course it's not, as long as you're careful, and I promise you I will be. Don't you think you ought to go and look at Quassy now, and see if she's any quieter?'

'If the Prince's potion is anything like his stories,' Anne said mildly, getting to her feet, 'she'll probably have turned into an elephant, or grown wings.'

But the first glance told her that Quassy was better. Still wearing her garland of aromatic leaves, she was pulling quietly at her hay rack, completely relaxed and evidently at peace. She turned and knuckered a friendly greeting as Anne appeared, but showed no disposition for trying to jump out of her box, or call for the herd. She even had one hind foot cocked, inelegant, but comfortable.

'Well,' Anne said, leaning over the box door, 'what a difference! The Prince's potion worked!'

'You don't really believe all that nonsense, do you?'

'But just look at her. The evidence is there before your eyes.'

'Those herbs couldn't have made any difference. Don't you think everyone would have known about them long ago, if they were good horse medicine?'

Anne turned to him with a smile. 'I don't know why you are so determined to be unkind to the Prince. He went to a lot of trouble to cure Quassy, out of the kindess of his heart.'

Sergei looked a little warm. 'It wasn't kindness, Anna Petrovna. Don't you see that? He wanted to marry you – he said so himself. Or something worse.'

'Nothing could be worse than being married to him,' Anne laughed. 'But all the same, he's cured my poor Quassy, and I'm grateful.'

They turned away to go back to the house. 'You realise, don't you, that the difference is probably because the herd is out of range now? Since she can't hear them or smell them, she's not upset any more.'

'Ungenerous! The Prince said she wouldn't even be interested in the stallion.'

'Yes, but she was evidently on heat before. Now she's been mated, of course she wouldn't be interested,' Sergei said unguardedly.

It was the kind of thing that no-one would have dreamed of saying to a young woman in England, least of all an unmarried woman; fortunately, the four years she had already spent in Russia enabled her to take such things in her stride.

Chapter Sixteen

They made an early start, while the air was cool and the dew still on the grass. Sergei had a packet of bread and meat and a bottle of wine packed into one saddlebag, a box of ammunition in the other, a blanket to sit on rolled behind the saddle, and his gun slung over his shoulder.

'That should cover all eventualities,' Anne remarked wryly. Quassy was fresh, and curvetted about as Stefan flung her up into the saddle; but it was only her normal high spirits. She showed no sign of distress, or of wanting to be off after the herd.

'All the same,' Sergei said, 'we'll go the other way to begin with, up through the beech woods, to give her time to settle down.'

It was a beautiful day, clear with the promise of heat. The air was already spicy with thuja and juniper, and the smell of damp, crushed grass rose from under the horses' quiet feet. In the distance the hills were lavender with shadow, and above them arched the dark-blue sky, decorated here and there with the little clouds of Russian summer – blinding white above and blue underneath.

They passed through the arable fields, where already the women were at work, bending between the rows of pale-green bean plants, their rumps broad with a multitude of petticoats. They straightened up as the two horses came by, resting their hands on their hips to ease their backs. A young woman with a red kerchief round her head was carrying a baby in a sling on her hip, and she waved its fat brown starfish of a hand lightheartedly at the *dvoriane* as they passed.

Anne was at peace with the world. How lucky I am, she thought, to have this perfect day before me, a beautiful horse to ride, a pleasant companion beside me, and all this glorious country to explore. Even the wistfulness, which is a quality of all happiness, was pleasant just then. She felt young, free, full of natural high spirits. She was twenty-seven years old, and in England she would have been considered already upon the shelf, perfectly old-cattish. She had never had the youthful pleasures that her birth ought to have entitled her to, the opportunities to enjoy her girlhood and secure herself a comfortable establishment; yet at a moment like this she could forget such things. She could forget that she was an orphan, a dependant, without security, without a home of her own, without love. For this one day she might have been ten years younger, in the first springing of youth, and riding beside a companion of her own rank, with a future of endless possibilities all before her. That was how life would have been for her, if her father had not died: today, she felt, had been given to her in compensation for what she had missed.

The beech woods were before them, lilac-shadowed in the early sun. The smooth, mysterious boles rose up like pillars in a cathedral to the canopy far above, where the leaves seemed almost transparent, quivering in the golden light. The feeling of tranquility was so strong that the riders fell silent, and rode side by side almost without breathing, as though they dared not make any sound which might disturb the majestic presences about them. When they came out at the top of the woods, the riant sunshine was suddenly hot, fell on them like a holiday blessing, and they glanced at each other and smiled almost with relief.

Above the beech trees, the view opened out all about them, a vista of green foothills rising to rocky heights, and in the distance the striding mountain chain, misty in the heat. There were skylarks high above them in the crystal air, and the sunshine fell so straight and clean and pure it seemed almost heatless.

'Where is the house from here?' Anne said some time later, when the windings of the path brought it to the edge of the hillside. They halted the horses to gaze out over the country; their shadows were short, now, and sharply black on the turf beneath them.

'You can't see it from here,' Sergei said at last. 'It's over there, beyond that slope. You see where those trees are? Below that, under the flank of the hill.'

'So far away?' Anne was impressed. 'I hadn't thought we had come such a distance.'

'It's easy to lose track of where you are up in the hills. We've probably come thirty versts. It's getting on for noon, you know.'

'I didn't know,' Anne said. At once she began to feel hungry and thirsty. 'I wish we'd brought some water with us, as well as wine,' she said.

'Bring water to a place like this? That's like taking salt to the sea,' Sergei laughed. 'There's water everywhere in the mountains – cleaner, sweeter water than anywhere down below. We'll ride on a bit, and stop at the first stream we see.'

Round the next curve in the path, they came upon a crop of sunflowers growing in a sheltered pocket of land, between rocky outcrops like short, knobbed grey cliffs tufted with gorse bushes and stunted thorn trees. The sunflowers, which Anne had grown used to as a cottage-garden crop, looked fantastic in such profusion, and in this unexpected place: so tall, and with their round black faces and golden halos, like strange Nubian saints.

Suddenly Quassy stopped dead, quivering, her ears almost crossed with excitement. Sergei halted his horse too, his hand moving round automatically for his gun, and he searched for whatever it was that had alerted the mare. Then he put out a hand to Anne, and whispered urgently, 'Anna! Look!'

She followed the direction of his pointing finger, and saw the brown plush coat and spreading antlers of a stag, basking amongst the sunflowers. They were downwind of him, and he hadn't yet become aware of them. He leaned back, resting on his shoulder, his eyes half-closed with pleasure, his white throat a little stretched, like a contented cat, while above him the giant plants waved in the gentle breeze, passing their faint shadows back and forth across his red-brown coat.

'Oh lovely!' Anne breathed; and then Quassy whickered her excitement, and in an instant the stag had sprung to his feet and leapt away over the side of the hill towards the beech woods, taking the steep slope in great heedless bounds.

'What antlers! A pity I couldn't get a shot at him,' Sergei said.

'You wouldn't shoot such a lovely creature!' Anne said reproachfully. 'How could you?'

He looked at her sympathetically. 'You're too tender-hearted. We call the stag the Tsar of the Forest; but they do a great deal of damage to the crops, and they're impossible to keep out even with fences. They eat and trample everything, and kill the fruit trees by chewing off the bark.' Anne looked unconvinced, and he added, 'Besides, you enjoy venison, don't you?'

She sighed. 'Yes, of course. I'm being foolish. It's just hard that having good things to eat should involve destroying something so lovely. When I was a child, I remember crying dreadfully the first time I realised that the lamb I ate was the same as those dear little knock-kneed creatures on the hillside.'

'Where was home? Tell me about it,' he said eagerly as they rode on.

'I was born in Hampshire – '

'Is that a city?'

'No, a county – a region. I was born in a house by a stream in a small village.'

'And what is Hampshire like?'

'Green, and fertile – soft hills, a little like these, but smaller and closer together. You would think it very small and cramped, I expect. And rivers full of fish, and woods full of birds. Narrow lanes deep with mud in the winter and dust in the summer. Flowers in the hedgerows and sheep on the hills.'

'I should love to see it some day,' Sergei said. 'I've always wanted to go to England. When this war is over, I *shall* go.' He glanced at her sideways, shyly, from under his thick lashes. 'It would be wonderful to go there with you, and then you could show me everything.'

'To see England again,' she said softly, and then she sighed. 'But it doesn't seem as though this war will ever end. Your father has been away so long already, I don't suppose Sashka would even recognise him.'

Sergei had nothing to say to that. They rode in silence for a while, and the path climbed higher, towards the blue sky and nearer the sun. They came to a place where a tiny stream of clear water fell down the face of a rocky outcrop, making a miniature waterfall, and Sergei jumped down and helped Anne to dismount, and held Quassy while she knelt on the springy turf to drink. The water was icy cold in her cupped hands, and tasted delicious. At the foot of the rock the stream ran away between deep, narrow lips of peat. They offered the horses a drink, but they only blew at it.

'Shall we stop here and eat?' Sergei said, looking around him. 'It seems as good a place as any.'

They tied the horses to a thorn tree, and spread the blanket beside a rock, to give them something to lean against. Anne pulled off her hat, and felt the smooth heat of the sun against the top of her head; and after a moment, she took off her jacket too. Sergei did likewise, and rolled up his shirtsleeves, and flung himself down gracefully full-length, to lean on one elbow and gaze at her while she unpacked the food.

Anne found herself not quite at ease with that bright stare, so disconcertingly like the Count's, and yet so unlike; and to distract him she engaged him in conversation. Once begun, it continued quite naturally; they were of a similar turn of mind, and the difference in their ages was not as great as before. They chatted comfortably while they ate, about horses and hunting and food, and the war and foreign travel and paintings, like old, tried friends.

When they had finished eating and drinking, a pleasant, mid-day somnolence came over them. Now Anne, too, reclined on one elbow, listening to Sergei's inconsequential account of a long-ago picnic with his cousins, gazing out into the distance towards the mountains, lilac in the heat-haze, peaked and spired and fantastic.

He was lying on his back now, his arms folded under his head, staring into the blue zenith. 'Anna, look there,' he said suddenly, breaking into his own narrative, releasing one hand to point upwards. She craned her head back.

'Where? What is it?'

'An eagle – look, he's wondering what we are, and whether we're good to eat.'

'Where? I can't see.'

Sergei laughed, and caught the arm that was supporting her and pulled it away, so that she fell onto her back, and then wriggling close to her held her hand up with his, pointing her forefinger directly above her head.

'There,' he said. 'Follow the line of your finger. Don't you see now? See his wings, like spread fingers? He flies so effortlessly.' He allowed her hand to drop down, but somehow, absently, kept hold of it. His body was resting against hers for its whole length, his head so close to hers that she could feel the warmth of his cheek.

Staring up at the black speck of the circling eagle in the deep blue, Anne felt a little light-headed. Suddenly she had the strange feeling that the sky was below her rather than above her, that she was somehow suspended face downwards, looking down into the crystal depths of space. What kept her there? She might tumble off at any moment! She pressed her back up against the earth, and tried to cling on to stop herself falling. The fingers of her left hand hooked into the short turf beside her, while her right hand clenched round Sergei's, and her head seemed to spin.

'Wouldn't you like to be able to do that?' Sergei murmured. His face came closer, was resting against hers now: she felt the softness of his skin, and the light prickle of golden hairs. 'To ride the air like that – he never beats his wings, look, just drifts – '

She tore her eyes away from the dizzying depths, and found herself looking instead into the hypnotic shine of Sergei's gold-green gaze.

'Anna,' he said softly. He turned over onto his side, facing her, moving very carefully, as though not to frighten her, never releasing her gaze. His free arm passed across her body, and at the touch of it, though it was so light, she shuddered. 'Annushka,' he whispered. His face was close to hers, she smelt his sweet breath, lightly fragranced with wine, his sun-warmed skin, the young-man smell of his body. His hand came up to touch her face, stroke the hair from her brow, trace the line of her jaw, her lips.

Stop: you must stop him, her mind protested; but from so far away, the warning was almost inaudible. She was held, mesmerised, by the warmth, the wine, the familiarity, the friendship, the natural longing of her body for love. His strong, gentle fingers brushed her lips and then took hold of her chin, holding her face still. His face came closer, blurring, and she closed her eyes as something inside her gave a desperate lurch, and his mouth was on hers, kissing her.

Tenderly, then avidly: young, passionate, impatient. She lay as though stunned; and then all the feelings that had been so long held in check – terrible, potent mixture of different affections, longings, and desires – rose up in her, and she yielded to him, her lips parting in response, her hand fluttering up to touch the back of his head. Sergei said something against her lips, and then he was pressing against her, out of control. She felt the young hard strength of him – a boy's strength allied with a man's desire. And then she was struggling, her dizziness gone as if she had been plunged into icy water.

What was she doing? This was Sergei, the Count's son! The son of the house, her mistress' step-son, her charges' brother, and therefore, surely, almost himself her charge? This was wrong, wicked, almost incestuous! She struggled madly against him, and after one moment of resistance, he allowed her to push him back, and looked down at her with a flushed and puzzled face, his hand still resting on her shoulder.

'What is it? Anna – Annushka!'

'No, no, you mustn't! Let me go!' She pushed at him, struggled to sit up, feeling her cheeks burning with distress. He stared, evidently not understanding, seeing nothing wrong yet in anything they had done.

'Did I hurt you? I didn't mean to, *doushka*,' he said.

She felt her heart contract. 'You mustn't call me that.'

'What? *Doushka*?' He laughed, and tilted his head quizzically. 'But why not? You are my darling! You must know that by now! What's the matter, Annushka? Did I startle you? It's all right, you know – it isn't wrong if we love each other. And I would never do anything to harm you.'

'Seryosha, stop! Don't say any more! This is all wrong – you must see that it is!'

'Wrong?'

'Impossible!'

'But why? I love you, Anna.' His face cleared as he had a sudden thought. 'You didn't think I meant to – to dishonour you? You

274

couldn't have! I want to marry you, Anna Petrovna. I mean everything that's honourable and good by you. When I said I wished you could go to England with me, I meant as my wife, my countess! The Countess Anna Petrovna Kirova – how good it sounds!' he said exultantly.

Anne felt close to tears. The name he had given her – the name she had secretly, wickedly, longed to bear – but in other circumstances from those he meant! She could not meet his eyes, and yet saw all too plainly his young, handsome, flushed face, the generous love in his eyes, the first outpouring of a warm and untouched heart, offered trustingly to her – to *her*. What could she say? How could she bear to hurt him? But she must – she must.

'Sergei, it's impossible. You cannot marry me. Please – you must put it from your mind. You must forget – *we* must forget that this ever happened.'

Now there was hurt as well as bewilderment in his expression. 'But why? Anna, why?' She might have known that he would not simply accept it – what man would? 'Why can't I marry you? I don't understand.'

'My dear,' she began desperately – mistakenly: he seized on the word, and her hand, lifting her fingers to his lips.

'Your dear – I am your dear, aren't I? You do love me, Anna – you do, don't you? I know you do.'

'Of course I do,' she said, 'but not – not as a wife.'

'What then?'

'I am a great deal older than you,' she said, fumbling for words. 'I knew you as a child, don't you see? To me you are still – '

'A child?' Now more puzzled than hurt. 'Not true! When I kissed you just then, you kissed me too – and not like a child. You can't deny it! You love me as a man.'

Impossible to explain. She could only shake her head dumbly.

He kept hold of her hand, looking earnestly into her face. 'There's something else, isn't there? What is it, Anna? Not your age, surely? The difference between us is nothing!'

'Others wouldn't say so.'

'You can't be so foolish as to care what other people think? If we don't mind it, why should they?'

'I am your sisters' governess,' she said desperately. 'Your father's employee – a trusted servant in his house. How can I – how could I – so abuse – '

'Abuse?' he cried dangerously.

'Abuse his trust – '

'But you didn't – you haven't! How can you say that? You have done nothing wrong! It was I who – made things happen. And Papa would not think so, either. He holds you in the greatest respect. You are not a servant,' he said hotly, 'and you never have been. You are more like a – a guest in our house. Papa would be proud and happy to have you as a daughter-in-law, I know he would. He has so often spoken to me about you, about how intelligent and cultured you are, how you are a gentlewoman by birth. He really likes you, Anna – you must believe me.'

She looked at him sadly, knowing she could not make him see. Since he thought of her as being of the same generation with him, he assumed she regarded the Count as he did – as one of an older generation, out of the question as far as romantic affection was concerned. He could no more have imagined Anne being in love with the Count, than himself being in love with someone of his grandmother's generation.

And besides, her feelings for the Count were something she could not admit to anyone. She tried not to admit them even to herself. What reason could she give Sergei for rejecting him, that he would accept? How explain that moment in his arms when her whole being had longed for love, for a lover, for caresses and warmth and belonging, for a mate? There was one part of her still that wanted, crazily, to accept him: it would be an escape from the impasse of her life, a way out of the weary, repetitive sin of loving another woman's husband. It would give her security and love; and she did love him, in a confused and complex way. But she could not do such a thing to Sergei, who deserved nothing but the best; and she could not do it to the Count.

She met his eyes as steadily as she could, and gently withdrew her captive fingers. 'Sergei, I cannot marry you,' she said. 'I am deeply honoured, and grateful – '

'Grateful! I don't want you to be grateful!' he said, his face flushed with mortification, his eyes too bright.

'Please try not to mind,' she said desperately. 'In a little while, in a few months, you'll see I was right. You'll meet someone else nearer your own age, someone of your own station in life – '

'Someone like Zinochka, I suppose,' he said angrily. 'A young, pretty, empty-headed girl – and she will drive you out of my heart – you, who are everything a man could want – kind, intelligent, gentle – '

Anne turned her face away. 'Don't. Please don't.'

He came close to her, put his mouth to her ear. 'Anna, listen to me! I think I understand – you think this is just a passing fancy of mine, that I will fall out of love with you in a little while, and go off after someone else. Well, I won't! You'll see. I love you, and I know you love me, and I will prove to you that it's a real, lasting thing! No, don't argue with me!' he said quickly as she drew breath to protest. 'There is no reason in the world why I may not try to win you, is there?'

Only reasons I cannot explain to you, she thought.

'I don't love you in that way,' she said again.

He smiled, and rested his forehead against her hair. 'So you say. Very well; but you will some day. I will *make* you love me.'

I shall have to go away, she thought desperately; and as if he heard her thought, he kissed the tip of her ear and straightened up, saying, 'Don't worry, *milienkaya*, I shan't do anything to embarrass you, or to shame you. In front of the others, I shall be just as I have been before; but privately, I shall try to win you. You will not deny me the right to court you, surely? Everyone has that right.'

She had no answer for him. He smiled – a lovely, warm, confident smile, which made her feel just for an instant younger than him, and under his protection. 'You'll enjoy it, Anna Petrovna. I promise you!'

She wouldn't have thought, after such a scene, and such spilling of emotions, that it would be possible for them to continue with the ride, to spend the rest of the day together, without awkwardness. But Sergei took charge, not only directing their activities and choosing their route, but setting the tone of their conversation and introducing topics when Anne's sad, confused mind refused to co-operate. His life-long social training as a cadet both of the Guards and a noble house had given him the skills; and he seemed happy enough with the promise he felt he had extracted from her to be able to be cheerful. Gradually his mood affected Anne, too, and she began to respond more naturally to his comments and questions, until at last they were chatting almost as easily on the ride home, as they had on the way out.

Anne was grateful to him, as well as a little surprised by his self-possession. Perhaps it would be all right, she thought. If he behaved like this, she could cope with the situation; and in any case, he would have to return to his regiment soon, in another week or ten days. By the time she saw him again, everything would be changed. At his age, surely, such a mistaken love could not last very long? Some pretty girl would take his fancy, and she would be forgotten.

From the picnic place they rounded the hill and began to descend, climbed again, and passed through a small wood to come out at the other side of the Valley of the Horses, having covered three quarters of the circular route Sergei had planned for them. The herd was down below, but Quassy paid them no attention beyond a sharp pricking of the ears and an intent look when she first spotted them. The stallion was out of sight, and the mares and foals were grazing peacefully, drifting westerly to the sheltered end of the valley where they would spend the night.

'I wonder if Quassy will prove to be in foal,' Anne wondered aloud; but Sergei's attention was not on her. He was staring away across the valley and to the east, away from home, a frown between his brows. 'What is it?' Anne asked. 'Have you seen something?'

He didn't answer at once; and then he said, 'I'm not sure. Look, across there, there's something moving. Can you see it? I thought at first it was a deer, but now I think it looks like someone on horseback.'

Anne stared. 'I don't see what you mean.'

'You see the whitish patch of rock, with the thorn trees above it? Well, just to the left, and below. No, it's gone behind some bushes. There, now — it is a rider, isn't it?'

'It looks like it,' Anne said. 'But who could it be? Someone from Chastnaya?'

'Too far away. And no-one from there would ride alone.' He paused, watching. 'It must be one of the tribespeople — see how small he is? And he's riding bareback, I think. But why is he on his own? The Tcherkess don't ride alone on raids, and there's no other reason for one of them to be here.'

'He's not alone,' Anne said suddenly. 'Look, higher up, against the skyline.'

Sergei breathed out. 'Yes! Quite a party of them. What would you say — six? Ten?' His hand drifted automatically towards his gun, and then he said, 'I think we'd better get back home as quickly as possible, and alert the men. If they mean trouble, we had best be prepared.'

They turned their horses towards home. Nabat pricked his ears eagerly, and Quassy put in a dancing step or two, and both were only too willing to increase pace. Anne glanced back just before they passed out of sight. The party on the skyline were gone, but the small figure was still moving on the path below, picking a dogged way along what must have been a narrow and precipitous track. There was something naggingly familiar about the figure, she thought; and then smiled at herself for her absurdity. At that distance, it was impossible to recognise anything more than that it was a human on a horse.

They met Mishka on horseback about half a mile from the house. He waved and changed direction when he saw them, and galloped towards them, shouting something they couldn't understand. Nabat and Quassy shied excitedly as he came up, circling his horse around them as he overshot.

'Have you seen her?' he shouted, hauling the reins of his sweating horse.

'Seen who?' Sergei asked. 'We saw some Tcherkess on the ridge above the valley – looked like a raiding party.'

'Natasha,' Mishka replied automatically; and then, 'What's that? Tcherkess?' He dragged his horse to a halt at last in a cloud of dust. Anne felt its grittiness in her mouth as she spoke.

'Mishka, what are you saying? What about Natasha? Where is she?'

'That's what we don't know. She's gone. She took a horse and slipped away some time this morning. No-one missed her until she didn't come in for dinner – well, you know what she's like, always doing things on her own. But then one of the serfs found a horse was missing from the stable, and one of the women came in from the fields to say she'd seen Nasha riding alone, and didn't think it was right. We've got everyone out looking for her.'

Sergei and Anne exchanged a glance; Anne's mouth flooded with the coppery taste of fear.

'We've just seen her,' Sergei said grimly. 'On the valley side, going east. She was so far away, I didn't recognise her – I thought she was one of the Tcherkess.'

Mishka's face was pale, not only with dust. 'But you just said you'd seen a raiding party.'

'Yes, on the skyline above the path where Nasha was. About six or eight of them, I suppose.'

Mishka's eyes were wide as he tried to assimilate the facts. 'What were they doing? Had they seen her? Did they know she was there?'

'They were just sitting there – watching her, I think,' Sergei said, and his voice sounded like a sentence of death.

'We must go after her,' Mishka cried, turning his horse so sharply that it snorted and gave a half-rear.

'Yes,' Sergei said. His voice sharpened into an officer's as he gave his orders. 'Anna, go back to the house, tell them what you know, get Feodor to turn out an armed party, as many as he can, and send them after us. Mishka will come with me. We'll go back to the valley and see if she's still in sight. If she is, I'll go after her and leave him somewhere to pass on the message. Do you understand? Then go!'

Anne made no argument, turning Quassy and kicking her into a canter even as Sergei finished speaking. A glance over her shoulder a moment later saw the two men already at some distance, galloping hard back towards the valley.

The women had the hardest part to bear. For the men there was at least the satisfaction of activity, to ease the ache of anxiety; but the women had nothing to do but wait, and think. Nyanka alternated between wailing and prayers, beat her breast with a gnarled fist clenched about her wooden crucifix, offered God her life in exchange for Natasha's. But behind this noisy and theatrical outcry, it was not hard to see the genuine, black fear in her eyes: not for the retribution she might expect if anything should happen to the child, but simply for Natasha herself. The child had been left in her charge: she should not have allowed her out of her sight; and if Nasha were not returned to them unharmed, Nyanka would never forgive herself.

It was not hard to discover how it had come about. At Chastnaya, the children enjoyed a greater degree of licence than in Petersburg, greater even that at Schwartzenturm. They were all well aware of the dangers of wandering too far from the house, and as long as they were somewhere nearby, everyone was happy enough to let them romp and play, and merely glance out at them from time to time to see that all was well.

Nyanka had had other things on her mind that day. Irina's maid, Marie, had come storming into the kitchen quarters that morning complaining bitterly that a pair of her ladyship's silk stockings was missing, and that someone must have stolen them. The Chastnaya servants had naturally resented the implication that there was a thief in their number, and counter-accused Marie of not knowing her own business. The Kirov servants rallied to Marie, and warfare had broken out, as all the frictions of the past weeks and the mixing of two households came to the surface.

Nyanka had tried to mediate, feeling herself to have loyalties on both sides – a Kirov servant, but Chastnaya bred. When Zina had come to find out what all the noise was about, Nyanka had tried to represent both sides of the argument fairly, and had her nose bitten off by Zina for her pains. She retired in high dudgeon to her sewing, and bid Tanya go and see if the children were all right.

Tanya, who had been given some mending to do which she did not believe was rightly her job, since the articles in question were the property of Danil's children, and should therefore have been mended by a Chastnaya servant, flounced off to poke her head out onto the verandah. Sashka was there, playing with some wooden soldiers, and seeing some of the other children run past engaged in a game of hide-and-go-seek, she found it convenient to assume Nasha was of their number.

Thus it was that no-one had noticed Nasha had gone until the children were called in for their dinner, by which time she had been gone several hours.

But gone where? And why? And why so far? To take a horse suggested some serious purpose, not just a lark, or a legitimate ride. If she had wanted to go for a ride, there was no reason why she should not have asked for the pony given to her use to be saddled up for her. A groom would have gone with her then, of course; that she had taken a horse suggested she wanted to go somewhere she thought would be denied her.

But where? Sitting in silence on the verandah through that long, airless afternoon, the women racked their brains, each silently blaming herself, and each trying desperately not to think of what might have happened to the little girl. It was not likely that any of the Tcherkess would lose the opportunity of capturing the fair-skinned, light-haired daughter of a Russian *Dvorian*. The best of them might simply return her in the hope of a reward – which they would undoubtedly receive. Others might kidnap her and hold her to ransom; and there were yet other possibilities too horrible to contemplate.

Nyanka might wail and croon her hysterical fear, while looking inwardly at her unforgiveable sin; Irina might sit in stunned silence, contemplating the loss of her dearest child, the child likest to her, knowing that she was ultimately responsible for Nyanka and Nyanka's failings, and for bringing the children here in the first place; but Anne knew that the final responsibility was hers. Nyanka was only a servant, and a serf at that; Irina had a mother's cares, but a high-born mother's detachment too. Anne was the person employed by the Count to take care of the children, to bring them up *in loco parentis*, and she should not have gone off on a pleasure-jaunt and left them unguarded.

She, above all, knew what Natasha was like – how unpredictable she could be – how little regard she had for physical danger. The child was strange, there was no escaping the fact. Anne remembered old Marya's warning – *the little one may walk away one day . . . don't let her stray too far . . .* There was no doubt that Nasha had deliberately taken a horse and ridden away, of her own will, for some purpose of her own. But where? And why? Her thoughts trod the weary circle again.

The men came back after dark, exhausted, silent with their failure to find her, or any trace of her.

'But you can't leave her out there in the dark!' Ekaterina cried, clutching her own daughter uncomfortably against her bosom. 'Think how frightened she will be! You must keep looking for her!'

'We can't search in the dark, Katya,' Feodor said, defeat heavy in his voice. 'We'll begin again at first light tomorrow, but there's nothing more we can do now.'

'We've left lookouts to bivouac at various vantage points,' Mishka added. 'It was Seryosha's idea. She may be trying to make her way back home by now, and she'll see their camp fires. If she comes across any of them, they'll bring her straight back here. It's the best we can do.'

'What about the tribesmen we saw?' Anne asked quietly. She saw the same reluctance in the eyes of the men to answer, as she felt in asking.

'We found the place where we saw them,' Sergei said. 'They must have been there quite a while, judging by the dung. But what they were doing . . . ' He shrugged.

'They came from the east and made off that way,' Mishka added, 'to judge from the few tracks we could find. But there was no possibility of following them. As to Nasha – well, the path she was following is bare rock. The only trace is a scratch here and there, and there's no knowing if that was made by her horse, or any other.'

There was a silence.

'But what did she go *for*?' Ekaterina asked, as if exasperated by the illogicality of the situation.

Feodor looked at his sister helplessly. 'God, if we knew that . . . ! Perhaps she went to look at the horses in the valley, and then wandered too far to get back before dark. She'll probably make her own way back,' he said unconvincingly. 'She's probably hiding up somewhere, waiting for it to get light. She'll turn up safe and sound tomorrow morning.'

No-one agreed or disagreed.

'I'd better see about supper,' Zina said dully. 'Come with me, Katya. There's water hot for you men. Go on to your rooms, I'll send it in.'

The next day, as soon as it got light, the men went out again in four parties, armed, and equipped with ropes, blankets, food, aquavit, and anything else they thought might conceivably be useful; and the women settled down to another day of waiting. Anne took Sashka away and taught him his letters, in an attempt to keep her mind from the fruitless anxiety that was wearing them all down. Nyanka, probably similarly inspired, washed, starched and ironed every item of children's clothing she could lay hands on. Irina merely sat on the verandah, rocking a little, staring at nothing, her long, golden eyes blank. Her hands were folded, motionless in her lap; under them, though no-one knew it but Anne, she held one of Nasha's shoes, a pink sandal she had worn on the night of the feast, to dance in.

The day's search revealed nothing. 'There are so many places she might be – woods, ravines, caves,' Danil said defeatedly. 'It will take for ever to search them all. It's hopeless.'

'We need more help,' Feodor said, giving his brother a warning look. 'Tomorrow I shall call out every serf, and comb the whole valley inch by inch. We'll find her, don't worry,' he added to Irina, trying to sound confident; but she only looked at him blankly. Anne, with Sashka in her arms for comfort, visualised the size of the area they were searching, thought of Nasha lying hurt and helpless in some hidden gully.

'If she had fallen from her horse, wouldn't it have made its own way home?' she asked.

'Not necessarily. If it were very far away, it might just wander,' Mishka said briefly. 'Or it might have got caught up somewhere – trailing reins.'

'If there were a fall, the horse might be hurt,' Grishka suggested.

'You'd better hope that the horse is still with her,' Danil said. 'A lone child will be even harder to find.'

Irina took Sashka from Anne to put him to bed, and the others drifted away, leaving Sergei, Feodor and Anne alone on the verandah. The darkness was the black velvet of before moonrise, and they instinctively turned their faces to it. It was easier to talk and hope, when you could not see the despair in other people's eyes.

'Tomorrow I will send out a message to the tribes,' Feodor said. 'If anyone has seen her . . . And they can search the hills beyond the estate better than we can. They know every inch.'

A silence. 'I don't know whether I ought to write to my father,' Sergei said, sounding for once very young, in need of reassurance. 'It will take so long for the message to reach him, and if she were found meanwhile, he would be worried for nothing.'

'Perhaps you might wait another day or two,' Anne said, knowing it was the answer he wanted. 'If she has had a fall . . . It's a large area to search.'

'If only we hadn't gone out for the day!' Sergei cried out, his guilt rising to the surface at last.

'My dear, it isn't your fault,' Anne said. 'It was never your business to take care of her. It is I who – ' She stopped abruptly. To voice her guilt was to court denials from the two men. She turned to look at Feodor's dark shadow beside her, leaning on the verandah rail. 'You don't think she's on the estate, do you? You think the Tcherkess took her.'

He was long answering; then he said quietly, 'It seems likely. But there's always hope. Let's not talk about it.' He pushed himself upright, the heavy movement of a tired man. 'We'll do everything we can – search, ask questions – and pray besides. But talking and thinking won't help.'

'How can any of us help thinking,' Anne said helplessly.

Feodor touched her shoulder as he walked away. 'We can try.'

Chapter Seventeen

Anne woke from a restless and tangled dream to find Sashka beside her bed, tugging urgently at her arm.

'Anna! Anna! Come quick!'

She struggled up onto one elbow. Moonlight filled the room: her bed here at Chastnaya was uncurtained, and the window drapes had not been pulled quite together. Sashka was brightly illuminated in his white nightgown, his fair hair ruffled into a crest.

'Sashka? What is it?'

'Mama's not well! Come and make her better, oh please, Anna!'

She was out of bed on the instant, reaching for her wrapper. 'Did you wake Nyanka?'

Sashka shook his head. 'She was snoring,' he said succinctly. Anne took his hand and hurried out of her room and along the passage towards Irina's. She had been watching the Countess carefully over the last few days, worried about her increasing withdrawal. Irina sat all day staring at nothing, or walked back and forth along the verandah, always holding Nasha's shoe tight against her like a talisman. She did not cry or speak, barely seemed to understand when she was spoken to, ate little and without interest when food was placed before her. The only change in her came when the men returned at night, and her focus would suddenly sharpen as she looked at them for their report.

Negative: they were always negative. It was as if Natasha had disappeared from the face of the earth; and though the words had never been spoken, everyone had gradually relinquished any hope of finding her alive. The Kiriakov men left at first light every day on an increasingly hopeless search, and the unvoiced thought that they were now only seeking the final proof of her death made the days longer and more weary for everyone.

Irina's door was ajar, and Anne saw that the room was even brighter than her own had been. Once inside, she could see why: the curtains had been drawn right back, and Irina was standing at the window, looking up at the moon. The sky outside was clear, and the moon was high and hard, a white-hot disc whose light was so bright it might almost have burnt.

285

In her nightdress and with her long plait hanging straight down her back, Irina looked like a child. She held the pink slipper in both hands against her breast; her eyes were wide and blank, her lips were moving soundlessly. She did not seem to notice when Anne came towards her.

'Is she ill, Anna?' Sashka whispered anxiously. 'I called her but she didn't answer, and she looks so strange.'

Anne squeezed his hand reassuringly, and then relinquished it and approached the Countess, saying quietly, 'Irina Pavlovna, are you all right? Is anything the matter?' There was no response. 'Can't you sleep? The moon is very bright.'

Close beside her mistress, Anne could hear now that she was whispering rapidly, and thought at first that she was praying. She touched Irina's hand cautiously, and was shocked to feel that, in spite of the warmth of the midsummer night, it was icy cold. 'Madame, come back to bed,' she said gently. 'You're cold.'

The rapid whisper went on unheedingly; Anne saw that her pupils were dilated, too. Anne turned to Sashka and murmured, 'Go quietly and wake Nyanka, my love, and bring her here. Try not to wake anyone else.'

He gave one wide-eyed look, and scurried away. Anne placed her hand over Irina's icy one, and tried to turn her from the window, but her whole body was rigid, and her resistance was so powerful that Anne could not make any impression on her, nor unclasp so much as one finger from around the shoe. She was either in a trance, or sleepwalking.

'Irina Pavlovna!' she said more urgently. 'Can you hear me? Wake up!'

The whisper became distinguishable. 'So cold . . . so cold. Dark, here . . . No light anywhere. Cold.'

'Wake up, madame. You're dreaming.'

'Cold,' Irina said. 'No more voices . . . you promised . . . so alone.' Out of the corner of her eye, Anne saw Nyanka appear in the doorway, clasping a crucifix a little before her as if to ward off evil. Irina's voice rose. 'Don't leave me alone . . . Lonely . . . So lonely . . . ' Suddenly she cried out. 'Mama! Mama! Mama, help me!'

Nyanka had been advancing across the room, but at the last words she stopped as though shot through the heart, and her eyes met Anne's, wide with horror. The voice which had issued from Irina's lips was not her own. It was higher, younger, a child's voice – Natasha's voice.

'Dear God alive!' Nyanka cried, crossing herself.

'Quick, Nyanka,' Anne said sharply, 'what must we do?'

But Nyanka was too frightened to be of any help. Irina's voice had risen again both in volume and pitch, but the words were now incomprehensible. She was rigid and shaking, and Anne feared she might actually injure herself, and yet feared to wake her by violent means, in case it should be harmful. Sashka was hiding behind Nyanka, clutching her skirt and peeping out in fear; and into the midst of this came Zina in a sensible wrapper, with Zinochka in curl-papers behind her, and strode across the room, grim-faced. She brushed Anne out of the way, took hold of Irina by one shoulder, and slapped her calculatedly, first on one cheek and then the other.

The high babbling voice was cut off; Irina's eyes widened even further in shock as she stared at Zina for an instant; and then she collapsed bonelessly against her sister.

'Help me put her to bed,' Zina snapped at Anne. 'Zinochka, turn back the covers. You, Nyanka, don't stand there like a stock! Fetch her smelling-bottle, and go and wake up her maid. Go, for God's sake – and stop crossing yourself like that! She's not possessed by evil spirits. She's just been sleepwalking again.'

While she was speaking, Anne had come round to the other side of her mistress, and between them they half-carried, half-dragged the inert form back to the bed, where Zinochka had pulled back the covers and was hovering anxiously. Nyanka had left the room. Out of the corner of her eye, Anne knew that Sashka was still somewhere near, and ought to be taken back to bed, but she hadn't any attention to spare for him at the moment.

They got Irina into bed, pulled the covers over her. She lay limp against the pillows, her eyes closed, her face white except for the reddening imprint of Zina's fingers. Zina lifted one fragile wrist to test the pulse. Anne saw that the Countess had dropped the shoe by the window, the first time it had been out of her hands since Nasha went missing.

'I was afraid of this,' Zina said grimly. 'I've seen it building up. She used to have these fits when she was a girl, especially when the moon was bright like tonight.'

'Fits?' Anne queried.

'Sleepwalking – or whatever you want to call it. A sort of trance, I suppose,' Zina said. 'Our mother was the same way, so I'm told – I don't really remember. She was thought to have second sight. The serfs believed it, anyway. She was a seventh child – and Irina was *her* seventh, if you count the stillbirth between Feodor and me.'

Marie came in, voluble with anxiety and questions, but bearing the vital smelling-bottle, while Nyanka hovered in the doorway, evidently torn between her desire to attend her nurseling, and her fear of things supernatural. Almost irrelevantly, in the back of her mind, Anne heard the Count's voice: *We all see visions. There's a magic in Russia that we breathe in all the time* . . . Well, but this was something a little different, a little out of Anne's experience. Yet four years in Russia had changed her. The sensible English governess would have dismissed what she had heard as imagination; but this Anna Petrovna was not so sure.

'Zina, did you hear?' she asked now, as Zina plied the bottle under Irina's nose. 'When she spoke – it sounded like Natasha's voice.'

Irina coughed, struggled a little, lifted a hand to ward off the bottle. Zina pushed it down firmly and said, 'One more sniff, there's a good girl.' Irina gasped, and her eyes fluttered open. She looked around her at the ring of faces hovering over her, and then closed her eyes and moaned.

'What happened?'

Zina's fingers were firm on the wrist again. 'You took one of your turns,' she said. 'Don't you remember?'

'No,' Irina moaned. 'My head hurts . . . What happened?'

'She's like this,' Zina explained to Anne. 'She'll be better in a minute or two.' She stroked Irina's forehead, her work-hardened hand unexpectedly gentle. 'There, little 'Rushka, there. It's all right now. Zina's here.' She looked over her shoulder and saw Sashka at the end of the bed watching, and frowned. 'Nyanka, take that child and put him to bed! What are you thinking of? Your mistress is all right now. Marie and I will stay with her. You go back to bed too, Zinochka. You need your sleep. And send those servants away,' she added, aware of some hovering outside the door.

When the room was cleared, Anne walked over to the window and picked up the shoe, noting as she did that it felt unexpectedly cold, though the soft leather soon warmed in her hand. Imagination, perhaps? She went back to the bed, and stood quietly. After a while Irina opened her eyes again, and Zina said, 'Take a sip of wine. You'll feel better soon.'

Marie helped her prop up Irina's head while Zina held a wineglass to her lips. When she was resting against the pillows again, Irina said, 'I saw her. I saw Nasha.' Her voice was weak, but clear.

'Of course you did,' Zina said soothingly. 'What else would you expect, the way you've been carrying on? I've seen this coming these two days. You must eat properly, Irushka, or you'll make yourself ill.'

Irina caught her sister's wrist, and her knuckles showed white. 'Don't baby me! You know what I'm saying! You know my visions are true ones! I saw her – I saw my child. She's alive!'

Zina did not deny it, but she could not help a tiny shake of her head in disbelief. Irina's eyes came round pleadingly to Anne's.

'She's alive. I saw the place.' She frowned with concentration. 'A high place. Very high. And very cold.'

'Do you know where it is?' Anne asked tentatively.

Irina stared through her. 'A long way away. Further away than we've been searching. A high place . . . '

'In the mountains?' Anne asked.

'Yes! High in the mountains!' She closed her eyes, plainly exhausted.

'Leave her alone, now,' Zina interposed quietly. 'Don't excite her again – she needs to sleep. You'd better go back to bed – Marie and I can cope. Goodnight, Anna Petrovna.'

Anne was dismissed too firmly to resist, and with a final, doubtful glance at the Countess, she went away. She looked in to see that Sashka had settled, and found him half asleep, with Nyanka sitting beside his bed. The old woman nodded to her, and Sashka turned his face drowsily for Anne's kiss.

'Is Mama all right now?'

'Yes, she's all right. She's sleeping now – and so must you. Goodnight, Sashka.'

'Goodnight, Anna,' he murmured. He was almost asleep. 'I'm glad Nasha's all right.'

Anne went quietly away, leaving him to Nyanka. In her own room, she went to the window to pull the curtains closed, and found Nasha's shoe still in her hand. It was so small, and so soft. She remembered the strange voice that had come from Irina's mouth, remembered the bleak, pitiful words, and suddenly she was crying – for the first time since Nasha had been lost. Whatever had been the truth of Irina's 'vision', it brought home to her the stark reality: wherever Natasha was, she was alone, facing either life or death without anyone to help or comfort her, and she was only seven years old.

Anne lay on her bed and cradled her head in her arms and wept; and weeping, she finally fell asleep.

It was a very different Irina who faced her brothers the next morning. Her face was pale, beginning to be a little gaunt, smudged here and there with violet shadow, and yet alert and alive, taut with eagerness, her eyes like gold flame as she told of her vision.

'You must search further afield. She's not nearby – not on Chastnaya at all. But she's alive.'

'Can't you tell us where, Rushka?' Feodor asked. He looked grey with fatigue; if he believed that his sister's vision was true, he hadn't enough energy to spare to show it.

'A high place,' she said. 'Cold and high.'

'But where? Which direction?' Dmitri asked. 'North, south, east or west?'

'If it's a high place, it can't be north or east,' Danil pointed out. 'The mountains are south and west.'

'Depends how high. It needn't be as high as a mountain.'

'Cold means high, doesn't it? Was there snow, Rushka? Did you see snow?'

'Maybe it's Mount Kazbek. Could you see that?'

Sergei had been listening to this with scant patience. Now he said, 'For God's sake, how could a little child get up Mount Kazbek? Or get as far as that, for that matter? It must be more than a hundred versts.'

Irina turned on him. 'You don't believe me? You don't believe I saw her?'

'It doesn't matter whether I believe it or not, Mama,' Sergei said impatiently. 'Unless you can describe the place in more detail . . . high and cold doesn't help us much, does it? It could be anywhere.'

'One thing we know,' Danil said, frowning at Sergei, 'is that it is *somewhere*. You don't understand – they run in the family, these visions, and they never lie.'

Sergei made a dismissing movement with his hand. 'All I said was a child of that age couldn't have got that far on her own.'

They looked at each other with hostility; and Anne, feeling sympathy on both sides, said, 'How far is it to the nearest mountains? High ones, I mean?'

'Fifty versts, perhaps, going south-west,' Feodor said. Sergei looked at him sharply.

'That's Chechen country,' he said.

'Those tribesmen you saw – could they have been Chechen?' Feodor asked cautiously.

Sergei shrugged. 'They were against the light, and a long way off. They could have been anything.' He looked uncomfortable, not wanting to say what he had to say next. 'But – look, if the Chechen took her, it's highly unlikely – well, that she'd still be in the mountains, and alive. Either they'd have killed her, or sold her south.' He flickered a glance at Irina. 'I'm sorry, Mama, but it's true.'

She rounded on him like a tigress. 'I saw what I saw! You don't believe me – you Moscow-bred, you city-bred nothing – but what do you know about it? You only believe what you can see and touch. But my brothers believe me! They know! I saw her – she's alive!'

'Please, Mama – ' Sergei began to protest; and Irina actually lifted both hands, clenched into fists, and brought them down violently against his breast.

'Find her!' she cried fiercely. 'Find your sister! *Find my child*!'

They pored over maps, they pondered, they discussed. None of the enquiries they had pursued outside the estate had produced any result, though they had hardly expected them to, even though they had offered a reward for information: the loyalty of the Tcherkess to each other was usually stronger than their sympathy for their Russian overlords, even when the latter was bolstered with money.

Anne looked from face to face, trying to guess what they were thinking. Dmitri and Danil believed wholeheartedly in Irina's vision; Sergei was openly sceptical, though he said no more about it. Between the extremes, Mishka and Grishka probably believed it with their stomachs, but rejected it with their minds, knowing that the chances of finding Nasha alive had diminished with every passing day, of which there had already been too many.

As to Feodor, it was impossible to judge what he believed: he knew what his duty was and did it, without comment or explanation; he was the patriarch, and responsible for the estate and everyone on it; but he loved his younger brothers and sisters with a warm-blooded Russian fervour, and not for anything would he have hurt Irina, or tried to destroy a faith which she evidently found sustaining.

It was while she was looking at his long, grey face that Anne had her idea. Her mind had been drifting a little; and suddenly, far away in the back of her thoughts, she heard the Tartar Prince saying *Akim Shan Kalmuck knows everything; it is his business to know everything*. She thought of him, of his dark, bright, feral eyes, his calculating looks, his seemingly genuine admiration for her. If anyone could obtain information from the tribes, surely it must be him? She wondered she hadn't thought of it before.

In dealing with the tribesmen they had had no weapon but money to use against the natural hostility of the wild mountain men for the *dvoriane* from the north. Why should they betray their own to the interlopers, the conquerors? But Akim Shan Kalmuck, besides being the Prince of one of the 'tame' tribes – for what that was worth – called himself her friend. He had placed himself at her service, and that, surely, must count for something?

She put it to Feodor. 'Do you know where he lives – where he is to be found? I imagine he is quite an important man, and therefore well known?'

Feodor considered, and his face lightened a little at the prospect of a new avenue to explore, which perhaps offered more of a chance than the search for an unidentified high, cold place. 'I don't know exactly,' he said, 'but it will be easy enough to find out. He comes from somewhere near Vladikavkaz, between there and the Pass of Dariel – on this side of the mountains, anyway.'

Sergei frowned. 'I didn't like the look of him,' he said. 'Why should he help us, any more than any of the other tribes?'

'Because he likes me,' Anne said shortly.

Feodor glanced at Sergei. 'It isn't much, but it's better than nothing. Besides, he has bought our horses more than once, and that makes a bond between us. And I believe he does a great deal of business with the regional agent in Vladikavkaz, which makes him almost civilised.' Sergei looked sceptical, and Feodor added with a shrug, 'It's worth trying, anyway.'

'Oh, yes, by all means,' Sergei said neutrally. 'I'm willing to go, if you like to trust me with the business.'

Anne fixed him with a hard look. 'Whoever else goes, I must.'

'Nonsense!' Sergei said quickly. 'It's out of the question – much too dangerous.'

'Sergei, consider – no-one but me can put a personal request to him on my behalf. Put yourself in his place – would you lift a finger to help, unless approached in person?'

Danil said slowly, 'She's right, Seryosha. Why, I'll bet he wouldn't even listen to us.'

'But it isn't seemly. Anna's a gentlewoman. Quite apart from the danger, there's no knowing what sights she might be called upon to witness.'

Anne shrugged. 'None of that matters. I must go. You know I must.'

'Then I will go with you. I owe it to my father,' Sergei said. 'While he's away, I am responsible for his household.'

Feodor had passed beyond that stage of the argument, and was already planning details. 'We'll have to take him gifts, to sweeten him; and armed men, to let him see we're not in his power. It's a delicate business.'

'A show of strength that isn't a threat – a present that isn't a bribe?' Anne said with a faint smile. 'Yes, delicate – and from what I know of him, he will be more adept at the game than any of us could ever hope to be.'

'That's a certainty,' Feodor said.

There was no time to be lost, and they set out just before noon for Vladikavkaz. The party consisted of Feodor, Dmitri, Grishka, Sergei, Anne, and ten armed men. Ekaterina was both worried and disapproving that Anne should have no woman to attend her: it was indecent, and dangerous, she thought. But Anne would not oblige anyone to come on such a mission against their will, and there were no volunteers. Besides, speed was of the essence, and none of the female servants could ride well enough to travel fast, and stay in the saddle all day long. When Katya went on protesting, Irina interrupted on Anne's behalf.

'Nonsense, Katya, hold your tongue. What do such things matter at a time like this? They are going to rescue my child, not to have a picnic at Pyatigorsk.'

Anne had been afraid that Irina would want to go herself, but she seemed to understand that she would only be a hindrance. However hard it would be to remain at home waiting for news, she accepted it without protest, only showing her emotions at the moment of departure by putting her arms round Anne and hugging her briefly.

'God bless you, Anna Petrovna,' she whispered into her ear; and stepping back a little, added, '*Find her!*'

They took with them a mule laden with gifts: sunflower seeds, oil, fine cloth, skins, and a jar of perfume – not overwhelmingly expensive things, which might look too much like the bribe of desperate men, but the sort of pleasant gifts that might be exchanged between friends. Anne dressed in her best habit, for she would need to impress – though probably Quassy would do that for her well enough. Anne had already decided that if all else failed, she would offer the Prince the mare in return for his help. As he believed Quassy to be in foal, she would now be twice as valuable to the man who had long coveted her.

It was fifty versts – about forty miles – from Chastnaya to Vladikavkaz; but the days were long, and the roads dry and hard, and they were able to reach the city long enough before dark for enquiries to be made by Feodor and Sergei, while the others looked for lodgings, saw to the horses, and bespoke a dinner. It was after dark when Feodor and Sergei joined them, but from their expression it was plain that they had achieved their object.

'We know where he is,' Sergei said the instant he came through the door. 'It's a village up in the hills about eight versts along the road towards Kazbek. It's called Karzerum, and he's the chief man of the whole area. A very important person, your admirer, Anna Petrovna.'

'We'll set off at sun-up,' Feodor said. 'We can't approach a man like that in the dark – open to misinterpretation.'

'If we left before dawn, we could be there at first light,' Sergei suggested. 'It might be better for us if we arrive unexpectedly.'

'Unexpectedly?' Feodor said.

'Throw him off balance – it would give us the upper hand.'

Feodor gave a tired smile. 'My dear Seryosha, you don't know the kind of people you're dealing with. It's two hours since we began asking questions about Akim Shan Kalmuck, and he lives only eight versts away. If he does not know by now that we are come looking for him, I promise you I'll eat my hat – new ribbon and all.'

Anne slept heavily, tired from the long ride and the emotions and worries of the day, but woke feeling refreshed, with the consciousness that at last she was doing something positive to try to find Natasha. Despite the arguments of her reason, she could not help feeling absurdly hopeful. Irina believed her daughter was alive. Anne saw now what she had been doing all those days when she walked up and down holding Nasha's shoe: not brooding, but searching – letting loose her mind to cover those distances impossible for her body. Akim Shan Kalmuck would help them; he *must* help them.

It was a fine day, but humid, and there were clouds covering the high jagged peaks of Mount Kazbek and the Mountain of the Cross, so that they looked mysterious and withdrawn, like inaccessible judges withholding their counsel, waiting to pass sentence. The road out of the town was steep, and the horses were soon sweating, early though it was, and clouds of little black flies descended to torment them. Sergei and Grishka got off and walked, leading their horses, and Anne would have liked to do the same, to save Quassy, but dared not: she could not remount quickly, as they could, in case of sudden need.

The village of Karzerum was built above the road, on a hilltop which was a natural fortress, a flat, green plateau above bare cliffs, impossible to scale. Above it the mountains rose sheer, uncolonised except for the gorse and thorn clinging to ledges. The village was dominated by a stone-built fortified house, presumably the Prince's, behind which was a cluster of wooden and daub cottages, sheltered from the north by a stand of trees. A little apart, on rising ground, stood the inevitable little white church, its Byzantine dome just catching the rising sun.

The path to the village left the main road and climbed in a winding way between natural cliffs. Anyone using it would be kept in view, and at a disadvantage, by lookouts on the top; and Anne, riding well to the front to emphasise the peaceful nature of their approach, thought that Akim Shan Kalmuck would be a hard man to take by surprise. She felt that they were being watched, but her occasional glances upwards could not discover anyone; only once there was a flash from amongst the bushes high overhead, as though something metallic had caught and reflected the sun's rays.

Yet when they emerged from the gully and out onto the hilltop, there was a party of horsemen waiting for them, dark, hook-nosed tribesmen in striped coats, with guns held upright before them, not threatening, but at the ready. The Prince was in the centre of them, on a white Kabardin stallion whose restless sidlings he sat effortlessly. The champing of its bit and the ringing of the gold discs on its browband were the only sounds on that silent hilltop.

The Chastnaya party halted, and Feodor raised his hand in the universal, palm-outwards gesture of greeting.

'Peace be with you, Akim Shan Kalmuck,' he said. 'Peace and prosperity to your tribe.'

The Prince gave a courteous bow, and raised his own hand, his eyes flicking over the group speculatively. 'Peace be with you, Feodor Pavlovitch,' he said in the Russian form. 'You are a long way from Chastnaya of the Horses.'

'We have come to visit you,' Feodor said. 'We bring gifts – ' he made a superbly throwaway gesture, as though the gifts were hardly worth mentioning between gentlemen of standing – 'so that we shall not leave your house poorer than we found it.'

The Prince inclined his head slightly. 'The guest who comes in friendship can never leave the house poorer,' he replied in kind. He surveyed them again. 'You will come and drink wine with me! Your men will be taken care of.'

It was not quite an invitation. The men surrounding the Prince performed a neat manoeuvre which put them between the Kiriakovs and their men, cutting off master from servant, ushering the former forward, and retaining the latter behind. But the Prince smiled as though he were in the Tsar's drawing-room, and turned his fretting stallion to walk him alongside Anne, holding him in with the curved spring of a wrist so that he kept perfect pace with Quassy. He was, Anne acknowledged to herself, a superb rider.

'I had not thought,' the Prince said, 'to have the honour of receiving you into my house, Anna Petrovna.'

'You know my name,' she said in surprise. Always before he had called her 'English Lady'.

He bowed. 'I think it must be some very important thing that brings you such a long way on horseback, in this wild country. I wonder what it may be?'

His bright eyes were watchful, and Anne felt she was being tested, though she had no idea what was the nature of the test. She tried to smile. 'I have come to see the tiger, of course,' she said. 'When you told me you had a tame tiger with an emerald collar, I felt my days would be weary until I had seen it for myself, with my own eyes.'

She seemed to have said the right thing. He relaxed a little, and laughed, showing all his teeth.

'You shall see it!' he cried.

'It exists, then?' she said demurely.

'It exists. Did you doubt it?'

'Entirely. And it has an emerald collar?'

'A collar of the most fabulous emeralds in the world, the bright green emeralds that are found nowhere but in the waters of the Ganges River. That also you shall see.' He looked pleased with himself, and allowed the stallion to dance a little. 'I have never entertained an English lady in my house before. This is indeed a special day.'

They were approaching the stone house, whose single door was a black cave in the shadowed side away from the sun. Servants in white robes came running out to take the horses' heads, and the Prince leapt down to come to Quassy's side and hold out his hands to Anne. Sergei was there at the same instant, ready to be angry and push the Prince aside; and though she looked at those hands with fear, and was loath to let them touch her, she knew he must not be offended. She stilled Sergei with a ferocious glance, and allowed the Prince to jump her down.

Close to he smelled of oil and strong perfume and meat and garlic, a smell like sheep yolk from the raw wool of his sleeveless coat, and a musky animal smell which she supposed was his body. He terrified her, but she forced herself not to struggle away from him as soon as her feet touched the ground; forced herself to meet his eyes steadily as he towered over her.

She saw his lower lip, pink and naked-looking amongst the curled and oiled hairs of his beard; the brown edges of his lower teeth; the dark pitted skin of his cheeks above his beard; the black hairs in his nostrils; the little white scar across the bridge of his beaked nose; and then the bright, black, unfathomable eyes with their yellowish whites under the jutting black cliffs of his eyebrows. She saw his tongue move like an animal in its cave behind his teeth, and felt his breath warm and moist on her face, as he said, 'The mare is tired. I shall order my men to give her a cooling feed while you drink wine with me. She must be taken care of, the beautiful one.'

'Thank you, sir,' Anne managed to say. She felt faint, and longed to break the gaze and put her head down, but she would not before he did. Minutes later, it seemed, though it must really have been almost instantly, he released her and stepped away, snapping an order to the servant who held Quassy's head. At the door he turned and spread his hands to all of them.

'Please enter, and be welcome. My house is yours.'

He turned and led the way, and they followed him, as the servants led away their horses. Now by stages they had been divested of men, arms, and means of escape. Inside his house he might have them all murdered if he chose, and no-one would ever be any the wiser. They knew it, and they knew he knew it, and the air around them seemed almost briny with tension. But Anne trusted him. He terrified her, but she did not believe he would strike without a reason.

Sergei jostled up beside her. 'Are you all right, Anna?' he murmured. 'When I saw him put his hands on you, by God, I wanted to – '

'Hush,' she whispered urgently. 'It's all right, Seryosha. For God's sake try to act like a guest – be friendly, don't provoke him. We're in his power now.'

'Don't I know it!' he muttered. 'I should have come here with a company of the Independents . . . '

'Then we should never have found out anything. Now be quiet – and smile!'

Inside the house was very dark, from the lack of windows – partly the result of fortification, she guessed, and partly to keep out the burning sun in summer, and the bitter wind in winter. Burning incense sticks smouldered in brass holders at every corner, wreathing faint blue smoke up into the shadows of the roof. Their choking sweetness did not disguise an unpleasant smell underneath. Anne did not know what it was, could catch it only in brief snatches, and unwillingly.

The floor was stone, and its unevenness suggested that they were walking on the living rock, which had been roughly levelled when the house was built. The walls were plastered white, and again looked rough, as if the plaster had been laid on bare rock. They were decorated with painted designs in bright, clear colours, though the true beauty of them was only evident where a shaft of sunlight from a slit window suddenly illuminated them. There was a frieze of twined flowers and fruit; there were hunting scenes, and feasting scenes, dancers and dogs and horses and hawks; a parade of serfs carrying baskets of produce on their shoulders; a young warrior leading his war horse; a slender girl feeding a bird from the palm of her hand.

The passage in which they were walking opened out into a large room. It was furnished with several handsome chests and tables, elaborately carved, wooden chairs with slung leather seats, and bare wooden stools. A number of icons, elaborately framed in jewel-studded gold, spoke to the household's being at least nominally Christian. As well as the plaster paintings, there were handsome Persian and Chinese carpets hung on the walls for decoration, and woven, patterned rugs on the floor. At one end of the room, on a slightly raised dais, there was a heap of sheepskins, some of them dyed, and brightly-coloured cushions decorated with knotted fringes, beads and discs, and it was towards this that Akim Shan walked. He turned, spread his hands again in a welcoming gesture, and folded himself gracefully to recline in the soft depths of the heap.

'My humble house,' he said. He gestured to the chairs. 'Please, be comfortable. English Lady, you will sit beside me, as my guest of honour.'

There were many things Anne would have preferred, but again she saw that it was inevitable, and took her place beside him, doing her best to sink gracefully as he had, though her clothes were not designed for it as his were. The prickly, caged-animal smell rose from the cushions as she sat, and was all around her, emanating, she felt, from the Prince himself. She didn't like to be so near him, especially as she could not now look at him without turning her head, which was too deliberate an act, calling attention to itself; and she very much wanted to keep him in sight.

The others took seats, and servants came in with jugs and cups and bowls of fruit and sweetmeats, and disposed them about the guests on little tables. The Prince himself poured a cup of wine for Anne, and held it out to her, with a courtly bow. She accepted, looked briefly at the others, and drank. There was absolutely no point in wondering whether it were poisoned or not. If he wanted to kill them, he would do it, and there was nothing they could do to stop him. On the other hand, there was everything to be gained by being bold. She drank deep, lowered the cup, and smiled at the Prince.

'Thank you, sir. An excellent wine.'

He looked as if he had known everything that had just gone through her head. 'From the Black Sea,' he said. 'The wines from there grow sweet and heavy with age, like a lovely woman; but when they are young, they are vigorous and not always to be trusted. Also like a lovely woman.'

Anne laughed dutifully, and the men smiled uneasily and sipped. Akim Shan looked from one to another, evidently enjoying the situation and his power over it. He plied them with sweetmeats and trivial talk, and seemed particularly to enjoy Sergei's discomfiture, though Anne did her best to draw attention away from him. Then at last the Prince seemed to tire of the game. He straightened up perceptibly, and fixed Feodor with an eye as hard and bright as polished jet.

'So, you have come to ask for my help,' he said abruptly. 'There is something you seek – some knowledge, perhaps?'

Feodor met his gaze. 'If you know that much, Akim Shan, then you must know what it is we seek.'

'I know what it is you seek,' he said, matching Feodor's inflection so exactly that it was neither question nor statement. 'You came last night to Vladikavkaz asking where you might find me. Yes, I knew that – I was told you had arrived. I knew also, long before, that you had left Chastnaya of the Horses. Between Eborus and Petrovsk, nothing moves that I do not know about.'

'If that is true, sir,' Anne said quickly, 'then you must know something of the whereabouts of the child.'

He looked at her, and his eyes were unfathomable; and then he turned away and said, 'The gifts you brought with you – shall I have them carried in? It would amuse me to see them.'

'Sir – ' Sergei began angrily, but Dmitri kicked him sharply to silence.

'They are small things, sir,' Feodor said. 'Mere trifles, to signify the common trust and friendship between gentlemen.'

Akim Shan looked amused. 'Gentlemen,' he mused, and then he chuckled. 'And yet, I might have you all cut into little pieces, there where you sit, just to amuse myself. I need only give the order. Are you not afraid?'

Anne answered. 'You have tasted our hospitality at Chastnaya,' she said, trying to sound offhand, as Feodor had. 'You have bought horses of the Kiriakov herd. Therefore no Kiriakov – and no friend of Kiriakov – can be afraid in your house.' He looked at her, and she made herself continue. 'In particular, you treated my mare, and made her well again, and I am in your debt. It would be impossible, would it not, to kill one who owes you so much – and means to owe you more?'

The Prince stared a moment longer, and then burst into wild laughter. 'English Lady, you are very clever! You have the wisdom of more than your years! For your sake I will listen to your request, and consider whether I may be able to help you.'

He turned his attention then to Feodor, who gave the history of the loss of Natasha as concisely as possible. Akim Shan asked one or two questions, and then sank into a thoughtful silence, which went on so long they all began to feel restless and nervous again. At last he roused himself and said, 'I tell you at once, I do not know where the child is.' Sergei drew a breath of mingled disappointment and anger, but the Prince went on almost without a pause, 'Yet I have ways of finding out what I wish to know. If the knowledge exists, I shall obtain it. By this hour tomorrow, I shall have information for you.'

'We are most immeasurably grateful,' Feodor began, and the Prince cut him short.

'It may not be the information you desire.'

'Nevertheless, we are grateful,' Feodor insisted. 'To know is better than not to know.

The Prince bared his teeth. 'You may have cause to change that opinion. But I do not perform this task for your gratitude, but for the sake of the English Lady who is in my debt, and wishes to be more so.' He turned the grin on Anne, and she felt a sinking sensation as she wondered what was going to be asked of her. She had been prepared to give up Quassy – but what if she herself were the price? He had wanted to marry her – what if he insisted on that in exchange for the information about Nasha? Could she bear it? She knew she could not – and yet if that were the only way . . .

She forced herself to meet his eyes, though her flesh felt as though it were shrinking on her bones in the effort to be further from him. Something was about to be asked of her. Out of the corner of her eye she saw the stirring amongst the men as they, too, wondered what the Prince was going to say; and in the Prince's eyes, she read his perfect knowledge of everything that was happening, and his enjoyment of it.

'The price, English Lady – do you not wish to know the price?'

Through the pounding of her own blood in her ears, Anne heard Sergei growl; she heard herself ask faintly, 'The price, sir?'

'The price for my services,' the Prince said, with patient enjoyment. 'Everything has its price. So life must have taught you, English Lady. Yes, I see it in your eyes – your eyes which do not flinch to look into mine.'

They did, but she controlled them as best she could. 'Well, then, sir – the price. What is it?'

His smile became infinitesimally more gentle, and yet it was not reassuring. It was the tenderness with which a great cat licks the piece of meat it is about to devour.

'The price,' he said slowly, 'is that you remain here until tomorrow as my guests – all of you.' Anne stared, feeling as though she had braced herself against something which had suddenly given way. 'I shall entertain you, and give you a dinner such as you have never eaten before and will never eat again, and you shall be ever deeper in my debt. And tomorrow morning, I will have the information for you. Is it agreed?'

Anne had no idea what she was going to say until she heard her own voice. 'Unfortunately, sir, because of the urgency of our quest, I did not bring a waiting woman with me. It would not be proper for me to remain under your roof, unattended by any female.'

She saw Dmitri staring at her as though she had run mad. She rather thought she had run mad; but the Prince seemed delighted with the inconsequence of her answer, enchanted by its incongruity.

'It is no matter,' he said, and the gentleness was real now. 'I shall appoint a woman of my own people to wait on you. You are my honoured guest. No harm shall come to you.'

Anne could only bow her consent, momentarily exhausted by the tension of the last few minutes.

The Prince gave a rapid string of orders to the waiting servants, who scattered to obey them with a speed which spoke of either great devotion or great fear.

'And now, you shall come and see the tiger,' he said, rising gracefully to his feet, and holding out a hand to raise Anne. When she was on her feet, he bent over her conspiratorially, and she smelt the feral sweetness of his breath. 'The interesting thing about the tiger is that if you fear it, it will tear out your throat; but if you do not fear, it will not harm you.' He smiled beguilingly. 'But of course you must be *genuinely* without fear. The tiger will always know the difference.'

'Always, sir?' Anne said faintly.

'Always. But you may comfort yourself with the thought that if it does kill you, it is a swift and noble death.' Anne walked with him, beyond fear, beyond even surprise now. 'The tiger's death, and not the jackal's,' the Prince said reflectively, leading her to the door. 'Perhaps, at last, that is the best any of us can wish for.'

Chapter Eighteen

Anne drifted upwards towards wakefulness, her thoughts hazy and confused. Where was she? Something had happened. Had she been ill? Half asleep, she thought she was in the sick-room at Miss Oliver's school. She had been there once, when she had influenza: a small room under the roof, with a hard and narrow bed, and a skylight through which you could see the clouds passing, and the shadows of birds. It had a dusty, unused smell, the smell of dry attics everywhere.

She drifted away again. The influenza had left her tired, weak and confused. She was too hot. The blanket was rough, and prickled her skin wherever it touched. Later the doctor would come and give her a draught, dark and foul-tasting, like thin tar. She didn't want to take it. He hung over her, menacing, his aquiline nose coming closer to her face . . . and closer . . . his teeth were white and sharp, his eyes yellow, a beast's eyes with slit pupils . . .

She woke with a start, opening her eyes to stare at the beams of the vaulted wooden ceiling in utter confusion, not knowing where she was, who she was, what had happened. For a moment she panicked, straining her head up from the pillow, staring at the wooden walls around her, her mind empty of the usual comfortable certainties of time and space, trying to make sense of what she saw.

Then knowledge seeped slowly back. She remembered. She was in the Prince's house, in the mountains, in the Caucasus, in Russia. Last night there had been a feast and dancing, and she had gone late to bed – to this unexpectedly hard bed with the coarse, striped blanket which had rubbed a sore place on her neck.

She lay looking at the roof and reflecting. It was utterly fantastic, of course. Five years ago – only five – she had been a governess in a house in Margaret Street; she had never been outside England; she had never even seen the sea. Her life had been ordered and monotonous, safe, filled with the familiar and trivial, with small vexations and small pleasures. A new book from the circulating library in Wigmore Street had been something to look forward to; mending stockings had been a chore to be put off.

She thought of last night, of the banquet in the smoky, dark hall: the air had been hard to breathe, with a mixture of incense and torch smoke, and the reek of charred meat and the Prince's civet-sweet perfume, and another pungent, almost herbal smell from the aromatic leaf which the Prince and his male guests smoked, which was not tobacco, and which, even breathed in second-hand, made Anne feel dizzy.

She thought of the strange things she had eaten and drunk. Most of the time she had no idea what she was putting into her mouth, and perhaps it was just as well. A seemingly endless procession of dishes had come from the kitchens, each borne by a servant to the Prince, who sniffed, tasted, and then with his own hands served a small amount into a bowl which he gave to Anne.

Many were spicy, all strange, some unpleasant. Sometimes she asked what it was, and sometimes she was told. A charred, strong meat was wild boar, the spiky flavouring of it rosemary; thin flexible strips with little taste at all was octopus; small joints full of bones were some kind of rabbit. At one point there was a chunk of lamb, moist and delicious, flavoured with coriander leaves. A soup with a grainy texture was presumably made with lentils; a dark stew might have been anything, and Anne did not recognise the name of the spice the Prince mentioned. There were some things that might have been oysters but weren't, and which she tried to swallow without thinking, because she was told they were a great speciality, and always given to the honoured guest. There were sweet things, too – cakes running with thin honey, sweet curds with nuts, sticky white gritty balls a little like marzipan – too many sweet things. Then more meats, and fish, and fowl. And more sweets. The feast went on until Anne had exhausted all capacity for surprise, and any desire ever to eat again.

While they ate there was entertainment, music and dancing. Some of the music was pleasant and familiar, the sort of thing she had grown used to since coming to Russia: country music, sweet and plaintive, or fast and jolly. But some seemed monotonous and hard to listen to, played on strange instruments with a penetrating, jangling sound which got into her head and hurt. The dancing was easy to watch, but made her feel dizzy, though that might have been something to do with the smoke in the air, and the quantities of wine she had been obliged to drink. Though she was tormented with thirst, it was beyond her even to contemplate lemonade or water in such fantastic surroundings. At the end of the feast, great bowls of fruit were brought in, and Anne fell on them with the first eagerness she had felt for hours, and quenched her thirst on figs and kumquats.

And even then they were not done. The servants brought in a small brazier, a brass pot with a long neck, and some other equipment, and proceeded to make coffee, which was served to the guests in cups so small and so fragile they were like the blown shells of robin's eggs. With the coffee they were served spirits – kumiss, made from fermented mare's milk, and kummel, flavoured with carraway seeds, and a variety of thick, sticky liquors made from fruit – and more sweetmeats. And there was more entertainment – music of the eastern sort, and singing, tuneless to western ears and wearisome.

Anne picked through her confused, whirling, multicoloured memories. Running through them all, the constant thread, was the Prince, the smell and sound of him, his presence, impossible to ignore, his character, impossible to understand. They talked all evening, and Anne felt exhausted at the very memory of it. It was like conversing with a lunatic: no ease, no surety, no knowing from moment to moment what he would say or how he could react, which words would spell life and which death. His Russian was difficult and idiosyncratic, and sometimes he used dialect words she didn't know, and there was no-one nearby to translate for her, or advise her.

The Prince; and the tiger. If the Prince was the thread running through the cloth, then the tiger was the jewel in the centre. Sifting back through the day, before the feast, she came to the moment when he had led her away after that first interview to see the tiger. She hadn't really believed in it, and her scepticism lasted right up until the moment she first saw it. The Prince took her to a small room at one end of the house, bare of decoration, with one small window high up, through which the only light came. It was empty except for the cage containing the tiger.

She had never seen one before, except for a drawing in a book, and that was no preparation for the reality. To begin with, a picture gave no idea of the sheer size of it. She had been supposing a large creature, the size of a big dog, perhaps; but the tiger was huge. If it had stood upright like a man, it would have been as tall as a man, but much, much more massive.

Then there was its beauty: the strong, fantastic markings, the wide, delicate, wild face, the luminous green-gold eyes. Round its neck it wore a collar of strong gold, studded with the fabulous emeralds, and their colour might have been just that instant created by God to complement the fawns and golds and browns of its coat: they glimmered amongst the deep fur as the beast padded back and forth in its cage, twitching the black tip of its striped tail at every turn.

The air was thick with the prickly, caged-animal smell Anne

had caught before, which hung about the Prince, and which she had thought was – which might still be – his own smell. The musky smell of the tiger's body, the rank carnivorous reek of its breath, the power and danger of it: there was death in those paws and those teeth, the knowledge of power in the unwinking eyes. The Prince stood and stared at the tiger reflectively, and the tiger stared back balefully, hating its captivity, hating its captor. Anne could not believe that it would feed from his hand, and said so.

'But all things have their price,' the Prince said, and he sounded sad that it should be so. 'She is my captive, and I feed her. So she must eat at my pleasure and according to my whim. Yet every time I go into the cage, I know that she has never surrendered, and that this time she may rise up and strike me down. I am unarmed, and she has her nails and her teeth. My flesh would rend easily. She knows it, and I know it.'

'Then why do you do it?' Anne asked, surprised, and a little disgusted.

He didn't answer for a long time, continuing to gaze into the tiger's eyes, almost as if in a dream. 'I am a prince from a long line of princes. I have ridden to war since I was eight years old. I have killed thousands of men: hundreds with my own hands. I kill them, and then I have their women, and burn their villages, and take their children to be my serfs. Men go in fear of me. Servants bow to my every caprice. I can have whatever I want. I have only to speak the word, and whatever I wish done will be done, whatever I wish to possess will be brought to me.'

He said these things not precisely with pride, but with satisfaction, which made Anne think what a barbarian he was. And then he put out his hand and moved it through the air, as though he were caressing the tiger's head; a small movement, repeated over and over.

'But her I can never possess. Yes, I know what you will say – that I do possess her, that I have her in a cage from which she can never escape; from which she *will* never escape until her dying day. And yet she is not mine. That part inside her, which animals have instead of a soul, is hers, and does not yield to me. And every day I go into her cage and feed her from my hand with the knowledge that this time she may kill me. She is free inside herself, and proud, and unconquerable. That is why I love her and respect her as I have never done any human being.'

Anne stared at him, appalled. 'If you love and respect her, why don't you let her go? For pity's sake –'

'Pity? There is no pity in her – she does not wish pity from me. No, she will never be allowed to go free. If she kills me, I have left orders that she is to be destroyed instantly. If I die naturally, or in battle, the same will be the case. She will die in that cage. But that is the price, and all things have a price. If she were not caged, where would be the merit in her pride? Anything that walks free can be proud; and anything that is caged can submit.'

Anne clenched her fists in frustration at his twisted reasoning. 'But it's monstrous! How can you talk of merit? Such a test can mean nothing to her. She didn't ask to be captured.'

He merely shrugged. 'Did we ask to be born?' He made the caressing movement again, and the tiger lifted her lips a little over her teeth. 'We are all captives. She is mine, but I am hers – I cannot let her go, and it breaks my heart.'

Then abruptly his mood seemed to change. His expression hardened, and he took Anne's arm and turned her towards the door. 'You must go. I wish to be alone with her. Go through the door, and the servant will conduct you to your friends.'

Anne left, deeply distressed, and yet not knowing precisely why, or for whom. Even as the servant conducted her back to the others, she wondered whether this might be the day when the tiger finally struck back. Perhaps the Prince would never emerge from that room again. It was monstrous that he should have left orders for the tiger to be killed on his death – poor, pitiful caged thing. It would serve him right if he were killed. But of course she must hope he wouldn't be, or where were their chances of finding Natasha? When she rejoined the others, they looked at her pallor and evident distress, and clustered round her, demanding to know what that devil had done to her.

But 'Nothing, nothing,' she said. She could not explain to them; she could hardly have explained to herself. 'I didn't like to see the poor creature in a cage, that's all.'

She returned from her memories of the tiger to the present. It was necessary to get up, and find where she was, and where the others were. At the feast, the rest of the Kiriakov party had been like distant figures in a fever dream, moving on the edge of vision, eating, drinking, lolling on cushions and watching the dancing just as she was, and yet as separate from her as if they were in another universe – parallel perhaps, but not touching. She had no memory of how the evening had ended, or indeed of how she had finally got to bed. At what point had she parted from the Prince, from the rest of the company? And where, indeed, were they?

There had been a woman at some stage, helping her to undress – an old woman in a black robe, who smelt; presumably a servant told to take care of her. Perhaps if she shouted, someone would come. Anne sat up, and a pain which had been lying loose in her head jolted into place and made her close her eyes in momentary agony. Too much wine, and too little air, she thought. She ran her tongue across her teeth, and it was hard to tell which was the more furry.

She groaned; and almost immediately the old woman appeared beside her bed, said something incomprehensible, bared her gums and cackled. The shrill sound hurt her head, and Anne groaned again, and the old woman nodded and touched her own forehead and said something in which the word 'kumiss' was distinguishable.

'I'm sure you find it very amusing,' Anne said distantly, 'but I must get up.'

The old woman bustled away, disappearing behind a coarse, striped blanket hung on the wall, which Anne realised now must conceal the doorway. She pushed back the bedclothes and swung her legs over the side of the bed. Her pulse seemed to be beating in different rhythms all over her body, a most unpleasant sensation. Now the old woman reappeared carrying a jug in one hand, and a cup in the other. She put down the jug and proferred the cup, and Anne took it suspiciously, but it proved to contain only strong, hot coffee, which she sipped gratefully.

The old woman nodded, and took the jug over to a chest in the corner, where she set it down beside a large earthenware bowl. Then she began moving about the room, tidying things, talking all the while, though her dialect was so strange and her accent so strong, Anne could understand only the occasional word of what she said. The coffee finished, Anne got up and washed herself, drying herself on the cloth the old woman held out. The sanitary arrangements, as she had anticipated, were of the most primitive sort, and to her distress, she found that the old woman expected to remain present while she used them. Through sheer vehemence, Anne managed to make herself understood, but had to resort to stamping her foot and making threatening gestures before her attendant would even go to the other end of the room and turn her back. She evidently found Anne's modesty highly diverting, and stood with hands on hips, cackling and shaking her head in amused disbelief, looking back over her shoulder from time to time for the sole purpose, it seemed, of refuelling her mirth.

When it came to dressing, Anne refused assistance with a firm gesture which produced only a resigned shrug, though the old woman insisted on handing her each garment, running her fingers appreciatively over the fabric and making what were evidently admiring comments. The clothes smelled of smoke and food, and it was disagreeable putting them on for the third day running. The realisation that it was the third day dispelled the last of the night's confusion and restored a sobered sense of reality: so much time had been wasted already in the search for Natasha. Anne brushed her hair quickly and twisted it up behind as neatly as possible, and then turned to the old woman.

'I must go to my friends at once. Will you take me to them?' she said clearly. The old woman grinned again and nodded, evidently not understanding. Anne pointed to the door, to the old woman, and to herself, and this seemed to work. The old woman beckoned with a bony finger, and led the way out of the room, chattering all the time, but in an undertone, as if to herself. Anne followed her through a labyrinth of stone corridors, until she stopped at a doorway and stepped aside, gesturing Anne to go through. Anne did so, and found herself in the banqueting hall of the previous night. It was quite empty; and when she turned to ask the old woman where her friends were, she found she had gone.

There followed a long and anxious wait. She expected someone to come from moment to moment, and moment by moment her anxieties grew. Did anyone know she was here? She imagined the others assembled in some other place, waiting for her as she was waiting for them, the precious hours ticking away uselessly. She had no idea of the time. She possessed no watch, and in this shadowy place with the small, high windows, there was no way to judge the time of day. The thickness of the walls also prevented any sound from penetrating: it was so quiet, she might have been alone in the world.

She considered going in search of someone, but was afraid of losing her way, or of leaving the room a moment before everyone else arrived in it. They might look for each other fruitlessly all over the house. Better, surely, that she stay put; yet they were wasting time! Why didn't someone come? Had the old woman told anyone she was here?

Her thoughts had time to tread the same circle many times. She had time to worry about everything: her safety, that of the others – was she a prisoner? would they be allowed to leave? The horses – would Quassy be returned to her? About Natasha, in self-defence, she would not think. Hope would be too painful until there were cause; despair too easy, too debilitating. The headache she had woken with had not gone away, and she was very thirsty too: the cup of coffee the old woman had given her had gone nowhere towards slaking the throbbing desert inside her.

And then at last, after she had despaired several times of ever being rescued, there was a sound of footsteps, and voices which quickly resolved themselves into familiarity. The men, led by Sergei, came into the room by the far door, and she turned to greet them with enormous relief.

Sergei ran to her and took her hands.

'Anna! Are you all right? I was so afraid we wouldn't see you again! We've been waiting for ages in a sort of ante-room, and no-one came, and we didn't know where they'd taken you.'

The others crowded round, and there was a moment of confused explanation and useless questioning. In the midst of it, Anne felt a chill sensation which made the hair rise on the back of her neck, and turning abruptly, she saw that the Prince had come in by the door at the back of the dais, and was standing watching them with a smile of dark amusement. Following the direction of her eyes, the others fell silent. The Prince advanced a few steps, and his eyes gathered their attention.

'Good morning, my guests. I trust you slept well,' he said neutrally.

Feodor spoke for them. 'Sir, we are grateful for your hospitality, but the day is already far advanced, and we have been waiting since sunrise for the news you promised us.'

The Prince's brows drew together a little. 'You are impatient,' he said.

Sergei growled, but Feodor restrained him with a glance, and managed to say calmly, 'Understandably so, I hope, sir. It is a matter of the gravest importance to us. Have you news for us? We should be grateful to hear it without delay.'

The Prince was silent a moment, almost as if he were debating whether to answer or not. Anne watched him with doubt and apprehension. In the gathering strangeness of last evening, she had become used enough to him to accept him almost as normal; now in the light of a new day, he seemed more darkly alien than ever – incalculable and unapproachable.

'Yes,' he said at last, 'I have news for you.'

Feodor looked at him with mingled hope and apprehension.

'You know where she is? You know where Natasha is?'

'I know where she is,' the Prince said indifferently. 'At least,' he corrected himself, 'I know where she was two days ago. It is a place called Kourayashour, about forty versts from here to the southeast, high in the mountains.'

Anne thought briefly of Irina's 'vision' – a high place, she had said, and cold. The Prince went on.

'My people made enquiries, as I promised, and one of them found a tribesman who had heard of the child being in that place. He knows it well – he trades with the people of that region. He agrees to take you there. He waits outside.'

The inflection of his voice plainly indicated that he had finished, that this was all the information he wished, or was able, to give them; but the Kiriakovs looked at each other a little helplessly, unable to absorb the implications so rapidly.

'But has he seen her? Is she safe? What sort of a place is it?' Feodor asked.

'It is a village of the Chechen people,' the Prince answered a little impatiently, as if that question alone were worth answering.

'But how did she get there? Have they captured her? Is she their prisoner?' Feodor persisted.

The Prince made a small, brushing-away gesture with his hand. 'I have kept my part of the bargain, and more,' he said. 'I promised you information – I provide you also with a guide. I can tell you nothing more.'

'But – '

'Consider this – that nothing moves in my village or in the mountains around it without my permission. If she is in Kourayashour, it must be by the will of the chief man of those people. Now go – you waste time.' He began to turn away, clearly indicating that he had finished with them.

Feodor bowed. 'We are truly grateful for what you have done, Akim Shan Kalmuck. The Kiriakovs of Chastnaya are in your debt. We will go now with all speed. I hope to God the child is still alive.'

The Prince paused at those words, his teeth bared in what was not quite a smile. 'I think you do not perfectly understand. The people of Kourayshour are Chechen. I myself am a Christian, and a most civilised man, as you have seen. But the Chechen belong to the Prophet, whose name be honoured! Such people have no respect for women. The women of their own faith they regard merely as – *useful*. But other women, women not of the Faith . . . '

He shrugged, and it was an unlovely thing to see. His eye was quite expressionless, and Anne felt a cold chill settle in her stomach. 'You hope that she is alive,' he concluded, 'but if the Chechen have her, you had far better hope that she died quickly.'

A servant led them through the passages and out into the hot sunshine of the courtyard before the house, where their men and the horses and the guide all awaited them. The guide said that his name was Kizka. He was a short, broad-faced, yellow-skinned man with straight black hair and

310

a drooping black moustache, and he sat astride a strong, thick-coated, mouse-grey mountain pony with the patience of a rock. Feodor and Sergei engaged him in a brief conversation, and then gathered round the others to discuss their plans.

'Anne must go home,' Dmitri said at once. 'That is plain. And you too, Feodor. The estate needs you.'

'You also,' Grishka pointed out. 'You are a married man with children – the risk is too great. This is a mission for unmarried men. Seryosha and I will take the men and go to this place, while you and Feodor escort Anna Petrovna back to Chastnaya.'

Sergei interrupted impatiently. 'None of you has listened to a word that has been spoken! Don't you understand how dangerous this is likely to be? If the Chechen have kidnapped Nasha, they will not tamely let her go because her uncles come and ask politely for her! They are fighting men, bandits; they live by war and pillage.'

His bright eye swept over them; his cheeks were flushed with the prospect of action. 'You, all of you – and the men – are to go back to Chastnaya. I shall go with this Kizka to the village – but not alone, I promise you! First we will go back to Vladikavkaz, and I will use my authority to call out a platoon of the Guards. Armed and trained soldiers will be a match for these tribesmen. I wish to God I could call out the Independents, but there isn't the time to spare to ride to Grozny and back. We've wasted enough time as it is.'

Grishka began to argue, but Sergei cut him short. 'I have the best right to decide. She is my sister, and I am my father's representative while he is away. For God's sake, don't waste any more time. See that Anna is safe. I will send word as soon as I can.'

Seeing some of them still not convinced, Anne intervened. 'He's right – it's the best way. Go, Seryosha. Don't worry about us. Do what ever you have to.'

He gave her one burning, grateful look, nodded briefly to the others, and then swung himself into the saddle, and with the tribesman beside him, clattered away towards the path down the hillside.

The others watched him go, aware that however much danger he might be called upon to face, he still had the easier part. For them, there remained only the ride home to Chastnaya, and the wait for news. They watched until the two figures were out of sight and then prepared to take their leave. A serf brought Quassy out for Anne, and the mare whickered eagerly, looking bright-eyed and well rested. Someone had groomed her very thoroughly, even to the extent of crimping her mane into handsome parallel waves.

Anne felt a sudden surge of gratitude and warmth towards the Prince, who had been kind to them, entertained them, helped them, without any need to do so. He might so easily have behaved otherwise – at best, merely refused to listen to them, at worst had them put to death, without anyone being the wiser. As she settled herself in the saddle for the long ride back to Chastnaya, she looked towards the house, wondering whether he were watching, wishing there were some way for her to show him her gratitude. Her feelings about him were very confused: in her mind he was ineradicably tangled with the image of the tiger – a barely contained savagery, with only the appearance of being civilised.

Now that he had something to do at last, some proper action to perform, Sergei was full of restless energy. Every delay frustrated him, and no-one and nothing could possibly have moved quickly enough to satisfy his desire to get on.

On the way down to Vladikavkaz he questioned Kizka closely, and came up against the maddening propensity, of which he had heard, of tribesmen lying to Russians, even when the truth would serve them better. 'To lie like a tribesman' was a common adage amongst the Independents; and it was not an indication of general untruthfulness – to each other, he believed, they were as true as any people – but rather an unwillingness to give anything away to the hated invaders. When the Russian masters asked a question, they were requesting a commodity which they did not propose to pay for; it was the natural, the obvious thing to do, to deny them what they wanted.

Kizka, he discovered, was a half-bred Nogay, and something of an outsider, belonging to no clan, making his living by trading amongst the tribesmen of the hills, who tolerated him because of his usefulness. He spoke in a strange patois which was a mingling of many different dialects; and though he said a great deal in answer to Sergei's many questions, what exactly he knew about Natasha remained maddeningly vague.

Through a mass of evasions and contradictions, Sergei elicited the information that Kizka had been at Kourayashour some days ago – Sergei could not determine exactly when, and gained the impression that Kizka's notions of time were no more definite than they needed to be. A mountain peddler, wandering his own way and answerable to no-one, would probably count time in generous measure, by the month and the season, rather than the hour and the day.

However, at Kourayashour he had been, and there had heard talk of the golden-haired child who had come to the village with an armed party returning from a raiding expedition on the Valley of the Horses. Sergei puzzled a little over this, for though he questioned Kizka closely, he could not get him to define 'with' any more precisely. Was it in the company of, or as a prisoner of the raiding party? Kizka only nodded. With the raiding party, he reaffirmed unhelpfully.

Had Kizka seen the golden-haired child himself?

'No – only heard speak of her. She had already gone to the Holy Place, high up in the sky.

Those words chilled Sergei's blood, for he took them to mean that Natasha was dead; but as he pressed Kizka further, there seemed some doubt about it. The Holy Place – was it of this earth? Both of this earth, Kizka said wisely, and not of it – as all Holy Places were. He had never been there himself, but he understood it to be a place of great power, where the sky was very thin.

A dangerous place, then?

Assuredly a dangerous place. Kizka suggested all Holy Places were dangerous; and then affirmed that there could be nowhere safer for one of the Faithful, than in the shadow of the Prophet's beard.

Sergei struggled with the notion. Was the child still there, then?

Kizka shrugged and would not commit himself further.

The Governor of Vladikavkaz made no difficulties about Sergei's request. Though he outranked Sergei himself, he knew that the Count Kirov was a senior member of the Diplomatic Service, and a prominent courtier, a favourite of the Emperor, and at present fulfilling a mission for which he had been personally chosen by the Little Father himself. That the Count's daughter should have been kidnapped and was at present in Chechen hands was a horrible thing to contemplate, but not nearly so horrible as the thought of what would happen to the Governor's career, if it ever emerged that he had done less than his utmost to help the Count's son to recover her.

Within two hours of Sergei's arrival in Vladikavkaz, he was on his way again, this time accompanied by a troop of regular Cossacks under their own lieutenant, with instructions to accept Sergei's orders without question. The two hours had been twice too long for Sergei, but he was aware that he was lucky not to have been delayed longer, for the Governor thought it would be much more sensible for him to dine and stay the night at his house, and set off on the morrow for what was – his eye plainly said, though he didn't speak the words – after all, a hopeless mission.

Feeling much happier with a disciplined force of armed men at his back, Sergei rode beside his guide up the road into the mountains. Kizka eyed the Cossacks a little nervously, aware that most of them hated the tribesmen of the Caucasus as a traveller hates bedbugs, and would relish the opportunity to reduce their number even by one.

'They are under my command,' Sergei told him sharply. 'Do your job, and no harm will come to you. My word on it.'

Kizka only looked unhappy, evidently doubting the word of a Russian as sincerely as he woud have expected a Russian to doubt his.

Their route led at first along the Georgian Military Highway, and the travelling was fast on the well-maintained surface. The road climbed rapidly, and soon they were far above the green of the valleys, in a land of strange and awesome peaks, spires and minarets reaching up into the clouds, like the skyline of a roughly-hewn, gigantic city. The unmistakable triangle of Mount Kazbek was on their right, and the Mountain of the Cross on their left, as the road climbed dizzily between the great peaks. Despite the bright sunshine, the air struck cool and thin so high up; and still the road climbed, up towards the Kayshaour Pass, after which it fell away again down the other side of the Caucasus backbone, into the green land of Georgia far below, and the plains which ran down to the shores of the Black Sea.

Before they reached the pass, however, Kizka halted, and pointed away up the mountain slope to his left.

'Our way lies there,' he said.

Sergei looked. 'I see no road,' he said sternly, wondering if his guide were about to lead them astray, the more easily to abandon them in a wild and rocky place. 'Do you expect us to scramble over the rocks like mountain goats?'

Kizka looked pityingly. '*There* is the path – don't you see? I will show you – follow me, but keep close. It is rough in places.'

Kizka's little tough pony made nothing of the scramble up the almost sheer mountain side, and the Cossacks drove their mounts upwards with a will, but poor Nabat was a cavalry horse, and resented the supposition that he had somehow of late grown wings. His iron-shod hooves slipped, and he scrabbled for foothold, sweating with anxiety, his ears laid back in protest. Had it not been for the round, mousey rump ahead of him, and Sergei's spurs digging suggestively into his flanks, he would have refused altogether; but after the first precipitous climb, something resembling a path appeared, a narrow way winding with the shape of the mountain, but evidently well worn.

When at last the path stopped climbing and widened out, Kizka stopped and slipped down from the saddle.

'We rest the horses here for a while,' he said.

Anxious though he was to get on, Sergei saw the sense of it, jumped down, and loosened Nabat's girth. The gelding sighed and stretched his neck gratefully, and dragged in the thin mountain air through stretched nostrils. Sergei looked around. They were almost at the top of the world. There were still peaks higher, but they were wreathed in cloud and invisible. The lower edges of the cloud blurred into mist, drifting with the light breeze, and occasional wisps of it brushed his skin with a damp chill. The Caucasus ran in a long ridge northwest to southeast, dividing Daghestan from Georgia, the Caspian plain from the Black Sea plain. From this vantage point, Sergei thought, on a clear day it ought almost to be possible to see both shores. Above them there was nothing but the blue sky, through which the sunshine fell clear and clean; stepping to a rock over the drop, Sergei looked down and saw a colony of jackdaws far below him, and the spread-fingered shape of an eagle, drifting out over the valleys on the warm air.

The horses had gained their breath, and were now nosing about in search of something to nibble, so Sergei nodded to Kizka, and ordered the remount. They rode on, climbing at first, and then beginning to descend. Time had worn the sharpness from this part of the mountain ridge, breaking it into small, subsidiary peaks. The track was clearly marked now, and here and there Sergei saw traces of previous travellers, horse dung at least several days old, and other tracks branching off downhill. Automatically he reached round to make sure his sword was loose in the sheath. A frequented path suggested lookouts, guards, danger.

Suddenly Kizka stopped.

'I go no further,' he announced firmly.

Sergei frowned at him. 'What are you talking about? You are to take us to Kourayashour.'

Kizka nodded ahead. 'This path goes nowhere else. Follow it, and you will come to the place, without fail.'

'You will come with us,' Sergei said, laying a threatening hand on his sword-hilt. Kizka's eyes followed the movement, and then flickered nervously about the horizon.

'I dare not,' he said. He dropped his reins and spread both hands in an unexpected gesture of appeal. 'Understand, master, I do business with these people. If they know I bring you here, next time they will kill me. For Akim Shan Kalmuck I bring you this far, because I am obliged to, but I must not be seen. It must not be known I am your guide.' He looked around again, his eyes showing white. 'Already perhaps I have come too far. I must go now, quickly.'

'You'll do nothing of the kind,' Sergei said, reaching out. 'You'll take us to the village as agreed.'

But Kizka was too quick for him. He turned his pony with a jab of the heel, picking up the reins as he did so, and drove it straight down the mountainside in a scurry of dislodged stones. 'Follow the path,' he called over his shoulder. Sergei gave a curse, and looking down, saw the tribesman reach a path lower down, turn onto it, and kick his pony into a trot.

'Shall I go after him, sir?' the Cossack officer asked.

'No – you'd never catch him. And what's the use? He'd only slip away again.'

'Do you think it's a trap, sir? Maybe he was leading us into an ambush.'

Sergei had already considered the likelihood. 'Anything is possible. Tell your men to be on the alert. But unless they take us by surprise, we ought to be a match for any undisciplined tribesman, even in their own country.'

He felt they were drawing near. The signs of frequentation were everywhere, dung both old and fresh, the scars of horseshoes on exposed rock, the print of bare hooves on the turf where the path crossed a stream. They had been going gradually downhill, and there was more greenery around them, moss and bushes and even the occasional stunted tree. More cover, too, and all the men were nervous and alert now, riding in absolute silence, hands ready on their rifles, eyes flicking back and forth for any sign of an ambush.

The path rounded a big, smooth outcrop of rock, and suddenly they were there. The path widened, crossed a stream, and opened out into a flat area on which had been built a corral for horses. Beyond that was the village itself, a jumble of *izby* of various sizes, built of wood, interspersed with huts made of daub and roofed with turf. Behind the village rose a cliff, on top of which they could see the silhouettes of armed lookouts. Between them and the corral was a party of mounted tribesmen, a few with rifles, others with arrows ready nocked on their short, lethal bows.

Sergei called the halt. He was not surprised to see the armed party, only surprised that they had not been challenged before, and his eye rapidly summed up their number and strength. The arrows and the guns were not pointing directly at them; that, and the fact

316

that they had been allowed to come thus far without attack, suggested an unexpected willingness to parley.

He turned to the lieutenant. 'Don't let anyone make a hostile movement until I give the command. It looks as though they don't want a fight – God knows why – and I should like to get out of this without bloodshed if we can.'

'Yes, sir. You're going to parley with them, sir?'

'Yes. Cover me. If they kill me, wipe them out.'

'Be careful, sir. They're Chechen,' the lieutenant said anxiously.

Sergei looked at his men, barely held back, like fighting dogs on a leash, and gave a grim little smile.

'And those are Cossacks,' he said.

His eye swept the waiting group of tribesmen, and picked out the man near the centre whose eye sought his. He wore a striped robe, which was edged with scarlet – usually among the Tcherkess a colour reserved for princes. There was a short hatchet as well as a long knife and a powder-horn hanging from his broad leather belt, and he carried a spear instead of a gun. His pointed cap was of leather dyed deep blue, and edged with a ring of fine, black fur – some kind of fox, Sergei thought – which seemed to ripple as the breeze stirred the long hairs. He looked young, not much older than Sergei himself, though it was hard to tell with the Tcherkess; he was dark haired and dark-skinned, with high cheekbones, and he sat very still on his pony, and very straight, head up. A young man, in the pride of his strength: evidently the war leader rather than the village elder, perhaps the chief of the clan, or the chief's son. It might make him easier to deal with, Sergei thought.

Slowly moving his hands so that they were in full view, he pressed his heels gently to Nabat's flanks, and walked forward, clear of his men. The Chechen leader let him advance five steps before he lifted his hand and held it up, palm forward, in a halting gesture. At the same moment the point of the arrow of the man next to him lifted almost lazily to the horizontal, so that it was pointing directly at Sergei's breast.

'Stop,' said the leader.

Sergei stopped.

Chapter Nineteen

There was a long, tense moment of silence. Sergei, stranded out in the open between the two armies, was aware of how perilous the moment was. All the men on both sides were poised on a knife edge of tension, and if any one allowed his excitement to overcome him, indiscriminate firing would break out, and he would be caught in it.

He sat very still, never allowing his eye to waver from that of the man with the spear. The sun was behind him; the tribesman frowned a little against it. The light breeze ruffled the fur of his cap, and lifted the fine ends of Nabat's mane. There was a sound somewhere of a crow yarking, and more distantly the chack of jackdaws, and below that the singing upland silence; the mountain air was cool and utterly without smell. Sergei waited. The tribesmen had already showed that they did not want to fight, which put him in the stronger position. Let their leader make the first move.

He did so at last by kicking his pony forward, advancing a few paces clear of the group and halting again. He held his spear like a badge of office rather than a weapon. Sergei sensed uncertainty in him, and his heart rose a little. If they had killed Natasha, or sold her south, they would surely expect retribution, and anticipate it by attacking. A desire to parley suggested a desire to trade, which in turn suggested that she was still alive and in their power.

The leader spoke at last. 'Turn around and go back,' he said in the strong, harsh accents of Chechniya. The dialect was similar to that which Sergei heard most often around Grozny, and he thanked God for it. If there were to be negotiation, it was important that they understood each other.

'I come seeking the village of Kourayashour,' Sergei said, 'and the chief man of that village.'

'I speak for Kourayashour,' said the tribesman. 'You have come to our village with armed men, but we will let you go in peace, provided you turn round and go now. Otherwise . . .' He shrugged, and let the threat suggest itself.

Sergei ignored it. 'I am Sergei Nikolayevitch Kirov, and I seek the chief man of Kourayashour. If you are he, name yourself. Otherwise, let him come forward.'

The tribesman lifted his head a little, stung by the tone. 'I am Tatvar Khoi Zaktal, and I speak for my people. Why do you come here with armed men? We are men of peace. Go now, that there may be no bloodshed.'

Sergei smiled a little. 'I have never heard that the Chechen people dislike the shedding of blood. Yet we do not come here for blood, but to take back what has been stolen. Restore it to us, and we will go in peace.'

Zaktal did not flinch. 'We have nothing that is yours,' he said. 'What is it that you seek?'

'You know what I seek,' Sergei said, his voice rising angrily. 'Bring forward the golden-haired child, restore her to me unharmed, and I will spare you and your village. Bring her to me now!'

There was a slight stir amongst the tribesmen, hardly more than the ripple of a light breeze through a barley field, but it filled Sergei with triumph. It was the right place, then! Kizka had not lied, not cheated him. He had brought them to the right place.

'I know nothing of any golden-haired child,' Zaktal declared, looking past Sergei aloofly. 'The children of my people belong to the Prophet, whose name be honoured, and they are dark-haired, as all of the Faith should be.'

'The child was here,' Sergei said, ignoring the jibe at his own fair colouring. 'Many have spoken of her. It is known all over the Caucasus that she was here.'

'Nevertheless, *I* do not know it,' Zaktal said.

Sergei was a little puzzled: it was not the best way to begin negotiations, by denying that you had the goods. His eyes flickered over the other tribesmen, trying to determine the purpose of the lie; and then he caught sight of something in the corral beyond them which made him stiffen. His blood coursed angrily through his veins, but he spoke with icy calm.

'It surprises me that you do not know. I would have thought one who spoke for his people would know everything that happens in his village. Perhaps there is someone else who knows more than Zaktal? If so, let me speak to him about the child.'

Zaktal was young enough, at all events, to be proud. His eyes narrowed and brightened, and there was another stirring amongst the field of arrows, mirrored by a stirring amongst the Cossacks behind Sergei. But before he could speak, Sergei went on.

319

'You say you know nothing about the child: yet the horse she rode is there in your corral, amongst your mountain ponies. How do you explain that?'

The Cossacks broke into a muted cheer, and Nabat waltzed restlessly sideways. Sergei checked him, and anxious that nothing should precipitate firing, raised his hand to quiet his men. The silence fell again, and Zaktal subjected Sergei to a long, thoughtful examination. Finally he said.

'By what right do you demand to know about the child?'

'I am her brother,' Sergei said simply.

The arrow that was pointing at him was lowered a little.

After a moment, Zaktal spoke. 'You and I will go apart from the rest,' he said, 'and I will speak with you.'

Zaktal wanted Sergei to leave his arms and his men behind and go into the village with him, but Sergei would not trust him quite as far as that. Eventually both men dismounted and walked to a little distance where they could not be overheard, but could be seen clearly by both sides. Zaktal seemed ill at ease, almost embarrassed, and Sergei wavered between hope and dread. This was not the behaviour of a man with a hostage to sell. He could not make sense of it.

When Zaktal finally began to speak, the story was long and rambling, and Sergei picked his way through it with difficulty. It seemed that the news of the Chastnaya horse fair had, as expected, fired some of the outlying tribes with the idea of using the occasion, with all its comings and goings, as a cover for a little horse stealing. Zaktal did not admit this in so many words, but it was obvious that the 'war party' he spoke of, which had happened to be passing along the ridge of the Valley of the Horses that day, was not there by accident, or for any innocent purpose.

'Yes, I saw you,' Sergei said, trying to cut through the evasions. 'I was riding along the other side of the valley, and I saw your men against the skyline. You were a long way out of your usual runs, surely?'

Zaktal shrugged. 'We are horsemen, travelling people. We go where necessity takes us.'

Sergei brushed that aside. 'No matter what you were doing there. Speak of the child.'

Zaktal looked embarrassed. 'We saw her — alone, unguarded. The children of the dvoriane do not customarily ride alone.'

'So you decided to kidnap her — seize here — hold her to ransom,'

Sergei said, hoping to quicken the tale. 'I beg you will tell me the truth. If she is unharmed, I will not exact revenge. I wish only for her return.'

Zaktal eyed him consideringly, and then said, 'So, I will tell you plainly. My brother saw her first, and thought to seize her, as you say. But I saw you on the other side of the valley, and so I counselled caution. Let us follow, I said, and see what comes.'

And seize her when it was safe to do so, Sergei thought angrily, but he held his tongue.

'We followed at a distance. The golden-haired one went on as though she were following a line drawn along the earth – she never hesitated, nor looked to left or right. Assuredly, she knew where she was going. When we had gone some way from the Valley of the Horses, we drew closer, and my brother said, Now is the time.' He looked sideways at Sergei, noting the tension in every line of his body. 'I tell you frankly, hiding nothing,' he said defensively. 'Soon you will see why.'

'Very well,' Sergei said grimly, 'but be quick, for my men are restless.'

The eyes slid away, and rested on the middle distance. A little frown puckered Zaktal's brows as he remembered. 'We rode up close, and the golden one heard us coming and stopped, and turned to face us. She had no fear, truly, though she was so young, and we were many, and armed. She waited for us to approach; and when we were a few horse's lengths away, I held up my hand and stopped my men. For I saw – ' He hesitated. 'I saw she was not for us.'

'What do you mean?' Sergei said impatiently.

Zaktal's frown deepened. 'I saw at once that she was in the hand of some god, and that it would be ill-luck to touch her,' he said. 'There was a shining about her. We all saw it. She did not speak to us, and when she saw that we would not come near, she turned her horse and went on. We followed, and she rode before us all the way to Kourayashour.'

Barbarian lies, Sergei thought angrily: they had seized her and brought her here, and now he was spinning this web to deceive, and to excuse himself. Yet something deep in him was uneasy. It was not the usual sort of lie; and Zaktal did not look like a tribesman lying. He looked disturbed, anxious – even afraid, but not of Sergei.

'So she is here, then? She is in this village?' Sergei demanded, going to the heart of it.

But Zaktal shook his head. 'No, she went on. She would not stay here.'

Sergei took a step nearer, in spite of the watching, hostile eyes. 'What are you talking about? My sister came to this village – you have admitted it. Where is she now? What have you done with her?'

Zaktal did not step back, or flinch. Instead he met Sergei's eyes directly, and looked back at him steadily, something so unusual amongst the Tcherkess when talking to Russians that Sergei felt a flicker of panic.

'Listen,' Zaktal said quietly, 'and I will tell you all. When the golden-haired one reached this place, she would have ridden on at once. But I called out to her, for her horse was lame, and she had not noticed it. So she stopped. The men of the village came out to meet us, but when they saw her, they drew back – they also, for they could see what she was. I asked her to come into our village and take refreshment, for in spite of all, her body was only that of a child. My brothers and the other men of the council were against it, wanting nothing to do with her, but still I asked. But she would not go with me. She asked that the horse be looked after, and went on, on foot, alone.'

'Went on?' Sergei asked desperately. 'Went on where?'

'Up the mountain,' Zaktal said simply.

Sergei remembered that Kizka had said the same thing. 'You mean she left her horse here and walked on alone? And did no-one follow her?'

The tribesman looked pitying. 'She was going to the Holy Place. None of us would go there, unless we were called. It is a place of great power.'

'And where is she now?'

He shrugged. 'She did not come back. She is still there or – or she has gone beyond.'

Sergei struggled to make sense of it. They had captured Nasha and brought her to the village, he thought, but for some reason she was no longer there. They had sold her, perhaps, or killed her and disposed of the body. Or they were holding her captive in some safer, more remote place. But why, in any of those cases, had they allowed Sergei to bring his men up here? Why hadn't they ambushed them, or picked them off on the way up the mountain, or even attacked at first sight? Was it just the superiority of numbers on Sergei's side? But to do them justice, the Chechen had never been cowards.

And this story that Zaktal was spinning: he didn't understand it. He told it with simplicity, with conviction – so much so that the dark, atavistic part of Sergei's mind wanted to believe it. But this was Natasha he was talking about, his little sister, a warm-blooded, mischievous seven-year-old, and ordinary little girl.

Still, it seemed that there was only one thing to do, only one way to find out more: he must go along with it.

'Take me there,' he said.

Zaktal's eyes widened a little. 'Take you to the Holy Place?'

'Yes, so that I may see for myself, and bring back my sister, if she is still there.'

'I cannot. I cannot go to that place.'

'Why not? Is it so far away? Where is it?'

Zaktal pointed upwards. 'Up the mountain. A cave, near the peak. I have never been there, but there is a path. Sometimes people go there, when they are called, but they do not come back. The child – your sister – went. It is the truth I tell you,' he added a little angrily, seeing the scepticism.

Sergei's eyes narrowed. 'You will come with me and show me. Either that, or I will tell my men to open fire. We outnumber you. We will kill every man in the village, and burn it to the ground. Take me to my sister, or I will give the order.'

There was a long silence. Zaktal stared at him, his mind evidently weighing the alternatives. 'Very well,' he said at last. 'I will take you. But it must be you alone, and you must go unarmed. I will show you where it is, but I will not go in with you, for that would be a blasphemy. And when you have seen for yourself, you will go away, with your men, and not return.'

Now Sergei considered. If there were another fortress higher up, a more secure one, where they were holding Natasha, all that would happen was that he would either be killed by the guards, or taken prisoner too. But what could he do? It was either that, or attack, and if he attacked, they would fight to the death, and he might never find out where she was. He felt he would have to go with the current, and trust that a course of action would become apparent.

'I agree,' he said at last, watching Zaktal closely for the tell-tale gleam of triumph in the eyes.

But Zaktal only nodded, seeming almost indifferent, as if he had made up his mind to perform some distasteful task, and wanted simply to have done with it. Sergei had the oddest feeling that he had not submitted to a threat, but decided to co-operate for entirely different, personal reasons.

'You had better tell your people, then,' he said. They walked back, and parted, each to his own side. Sergei explained to the lieutenant what he had agreed, and the lieutenant looked at him as though he were mad.

'Sir, they'll surprise you as soon as you are beyond our help, and kill you, for sure! Don't go, sir. It's madness!'

Sergei looked at him steadily. 'I don't believe this crack-brained tale any more than you do, but I don't see what else I can do. You will wait here with the men, and if I don't return, you must use your own judgement about what to do next. The thing is, the guide, Kizka, spoke about a holy place too,' Sergei added musingly. 'There may be some grain of truth in it.'

The lieutenant raised a brow. 'Oh, but there is a holy place up there, sir. It's famous amongst the tribesmen. The Lesghians call it the Cave in the Sky: it's sacred to them, though it's actually just in Chechen country. They say the sky is so thin there, you can step through into Heaven. Even some of my boys have heard of it.' He laughed, uneasily, seeing Sergei's look. 'A lot of nonsense, of course, sir, but the Tcherkess believe it all right.'

Sergei heard him with a sense of shock. He looked around, and everything seemed suddenly sharply etched, the colours bright and clean, as though he were seeing this place for the first time – or was it the last? Even the distances were clear, every detail outlined, small but distinct, as if seen through a perspective-glass.

'Wait for me here,' he said at last. 'Use your wits, and don't provoke anything unless you're sure I'm lost.'

Zaktal was waiting for him at a little distance, patient, resigned.

'I'm ready,' Sergei said.

It was a stiff climb, and Sergei's riding boots were not made for the exercise. Zaktal went on upwards lightly, only pausing from time to time to take his bearings. It was true there was a path, of sorts, but it petered out here and there, where there had been an earthslip, or there was a rock too big and hard to move. It did not seem to have been much used, and that reassured Sergei. No armed party could inhabit the higher place, and be supplied with their needs, without leaving a well-worn track behind them; if there were to be an ambush, it would be by one or two men only, and against a few he might give a good account of himself.

He climbed a little further. Unless, he suddenly thought, his spirits sinking again, there were another path going up from another direction. Well, if he was going to die, he'd take a few of them with him. He struggled on, his sense bristling.

It was getting harder to breathe, and the exertion was making him breathless. Though the air was no more than pleasantly cool in the sunshine, there was a scattering of snow here and there, and he imagined it would be very cold at night. They were climbing towards the cloud, but Sergei, his eyes on his footholds, didn't notice until he suddenly stepped into it, and it closed down around him, chill and grey, shutting out the sun, and cutting off the warmth of the day as abruptly as snuffing out a light.

Zaktal climbed on steadily, without slowing. Now there was only one way to go, and the path ran deep like a furrow between knee-high rocks, as though it had been worn away by thousands of years of devout footsteps. An old water course, perhaps, Sergei thought. The rock was smooth under his feet, and glistening-damp from the mist. His foot slipped a little; he put out a hand to save himself, and a big, irridescent green-gold beetle scurried away almost from under his fingers.

They came out at last onto level ground, and now Zaktal stopped.

'I go no further,' he said. 'The cave is straight ahead – you will not miss it. I wait here for you.'

The milky mist was all around them, opaque, shutting out everything further than a few feet away.

'You come with me,' Sergei said firmly.

'No, I cannot.'

Sergei drew out from inside his jacket the knife he had not given up with the rest of his arms. 'We live together or die together,' he said. He seized and twisted Zaktal's arm round behind him, and put the point of the knife to his neck, pricking the skin over the great vein lightly. 'Go on, now, if you wish to live. Take me to the place.'

Zaktal wriggled lightly, to test the strength of the grip, and then relaxed. He bowed his head a moment, and then sighed.

'Very well. But go quietly, and be careful what you say. This is a powerful place. It does not do to anger the spirits of such a place.'

They walked forward, and the mouth of the cave appeared suddenly out of the mist like the yawn of a monster. It was huge, as tall as a cathedral. Sergei had imagined some little, man-sized cave, and saw easily how the ignorant mountain people might be afraid of it, and weave some magical story about it. But it was only, he told himself comfortingly, a natural phenomenon, nothing to be afraid of.

Zaktal was hanging more and more heavily on his arm, though it must have hurt him, and Sergei got the odd impression that the man's body was shrinking back in spite of his mind; that he had resigned himself to going in, but that his body was refusing all on its own.

They stepped into the entrance. Beyond the grey slick of light from the cave-mouth, it was dark, and it smelled cold and utterly unused. No higher garrison this – no armed guard would jump out on him. Why, then, had the man brought him here? To abandon him? Or had Natasha really come here? He shivered.

'We should have brought a torch,' he said, and his voice sounded shockingly loud.

Zaktal made a little whimpering sound of protest, and pulled a little, desisting at once with a gasp of pain.

'Walk,' Sergei said – but he whispered this time. 'I don't wish to hurt you.'

'Let me go,' Zaktal muttered. 'Let me wait outside. This is a bad place.'

'It's a cave, like any other,' Sergei said determinedly. 'Take me to my sister.'

'I don't know where she is.'

But they walked forward into the blackness. Sergei strained his eyes forward, waiting to become accustomed to the dark; sliding his feet cautiously in case of potholes; feeling his way, almost as unwillingly as his companion. He began to feel that it was pointless to go on without a torch. Why hadn't he thought of it? He thought of going back down to the village for one, and the notion wearied him. What was he doing here? Nasha could not be here. Zaktal was wasting his time, leading him away from the scent.

But now the darkness before him was not so utterly black: there was a greyness of light somewhere ahead. He stopped, thinking he must have wandered round in a circle in the darkness. He looked over his shoulder, and saw the dim light of the cave entrance behind them. He walked forward again, and now, oddly, the sense of position the two sources of light had given him made him more reluctant to move on, made his stepping into the blackness seem even more dangerous than before.

The hair rose on his scalp at the sensation of space all around him, the cold deadness of the air, the fear that there might be something in the dark that could see better than him. No, that was not it. There was no sense of any living creature near them: if there had been – bear or bat or snake or lizard – it would have been in a strange way comforting. What was so terrible was the feeling that there was no life anywhere in the darkness, that no living thing could survive here.

The source of light grew nearer, illuminated a rock wall, massive, impossibly high, reaching up into the fluted vaults of the mountain top. The light came from behind it: the cave turned a corner, that was it. Sergei shuffled towards it, laid his hands on the vertical plane, stepped round it; and there suddenly was the light. He drew in a breath of astonished awe. It was a perfect column of sunlight falling from a gap in the roof of the cave, far, far above: extraordinary, eerie in the blackness, its sides too regular to seem natural. It was like a finger of light pointing down from Heaven.

At some point, without knowing, he had let go of Zaktal's arm, but Zaktal was beyond running away. He crept at Sergei's heels, more afraid of being left alone now than Sergei was. Closer to, they could see that it was a natural fissure in the rock which went all the way up to the top of the mountain. The peak must have been clear of the cloud they had climbed up through: high above there was a strip of heavenly blue sky, and the sunlight fell into the cave like liquid gold.

'Where the sky is so thin,' Sergei murmured, remembering, 'that you can step through into Heaven.' After all, it was nothing but a natural phenomenon, a trick of light and rock and space; but to a receptive mind, it would seem much more, in some way significant. Sergei stared, fascinated; even he felt a reluctance to go closer, as though that strange golden beam might have some supernatural power, might burn him up like paper, or transport him upwards like a whirlwind into the upper air. It looked unnatural, strange, eerie – dangerous.

The Holy Place! He tried to mock with his mind; but he didn't want to go on. He wanted to go back, and be safe.

And then Zaktal gave a little gasp and gripped his arm; and he saw Natasha. She was sitting at the edge of the band of light, looking so small in that vastness, less than a child. Her back was to the rock wall, her knees drawn up, and she was staring upwards through the fissure into the blue sky above.

Sergei's heart leapt. 'Nasha! Nashka!' he cried out.

The echo jumped and boomed and reverberated, flicking from rock to rock high up like mocking goblin voices. Zaktal whimpered, and pulled at his arm, trying to hold him back.

'Come away,' he begged. 'Come back. It's not safe.'

Sergei shook him free. 'It's her,' he said. 'It's my sister.'

'Don't touch her! It's unlucky!'

But Sergei ran forward, heedless of everything but his having found Natasha after so long, and against all hope. He flung himself down by her, hurting his knees on the hard rock, crying, 'Doushenka, it's me! Thank God I've found you!'

And he took her by the shoulders; and his words were cut off.

She was cold, as cold as the stones on which she sat. Her knees were drawn up and her arms locked around her knees, locked with a rigidity that defied his fingers. Her head was tilted back, her eyes open and fixed on that patch of blue sky far, far above, where the light came from, and her lips were curved in a smile. But she saw nothing. The first touch told Sergei that his sister was not here. She heard nothing, smiled at nothing, felt nothing.

'God,' he said. He drew back from her in horror. He looked around, looking for escape, escape from those blank, staring eyes and that terrible smile. His fists clenched. 'God. God.'

Zaktal was whispering, retreating. 'Come away. Leave her. It's not lucky. Come away.'

'God!' cried Sergei. His mind felt close to bursting. There was too much space, inside and outside, pouring through him as though he were hardly there, transparent as air; and that terrible, burning light, and the madness of that small smile, burning his brain. Get out, get out, get out.

'God!'

Natasha, said a voice somewhere. Not without Natasha. He forced himself to stoop and pick her up, and she came up all-of-a-piece, light as a starveling bird, stiff and cold with the loathsome cold of death. The madness expanded like an indrawn breath in his mind as he made himself hold on to her, and turned and stumbled away from the light, with the horrified, retreating Zaktal before him; into the darkness, blacker than before, too black, going on for ever, into the eternity of death, going on into the nothing of Hell itself. They would never get out. He held death in his arms, and it was inside him and outside him, filling him with its emptiness.

And then, thank God, there was a little grey light. With a sob of relief he went towards it, dragging his breath as though he had been running. Grey, drab light from the misty cave mouth, dank, damp, chill light, but oh! the light of sanity! He stumbled towards it; and then they were out of the cave mouth, and he felt earth under his feet, and tendrils of damp cloud on his face. He stopped and turned his face up into it, and gulped at it like a man saved from drowning.

When at last he looked unwillingly down at what he held in his arms, he saw it was only pitiful, a frail little husk of humanity. There was no horror there, only a great overmastering sorrow. Natasha, his sister, was dead. He set her down carefully on the grass, as though she could still feel, and knelt beside her. Her empty eyes were frozen open, and her lips had drawn back a little with the stiffening of death, but there was no glare, no horrible smile. She had died of cold and hunger in that remote cave to which somehow she had been brought, or wandered; small and alone and lost, she had died.

Zaktal stood near. Sergei looked up and met his eyes. 'I am sorry for your grief,' the tribesman said with dignity, 'but it was between her and God. She was called, and she went. We did not harm her. I knew when I saw her that she had been called, and I suffered no-one to touch her. This I swear, by all that is holy.'

Sergei tried to speak, but nothing emerged but a shapeless sob.

He brought Natasha's body home from Vladikavkaz three days later. When the stiffness of death had passed away, the women of the Governor's house had straightened her limbs and washed her, and made a decent robe for her from one of the Governor's wife's nightgowns. A coffin had been hastily fashioned for her, and they laid her in it. Sergei hired a cart, and drove it himself, and the Governor authorised an armed guard to ride with him, to see him safe home to Chastnaya. He offered also to start a message on its way to the Count by official courier, and Sergei accepted the offer bleakly.

Torn with anxiety, the family had waited, hardly daring to think that Natasha would be found alive after all that time, yet unable to believe that she would not be. The first sign of that melancholy procession told all, spelled the death of hope. That common little *telega*, drawn by a gaunt, bewhiskered dray horse, with the weary Nabat nodding behind; the plain wooden coffin in the back; Sergei on the box, the reins slack in his hands, his shoulders bowed as though with great age; these were sights no mother ought to witness. Irina and Anne came out on the verandah as the cart drew near. Irina's eyes widened; she stood as though she had been turned to stone, and only one small sound escaped her, but it was a sound Anne could never forget, a cry of unbearable pain, of something wounded to death. The horse halted of its own accord; Sergei managed to remember to put on the brake; and then he simply sat, his head bowed, his hands in his lap, unable to do more, unwilling to meet anyone's eye.

Others took over, others less intimately involved with the anguish. Death had its dues and its rituals, which must be observed, and Anne perceived dimly through her grief how they were a comfort. Perhaps the worst thing about death, she thought, was its passivity. There was nothing to do about it, nothing to distract the mind from it: the rituals gave the bereaved some action to perform, to fill the vast empty spaces of time.

A new coffin was made, lovingly, with their own hands, by Mishka and Grishka. Nyanka and Tanya made a new robe of white silk, rocking and weeping over it: Tanya with the easy, healing tears of youth; Nyanka, grey-faced and red-eyed, with sobs that tore her painfully. With her own shaking hands, the old woman dressed her nursling and lifted her into the coffin. 'There's so little of her!' she cried out in pity. 'She weighs no more than a dead leaf.'

The coffin was placed on a trestle in the best parlour, draped with a white pall, turned back to show the face, and the hands crossed high on the breast over an icon of St Catharine, her birth saint. Candles burned at the four corners, and more were set all round the room, so that their blaze almost challenged the daylight. Juniper sprays were spread about the floor; the chanter sat in the corner, reading psalms, while members of the family prayed, and neighbours came in to pay their respects. The village priest came in every hour to say the *panihida*, the prayers for the dead, and prudently made great play with his censer: despite the juniper and the candles, it was noticeable that the body had been dead four or five days.

As soon as darkness fell, the bells began to toll monotonously, and the funeral took place. Anne did not consider for a moment absenting herself, knowing Irina needed her. Irina was as inert as a china doll. Anne helped Marie to dress her, and then drew her arm through her own and led her like a blind woman to take her place in the procession.

The flaming torches turned the dusk to darkness, stretching like a bright snake all the way from the house to the church, as the servants lined the route, ready to fall in behind as the coffin passed. Dmitri, Danil, Mishka and Grishka carried the coffin; Feodor walked before, bearing Irina on his arm; Sergei supported Anna, who led the bewildered Sashka by the hand; the rest of the family walked behind. It seemed a long way, between the darkness and the wavering torchlight; Anne stumbled a little on the uneven ground, and Sergei bore her up. She kept thinking of Natasha's pink kid slipper. She could not associate her with the coffin; it could not be Natasha in there, not possibly.

The church was a cave full of jewels, a treasure-trove, filled with winking diamond points of light, and the glimmer of gold, and the jewel-bright colours of the icons and the priest's robes. It was filled with singing, too, and the sweet harmony of the massed voices was too beautiful to be melancholy: it bore the coffin forward as though to some joyful celebration. The altar was so weighted with candles it looked like a fire-ship; before it stood the priest in white and purple, and the attendants swinging the censers, filling the air with lilac clouds of incense which drifted across the golden candle light, and wreathed the sad, dark brow of the Byzantine Christ painted on the tall panel behind.

More and more people came in, packing the crowd ever tighter. Anne thought briefly of the churches of England: the cool, elegant spaces, the careful distance maintained between the clergy and the people, and between the people themselves; the restraint, the civilised lack of emotion. Crushed between so many bodies, Anne thought of England longingly, deplored this barbarous proximity, the heat, the smells, the lights, the childish colours.

But it was a brief rebellion. The singing worked its way past her defences, unlocked her heart, set free the tears she longed to cry. The long, dark faces of the saints, transfixed in mortal agony, looked back at her from their golden frames, telling her that they understood, that they had surmounted human sorrow, that ease was possible, that wounds could be healed. The colours were not crude, but pure and beautiful and comforting; the cloudy incense blurred the edges of pain; the bright dancing flames spoke of life and hope.

The service was long, the rites complicated, the responses unknown; but as weariness increasingly blunted her sense of reality, Anne found herself yielding more and more to the dark earth-magic of the old religion. The sounds and the rhythms sank deep into her soul like water penetrating the earth, bringing things to life that had laid dormant year after dry year, making them spring up green and living and juicy. She began to murmur responses, learning them as she went, finding they fell into place as though she had known them already, long ago, but had forgotten. Her hand of its own accord made the sign of the cross, and she felt a joy of release. She looked up at the narrow, Byzantine face of Christ, and He, too, seemed familiar; the sad smile was for her; He seemed to say *I know you: welcome home.*

Idolatry, said a warning voice in her mind; but it was a small voice, and very far away. All that was here was love: there was nothing bad or wrong. She gazed and gazed, and the candle flames wavered and blurred into each other until they became one single light, a burning golden light, at the heart of which was the dark face, itself more full of light than a hundred thousand candles, than the sun itself: a darkness that was light. *There is in God a deep but dazzling darkness . . .* I understand, she thought gladly, humbly. It was a thing to be understood not with the mind, but wordlessly, with what was older by millennia than the mind: the first part God made – primitive, blind, dumb, but turning always, instinctively, towards the light; knowing nothing, and so knowing better.

The service was over, the rites completed. The lid was screwed down on the coffin, and the congregation streamed out into the darkness. The torches massed to make a new path, round the side of the church to the little burying plot behind, fenced for decency, shaded by tall trees invisible in the darkness. The coffin was born aloft again, floated down a stream of fire on its last journey. Now they were by the graveside, an oblong hole in the solid earth, the cast-out soil heaped beside it, horribly real. Anne saw the colours of the strata, heaped in the reverse order from Nature's: the black topsoil, the greyish clay, and on top the yellow sandy subsoil. She saw in the fluctuating light the crumbled sides of the hole, with severed rootlets protruding. The incense clouds were dispersing from her mind. Oh don't let the magic stop now, she prayed. I don't want to see this.

But the grass was dew-cold under her feet, the night air drifted the smell of bodies and tar and smoke and the soured, turned earth across her senses. Sergei beside her was grey with fatigue, taking no nourishment from the rites of passage; beyond him was Irina, and as their eyes met, Anne saw her despair and pain as the numbness of shock wore off, and the reality of the graveside brought her, too, wide awake.

The clamour of the bells filled the air, almost drowning the priest's words. The four serfs at the ropes' ends swung the coffin over the open grave and began to lower it. It swung a little, dislodging a shower of stones and earth as it struck the side. It was all too real: a child's body in the coffin, being buried deep in the cold earth. Natasha was dead. To outlive a child seemed monstrous, an affront to nature.

The ropes went slack. The coffin was at the bottom of the hole. The priest stooped and took a handful of soil, and pressed it into Irina's hand. She looked at him, bewildered, and then at her hand, and then threw the soil into the grave with a jerky movement, as though of disgust. It struck the coffin lid with a hollow thud, a sound so like a hand knocking at a closed door that Anne's heart jumped; and at the same instant Irina cried out, and flung herself down as though she would jump into the grave. Dmitri and Sergei, to either side of her, grabbed her arms, pulled her back, and to her feet. She struggled ineffectually, like a trapped bird; she looked around from face to face. 'Give me my child!' she cried out. 'Give me back my child!' Dmitri said something; Zena and Katya came close, murmuring; but she went on crying out her useless appeal, over and over with the monotony of madness, until the last words had been said, the gravediggers reached for their shovels, and her sisters drew her away.

The serfs worked quickly, as though in a race against time, and within minutes the coffin had disappeared, and the grave was only a hole in the ground. After the first few spadefuls, most people moved quietly away; but Anne stayed to the very end, not so much from a need to pay her respects, but from not really knowing what to do next.

The following day was worse, by far the worst day since Natasha had disappeared, for now all doubts were resolved, and there was nothing left to do. The Kiriakov men went, a little apologetically, back to their work about the estate. Zena went back to her work without apology, and dragged Katya, who had been weeping on and off since she woke up, with her, and spent the rest of the day bullying her so unmercifully that she forgot her grief in a burning resentment against her heartless sister. Irina did not emerge from her room, and Nyanka had taken charge of Sashka with such an evident need to fill her empty arms that it would have been cruel to deprive her of him, which left Anne with nothing to do but think.

There was nothing she wanted to do; she suffered from the listlessness of the convalescent, the boredom of pain. It was a dry, hot day, unfeelingly bright, too hot to ride, even had she been able to bring herself to make the effort. She wandered out onto the verandah and sat in Irina's rocking chair, and rocked herself, and thought.

All her memories of Natasha were there to hand: she remembered the moment she had first seen her, when she had run in to Anne's room in her white nightshirt, her toffee-coloured curls disordered from sleep, her eyes bright with unspoken thoughts. Little Nemetzka, the strange one, seeing so much and saying so little! She remembered her at her lessons, so quick in some ways, so blankly withdrawn in others. She remembered the day at the fair when she had first spoken – a precious memory, mixed up with her feelings for the Count. Oh, God, what would he suffer when he heard the news? To have missed so much of his child's life, and to have lost her at such a distance!

But why had she been lost? That had not been at all clear from Sergei's confused narrative of the night before. He had been too exhausted, and everyone else too shocked, for a detailed exposition; and after the funeral, he had sat apart in grey silence, locked into a world of his own bitter thoughts. Anne had watched him from the corner of her eye, longing to be able to comfort him, but knowing that she could not have reached him then. He would come to her in his own time, she thought, and she would give him what comfort she could – though, God knew, that would be little enough, her own store being so depleted.

The sun slid over the zenith; other members of the family came and sat a while, and went away again, and Anne stayed, too lethargic to do anything about her discomfort. The afternoon heat softened and broadened, the shadows moved round, dogs and chickens sought shade and slept. Anne was alone again on the verandah when Sergei came out at last, and stared about him like a sleepwalker suddenly woken. She looked towards him and smiled encouragingly. He avoided her eye, as though he were embarrassed, but he came towards her all the same, and drew out a chair to place it beside hers, and sat down.

For a long time they sat side by side, not speaking or touching, staring out past the hanging flowers of the jacmanna towards the dusty shade-trees. Then at last Sergei said, 'I want to tell you what happened. I must tell someone, just once. Then I shall have done.'

'Yes,' Anne said neutrally.

'It's fantastic,' he said. His voice was weary, as though he were past all surprise. 'I hardly know what to believe. I couldn't tell it to the others, not everything.'

'You can tell me.'

'Yes, I know. I must tell you – you ought to know everything.'

Slowly, with many pauses, he told her everything that had happened since they parted at Akim Shan's house. He spoke without inflexion, as though he were reading someone else's narrative, as if he neither believed nor disbelieved. Anne listened, seeing through the eyes of his unemphatic words as if through a magic window onto past events.

She remembered the distant figure of Nasha riding purposefully along the side of the Valley of the Horses; she rememberd Marya Petrovna's words: *She dances to a music we cannot hear.* It was not difficult, at least today, and in this state of shock and emotional exhaustion, to believe that Natasha had ridden away to a Holy Place she could only know of, if she knew of it at all, by the most distant heresay.

'Do you remember, the day of the picnic?' she said at one point. 'She talked about hearing voices.' The evidence had been there, if she had only taken notice. She ought to have stopped her: she alone had all the clues. 'She asked me if a person who heard voices was mad.'

Sergei looked at her for the first time. His eyes were red-rimmed, his skin grey with weariness. 'She was talking about Kerim.'

'Yes, so she said. So I thought.'

He looked away again. 'God,' he said. 'God.' If it was an appeal, it was for oblivion. After a while, he took up the narrative again, describing the climb up the mountain, the cave, the finding of Natasha. There were tears on his cheeks when he reached that point, but he did not seem to notice them. He spoke of carrying the body out of the cave to the hillside, and of Zaktal's words to him, how he swore that no-one had harmed Natasha. Then he stopped.

Anne looked at him. His head was hanging, as if he were exhausted almost to death; his face bore the lines of a man who had seen what no man should ever see. After a moment he went on. 'I believed him, God help me; somehow, at the time, I believed him. But we burned the village anyway. I carried her down the hill to where my men were waiting, and then I gave the order. We killed everyone – every man, every woman, every child – we even killed the dogs. I killed Zaktal with my own hand. And then we burned the village.'

He looked at Anne, but not as if he saw her. 'What else could I do? If the other tribes had heard that she was dead and we had done nothing . . . ' He stopped again.

Anne was shocked beyond speech. She tried to think of something to say, but her mind baulked at the images he had conjured for her, shied away like a frightened horse.

When he spoke again, it was in a faint voice, as if to himself. 'There's nothing left there now. I suppose eventually others will come and build over it again – a place such as that. But until then, it will be her monument . . . '

His voice faded and stopped, and did not begin again. Anne gathered herself together and looked at him. He was sitting forward, his elbows on his knees, his hands dangling loosely between them. His face looked old: he looked older, just then, than his father.

Anne, who knew the truth of it – about Natasha, as about him – saw that what he had done, up there in the mountains, had violated his soul. He was a boy no longer. He himself had killed the boy he had been, and there was not yet a man to take his place: there was only this killing exhaustion. He might die, she saw, if he did not find himself again, because he had done what he could not regret, and could not live with. But she couldn't help him. It was the boy she had loved: there was nothing she could love in this old man.

Chapter Twenty

In August, the Kiriakovs, like other wealthy families of the region, usually travelled to Pyatigorsk, a town whose natural sulphur springs had made it into a spa rivalling England's Bath or Tunbridge Wells. It attracted invalids and valetudinarians from all over Russia, and as the facilities and entertainments of the town expanded to accommodate them, it became also a fashionable place for summer houses for the aristocracy. The young and the wealthy went there to dance and to flirt; and mamas took their marriageable daughters for the Pyatigorsk Season, for it was a favourite resort for officers on leave and convalescing from wounds.

The proposition was raised at Chastnaya and listlessly rejected; but Ekaterina, who had a tendency to fancy herself sickly when she was bored, wanted diversion and decided the baths would do her good. She began canvassing for support with Zinaidia.

'I know we have had all this sadness, but it doesn't seem fair to make you miss the balls at Pyatigorsk. It's different for Nadya, after all – she's already betrothed – but you ought to have your chance too. My own health is very indifferent, Zinochka dear, but I would undertake to chaperone you if dear Zina didn't care to go.'

'That's very kind of you, Aunt Katya,' Zinochka said with a frightened look, 'but I couldn't think of dancing at a time like this. I'm sure Uncle Feodor wouldn't allow me to go.'

So Ekaterina went to Feodor's wife, Galina. 'You know, Galishka, I do think in spite of everything that it would be a good idea for your poor Masha to be allowed to go to Pyatigorsk this year. After all, a girl is only young once, and if she doesn't have her Season, you'll never be able to get a good husband for her – and why should she be made to suffer for something which isn't her fault? She's such a pretty girl, she ought to have her chance.'

'I don't think Feodor will want to go at a time like this,' Galina said.

'No, perhaps not. But then, I was thinking of going myself, for the baths – I'm such a wretched invalid, you know – and if I do, I could chaperone Masha for you. She's such a good girl, it wouldn't be any trouble, I'm sure.'

'Well, I don't know,' Galina said doubtfully. 'I'll have to speak to Feodor about it.'

To Zina, Ekaterina said, 'I'm so worried about poor 'Rushka. I think her health will break down entirely if she isn't taken out of herself. It can't be good for her to stay in her room all day long, brooding. Don't you think, Zina dear, it would be a good idea if we were to persuade her to go to Pyatigorsk for a month or six weeks, to take the baths? It would be a change of scene for her, too, help her to forget. I'm sure if you suggested it, she would go – you always had great influence over her.'

Zina, who had been really worried about her sister in the weeks since Natasha's death, frowned and said, 'I don't suppose for an instant she would listen. But she could be *made* to go.'

'You could make her, Zina dear. And perhaps I ought to go too,' she added with a wistful sigh. 'My own health has suffered so these past weeks, and it would not do for me to become a burden on you. But at least,' she brightened, 'if I went, I could save you the trouble of escorting poor 'Rushka, for I'm sure you will not feel like going there at a time like this.'

As a result of these campaigns, Feodor, Galina and Zina got together, and decided that the summer house at Pyatigorsk should be opened after all. None of the younger brothers wanted to leave Chastnaya, but Dmitri insisted they could manage very well without Feodor, and that he ought to have a break from his cares, which seemed of late to be bowing his shoulders and greying his hair. So it was decided that he and Galina should go, and chaperone their own Masha, a plump merry sixteen-year-old, and Zinochka; and that Katya and Irushka should go along for the baths.

'What about Anna?' Zina said. 'She is looking pale, too. Perhaps a change of scene would do her good.'

Anne, when asked, thanked them, but declined. She had no desire for the bright lights and music of a fashionable resort. She would prefer to stay quietly at Chastnaya teaching Sashka, from whom, now she had got him back from Nyanka, she was rarely parted. And she had begun in the evenings to have regular talks with Father Gregory, the priest from the estate church, who was helping her to come to terms with her guilt over Natasha's death. He was also, she knew, trying to convert her to the Old Faith, but she didn't mind that. She was beginning to feel that the English prejudice against Idolatry was not so age-old and deep-seated, nor even necessarily so absolutely reasonable as it had once seemed to her; that God could not be entirely averse from a little magic, since He had put so much of it into His world in the making. Little by little, she was coming closer to her adopted country; but where the realisation would once have alarmed, now it pleased her.

However, when it came to it, Irina refused to go to Pyatigorsk without her. She was indeed looking very ill, and the cough which had troubled her last winter had returned. She was listless, unable to be interested in anything, sleeping a great deal, and when she was awake, lying on her bed or on a sofa staring at nothing. Anne tried to involve her with Sashka, feeling that if the boy could draw his mother back from the darkness, it would be worth losing him to her; but Irina didn't seem to be able to care about him. She tried, politely, but she looked at him like a stranger, and Sashka's lip began to tremble ominously. She had nothing to give her son. Nasha had been everything to her; she could care for nothing else, not now.

So when Zina and Feodor insisted she went to Pyatigorsk, she made little resistance, and sat and watched Marie packing for her with dull but resigned eyes. When she understood that Anne meant to stay, she suddenly roused herself and issued an ultimatum. She would go if Anna went, or stay if Anna stayed. They might take their choice.

So when the party set off from Chastnaya to travel back along the Cossack line, westwards along the River Terek, and then north-west to Pyatigorsk of the Five Hills, Anne went with them, leaving Sashka behind in Nyanka's charge. It tugged at her heart dreadfully to leave him, though it would only be for a few weeks, and though, after what had happened, there was no danger that Nyanka would let him out of her sight for a second. He waved goodbye to her bravely from the verandah as the carriage pulled away, and Anne leaned out of the window and waved back as long as his small figure was in sight.

The Kiriakovs' summer house was a pretty, modern building of white-painted wood and pink shingles, sitting in an extensive and rather overgrown pleasure ground just outside the town, on the road which led from Pyatigorsk to Karras and Mount Besh Tau. It had a large verandah – an essential feature of any house in those parts – over which clambered a riot of white and palest pink roses and white summer jasmine, whose scent filled the air all day and through the long pale twilight.

The area around Pyatigorsk had always been famous for horses, and there were well-marked bridle paths to all the best viewpoints, interesting ruins, and 'safe' villages. Expeditions on horseback to tribal villages to see displays of horsemanship and charming Tartar customs, to buy native souvenirs, and to witness the strange ceremonies of the Moslem feasts, were an integral part of the Pyatigorsk 'Season'. Anne felt she had seen as much of these things as she wanted. Fortunately, after Feodor's curt refusal of the first such invitation, the story was quickly passed around as to the circumstances of Natasha's death, and the Russian community tactfully refrained from asking again.

But there were still picnic rides, and expeditions to other places of interest, such as the famous stud farm in the foothills of Mount Mashuk, and to the great St Eusignius' Day Fair at Karras. And then, of course, there was the life of the town itself. It was evidently in a state of rapid expansion, new houses and public buildings going up along the main street, and the dachas of the rich being built at the edges of the town in their own pleasure gardens. The houses were mostly of wood, but painted bright, cheerful colours — blue and raspberry and rust-red and woodland green — and they had breath-taking views of the blue-green foothills rising up to darker mountain peaks, and in the far distance the misty silver chain of the Caucasus.

As well as the sulphur baths, on which, of course, a great deal of the town's activities centred, and the chalybeate springs, there were newly-laid-out public gardens for walking in, and an open-air theatre; and the main street was in a state of improvement, with new shops opening every month, and a raised footpath along which had been planted an avenue of spindly saplings which would one day be scented limes. There were numerous public and private balls, for the Season was now at its height; and routs, picnics, masks, dinner parties, card evenings and every other sort of occasion that the fashionable people could invent for dressing-up and getting together to gossip and flirt.

Besides the invalids and the pleasure-seekers, Pyatigorsk always had a large and fluctuating population of military personnel, for it was strategically placed on the route between Stavropol, and Tiflis in Georgia and Petrovsk on the Caspian shore. It was a cheerful town, and Anne could not help her spirits being raised, though she had anticipated little pleasure from the visit. Masha and Zinochka, after a brief struggle with sadness, flung themselves whole-heartedly into the gaiety which inevitably surrounds a large number of handsome young officers on leave, and only occasionally looked guilty when they discovered they were enjoying themselves. Feodor encouraged them. They had loved little Nashka as much as anyone could in the short time they had known her; but they were young, and life must go on.

Katya soon found a circle of matrons who were just to her taste, and when she was not subjecting herself to the malodorous baths, she was usually to be found sipping coffee or soda water with two or three women of her own age and status, and chatting luxuriously about ailments, confinements, the delightfulness of one's own children, the wickedness of servants, and the expense of everything in particular.

Irina, however, did not revive. She went dutifully to the baths every day, accompanied by one or other of the women, drank her glass of the stinking water, and immersed herself in the communal pool. Thereafter she sat on the verandah, just as she did at Chastnaya, her eyes fixed on some invisible distance, rocking and rocking herself, as if the movement were putting distance between herself and her pain. She seemed to Anne somehow to be fading, becoming transparent, as though the stuff of her were wearing thin, and time were beginning to show through here and there. She rocked and rocked, travelling every day further from them, her blue-shadowed eyes focused elsewhere, on what alone now could brighten them.

Anne tried to talk to her, to make her discuss what she felt and thought, but it was a hopeless task. Sometimes she would talk about things that had happened in her childhood – some incident which had intrigued or pleased or frightened her – but nothing more recent seemed to interest her; and even then she would sometimes stop in the middle of what she was saying, as though she simply could not care enough to go on.

Anne wished fervently that Zina, with her strong mind and determined views, were here; in lieu of her, she tried talking to Feodor, who she knew was as worried about his sister as she was.

'We must just wait until she gets over it,' he said helplessly. 'Irushka was always the strange one. She feels things differently from the rest of us. She'll work it out in her own way, I suppose.'

'I'm afraid,' Anne said hesitantly, 'that if she loses interest in life she may . . . ' She stopped. 'She's too thin. She doesn't eat enough.'

Feodor met her eyes. 'I know. I don't know what to do about it. I'll try talking to her tonight.'

He spent a long time with her on the verandah that evening, talking about their childhood together at Chastnaya. Irina seemed to be listening; sometimes she responded; and once, miraculously, she smiled when Feodor reminded her of some childhood prank of Dmitri's. But as soon as he left her, her face went blank again, and she resumed her rocking, rocking journey away from reality.

In the second week of the visit, Anne was walking one day with Zinochka in the Tsarskoye Gardens, where there was shortly to be a concert on the bandstand by the band of the Caucasian Highland Guards. The handsome young captain who conducted them had danced with Zinochka at two balls, and a promising inclination on his part deserved the encouragement of her attendance at his performance.

Galina had taken Masha to visit a mantuamaker, and Katya had gone to the baths with a friend, but Anne had been quite happy to take a turn at chaperoning Zinochka. She liked music, and felt that it was one of the few pleasures she was able to enjoy at the moment. Zinochka had been so anxious not to miss the start that they had arrived much too early, and they had been occupying the time by strolling along the formal walks, between the dazzling displays of roses, while Zinochka told Anne what a superb musician Captain Orlov was, and how gracefully he danced.

Anne was listening amusedly but with only half her attention. There was something unexpectedly familiar about a figure approaching on a path at right angles to the one they were walking along. Thin, dark, with a dark moustache which suggested the military; but his was not a military gait. Smart, city clothes; a silver-headed cane – but of course! He turned the corner, started as he saw her, and hastened towards her with outstretched hands, and a smile of welcome.

'Anna Petrovna! Oh, how good it is to see you!'

Her hands were engulfed, and she looked up into Count Tchaikovsky's face with unexpected pleasure. The spontaneous warmth of his greeting had touched a loneliness she had not been fully aware of; the thin nose and protuberant eyes did not, for once, seem either ugly or ridiculous, only comfortingly familiar.

'Basil Andreyevitch, what a surprise to see you here!'

'I heard you were in Pyatigorsk, and I was intending to call on you tomorrow. I arrived only this morning, from Georgievsk. But what a pleasant coincidence that you should choose to walk here this morning! I think Fate must be wanting to bring us together.'

She was surprised at the directness of his speech, but smiled and introduced him to Zinochka. 'We have come for the concert – which I believe is about to begin,' she added, intercepting an urgent fidget from Zinochka.

'Will you then allow me to escort you?' he asked at once. 'I have so much to tell you, so much to ask.' He offered an arm to each of them.

'What a pleasant town this! Though the smell of the sulphur baths is something one has to get used to.'

'The officers say that the sulphur in the air turns their silver epaulettes quite yellow if they are here more than a day or two,' Anne said.

They walked as briskly as Zinochka could make them along the gravel path to the centre of the park, where the pagoda-shaped bandstand was ringed with wooden chairs, and already a considerable audience was assembling. Once Basil Andreyevitch had secured them seats from which Zinochka could admire Captain Orlov's undeniably distinctive profile, he was able to claim Anne's attention and converse with her in reasonable privacy under cover of the music.

'I heard about your dreadful loss,' he said. 'The shock must have been terrible for you. To lose a child is always a tragedy – but in such a way! I wish there were some way in which I could offer you comfort.'

'Thank you,' Anne said bleakly; but his sympathy was so genuine, it did comfort a little.

'Has Kirov been informed?'

'Sergei wrote to him. We haven't yet had a reply.'

'He will come home, I imagine. The situation in Paris is surely not so grave that they will deny him compassionate leave. And Sergei Nikolayevitch – he is back with his regiment?'

'Yes, at Grozny.' Anne frowned. 'He of all people ought to have had leave. He was very shocked. Nasha was a great favourite with him, and of course, he was the one who witnessed it all at first hand. In some ways, it was worst of all for him.'

'Yes – poor young man! But at least he was able to take revenge.'

'Oh, but you don't understand – that was part of what was so shocking! Poor Seryosha – to witness, to take part in such killing . . .'

Basil Andreyevitch eyed her curiously. 'But he is a soldier; it is his trade! He would not feel about it as you do. He has not a woman's tender feelings. And besides, surely the barbarians deserved it? You would not have had them go unpunished?'

Anne avoided the question. Sergei had told the whole truth to no-one but her, and it was not her secret to impart to anyone else. She said, 'No, I suppose not. But now there is trouble along the Chechen line – some of the tribes have risen up in protest against the burning of the village, and so the Independents are called out to contain them, and all leave is cancelled.'

'Action of that sort may be the best thing for him,' Basil said wisely. 'It will leave him no time to brood. But you, Anna Petrovna – you are looking pale, and tired. I think you have been bearing the whole burden for too long.'

Anne was embarrassed. 'Nonsense – how can you say so? It is not my bereavement alone; indeed, the family is more involved than I.'

For answer he took her hand and pressed it. 'I know you,' he said. 'You have more feeling than the rest put together.'

She drew back her hand, wondering at his behaviour. She could not believe that he would flirt with her at a time like this; yet this warmth was more particular than their previous acquaintance would have led her to expect. She sought to change the subject.

'Your sister is well, I hope? Is she with you? Shall I have the pleasure of meeting her again?'

'No, Olga is at Odessa. In fact, I have just come from there. We have been there all summer, staying with my aunt. My uncle died in March.'

'Oh, I'm sorry – I didn't know.'

'No, how should you? We were in time to see him before he died, which was the important thing.'

'And what brings you to Pyatigorsk? I should have thought, from what I've heard, that Odessa would be the most pleasant place to be at this time of year. Have you come here on business?'

'You might call it that,' he said, watching her with a curious expression in his softly bulging eyes. 'In fact, I came partly to put a distance between me and Olga. She and I have been quarrelling for the last six weeks.'

Anne was surprised – the closeness of the brother and sister was legendary – but she did not feel she had any right to ask questions. Basil Andreyevitch, however, seemed to want to tell her.

'My uncle, you see, had always given us to understand that when he died, he would leave us his fortune between us. However, when the will was proved, it came out that he had left the bulk of his fortune to me, with no more than a pension to Olga and my aunt. Quite a generous pension to each of them, but it's not quite the same.'

Anne looked concerned. 'It is a pity that something like that should come between you,' she murmured.

'Oh, Olga is being perfectly unreasonable! She and my aunt have been stirring each other up, and attacking me in the most absurd way. My uncle, being childless, was entitled to leave his estate where he liked. And if he wanted to leave it to me, why shouldn't I accept it?' Anne could not answer that, of course; but Tchaikovsky evidently didn't mean her to. He was smiling at some pleasing inner landscape, and went on with a chuckle. 'The best part about it is that it makes me independent of my father! Now I may do as I please, instead of being forced to tow the line so as not to jeopardise my allowance!'

'But I hope you will be able to make it up with your sister,' Anne said.

'I don't care if I do or not – and neither should you. She's no friend of yours, Anna Petrovna – but I suppose you know that?'

Anne was upset. 'I'm sure I have never done anything willingly to offend your sister – ' she began.

'You didn't need to,' Tchaikovsky interrupted, smiling at her in a way that made her begin to blush. 'You put poor Olga's nose out of joint the first time you were ever in company with her. Mine too, I must confess. I shall never forget the way you looked at me – so coolly! – when I exercised my wit on you! I was used to Kirov laughing at me, and I thought he had corrupted you to his cynical view of the world, but of course, it was just you, Anna Petrovna, and your superior intelligence.'

'Please, Basil Andreyevitch,' Anne said, hardly knowing where to look, 'you shouldn't be talking to me like this . . . '

'Why not? Can't you bear a compliment? It's the truth, and you know it – you are superior, though it took me a while to acknowledge it. I had been used to being regarded as the leader of intellectual society, and I didn't care to be unseated! But I'm wise enough, at least, to acknowledge myself bested.' He eyed her averted profile. 'I must say, that colour becomes you, Anna Petrovna.'

'Please,' she said in confusion, 'don't say any more. I can't bear – at a time like this – '

He was instantly contrite. 'No, of course not! How thoughtless of me! I beg your pardon. I have allowed my tongue to run away with me. I'll say no more – only I beg you to remember that you have no more sincere admirer in the world, and to regard me as your friend to command. Now, don't turn your face away any longer – I shan't embarrass you again! What a jolly band this is! Did you know Orlov, the conductor, is a very fine violinist? I heard him at Princess Arsineva's in Moscow. He doesn't give public performances, so it's considerd a great coup for any hostess who can persuade him to play for her guests.'

He chatted in a light and pleasant way about music and Society in general, allowing Anne to recover her countenance, and neither said nor did anything else to embarrass her. The admiration and warmth he had expressed, combined with this evidence of tact and genuine consideration, made her like him more than she had thought possible; and when, after the concert, he asked permission to escort them home, and to be allowed to take Anne out riding the following day, she was happy to accept on both counts. She had been lonely in her grief, and it was good to have someone whose sympathy was particularly her own.

But it was more than that: she had been lonely for a long time, simply as a woman. The unfortunate incident with Sergei had been precipitated by that loneliness: he had misinterpreted it, and responded to it. The dreadful tragedy which had followed had driven any thought of courting her from his mind, of course; and Anne was confident that when they next met, he would have forgotten all about it, and would regard her again as his father's employee, his siblings' governess.

Over the next few days, Count Tchaikovsky proved himself both kind and sensitive, placing himself at Anne's disposal, escorting her, arranging diversions for her, talking amusingly to distract her from her sadness, but with such delicacy that she never felt in any way threatened by it. He did not flirt: he behaved like a friend; and though she did not understand why he should go to so much trouble on her behalf, or even, indeed, why he was here at all, she found herself eased and comforted, and was grateful to him. He was, she thought, a much better person than she had ever given him credit for.

Anne had walked into the town on an errand for Galina, and as she was returning along the dusty road, she heard a carriage coming up fast behind her, and stepped up onto the grass to be out of the way. It went past her very fast, and then to her surprise slowed and came to a jerky halt up ahead of her. She started towards it doubtfully, thinking it must be some lost traveller needing directions; but before she had gone more than a step, the door opened, a hand appeared and then a boot, and Count Kirov jumped down into the road and strode towards her through the swirling dust from the carriage wheels, his hands outstretched.

She must have run to him, though she didn't remember covering the distance between them. She had one vivid, confused glimpse of his face, white under his tan, his eyes burning with emotion, and then she was in his arms, being strained against his lean, hard body. Her own arms were round him, and such joy and relief and love fountained up in her that she could not have spoken just then, even had the force of his embrace allowed her breath enough.

It lasted only seconds. She was released, swayed a little, found her balance. She looked up at him, and saw the intense, troubled look in his eyes, the marks of grief and anxiety in his face, and realised that she was probably revealing all too much in her own expression – and in a public place! Shocked at herself, she looked down and conducted a brief, desperate struggle to control her feelings.

'Anna Petrovna,' he said hoarsely, as though the dust had got into his throat. 'It's so good to see you! I hadn't expected . . . Dear God, what you must have been suffering, all of you! I came as soon as I got the letter. I couldn't believe it. My poor little darling! My Natasha!'

Anne felt her eyes hot with tears, and tried to blink them back. She was ashamed of what she had felt, when he must be riven with grief for his child; ashamed that she had not thought first of that; ashamed that her heart had jumped when he said 'My poor little darling,' as if she could have supposed those words were meant for her.

'I'm so glad you've come,' she said, and tried to mean it only as she was allowed to mean it; but her treacherous heart kept on singing with his presence, and yearning towards him with almost a physical tug.

'Thank God they had you!' he said, and at the warmth in his voice, the tears spilled over helplessly, and one awkward, sobbing gasp escaped her control. 'Yes, yes,' he said, taking her hand – oh, the touch of him! – and leading her towards the carriage, 'I know how much you will have supported them all! I did better than I knew when I rescued you in Paris! How is she? How is Irushka?'

They were at the carriage door, and she was able to let him help her to climb up, and to settle herself on the seat before being obliged to answer. By then she was calm, the rushing, flooding, blood-hot joy of love for him shut down again; duty, propriety rolled like a boulder over the mouth of the spring to keep it from gushing forth.

'She is far from well,' she answered him as he closed the door and the carriage rolled forward again. 'She grieves terribly, but she's so withdrawn it's impossible to comfort her. I'm glad you're here. I hoped you would come. Nothing else can help her – but you will bring her back.'

She kept her eyes forward, not allowing herself to look at him again. Out of the corner of her eye, she saw him put his hands over his face, and rub it wearily.

'It's so hard to believe,' he said. 'Little Nasha! How could it happen? I can't make myself understand that she's dead, that she won't come running to me when the carriage stops, and look up at me in that way – '

He stopped abruptly, and said nothing more until they reached the house. The carried stopped, but he sat still for a moment, thinking. Then in a low voice he said, 'What in God's name can I say to her? I can't even comfort myself.'

346

Anne absented herself all day, took herself off to the remotest corner of the tangled gardens with a book she was quite unequal to reading. It was inexpressibly painful to think of them together, painful and shocking to discover how much she still felt for him, how little control she had over her mind and her feelings. She had not even been able to bring herself to witness the first reunion between them. As soon as he had handed her down from the carriage, she had hurried away round the side of the house before anyone had time to emerge from it.

When the hour for dinner approached, however, she had to go back. To stay away any longer would be to court the very attention she wanted to avoid, and lay herself open to being searched for. When she got back to the house, Galina told her that Count Tchaikovsky had been there asking for her, and she remembered belatedly that he had promised to bring a book they had been discussing. He had left the book, and a kindly message to say that he would call the next day, as he didn't suppose she would be at leisure to receive him that evening, in view of the Count's arrival.

Dinner proved not to be the ordeal she had expected, for neither the Count nor Irina emerged from their rooms for it. The mood of the assembled company was subdued, and there was little conversation over the meal, for which Anne was grateful: she didn't want to know how the Count had greeted Irina, nor she him. After dinner, Galina was obliged to chaperone Masha and Zinochka to a ball, and Katya was engaged to drink tea with a friend. Feodor sat with Anne on the verandah for a while, smoking a cigar in silence, and then smiled apologetically.

'I don't seem to be much company tonight, do I?'

'It's all right,' she said. 'I don't really feel like talking myself.' She glanced at him. 'Don't feel you have to bear me company. I had just as soon be alone. I think I'll go to bed early.'

'Well, if you don't mind . . . Feodor said, pushing himself up out of his chair. 'I've some letters I ought to be writing.'

Left alone, Anne sat by the verandah rail and watched the light fade from the pale-green evening sky, and the soft, moth-winged dusk creep in. She was too tired even to think, and she listened to the sounds of evening and smelled the emerging twilight fragrance of the jasmine with her mind blessedly blank.

Some time later – she didn't know how long – the Count came out from the house. She felt his presence before she saw or heard him, felt it like a weight on the back of her neck, and turned to see him standing in the doorway, one hand against the upright as though he needed its support. He didn't look at her, but he crossed the verandah and took the chair next to hers, and leaned back in it, sighing like a weary man come home after a day in the fields.

Anne sat very still, feeling his ease with her – the treacherous way he had come to her as to a place of comfort – and worse, hers with him. After a while she heard herself ask him calmly if he had eaten, and the sound of her own voice amazed her. It was like a question passing between husband and wife of long standing: unemphatic, almost needing no words.

'No,' he said. 'They sent in dinner on a tray, but I couldn't eat it. Too tired,' he added, and she heard the deprecatory smile in his voice. She was putting off the moment of looking at him – half in fear, but half as a child postpones a treat.

'I expect they sent you the wrong things,' she said, and the smile was in the sound of her voice too. 'Let me get you some fruit, and some wine.'

'Fruit – yes. I could eat fruit.'

'And wine.' She rose to her feet to ring the bell.

'Only if you will drink with me. It's poor sport to drink wine alone.' She nodded consent, and he added suddenly, 'Champagne – let it be champagne! Did you know the best champagne in the world comes from just across the mountains, in Kakhetia?' She looked at him, startled, but the servant had come out in answer to the bell, and he gave him the order. When they were alone again, he turned to her and said gently, 'He thinks I'm mad too. But champagne is not only good for celebrations, you know. It's a medicine to. They gave it to Yelena Vassilovna when she was dying. I should like to be sure I will die with something so good on my tongue.'

It was the first time he had ever spoken of his first wife to Anne. He was looking away from her now, out into the evening, and she was free to study his face. It was tired, drawn, grey with fatigue and, probably, hunger; but there was a burning, luminous look in his eyes, which she didn't understand.

The servant came back with the wine, and a bowl of fruit, which he placed on a small table before them. The Count poured two glasses.

'This is Tsinandali, the best of the Kakhetian champagnes. Drink, Anna – the first toast I taught you, do you remember? *Za vasha zdarovia*! How long ago it seems! I feel as though I have known you all my life.'

She was unable to speak, and drank the toast in silence; but he went on without seeming to need more encouragement.

'I came across Kakhetian champagne for the first time when I was about Sergei's age. Like him, I served in the Caucasus against the Tcherkess, but I was stationed with the Dragoons in Tiflis, protecting the vineyards of the foothills against the wild mountain beys. They used to come down like sudden hail storms from the mountains, and we had to drive them back, and kill enough of them to discourage them for a while. It was hard, dangerous living – and how hard we celebrated in the mess every night, those of us who had survived the day!'

He drank again, and then took a glowing, Crimean apple from the bowl and lifted it to his nose to sniff it delicately; but then he seemed to forget it, put it down absently, and said, 'So beautiful, the Caucasus – ice blue and brown and white and blood red – have you seen the "bloody snows" of the Caucasian mountains? Something to do with iron in the rock, I believe. Beautiful and sinister.' He was silent a moment. 'When I came again, years later, I was seconded to the Independents, as Sergei is now. That's when I met Irina.'

'Yes,' Anne said. 'I've heard the story.'

He put his glass down abruptly. 'I can't reach her,' he said. 'I don't know what to do. Tell me, Anna, tell me what happened.'

'You know what happened,' she said warily. 'Sergei must have told you in his letter.'

'His letter made no sense; and she won't tell me the real story.'

'She doesn't know it,' Anne said quickly. 'For God's sake, don't say anything to her!'

Triumph bloomed in his eyes. 'So there is another story. I knew it! And I knew you would know the truth of it. You must tell me, Anna, I must know.'

She was distressed. 'I can't. It's for Sergei to tell you. The story is his.'

'No, the story is mine. Tell me the truth – what really happened?' She looked at him, wide-eyed, miserable, and he added gently, 'It could not have been as Sergei said. There could not have been so much dereliction of duty in the whole household that the Tcherkess could come down to the very threshold and snatch her away. There is a story, isn't there?'

She saw the impossibility – and worse, the impropriety – of holding back the truth from him, the child's father. But would he believe? Would he understand? Sergei's letter must have been incomprehensible because he did neither – and how could she explain that to him?

Stumblingly, she began the story; but as it progressed, she began to tell it not to his face, but past his eyes, into his mind, and saw the words sink into place without effort or translation. She wondered

349

how she could ever have been so stupid as to think he would not understand. She had been apart from him too long, had forgotten that all she knew, he knew; that they were not different from each other except unimportantly, on the outside.

When she came to the last part, she trembled; and without breaking her rhythm, he reached across and took her hand, and it made a warm bridge across which the communication could flow, half thought, half feeling. She told Sergei's part of the story too, remembering that Sergei was his child, and that he had a right to know what he could know; and she saw that he did not understand that part directly, but only through the medium of her sympathy. She thought that had it been he who had found Natasha, and heard Zaktal's words, he would have found some way not to do what Sergei had done. He would have been stronger, strong enough to have spared the village; or weaker, perhaps, in his grief, enough to have killed without the remorse. He did not understand why Sergei was suffering, could only accept it because she said it was so.

When she stopped at last, there was a silence, filled only with night noises – the chirp of cicada, the rustle of the breeze in the leaves, the thin high squeak of a hunting bat. A servant came out to close the screens on the windows, so that the lamps could be lit inside, and their butter-yellow light made the dusk suddenly blue as steel. When the servant had gone, leaving them alone, the Count lit a cigar. Anne watched the movements of his hands until the task was completed, and then said, 'She doesn't know the true story. Sergei didn't tell her, and it was not for me to do so, if he did not.'

'You're wrong,' he said. 'She does know. Perhaps not in detail, but she knows something. Natasha was her child, more than anyone's. She knows, at least, that Nasha went away of her own accord.'

Anne watched him draw on the cigar, making the tip glow with sudden jewels, sending the smoke wreathing out into the twilight through the tangled, nodding roses. And suddenly she thought how the accoutrements of the scene were utterly fantastic, like details in the dream of a lunatic: cigar, champagne, roses, glowing fruit in a deep lapis-blue bowl – so completely incongruous with what was happening and what was being said. If this were a dream, it could only be her dream, and there was nowhere to hide in it. She felt utterly exposed to him, as though all her nerve endings were uncovered and unprotected, as though he would be able to hear her thoughts as she thought them.

At last the Count put down the cigar on the edge of the table, and looked down at his hands, and said wearily, 'I wish to God I had

350

never allowed you all to come here! This place! I rescued her from it –
why did I let her come back? It's like an evil monster in a fairy-story,
weaving bad spells, stealing life away.'

'I thought you would blame me,' Anne said. 'I blame myself.
I shouldn't have left her unguarded.'

'Blame is useless,' he said. 'Nothing can bring her back. What
we have to do now is to find some way of going on. But just now,
I can't think what it could be. Perhaps it's too soon.' His hand went
up to this face as if it didn't know what to do with itself; he rubbed
his eyes, and then dropped both hands to his knees. 'Help me, Anna,'
he said quietly.

'I'll try. Only tell me what to do.'

He gave a small, quirky smile. 'I was hoping you would tell
me.' He looked down at his hands, and then at her, and the smile
warmed into something without pain in it. 'Well, you can help me
finish the bottle, to begin with. Fill the glasses, would you? I think I'm
too tired to reach for it.' She hesitated, and he met her eyes with faint,
humorous reproachfulness. 'What, you won't even do that for me? Do
I ask so much of you, Anna Petrovna?'

She felt the tears close behind her eyes, and wanted to look away,
so that he shouldn't see them; but his gaze was too bright and close,
and that faint smile told her that he knew everything she was thinking,
understood all and forgave all.

'No, sir,' she said at last. 'Nothing you ask of me could be too much.'

'Then drink with me.'

He released her gaze, and watched her fill the glasses, and took his
from her hand with an odd grimace, his mood changing again. 'It will
at least make us both sleep,' he said.

Chapter Twenty-One

The next few days were hard for Anne. She couldn't bear to see the Count and Irina together; she hated his care for her, the absolute concentration he bestowed on her. At dinner he sat beside her, served her with his own hands, poured her wine, coaxed her to eat and obliged her to drink. After dinner he sat beside her on the verandah, talking and talking to her in a low voice while she rocked. Anne sat apart with a book, trying not to overhear, but her ear seemed especially tuned to the pitch and timbre of his voice. She wished, desperately, that there were a piano here, so that she could keep out his voice with music; she talked to Galina about household matters, even surprised Katya by asking after her various matronly friends.

By day, the Count walked with Irina in the gardens, accompanied her to the baths, was with her every moment. By night he retired to her room with her, and Anne shut her mind resolutely to that. Unable to sleep, she would stand by her window for air, and see the light burning in their room at all hours. It didn't seem to matter how much she told herself that she was both foolish and wicked: she had felt, that evening on the verandah, how close they were to each other, and how alike, in a way she could not believe was true of him and Irina. She could not bear that he loved his wife, cared for her, gave her all the product of his remarkable mind – that woman who could not begin to appreciate it. And yet she cared for Irina too, grieved for her grief, wanted to comfort and restore her, and was bitterly ashamed of her jealousy. The dichotomy in her own feelings was doubly hard to bear.

She turned to Count Tchaikovsky for respite from the impossible situation, and was grateful that he seemed ready at all hours to escort and distract her. He took her riding, strolled with her in the gardens or along the main boulevard to look at the shops, and talked to her endlessly: social small talk, gossip, long discussions about the political situation – it didn't matter what he said, she responded with all the eagerness of one trying to escape from her own thoughts.

She met him in the evenings, too, for though she would not attend entertainments on her own behalf, she offered with a firmness that would not be denied to chaperone Masha and Zinochka, to save

352

Galina the trouble. At balls and routs and social evenings, she sat in a corner, protected by her cap and her black gloves from being asked to take part in the amusements, and Basil Andreyevitch would come and sit by her and talk. From time to time she intercepted odd looks from some of the matrons, and knew that they were being talked about. The particularity of his attentions to her was bound to cause comment, but she was beyond caring about that. She began almost to wish that the Count would be recalled to Paris: at least there he would be as much hers as Irina's.

One day, when they were out riding on the lower slopes of Mount Mashuk, she asked Tchaikovsky, diffidently, what chance there was of it. They had reined in their horses at a natural vantage point. Below them the town was spread out, humming with morning life in the clean sunshine; to the west, Mount Besh-Tau rose up to jab the sky with its five peaks; and to the south, just visible against the skyline, were the twin peaks of Mount Elborus, between which Noah's Ark was supposed to have lodged when the Flood subsided. It was a lovely day, the sky clear blue, the air fresh, the sunshine bright. Anne was aware of these things outside her unhappiness, close but not touching her, like something seen beyond a window.

'Recalled to Paris?' mused Basil Andreyevitch. 'It's hard to say. The situation is tense, but not critical, from what I hear. Of course, Napoleon's had to go to Spain to take charge of the campaign his brother's bungled, and the life of Paris always drops from a canter to a trot when he's away.'

'Do you know Paris so well?' Anne asked, surprised.

He looked embarrassed. 'I'm reporting what I hear at mess dinners: there are plenty of officers who have been there since Napoleon took it over. Anyway, he won't beat the Spanish in five minutes, so Paris will be quiet at least until after the harvest.'

Anne frowned. 'I can't think why Boney should want to conquer Spain. From my geography lessons, I learnt that it was just a trackless wilderness.'

Basil Andreyevitch shrugged. 'So it is — but it's the last piece of Europe he doesn't control, and naturally any conqueror worth his salt will not be satisfied with less than everything. He can't move north, because Russia stops him, and so he must move south.'

'Well, at least he is leaving England alone,' Anne said.

Tchaikovsky smiled. 'But will England leave him alone? Your country has already sent an army to Portugal, and rescued the Spanish royal family from under Murat's nose. Napoleon won't like that piece of interference.'

'Portugal is our oldest ally,' Anne said.

'And Lisbon is the only port in Europe open to English ships, now that we have been obliged to fall in with Napoleon's embargo,' Tchaikovsky said. 'He means to starve England into submission.'

'He won't do that.'

'No, I don't think he will,' Tchaikovsky said thoughtfully. 'From what I hear, the embargo is causing as much hardship in France as it's meant to cause in England. It cuts both ways, you know. There's all sorts of things that can't be got except in English ships – coffee, sugar, spices. I shouldn't be surprised if the embargo doesn't bring down the alliance between us and France in the end. I don't think the Tsar was ever too keen on it, and if the Imperial Court can't get its little luxuries, life in Petersburg will be hardly worth living.'

'You think Russia will change sides again – ally with England?'

'It seems more natural somehow. And I don't see how anyone can trust a man like Napoleon. He won't be satisfied until he rules the whole world.'

'Including Russia?' Anne said innocently.

'No-one can conquer Russia,' Tchaikovsky said airily. 'No-one would be fool enough to try.' He looked sideways at her. 'Come, that's better – you actually smiled then!'

'I see now why you think England and Russia are natural allies – both countries have that same belief that they cannot possibly be conquered.'

'You speak as though you belonged to neither.'

'In a way, I don't. I belonged entirely to England for most of my life; now I am half-way between England and Russia, I seem to be without a country.'

He looked at her with keen sympathy. 'Move closer to Russia, then. Become wholly Russian.'

'I don't know if that's possible,' she said.

'There is a way.' He reached across the space between them and touched her hand, and she looked a him startled at the tone of his voice.

'What – what do you mean?'

'Is it so hard to guess? Have I not made my feelings clear to you these last weeks?' he said gently. 'Please, don't speak yet – let me finish! I know that you are deeply grieved by the poor little girl's death, and I would not have spoken, except that I can't help feeling you need comforting – a special sort of comforting, that can only be given by someone closer than a mere friend.'

'You have been everything that is kind – I am truly grateful for all your attentions to me – '

'It wasn't kindness, Anna Petrovna!'

'Yes, it was,' she said hastily.

'Well, if you insist – only in that case, let me be kinder still. Will you marry me?'

Despite her recent observations, she was still taken by surprise, so much so that she could not find any words to answer him.

'You look surprised – but surely you must have known what was in my mind?'

'I – I didn't think about it. I thought – '

'You thought I was only flirting with you?' he said with a hint of reproach. 'Am I such a scoundrel in your eyes?'

'No – indeed not. I didn't think that.'

'Well, then? We have been friends for many years, have we not? I have grown to admire you more than anyone I have ever met. But lately, it has become more than that. I will confess to you – I came to Pyatigorsk on purpose to ask you to marry me.'

'Oh, surely not!' she protested at such an extravagant idea. 'You could not have known I was here.'

'To be sure I did! News travels faster here than in the north, where there's little else to talk about. I have told you that my uncle's death leaves me independent. I've remained unmarried all these years, despite my parents' pleadings, because I didn't want the sort of wife they wanted for me. But now I'm independent, I can choose for myself. That's why I came here.'

Still she looked unbelieving. 'But why me? How can you possibly want to marry me?'

'I want an intelligent wife.' He spread his hands in a disarming gesture of honesty. 'I've long had the reputation of leading intellectual society – yes, and I know you've laughed at me secretly. Well, I want to do in fact what I've already done in reputation. With you as my wife, I can do it. We shall have a salon: all the great thinkers, the writers, the reformists – artists and musicians, too – they will all come. We'll be famous. We'll go down in history – more than that, we'll *make* history!'

Anne tried to stem the torrent of his enthusiasm. 'Sir, you do me too much honour! I'm no intellectual – I'm an English governess. I am far beneath your touch – '

355

'No! Don't say that!' His pale eyes glowed with fervour. 'I won't allow anyone to say you are beneath me. You are gently born, and better educated even than most of the men I've ever met, and besides that, you have something else that makes you worth ten of every other woman in Russia. I don't know what to call it, except intelligence, but it isn't only that.'

He held out his hand to her. 'Anna Petrovna, listen to me! I came to Pyatigorsk in all arrogance to ask you to marry me, thinking you would jump at the offer – for I can offer you security, position, rank, fortune, all those things. But meeting you again after so long, I remembered what you were really like. Now I ask not as one conferring a favour, but as one asking it. You are by far my superior in everything that matters – I know that! But I do sincerely love you, and I will try with all my heart to make you happy, if you will honour me with your hand.'

She looked at him with sad astonishment; flattered by his preference, deeply touched by his unselfish offer, unhappy that she must be the cause of wounding him.

'I can't tell you how grateful I am for your good opinion,' she began, but he interrupted her.

'Oh, I don't want your gratitude! I can see from your face that you mean to refuse me – but please, won't you take a little time to consider? I don't need your answer this minute! You are not yourself, you are still in mourning for little Natasha, I know that. Wait, please wait, until you are calmer, and think about it. There is a great deal I can offer you.'

'I know that. I am truly honoured to be your choice, Basil Andreyevitch. Any woman would be.'

'You didn't used to think so,' he said wryly. 'You used to laugh at me.'

'No-one could laugh at such generous feelings as you have expressed,' she said seriously.

'Well, then, what is the impediment?' he asked anxiously.

She hesitated, and then said as gently as possible, 'I don't love you.'

His face cleared. 'Oh, is that all? But that is nothing! I didn't expect you to have a heart ready for me the moment I asked for it! Don't refuse me on that account. We have been good friends these last two weeks, have we not? You don't *dis*like me?'

'No, of course not – but – '

'Then it's all right. People can be very happily married with no more than liking. Half the married people in Russia no more than tolerate each other.'

'I should not wish you to have so little in return for all you offer,' she said.

'Well, I would settle for it. And love will probably follow in time. *I* love *you* all right. Please, Anna Petrovna, say you will think about it. At least don't refuse the first moment I speak.'

She felt her lip trembling, and was aware of an absurd desire to laugh and cry, both together. He was ludicrous, he was kind, he was touching and sad, he was a friend, he was more generous than she deserved.

'Say you'll think about it,' he pressed her again.

'I'll think about it,' she said, feeling ungracious and unkind. 'I do *thank* you,' she added, and he smiled.

'No need for thanks. Come, let's ride on. Have I taken you to the Elizavyetinski spring yet? No? We'll go round that way, then. It's a pleasant ride, and everyone goes to the springs at this time of the morning. There's sure to be someone agreeable to chat to. We'll gather up all the latest gossip, and then go back by the gallery, and stop for a glass of coffee, for it will be noon by then.'

A new Governor of Georgia was on his way to take up his duties, and as he was to break his journey in Pyatigorsk, there was to be a grand reception and ball to which everyone would be going.

The occasion also brought Sergei to Pyatigorsk, as part of a detachment representing the Grozny garrison. He arrived the day before the Governor was expected, and as soon as he had made his report, he rode out to the Kiriakov dacha to meet his father.

He arrived just after noon, when the family was gathered on the verandah eating a nuncheon of fruit, sweet buns, and coffee. Galina had ordered a coddled egg with spinach for Irina, who was looking more wasted every day, and the Count was trying to persuade her to eat it, when Sergei came striding down the path between the oleanders, his spurs clinking, his boots white with dust.

Anne thought at once that he looked ten years older, no longer the handsome, light-hearted boy who had boasted to her only two months ago about breakfasting on quails and champagne. The boyish fullness had gone from his cheeks, and their high colour: his face was stern, his lips thinner, his eyes harder. His fair brows were drawn down in a sun frown, which she could see would soon become a permanent mark. As he halted before the step, he pulled off his hat, and she saw that he had cut his hair shorter, so that even its barley-fair softness could not lighten the impression of grimness about him. His temples and brow, newly exposed, were paler than the rest of his face.

His eyes went straight to Irina, who sat looking at nothing, her hands hanging like dead leaves from her thin wrists, as though she had no strength to use them; and then jumped to his father. He coloured under his tan and his mouth grew uncertain, and just for a moment he looked a boy again. The Count had risen to his feet, was staring at his son with painful love and longing.

'Papa – ' Sergei said, his voice light with hesitancy.

'Seryosha! Oh my dear boy!' The Count crossed the space between them in three strides, and took his son in his arms. It was customary in Russia for men to embrace, and Anne, brought up amongst undemonstrative Englishmen, had at last grown used to it; but the Count held Sergei not as men embrace, but as he might have held a woman, one arm round his shoulders, the other hand on the back of Sergei's head, holding him close against him.

Anne heard Sergei's muffled voice say, 'Papa, I'm sorry!' – the apology pitiful in its inadequacy; and she looked away, biting her lip.

The Count released him, took hold of his shoulders instead, looking into his eyes. There was little physical difference between them now; in the year since he had graduated, Sergei had filled out, and grown the half-inch he had lacked of his father. They looked more than ever alike; yet the difference between them was greater than it had ever been. The lightness, the inner glow had gone out of Sergei: it was no longer in this young man to grow into one such as his father was.

'Papa, I loved her,' he said now. There were tears on his eyelashes, but he would not look away, or hide them: he was a soldier on report. His pride was the only young thing about him. 'I would never have let anything harm her. I loved her.'

'Oh, my dear,' the Count said helplessly.

Sergei met his eyes with a look of desperate pain. 'I'm sorry,' he said again.

'It wasn't your fault. You can't think I blame you?'

'It was my responsibility,' he said, his voice flattening with inevitability. 'I was *in loco parentis* – I was your representative.'

'You couldn't have prevented it!'

Still Sergei looked into his eyes. 'If you had been there, it would still have happened. And you would have taken the responsibility, wouldn't you, sir?'

There was a long moment of silence. Father and son stared at each other; then the Count dropped his hands to his sides. 'Yes,' he said quietly. 'But now I am here, it is mine again. You must not punish yourself over this, Seryosha. You did all you could. Your little sister is dead, and nothing can bring her back. You have your own life to lead, and it's as precious as hers was.'

'Yes, sir, I know,' Sergei said. 'And I shan't waste it, I promise you.'

The Count stared at him helplessly, and Anne saw that he was looking for some sign of the lightsome, merry boy he had left behind. He and Sergei meant different things by the same words. Sergei would live his life, but not as the Count would have wanted him to live it. Things were changed; they could not be changed back.

'Come,' the Count said at last, 'come and have something to eat and drink. You must have had a long journey this morning.' It was the only thing to do – to fall back on social form, when everything else became impossible to bear – but Anne could see that Sergei didn't understand that, and thought his father unfeeling, frivolous. Suddenly she couldn't bear any more. With a muttered excuse, she got up and almost ran into the house, before she could be obliged to join in the painful ritual.

There was no opportunity for Sergei to talk to her for the rest of that day, and Anne was glad of it. As she felt the Count's pain, so she felt Sergei's; and when he and his father were together, and their wounded minds rubbed against each other, it became intolerable. She exchanged only a distant, polite greeting with the young man, and for the rest, avoided them both as much as possible.

She managed to be out of he way when Sergei left that evening, being obliged by the call of duty to return to the military headquarters. She hoped that the arrival of the Governor would keep him out of the way the following day. All the family was going to the reception and ball, and no doubt she would meet him there, but at a social occasion of that sort, they would be cushioned from each other by etiquette. Basil Andreyevitch would be there, of course, and would no doubt constitute himself as her escort, and she looked forward to that with a kind of relief. More and more she appreciated his good manners, his gentlemanly restraint. Since proposing to her, he had not mentioned the matter again, nor behaved with any greater particularity towards her, except that his manner was a little softer – to which she could hardly object. Indeed, fraught as that situation was, it was still easier to be with her hopeful suitor than with either of the Kirovs.

The following day was cooler and hazy, a thin, high cloud covering the sky like gauze, through which the sun shone distantly, muted. Anne walked about the gardens all morning. Whenever she sat down anywhere for a moment, her restlessness drove her to her feet again within minutes. Sitting down, she felt vulnerable, as though someone might come upon her and demand something of her. She walked and walked under that mazy sun, and by the time everyone gathered for a nuncheon at noon, she was weary with the exercise. She drank a little coffee, crumbled a cake on her plate to look as if she had eaten, heard from a distance Galina ask her if she had a headache, and herself answer no, she was quite well. She was aware of the Count looking at her, and would not meet his eyes.

The meal over, everyone retired to their room to dress for the Governor's reception, while the servants went to their quarters for their dinner.Gradually the house grew quiet, and Anne, sitting on the edge of her bed, felt her restlessness and anxiety dissipating into simple tiredness. She supposed, wearily, that she ought to dress. Marie would probably come later, when she had finished with her mistress, and offer to dress Anne's hair, as she usually did for parties or balls. She had better be ready. She got up from the bed, took off her sandals, and then remembered she had left her reticule on the verandah. She would just slip out and get it before she changed.

She opened the door to her room and stepped out into the passage, and at the same instant the Count appeared round the corner of the passage and came face to face with her. He stopped in front of her, blocking her path, and she looked up at him nervously. His mouth was curved into an enigmatic smile, and his bright eyes, more gold than green today, looked directly into hers, dazzling and confusing her.

'I was just – just going – ' She waved a foolish hand towards the verandah, the direction from which he had come. With his arms folded across his chest, he seemed to fill the narrow passage completely.

'You've been avoiding me,' he said.

'No, sir, of course not,' she said, lowering her eyes. 'Would you please let me past? I want to fetch my reticule.'

'Not until I have an explanation,' he said.

'There's nothing to explain.'

'Yes, there is.' He unfolded his arms, and rested one elbow against the jamb of her open door. 'What's the matter, Anna? I thought you were my friend – my dear friend. Yet you avoid me, you won't talk to me – you won't even look at me. Don't deny it! Where are your eyes this minute?'

She looked up, and it was a mistake. Their eyes met, and she felt her scalp shrink and her stomach clench at what she saw in his face, what she knew was mirrored in hers. 'No,' she whispered. She stepped back from him defensively into her own room, and he followed her step for step, closed the door behind them. The small click of the latch sounded too loud in the quiet – accusing, dangerous. He stood against the closed door. She could hear his breathing, too loud, as though he had been running. His lips were parted, his eyes narrowed with some fierce emotion.

No, she had said; but in the end it was she who led them. He made a small movement towards her, and half in terror at her own insane daring she stepped close to him, and her arms went up about his neck as eagerly as a child's. There was no thought but to have what she wanted so much. She put her body against his hungrily, quivering at the forbidden touch of it, alien, and yet already, somehow, known to her.

His response was instant; his hand rose to stroke her cheek; he cupped her face with his hands. 'Anna! Annushka!' he whispered. His eyes closed, and he kissed her brow, touched her lips with his; her mouth opened hungrily, and then they were kissing like lovers, with the utter abandon of long desire let loose at last. His arms were round her, his hands behind her shoulders pressing her against him.

For once in her life she abandoned herself completely, her inner voices silenced. She leaned against him avidly, revelling in the exotic hardness of his male body, the warm smell of his skin, the touch of his strong hands on her body. Her whole body, every nerve ending, sang with the joy of him. Love welled up in her, and a huge desire that, innocent as she was, she hardly knew what to do with; the knowledge that he wanted her, loved her equally, made a hard knot of passion in her stomach that would not be ignored.

He pulled his mouth away, panting. 'Annushka! My own, my love.' He kissed her throat and the upper curves of her breasts. She slid her hands up into his hair, loving the hard curve of his skull that her eyes had so often caressed. His hands were hard about her waist, slipped upwards and spanned her breasts, and she trembled and felt sick with the force of wanting him. 'I love you.'

'I love you, too,' she whispered. His lips came back to hers, and they kissed again, feeding on each other.

'*Je te veux!*' he said against her mouth, and she quivered with response. He was strong; he lifted her with one arm round her waist, stepped with her away from the door, reached out one-handed for a chair and swung it round and under the door handle, to jam the door closed. It was enough to break the spell.

'No,' she said, more urgently this time. 'We can't. We mustn't'.

He set her feet to the ground but did not release her; he looked down at her, his face flushed, his eyes bright, his hair ruffled.

'Anna!' he said.

'It's wrong,' she said desperately, growing colder, more sober with every breath.

'I love you,' he said, but she heard the change in his voice, too.

'You have a wife.' She said the deadly words.

'Yes,' he said helplessly. Anne, in his arms, knew she should withdraw from him, but could not, not yet. He felt the thought in her mind, and snatched her tighter to him. 'I can't reach her. Anna, I have nothing for her, nor she for me. We should never have married. It was a dreadful mistake.'

'These past few days – I've watched you together – '

'Yes, I've tried, God knows I've tried! But I can't love her. I don't know why. Poor woman, she has never done me any harm, but – Anna – *she fills me with horror!*'

'No,' Anne pleaded.

'It's true. But you – Oh God, I love you! I've loved you since the first moment I met you. You are like me – you are my image, my match, my soul!' He kissed her again, her brow and her eyes and her lips, and she whimpered, but could not struggle. 'If you knew how often I've wanted to do this! How I've stopped myself! Anna, Anna!'

'Don't – please – '

'You feel it too. We're alike, you and I, we belong together. When I arrived here, and I saw you standing there in the road, it was like – like coming home! I swear to you I felt more as though you were my wife than I have ever felt with Irina.'

'Yes, I know,' she said. The fever was mounting again. She saw his eyes narrow.

'I can't let you go. I must have you. I want to possess you utterly – to fill you up with myself – '

She gave up her mouth to him again, and felt the sweetness flowing between them, and knew how easy it would be to give way to the madness, to have what she wanted, what they wanted, so much. But it would be at too great a cost. If she lost herself, she would lose him too, and the more completely. She sighed as she kissed him, and he felt it, and their lips parted.

'It's not possible,' she said.

He resisted the words, but she pushed him back firmly – not completely away, but enough to stop him kissing her. She looked into his eyes, saw the knowledge of their plight reflected there. He knew as well as she did that this was a moment outside of time, that real life was waiting for them only a shadow away, ready to part them, ready to break their hearts.

'I love you,' he said again.

'I know,' she said. 'I love you too – '

'Say my name,' he begged. 'Just once, let me hear it on your lips.'

'Nikolai,' she said, and the sound of it made her feel shy. 'Nikolai, Nikolasha.'

He drew her against him as she said it, and cradled her close, the fierce passion gone now, only the tenderness, the dearness between them, binding them together with frail, indestructible ropes. She rested against him, knowing in this one moment of perfect wholeness, that she had found the place where she belonged, the other half of herself for which each person searches all their life. How could this be wrong? How could anything part them? The vitality of life itself flowed between them, unhindered by their separate flesh.

There was a light scratching at the door, and they both grew very still. Marie's voice came quietly from the passage. *'Mademoiselle? Puis-je vous coiffer maintenant?'*

The world had caught up with them. He looked down blankly into her eyes, and she heard her own voice call out with amazing calmness, 'Go away Marie. I will do my hair myself.'

There was no further sound from the passageway; but the mood was broken. They released themselves by common consent, and stood a little apart. His arms were down uselessly by his sides. He was all too aware, now, of the other view, the one any person other than themselves would have of the matter.

It was Anne who spoke first. 'You had better go and dress.'

He nodded, turned to go, and then turned back, unable to leave something so important so lightly.

'Don't worry,' he said. 'Everything will be all right.'

No, she thought; nothing will ever be all right again. He must have seen something of that thought in her eyes, for he gave a small, crooked smile, and said, 'Trust me, Anna.'

She could not see any way forward, anything to come but pain; but she said, 'Yes,' as if it were an answer to his question – no, his demand – and he seemed satisfied, for the moment, with that. He nodded again, and after a brief hesitation, left her.

*

By the time she arrived at the reception, Anne felt exhausted, as if she had not slept for two nights. She travelled in the second carriage with Katya and the two girls; the Count and Irina had gone on ahead in the first carriage with Feodor and Galina, and when Anne stepped into the commandant's house, the Count was already established and out of reach in conversation with a group of senior military and diplomatic personnel.

Feodor had waited, so that they should have someone to present them, but he was not obliged to trouble himself on Anne's behalf, for her hand was at once claimed by Basil Andreyevitch, who begged to be allowed to present her to the Governor, who was an old friend of his mother's. Feodor met Anne's eyes and raised an interrogative eyebrow, and she shrugged minutely. If she were not to be allowed to lie down and die of her misery, she didn't much care what happened to her.

Tchaikovsky presented her as the daughter of the English Admiral Peters, and in that flattering light the Governor bowed over her hand most graciously. They moved on, and other members of his staff came forward to be introduced to her. Tchaikovsky was expert, if in nothing else, in manipulating conversation, and before long there was a lively discussion going on around Anne, which she could not help but join in.

The thing which had happened to her was shut away in a separate part of her mind: for the moment she could not think about it, and her physical tiredness helped her to stand outside herself, and regard the present in a detached way. Servants drifted up at regular intervals with glasses of champagne and trays of *zakuska*, and in the background an orchestra played quietly. It really was a very good reception. She discovered that she was actually deriving pleasure from it, and regarded herself with detached astonishment. Then realising that it was to a great extent her escort's doing, she had the grace to repeat the thought to him.

He looked pleased. 'Mess hospitality!' he said. 'In Russia, it's the best in the world! Have some of this caviar – the red is best – and some more champagne.'

'Tsinandali?' she said, remembering. They had sat on the verandah together in another world, long ago, drinking champagne. On top of the tiredness, the wine was filling her with a pleasant sense of unreality. The edges of things were just a little softened. The wounded place inside her seemed far away; the pain quiescent for the moment, like a fierce animal sleeping. 'I like you, Basil Andreyevitch,' she said. 'You're so restful.'

He smiled uncertainly. 'I suppose you mean that as a compliment.'

During the progress of the reception, Anne saw Sergei only at a distance, talking to various officials and dignitaries. She knew that he had seen her: he bowed the first time she caught his eye, and several times she saw him look her way, but he was in uniform and on duty, and could not excuse himself to come to talk to her.

Basil Andreyevitch had brought her a Colonel of Hussars who had recently come from Spain, where he had been liaising with Murat's army in Madrid. He was able to give fascinating details of the situation there. Napoleon had made his brother Joseph king in place of the deposed Bourbon, and Joseph had embarked on a programme of reform and public building. But the Bonapartes had underestimated the strength of the Spanish church, which regarded the Revolution with horror, and Napoleon as the Anti Christ. Urged on by the priesthood, the Spanish people themselves, though betrayed by their queen and abandoned by their king, had risen up against the French occupation, and had driven the army out of Madrid.

'When I left, the news was that your General Wellesley was marching through Portugal to head off Junot's army,' the Colonel added. 'Do you know him? He has done great things in India, so it's said.'

Anne contemplated the idea of her 'knowing' Sir Arthur Wellesley, the proud son of an Anglo-Irish peer and brother of a minister of the realm. 'I've heard of him, of course,' she said.

The Colonel nodded. 'An able man. I think France may have more trouble than she looks for in the Peninsular. Napoleon invaded Spain in a frivolous mood – but he may find it a sobering experience.'

Tchaikovsky said, 'You seem not to mind the idea of our ally being bested by the Spanish, Boris Feodorovitch. Can it be that you have no great love for the French?'

The Colonel shrugged. 'France or Spain, it is not our quarrel. And Napoleon – who is he? A commoner, when all's said and done. It is not for our Emperor to ally himself with a brigand. We ought to be opposing him, and helping England. The English are our natural allies,' he said with a bow to Anne.

Tchaikovsky gave Anne a conspiratorial glance, and said innocently, 'What you mean, Borya, is that England has no Continental ambitions to clash with ours. Provided she rules the sea, she will let us rule Europe as we please.'

The Colonel looked dignified. 'You may laugh if you will, but a clash is bound to come sooner or later, between us and a mushroom like Napoleon. What about Poland? What about Sweden? What about the Levant? Do you think he will stand back and let us have them? And do you think we will let him take them from us? Let France have her natural frontiers, and we ours, that's what I say. The ancient empire of Byzantium – '

'No no!' Tchaikovsky protested, holding up his hands. 'I cannot permit you to start on Byzantium. Once he mounts that horse, Anna Petrovna, nothing can throw him.'

The Colonel grinned good-naturedly. 'Very well. But I don't scruple to say this before you, Vasya – or before Mademoiselle, your friend: the idea of a marriage alliance between Russia and France is going a great deal too far, and so it will appear.'

'A marriage alliance?' Anne said in surprise.

Tchaikovsky lowered his eyelids. 'It seems Napoleon is thinking of divorcing Madame Josephine – '

'That sweet woman!' the Colonel added indignantly.

'But I thought it was a love match,' Anne said. 'Everyone talked of it so. When I was in Paris – '

'Napoleon wants a son, and she cannot give him one,' Tchaikovsky said. 'Now he has a throne, he must have a son to pass it on to.'

The Colonel nodded. 'That's right. And at the conference in Erfurt next month, he plans to suggest a marriage between himself and one of the Grand Duchesses,' he said indignantly. 'He does not know his man. The Tsar may sign a pact with the Devil, if he is driven to it, in order to gain time; but he will not sell one of his sisters to him.'

A general disturbance at that point, as everyone began moving towards the ballroom for the opening of the ball, interrupted the conversation. The Colonel bowed to Anne, and excused himself to go and find the lady he was engaged to escort; and Basil Andreyevich offered Anne his arm and smiled down at her with a certain satisfaction.

'You see, Anna Petrovna, how it would be? I can offer you not only wealth and position – any rich nobleman could do the same. But I have the entrée at Court. I know the Imperial family, and I know the ministers and the generals. You could hold a central position in the wheel of power – you could know what is happening before it happens.'

She looked at him, a little bemused. 'Why should you think I want to?' she asked.

'Because knowledge is power. Because for the intelligent mind, to *know* is everything.' He read her expression. 'Yes, I have seen that hunger in you, mademoiselle! Now, visualise yourself at the heart of matters, mistress of the salon where the fate of nations is decided: the *intriguante sans pareil*! Yes, it attracts you, doesn't it?'

'You talk such nonsense, Basil Andreyevitch,' she said; but he was not put out. He smiled that same, satisfied smile and led her towards the ballroom without pressing the matter further.

Sergei came up to her at last, where she was sitting on a sofa a little out of the way, in a sort of alcove in a corner of the ballroom. She could not dance, of course, but apart from Tchaikovsky, several people had come up to sit beside her and talked for a while, and she had got through the evening more pleasantly than she had thought possible.

The Count had not come near her, though she had seen him looking at her from time to time. She saw aware of him wherever he was in the room, even if she was not looking at him; she could feel him on her skin like a radiance. The memory of his love, their passion, the touch of him, was small and secret in her mind, something she would take out later, when she was alone, and examine, for pleasure or pain, probably both. What to do about it was beyond her to consider for the moment. She was tired; she wanted nothing, only to be left alone.

Count Tchaikovsky was obliged to dance one or two duty dances, and it was while he was thus away from her side that Sergei took the opportunity to approach her. She was engaged in the delicate task of untangling the clasp of her fan from the net-mesh of her reticule into which it had hooked itself in her lap, and noticing at last that a pair of white breeches and silk stockings had been stationary in front of her for some moments, she looked up to encounter Sergei's flushed face and over-bright eyes. He was, she realised with a sinking heart, not sober.

'So, I have you to myself at last,' he began unpromisingly. 'I began to think if that dog Tchaikovsky didn't go away and leave you alone, I should be obliged to come over and let some of the air out of him.'

She met his eye questioningly, and he gave a twisted grin. 'Yes, I am a little foxed,' he said, reading her thoughts. 'Well, it's expected on occasions like this, when the champagne flows. Every man in uniform will be drinking himself into a stupor tonight, if he can. Mess hospitality, you know!'

She made a small gesture of dismissal. 'Don't let me prevent you from enjoying yourself.'

He flung himself down at her side. 'Don't be angry with me, Anna! Why have you been so distant with me? What have I done to upset you?'

'Nothing – nothing in the world.'

'It must be something. Is it because I haven't come to Pyatigorsk before now? But you must have known that I would have come if I could. We've been at full stretch, every man, trying to hold back the Chechen – raids every day, and at night too. I couldn't have come before.'

'I didn't expect you,' she said truthfully.

'Then what is it? Why are you offended?'

'I'm not offended, Seryosha. I'm just tired,' she said. She looked at him rather blankly, having no feelings to spare for him at the moment, one way or the other. 'Just leave me be.'

His eyes showed hurt. 'You've changed,' he said abruptly. 'What is it? It can't be that Tchaikovsky creature! Why, he's hardly a man at all – he's just a clothes-wearer. Why do you let him hang around you so?'

'He's very kind to me.'

'Kind! It's not kindness! Can't you see the fool is flirting with you? I wish you may not be taken in by him, Annushka! You're too trusting.'

This was exhausting. 'Basil Andreyevitch has asked me to marry him,' she said. 'He is perfectly honourable.'

'Marry him? You can't marry him! What have you told him? Why is he still hanging about you? You haven't accepted him, have you?'

'No – '

'Then he has no right to plague you. I'll have to teach him some manners,' Sergei said triumphantly. 'If he comes near you again, I'll settle him for you, don't worry.'

'Please, Sergei, I can't bear this,' Anne said, putting a hand to her brow; but he caught it in both his and lifted it to his lips, kissing it fervently.

'I know, my darling! I've been away from you too long, and you've had to bear the sorrow all alone. But everything will be all right, you'll see. Don't be angry with me, Annushka! I didn't neglect you on purpose.'

Anne tried to pull her hand away. *Everything will be all right!* How many more people would promise her that, when it was plain that everything was coming to pieces, would never be all right again? 'Don't, Seryosha! People are looking.'

'Let them look! I don't care! I want the world to know about us!' He kissed her hand again, and then turned it over and began to kiss her wrist. 'Angel!'

She struggled, half tearful, half angry, pushing at his hard, muscular shoulder with her free hand, and making no more impression on it than on a rock. His fingers were making red marks on her arm.

And then out of nowhere the Count was standing before them, his voice cool and cutting.

'What is happening here? Sergei Nikolayevitch, can it be that you are drunk so early in the evening? Release Anna's hand at once. You're annoying her.'

The hard tone, the formal appellation, acted like cold water on Sergei's passion. He dropped Anne's hand, and started up, and then his face began slowly to colour. He straightened to attention before his father and said with dignity, 'You are under a misapprehension, sir. I am not drunk, and I was not annoying Anna Petrovna.'

'Forgive me,' the Count said with cutting irony. 'I was judging by appearances. When a young man is trying to kiss a woman in a public place, and she is struggling to prevent him, I can only suppose she finds it an annoyance. And when that young man is my son, I assume that only excess of drink could lead him so to forget himself as to behave so improperly.'

Sergei glowed with anger. 'Appearances can deceive, sir. There is nothing improper in my attentions. I am going to marry Anna – she and I are promised to each other.'

If it weren't so horrible and so tragic, Anne might have laughed, to see the look of shock and disbelief on the Count's face, rapidly followed by bewilderment and doubt. Knowing his son, he must immediately have realised that Sergei would not tell such an outrageous lie without some reason. He stared at Sergei, and then looked to Anne for enlightenment, and read some consciousness in her eye. His expression changed. Knowing he had no right to her only made his jealousy the more bitter.

'Perhaps I have been deceived,' he said in a hard voice. 'Must I congratulate you, mademoiselle?'

Don't be a fool, she thought wearily, but those were not words she could say to him, not in public, not in front of Sergei.

'No,' she said. 'I am not going to marry Sergei.' Out of the corner of her eye she saw the young man's start of protest, but she could not spare him her attention at the moment. She was looking into the Count's eyes, holding his gaze steadily.

'Do you mean to tell me there is nothing between you?'

He wanted, needed her denial; yet she felt Sergei like a weight on her consciousness. There had been nothing between them, in the sense that his father meant; yet she could not quite do that to Sergei. She had done such wrong by him already: who knew what harm her moment of weakness, when she had responded to his embrace, had caused? She said, 'I am not promised to him. He is mistaken.'

'But Anna – ' cried Sergei.

Now she flung him a look. 'I did not accept you,' she said firmly. 'I told you it was impossible.'

'Nevertheless,' the Count said in a voice of bitter darkness, 'it seems he did ask you. I had no idea – how long has it been going on? There must have been a great deal more – *affection* – between you than I ever imagined possible between a governess and her charge.'

He was being unfair, and he knew it: Sergei had never been her charge; in that respect at least, there was no wrong. But he wanted to punish her, to hurt her, and she understood, though the words did wound.

She looked at him sadly. 'Ah, no,' she protested softly.

The anger drained from his face, leaving him only puzzled. 'Anna, what happened? You didn't love him, did you?'

'How could I help loving him? He's your son,' she said.

Sergei looked from one to the other, hearing the warmth, the unmistakable intimacy of the exchange. They were not words spoken merely between employer and employee. The wine flush drained out of him. He was suddenly horribly sober.

'Papa – not you and Anna?' He met Anne's reluctant eyes. 'Was that why you said it was impossible?' She didn't answer. His fists suddenly clenched themselves, and the words burst out of him. 'You and Papa? God, it's disgusting!'

'Seryosha – !'

'How could you? The two of you? It's – it's obscene!'

Anne could bear no more. She got to her feet, desperate to escape. She felt sick, she swayed, putting out her hands dizzily. The Count was there; she felt his firm hands catch her arms, steadying her, supporting her. He would always do that – he loved her, he understood.

'It's all right,' he said. 'Go out onto the terrace. No-one will follow you.'

She looked up at him blindly, and then stumbled away.

The warm evening air seemed hard to breathe. The terrace was empty, thank God! She leaned against the balustrade and stared into the shadows of the shrubbery beyond. Before her the darkness sang with a monotony of cicadas; behind her the strains of music drifted out from the brightly-lit ballroom; between the two she was suspended in a world of anguish. The pain was awake now, tearing at her sickeningly. She contemplated the devastation of her life; she hung her head, and the hot, bitter tears began to fall.

Some time later, she was aware that someone was near her. She tried to stop herself crying. Her reticule was left behind on the sofa in the ballroom: she had no handkerchief, and wiped at her wet face uselessly with her fingers; but the tears were still flowing, too many to be staunched that way. She struggled for control, not wanting to expose herself to impertinent curiosity, perhaps to scandal. Then someone put clean linen into her hand, pleasantly scented. She recognised the scent. It was Basil Tchaikovsky – only him.

'Here', he said kindly. 'Go on – it's a good, big one.'

She took it, dried her face, pressed it to her eyes. He was standing beside her, shielding her from anyone who might be looking from the ballroom, his eyes full of sympathy. She tried to thank him, and began crying again.

'Oh dear,' he said, and took her in his arms. There was nothing of the lover in the gesture – he held her against his shoulder in pure kindness, simply to let her cry more comfortably. He was almost motherly. At first the very quality of his kindness made her cry harder; but at last the sobs began to ease, and after a while she was able to draw a long, shuddering breath and mumble, 'I'm sorry.'

He held her a moment longer, and then put her gently away. 'All done now?' he said. She uncrumpled his handkerchief – damp now – from her clutch, and wiped her face again.

'I think so,' she said unsteadily.

'I saw something of what happened from across the room,' he said, and then gave her a rueful smile. 'Fascinating people, these Kirov men! I'm not surprised you fell victim. Which one was it? Or was it both?'

She looked at him in blind misery, hardly hearing what he said. 'What am I to do?' she said. 'What am I to do?' The tears welled up again helplessly. 'My life is ruined.'

'Oh, surely not,' he said gently. 'A little *contretemps* – it will blow over. It will all be forgotten in a day or two. Lives are not ruined in ballrooms – it doesn't happen, you know.'

She shook her head dumbly. He didn't know the full gravity of it. 'I shall have to go away. But what can I do? Where can I go?' she said. She couldn't see even one step ahead. She was utterly lost, helpless, bewildered.

Tchaikovsky looked at her carefully. 'There is something you can do,' he said. 'I don't mean to press you when you are obviously upset – but if you want to get away from them, you could marry me. My offer still stands.' She said nothing, and he wasn't sure if she had heard him. 'I wouldn't blame you for wanting to escape them. They are rather larger than life, aren't they? And they tend to engulf everything around them, like octopuses – well, Nikolai Sergeyevitch does, at any rate, and I imagine young Sergei is going to be just the same one day.'

His light voice, easy as the little night breeze, drifted on past her, soothing her, dispersing the fog of pain, leaving her feeling weak, tired, empty, beyond emotion. She wanted to lean against him, to close her eyes and sleep; but she knew it was not fair.

'You know that I don't love you,' she said. 'Can you really want me to marry you on those terms?'

'I don't mind why you marry me, so long as you marry me,' he said lightly. 'It will be all right, you'll see.'

Running away, she thought. Cowardly. But what else could she do? She must escape, and she had nowhere else to go. She was worn out, and he offered her a haven; as long as she was not deceiving him, there could be no harm – could there?

'Yes,' she said.

'Does that mean you will marry me?' he said cautiously.

She hardly knew what she had meant by it; but she said again, 'Yes.'

She heard him draw a deep breath of relief and triumph, and then, permitted now, he drew her against him again. 'Thank you,' he said quietly into her hair. 'You won't regret it. I'll make you happy, you'll see. Everything will be all right.'

Anne stared over his shoulder at the ground. I feel nothing, she thought, nothing at all.

BOOK THREE – 1811

Chapter Twenty-Two

The barouche which waited before the steps of the Byeloskoye Palace, one June day in 1811, was new, glossy, and very smart. It was French-hung, painted black with scarlet trim on the wheels, and the upholstery was of the shade of pale blue known as Ecstasy, which was all the kick in Moscow that year. Between the shafts were two white English carriage horses, brought all the way from Yorkshire at enormous expense. The black leather harness which lay so vividly against their milky coats was decorated with tasselled Turkish knots of scarlet silk, and their plaited manes were tagged with little scarlet hackles, which stood in a ridge above their proudly-arched necks.

It was an outfit which spoke not only wealth and high fashion, but imagination too; and the building before which it stood presented the same sort of image. Faced all in white marble, it had the appearance of an enormous Greek temple, complete with soaring, fluted Corinthian columns. These supported a massive triangular pediment on which, in a mood of frivolity, not to mention irreligion, was depicted the Rape of Europa, in bas-relief and considerable detail.

The carriage had not been waiting more than five minutes before there was a movement in the shadows under the portico, and the chateliane of Byeloskoye came out into the sunshine, pulling on her gloves of lavender French suede, and closely followed by a diminutive French maid holding a lace parasol above her mistress's head. The groom caught the coachman's eye and nodded approval. One thing about the Countess Anna Petrovna Tchaikovskova: she appreciated fine horseflesh, and never kept her horses standing about unnecessarily.

The liveried footman handed her up into the carriage, folded up the step and closed the door, while the maid slipped in on the other side. The footman climbed onto the step behind, the groom stood away from the horses' heads, the coachman gave the office, and the barouche rolled away from the house, crunching over the gravel forecourt towards the wrought-iron gates.

As they moved away, Anne looked back as she always did at the gigantic, tongue-in-cheek replica of the Temple of Hephaistos which she now inhabited when she was in Moscow. She never knew whether to admire or deride, as the remnants of her English conservatism struggled with the romantic flamboyance she had learned from her adoptive country. Moscow itself was a strange mixture of such contrasts: at once Oriental and fiercely Russian, patriotic and cosmopolitan, flamboyant and conservative. Perhaps that was why she felt at home there.

They had only lived in the Byeloskoye Palace for a year, since Basil's father had died. Before that they had lived in a modest but attractive townhouse in Tver Square; but once Basil had inherited his father's fortune, he had taken Anne on a tour of all the vacant palaces and great houses in Moscow, to select their new home.

'The choice is yours,' he said. 'I leave it to your taste – only make it large enough, and impressive enough.'

It was not exactly that she had fallen in love with Byeloskoye – she never knew whether she was more amused or appalled by it – but it was certain that after seeing it, everything else was an anticlimax. Moscow was full of oddities, and of the spectacular edifices of Russia's leading families, many stood, like Byeloskoye, in extensive grounds. The number and extent of these parks, as well as gardens, orchards, and ornamental squares meant that Moscow, city of around three hundred thousand souls, sprawled over a vast area, more like a province than a city.

The area it covered was roughly circular, with the River Moskva winding a sinuous course through the bottom third of it. The main streets radiated outwards like the spokes of a wheel from the hub of the Kremlin – fortress, arsenal, royal palace, barracks, and urban grainstore – whose dark red walls and glittering, spiralled onion-domes dominated the vast market-place of the Krasnaya Ploshchad – the Beautiful Square. Here every day the peasant carts from outside the city trundled in their freight of vegetables, fruit, poultry, eggs, butter, grain, and sunflower seeds; and peddlars, trappers, and merchants from all over the empire and beyond set out their wares: Kashmir shawls, Chinese silks, Indian muslins, Persian carpets, Turkish bronze and copperware; sable and mink from Siberia, spider-web lace from Azerbaijan, dried flowers and herbs from the Crimea, enamel bracelets and earrings from Kiev.

When Peter the Great had built his new capital of St Petersburg almost a hundred years ago, he had issued a decree forbidding the use of stone for building in any other city. Though this decree had been rescinded fifty years later by a successor to the imperial throne, it meant that many of the great houses in Moscow, and all the lesser ones, were built of wood. The Muscovites had made up for it, however, by painting them in bright colours – yellow and pink and leaf green and sky blue – and by adding carved decorations, porches, fancy shutters, even columns and gables, all of wood. The rich went one better, and behind many a noble facade of white marble or pink granite or honey-coloured Portland stone, was concealed the lowly reality of common timber.

Perhaps, Anne thought, that was another reason that she felt at home in Moscow. Her life, like the great buildings, was not all it seemed: a splendid and eye-catching affair which concealed a hollowness. The succession of violent emotional shocks which had driven her into marriage with Basil Tchaikovsky seemed, like a fierce fire, to have burned out her capacity to feel. They had left her quite numb, and she had longed only to escape to some place where nothing would be demanded of her that would plumb those painful depths again.

At first she had succeeded. Basil was a kind, pleasant, and undemanding companion, and within a short time of their marriage, he had brought her to that place in society which he had promised her. She was 'Madame Tchaikovsky' the society hostess: wealthy, handsome, fashionable, with a following of the best of the *intelligentsia*. She was mistress of a large house and a small army of servants, co-spender of a large fortune, with a family name to respect. It was a very different life from that of a governess, however well treated or highly paid, and it was only to be expected that it had changed her. She knew that she was much more assured in her manner, more poised and confident, more authoritative; inevitably she was also less confiding, more formal, more careful of how she appeared to others. She had been brought up to be a gentlewoman, but a great lady was quite another matter.

Informality and gaiety were now social devices to be calculated for their effect; but if she had lost some spontaneity, it was certain that there was no-one to desire it of her, or to regret its passing. What she had become was what was required; and she and Basil were a success. They were invited everywhere, and their invitations were prized; their taste was consulted, their opinions repeated, their approval sought; they were accepted by everyone, and liked almost as universally. Theirs was a winning combination: Basil had the old name, the family fortune, and his own social expertise and charm to recommend him; Anne was clever, well educated, shrewd, and unpretentious. She was also English, and since, after Tilsit, Anglophilia had replaced the rabid Francomania which had invested all things fashionable in Russia, that counted for a great deal.

The Kirovs, who had so filled and dominated and changed her

life, had dropped away from it as completely as a shed garment, and in her state of exhausted numbness and shock, she was content that it should be so: to remember them would be to raise unwelcome speculations about their states of mind. She heard of them only at a great distance, very much at third hand, when the name came up in conversation at this or that great house. The Count's status as a Special Envoy to the Emperor earned him occasional honourable mention on the dinner-party circuit, and from time to time his wife's continued ill health was deplored as a hardship for a man so much abroad: Irina had never recovered from the loss of her best-loved child. Seryosha's military career cropped up less often, but from what she heard of his dedication and single-mindedness in pursuing it, Anne guessed that he would never get over Natasha's death either.

Lolya was merely a child, and her visiting her Grandmama in Moscow was the only reason Anne ever heard of her at all. Of Sashka she never heard, and she was glad of it. The ache in her heart where he had been torn from it was something from which she resolutely turned away: her numbness was not quite so deep as to prevent her from grieving for him, if she allowed herself ever to think of him.

The barouche was now turning into the Kuznetsky Most, the main boulevard in Moscow's most fashionable quarter. It was a wide street paved with closely fitting, solid wood planks, and lined with the most delicious shops, filled with fashions and luxuries, silk and lace and leather, French lingerie and perfume, imported wine, English worsted, hand-made shoes, books, song sheets, and jewellery: everything, in fact, that the rich and fashionable Muscovite could want. Here you could buy a tame nightingale from Moldavia, and a golden cage to keep it in; perfume to attract a new lover, or a book of French lewd engravings to revive an old one – and a silk chemise from Paris, trimmed with Mechlin lace, to entertain either in.

The Kuznetsky Most was also the place to be seen, either walking or driving – the Bond Street of Moscow, Anne thought of it to herself. Even for a shopping trip, therefore, Madame Tchaikovsky had to present a smart appearance, and maintain her reputation for leading fashion. Today she was wearing a sleeveless pelisse of her own design, of very light, ruched velvet trimmed with gold loop braiding, rather in the style of the Hussar uniform, and a small hat decorated with three curled cock's feathers and a half-veil. Her suede gloves were elbow-length, and clasped round each wrist was a heavy gold and enamel bracelet showing Basil's family device of a chained swan. A four-strand pearl collar and pearl earrings completed the ensemble. She looked smart, *tonnish*, very much a leader of society.

To maintain that position required endless work and attention to detail. Anne would never have thought that mere social life could so have used up so much of her time, that it could be such hard work to remain at the top of the tree. Clothes, alone, took up hours of every day, what with designing, choosing fabrics, making-up, and having fittings — not to mention hats, gloves, shoes, stockings, pelisses, capes, cloaks, furs and shawls. Then she must read all the newspapers, and the books people were talking about, as well as those she intended they should talk about. She had to see all the plays, good and bad, and attend all the concerts, in order to have an opinion about them; keep up with political matters, both domestic and international, and the social gossip about who was having an affair with whom; and she had to find time to practise her pianoforte and singing, both of which were much in demand at parties.

Then there were the parties themselves: she and Basil had invitations every day to dinners, masks, routs, balls, card evenings, musical soirées, theatre parties, picnics, water picnics, and rides; and when they took their turn at entertaining, the work involved was almost inconceivable. Over the years she had built up an efficient staff of free, and therefore mostly foreign, labour, on whom she could rely, but there was still all the planning and deciding and supervision to do.

It ought, she reflected, to have left her no time in which to be unhappy; and she arranged her routines in order to leave herself no dangerous idle moments when reflection might ambush her. She was woken in the morning by Pauline, her maid, who brought her bread and fruit and coffee on a tray, together with the newspapers, letters, and the day's crop of invitations to sift. When she had eaten, she had her bath, and then various members of her staff were admitted while Pauline dressed her hair.

Her secretary, Miss Penkridge, who came from the same part of Yorkshire as her carriage-horses, would arrive first with her diary to remind her of her engagements, and to take instructions over which invitations to accept, and how to reply to the various other letters which had arrived that day. It was also Miss Penkridge's duty to be aware of what plays, concerts, military reviews, exhibitions and other public entertainments were going on, and to acquire tickets when necessary; and to know what new books had been published, and to buy copies on her mistress's behalf.

After the all-important Miss Penkridge the butler, housekeeper, cook, and mantuamaker all had their consultation, and then Pauline would dress her for her morning engagements. If Basil was at home, he would usually call on her at that time in his dressing-gown, yawning and gum-eyed after the previous night's all-male dissipation, and discuss the day's programme and the new invitations. If he was not at home, or had been unusually late to bed and was not yet awake, she would not normally see him until they met for the evening's engagement. They spent most evenings together – or at least, under the same roof, be it their own or someone else's – but when the evening engagement was over, Basil usually went off to some club or mess to drink vodka and play cards until the early hours of the morning. Within Byeloskoye he had his own suite of apartments, and Anne hers.

A busy life, certainly; but, she was aware, lacking some essential ingredient. It was hollow, false, a mere shadow of real life; it wearied, but did not satisfy her. She and Basil had not slept together for over a year, she reflected. It was not that she missed his physical advances, or had relished them when she had them; but it was the most obvious symptom of the fact that their marriage was not what she would have wanted or expected. She had married him as a means of escape, and to acquire security for herself, and if they were not good reasons, they were at least the reasons for which a great many women married. Basil had loved her – so he said, and so she believed. She had thought her numbness would last for ever, that she would never be able to feel anything deeply again; but the pleasure of being beloved would have warmed her practical sentiments into something better. Theirs might have been a contented, if not a passionate, partnership.

But the love, if it ever existed, did not last long. Anne went a virgin to her wedding bed, knowing nothing of the facts, and little of the feelings beyond the undefined yearnings she had felt in Kirov's arms. She found it deeply, distressingly embarrassing to get into the same bed with Basil Andreyevitch, both of them in their nightgowns and caps; and what happened after the candles were snuffed and the bed curtains drawn was astonishing, painful, and repellant.

She could not believe that he had got it right. Surely no all-knowing, all-forgiving Deity could have designed it that way? And yet Basil Andreyevitch had something of a reputation as a gallant – ought he not to know? Perhaps, she pondered, his reputation for gallantry had been like his reputation for wit – going a long way before the truth. Certainly he seemed to find almost as little gratification in what he did to her unwilling body as she did.

To her relief, his attempts on her grew less frequent after the first few weeks, and she rewarded his restraint by being more pleasant and attentive towards him on the mornings after nights when they had simply gone to sleep. When the thing had been done, she found it hard to meet his eye in the morning, and her embarrassment made her cool and distant with him; and sometimes she felt guilty about it, for if he really did love her, and his love drove him to want to do that extraordinary thing, ought she not to be more accommodating?

But it transpired at last that he must have been doing something right, for she became pregnant. As soon as her condition was confirmed, Basil moved out of her bed to his own apartments, with what seemed like relief on both sides; and they had never slept together since. Eleven months after their wedding, Anne had given birth to his child.

Marya Vassilievna had arrived on the 8th of September with very little difficulty, a tiny, pink and white and gold baby, who had almost from the moment of her birth been nicknamed simply Rose. It was then that Anne discovered that all was not dead inside her. She would never have believed that she could feel so much for such a tiny scrap of humanity, but when her baby was first placed in her arms, and she gazed down on the soft, unused face, the perfect miniature fingers, the fragile skull with its delicate fronds of hair – her child, her own child born out of her own flesh! – she knew a love as powerful as it was complete and perfect.

Basil adored Rose on first sight, and the baby should have brought Anne and Basil together, a shared concern to make a bond between them; but two things prevented that from happening. Firstly, there was her sex. Basil's parents had been deeply upset over his choice of Anne as a wife. They had liked her well enough as Kirov's governess, but it was mortifying to have their only – and staggeringly eligible – son marry her, especially when she had neither family nor fortune. Had Basil not taken the precaution of marrying her first and telling them afterwards, they would probably never have accepted her. As it was, there was nothing they could do about it but put on a good face in public, though in private they remained cool towards her, and vented disappointed sighs whenever marriage arose as a topic of conversation.

In this they had the support, and more, of Olga, who could never forgive Anne for usurping her place at Basil's side, and for outshining her in intellectual society. Olga would have done anything she could to destroy Anne. As it was, she was quick to make profit out of it, when Anne destroyed herself by producing a female child. It was she who pointed out to her parents that Anna Petrovna had failed in her primary duty; who induced her mother to believe that Anna was probably incapable of bearing a son; and when her mother died only a week after Rose's christening, convinced her father that she had died of a broken heart, consequent upon the reflection that Basil was tied irrevocably to a barren woman.

Basil was in an unenviable position. Having chosen Anne knowing she would not meet with his parents' approval, he ought to have stood by her and forced them to accept her fully. But he had been single, and their darling, for too long. He and Olga had long preserved for each other the illusion of childhood, and with it went a dependancy on their parents' opinion and a need for their approval and love. His loyalty to Anne was too new and uncertain to outweigh the old love and loyalty; he was their child first, and Anne's husband only second. He equivocated, tried to mediate, attempted to please both sides and ended by pleasing neither; and Anne, disappointed and angry that he did not protect her from his parents' disapprobation, felt the first coolness, the first shadow of contempt for the man whom all her early upbringing had taught her she should trust and respect.

When his father died, leaving him both rich and an orphan, the moment might have arrived for the new ties to strengthen, for Rose to become the centre of his universe and the cement that bound him to Anne. But what had happened in the meantime made that impossible – indeed, made it difficult for him even to think about his daughter without pain.

Rose, so enchantingly pink and white that she was nicknamed after the loveliest flower of all, was a healthy, happy baby – small, but perfectly formed, with pale golden hair and pale blue eyes. She hardly ever cried, and had a smile for everyone, and everyone who hung over her cot became her willing slave. In February 1810, when she was five months old, she was taken to St Basil's Cathedral for her Christening. It was a very grand and fashionable affair: the Grand Duchess Catherine herself – the Tsar's sister – had agreed to be godmother to the baby, and Prince Yussupov, a close neighbour whose Arkhangelskoye Palace was one of the wonders of Moscow, was the godfather.

The cathedral was packed – everyone who was anyone was there. An anthem was sung by the choir, and the trumpeters of the Preobrazhensky Guards played a fanfare. The Metropolitan himself conducted the service, annointing the baby's hands and feet with holy oil from the tip of a new goosefeather. The godfather carried her round the font for everyone to see, while the solemn prayers were said, and the godmother held the lighted taper, representing the light which would lead the infant on the safe path. Lastly, the priest cut off a small piece of the baby's hair, and stuck it with a drop of wax from the taper. When it had hardened, he dropped it into the font, where it should have floated, signifying good luck.

But the wax didn't float: because of some defect, it sank to the bottom, taking the tuft of fine golden hair with it. An awful silence fell, rippling outwards from the font as the word of what had happened was passed back; and Rose, who until that moment had borne everything with a calm smile, suddenly screwed up her face and wailed. It was a dreadful omen. Deeply embarrassed and upset, the Metropolitan hastily repeated the ritual, and this time the wax floated as it should; the baby was soothed and the crying stopped; and the assembled company trooped off to enjoy the enormous Christening feast, where quantities of French champagne soon restored the smiles to their faces.

Probably few people afterwards remembered the unfortunate incident; but a week later old Countess Tchaikovskova caught a fever and died, and on the following day baby Marya Vassilievna fell victim to a mysterious illness. The best doctors in Moscow were called in, and confessed themselves baffled. The baby was feverish, vomited, wailed, jerked her limbs in spasm: they had never seen anything quite like it, they said, and could only apply the old remedies of bleeding and purging in the hope that they would work.

Anne never left the baby day or night, snatching sleep sitting upright in a chair placed beside the crib, despite Basil's attempts to persuade her to go to bed, and his urgent requests to take her place in the vigil. She would only shake her head, too weary even to speak. She could not go; how could he even ask it? Everything in the world that she loved, that was precious to her – dear God, it was her baby lying there, suffering! How could she leave her side? The doctors sighed and shook their heads, and Anne stared at them with anger and despair, with an anguish that burned her as the fever burned her baby. Days and nights ran into one another, and Anne hung over the crib, all of life condensed to that one point, the tiny flame that struggled and flickered and dimmed. As great as had been the joy of bringing Rose into the world, so great was the pain of watching her die.

Everything was done that could be done. Three priests took it in turn to remain in the room reciting prayers for deliverance, and Basil made offerings to every saint who could conceivably have any influence in the case; but still the fever mounted, and now the baby no longer cried or jerked, but simply lay motionless. How could so small a life bear so much? There was so little of her: Anne, tearless with so great a suffering, waited in helpless pity, and prayed to God in the new form she had learned when she converted to the Old Faith for her marriage. If you must take her, she prayed, take her quickly. Don't make my baby suffer any more – let her die.

But Rose didn't die. When her tiny spark of life was dimmed almost to quenching, like a miracle the fever broke, and she fell into a natural, healing sleep. After a further week, the doctors pronounced her out of immediate danger. There was no reason, they said cautiously, why she should not live to adulthood; oh, but here was a bitter, bitter price to pay! Many had been the times since that Anne had wished Rose had died. Why had God left this pathetically thin scrap of a child with stick-like arms and legs to lie motionless in her crib, too sickly even to cry, only uttering sometimes a frail whimper of pain? The enchanting pink and white baby was no more. Rose's hair fell out after the fever, and what grew back was not golden and curly like before, but barley brown and limp, lying across the fragile skull as if devoid of any vitality. The thin little face did not smile, and one pale eye was turned up and to the side in an ugly squint.

The doctors said that the power might come back to her limbs in time, that with careful nursing she might grow up to be almost normal. Almost normal! Her child, Anne had brooded blackly, to have no more than a hope of almost-normality; the golden future that should have been hers snatched away. Anne remained in the sickroom day after day, staring at the baby; Basil had absented himself, almost lived at his club, sent word merely each evening, a formal enquiry after the progress of Marya Vassilievna to which the brooding mother never replied.

Then one day Anne emerged from her darkness, became brisk and business-like and determined. She engaged a full nursery staff to take care of Rose – a wet-nurse, a day nurse, a physician, and a governess – Mlle Parmoutier, a quiet, sensible Belgian woman. Rose should have everything she could possibly need, anything that might in any way give her comfort or improve her condition. Anne went every morning to visit the nursery before she went out, and again in the evening when she had dressed for dinner; and for the rest of the time, she tried to forget what she could not endure to think about. She loved Rose so much, and it was an agony that she could do nothing for her. The sight of her child so stricken, so thin, partly paralysed, a dreadful parody of herself, tore so badly at her heart that she must shut her mind to it or be destroyed.

Basil, she guessed, felt much the same, and the knowledge of his anguish only made hers worse. Though he had wanted a son, and had allowed himself to join with his parents in disappointment when Rose was born, his first sight of her had converted him. He had adored her extravagantly. It was by his desire that the Christening party had been such a grand occasion; he had bought her extravagant gifts – a Christening gown of exquisite lace, a silk shawl more costly than any gown Anne had ever worn, a solid gold teething ring to suck on. He had planned ahead for her growing-up, her first puppy, her first pony, her first grown-up gown, her first ball, the match he would make for her – though who could be good enough? Many a time Anne had found him hanging over the crib, one forefinger firmly encircled by Rose's diminutive fist, telling her all his plans, while the golden baby gazed up at him and smiled and smiled.

He never visited the nursery now, and Rose was never mentioned between them. The common love which might have brought them together turned into a pain which drove them apart simply in self-preservation. They pursued their social careers more intently than ever, filling every moment with activity, allowing their minds no instant of repose where pain might settle. Outwardly their life seemed quite normal, and since children were not usually spoken about socially until they were old enough to be brought down to the drawing-room, there was nothing in their daily round to suggest that it was not. The Tchaikovskys remained courteous to each other, presented to the world a united front of sophisticated partnership; but never quite met each other's eyes.

Anne's mission in Kuznetsky Most that morning was to buy a present for Basil, whose fortieth birthday was to be celebrated in a few days' time. She wanted to get something suitably remarkable, for everyone who came to the dinner and ball they were giving for the occasion would want to know what present she had given him. It must be a talking-point for the evening, something sufficiently valuable, unusual, and tasteful to fit in with the Tchaikovsky style. Yet what was there, she wondered with a frown, that you could buy for a rich man who could have anything he wanted for the asking? A man who wants nothing, wants nothing. She had already had three abortive outings, and had spent a month racking her brains in vain. Today, she was determined she would get something, even if it took all day – and to that end she had made no daytime appointments. She was free until the dressing-bell tonight.

On her orders, the coachman drove very slowly along the Kuznetsky Most, while she looked from side to side at the various shops, hoping an idea would strike her. People on the footpath stopped to stare as she passed, for everyone knew the Countess Tchaikovskova's white English horses, and now and then an acquaintance bowed or waved. Anne responded absently, her mind occupied elsewhere. A piano? A fur coat? A clock? A marble statue? Actually, now she thought of it, a marble bust of himself would have been a suitable present, but it was much too late to get one done now – and of course since he would have had to go to sittings, it could never have been kept a secret. Jewellery? Well, it had the advantage of being obviously expensive, and Basil, like most Russians, liked wearing jewels.

'Drive to Fontenardes,' she told the coachman, who lifted his whip in acknowledgement. Fontenardes, the court jewellers, had a large shop at the end of the boulevard, where not only did they design and make modern jewellery, but also sold antiques: Russian, Oriental, Egyptian, Persian, and of course French – the spoils of the Revolution. It was a shop she liked visiting in any case, for there was an oddly informal atmosphere, generated by the affectionate way Russians regarded their jewels – almost as if they were pet animals, or favourite children.

When she went in, there was no-one immediately to attend her. Monsieur D'Avila, the manager, was engaged in conversation with Count Razumovsky. He begged the Countess to excuse him, and invited her to sit down for a few moments until he was at liberty. Anne preferred to wander about the shop, looking at the various items displayed in glass cases, some of which were for sale, others simply exhibits – items of antiquity or curiosity.

Amongst the former, Anne was most attracted to a diamond necklace, and she stood in contemplation of it for some time. It was displayed all alone in its cabinet on a bed of dark blue velvet: a beautifully simple thing, the centrepiece being an enormous oval diamond of breathtaking size and quality. It was set in a frame of gold wires, in the centre of a gold chain; and to either side, at intervals along the chain, smaller, brilliant-cut diamonds were also suspended, hanging at the ends of fine chains like droplets of sparkling water gathered for an instant before they fell.

It was beautiful – simple and beautiful; and it would suit her perfectly, she knew. She imagined how it would look, with a décolleté evening gown, very simple, of white silk embroidered with gold threads. Yes! And then suddenly she rememberd the Embassy Ball in Paris, so long ago, when Count Kirov had said to her that she ought to wear diamonds, and she had laughed inwardly at the very idea. How long ago it seemed! She hadn't thought of him for a long time – consciously, that is, for sometimes he would invade her dreams, and she would wake with tears on her cheeks. She would dream of him, always just out of reach, turning away from her, perhaps, or glimpsed from the window of a speeding carriage; a hand stretched out, just beyond her grasp, and a sad, reproachful look. She would dream of Nasha, too, and Nasha would become Rose, cold and white and dead; her fault, oh God, her fault! In her dream old spectres were raised, old griefs relived, deep wounds forgotten or set aside in daylight proved themselves unhealed. Her dreams were beyond her control: sometimes she dreaded going to sleep.

She shook her head a little, to shake away the unwelcome thoughts which had suddenly evaded her defences, and as if in answer to that shake of the head, she heard his voice saying, 'But yes, it would look very well. It would suit you entirely.'

I imagined it, she thought; and yet how real it seemed. She turned slowly, and he was there, standing just behind her, looking down at her with a painful intensity, as though it hurt him. I'm dreaming, she thought; it must be a vivid dream. And then she saw behind him the ravaged, one-eyed face of Adonis, emerging from the collar of the cavalry trooper's uniform in which his stocky, muscular body was incongruously confined.

'I would never have dreamed that,' she said aloud. 'It is you.'

'It is you,' he repeated, as if he hadn't been sure until she spoke. 'Anna Petrovna.'

'Yes,' she said foolishly. She stared at him, unable to think of anything to say. His face looked thinner and browner than when she had last seen him, almost three years ago; and she saw that there were some silver hairs mixed in with the soft brown. It touched her unbearably that he should have silver hairs, and she had to bit her lower lip for a moment. Time should not touch him. It wasn't fair.

'What are you doing here?' she said at last. It was, at least, no more foolish than anything else she might have asked.

'I'm on my way to Tula, to see Lolya,' he said.

When Anne had left his employ he had no desire to search for another governess, so Yelena had stayed on with her aunt and uncle Davidov, sharing her cousin Kira's education and regularly visiting her grandmother in Moscow. A young woman not yet out did not come much in Anne's way, but she had seen her at a distance, passing in a carriage, or coming out of a shop. Once they had come face to face at a military review, Lolya in the company of her grandmother and one of Vera Borisovna's elderly military beaux. Lolya's face had lit up, and she had been on the brink of uttering a glad welcome, but the Dowager had frozen the words with a look before they reached the air, and hurried Lolya away with the hint of a pinch in her stiff, shiny fingers on Lolya's arm. She had never forgiven Anne for calling her interfering, and above all, for marrying into the aristocracy and thus obliging Vera Borisovna to acknowledge her in her own friends' drawing-rooms.

'I called in here to try to find a present for her,' the Count went on. He glanced around, but his eyes would only stay an instant away from Anne's. He gave a rueful smile. 'I come from Paris, where I could have bought any number of charming things; but foolishly I left it until I got to Moscow.'

'You've come from Paris?'

'Just this instant arrived.' He spread his hands. 'You see me in my travelling dirt. But what are you doing here?'

'I live here,' she said. There was no reason, after all, that he should know anything about her life since she had left him. It was far less likely that she would be spoken of in Paris than he in Moscow.

But he smiled, and all sorts of things inside her loosened and melted; her body obeying the atavistic commands, in spite of her sophisticated mind. Not dead, but asleep, all those old, lovely, painful things! Peace, heart – lie down. This is not for you.

'I meant,' he said, 'what are you doing in this shop? Foolish!'

'Oh – I came to buy a present, too.'

'For whom?'

She didn't want to speak of her husband to the Count. Reluctantly she said, 'For Basil Andreyevitch. It's his birthday next week. His fortieth birthday.'

Yes, he minded, she could see. 'Ah, then it must be something special,' he said lightly, looking away from her. 'I had better not interrupt you.'

But I don't love him, she wanted to cry out. Don't shut yourself away from me! Don't be distant! She mustn't, she mustn't – and yet he was so much to her, he fitted so naturally into the place inside her that was his, always.

'Please,' was what came out, and a little fluttering movement of the hand went with it, which halted Kirov like a bullet through the heart. 'Help me.'

He caught the hand; her fingers closed around his; their eyes met, and everything flowed between them, everything they felt, everything they had suffered, and would suffer. 'Yes,' he said in a low, passionate voice. 'Anything – I would do anything for you! You know that!'

Her whole body trembled towards him; her mind, running ahead, had put her in his arms, held close against him, safe, belonging, loved, warm; was holding him with all her strength, never to let go again. It would have been impossible then for either of them to have done or said anything remotely resembling a normal social exchange in a jeweller's shop, had not Adonis at that moment barked a warning cough; and the next instant D'Avila, having finished with Count Razumovsky, was beside them, inclining his head in a way that was part courteous greeting, and part a tactful way of not noticing that they had been holding hands.

'Madame Tchaikovsky,' he said in his curious Castilian French, 'what a pleasure and privilege to see you here! I am so sorry to have kept you waiting. How may I help you? And Monsieur de Kirov — a rare pleasure indeed, monseigneur!'

Their hands had parted. Anne faced D'Avila with astonishing calm.

'I have come to try to choose a present for the Count,' she said graciously. 'Something unusual — something special — to mark a special occasion.'

D'Avila looked intelligent, almost conspiratorial. He nodded attentively. '*Bien sûr*, Madame! And what form shall this present take? A ring, perhaps? Monseigneur has just the kind of hands that most elegantly display a ring to the best advantage!'

Anne saw just in time the direction of his eyes; met the Count's wicked gleam of amusement at the misunderstanding, and stifled the laughter that suddenly, for the first time in so very long, welled up inside her. 'That is true,' she said in a voice which barely trembled, 'but I think my husband already has more rings than he can wear.'

The tips of D'Avila's ears grew pink. 'Then madame,' he readjusted almost without pausing, 'perhaps a snuffbox? I have some quite delightful boxes — one with the most exquisite grisaille paintings on the panels — quite *curious* scenes . . . ' His emphasis on the word revealed that curious in this case meant obscene. 'There is not another like it in the world, I assure you, madame!'

Yes, it was the sort of thing Basil would like, she thought; and it would make a talking point, and be a daring present from a wife to a husband. But she could not buy such a thing in front of Kirov, admit her husband's taste in front of him, allow him to think what he would inevitably think from the choice of such a present. 'A snuffbox? I don't know,' she said as if musingly; and then out of the corner of her eyes, saw Kirov smiling at her predicament, knowing perfectly well what D'Avila, the old sinner, meant by *curious*. 'No,' she said defiantly, 'I think something more unusual – something exotic, perhaps. You had a jewelled dragon once, Monsieur D'Avila, as I remember, that came from Cathay . . . '

'Ah yes, I remember it well, madame! A rare piece – the property of a Chinese Emperor. Unfortunately, too expensive for the private purse. We were quite in a worry what to do with it. When a thing becomes priceless, madame, it becomes, in a curious way, worthless.' He looked reflective.

'And what did you do with it?' Kirov asked.

'I suggested to Monsieur Fontenarde that it had better be broken up and melted down to be used again, though that would have been a great shame.'

'Indeed,' Kirov murmured.

'Oh yes – it was a remarkable piece. So Monsieur Fontenarde decided in the end to present it to the Emperor.' He sighed. 'A fitting end for such a remarkable piece,' he concluded glumly.

'Well, I have no desire for something beyond price,' Anne said. The absurd laughter was still bubbling up inside her, and she knew it was simply because *he* was here, standing beside her, sharing her thoughts and her amusements – simple, unreasoning reaction to his presence. 'Have you no smaller dragon? One that it is possible to value?'

D'Avila knew he was being laughed at, and drew on his dignity like a coat. 'No, madame, I regret absolutely – ' he began, and then stopped, thought, and lifted a finger. '*Attendez!* There is something – it came in yesterday from a merchant we sometimes deal with – widely travelled – it was part of a horde of treasure left by a Persian warlord. It is not new, you understand, madame – by way of being an antiquity, in fact, but unusual, and quite fine, quite fine. Perhaps . . . ?'

'Please,' said Anne graciously.

'Then, if you would step this way,' D'Avila said, extending his hand towards the back room. Anne flickered a glance at Kirov, asking him to stay with her, and he answered it with a glint of the eye which said he wouldn't miss it for the world.

In the small back room, D'Avila sat her at the table, and drew out a bunch of keys from his fob. Selecting one, he opened a cupboard in the corner, and took out a bundle wrapped in green cloths, which he brought over and placed on the table in front of Anne. It was evidently heavy – he carried it in both hands, and it filled them. Reverently, he pulled the cloths away, and stepped back to allow Anne to look her fill.

'Persian work,' he said at last when she didn't speak. 'The treatment is a little primitive perhaps, to our eyes, but the work is very fine.'

It was a tiger. About eight inches long and four high, made of gold; head low between its shoulders, it prowled, the mouth open, the tip of the tail just curling up alertly. The gold of its solid yet sinuous body was of two colours, the darker gold making the stripes, and the eyes were emeralds. It was a beautiful thing, alive, full of power.

'I have other things,' D'Avila began, feeling Anne's silence must be disapproving, but she interrupted him.

'How much is it?' she asked, and then, without waiting for him to answer, 'I must have it. It's perfect!'

D'Avila, who had opened his mouth to name a preposterous price, was so taken aback he closed it again. This was not the way the game was supposed to go: there should be at least half an hour of delicate, oblique bargaining ahead before they closed on a price a little more than half the first one he named. But she had taken the pleasure out of it for him now. Almost sulkily, he named the price he had expected to get in the end, and though it was very high indeed, Anne agreed to it almost absently.

'I'll have it sent to Byeloskoye, madame,' D'Avila said gloomily.

'No, I'll take it with me,' Anne said quickly. She did not want to part with it; but now Kirov intervened, touching her wrist lightly.

'Have it sent,' he said. She looked up into his eyes. 'It's inconveniently heavy, you'll find,' he murmured. Her heart stopped and started again.

'Very well,' she said to D'Avila, 'send it; but make sure it is given to no-one but my secretary or my maid. I wish it to remain a surprise until the Count's birthday.'

They stepped outside into the sunshine. Anne was astonished that it was the same day, that the sun was almost in the same position. So much time seemed to have passed: she hardly felt like the same person. So few words had passed between her and Kirov, and yet the brief transaction had rolled back the intervening years, had placed them on a footing of intimacy they had done nothing to deserve: she was at ease with him, as though they had been married twenty years. All the same, her blood seemed to be singing in her veins, and every breath she took seemed to expand her lungs with astonishment; exhilarating, like the air at the top of a mountain.

She looked up at him and said simply, 'What now?'

He regarded her in silence for a moment. His eyes seemed to penetrate past hers and into her mind, as if seeking information, or perhaps assurance.

391

'Can you trust your maid?' he asked abruptly.

'Yes,' she said doubtfully – not because she was unsure of Pauline, but because she didn't know what he was planning.

'Send your carriage home,' he said, 'and come for a drive with me. Your maid will ride with us, and Adonis will drive us.'

Yes, she thought, I can trust Adonis, I see that. 'Very well,' she said, and beckoned her footman to her.

The Count's carriage – an elderly landaulette, obviously a hired coach, but with a decent, if unremarkable pair of horses – was standing a little further down the road, with a driver dozing on the box. While Anne dismissed her own carriage, the Count paid off the driver, and Adonis climbed up and took over the reins. There was not room for three inside the carriage, and Pauline, with a doubtful look at Adonis, was obliged to sit on the box beside him.

Anne heard no command pass between the Count and his body servant as to their destination, but he seemed to know well enough, and sent the horses forward into a confident trot. He must have told him where to go while I was talking to my coachman, Anne thought; noticing with the only small, unaffected part of her brain that she had been noticed by someone on the footpath – Madame Gagarin, she thought it was – who was bowing to her, but with eyebrows raised in mild surpirse.

Adonis left the main thoroughfares, and Anne soon lost her bearings, only regaining them when they passed out of the city over the Dorogomilov Bridge. She didn't ask where they were going: she was only happy to be with him again. For the moment, he didn't seem to need to talk, either. He sat beside her, not looking nor touching, his hands resting in his lap, seeming utterly relaxed.

The journey didn't take very long; soon the carriage turned into a gateway, passed along a drive between tall, overgrown hedges, and pulled up before a large wooden house, painted terracotta red. It was very quiet – nothing but the sound of birds rioting in the overgrown shrubbery – and the house had an air of neglect. The paint was peeling here and there, silvery and sun-blistered on the shutters, and a creeper had grown over the upstairs windows.

'Whose house is this?' she asked at last, mildly.

'It's mine,' he said. 'It belonged to my first wife. I hardly ever come here now – when I'm in Moscow I usually stay with Mother – but I always kept it, just in case.'

'Is it empty?'

He was examining the façade and the garden with a critical eye. 'There's a housekeeper, and her husband tends the grounds. Not very well, by the look of it. If ever I come here, I send word ahead, and they hire extra servants and get things ready.'

Now he looked at her, perhaps a little apologetically. 'I thought we ought to go somewhere where we could talk privately. Where we wouldn't be overheard.'

'Yes,' Anne said, seeing the sense of it. They needed to talk, although she felt that it didn't much matter what they talked about. But was there more? She looked up at the façade of the house, and it seemed like a face – patient, dumb, watchful, the half-shuttered eyes, the closed, secretive mouth. Was it sin? she wondered, with distant curiosity. Was it the face of sin?

'Are you expected anywhere? When do you have to be back?'

She hadn't even considered that aspect of it, but now the thought came to her gloriously, obliterating all other considerations. Her formal, organised, careful and empty life had looked away for a moment, had inadvertently set her loose; no-one knew where she was, and no-one would wonder.

She smiled, lighting her whole face. 'I have all day,' she said.

Chapter Twenty-Three

Inside the house smelled of dusty carpets. The housekeeper was evidently taken aback, wringing her hands and glancing back at her silent husband, who had emerged behind her from the kitchen with a line of foam on his upper lip. 'If you had only let me know, master!' she cried again and again. 'I could have had everything ready for you.'

'It doesn't matter, Yasmin,' he said patiently. 'Go and make us some tea, and bring it up to the green drawing-room. And see our servants are made comfortable.' He turned to Anne. 'Everything will be in dust-sheets, I expect.'

The drawing-room was on the first floor, and Anne soon saw why he had chosen it. It had long French windows all along one side, beyond which was a narrow balcony with a pierced-work rail, looking over the tangled garden. The Count opened all the windows, and at once the fresh, green-scented air flooded in, driving away the mustiness and gloom. He stripped the Holland covers off some chairs and a table, and dragged them out onto the balcony, and then invited Anne to come out and sit down.

The sun had gone round enough for the balcony to be in the shade, and the view was glorious: beyond the overgrown garden, which sloped gently away downhill, the prospect opened up, and the whole of Moscow was spread out in the sunshine in a magnificent Oriental tangle of shapes and colours. Embraced by the long, low honey-coloured sweep of the city walls, the houses sprawled maroon and egg yellow, rose pink and holly green, interspersed with the blue spires and glinting golden cupolas of innumerable churches, and the brilliant white walls and blood-red roofs of the great palaces. The spaces between were filled with the dark, satisfying green of summer vegetation; the Moskva coiled in a silvery loop across the smiling land; and the whole was presided over by the red walls and multicoloured, spiralled and gold-tipped domes of the Kremlin.

They sat in silence for a while. Anne felt at peace, unhurried. All the things were there between them to be said, but it didn't need to be yet; difficult things, many of them, but lying peacefully asleep in the corner of her mind – no need to disturb them now.

'What a place!' she said at last, softly. 'I still find it hard sometimes to believe that I'm here.'

He grunted, seeing what she saw, and what she remembered, side by side in astonishing contrast. 'You are very much at home here now, by all accounts: Madame Tchaikovsky, they say, is the leader of the *ton*! Oh yes, even in Paris we get news of home – the gossip comes in the diplomatic bag! You've done well for yourself, Anna Petrovna – just as I always said you would.'

So he had heard of her since they last met. Somehow it disturbed her, as if some cord that connected them had not been severed along with the others, without her knowing about it. She did not want him to be approving of her hollow success, to applaud her sham of a victory. She wanted him to mind, but could not bear it if he did; and this was all too close to the difficult things that ought not yet to be disturbed. She sought for a neutral topic, one which would sufficiently engage them both. 'Have you seen Caulaincourt?' she asked. 'You know he was recalled to Paris? Did he arrive before you left?'

'Yes, indeed. I had a long talk with him on the day he arrived from Petersburg. He thinks his being replaced is an ominous sign – indeed, as I do – especially as his replacement is Jacques de Lauriston.'

'I haven't had a chance to meet him yet. I liked Caulaincourt very much. What is Lauriston like?'

'Oh, he's a good man – but you see it's a military appointment, rather than a purely civilian one. Lauriston is a general, an experienced soldier. It's all of a piece with Napoleon's state of mind.'

'So you think war is likely?' Anne asked.

The relationship between Russia and France had been worsening steadily year by year, incident by incident. There had been that business over Napoleon's second marriage, for instance. When Grand Duchess Catherine had refused him, Napoleon had offered instead for the Tsar's younger sister Anna, who was just fifteen. By a clause in the previous Tsar's will, the Empress-Dowager had been given final veto over the choice of husband for her daughters; and hating the Corsican Anti-Christ with an utterly Russian fervour, she refused absolutely to consider the match. The Tsar had hesitated to offend such a powerful ally, and after stalling for a number of weeks, finally told Napoleon that Anna was too young, and could not be married until she was eighteen.

Napoleon had then concluded a marriage treaty with the Emperor of

Austria for his daughter Marie-Louise, but with a speed which suggested he had been carrying on negotiations all along, even while waiting for Alexander's reply. This infuriated the Tsar, but also alarmed him. Russia and Austria were old rivals, having been the most interested parties in the partition of Poland. The Tsar was always afraid that a closer relationship between France and Austria would result in an expansion of Austrian control over former Polish territories.

The new Empress Marie-Louise had presented Napoleon with a healthy son in March 1811, only a year after their marriage, which must have been galling for Alexander, whose frail wife had only managed to give him two daughters, both of whom had died. The birth of the baby was attended by great pomp and celebration, and Napoleon immediately created him King of Rome – a title which annoyed the old established royal houses.

But the greatest cause of contention between the two Emperors was undoubtedly the embargo – the Continental System, as it was called. Napoleon was still determined to defeat England by crippling her trade, closing the Continent absolutely to her goods; and for a while it had looked as though it would work. News from England had been alarming – of bankruptcies, of factories working only half the week, of warehouses choked with unsaleable goods, of soaring prices and starvation. But the Continent could not do without England either, especially as her navy controlled the carrying trade. No imports meant no exports; stagnation entered the veins of European commerce. Inflation was rife, currencies were devalued, the unemployed roamed the streets and lanes in starving mobs, and smuggling grew to epidemic proportions.

So the previous year, in July, Napoleon had eased the situation by granting licences to trade with England to certain French companies, by which they could import necessities such as sugar and soda and clothing, and export French corn and wine. A secondary effect of the policy was a vast increase to French treasury resources from the duties; but the rest of Europe looked on sourly, and commented that since Napoleon could not suppress the smuggling, he had resorted to running the trade himself, while other nations were still obliged to keep their ports closed.

The Tsar, in protest, had begun to allow neutral ships to unload their cargoes in Baltic ports, easing the situation in Russia, where the stagnation of trade had caused severe hardship. In October Napoleon wrote him a furious letter of protest, saying that the 'neutral' ships were really English ships, disguising themselves by flying a flag of convenience, and he ordered the Tsar to confiscate the goods he had allowed to be landed. The Tsar refused; and Napoleon responded by annexing the rest of the Baltic coastal countries, and closing off the loophole.

Included in the annexation was the Duchy of Oldenburg. Oldenburg was a tiny, marshy flatland sovereignty of no great importance, except that its present incumbent, Duke Peter, was married to the Empress-Dowager's favourite sister; and his second son Prince George was married to the Grand Duchess Catherine, the Tsar's favourite sister. Relations between Alexander and Napoleon deteriorated still further.

Then in December the Tsar issued a decree imposing a heavy tax on the import into Russia of luxuries. This was done to try to protect the rouble, whose exchange rate had declined dangerously because of the Continental System. All luxury goods were included, but the worst affected were French silks, lace, and wine, which had been flooding into the country since 1807. It was a blow which Napoleon took personally. The relationship between the two Emperors was now at its lowest ebb, and in countries like Russia and France, virtual dictatorships, that was ominous.

'From what Caulaincourt told me, war is inevitable,' Kirov said. 'Napoleon saw him straight away, the moment he arrived in Paris, but he said there was nothing like the warmth and affection Napoleon usually showed him. He seemd to think Caulaincourt had been seduced by the Tsar and was no longer to be trusted, and you know nothing could more incense Armand than to have his loyalty impugned.'

'I can imagine. He's the most honest man in Europe.'

'Just so. At all events, he did his best to explain Russian grievances. When Napoleon complained that the Tsar wasn't honouring his promise to uphold the Continental System, he said that Russia could hardly be expected to sustain hardships which France was now avoiding by the issue of licences.'

The servants came in with the samovar and the tray of cups, spoons and sugar bowl. Kirov stopped and waited until they had arranged everything and withdrawn. Anne performed the ritual with accustomed ease, aware that he was watching the movements of her hands with a faint smile: the English governess was very far from home. She handed his cup, and he resumed.

'Thank you. Then Napoleon complained that Russian troops had been moved up as far as the Dvina river, which he said was an aggressive move. Caulaincourt pointed out that Napoleon had been moving troops up to Danzig and Prussia for weeks, and that the Tsar was naturally worried that this meant the Kingdom of Poland was about to be recreated.' He stirred his tea thoughtfully. 'Poland's a little of a sore point with Caulaincourt anyway, because he was the one who drew up the document – which Napoleon eventually refused to sign – agreeing to expunge the name of Poland from all official documents for ever.'

'Yes, I remember. It was supposed to be a guarantee that Poland would never be reinstated. Everyone was quite excited about it.'

'I don't think Napoleon ever meant to ratify it: it's all a part of his policy of *reculer pour mieux sauter*. Perhaps Armand was beginning to realise that: he must have shown his resentment at that point, because Napoleon apparently lost his temper, and shouted that Armand was the dupe and tool of the Russians. Armand flared up, and said that he was willing to be arrested on the spot and place his head on the block if Lauriston didn't confirm every word of what he'd said.'

Anne took his cup to refill it. 'He must have been deeply hurt to react so strongly. He is always so restrained.'

'Yes. It must have been a surprise for the Emperor, too, because he calmed down after that; but Armand said the rest of the conversation – and it went on for five hours – was utterly frustrating. Napoleon was convinced – or claimed to be – that Russia was the aggressor, and wanted war, and was trying to frustrate his plans to defeat England. Then when Armand insisted that Alexander didn't want war, Napoleon said it must be because he was afraid of him. He seemed convinced that a short campaign and one good battle would have the cowardly Russians running for cover and begging for peace.'

Anne noticed with amusement that even the rational, cosmopolitan Kirov was annoyed by this insulting view of his people.

'Caulaincourt did his best to persuade Napoleon that Alexander wasn't afraid of invasion, told him the sheer size of the country, the difficulties of the terrain, and the climate would defeat the French without any need for battle. But to every point the Emperor simply replied that Caulaincourt had been deceived by his love of St Petersburg and by Alexander's charm. When I spoke to him afterwards, he was almost in tears at the impossibility of persuading the Emperor that to invade Russia would be a monstrous error. But as I told him, Napoleon simply has no concept of the size of Russia. He never was very good at distances.'

'Poor Caulaincourt. It would be hard, I imagine, for anyone to persuade Bonaparte he could be beaten.'

The Count grunted. 'He had no chance anyway. What he couldn't know was that Napoleon has already decided on war.' Anne looked her surprise. 'Oh yes – the movement of troops into northern territories is all part of a vast and careful plan. He's gathered huge quantities of military supplies secretly into depots at key points – Mainz and Danzig, for example – ready for invasion.'

'How do you know that, if it is a secret?'

He smiled. 'I told you once before, did I not, that we Russians know everything? But look – he's replaced Caulaincourt with a soldier, who can send him information about the Tsar's military preparedness, which dear Armand could never do! He's had new and better maps of Russia made and sent to his chief of staff, along with large-scale maps of Poland and Livonia. And – what few people know – he's told Lauriston to send back detailed maps of both Moscow and St Petersburg, to be engraved and copied.'

Anne stared. 'And how can you know that?'

'I have a good friend within the *Depot de la Guerre*,' he shrugged.

'But – surely – if it's true, shouldn't you tell someone, try to stop Lauriston? If Bonaparte has maps of Moscow and Petersburg . . . '

He put down his cup. 'Listen, Anna, listen! There's no chance in the world of Napoleon's defeating Russia. He has no concept, no concept at all of how great the distances are, how short the summer, how bitter the winter! He's given no orders for winter clothing for the army, you know, or extra footwear for the infantry.'

'Perhaps he means to be finished before winter starts.'

'He can't begin the campaign – and he knows this – until the field crops in Russia have ripened, because he'll need them to feed the horses as he advances. That means he can't begin until June at least. That gives him a maximum of five months before his army is hopelessly trapped by the onset of winter, and it will take him four months – with an ever-lengthening chain of supply – to get his army from the borders to Moscow.' He gave a curious grimace. 'If he ever gets that far. He hasn't taken the Cossacks into account. Oddly enough, no-one's told him about them; and if they had, he wouldn't believe them. Napoleon is a great man in his way – he can perform miracles on the field of battle by his sheer presence – but like all dictators, his vision is very narrow. He has no imagination, and that is one thing you cannot do without when you are dealing with Russia. He doesn't understand the country or the people – and he doesn't want to.'

'You *want* him to invade Russia? You think we can beat him?'

If he noticed that tell-tale 'we', he didn't refer to it. 'We won't need to. Russia will defend herself, as she always has. Nothing – *nothing* – can destroy Russia. She cannot die, unless she loses the will to live. And as to wanting the war – don't you see, this is the only chance there may ever be of destroying Napoleon? He has been growing year by year, swallowing whole nations, swelling up into monstrous proportions. Your own country has been at war with France for almost *twenty years* – '

'Undefeated,' Anne said quickly, stung by the implication.

'But without defeating him,' the Count pointed out. 'Now he is about to overreach himself. He will defeat himself – all we have to do is to let him.'

'But men will die!'

'They are dying already, by the thousand. How many lives have already been sacrificed to Napoleon's ambition? Only God could count them.'

There was a silence. Anne contemplated the prospect of war between Russia and France, of an invasion, of battles and bloodshed and death.

'When, do you think?'

'Next year. It is too late now, to begin this year. By next summer he will be ready.'

'Oh God,' Anne said, and reached out for his hand. 'It's like the end of the world.'

His strong, warm fingers closed round hers. 'No, no, *dushenka*, not the end, the beginning! God, I'm weary of this war. Since I met you eight years ago – eight years, little Anna – I have been longing for peace.' He transferred his grip to her wrist and pulled at her gently, drawing her from her seat and onto his lap, and she came, half reluctant, half longing, feeling how natural it was to be in his arms, knowing it was wrong. She trembled as he closed his arms round her, folded her close, resting his face against her hair. 'Peace, Anna – to stay home, and watch my crops grow, and be with those I love . . . '

He stopped, realising where that sentence led. There was a long silence as they both contemplated the impossibility of the situation. Suddenly he cried out, 'Oh Anna, why did you do it? Why?'

'You know why,' she said, muffled, against his neck.

'There was no need! My love, my love, I would never have harmed you! Why didn't you trust me?'

She raised her head to look at him, a long, clear look which cut to his heart. 'Trust you to do what? There was nothing you could do. If I had not married, we would be no better off. *You* are married – or had you forgotten?'

He looked broodingly into her eyes. 'No, I hadn't forgotten. But it does make a difference – two barriers instead of one.' He tightened his arms around her convulsively. 'I can't bear you to belong to anyone else! Oh Anna, *mylienkaya*, you do love me, don't you? Say you love me.'

'Yes, I love you, Nikolasha.'

He kissed her, brow and cheek and lips. 'Yes, yes, you love me,' he murmured, punctuating the words with kisses. 'It's been so long since I was with you – so hard to be away from you – and yet I never felt separated from you. Is that foolish? But you are so close to me in my mind – I understand you as no-one else in the world – and minds cannot be separated by mere distance. Do you feel it too?'

She understood what he meant, but it was different, always different, for a woman. A woman, her being so much more closely tied to the earth and the seasons, the rise and fall of the tides of life, needed the physical reassurance of love's presence. And a woman had not man's activity in the world to fulfil her days. He could say that he never felt separated from her and mean it – she knew he meant it; but she would never be able to make him understand her own isolation, and the loneliness – yes, she saw now that she had been appallingly lonely – of being married to the wrong person.

Yet there was something still to say that he would understand. 'I needed you,' she said. 'And yet as soon as you were near me again, I felt as if we had never been apart.'

'Yes, yes, that's it! Oh Anna, we belong together.' He kissed her again, and this time his lips lingered on hers, and her mouth yielded to his as their hunger suddenly flowered. She clung to him, and they kissed more and more avidly, until the moment came when she knew that this time there could be no drawing back. And she didn't want to. She was coming alive after the long dead season, feeling things she never thought to feel again. She wanted everything – all there was – all she could have – no matter what the cost. If there were suffering afterwards, so be it. She wanted it too much now to turn back, and she shut her mind resolutely to everything but the sensation of his mouth and his hands and his warm body and breath.

He knew: sensitive to her every reaction, he knew when – and what – she had yielded. He drew back his head to look into her eyes, but it was only for confirmation of what he already knew.

'Now?' he asked softly.

'Is it safe?' she asked; but she would not draw back, whatever his answer.

'No-one will disturb us. The servants will not come until we call them,' he said. He set her gently on her feet, took her hand, led her into the house, and she followed like a child, trusting beyond thought, feeling his strength and resolve in the grasp of his hand. The things from which he could not protect her were the only important things; yet she trusted him all the same, with her self, with her life. It was what she was for.

Along the passage, up a flight of broad, carpeted stairs, into a bedroom. The furniture was shrouded, the bed curtainless, but covered by a gold silk counterpane. The air was stuffy, for the sun was still slanting against the window, its strength hardly impeded by the white blind, which made a curious muted daylight in the room. He led her to the bed, and then took her in his arms again, to look down at her face and be sure. For answer she lifted her hands and took out the pin from his neck-cloth, and loosened the starched muslin. She could feel the urgency of his need pressing against her, and was beginning to be light-headed with desire. She wanted no delay. She must have him, and now.

He unhooked her gown, and would have helped her take it off, but she pushed his hands away, knowing she would do it quicker herself, freeing him to undress himself. Women's clothes were so simple these days, that there was very little for her to remove. The muslin gown; the little laced busk-bodice – no stays or corsets for the modern woman; the chemise; the gartered stockings; and then she was done.

Her body tingled, enjoying the unaccustomed sensation of air and light touching it, revelling in the freedom of nakedness. It was a release; surprisingly, wonderfully, it was even a security. She could feel herself stretching confidently, feel her skin glowing, and knew she was beautiful. Never in her life, since she was a very small child, had she been completely naked – never would she have imagined that she could stand naked before another human being – least of all a man – without suffering the deepest, most crippling embarrassment. Yet she stood watching Kirov coping with his far more complicated clothing, making no attempt to cover herself, wanting him to look at her, wanting to look at him.

When he let his last garment fall, and stood before her naked, she felt a strange, heady sense of wonder, almost awe, at the sight of his male body. She had never seen one before; she had known nothing of how it would look. Now she saw the great beauty of it: hard, smooth-contoured, unlike a woman's body; long bones and wide shoulders, the muscles designed for strength and endurance. His skin was milky white except for his face and hands, and smooth; hairless except for the dark crop at the base of his smooth belly, from which his penis arched strongly, as if with a life of its own.

She looked at the miraculous delicacy of his collar-bones, the tiny, mute nipples, pale pink as a child's, and she found him a thing of wonderful completeness, and yet curiously unfinished. Man, the bestrider of the world, the proud wielder of weapons, the subduer, when stripped naked was so vulnerable – not strong in nakedness, as she now perceived she was.

She looked into his eyes, and saw that he knew it, too. His desire for her made him weak, as it made her strong.

'You're beautiful,' she said. She looked again at his penis, and it seemed as though it were a separate thing from him, possessed of a primitive force that he could not control, drawing strength from the vitality of the earth, without reference to him. She understood now how men could be governed by it, driven by those desires which before had seemed to her incomprehensible. 'That's beautiful too,' she said. 'I've never seen a man before.'

He nodded, his eyes fixed on her; and then, in helpless appeal, he put out his hands to her, and she took them and lay down on the bed, drawing him with her. She was not the petitioner now: she had a great wealth to give him.

'Come, then,' she whispered.

He lay down beside her, and she felt his hands on her, and was filled with an unbearable excitement, though she hardly understood for what. He bent his head and kissed her breast, and she felt that same loosening, weakening sensation that she had known before with him, as if everything inside her were turning to liquid. He moved across her, she felt his penis hot and hard like a brand between them, and she put her arms round him to draw him closer.

Then it was – but not like anything she had known before. He entered her as though she were his home, and it was easy and good, with the goodness of something completely natural, something that was meant to be; like cool water after a long day's thirst. What with Basil had been a painful intrusion, with Nikolai was lovely, ravishing to the senses, utterly satisfying: her whole body sighed with relief at being completed at last. She felt him inside her – strange! wonderful! – and only wanted more, more of him, wanted to take the whole of him inside her and keep him folded in the warm darkness under her heart for ever.

She was unaware of anything but him, the touch of him, the smell of his skin the pulse of his life around her and inside her. She moved with him, towards him, wanting always more, to be closer, to yield up her separateness absolutely and be one thing, indivisible. And the life of their bodies quickened and caught each other's rhythm, and then they were absolutely together, no difference between them, one person. The thing was not part of them, they were part of it, carried along by it towards the place – oh, she wanted to be there, but she didn't want this to end, her soul would step out of her body and she would die if it should end!

She had not known there could be such feeling. Then for one beat of the heart everything stopped; they were suspended out of time in a miracle of light and sensation, soundless and breathless, as though the very stuff of the universe were streaming through them. Anne opened her eyes wide, and her mouth stretched in a soundless cry of ecstasy as she felt deep inside her the double convulsion of their accomplishment.

Years, aeons later he lifted his head and looked down at her, and saw she was crying; at least, her cheeks were wet, her eyelashes spiked and dark with tears.

'My love,' he said tenderly.

'How could I have known?' she whispered. 'How could I possibly have known?'

All the long, hot June afternoon they lay on the bed and talked. Anne found a new pleasure, the greatest pleasure she could imagine – to lie curled against her lover, her head in the hollow of his shoulder, and talk, utterly without restraint, with perfect trust and understanding. It seemed very natural – their intellectual companionship had, after all, long preceded any other relationship between them; but there was an extra dimension of intimacy now added, and the thoughts and ideas flowed more easily than ever between them, as their entwined bodies made a perfect conduit.

Their conversation ranged comfortably, circling and always coming back to what had happened between them. It seemed, at the last, all right.

'I can't feel guilty about it,' she said. 'Not yet, at all events.'

He stroked her hair. 'I can't believe you have ever been anyone else's. When I saw you in Fontenarde's, I thought you had changed. You seemed harder – so assured and sophisticated – very much the Madame Tchaikovsky I had heard about – and oh, my love, how that hurt! When I heard the gossip about you in Paris, I hated to think of your being spoilt, becoming a brittle-smiling, autocratic society hostess.

404

But now I see that you are still the same, my Annushka – underneath, you are the same, innocent girl I brought to Russia all those years ago. What sort of a man can you have married, to have left so little mark on you?'

She didn't want to talk about that. 'I didn't know what – marriage – would mean. Now I see this is what it ought to be like. Is it like this for everyone – for all lovers, I mean?' She tilted her face up enquiringly.

He smiled. 'How would I know that? You attribute me with a vastly flattering experience, *doushka*.'

'I love it when you call me that! But there have been others, haven't there? You've spent so long away – in Paris, particularly. There've been lots of others?'

He was touched, but wary. 'There were others; but never anything like this.'

'No,' she said, with satisfaction. 'I love you.'

'I love you, too. This was something that was due to us, Annushka; something we ought to have had, but was denied us.'

'It's a moment out of time – it doesn't count, does it? It's outside of real life.'

He pulled her against him. 'It's real – it's the most real thing of all. Don't doubt that.'

She was silent for a while, and then, measure of her ease, her confidence, she said, 'Tell me about them. I hear so little now. How is Irina?'

He did not immediately answer, and after a while she lifted her head to look at him. His eyes were distant; but she was not separate from him – she was where he was, looking outwards.

'She's not well. It's part of the reason I came home. My tour of duty doesn't end until September, but the good Fraulein Hoffnung wrote to me to say she was worried about her mistress. Since – since the death of Natasha – ' She saw that it was difficult for him to talk of it. The horror of the child's lonely death had changed everyone whom it touched. 'Irina just withdrew into herself. It was always her way to cope with things that troubled her, but now Fraulein Hoffnung says she is afraid her health is breaking down under the strain. I wrote to the Emperor, asking to be relieved. I can be of more use to him in Petersburg now, than in Paris, in any case.'

She saw that the tangle of reasons, personal and political, was not evenly balanced, but she didn't wonder at it. She knew a little of what he felt about his wife – more, really, than she wanted to know.

'So you've been to Schwartzenturm already? I thought you said you'd come straight from Paris.'

'I did – I have. I'm going to Petersburg after I've seen Lolya, and then to Schwartzenturm.'

'Ah, then it isn't serious? She isn't seriously ill?'

'I don't know.' He looked at her with a wry expression. 'Do you think I should have gone directly to her?' Anne couldn't help feeling a little shocked, and though she tried not to show it, he knew her too well for her to be able to disguise it from him. 'You're a strange one, Anna! You should rather want to keep me from her, keep me with you.'

She flinched. 'Ah, don't! You know –' Impossible to go on. There was too much guilt in her own heart – of thoughts, if not of deeds – to speak of it. Instead, with a painful eagerness, she said, 'Tell me about Sashka. God, how I've missed him! It was so terrible, Nikolasha, when I left. I waved goodbye to him at Chastnaya, saying that it was for a few weeks, and I never went back again. I dreamed of him for months, waving goodbye. I dreamed of him looking at me reproachfully.' She frowned, biting her lip, her eyes dark. 'He was like a son to me . . . '

'More than he has ever been to me,' Kirov said quietly. 'How can I tell you anything about him? Since he was born, I've hardly spent six months with him.'

'He must be – almost seven. Seven in August,' Anne mused. 'I don't suppose he would remember me now. Well, it's for the best, I suppose, as things are. And Lolya I know about – I see her now and then, and a very beautiful young lady she's grown into. I've heard she's the toast of the Cadets' mess – in a very discreet way, of course, since she's not out yet. When do you mean to bring her out? She's old enough now.'

'Next Season, in Petersburg. In November, I expect, if Irina's well enough. She can be presented at Court at the same time. It's another thing I had to come home for – my mother was beginning to write stern letters to me. She longs for Lolya to dazzle society –'

'*La belle Hélène*,' Anne murmured.

'Just so. Of course, it's really that Mama wants to be the toast herself, as she was when she was young, and hopes to do it vicariously through Lolya. I'm afraid she will make her very vain and silly, with her talk of breaking hearts and such female nonsense.' He kissed her brow. 'She doesn't have you, now, to keep her sensible.'

'Your sister is a sensible woman.'

'Shoora's a dear, but not clever. However, it was in the hope of mitigating the worst effects of Mama's flattery that I've left her in the

406

country, at Tula. My mother would have loved to have her in Moscow, but I refused to allow it. I wanted my little girl to grow up modest and natural.'

'Will you take her back with you when you go to Petersburg?'

'No – let her have one last summer of romping in the fields. I'll fetch her in October. That will be soon enough.'

Anne mused. 'I always thought you didn't understand about your mother.' He raised an eyebrow. 'I mean, I thought you were blind to her real character.'

'To her faults, you mean? No, dear love, I knew all about her – I grew up with her, don't forget, and watched what she did to my sisters. But what could I do? You can't change a grown woman, particularly a widow who's had the command of her own fortune all her life. And I could never bear to have to take sides between her and Irina. I owed a loyalty to both of them, and how could I choose? So I stood aside, and tried to make light of it.'

Anne's mind cried a protest: but you were wrong! You left Irina victim to your mother, who was twice as strong as she. You should have defended your wife – that was where your loyalty lay! She felt he had been at fault, and that it was a weakness on his part; and probably he knew he had been wrong, but hid the knowledge from himself. He was not perfect, she saw that; her love for him did not make her blind to his faults. But she said nothing. In the first place, it was not her business; and in the second, she had no desire to argue with him about Irina – that was the last thing that should come between them.

Instead she said, 'And Sergei? How is he? Have you heard from him?'

'He's with his regiment, fighting the Persians in Azerbaijan. He writes to me regularly, but he never says much about himself – just about the campaign, and occasionally about hunting or fishing trips.' He sighed. 'Mama complains that he never writes to her, or goes to visit her. When he has leave, he spends it in the Caucasus. I tell her it's only natural that he shouldn't want to spend half his leave travelling, but she suspects there are other reasons.'

'And are there? What does he do in the Caucasus?'

'Rides, hunts.' He frowned. 'That place has an unholy fascination. I felt it myself, and tried to resist it. I think you felt it too, didn't you?'

'It's not like anywhere else in the world. But I have unhappy memories connected with it,' she said quietly.

'So do we all. Seryosha too. That's what makes it all the more strange that he should keep going back – and particularly that he should spend so much time at Chastnaya. I think it's unhealthy – obsessive. He keeps going over and over the ground. He blames himself for Nasha's death, I think, which is absurd.'

Anne thought of the grim young man she had last seen at Pyatigorsk. Yes, obsessive was a word that fitted. But there was more to it than that, she thought. There was her own part in his ruin, which she could not calculate; and his complicated feelings about his step-mother and about her relationship with his father. In the Caucasus, she thought, in that place of light and shade, of dark magic and brooding mystery, Sergei might well be able to bring himself to believe that nothing at all was real, beyond the sword in his hand and the dust in his throat.

'I wish he'd find a girl and get married,' Kirov said. Anne, coming back from her thoughts, almost smiled.

'How can you, of all people, recommend that as a cure-all?'

'Unfair, Anna! But I do think it would be more natural if he were to marry. There are girls enough in Pyatigorsk, but he doesn't seem to care for any of them.'

'He may not tell you everything. Perhaps he has dozens of women. Would you tell him everything?'

'*Women* is not the same as *woman*,' he said succinctly. He leaned up on one elbow and looked down at her. 'You don't suppose he's still thinking of you? I though at the time that it was just an absurd infatuation – but feeling as I do about you, I could hardly blame him if it were more than that.' He stroked her cheek.

'I don't think he ever really saw me,' she said evenly. Her eyes met his, and something clenched inside her. 'Nikólasha – ' she said in supplication.

It was different this time, slower, gentler, full of tenderness. She felt so close to him, pressing her cheek against his and cradling his head with her hands as they moved; yet the passion was filled with sadness. Afterwards they lay in silence, watching the shadows move across the walls. Time was running out. I shall never forget this place, she thought, not one detail of this room, of what happened, of what was said; yet it was not true. Already things were slipping away. The wholeness was so important, that it was impossible to hold on to the detail. It mattered so much, that it dispersed like mist when she tried to grasp it.

'I love you,' she said, nudging closer to him. He knew what she was saying.

'Anna, afterwards – '

'There is no afterwards for us. We're both married. This is all there is.'

'*Doushka*, don't. I can't bear to be apart from you.'

408

She grew angry. 'What do you propose? Let me hear your plans, then! How are we to be together, Nikolai Sergeyevitch? Tell me what you mean to do with your wife and my husband.'

'I hadn't begun to – '

'You thought perhaps I would be your mistress? That might be a little hard to arrange, perhaps, for two such public figures – especially if we are not even living in the same city.'

'Annushka, don't tear at me,' he said gently. 'We must never hurt each other.'

Her eyes filled with tears. 'You don't know, you don't know . . . '

He gathered her close. 'Something will happen. I can't believe that God gave us so much, meaning to deny us the rest. Somehow, we will be together.'

'Nikolasha – !'

'I'm not going away from Russia again. I've done my duty to the Emperor. In Petersburg or in Moscow, somehow we'll be together. We must be practical.'

She wiped her eyes with her fingers, a childish gesture that disarmed him. 'Practical,' she said, and he didn't know if she were agreeing or deriding.

'Yes, love. I must be in Petersburg this winter, for various reasons. Can't you come too? Do you have to stay in Moscow? You could persuade your husband to come for the Season, couldn't you?' It seemed strange to hear him refer to Basil like that, while she was lying in his arms.

'It may be possible, provided he doesn't guess the real reason. We have a house there.'

'What are your immediate plans?'

'We go to the *dacha* at the end of the month. Everyone will be going out of town, of course. We usually spend the summer there, entertaining and riding – '

'You still have Quassy?'

'Yes, of course – and her colt. He's two years old, now. I meant to begin breaking him this summer. I wanted to do it myself. I had thought – ' She stopped. When Rose was born, she had thought of training the colt to carry her daughter; she had imagined herself and Rose one day riding together on Quassy and Image. It was a picture that remained locked away in the back of her mind, which presented itself now and then to torment her. 'In the autumn, we go back to the city for the Season.'

'Try to persuade him to make it Petersburg instead.'

'But even if I do – how shall we see each other?'

'Publicly, I suppose.' Her pain was reflected in his eyes. 'It is better than nothing.'

Is it? she wondered; but she didn't say it aloud.

Now, at home again at Byeloskoye, she was alone with her thoughts of what had passed that day, with tormenting speculation, with fragile memories. The long day was ending. She felt almost dazed. There seemed no substance to her, as though she had left her real self in that bare bed-chamber, and what had come home to walk about the house was a dry husk, like the discarded snake-skins she sometimes found on hot stones in the garden. She half expected the light to pass through her unhindered; she felt that if anything touched her, she would crumble into dust.

Did the servants give her odd looks? Would they wheedle out of Pauline what had happened? Russian servants were the worst gossips in the world, but Pauline was not Russian, of course, and held herself aloof from them. Miss Penkridge, stern Yorkshire virgin, would never stoop to gossip; and between Pauline and Mlle Parmoutier there was the deep reserve of suspicion that you would expect between a Belgian and a Frenchwoman. No, probably Pauline would not gossip.

Provided she thought of some way to account for having sent the carriage home . . . She could not, just at the moment, make herself care. She knew that it was heat and exhaustion, physical and emotional, and that she would care very much later on. To be discovered in her misconduct – recriminations from her husband – would be beyond bearing. Misconduct? Sin? How could it be that? She could not feel it to be wrong, and knew that it was. It seemed a thing separate from the flow of real events, but she knew intellectually that nothing one does is without its effect on others.

Her husband – his wife. The appalling complication of her feelings about Irina were a hopelessly tangled skein, beyond unwinding. She liked her, pitied her, was frantic with jealousy towards her. It was impossible, perhaps, to hate a woman whose children one had loved and cared for, and yet she wished those children had been hers, that Irina had never existed. Unwell, grieving, ignored by her husband . . . he should have hurried there at once! How cruel, no, how thoughtless of him! Irina . . . It was strange that she had so often felt racked with guilt when her crime was no more than a sin of thought, an imagination. Now, when the crime was of commission, she could feel no guilt at all, only a low singing of joy, and an intolerable ache of loss.

Would she see him again? They could never have another day like today, never again be lovers; but if she could just see him . . . But to see him without being able to touch him, talk freely to him, how could she endure that? It would be worse . . . better than nothing . . . unendurable . . . She wandered through the house, and the air felt dry and used, and the floor felt swollen under her feet, and the walls bulged softly like uncooked pastry, as if she were in a fever.

There was a little time before the dressing bell summoned her to her bath. Tonight she and Basil were going to the Grand Théâtre to see the new French comedy; a new actor had just arrived from Paris, who promised to become the *succes fou* of the year, a slender and apparently startlingly beautiful young man who portrayed women so perfectly that he could not be told apart from the real thing. If he were all he was reputed to be, she and Basil would have to make sure he was their dinner guest before anyone else's.

The thought wearied and depressed her. Hollow! Is this what your life has become, trying to succeed at a game that isn't even worth playing? To sustain an illusion when even the original would be worthless? She thought of Nikolai, and suddenly missed him dreadfully, like a physical ache. Half an hour to be got through before the dressing-bell; and all the rest of her life after that.

She walked across the hall and started up the stairs. On the first floor she met Miss Penkridge, who told her that a package had arrived for her from Fontenarde's.

'Yes, that will be the Count's birthday present. Put it away somewhere, will you? I wish it to remain a secret.'

'I conclude, my lady, that it is valuable? Should I put it in the safe-box?'

'Yes – do.'

'Also the Dowager Countess Gagarin called, my lady,' Penkridge went on. Did her flat eye convey a warning? 'She wished to see you, but she did not leave a message.'

Already, Anne thought. Of course, she must have been seen by many people, riding in Kirov's carriage. She would have to tell Basil she had met him, that they had gone for a drive together. Would he ask questions? She didn't want to think about that now. 'Very well,' she said, turning away. 'I'm going up to the nursery.'

Aware of Penkridge's eyes on her back, she went on slowly up the stairs, keeping her shoulders straight, though they wanted to slump forward wearily.

The nursery was on the top floor at the back, the nicest, sunniest suite of rooms in the house. Here the Countess Marya Vassilievna's household lived their private and separate lives, all their needs catered for without ever encountering the rest of the world. Here, there were bedrooms and sitting rooms, a schoolroom and a playroom, closets and storerooms, even a large balcony on which to take the air. The views from the windows were lovely; the rooms were decorated in the best style, with light modern furniture and drapes. The meals that were brought up were of the first quality; there was no need for anyone ever to leave the upper floor.

It all looked as little like a hospital as was possible. In fact, Anne thought painfully, it was a prison. Here Rose was imprisoned in the cage of her illness, and the staff who had too little to do to attend her few wants were her gentle gaolers.

Mlle Parmoutier, forewarned in some way of her approach, met Anne at the door of the day-nursery, the large, handsome apartment in which Rose spent the most of her time. It was from this room that glass doors led onto the balcony, from which one could look across the English lawns to the plantation which divided Byeloskoye from the park of the next-door palace. It was all so verdant, you would hardly know you were in the city at all.

There were wheels fixed to the legs of Rose's bed, so that she could be moved from room to room without having to lift and carry her – a process which caused her some pain. Grubernik, the doctor in charge of the case, had advised that she should be given as much stimulation as possible, by changing her position, placing different objects within her field of vision, talking, even reading to her. Only by means of continuous stimulation to her mind, and massage and forcible exercise to her limbs, could she be helped towards normality.

So in the mornings her bed was wheeled from the night-nursery to the day-nursery, and moved from one part of the room to another during the day. Parmoutier had *carte blanche* to ask for anything she needed – books, toys, clothes, furniture, food – to help her in taking care of Rose. She was a dedicated woman, and spent almost every waking moment with her charge. Anne was aware in the back of her mind how ironic it was that she, who had dedicated years of her life to the upbringing of another person's daughters, should employ someone else to do the same thing for her own child. She thought perhaps Parmoutier also considered it ironic and regarded her employer oddly from time to time; but Anne knew really that this was just morbid imagination. Women in her position in society did not look after their own children – any more than Irina had, or why had Anne been brought to Russia at all?

412

'Madame,' Parmoutier said now, coming forward eagerly.

'How is she?' Anne asked abruptly. It was a question that was hardly ever answered directly: Rose's condition did not vary from day to day.

'I was just going to read to her,' Parmoutier said. 'Perhaps you would like to do it instead, Madame?'

Anne looked past her into the room. The floorboards were painted amber, and when the sun shone on them, they glowed like honey. The walls were papered with a gold and white stripe, and the furniture was French mahogany, the seats upholstered in straw-coloured silk. On the far side, by the open glass doors, was the only jarring note – the narrow, wheeled bed with the embroidered Chinese silk counterpane on which lay what looked like a badly-made little wooden effigy.

Anne's heart contracted with love and pity, as it always did, at the sight of her child. Rose, she cried inwardly, how could God have done this to you? The child had been dressed that day, by her nurse or by her governess, Anne didn't know which, in a loose-fitting robe of the fashionable *bleu d'extase* – a choice which might have been a horrible and spiteful jest, but in fact had been generated by uncritical love. Suddenly Anne could not bear the presence of the governess, or of anyone of Rose's court. The quality of their pity tore through her defences like claws.

'Yes,' she said. 'Yes, I'll read to her. Give me the book and go away. I want to be alone with her.'

She crossed the room to the bedside, and drew up the chair which had been placed ready, and sat looking at her child. She remembered Sashka at that age; and Nasha, just a little older, when she had first seen her, a little bright-eyed tangle-head in a nightshirt. Rose was lying on her back, propped from the shoulders upwards by a heap of pillows, her head turned towards the window. Her pinched face was white, with the almost transparent pallor of the invalid; in her broad, hight forehead the blue veins were visible under the thin skin. Her eyelids were blue, too, as if touched by a delicate brush, and her eyelashes were long and tipped with gold. Her left eye was a pale, bright blue, the pupil seeming unusually large and black; her right eye was mostly white, turned so far away that the iris was almost hidden.

She lay motionless as no child ever should, her large head and brittle limbs giving her the look of an unfledged bird, the sort one finds on the ground in early summer, fallen from the nest before life has fairly begun. Her hair, the colour of cooked barley, lay thin and soft against her fragile skull, brushed to a shine by some loving hand, tied back from her face with a bit of blue ribbon to match her gown.

Anne's throat tightened painfully. A little girl with a ribbon in her hair: it was such a natural, such a universal thing! But this little girl would never prance in front of a mirror to admire herself, try on her mother's shoes and pretend to be a lady. She might die; Anne had wished often enough that she would; but now, today, after what had happened, she found she could not want that any more. Her child, her only child, grown and nurtured within her body, part of her; whatever there was of life, Rose should have her share. Life was strong, determined. Against all expectations, today it had nourished her, woken her from sleep – who could say it would not happen also for the child?

'I love you, Rose,' she said. The sound of her own voice startled her. You shall live, she went on, but inwardly. You shall grow up and be a lady – I swear it! Forgive me, my darling girl – I haven't known how to give you anything. The thought stopped her, made her examine it, original in its truth. Here was unpalatable fact. She had felt rejected by her daughter's immobility, lack of response, by the impossibility of doing anything for her. But now, today, it was different. She was richer; something was unlocked, something healed. Today – being with Nikolai – had helped. Loving and being loved had shown her how to do it. Whatever happened afterwards, today had been important: she had learned a little of how to give.

So much of giving, she thought, was a selfishness; a desire for recognition. When we say *I love you*, it is not a statement but a question: *Do you love me?* She took Rose's hand, and the little cold bird-claw lay unresponsive in hers, neither accepting nor rejecting. I love you, Rose, she said inwardly. I love you enough not to need a response. I love you enough to give, even if the gift will never be acknowledged. Live, and grow into a lady, with ribbon in your hair, and the kiss of the sun against your skin.

My love, little bird. She kissed Rose's cheek, hung over her, smiled and talked to her, watching for any sign of reaction. Rose lay mute, unmoving; but perhaps, Anne thought, in some way, the poor parched soul trapped within, or hovering near, might hear and know, and grow a little fuller, and feel a little peace.

She did not hear the dressing bell, and since Mlle Parmoutier didn't like to disturb her, Pauline had to come upstairs and fetch her. As a consequence, Basil was ready before her, and waiting in the drawing-room with a glass of wine in his hand by the time Anne appeared.

414

She began to apologise, but Basil, seeming unusually genial, said, 'There's no need. I understand you were visiting the nursery. That duty must come before everything.'

She eyed him cautiously, wondering why he looked so pleased with himself. Was there a trap here?

'Have you had an agreeable day?' she asked.

'Most agreeable,' he said with a private smile of satisfaction. 'Vanya Golitsin took me along to the Grand Théâtre to watch the rehearsal of the play, and afterwards we entertained the entire cast at the Muscovy Club.'

Ah, thought Anne, so that's all it is: a wine-flush. 'Did you meet the new actor? What's his name?'

He turned his pale, full eyes on her. 'Jean-Luc de Berthier. Yes, I most certainly did. What a *drôle* he is! A fine actor, and, I must tell you, so ravishingly beautiful that he will put our belles to shame! I could not believe when I first saw him that he was a man. I thought Vanya must be teasing me. When I met him afterwards I begged him to take off his wig, but he wasn't wearing one – it was all his own hair! At the club I took him in on my arm, and no-one guessed. Vanya bet a hundred roubles we could not carry it off, but Jean-Luc wouldn't take the bet – he said it would be unfair, because he'd done it hundreds of times before. I never met a more honest man!'

Anne listened with only half her mind, surprised at his high good humour – he semed more lively than he had for months past – and glad that he had been well occupied for the day. She didn't want to feel guilty about her day; didn't want to say anything about it if she could help it. As long as Basil kept talking, there was a good chance he would not ask her any questions. She would prefer not to have to lie.

Pauline appeared through one door with her gloves just as the butler came in through another to say that the carriage was waiting.

'And there's a messenger here, my lady, from Madame Gagarin, with a letter.'

Anne paled inwardly. 'Tell him to go away. I haven't time to read it now,' she said quickly.

Basil looked round. 'Oh, by all means read it. There's no hurry. The play won't start on time. They never do the first night.'

'It's not important,' Anne began dismissively, but the butler, damn him, interrupted.

'The boy asked me to say, my lady, that it was most urgent, and he was instructed to wait for an answer.'

'Go and get the letter,' Basil said. 'I don't mind waiting.'

'I have it here, my lord,' said the butler.

'Give it to me,' Anne said angrily. He would be dismissed the very next morning, if she had her way. What did the old bitch Gagarin want? It was a conspiracy to betray her. Did Basil know? Was that why he was insisting she open the letter in front of him? Was there a gleam of malice in his eye? She broke the seal, and could not make her eyes focus on the black scrawl within – no secretary's hand, that. Madame Gagarin must be one of the few of her generation who could read and write.

'Well, what does she say?' Basil prompted.

Anne scanned the lines again, trying to make the sense go in and stay in. *Chère madame, when I saw you today in the Kuznetsky Most* – she was going to be betrayed! She would have to say something to Basil. What excuse could she give? Her mind worked feverishly – *I remembered that I had meant to ask you for the recipe for those delicious brandied cherries I tasted at your card party last week* –

Anne looked up, and Basil's face seemed to swim, blurred and wavering, before her. She licked her dry lips. A recipe! She wanted a recipe!

'By the way,' he said before she could speak, 'did you know your friend Kirov was back from Paris?' Her heart dropped sickeningly, like a stone. 'He's gone straight down to Tula to see his daughter, apparently. God knows why he didn't go to St Petersburg first. Vanya says there's a whole bag of letters that have been following him about from place to place for weeks, trying to catch up with him. I suppose he'll get them in Tula – the courier's gone after him, anyway.'

Anne could not find any words in her dry mouth. Basil was still talking, his face devoid of guile. 'It's going to be a bit of a shock for him, poor fellow. He'll blame himself for not going to Petersburg first, when he knows. He might have been in time to see her if he had.'

'See – her?'

'His wife. She's dead.'

Chapter Twenty-Four

Anne came down the stairs one day in March 1812 with a cautious smile of welcome stitched onto her lips. The Tchaikovskys were giving a ball tomorrow – the final ball of the Season – and she had not been pleased to be disturbed by her butler, who informed her that 'a lady' wished to see her, but would not give her name. There were all sorts of uninvited callers who demanded the time of a great lady during the St Petersburg Season, including beggars and troublemakers and petitioners, but the butler had assured her with an odd smile that the caller was none of these, and she had sighed and put down her pen resignedly.

However, as she reached the turn of the stairs and looked down into the hall, she saw a slender figure standing there, dressed in a magnificent long sable coat decorated with gold-tagged tails, and a very cunning little black hat, which sported a pair of crow's wings and a great many jet beads. A heavy black veil completely covered her face and was tied under her chin. She was accompanied by a very young and pretty maid in a plain brown *shooba* with a hood. Anne's artificial smile became genuine, if a little exasperated.

'Lolya,' she said, 'you absurd child! What is this? Another of your silly pranks?'

Yelena Nikolayevna turned at the sound of her voice, and unfastened the veil and threw it back. 'You recognised me!' she cried disappointedly. 'I thought I could surprise you.'

Anne advanced and kissed the rosy cheek offered up to her. Lolya had grown into a lovely young woman – not classically beautiful, but with an impish, charming face so full of life and fun that it was impossible not to love her. The death of her step-mother last year had delayed her come-out until two months ago, in January 1812; but since her presentation, she had been enjoying every instant of the Season, and was certainly one of the most popular debutantes of that year. A strong friendship had developed between Anne and her former charge, whose naturally open temper and generous heart had not forgotten the affection that had existed between them, nor the debt she owed Anne for her upbringing and education.

'If you want to go about incognito,' Anne advised her now

solemnly, 'you will have to wear a different coat! I should think everyone in Petersburg recognises your father's coming-out present to you.'

Lolya began pulling off her gloves. 'Oh, is that what gave me away? But I have to wear it – I love it so!' She stroked the sleeves with loving hands, and then threw the coat open to reveal a gown of fine, thin wool of a blue so dark it appeared almost black. Though officially out of mourning, Lolya had decided that dark colours suited her, and was attempting to start a fashion amongst her peers for discarding the pastel shades more usual for debutantes in their first season.

'I'd have know you anyway, darling; and you forgot to disguise your maid,' Anne said affectionately. 'What is all this about? Some mad freak of yours, I suppose?'

'I've come here secretly,' Lolya said importantly, 'to beg your help. No-one knows I'm here. Even your butler didn't recognise me.'

Anne thought of Mikhailo's secret smile, and suppressed one of her own. 'Where is your grandmother?' she asked, going to the heart of it.

'She's taken Sashka to the puppet theatre. I said I couldn't go, because I had to go to the mantuamaker's for a final adjustment, and I did call in there, though there wasn't really anything to do. But it did make it all right, and only a little of a lie, didn't it? Only I couldn't tell her what I really wanted to do, of course. Why does Gran'mère hate you so, Anna Petrovna?'

'It would take too long to explain. But do you think you ought to do things you know she will disapprove of?'

'Oh yes! It doesn't matter really what she thinks, though I don't like to upset her because it makes things so uncomfortable. But if Papa doesn't mind me visiting you, it can't be wrong, can it? I'd have asked him, only he went out too early this morning, before I was up. Anyway, he'll make it all right with Gran'mère. Since Mamochka died, he stands up to her a great deal more, and makes her mind him. He never did before.'

Anne looked into Lolya's wide brown eyes and read there an absolute innocence. She really had no notion of the dark streams of conflict that had run below the calm surface of her life. How Vera Borisova had received the news of Irina's death Anne had no way of knowing, but having seen some of the new coolness between Kirov and his mother, she could guess that the Dowager must have allowed to show a little of her triumph – whether by accident or design.

At all events, she had hastened to offer her services for Lolya's come-out, and lest her offer be refused, had followed her letter to Petersburg in person too closely for a reply of any sort even to have been thought out. Thus she had achieved her life's ambition, of being intimately involved in Lolya's undeniable social success. The one taste of gall in her honey had been Anne's presence in Petersburg: she must have hoped, poor creature, to have left her behind in Moscow!

'And what was it you wanted me to do for you? Am I going to regret deeply that I didn't tell Mikhailo I was not at home?'

Lolya grinned impulsively. 'You couldn't be not at home to me, darling Anna! And I know you must be very busy, and I'm sorry to disturb you, but you know Pinky can do everything for you just as well, and you'd be sorry to miss it, really you would.'

'Miss what?'

'The review at the Winter Palace, of course! Only do hurry, or we won't get a good place. We can go in your new calèche, can't we? It's so very smart, and Varvara Salkina is bound to be there, and I want her to see me riding in it.'

'Is that the only reason you have come disturbing me, you monkey? Just to ride in my carriage?'

'Oh no!' Lolya said, round-eyed. 'I must have you with me, because it wouldn't be at all proper for me to go to a review with only Sophie. She's so young and silly,' she added sotto voce, 'and I must have an older woman with me to give me credit.'

'Thank you,' Anne said. 'It's good to know I can still be useful in my dotage.'

Lolya stroked Anne's arm wheedlingly. 'But you'll enjoy it, Anna, you know you will! And you ought to go out and get some fresh air — it's bad for you to be indoors all the time. There's a whole regiment parading today, and they're marching off to the border, so it's our patriotic duty to go and cheer, and they'll look so splendid!'

At that moment Miss Penkridge appeared on the staircase. 'Excuse me, my lady, but should I – ' she began, as if she had come seeking Anne's guidance on some point, but Anne saw through her. In the few weeks that Lolya had had the run of Anne's household, she had wound every member of the staff around her pretty fingers. Miss Penkridge's granite face was as soft as *blancmanger* as her eyes crept irresistibly from her mistress's face towards Lolya's. 'Oh, I'm sorry, I didn't know you were engaged.'

'Darling Pinky,' Lolya said, going up two stairs to kiss her cheek. Miss Penkridge grew pinker. 'I'm so glad to see you! Won't you help me persuade Anna Petrovna she ought to go out and get some fresh air?'

'It isn't my place, my lady – ' Miss Penkridge began. Anne watched the manoeuvring with fascination. Anyone who could call the forbidding Miss Penkridge 'Pinky' and kiss her into submission was a force to be reckoned with. She foresaw a great future for Lolya; if only she had been born male instead of female she could have been a politician or a great general.

'But you can tell her,' Lolya went on persuasively, 'that you can manage without her, can't you? You can do all the preparations for tomorrow, can't you?'

'Of course, my lady. Her ladyship knows she can safely leave everything with me,' Penkridge said stoutly.

'There you are, you see!' Lolya said triumphantly. 'So *do* come, darling Anna! And put on your new hat, the one with the marabou trimming, because you look so lovely in it, and I want everyone to see how smart you are!'

Anne saw she could not win. 'Very well. I suppose I had better come with you, or you'll do something dreadful, and I shall feel guilty. Come upstairs with me, while I get ready.'

'Thank you! You can go home, now, Sophie. Madame Tchaikovsky will send me home in her carriage so I shall be quite safe.'

She followed Anne upstairs, chattering. 'I do like your house, Anna, much more than ours. Ours is so stuffy! I know it wouldn't have been proper to redecorate while we were in mourning, but there couldn't be any objection now, could there? I don't know why Papa won't let me order new drapes, at least. I saw the most gorgeous material in Zubin's the other day – cloth of gold, covered with peacocks and birds of paradise! You can't think how lovely! I described it to Papa and said it would be the very thing for the state drawing-room, but he only pretended to shudder and said I had taste to match my age. What d'you think he meant by that? But I think he just didn't want to spend the money,' she went on without waiting for an answer. 'He's got awfully mean since Mamochka died. He wouldn't even buy a new barouche for the Season, though ours is shockingly old. He said it would "do" for another year. I hate things to have to "do" – and so does Gran'mère. Why, she won't wear an evening gown more than twice – she gives them away to her maids to do over, once the trimming had been taken off. I heard Madame Kurakina say that Gran'mère had the best-dressed servants in Russia.'

Anne smiled. 'I don't think she meant that as a compliment, darling.'

'Oh,' said Lolya blankly, stopped in mid-flight. Her mind hopped to another subject. 'How is your darling baby? I do think she's the sweetest creature in the world! Would I have time to run up and see her, do you think, while you're putting on your hat?'

'No, love, you wouldn't. But in any case, she's out of the house at the moment. We can go and see her afterwards, if you like. Basil Andreyevitch and Jean-Luc have taken her out on a sledge into the garden. They spent all yesterday building a toboggan slope for her.'

Lolya cocked her head a little, quick to hear the undertone in Anne's voice.

'You don't like Jean-Luc, do you? But he's such fun, Anna, and you must admit he loves Rose! You aren't worried it will be dangerous for her, are you?'

'Oh no – it's a very gentle slope. Grubernik said she ought to go out more, and have gentle exercise. This was Jean-Luc's idea. They mean to take her out in the troika tomorrow, along the river to the fortress and back.'

'Oh, she'll like that! Is Jean-Luc coming to the ball tomorrow? Will he come dressed as a woman, the way he did to the rout at Countess Edling's? Oh, it was so funny when she discovered he was really a man and didn't know whether to have him thrown out or not! I laughed so much I thought I should choke, though Gran'mère didn't like it, and said it was an insult to the Empress-Dowager. Though what she had to do with it I don't know, because she wasn't even there.'

'Countess Edling is her lady-in-waiting.'

'I know, but it isn't as if it were meant to insult her. It was just a piece of fun! Oh, don't look so disapproving, Anna dear! I depend on you not to be like Gran'mère, who thinks anything jolly must be improper.'

Anne pulled herself together. 'I don't think that, love. I suppose there's no real harm in Jean-Luc. It's just that I see so much of him, the jest wears thin sometimes. Now, tell me what you're going to wear tomorrow,' she added, firmly changing the subject. Lolya at once launched into a passionate description of *mousseline de soie* and spider-gauze, crystal spars and spangled scarves, which left Anne free to pursue her own thoughts.

The truth was that she didn't like the little actor, and she wasn't entirely sure why. His friendship with Basil had grown apace since their first meeting in Moscow, so much so that Anne had a suspicion that Basil's eagerness to spend the Season in St Petersburg had a lot to do with the fact that Jean-Luc had been invited there to play with the French company before the Emperor.

De Berthier ran tame about the Tchaikovskys' town house, and was present – and extremely visible – at every entertainment they gave. He and Basil were inseparable: Basil went to his every performance, held court in his dressing-room, entertained the entire theatre company to expensive suppers at the English Club, and talked French Drama as an expert at dinner tables all over St Petersburg.

He and Jean-Luc were seen everywhere together, and more often than not drunk. The actor seemed to have had a deplorable effect on Basil, who behaved in his company more like a twenty-year-old cadet than the forty-year-old head of his family. Basil had taken to wearing very odd clothes, and indulging in strangely youthful horseplay, which was getting him talked about, and not always with indulgence. Olga had even broken her self-imposed rule of never stepping over Anne's threshold unless absolutely forced to by calling on her voluntarily to beg her to stop Basil making a spectacle of himself, and consequently of all of them.

She had not enjoyed Anne's assurance that she had no influence over her husband, which would once have given her great pleasure.

'If you had behaved as a wife should,' she said hotly, 'you would now have sufficient credit with my brother to stop him destroying himself. But I suppose you don't care about that. You always were a cold, hard, selfish woman, and I suppose it's too much to expect you to change now, now that you have the spending of Basil's fortune, which is evidently what you married him for.'

Anne did not care a jot for Olga's good opinion, but it was rather too much to be insulted in her own house, so she invited Olga to leave, and they had not spoken to each other since. In fact, Anne did not care any more than Olga to know that her husband was making a fool of himself. What Basil did inevitably reflected on her; but it was not only that. She was fond of Basil, and did not like to see him come under a bad influence. There was something sinister about Jean-Luc; something not quite right. She didn't like him and she didn't trust him, and if there had been any way she could have detached Basil from his new friend, she would have done it.

But the thing which troubled her most about Jean-Luc was his devotion to Rose; and the undeniable fact that Rose loved him and responded to him more than to anyone else. Since he had been visiting her regularly, she had improved by leaps and bounds. She would turn her head and smile the moment she heard his voice; she would endure the massages Grubernik recommended without a whimper if Jean-Luc held her hand; for him she would do her exercises and attempt things that no-one else could persuade her to try. By association, she had come to love Basil too, and the two of them frequently spent a whole afternoon playing with her, crawling about the floor to move the pieces of her toy farmyard at her command, dressing-up and play-acting, clowning to make her laugh.

Jean-Luc took Rose's condition very seriously, and often used their games to induce her to increase the range of her abilities. He taught her spillikins to improve her manual dexterity, for instance, and invented a picture game with icons to exercise her eyes and to try to straighten the crooked one. He played wounded soldiers with her, to persuade her to try to walk in the leg braces she so hated; and it was he who first got her, in the course of a farmyard game, to lie down on the floor with him and Basil, and to crawl by pulling herself along by her elbows, with her poor weak legs trailing behind.

All this, Anne knew, ought to make her like him – at the very least, to be grateful to him. Yet she could not help feeling that all was not as it seemed, that he was in fact using Rose as the most unexceptionable way to gain a firm foothold in the family; to gain power over them all through gratitude. Because she always tried to be honest with herself, she had also wondered whether she was merely suffering from plain jealousy, because her daughter seemed to prefer the Frenchman's company to hers, which was the unpalatable truth. Was it jealousy that made her feel Jean-Luc was trying to steal Rose from her, to shut her out from the nursery and transfer Rose's affection to himself and Basil? When that idea had first occurred to her, she tried very hard to fight it and to like Jean-Luc for Rose's sake, and for a while she had felt guilty that her reaction towards the Frenchman remained deeply, instinctively hostile.

Then came the day when she had gone to the nursery, and standing at the door had seen Jean-Luc, on one leg with his arms above his head and his face painted in primary colours, pretending to be a flower, while Basil in a gold-and-brown striped shawl taken from Anne's wardrobe buzzed around him as the bee. Rose, watching from her wheeled chair, was evidently some kind of fairy queen or woodland goddess, for she was draped in the green nursery table-cloth, with a crown of ivy round her soft, barley-brown hair and a wand clutched in her hand.

The flower's antics as it tried to prevent the bee from pollenating it, and its expression when the bee finally succeeded, were so funny that Rose was almost choking with laughter, her face brighter and more alive than Anne had ever seen it. The bee and the flower ended up in a heap on the floor, laughing and panting, while Rose clapped her hands and cried 'Again! Again!'

At that moment they all three caught sight of Anne at the door. The laughter died away, and five eyes regarded her, not precisely with hostility, but cautiously, and certainly without welcome.

'Carry on,' Anne had invited them. 'Don't let me stop the fun.'

But Rose's smiles had disappeared like the sun going behind a cloud. Jean-Luc got up politely and engaged her in small talk, but they were evidently waiting for her to go. They were like three small children subdued by the sudden presence of an over-strict parent. Eventually Anne had felt it would be cruel of her to remain, and took her leave; and turning at the door she had caught Jean-Luc's eyes on her with a bright, hard, speculative look. It was instantly veiled and withdrawn – so instantly, that afterwards she could tell herself she must have imagined it. But before she reached the bottom of the first flight of stairs, she heard Rose's infectious giggle floating out from the nursery behind her, and her eyes stung with tears. It hurt her profoundly to be so excluded from her beloved daughter's court – and from no fault of her own, but, she was sure, by another's design.

It was all made worse by the fact that she was sure Basil recognised her feelings and enjoyed watching her struggle with them. She did her best not to gratify him, and to behave always with absolute courtesy towards Jean-Luc; but she sometimes caught Basil watching her with a strange gleam in his eye. She was sure he was enjoying every moment, though she had no idea what she had ever done to cause him to wish to side with his friend against her.

Lolya had removed the absurd and melodramatic veil from her hat, was sitting very upright beside Anne in the winter calèche, her hands thrust deep into her muff, looking about her with enormous pleasure and hoping for someone to recognise and admire her. It had been a particularly severe winter, and there had been a great many snowfalls lately: the thaw would be late, by the look of things. Today was fine and bright, freezing hard, but with a blue sky and a thin sunshine like watered gold making deep, luminous blue shadows across the snow.

Anne's white horses trotted out well, and while their feet made no sound, the bells on their harness rang a thin, sweet carillon, and the runners of the calèche hissed against the packed snow and threw out a fine spray of diamonds.

'I always think, every winter,' Anne said, 'that travelling in the snow makes the best sound in the world. One could never be unhappy riding in a sleigh, don't you think?'

Lolya looked round with a relieved smile. 'Oh, you are happy! I'm so glad. You seemed so quiet before, I thought you were angry with me for interrupting you.'

'No, love. I had something on my mind, that's all. I'm not angry with you. How could I be?'

'Oh good! Because there is one other thing I wanted to ask you. Could we drive down the Nevsky Prospekt, do you think? There's something I want you to see.'

Anne looked at her suspiciously. 'What is it? This is another of your wheedles, isn't it?'

'Oh Anna! It's the most beautiful thing! And Papa's so mean, he won't let me wear a tiara, even though there are three of Mamochka's that are *meant* for me; and your ball *is* a formal one after all, and the last of the season, and everyone will be wearing tiaras. You will won't you?'

'Of course. But that's different: I'm a married woman.'

'But Papa says I must wear flowers in my hair,' she made an indescribable face, 'just as if I were a child of fifteen! Honestly, Anna, he seems to forget I'm almost eighteen, and a grown woman!'

'Flowers are perfectly suitable – the best thing for a girl in her first season.' Anne said what should be said, while inwardly understanding exactly how Lolya felt. Quite suddenly she remembered the earrings her father had sent her for her seventeenth birthday, her very first earrings, and how deliciously grown-up she had felt wearing them to dinner that night. She had more earrings now than she could calculate – diamond, emerald, ruby, pearl – but nothing, nothing would ever quite thrill her like that first pair!

'Well, it wouldn't be my first season if Papa hadn't had to be away so much,' Lolya was arguing absurdly. 'I'd have been out long ago. Kira came out when she was seventeen, and Varvara Salkina came out when she was *sixteen*, and she's betrothed now.'

Anne looked at her sadly. 'Oh Lolya, don't be in such a hurry to grow up! You only ever have one chance to be young and happy.'

Lolya looked sceptical. 'Old people always say that, just as if young people don't have anything at all to worry about! I dare say we have far more troubles – and more important ones, too! I think it's because you all have such fun being grown-up, you don't want to share it with us.'

Anne smiled. 'Do you think I have fun?'

'Yes, of course you do. You have your own house and your own carriage, and you can go anywhere you want, and wear what you like and eat what you like. And you have your husband and your darling baby. Well, I want all those things too! I don't want to wait for them. It's so stupid being too young for things, and having to behave oneself and be mimsy and silly and pretend to be shy! Oh, look – here it is!' Her attention was distracted and she flung out a hand. 'Please stop, Anna, and tell me if it isn't the handsomest thing you ever saw!'

It was the Court jeweller's shop to which Lolya was directing Anne's gaze. In the centre of the main window, artistically displayed on a fold of crimson velvet, was a pair of hair-clips in the shape of sprays of flowers. The blossoms were diamonds, the leaves cut from emerald, and the whole was exquisitely set in white gold.

'Please say you'll persuade Papa to buy them for me for your ball! If I have to wear flowers in my hair, well, those are flowers, aren't they? And one ought to be fine for the Emperor, you know.'

'Oh Lolya,' Anne laughed, 'of course I won't do any such thing! They must cost the earth. And besides, if your father wants you to wear flowers, then you must. It's not for me to try to overset his decisions, even if I could.'

'Of course you could,' Lolya said simply. 'Papa thinks the world of you. He's always talking about you, and about how clever you are and all that sort of thing. You could persuade him if you wanted to.'

'Well I don't want to,' Anne said, and told her coachman to drive on.

'Very well,' Lolya said with suspicious meekness. She didn't even sulk or pout, but began a new conversation in a perfectly cheerful, agreeable voice. Anne wondered what was coming next.

The open square before the Winter Palace was already thronged with people, the peasants on foot, the *dvoriane* in sleighs drawn up side by side to enable the occupants both to watch the parade and to gossip. They were only just in time. The coachman dextrously beat a lozenge-coach to the last space on the near side, and Lolya was still bowing and waving to the occupants of the neighbouring carriages when there was a burst of applause from the far side and the regiment marched into the square.

'Aren't they splendid!' Lolya cried with simple fervour. Anne had to agree they were. The officers rode out in full dress uniform, their fur-trimmed pelisses flashing with braid and loops, their hats splendid with plumes and gold lace rosettes; the horses stepped delicately, necks arched, with silver shells flashing on their bridles, and gold vandyking on their richly-coloured shabraques. The men marched behind proudly, arms reflecting the sun, their boots glinting as the legs swung forward all together, left and right, so that the ranks looked like strange insects, caterpillars rippling along a leaf.

They were parading in order to receive the Emperor's blessing before they marched off to the border, and Anne was aware from diplomatic sources that the public review was meant to calm fears that a war was imminent; curious reasoning, she thought. Suddenly a great double cheer went up, signifying that the Emperor and his train had appeared, and craning her neck, Anne saw he was in his favourite pale blue uniform of a colonel of Hussars. She had a good view of him now: tall, romantically handsome, ruddy-cheeked and fair-haired as he swept off his hat in acknowledgement of the cheers. His expression was one of great sweetness: above all it was possible to feel for this Emperor, as perhaps for none other, a great affection. He sat his horse well, as she had had cause before to remark; and his attention never seemed to waver as the soldiers marched and wheeled about the square before him.

Lolya had been silent for quite a while, when she drew a deep, heartfelt sigh, and said passionately, 'Isn't he the handsomest creature you ever saw? Honestly, Anna Petrovna, don't you think he's the most divinely handsome man in the world?'

'The Emperor?' Anne said, a little startled. She would have expected a much less personal adoration of the Emperor of all the Russias from a young girl like Lolya.

'No, no,' Lolya said, colouring. 'Of course the Emperor is very handsome too, but I was talking about Colonel Duvierge. That's him on the bay horse, next to General de Tolly. He's one of General de Lauriston's aides.'

'I know who Colonel Duvierge is,' Anne said drily. 'I've met him several times. What I can't understand is how you know him.'

Lolya looked pink and conscious. 'I know lots of diplomatic people. Why shouldn't I? I met Colonel Duvierge when Papa took me to the Embassy Ball. He's the most charming, intelligent, handsome – ' She caught Anne's amused look and said hastily, 'He likes me to. He danced with me twice, and twice again at the Salkins' the next evening.'

'I see,' Anne said neutrally. 'Well, he's certainly an agreeable young man, from the little I know of him.'

Lolya looked at her sidelong, cautiously. 'Are you sure you won't ask Papa to buy me the diamond sprays?'

'Certainly not.'

'Not even to please me?' Anne quelled her with a look. 'Well in that case, Anna Petrovna,' she went on, taking a deep breath, 'I have a great, *great* favour to ask you, and you have to say yes now, because you wouldn't do the other thing for me, and this favour is the really important one, because if you don't grant it, I shall really and truly die.'

'Nonsense. Of course you won't.'

'Well, then, I shall go into a decline, and become terribly religious and join a nunnery, and you'll have ruined my life and you'll be very sorry and that will ruin your life.'

Anne laughed and held up her hands defensively. 'Well, then, what is it? I warn you, if it's anything improper – '

'Oh no, darling Anna, of course it isn't! This is it: you have invited General de Lauriston to your ball tomorrow, haven't you? I know you have, because Gran'mère thinks it's disgraceful and says she wouldn't be surprised if a lot of people didn't *cut*; only of course they won't because the Emperor's coming.'

'It was the Emperor who asked me to invite him,' Anne said. 'He doesn't want Bonaparte to accuse him of ill-treating his ambassador.'

'I love the way you call him Bonaparte! That's because you're English, isn't it?' Lolya said. 'Anyway, Gran'mère said it was a disgrace that decent Russians should have to mix with the AntiChrist's agents; but Countess Edling said it was better to have him where you could see what he was up to. But the thing is, Anna dearest, if you are inviting General de Lauriston, could you please, *please* invite Colonel Duvierge as well? Because otherwise I don't see how I am ever to meet him without doing something improper, like making a secret assignation, which I don't want to do. Gran'mère would never let me meet him any other way.'

Anne felt herself being cornered. 'Lolya, my dear, even if I invited him to my ball, and even if he accepted, that wouldn't necessarily make him dance with you. Don't you think he's a little too old for you, anyway? There are lots of nice Russian boys who will rush for your hand tomorrow.'

Lolya's eyes grew bright. 'He will dance with me! You don't understand, Anna, how we feel about each other! And he's not a bit too old. In any case, young men are boring and insipid. Andrei is just right for me.'

'*Andrei?*'

Lolya looked defiant. 'It's how I think of him. We're in love, Anna, and it would be cruel not to help us.'

'Has he said he's in love with you?'

'Well, not *said*, not yet, but I know he is really. He hasn't had the chance to declare himself, that's all. Oh please invite him to the ball!'

Anne considered, looking at Lolya's hopeful face thoughtfully. She saw in this request all the symptoms of a hopeless crush of the sort young girls frequently developed for unsuitable or out-of-reach men.

It was a sort of practising to love, she thought, and probably the best way to cure it was to allow the victim to discover for herself that the object of her passion was entirely indifferent to her. Also, with a hight-spirited creature like Lolya, opposition was likely only to have the effect of making her mulish.

After all, there was no harm that could come to Lolya at a large, well-attended ball. Colonel Duvierge was a perfectly respectable young man, and probably didn't know Lolya existed. If he came to the ball and didn't ask her to dance, which was likely, she would be quickly, if painfully, cured of her sudden fancy.

'Very well,' Anne said. 'I'll invite him; but you must promise to behave yourself, and not shame me by making yourself obvious.'

'Oh I promise, I promise! I'll be as mimsy as you wish! I'll wear mittens and stand with my eyes cast down *so* until he asks me to dance! Thank you, darling Anna! I knew you wouldn't let me down!'

'Now what has she been persuading you to do, Anna Petrovna? You should know better by now than to agree to anything Lolya suggests.' The Count's voice startled Anne, and she turned to see that he had just ridden up behind them, and was sitting his horse and smiling at her with a warmth in his eyes which made her throat close up. Fortunately she was not obliged to speak at once, for Lolya answered him by launching into a description of her gown for Anne's ball, meaning to lead up to the question of the diamond sprays.

Nikolai listened, glancing from time to time at Lolya and smiling, but for the rest of the time looking at Anne as thought he were receiving some nourishment or refreshment through that medium. Their meetings since she came to Petersburg had been few, their conversations limited to brief exchanges snatched at public functions or private parties. His deep mourning had not ended until December, and he had remained during that time at Schwartzenturm, coming to St Petersburg only after Christmas, when he brought Lolya for her presentation.

Since that day in Moscow, he and Anne had had no opportunity to be alone together. Anne was almost glad of it. It would have been too grave a temptation. The memory of the afternoon they had spent together was too wonderful and painful to be taken out and looked at very often. She had not seen him again before he left Moscow; she had had no-one to turn to for help or comfort or advice a fortnight later, when her monthly flux had not begun on time.

It was only then that full enormity of her crime was brought home to her. If she were pregnant, there would be no more hope of concealment. Basil would know that it was not his child: she would be exposed, villified, punished. He might cast her out, penniless, to make her own way in the world, and she knew well enough what the fate of an unprotected pregnant woman would be. He would be perfectly within his rights to repudiate her; certainly he would refuse ever to let her see Rose again.

For ten days Anne contemplated, all alone, the most hideous ruin; and then on the eleventh day she began to bleed. A few moments of unspeakable relief and euphoria were followed by black reaction, and she locked herself in her room and wept and wept for her loss and her dreadful guilt. Now, much as she loved him, she was reluctant to go through that again; but she knew that if she were put in the position of being tempted, she might not be able to resist.

Oh, but she loved him, and missed him, and wanted him! It seemed so wrong for them to be separated by her farcical marriage. He lived only a few hundred yards away from her, at the Kirov Palace on the English Quay. She could slip out one day and simply never come back. He would keep her, protect her, love her, make her happy. Though he did not press her, she knew that it was what he wanted.

But if she did such wrong, how could she live with herself? And if she left Basil, she would never be allowed to see Rose again; and she could not, could not part with her own, only child.

Lolya had almost talked herself out, when Kirov interrupted her, saying, 'Did you know that Anastasia Kovanina is in the fourth carriage down from here? Ah, I didn't think you did! Why don't you pay a visit to her, a good long visit, so that I can have a talk with Mademoiselle de Pierre?'

'I don't call her that any more,' Lolya said with eighteen-year-old scorn, but she took the suggestion and went with the greatest good nature. Nikolai climbed up into the calèche beside Anne, and they sat for a moment or two enjoying the sensation simply of being close. Provided they spoke quietly, the coachman wouldn't hear them: the music from the regimental band would cover their voices.

'It's a fine display,' Anne said at last. 'I can't understand why Speransky thinks it will calm public fears, though. Everyone's counting how many regiments have left St Petersburg recently and drawing their own conclusions.'

'If they slipped away under cover of night it would be worse,' he said. 'People would be convinced that Napoleon was on our doorstep.'

'It's going to come, then? He will invade Russia?'

'Yes, this year, sooner or later. He's mad enough to do it. Thank God at least we have Barclay de Tolly as our Minister for War. He's been quietly working away at the Emperor, trying to convince him that the best policy if – when – Napoleon invades is to keep withdrawing in front of him, leading him further and further into our territory.'

'And is the Emperor convinced?'

'You know what he's like – he hates to make decisions, hates to offend people. He flows this way and that, listening first to Tolly, and then to the hotheads like Bagration.' He frowned. 'Worst of all is that his sister – Grand Duchess Catherine, I mean – keeps trying to push him to bold action, talks about cowardice and Our Beloved Russia, and heaps scorn on Napoleon as if he were some untried cadet! He has always listened to her; and of course Bagration's her tool, and he has the Emperor's ear, which makes it worse. But I add my voice to Tolly's, and he trusts me, so I don't despair of the outcome.'

'We called on the Grand Duchess at Tver on our way to Petersburg,' Anne said. 'She holds court there like a frustrated empress – but she's always been good to me, so I shouldn't speak slightingly of her. At all events, she thinks she's pregnant now, so that should give her something else to occupy her mind.'

'I wish it had. You won't know, of course, that she's been plotting busily against Speransky. I can't find out the details of the plot, but I'm afraid it's serious. There are too many people who want his downfall.'

'Why do people hate him so much? He's done so much good, reforming the government – and he works so hard, poor little man.'

'They hate him because he's a peasant, risen from the ranks by his own efforts. Lots of aristocrats can't forgive that – particularly those he's overtaken on the way up. For the son of a parish priest to become State Secretary – it's too much to be borne!'

'Well I like him,' Anne said stoutly.

'You like all sorts of odd people,' he said with a smile. 'What about those actors you have running tame about your house? Is it true that de Berthier is going to appear at your ball tomorrow dressed as Cleopatra and carrying a live asp?'

'Oh, don't,' she shuddered. 'I've heard so many tales of what he is going to do . . . Talk about something else! Did you know that Lolya has fallen in love?'

'She falls in love at least once a week. Who is it this time?'

'Duvierge. She seems to think he has your seal of approval.'

'Duvierge? But that was last week!' He pretended to be alarmed. 'If she's been in love with him for two whole weeks, it must be serious.'

'You had better hope it isn't,' Anne said severely. 'From what I hear, Lauriston himself is hardly safe from assassination. His carriage was stoned yesterday. If Lolya were to marry a Frenchman . . . '

'Don't worry,' he said with a smile. 'Duvierge doesn't know she exists. He's a thoroughly ambitious young man – and fanatically loyal to Napoleon, too. I have a fancy he's carrying on a secret correspondence with his Emperor, but I haven't been able to prove it.'

'He's a spy? But surely it isn't your job to expose him? Surely the Minister of Police, or the Minister of Secret Police – '

'Anna Petrovna!' he said, amused. 'You know perfectly well there are no secret police in Petersburg!'

'Oh – well,' she said, colouring a little. 'At all events, I have agreed to invite him to my ball tomorrow. I hope you approve? I thought the best way to cure Lolya was to give her the opportunity to see he didn't care for her.'

'I agree. What she's denied she only wants twice as much. Like a certain barouche in Landseer's warehouse, with so much gold plating on it, it would kill a pair of horses to move it ten feet!'

'Oh, it was *that* barouche, was it!' They regarded each other with amused understanding, and suddenly Kirov took her hand under cover of her muff and said.

'Anna, I must see you!' She turned her face away a little in pain. 'Don't, don't turn away. My love, the war will begin soon, and who knows what will happen?'

'You won't fight?' she said in alarm, turning back to him.

'I don't mean to – but who can tell? If the circumstances – or the Emperor – demand, I can't refuse. But I shall certainly be asked to advise at the front; I shall have to go away. Anna, I must see you privately – alone. I can't go on like this.'

'It's impossible,' she said.

'Not at all. We must be discreet, that's all. It can be managed.'

She bit her lip. Longing and guilt warred with each other. 'Where?' she said, despite herself. 'How?'

'Tomorrow morning. Yes, I know you have your ball to prepare for! That's why you have no engagements, why no-one will expect to see you anywhere about the town.'

'But my servants – '

'You must have a headache, stay in your room with the blinds drawn, forbid your servants to disturb you. They will all be too busy to think about it in any case. Then you can slip out and meet me, very early, before anyone's about. Wear a cloak with a hood, and keep it drawn forward to hide your face.'

She looked at him despairingly. 'Nikolai, I hate deceit, and subterfuge! I hate all this!'

'I know. Don't you think I hate it too? I want to love you openly – claim you before the world. If you would only come and live with me . . . Anna, won't you? We could go abroad – '

'I can't leave Rose.'

'We could take her with us.'

'Basil would never let her go. Besides,' she added, 'you wouldn't leave Russia now, not now, not on the brink of war.'

'Yes I would, for you,' he said, but she knew it was a lie.

'Napoleon would have you arrested and shot,' she said quietly, allowing him to save face. 'Your life would not be worth a day's purchase beyond the border. There's nowhere we could go. And there's nothing we can do.'

He was silent, facing the truth. Then, 'Only this one thing. Come to me tomorrow, Annushka. Let us have that much at least.'

She shook her head, dumb with misery; oh but she was weak, weak, and she knew she would give in, in the end.

It snowed again in the night, but froze before morning, and the day dawned clear, blue and gold and silver white like some heraldic device, and breathtakingly cold.

Anne had to take Pauline into her confidence, for how else was she to procure a cloak, or get out of the house unseen? But Pauline, in her quiet way, disliked Basil, and was glad to help her mistress, who had always been generous to her, to deceive him. She provided her mistress with a plain, coarse brown cloak, like the sort the serfs wore, with a hood, and voluminous enough to wear over her furs.

'Keep well covered up, madame,' she said as she fastened it. 'Today is a day for frostbite. Sunshine makes people careless.'

Anne remembered the words as she sat beside Nikolai in the troika, which he drove himself, as they left the city and dashed into the countryside. She almost felt as though she were dreaming. The sun shone bright and heatless from a deep blue sky, and the dazzling crystal snow rushed past with a sweet hissing sound under the runners, while the harness bells tinkled their sweet, secret language. Before her the necks of the three horses curved as they threw themselves willingly into their collars; their pricked ears bobbed, and their warm breath clouded on the bitter air as they cantered along, and formed icicles on the whiskers of their muzzles.

The whole world was white, with deep lavender shadows, except for the dark brown of tree trunks in the woods to the side of the road. Most of the trees were like fantastic confections of frozen sugar, but here and there, where the snow canopy had slipped and fallen, a branch would spring forth in deep and living green, like something shaking off an enchantment. But the enchantment held her deep, willing victim. She asked no questions, and wanted no answers; simply allowed the day to carry her forward where it would.

Their destination turned out to be a small inn on an unimportant side road. Anne looked askance as he drew up outside, thinking that a public house was not the best place to secure their secrecy. But they were evidently expected. When they stopped, Adonis – almost unrecognisable in his bundling clothes – ran out to take the horses, and when they entered the inn, the hostess greeted them with a quiet smile, and told them dinner would be ready whenever they rang for it. Anne looked at her curiously. There didn't seem to be any other customers. Business must be very bad, she thought, for even so small an inn to have no customers at all.

Kirov conducted her up the narrow wooden stairs, and into a private sitting room, where he began at once to help her off with her furs. He looked into her eyes, and read the question there.

'Yes, it's safe. No, there's no-one else here, and there won't be.'

'How can you be sure?'

'Because I own this place. I've told them they are to be closed for the day. They are my own people. They won't betray us.'

They were to be protected, then, in their wrongdoing, by the loyalty of his servants. Strange irony! And yet all one with the dreamlike quality of the day. To be snatching love like this, when the world – their world – was on the brink of war, was eccentric, and yet somehow right and logical. She dismissed all further speculation, and gave herself up to the pleasure of being with him.

Their time was all too brief. The short day was waning when he drove her back into the city, and clouds were beginning to gather, threatening more snow.

'The thaw's going to be late this year,' he said. 'That will be to our advantage. If the crops are sown late, they won't be ripe when Napoleon begins his advance. He'll have nothing to feed his horses on.'

The words dissolved the dream; reality closed round them abruptly. Anne wondered how she was going to be able to face him tonight as her guest without revealing everything in her eyes. Would Basil be back? Would she have difficult questions to answer? The toils of guilt and worry began to tangle themselves around her. Life is long, she thought, and pleasure brief.

'Put me down at the end of the Oblensky's garden,' she said. 'The house is empty. There's a gap in the hedge between their garden and ours; I can slip through, and then if anyone sees me, I can say I just went out for some fresh air to clear my head.'

He stopped the troika and kissed her face within the hood. 'Goodbye, then, my darling, my love. Thank you for today.'

He wanted to say more, but she was restless to be gone now, and pushed him away. He watched her anxiously, wondering about her state of mind, as she jumped down into the snow, and tramped away, opened the shrill and rusting iron gate, and disappeared into the garden.

Anne's mind was working rapidly now, woken from its enchantment, clicking like a machine through the things that had to be done and the things she had to worry about. Basil had been out all day – some kind of celebration at the Guards' mess, he had said, so he would probably arrive back late and fairly drunk. She was probably safe: as safe as she could be in the circumstances.

She pushed through the hedge into the garden of her own house, and felt at once a fraction safer. Now, on her own ground, she had a reasonable excuse. This part of the garden was rather unkempt, with overgrown shrubs and a little plantation, and a sort of summer-house, a little wooden garden house in the shape of an Alpine chalet. Basil and Jean-Luc had been using it recently, and had taken Rose there once or twice for picnics and play. Jean-Luc, with an amused exchange of glances with Basil, called it *Le Parc aux Cerfs*, which puzzled Anne a little for there were no deer here. Perhaps it was a reference to something; or a pun on the word *serfs*.

She passed it and was tramping on towards the house when something registered out of the corner of her eye made her turn back. Yes, there was a glimmer of light coming through the closed shutters. She stopped, puzzled, a little alarmed. Could the place be on fire? Ought she to fetch help? No, it was not that sort of light. Watching for a moment, she saw it was too steady and deliberate to be an accidental fire. Someone was in there. Burglars? Robbers? But surely they would not advertise their presence by lighting a fire? She went closer, stepped onto the verandah and walked cautiously up to the window, and put her eye to the crack in the shutter which had allowed the light to escape.

It was too small a gap for her to be able to see anything, but as her face was close to the window, she heard Jean-Luc's distinctive laugh. She felt a surge of indignation and triumph. So he was using the garden house without permission, was he? Probably entertaining some woman in there, some slut from the playhouse – and in the same place that he took her innocent daughter to play! This was her chance to discredit him, to get rid of him. Even Basil would not condone that sort of loose behaviour on his premises. She would catch him red-handed and be free of him at last.

Softly she crept to the door and tried it, but it was locked, as she had expected. Further proof that his presence there was unlawful! If he were there with permission, there'd be no need to lock the door. But she knew another way in. At the back there was a lean-to for storing fuel, and from there, behind the woodstacks, a little door led into the summer-house. The door, being well concealed, was never locked, and she doubted whether Jean-Luc would have thought about it.

He had not. Moments later she was trying the little door and finding it yielding; beyond it she heard the low murmur of voices, and soft laughter. She gathered herself, took a deep breath, and flung the door wide, stepping through that the same instant.

There was only one room in the summer house, square, with a stone-built fireplace, in which a fire was burning steadily. There seemed time in that first second to take in all the details. The fire had evidently been alight some time – the logs were burning on a bed of ashes. The summer furniture had been pushed back against the walls, and in front of the fire was a dark red Turkey carpet, on which, on a heap of cushions, lay Jean-Luc. He was quite naked, except for a gold chain about his neck, and with his long hair spilling down his back, his painted face, and his male body glowing in the firelight, he looked like some appalling hermaphrodite.

He was not alone. Lying with him – indeed, supporting him in his arms – was Basil. Basil, she saw with a dazed sense of unreality, was also naked. He had a glass of wine in one hand, while the other was draped over Jean-Luc's shoulder and across his chest, the long fingers toying with one of his nipples. Basil had been speaking; now as he saw Anne his voice stopped in a little squeak like a mouse caught by an owl. His eyes widened, his face drained of colour, went ash white, chalk white, cheese white. In her shock, Anne seemed to have time particularly to notice that; and the colour of the wine — deep, glowing red with the firelight shining through it. His hand must have shaken, for a little of it lipped over the rim and splashed onto Jean-Luc's chest. The drops looked dark and viscous against his fair skin, like blood. He had been looking up at Basil; now, seeing Basil's expression, and feeling the touch of wetness on his skin, he looked down at himself.

It all seemed to be happening very slowly, and without sound. There was a roaring in Anne's ears that was like a huge silence. She saw him look down at himself, and knew, as if she could read his thoughts, that he thought it was blood. He opened his mouth very slowly and cried out something, but the words were distorted and boomed soundlessly, as thought he were shouting underwater. He looked up again, and one white hand rose in protest; Basil's fingers opened, and the glass tumbled very slowly through the air, throwing an arc of blood across Jean-Luc's white belly, reddening his golden pubic curls, trickling like desperate revenge across his limp white penis and down his thighs.

Anne was already turning away, but she paused and looked back, and in the instant before life resumed its normal speed and she was running, running in desperation away across the garden and towards the house, she saw Jean-Luc turn to look at her at last. His eyes narrowed, but his expression was not of fear or shock; it was of *pleasure*. Arching a little, leaning back against Basil's body, he smiled the closed-mouthed, feline smile of triumph of the adored mistress at the despised wife.

Chapter Twenty-Five

The ball was over. It was almost four o'clock in the morning, and the last guests had been wrapped up in their furs and escorted to their carriages, and the purple-nosed coachmen had cracked their whips in the bitter black air and driven them away to their beds.

The ball had been an enormous success. The beautiful blue and cream and gold ballroom had been as full as it would hold of the pick of Petersburg society. The Emperor had come, as promised, intending only to look in briefly out of courtesy to Anne, and to be seen in company with de Lauriston; but Anne had had the foresight to invite Marya Antonovna Naryshkina, the wife of the Grand Master of the Imperial Hunt, who had been Alexander's mistress for ten years or more. She had been away for some time in Odessa, on the Black Sea, where she had been sent by her doctors, who feared she was consumptive. Now she was back and apparently in perfect health, and more beautiful than ever.

Anne liked Marya Antonovna: she had grace and style and composure, as well as discretion and an unexpected modesty. She dressed usually in white, which suited her alabaster skin and black hair, and preferred always to stand quietly in a corner, watching the world from within the remote fastness of her beauty. That the Emperor still adored her was plain from the glances of tenderness and intimacy he gave her from across the room; and having seen she was of the company, he seemed to forget to go away again. He didn't dance, but he took a little supper, and spent the rest of the time talking earnestly with a fluctuating group of courtiers and advisers in one of the ante-rooms, remaining always near the door so that he could watch the company, which appeared to amuse him.

It was a bold mix: a large number of courtiers, naturally, and the leaders of society; members of the governmental circle and the diplomatic set; handsome young hussars and Dragoons about to be sent off to the borders, and an equal number of lovely young women to console them; and a group of leading actors, ballet dancers, and opera singers to add a touch of the bizarre and the exotic to the evening.

Anne was everywhere, talking, dancing, introducing people, making sure everyone was entertained, drinking a great deal of champagne and laughing perhaps a little too much. Jean-Luc was subdued, dressed almost normally in breeches and coat – though his waistcoat was scarlet satin embroidered with blue and gold parrots – and with his long hair tied respectably behind in a queue. He chatted mostly with his friends from the company, did not dance, avoided Anne's eye, and spoke to Basil only once, when they snatched a brief, whispered conversation just before supper. Basil was being the perfect, charming host, flirting with the dowagers and dancing with the shyer young matrons just as he should. He, too, avoided Anne, and after they had danced the opening minuet together, made sure he was always at the other end of the ballroom from her.

Anne spoke to Kirov only once, for he was engaged the whole evening either with the Emperor, or with one of the satellite groups around him, talking now to Lauriston, now to Rumiantsev, the Chancellor, now to Barclay de Tolly. When everyone was on the move towards the supper-rooms, he managed to manoeuvre his way to Anne's side.

'You're very gay this evening,' he murmured. 'Is everything all right?'

She turned her face up to him; her cheeks were flushed, her eyes over-bright. 'Yes, of course.'

'There was no trouble? You got into the house all right?'

She laughed brittly. 'Oh, he made no trouble. There will be no trouble, I promise you!'

He looked concerned, touched her hand under cover of the crowd. 'Anna, what is it? Are you ill? You look fevered. What's happened, my love?'

She pulled her hand away. 'Not now. I can't talk about it now. But everything's all right, I promise. We are not discovered.'

'Nevertheless, something's disturbed you.'

'I'll tell you about it – tomorrow. I must go now. I have to go down to supper with Admiral Chicagov.'

He looked worried, but bowed and began to move away; then she called him back.

'Nikolai!' He turned enquiringly. 'What is *Le Parc aux Cerfs*?'

His brows went up. 'It was a house belonging to Louis XV of France, where he kept young women for pleasure. A private brothel, I suppose you might call it. Why do you want to know that?'

Her mouth bowed as though she had bitten an unripe olive; and then she turned away. 'No reason at all,' she said.

One of the surprises of the evening was the behaviour of Colonel Duvierge towards Lolya. Anne had received him as part of de Lauriston's suite, and he had bowed politely over her hand, and murmured his gratitude for the invitation.

'I am sorry it was sent somewhat at the last moment, Colonel,' Anne said. 'I am sure you will forgive the oversight.'

He straightened and smiled at her – an attractive smile, full of white teeth, except that it didn't touch his eyes, which remained distant and watchful. 'There is nothing to forgive, madame. An invitation to your house is an honour whenever it arrives.'

Studying him with new interest on Lolya's behalf, Anne found he was older than she had at first thought: thirty-two or -three, perhaps, certainly too old for Lolya, and too old, she would have thought, to be interested in her. His face was handsome in a mature way, strong-featured, firm with accustomed command, but rather harsh. There was experience in his eyes, and a certain cynicism, but no warmth or humour. A dedicated man, she thought – ambitious, likely to be ruthless in pursuit of his ends, and the sort who would inevitably regard women as dispensable aids to pleasure in the few moments of recreation he ever allowed himself.

Emphatically not the sort of man one would wish to see a warm-hearted, impulsive, trusting creature like Lolya throw herself at; but fortunately not the sort of man who would find anything to interest him in an untried girl. A discreet, experienced, beautiful, above all *safe*, married woman would be the choice of a man like Duvierge. He would not be willing to spend time on careful courtship, and would find emotional scenes a bore. He would want a woman who would serve his needs efficiently and cause him no trouble; and Anne was not surprised to intercept, during the course of the evening, a look which passed between Duvierge and Countess Sulovyeva – wife of a senior member of the War Ministry – which suggested very strongly that she was at present providing what was required.

Anne felt sorry for Lolya's inevitable disillusionment: but as she was still as volatile as she was young, Anne thought she would soon find another and, she hoped, more suitable object for her passion. Lolya was looking very lovely that evening. Someone – either her grandmother or her father – had persuaded her to wear a light-coloured gown, and she was all youth and freshness in almost transparent spider-gauze over a silk slip of *bleu d'extase* sewn with tiny crystal spars which caught the light and shimmered as she moved. She had pearls around her throat, and her piled dark hair was dressed with white silk flowers sewn with seed pearls. She wore her spangled shawl over her elbows with a natural grace, and stood with her head high and her bright, animated face alight with expectation of the highest happiness.

Anne braved the chill of her grandmother's gaze and went up to speak to her, took her hands and kissed her cheeks, and said, 'Dearest Lolya, you look so pretty! You'll dance every dance tonight, that's certain!'

Lolya smiled, but looked a little anxious. 'People keep asking me, and it's difficult to refuse them all without Gran'mère hearing. That beast Andrei Fralovsky asked me *twice*, and wouldn't believe I was engaged unless I told him with whom and then Pavelasha Tiranov came bothering me too! Oh Anna, I wish he'd come quickly and ask me! Don't you think he'll want to dance the first dance with me? The first is the important one, isn't it?'

Anne was startled. 'Lolya, you silly child, are you refusing to dance with your old friends because you hope Duvierge will ask you?'

Lolya's cheeks grew pink with vexation. 'I'm not a silly child! And he will ask me, he will! I'd ask him, only I promised you I wouldn't be bold, and Gran'mère would have forty fits.'

'I should think she would,' Anne began, but Vera Borisovna at that moment drifted nearer to hear what they were saying.

'*Ma belle Hélène*, you mustn't keep Madame Tchaikovsky from her duties.' She gave Anne a frigid bow. 'And besides, there are lots of young men waiting to ask you to dance. Have you any dances left, my sweet one? Because I think you ought to dance with Prince Straklov before supper. The dear Princess, his mother, told me he was going to ask you.'

Anne would have moved away at that point, but Lolya seized her arm and hold her back.

'I'd be happy to, Gran'mère, only Madame Tchaikovsky has just told me that there is someone Papa wants me to dance with, so I must go to him this instant and find out who it is. Come, Anna Petrovna, I'm ready now!'

And she curtseyed to her grandmother and hurried Anne away, gripping her arm in a way that was part command and part appeal. When they were out of earshot of the irate Dowager, Anne said, 'Now, Lolya, this is too bad of you! I don't wish to provoke your grandmother – and if you had any sense, you wouldn't either.'

Lolya looked despairing. 'Oh, but you don't understand! She wants to engage me for every dance with the sons and grandsons of her dreary old friends, and I must be free for Andrei when he asks!'

'Lolya darling, I don't think he is going to ask,' Anne said gently. 'He is much too old for you, you know, and probably interested in older women.'

'He isn't! Anyway, all the older women are married,' Lolya said, and Anne did not want to take the bloom off her innocence by telling her what interest a married woman might hold for her idol. Then Lolya went on, 'But the thing is, he may not be able to get away from General de Lauriston – you know how these old people think balls are for talking instead of dancing! – so I want you to take me to him, and then he's bound to ask me, isn't he?'

'No, you unscrupulous child, he isn't – and I won't. I'm taking you straight back to your grandmother.'

Lolya's face was despairing. 'Oh *please*, Anna! You can't be so cruel: I love him quite dreadfully!'

Anne looked at her unhappily. 'Lolya, you're so young and so pretty! Don't waste your loveliness on someone like that, who will never care for you, and could never make you happy.'

But Lolya had ceased to listen. Her eyes, restlessly wandering in search of her beloved, had at last found him – and by an infernal piece of luck, found him deep in conversation with his superior and Count Kirov. Lolya gave a little squeak, and before Anne could prevent her, had darted off to join the group, her cheeks extremely pink and her eyes extremely bright. Anne would have gone in pursuit, but at that moment Minister Kochubey claimed her attention, and she could not be so rude as to brush him off.

'So very brave of you, Madame Tchaikovsky, to invite our friends from the French Embassy! But as I've said to His Majesty, it's sometimes as well to keep the wolf where you can see him!'

In the intervals between nodding and agreeing, Anne watched the little tableau across the room distractedly: saw Lolya approach her father confidently and slip her hand through his arm; saw the three men look first annoyed and then polite; saw the two Frenchmen bow over Lolya's hand with restrained courtesy. Then the gap through which she was watching closed up, and she saw no more.

A few minutes later, she was called to dance the opening formal minuet with her husband; but when, after the minuets, the general dancing began, she was considerably startled to see Lolya being led into the set by Colonel Duvierge. Startled, and displeased – for Lolya was wearing her heart on her ecstatic face, while Duvierge was looking merely politely amused. Evidently he had been forced into asking her out of courtesy to her father.

Anne was glad to see after that, in the moments she could spare from her own concerns, that Lolya was dancing as she should be with a succession of suitable young men, and looking as though she were enjoying herself. Anne had ordered the new dances to be called from time to time during the evening – the lively mazurkas and polonaises, and the bold and increasingly popular waltz, which had gained ground over the last couple of years to the extent that it was now considered to be respectable by everyone except the very stickiest of dowagers. The last dance before the supper interval was a waltz, and Anne, circling politely in the restrained embrace of Count Chernyshov, was again startled and displeased to see Lolya whirling on the other side of the room with Colonel Andrei Duvierge's arm round her slender waist.

He had asked her a second time! How had she jockeyed him into that? But as Anne watched them over her partner's shoulder, she saw that Duvierge was not merely being polite. Lolya looked as though she had eaten Bliss whole, and leaned into his embrace as they danced, it had to be admitted, extremely gracefully together; while Duvierge looked down into his partner's sparkling black eyes with something like interest.

He had found her sufficiently amusing, it seemed, to have asked her a second time; but then Lolya had said that he had danced with her twice at two other balls. This was a situation to disquiet. She must warn Nikolai to take care of his daughter; though she could not believe that a man like Duvierge would waste much time on an inexperienced virgin like Lolya, and he could certainly not mean her any harm – that would be suicidal in the present climate. But he might encourage Lolya just enough to break her heart, and that would not do at all.

But now the ball was over, and the activities and concerns which had kept Anne preoccupied for so many hours were over, and there was nothing any longer to keep her from thinking about her husband. The last guests had gone; Basil was talking to Mikhailo, giving him instructions about callers the next day – or rather, later that same day – while the footmen went round putting out the lights. Jean-Luc had taken himself off with some of the other members of the company, wisely leaving husband and wife alone.

Anne sent Pauline to bed; and when Basil finished talking to the butler amd came up the stairs, Anne was waiting for him at the first landing. He just failed to meet her eyes, made a resigned gesture towards the small drawing-room, and preceeded her in.

'Would you care for something?' he said lightly, walking across to the cabinet on the far side of the room. 'I'm going to have one.'

The fire had died almost to nothing, and the room was cold. Anne went to it automatically, poked the ashes into redness and put on some more coal, and then just stood, staring at the tiny flames that began to flicker and pop as the coals warmed into life.

Basil poured himself a large brandy, and then, having had no reply from Anne, poured a second one and carried it over, putting down on the small table nearest her. He perched nervously on the arm of the sofa and looked at her back, trying to gauge her mood from her posture. At last, unable to bear the silence any more, he said, 'Well, I suppose there are things you want to say. For God's sake say them, and let's be done with it.'

She turned slowly and looked at him, and he flinched from the look. The shock which had been her first reaction was beginning to wear off, and exposing what was underneath, the disgust and contempt and rage. These were what he saw in her eyes now, and he flushed a little, looked away, and drank nervously from his glass.

Anne didn't at once know what to say. It was something so horrible, so horrifying, that instinct made her want to turn away from it, to deny that it had happened. It was something which had never been mentioned to her directly in all her life – naturally not – although in some oblique and largely wordless way, she had become aware of its existence. She knew, for instance, without precisely knowing how she knew, that in the King's Navy, it was punishable by death, and that the sentence was regularly, though infrequently, carried out against offenders.

Yet to discover it by her own experience, and in someone so close to her – someone with whom she had shared her bed – shared her body! – was like suddenly meeting the Devil face to face, curling horns and sulphur-breath and all. It was like pulling back the covers from one's safe and comfortable bed, and finding it full of crawling maggots. Even now, looking at Basil perched on the sofa's arm, swirling his brandy in his glass, and looking so ordinary, only a little flushed and embarrassed, as if he had been caught out in some minor misdemeanour, she could hardly believe that it was true.

There were things which she found, now, that she didn't want to know. One thing, however, she must ask.

'How long?' she said abruptly. He looked up. 'How long have you been – like that?'

He was stung by her choice of words. 'I don't know what you mean by "like that". I don't know what you suppose I am.'

'I know what you are,' she said with loathing. 'But how many others were there before Jean-Luc?'

'Is it any business of yours?' he retorted.

'Of course it is,' she said. 'I want to know if you were always like that, while you were sharing my bed – before me, even.'

'Jean-Luc was the first,' he said with dull anger. 'And you don't understand. I'm not "like" anything. I love him, that's all.'

'Is that why you didn't marry?' she asked, ignoring the second half of his reply. 'Was it that you didn't like women? You had a reputation as a gallant, I know – but from what I remember, you didn't seem very experienced. Was it always men you wanted?'

The brandy lipped over the edge of his glass with his angry swirling. 'I've told you, Jean-Luc was the first. Before that – ' The truth was that he had always been a little afraid of women, except for his mother and Olga. He had early developed a charming way of flirting with elderly dowagers, and a whole repertoire of near-outrageous compliments with which he kept younger women off-balance and at arm's length.

The truth was that when he had married Anne he had been a virgin, but he could not then, and certainly would not now, admit it. His pursuit of her had been at least partly because he felt safe with her, as with his sister. She was not coquettish like other women, not moved by dark and incomprehensible passions. Her open mind and straightforward speech had made her seem to him clear and plain like daylight, and he had become more and more attracted to her as other women seemed increasingly alien.

He had thought it would all be all right. But though Anne's mind might be like a man's, she still had a female body. The dark power, the earth magic, the animal smell of women, the secret eyes and the mystery, the bleeding and the pain and the exaltation: these things all attached to his familiar, safe Anne. In the daytime, he could love and admire her, but at night she filled him with horror; and after Rose was born, he found it easier to live apart from her, and to lavish on his daughter the love he had once given his wife.

And then came Jean-Luc, woman-like, yet with a safe, clean, smooth man's body; adoring Basil, admiring him flatteringly, regarding him as wise, witty, learned, mature – all the things he had hoped to be, and which Anne proved he was not. How could he help falling in love? And how could that love be wrong? Jean-Luc was simple and kind and good, and loved little Rose. When he and Jean-Luc took her out on a sledge or in a carriage or a boat, they were like a true family: man, woman, and child, loving each other, and safe together.

The truth was, that he had never felt himself to be married until he met Jean-Luc; but how could he tell her that? Besides, it was plain that she was not really listening to him. With a frown between her brows, she was pursuing her own train of thought, only a small part of which was emerging in words.

'How could you?' she said, more in wonder than anger now. 'How could you do such a thing? How could you bring yourself to touch – that creature – in that way? You – ' she shuddered. Thinking about the scene she had witnessed robbed her of words.

Basil stood up abruptly, driven by a mixture of guilt and resentment to defend himself. 'I don't know why you're being so pious about it. It's no more than you've done, after all, and I don't see you beating your breast.'

'What are you talking about?' She was astonished.

'I've taken a lover – very well, what's so wrong with that? You did the same thing. Oh yes, I know about you and Kirov – don't think I didn't! I know all your sordid little secrets! Don't forget I took you in the first place because you wanted to get away from him.'

'Don't,' she said, white with fury. 'Don't *dare* to speak his name – '

'Too holy for my profane lips, is it?' he sneered, whipping his pain and guilt into rage. 'Which of them seduced you first? Quite a family the Kirovs! Was it the father or the son? But I don't suppose you resisted too hard! And did you have them one after the other, or was it both together? Of course, Kirov *père* won in the end – he always does! Sent his son off to Azerbaijan for the Persians to kill! Putting him like Uriah in the forefront of battle, you might say!'

Anne felt nausea knotting itself in the pit of her stomach. She was trembling with rage – and worse than that, with a sort of horrified pity, as though she were witnessing the results of a terrible accident. This man, after all, had rescued her, married her, shared her bed, fathered her child.

'What you have done is different,' she managed to whisper at last. 'You know that it is.'

It was. Right or wrong, even putting aside the moral or religious implications, it was different. The fact was that society turned a blind eye on marital infidelity. People married each other mostly for financial, social or family reasons: they were not obliged to be in love, or even to like each other very much. If they later found someone more to their fancy, well, provided they were discreet about it, who was the worse for their little act of adultery?

But what Basil had done – there was no condoning that. It was unforgiveable, unspeakable, horrible. A man taken in adultery was regarded with amused toleration; the man discovered in the act of sodomy would be treated with horrified revulsion, become an outcast, would never be received in society again. She knew it and he knew it, and as she met his gaze steadily, his wavered and dropped.

'What do you mean to do about it?' he asked at last. She had not considered the implications. Now she saw that his act had placed the reins of her life back in her hands. He had placed himself in her power; he might make no further demands of any sort. But the realisation for the moment led nowhere.

'I don't know,' she said. All the excitement of anger had drained out of her. She felt now desperately tired, wishing most of all that she could sleep, and forget. 'I'll have to think about it.'

'If you want to leave me – set up your own establishment – I'll make you an allowance,' he said. He looked up. 'I suppose I owe you that much.'

It was an apology, and again she felt that terrible, unwelcome pity. This was a maimed creature, she thought – no devil, no colossus of evil, but a pathetic, pitiful thing, like a dog run down by a carriage. She could not hate him. Hate the sin, and love the sinner, the words came to her. Well, she could not quite love him; but she had known him a very long time.

'What about Rose?' she said at last.

'Yes,' he said. 'That's the question, isn't it?'

They looked at each other consideringly. Hers was the power. If he tried to prevent her from seeing Rose, tried to keep Rose from her, she could threaten to expose him. But would she really do that, either to him, or to her daughter? Should Rose grow up one day to discover what her father was? If Anne ever parted with the secret, it became common property; and one day someone, some helpful person, would tell it to Rose.

'She loves me,' he said.

'Yes,' she said.

She could go, leave him, be free of him; set up her own establishment, live with all the freedom of a widow; she might have Rose with her, have her love again. Have it by default – there was the rub! Rose would cry for her father and Jean-Luc, and even though she would gradually forget them – as Sashka had forgotten Anne – her love would only be Anne's for second best. It was a hard thing, she thought bitterly, to be jealous of such creatures.

But Rose must be protected – that was paramount. Anne must detach her affectionate heart from the Creature, before he could do her harm. The thought of that corrupt influence over her child made her tremble with fear and anger; what might he already have told her, shown her? How might he already have twisted that innocent, malleable mind? Jean-Luc must be eradicated from Rose's life – and perhaps Basil too. But it must be done carefully. She would not willingly inflict suffering on her already suffering child.

'What will you do?' Basil asked again.

She sighed, a long, difficult breath of acknowledgement and resignation. 'I don't know,' she said again. 'I don't know what I'll do in the long term. For the moment, I'll stay here. I must think carefully what will be best for Rose. I don't want to act hastily.'

'Then – '

'I'll keep your secret, Basil Andreyevitch. Provided you are discreet, and careful – provided no-one else ever finds out – I'll keep your secret, for Rose's sake.'

'Thank you,' he muttered awkwardly, resentful, relieved, embarrassed, grateful, all at once.

She straightened up, and looked at him coldly. 'In return, I don't expect you ever – *ever* – to get in my way, or question anything I do. You forfeit all right to know anything about me or my life or my concerns, where I am, what I'm doing. Is that clear?'

He sneered. 'Oh yes, perfectly clear. It means you can now continue with your affair with Kirov without having to sneak off into the country. So convenient! And no guilty conscience to spoil it, either!'

'My conscience is my own concern,' she said, turning away wearily. 'I leave you to the mercies of your own.' At the door she turned. 'Don't forget – discretion. I never want to notice you or your – *friend* – again.'

'My lover!' he retorted, jumping to his feet. 'You had a lover, too, don't forget!'

Anne thought for a moment resentfully of the agonies of guilt she had suffered over her – compared with his – small and unimportant sin. For this man she had suffered pangs of conscience, and all the time he was – but she didn't want to think of that. 'At least my lover was a real man,' she said coldly, and left him.

State Secretary Speransky's downfall was finally brought about by his enemies at the end of March, and his regime of reform, which threatened to raise people to positions in the government which they were competent to fill, regardless of their birth or rank, was ended with great relief on all sides. The Emperor, obliged to dismiss him, nevertheless loved him enough to save his life, by sending him and his family under armed guard to Nizhny Novgorod, where he would be safe from the assassin's hand which would doubtless reach out for him in St Petersburg.

April brought bad news and good – Austria, now tied by marriage to Napoleon, signed a formal treaty of alliance with France; but on the other hand, Sweden, lately a neutral power with good reason to be hostile to Russia, had signed a secret pact of alliance with the Tsar. April brought a change of command in the war against the Turks in the lower Danube: Admiral Chicagov was sent to replace the one-eyed, pleasure-loving veteran General Kutuzov, who, it was thought, had been living the life of a Pasha down there and achieving nothing. Chicagov had strict orders to get things moving and negotiate some form of peace with the Turks, in order to release the army there for service against the French.

April brought a formal letter of complaint from Napoleon to Alexander about his failure to keep to the terms of the Treaty of Tilsit: plainly, this was to be the official excuse for the invasion there was no doubt now was being prepared for. April brought the news that Napoleon, to release his own troops for the Russian venture, had offered to make peace in the Iberian Peninsular, provided his brother Joseph remained King of Spain – an offer the Spanish, Portuguese and British all indignantly rejected. Under the painstaking general Sir Arthur Wellesley – now Lord Wellington – the British troops and the indigenous guerillas had been tying up huge numbers of French soldiers for years, and wearing them down bit by bit; and it was plain that it was only a matter of time before they were defeated and driven back over the Pyranees.

April also brought – at last, and almost a month late, the thaw – *ottepel*! The late snowfalls provided a weight of frozen water over the land which threatened serious floods once it was loosened by the lengthening days: floods, fogs, and fathoms of mud; and at this unpropitious moment, the Emperor at last left St Petersburg.

Late in the evening on the 20th of April, Kirov came to call on Anne, who received him in her private sitting-room. Since the night of the ball, Anne had changed her conduct very little, except that she now met Nikolai openly, whenever she wanted to. She had not betrayed Basil's secret to him, had merely told him that she and her husband had come to an arrangement; and if Kirov, seeing her evident shock and distress, and having observed Basil's behaviour over a very long time, particularly recently with Jean-Luc, drew his own conclusions as to what had happened, he said nothing of it to her.

Her meetings with him so far since that day had been innocent. She was still too shocked to want to have any intimate contact with anyone; and she was too aware of their position in society, and Rose's vulnerability, to dare to risk it. She knew, of course, that some decision would have to be taken as to what their relationship was to be in the future, but for the moment she wanted only to be able to be near him and to talk to him. She needed time for the mental wounds to heal.

Time, however, was a luxury in short supply in the spring of 1812. When Kirov came into her room that day, she saw at once that something had happened, and got to her feet in alarm.

'Nikolai, what is it? Is it bad news? Is it – ' Though the word *war* was in everyone's mind, everyone was curiously reluctant for it to be on their lips. Turbaned dowagers nodded their heads together over tea, dashing young officers laughed and boasted at the mess table, handsome young women whispered in Zubin's across seven lengths of Indian muslin; but it was always The Situation they discussed, never that small and forbidding word. If it came, their sweet-faced, sweet-natured Emperor would be pitted against the cunning of the wicked Corsican bandit, who had already defeated him twice in campaign, and had conquered by his staggering military skills half the civilised world. There was no possibility, of course, that Russia could ever be overrun, but all the same, no-one really wanted to think about what might happen . . . And no-one wanted to mention That Word, in case voicing it might give it power.

'Not yet,' he said, understanding her, 'but soon. The call has come, at any rate. I am to leave St Petersburg in the morning.'

'Oh – ' She crossed the room to his arms, and he held her close, stroking her head automatically, his thoughts still running fast on other things. She felt his distraction, released herself, gestured him to a chair. Now that the light fell on his face, she could see how tired he was, how drawn. It was nine years since she had first met him – he was no longer a young man. I've been foolish and selfish, she thought. We must not waste time.

But for now she said, 'When did you eat?'

He smiled. 'I don't remember. I don't think I did. I've been at the palace all day, in meetings.'

'Then first I will get you supper. No, sit still, rest. I shan't be a moment.'

She went through into the next room and rang the bell, and when Mikhailo came, ordered a supper tray – bread and meat and whatever there was that was quick to prepare – and a bottle of good claret. When she returned to the inner room, she found that in her brief absence he had fallen asleep in the deep armchair before the fire with his chin sunk on his chest.

She didn't wake him, but sat quietly in the chair opposite and watched him thoughtfully. This was the man whose existence, whose character and actions, had directed her life and coloured her thoughts for nine years – most of her adult life. But why? What made him so different? It was not simply a case of loving him – the words meant little, hackneyed as they were. It was that he – the wholeness of him, the unique entity of flesh and nerve and mind and muscle, intellect and passions, experiences and prejudices, that made up Nikolai Sergeyevitch Kirov – was somehow a part of her life and experience that could not be removed or replaced. If he were to go away and never see her again, she would not stop knowing him, or living through her experience of him. It was as if a hundred thousand invisible threads issued from his body and penetrated hers, along which some vital power rushed and throbbed and sparked, carrying information beyond words, feelings beyond emotion.

She knew him completely and with every fibre of her being: they were not truly separate people any more. And yet here he was in his separate flesh, a tired middle-aged man in mud-splashed boots who had fallen asleep by the fire. She studied the long, mobile face, the humorous mouth fallen at the corners in sleep, the fine mesh of lines around the eyes, the soft light-brown hair, greying now, receding a little from the temples. His chin and cheeks were lightly stubbled since that morning's shave, and the stubble, she noticed with a pang, glinted silver like frost; the cheek muscles were growing a little slacker, and there was a fold of loose skin under the chin.

She looked down at his hands, lying unconscious in his lap – strong, long-fingered hands; neat, smooth nails; large veins across the backs of them, and skin beginning to be loose. A man's hands, not a boy's. Hands skilled to wield a sword or a pen, to control a horse, to cradle a child; hands that knew how to kill, and how to seek out pleasure for her; hands skilled to love.

She shivered, and returned her gaze to his face. This was the flesh of the man, the warm, human, vulnerable body, in which he lived, and knew pain and hunger and pleasure and weariness; the body which slept, and ate, and grew old and would one day die; the body which created her physical delight, which touched her and longed for her and possessed her and transformed her. She loved this body: and it was not profane love, it was not less than loving the mind or the soul, for this poor human flesh was the manifestation of those things, the outward and visible sign of those inward and intangible graces. And more, it was the frailness of human flesh which bound all human creatures together in one love and one pity and one understanding; which made it so easy to kill one other, and, in that knowledge, still to love and forgive. The flesh was the humility of humankind, and in transcending its frailty, the great, humble pride.

Fragments of old religious teaching passed through her mind in a tenuous cobweb of understanding. *God made man in his own image* – made the flesh to resemble the spirit, strong as the air, frail as the earth; *And the Word was made flesh and dwelt among us, and we beheld His glory* – beheld the glory through the flesh, naked under the sun; *Beloved, let us love one another: for love is of God, and everyone that loveth, knoweth God.* The sacred and the profane; but it was the intention which made the difference, not the act.

Nikolai! She had known from the beginning, from the first moment she saw him, that he would be important to her. How young she had been; how untried! Her experience since then had changed her – inevitably – but that one thing had remained constant. He was human, with humanity's faults – selfishness, indolence, greed, self-interest – but also with its great strengths – humour, courage, compassion. A flawed image, but an image all the same, of the Maker. She loved him; and she thought that perhaps to know and love one human being completely was the best and greatest thing life could teach.

The door opened, and Nikolai woke with the suddenness of the old campaigner. Mikhailo came in with the tray, and placed it on a low table by him, and withdrew.

'I'm sorry, did I sleep? Too bad of me!'

'You were tired,' Anne said. 'Now have your supper – but first, let me make you comfortable.' She slipped to her knees in front of him, and took hold of his boot, smiling up at his mute protest, 'Oh yes, I did it many a time for Papa. My wrists are quite strong, you know.'

He let her minister to him, seeing that she wished it. She pulled off his boots, poured his wine, arranged napkin and knife and plate within his reach, and then continued to sit on the floor in front of him in the firelight, and watched as he ate. Mikhailo had brought bread and cold chicken, cheesecake and dried figs, almonds and apples.

'Let me pour you some wine, too. I hate to drink alone.'

She consented, and sipped while he took his supper, and told her the news.

'The Emperor is going tomorrow to Lithuania, to the field headquarters at Vilna. I tell you this in confidence, however: for public consumption the bulletin will say that he has gone on a routine inspection of military camps. That's partly to calm the public, but mostly I suspect to throw dust in de Lauriston's eyes. His Majesty's taking Rumiantsev with him, and Kochubey – Arakcheyev, too, and Bennigsen.'

'And General Tolly?'

'Of course. Tolly and I are going on ahead, leaving tomorrow morning. The Emperor and his staff are to go in the afternoon, after a special service of blessing at the Holy Mother of Kazan – for public consumption, of course. The travelling will be bad because of the thaw, but it's important the Emperor moves now. I've heard from Kurakin that Napoleon is still in Paris, but there are four hundred and fifty thousand men on the move towards our border, and there's no time to loose if preparations are going to be complete before they are all assembled along the Nieman.'

'Four hundred and fifty thousand,' Anne said blankly. The number was colossal, unimaginable, a desert of humanity. She had had no idea before then of the scale of the operation Bonaparte was intending to stage against Russia. It was impossible to imagine an army of such a size.

'That's not including the crack troops he'll bring with him. It will be more than half a million men, when all's told.'

'Half a million . . . He's mad. Quite, quite mad! How can food be found for half such a number?'

Kirov looked grim. 'That's partly why we must move now. Napoleon's way has always been to live off the land – that's what's made his soldiers so hated throughout Europe. In this case, it will be more than ever essential. Imagine the size of a supply train for such a horde; imagine the numbers of men, of horses needed to move it; imagine how far it would have to bring the supplies, how slowly it would travel, how vulnerable it would be! No, Napoleon must make his men live off the land – and so we must get there ahead of him, remove everything that might be of use to him. Burn the crops in his path, herd off the animals, evacuate the people, destroy the buildings.'

'That's Tolly's plan?'

'An important part of it. My job, as always, is to try to persuade the Emperor not to change his mind. He is going to be surrounded by hotheads and fanatics and Old Russians, who will all argue that the good advice Tolly gives him is cowardly, even treacherous.'

'That will be your job, then,' she said carefully. 'Simply to advise?'

He smiled a little, reading her mind. 'There will be nothing for you to fear yet awhile, Annushka. I shall be helping to implement Tolly's plans – there's bound to be some resistance amongst the peasants to having their houses destroyed, but I shall have a troop of cavalry to help me persuade them of their duty. I've told you before, love, that Napoleon won't invade before June.'

'Because he needs the crops for his horses – but you will have burned them.'

'And what he does manage to find will not be ripe, because of the late thaw.'

'June,' she said. She picked a crumb of bread from his plate and rolled it unhappily between her fingers. He looked down at her bent head, and the firelight on her hair, and loved her so consumingly it was like a spasm of hunger. She was all he had ever wanted. 'And when will it all be over?' she asked, and then shook her head at her own foolishness. 'I suppose you can't know that.'

'Annushka, come with me,' he said suddenly. She looked up, relief and doubt in her eyes. 'Vilna is a pleasant town, and lots of people will be going. Where the Emperor goes, you know . . . It will be quite safe there for six weeks, maybe two months, and when Napoleon finally crosses, we can think of somewhere else to send you, somewhere safe, but near enough for me to reach you. Come with me! I need you, *doushka*.'

He pushed aside the tray and held out his arms to her, and she knelt up and put herself into the circle of them, and he held her close.

'I know it's a hard thing to ask you – that there are principles at stake,' he said. 'But lately I have felt . . . ' He paused and began again. 'I used to play fast and loose with life. When you are young, you think you're immortal. Then you have children, and you know that you're not. But it's only when you get to my age that time seems to run faster and faster, dragging you along with it, and you can only try to clutch at things as they pass, and they're whipped away from under your fingers.'

She nodded, her face pressed against his. He stroked her head. 'What

I mean to say is that life is uncertain at the best of times, and in time of war there is no certainty at all. My only sureness is that I love you, and I don't want to waste any of the time we have left in being apart from you.'

She nodded again, and he could feel her thinking; but she was not consenting, not yet. He went on gently, 'Annushka, I'd never ask you what happened between you and Basil Andreyevitch, but I have been in the world a lot longer than you, and I have seen a great deal more. I think I know what he is, and what he has done, and I ask you this: do you owe such a man any loyalty?'

She pulled herself back from him, and looked into his eyes.

'It isn't that, you see,' she said. 'At least, it isn't so simple. It's myself – what I owe myself.'

'Do you think you would do wrong by loving me?' he asked carefully, afraid of what her answer might be. Her mind he knew intimately – but her Faith he was unsure of. 'Do you think you have done wrong by loving me?'

She looked at him searchingly, and after a long moment, she said, 'No.'

'Then you'll come with me?'

She hesitated. 'I have to think of Rose.'

'You can leave her in Petersburg. She'll be quite safe.'

'No. I can't leave her with him – with them.'

'I meant with my household, with Sashka. My staff is perfectly reliable as you know. And once the roads are fit they can all go down to Schwartzenturm, and stay – '

But Anne was shaking her head before he had even finished.

'No. I can't leave her.' She opened her mouth to explain, and shut it again. There was simply too much to be said. He must understand without words.

He did. He thought a moment, and said, 'Then bring her with you. Yes, why not? Didn't Grubernik say she should have change, stimulation? Bring her nurse and her governess, yes, and Grubernik too, if you like, though there are some excellent doctors in Lithuania. We'll take a house, hire extra servants, make a home for her with us. It's lovely there in the spring. Why not? Say yes, Annushka. For God's sake say yes!'

'The roads will be too bad,' she said. 'Think of lurching through all that mud – it would be terrible for her.'

That was a point. 'Very well, then. I have to go now – I'm under orders – but in a fortnight's time, as soon as the roads are sound, I'll

455

send Adonis for you, to bring you to me. And meanwhile, I can have the house made ready for you, and everything prepared. You can send any special instructions to me in the diplomatic bag. We'll still have a month or six weeks there before we need to move on.'

He looked at her expectantly, and suddenly she laughed.

'It's madness,' she said, shaking her head; and he knew she would come to Vilna.

Chapter Twenty-Six

Anne's first sight of Vilna was a smiling one, as she approached it on a sunny day in May. It was built on a curve of the river Vilia, which ran in a deep, wooded ravine through gently hilly country. The town itself spread along the bank and climbed up the hillside, a pretty tangle of houses and narrow twisting streets. The soft red-tiled roofs were dominated by a forest of spires and golden cupolas, rising to the highest point where an octagonal red-brick tower was all that remained of the original mediaeval fortress. A single wooden bridge spanned the river at the foot of the town, and the hills above it were crowned with forests of birch and fir which protected it from the north and west.

From Vilna the road led westwards to Kovno on the River Nieman, about fifty miles away. Other roads came in from St Petersburg in the north, and from the vast and impassable area of the Pripet Marshes in the south: it was this area of marshland which limited Napoleon's choice of route for his invasion. The main road to the east was the long and winding one via Smolensk to Moscow, some six hundred and twenty-five miles away.

When Adonis had come to fetch her, Anne asked him anxiously about the town and the facilities.

'Oh, you'll like it,' he said ironically. 'It's not like military head-quarters at all. There's dancing and banquets and parties. The local gentry come in their best clothes, all smelling of mothballs, and fawn at the Emperor's feet, and he gives them medals, and makes their wives and daughters ladies-in-waiting to the Empress, who's here in Petersburg. You'll feel at home, all right.'

Anne looked concerned. 'But doesn't the Emperor do anything?'

'Oh yes. He rides here and he rides there, and he sits up all night writing letters. He never stops . . . Well, he's not my Emperor, thank God.' He shrugged. 'We'll have a good fast journey, anyway — the roads have hardened off nicely.'

Anne had hired a large berlin, across the seats of which a mattress could be placed on a board, so that Rose could lie down as well as sit. She had been a little worried as to how Rose would react to Adonis's ruined face, but Rose took to him at once, evidently having inherited her father's taste for the bizarre. At their first meeting they fixed each other with a solemn, one-eyed regard, and after a moment's judicious study, Rose favoured him with her most ravishing smile, and held out her hands to be picked up.

Adonis lifted her with skilled ease to his shoulder, and she studied his face at close quarters and finally put out a tentative finger to touch his scar. 'Does it hurt?' she asked in English.

Adonis touched her velvet cheek, and to Anne's surprise replied in the same language. 'No more than this does.'

'I didn't know you spoke English,' Anne said.

He shrugged. 'I speak a little of everything.'

And Rose, who at that time spoke English and French more or less at random, decided from then that the English language was peculiarly for Adonis.

Basil had received the news that Anne intended to go to Vilna without comment; and when she had said she was taking Rose with her, he had opened his mouth and then closed it again, knowing the weakness of his position. But for Rose's sake he made light of their separation, telling her that she would enjoy herself, and that they would meet again soon, and Rose had seemed to accept it without fuss. Anne was unspeakably glad to be removing her child from Jean-Luc's influence, even if only for a time. Now she would have the chance to win back Rose's love; and by the time she saw her father again, who knew but that Jean-Luc might have disappeared from the scene entirely? Rose parted from them at the carriage door with some tears, but once they were on the move, and Anne was pointing out things of interest to her from the window, and telling her of all the fun they would have together, the tears soon dried. At that age, Anne thought, a child's memory is short.

The journey was accomplished without difficulty, and Adonis's burly muscles and trained strength made light of Rose's disabilities. Anne's caravan included Quassy and Image, being led along between the carriages by grooms. On the first evening, when they stopped at an inn, Adonis went with the grooms to see the riding horses settled; and coming back to report to Anne, said to her thoughtfully, 'If you want her to ride the colt one day, you must begin soon.'

Anne began to ask how he knew what had been in her mind, but decided not to waste her time. Instead she said, 'How can she ride? She can't even walk.'

Adonis nodded. 'All the more reason. The one will help the other. I can teach her, mistress, if you want me to – but not on the colt. No, nor the mare. Give me the money, and I'll get a little Cossack pony for her – the cleverest and kindest horses in the world! Once she learns to ride, you'll see the difference!'

Anne looked at him gratefully, and close to tears. All that she had wanted for her daughter, and had put away, folded in a locked drawer in the back of her mind, came suddenly before her.

'Do you think she could? Do you think she could ever lead a normal life?'

Adonis's one eye was darkly understanding. 'In my village, when I was so big,' he offered a hand two feet from the floor, 'there was a girl a couple of years older than me, who got this same sickness, and they said she'd never walk or talk. She grew up into the prettiest girl in the village, and the best dancer, and everyone wanted to marry her. *I* wanted to marry her, but my brother got in first. So I left and went to be a soldier.'

Anne looked sceptical. 'This is just a story.'

He grinned. 'Her name was Marta, and before I left she gave my brother a big fat baby boy to leave his name to. She could ride any horse bareback, and danced the mazurka like a woman possessed.'

'But that's a Polish dance,' Anne objected.

'It's similar. You wouldn't know the name in my language,' he said with a shrug.

Kirov had taken a pretty little house on the outskirts of the town, with lawns that ran down to the river, property of an impoverished Lithuanian baron who was only too glad to let it and move his wife and too-numerous family to a smaller and cheaper house in the country. As soon as the carriage stopped, the Count was there to open the door and lift Anne down, to hold her hands and smile down at her in the sunshine.

Anne felt a mixture of excitement and peacefulness, a holiday feeling of having nothing more to worry about, of having time ahead filled only with pleasure. This was the beginning, she thought, of their married life together, though they were not, and could perhaps never be, married. But they were together now, and no-one could come between them. It was to her that he would return from whatever missions he was sent on, and if the world didn't like it – well, it could look away.

'I've missed you,' he said simply.

'Even busy as you were? I've missed you too. This is a pretty place.'

'You won't be bored – there are all sorts of things going on. It's as lively here as Moscow – parties every night.'

'So Adonis has been telling me. He doesn't approve. But I shouldn't be bored anyway: just walking and riding would keep me happy.'

Adonis came round the side of the carriage to lift out Rose, and from the safety of his arms she greeted Nikolai gravely. She didn't take to him as she did to Adonis, and he, long removed from that stage in his own children, and with the thought of Basil to come between them, was reserved with her.

'Come inside and see if you approve of my housekeeping,' he said, turning with relief to Anne. 'Tea will be brought in as soon as you're ready, and then you must tell me everything that's been going on in Petersburg since I left.'

A while later they were settled on the little terrace overlooking the lawns, and Anne was performing the ritual of the samovar. Mlle Parmoutier was pushing Rose around the garden in her wheeled chair, examining the shrubs and flowers and benches and urns, and the child's high-pitched exclamations mingled with the bird song and the distant murmur of the river to make a pleasant background to their conversation.

'The river looks high,' Anne said. 'Has there been much rain lately?'

'The weather's been terrible. This is the first really sunny day we've had. But tell me about Petersburg.'

'Well, de Lauriston's applied for permission to come here, for a private audience with the Emperor –'

'Yes, I know. He's been refused. Napoleon will take it as one more proof that Russia is the aggressor, but better that than have Lauriston send him detailed reports of our plans and state of readiness back to Paris. But I didn't mean that sort of news. Where's Basil Andreyevitch, to begin with?'

Anne passed his cup and said, 'Did you think I would bring him with me? Actually, he did toy with the idea of coming here. "*Everyone* is in Vilna," he said. But I think he only did it to torment me. In the end he and Jean-Luc decided to go back to Moscow. I think Jean-Luc felt ill at ease with the growing anti-French feeling; and Basil said that Petersburg was intolerably stuffy, and that Moscow was much more cosmopolitan. So I think they will stay there.'

'Unless Napoleon reaches it with his army,' Nikolai said drily.

'You don't think he will?' Anne was startled.

He didn't answer, only shook his head doubtfully. Anne went on, 'I thought, you see, that when I have to leave here, I ought to take Rose to Moscow, because she will want to see her father. I don't wish to separate her from him completely.'

'All we can do is wait and see. If Basil Andreyevitch has to leave Moscow, presumably he will tell you were he is going.' He sipped his tea, and changed the subject with obvious relief. 'Have you seen anything of Lolya? I didn't really like leaving her with my mother, but I couldn't bring her here without a chaperone – and in any case, I shouldn't have liked to expose her to the flattery of so many young officers with nothing to do!'

'You'd never have got her to come,' Anne said grimly. 'Where Duvierge is, there Lolya must stay!'

He looked alarmed. 'She isn't behaving improperly? Surely my mother wouldn't so far forget her duty as to – '

'Oh no, she doesn't admit him to the house, or have him to dinner. But he is better liked than de Lauriston, and when he's invited to the same function as Lolya, Vera Borisovna can't stop them talking to each other, since they were apparently introduced in the first place by you.'

'Don't remind me! If I had known . . . '

'He behaves very well, I have to say – perfectly proper in every respect. But I didn't like to see his interest in her. They always dance together, though never more than twice; and they talk together, though never apart from the company. I've seen him approach her when she's out shopping or walking with her maid, and stand talking to her for a minute or two. Nothing anyone could object to – but why does he do it at all?'

'And Lolya?'

Anne sighed. 'She wears her heart on her sleeve, I'm afraid, though I've warned her twice not to make her feelings so obvious. It's something of an *on-dit*, though at the moment people are tending to be amused by it rather than shocked. No-one, I'm glad to say, suspects Duvierge of having designs on her innocence. They seem to think he's interested in her as your daughter, and probing her for state secrets.'

'And is he?'

'Oh yes, but don't look so shocked! Lolya may be a wet goose where matters of the heart are concerned, but she hasn't been your daughter all her life for nothing. Discretion is fundamental to her. Even if she knew anything useful, she wouldn't tell him. I've overheard one or two of their conversations, and she wouldn't even tell him you had gone to Vilna, though he asked her very cleverly in the form of a statement. "Your Papa has gone to Vilna with the Emperor, of course," he said.'

'And what did Lolya say?'

'She shrugged and said, "Oh, Papa never tells me where he's going, and I never ask", and then she asked him wistfully if he would be at the puppet show the next day. I didn't know whether to hug her or shake her!'

Nikolai smiled at last. 'I shouldn't have left her to be exposed to that. She ought to go away from Petersburg, but it would be no good sending her to Schwartzenturm with Sashka – it's too close. Besides, Mama doesn't care for the country.'

'Perhaps you ought to send her to Tula?'

'Yes, I think I may. Shoora will keep an eye on her, and take her in to Moscow often enough to keep her amused. She'd be far enough away from her brave soldier hero then. I'll write to Shoora today, and Lolya can go down next month.'

'And what has been happening here?' Anne asked after a brief pause. 'I imagine you've been kept busy.'

'Busier than you know! The Emperor's brought that fool Shishkov with him – Speransky's replacement, you know – and he's busy trying to persuade His Majesty to ignore Tolly's and my advice. He's so insanely patriotic he thinks that to yield an inch of land to Napoleon is tantamount to high treason.'

'I've heard that he hates the French so much, he'll only converse in Old Church Slavonic,' Anne said, amused.

'Well, that's not quite true. But certainly he writes plays and poetry in it, which of course no-one can understand, since no-one but him and a few monks speak it! And then there's all the hothead amateur soldiers, like Armfelt and Yermolov, who talk grandly about making a stand – *making a stand*, you know, with a hundred thousand against five times that number! And Bennigsen and Phull, who hate each other cordially, keep coming up with the most insane and elaborate plans of campaign which couldn't possibly work, and His Majesty listens to them all gravely, and wavers first this way and then that way.'

He snorted in derision. 'The trouble is,' he went on, 'that they look so good on paper! There are maps and little drawings, and arrows, and little coloured squares with numbers in them, and the Emperor thinks it's all very clever, and he's really impressed, despite the fact that Phull has never won a battle in thirty years of soldiering, and Bennigsen's been retired since Friedland. But Tolly won't draw him any little pictures. He just says quietly, retreat, Your Majesty, harry the columns from the flanks, draw them on, and let the sheer size of Russia defeat them. What can a poor Emperor do?'

Anne smiled, but she could hear that he was worried. 'And you have to convince him that Tolly's right.'

'That's not my official task, of course. I'm supposed to advise him about the composition of the French army and Napoleon's state of mind.'

'And what is Bonaparte doing at the moment?'

'Still trying to organise supplies, I imagine. The problem is even thornier than he probably thought it would be. The last two years' harvests in Poland and Prussia have been poor, so the stocks of grain are low in any case. And to make it worse, it's taking all the troops different lengths of time to reach Poland from the corners of the Empire. The ones who are already assembled are swarming over the land like locusts, stripping it bare while they wait for the rest of the Grande Armée to come up. The latecomers are going to begin hungry; and the people who are being forced to support all these soldiers are not very happy.'

'Will they rise against him?'

He shook his head. 'Napoelon's put out a rumour that he intends to restore the old Kingdom of Poland and guarantee its independence, just to keep them sweet, and to keep the anti-Russian fervour at fever pitch.'

'Unscrupulous,' Anne said. 'I don't suppose he means a word of it.'

'It's just an expedient. Our Emperor has let it be thought that he means to grant Lithuania independence, for much the same reason.'

'Oh,' said Anne.

'But Napoleon's supply troubles are worse even than that. The spring weather has been bad not only in Russia, but everywhere in northern Europe, so the summer cereals went in late. He's going to have something like a hundred thousand horses, and no corn to feed them on – and army horses can't survive on grass for more than a day or two. The work just kills them without high feed. A man will go on and on, driven by fear or hope or patriotism or hero worship, when there's nothing in his belly – but the horses just lie down and die, and without horses there's no cavalry and no artillery.'

'Then Bonaparte really has no chance of winning?' Anne said hopefully. 'Things aren't so bad after all.'

He smiled at her eagerness. 'My love, the largest army the world has ever seen is knocking at our doors, led by the most successful soldier the world has ever known; and we are led by a young man who knows nothing about war, and prefers to repose his trust in those who know just about as little. Of course things are bad! I've told you about Napoleon's troubles – but there's no knowing what he might do to overcome them. He's ingenious, and he's determined.'

'I thought you said Russia could never be defeated,' she said in a small voice.

'So I believe. And if the Emperor can be brought to follow Tolly's plan, I think this invasion will fail. But no-one should ever underestimate Napoleon. There's always next year, and the next. And until Napoleon is dead, the world will not be safe from him.'

Despite Kirov's words, and despite her own intellectual understanding of the situation, Anne found it impossible to keep believing in the imminence of danger. Vilna was *en fête*, and there was a constant round of pleasure – balls, reviews, exhibitions, plays, and concerts. The houses of the rich were brilliantly lit every night; the taverns were filled to overflowing; the streets rang to the sound of horseshoes day and night, as dashing cavalry officers rode here, and carriageloads of fashionable ladies drove there; there was gaming and singing and drinking and not a few fights; and a brisk trade at a couple of unofficial brothels on the south side of the town.

The Emperor, too, seemed to have forgotten, at least with his public face, what he was doing at Vilna, and after the bustle of the first weeks, seemed to have settled down into an unhurried round of social engagements, smiling and nodding and charming the Lithuanian gentry, who responded by clamouring to entertain him.

The news came that Napoleon had left Paris on the 9th of May with his Empress, arriving a week later in Dresden where he held court. At splendid receptions, he received all the kings, princes, and dukes of Europe who were now his vassals. It was a display of power not entirely lost on the Imperial Court at Vilna; especially when it was followed, on the 18th of May, by a visit from the Comte de Narbonne, as a special emissary from Napoleon, to deliver an implicit threat, and to give the Emperor of all the Russias one last chance to come to heel.

The Emperor responded by unrolling before the Comte a huge map of Russia, and saying that though he believed Napoleon to be the greatest general in Europe, with the best-trained troops, yet space was a barrier, and that if he let time, deserts and climate defend Russia for him, he would still have the last word. Then he sent de Narbonne away, ordering him to be given food and wine for his journey back to Dresden.

Early in June the news arrived that Napoleon had left Dresden on the 29th of May, heading north again for the Nieman. Still the news did not seem to dismay the Emperor, who at that moment was negotiating to buy the house and estate of Zakret, close to the city, from General Bennigsen who had been using it in his retirement with his new young wife. Prince Volkonsky had persuaded the Emperor that in order properly to reciprocate the hospitality the local aristocracy had been showing him, he needed a house of his own; but the Emperor had not been hard to persuade. It was very pleasant in Vilna for everyone, and in buying Zakret, the Emperor looked as though he were intending to settle down for the summer.

Adonis acquired a suitable Cossack pony for Rose, and in his spare moments, began to teach her to ride, sitting her astride the patient back on a blanket rather than a saddle.

'She must learn to balance, since she can't grip,' he explained to Anne.

Rose had looked at the pony rather doubtfully at first, and Mlle Parmoutier had begged Anne to forbid what must be of the gravest danger to her Lamb. But Professor von Frank, of the University Medical Faculty, whom Kirov had engaged to take care of Rose's health, since Grubernik could not be tempted away from Petersburg, had said he thought there was no harm in it; and once Adonis had shown Rose how to feed the pony on bread and carrots, and how to brush its long mane and forelock, she had lost all fear of it, and was eager to ride.

Adonis merely held her round the waist and walked the pony round a few times; and when he lifted her off, saying that it was enough for a first time, Rose was eager for more. To Anne he said afterwards, 'Leave her always wanting more – that way she will learn quicker. Never let her go on until she's tired.'

'Why are you telling me this? You are her teacher,' Anne said, amused, but impressed with his wisdom, and with the gentleness of this tough mercenary towards the crippled child.

'I cannot always be here, mistress. You forget I am a soldier, and under command. The little one must ride regularly, every day, and when I am not here, it must be you who teaches her. But do as I do – don't try to make her do too much, out of your own pride.'

Little by little, but astonishingly quickly, Rose learnt. At first she had to be held on to the pony's back; then she could balance for herself, holding the neck strap; then she could balance without holding, and learnt to use the reins. The pony was ideally suited to the task: small and sure-footed, patient and obedient, yet remarkably intelligent. Anne had seen him sometimes look round and fix his small rider with a considering regard from those great brown eyes.

'I'm sure he knows that she's a child, and weak. Look how carefully he moves with her, and how he stops at once if she begins to lose her balance.'

'Of course he knows,' Adonis said, rubbing the mealy muzzle affectionately. 'He's taking care of her. You can trust him.'

Anne and Mlle Parmoutier between them made Rose a pair of Cossack trousers to ride in, and the Count had a pair of soft boots made for her in the town. Rose was delighted with her new outfit, because it hid her leg braces. The Count laughingly promised her a Cossack hat for her birthday, and she smiled at him shyly – the first time she had really warmed to him.

'She will always have to ride cross-saddle,' Adonis told Anne, watching her sideways for reaction. Anne merely nodded. 'And trotting I think will not be possible. When she is older and stronger, she may learn to canter. For now, walking, always walking.'

By the middle of June, Marya Vassilievna could ride her pony confidently round the field at the walk, and Adonis told Anne with tears of pride in his eyes, that his little English Rose was even beginning to hold on with her knees in the proper fashion.

'She's grown shockingly brown,' Anne said to Nikolai one night in bed, 'but it makes me so happy to see her, I can't mind it. I never thought she would be able to ride at all. Adonis is a wonderful man.'

The Count, holding her in his arms, smiled into the darkness above her head. 'I think he approves of you, too. He offered, when this campaign's over, to murder your husband for me so that I could marry you.'

Anne laughed nervously, not sure how far it was a joke. 'I wish we could be married,' she said after a moment. 'Then we could have Sashka with us, too.' She hated the fact that because she was, in effect, his mistress, she was no longer respectable enough to take care of the child she had once bathed and dressed and played with and taught his letters and his numbers.

He kissed the top of her head and held her closer. 'When this war is over, we'll find a way to marry, I promise you. Something will be done. Until then – '

'Until then,' she said, nudging closer and sighing contentedly, 'I am so happy just to be with you. If I have nothing else for the rest of my life, I shall have had this.'

'There's plenty more to come,' he said. 'It's only just beginning.'

Professor von Frank had a young wife, and the young wife had a fine operatic soprano voice. Though only an amateur, she was famed throughout Lithuania, and as the Emperor had graciously expressed an interest in hearing her sing, a concert was arranged for one evening in the middle of June. It was fortunate that the cellist, Bernhard Romberg, was also visiting friends nearby, and was delighted to receive an Imperial invitation; and with the addition of a tolerable pianist, and an excellent string quartet, a very good programme was arranged, quite as good, Anne thought, as anything she had heard in Moscow.

Nikolai was unable to attend, his duties having taken him to Novi Troki, a village about twelve miles or so closer to the border, where it was rumoured that a senior French officer had been taken prisoner and was being held in a barn. Though it seemed likely to prove false, it was necessary for someone to go and investigate; Anne had therefore gone to the concert in the company of Madame de Tolly, who was frequently without her hardworking husband on such occasions.

After the concert, the two women were waiting at the door for Madame de Tolly's carriage to be called. A prolonged clattering on the cobbles down the street heralded a troop of cavalry of some kind, and everyone hastily cleared the way for them. Troops were moving about Vilna all the time, arriving and departing with new orders, and Anne was paying no particular attention, until Madame de Tolly said, 'Oh, look, more Cossacks! I do love their clever little horses, don't you? Mikhail says they think with their feet.'

Anne smiled. Evidently the good Madame de Tolly thought that her husband had originated the phrase; but it was a commonplace that Cossack ponies thought with their feet, to which Nikolai had added pungently, 'Unlike certain members of the Emperor's staff, who usually think with their bottoms.'

'They're wonderful creatures,' she replied, thinking gratefully of Rose's pony Myelka, and turning to look at the troop, she saw a familiar tall bay horse with long ears, the mount of the officer commanding. 'Nabat!' she whispered in surprise; and her eyes travelled on upwards to meet, in the instant in which he passed, the startled gaze of Sergei.

He was gone, posting fast up the cobbled street at the head of his troop. The horses clattered past, ridden by brown-faced, hawk-nosed, Tartar-cheeked Cossacks, with the long moustaches of the Caucasus, and wearing the distinctive black *burkas* which Anne remembered so well – the mountainman's protection from heat, cold, rain, and the damp of the earth by night. The horses were all well splashed with mud, right up to their girths, and the Cossacks' boots were muddy too – they had travelled hard that day. Now they were past, Anne began to wonder if she really had seen Sergei at the head of the troop, or whether she had imagined it. There was nothing so very surprising about it really, she told herself as the carriage pulled up and she stood aside to let Madame de Tolly climb in: troops were being brought in from all over Russia; but she had thought he was far away in Azerbaijan with General Tormassov.

The next morning while she and Rose and Mlle Parmoutier were taking a late breakfast on the terrace, Sergei arrived to call on her. The butler showed him out to them, and hovered in case extra covers were required.

'Good morning, Madame Tchaikovsky,' Sergei began unpromisingly. 'I trust I don't disturb you? But I thought I ought at least to pay my respects, as I find you here so unexpectedly.'

Anne looked at him with guilt and pity. There was no trace any more of the laughing, fair boy who had teased Lolya, carried Natasha pick-a-back, played chess with his father and minded not winning, flung himself flushed and shy at her feet with an untouched heart for her taking. This Sergei was a solidly-built, muscular young man with a strong jaw, an uncompromising mouth, and hard eyes, which just now were looking flintily past her left ear. The sun frown between his brows had evidently become habitual even when there was no sun, and the lines at either side of his mouth were not good-humoured. His skin was very tanned, and the front of his hair was bleached fair, and above one temple it had been shaved back to the scalp, evidently in the treatment of a wound, which had left a jagged scar running out from his hairline and down his forehead.

Yet for all his coldness and the lack of a welcoming smile, he had come to see her, when he need not; and in the very fact that he would not meet her eyes, she read a hint that there was something inside him which was not yet as hard as everything outside.

'I'm glad you did − very glad,' she said warmly, rising and offering her hand. 'It's good to see you again.'

He hesitated, but took her hand. His was very brown, and as hard as a plank, and he gripped hers briefly, then let it go.

'Have you had breakfast? We're shockingly late, as you see. Will you take something?'

His eyes surveyed her table briefly, and he said, 'No, thank you.' But she had seen their hastily-suppressed glow of avidity, and thought that if they had been travelling at full speed from the Caucasus, they would have had little time for luxuries. Fresh wheaten bread, and cherry jam, and hot coffee probably had not featured much in his diet of late.

'Oh do have something,' she said lightly. 'Giorgy, bring fresh covers for my guest – then you can help yourself, if you change your mind,' she added to Sergei as the servant left. 'Do sit down. It was such a surprise to see you last night.'

'I was more surprised at seeing you. What brings you to Vilna?' he said harshly.

'My dear Sergei, everyone is at Vilna. Where the Emperor is, you know . . .' she said. 'How did you find out so soon where I lived?'

'I asked one of the Quartermaster General's staff. It's typical of our army that there were no billets assigned to my men – in fact, I couldn't find anyone who even knew we were coming; but the first person I asked knew where Madame Tchaikovsky was living.' He gave a wry look. 'Administration was always our weak spot. Monsieur Tchaikovsky is not here?'

Anne looked at him warily. Did he not know her circumstances? 'No, he is in Moscow,' she said. 'May I make my daughter known to you? This is Marya Vassilievna; and Mlle Parmoutier, her governess.' Sergei nodded in their direction. His eyes engaged briefly with Parmoutier's, but avoided Rose altogether, and Anne, always sensitive to her daughter's feelings, bristled a little. But perhaps it was the fact of her being Basil's child, rather than the leg braces and the white eye, she told herself sternly. She would offer him a second chance. 'We always call Marya Vassilievna "Rose", however. She's learning to ride at the moment on a Cossack pony of phenomenal beauty and intelligence – isn't that right, *ma poupée?*'

Rose nodded, her eyes going from her mother to the visitor warily. The old Sergei would have picked up the hint and entered into a discussion of the pony's merits, which would have won Rose's heart. All Russians seemed to love children, and Sergei had always had a particularly soft place for them in his heart. But the new Sergei merely nodded, cleared his throat, and looked away down the garden.

'A pleasant situation you have here,' he said. Rose's face closed up, and Parmoutier jumped instantly to the defence of her charge.

'I think, madame, if you will excuse us, we will go and get ready for our morning exercise,' she said.

When they had gone, Anne did not speak for a while, but continued to study the averted face of her guest, who was still staring down the garden expressionlessly. She felt a little embarrassed, and a little awkward. She had nothing to say to this Sergei; and if he came only to sit in silence, why did he come at all? At last she said, 'You arrived yesterday from the Caucasus I suppose? Had you travelled fast?'

He cleared his throat again, and flicked a glance at her. 'Yes, we came without stopping. There's a new regiment been raised – all volunteers – called the Pyatigorsk Cossacks, and I've been put in charge of a troop, and sent up here ahead of the rest of the regiment for special duties. Irregular cavalry, they call us.'

'That sounds like a joke,' Anne said. 'From what I remember of the Cossacks, they'd be very irregular.'

He looked at her blankly. Oh Sergei, she thought, what happened to you?

'You must have done well,' she went on hastily, 'to be singled out for such a command.'

'Yes,' he said, matter-of-factly. 'I've a good reputation; and my men trust me. It counts for a lot out there, in the wild country. We depend on each other. There wasn't one man in my troop who didn't owe his life to someone else a dozen times over. This,' he touched the healing scar on his forehead, 'was from a Persian javelin. One of my men saw it coming and pushed me out of the way just in time. I'd be dead if it weren't for him.'

And that's what you've filled yourself with, she thought; what you've put into the loneliness inside. The comradeship of soldiers, the warmth of the bivouac and the shared danger.

'It must be a hard life,' she said invitingly.

'Yes,' he said, and looked about him rather like a sleepwalker awakened. 'Nothing like this. You can't imagine.'

'No, I can't,' she said. 'What did you do with your free time, when you were off duty?'

'There was never time to do much, except drink a bottle of wine in the mess, and play cards perhaps. When we had a few days off, we'd go to Tiflis, for the baths. Have you ever had a Georgian bath? No, I don't suppose you would have. The baths in Tiflis are the best in the world. First the attendants rub you down with goat's-hair gloves and soap, and knead and pummell you and rinse you off, and then you lie down on a ttowel and they walk up and down your back in their bare feet.'

Anne laughed incredulously, and he looked at her, showing the first sign of animation – of humanity – so far. He almost smiled.

'It's true! It's the most exquisite feeling – I can't tell you! All your joints and muscles click and crack and you can feel all the aches of riding and sleeping rough being massaged away. You feel wonderful afterwards – and then you go down into a sort of cave, where there's a bath cut out of the mountain rock itself, and the hot mineral water pours into it constantly. And you just sit in that for as long as you like. There's lots to do in Tiflis, but mostly we just go there for the baths. It's worth the trip.'

He had grown almost expansive, tempting Anne to rashness. 'And are the girls of Tiflis pretty?' she asked.

He looked at her strangely. 'I suppose so,' he said, as though it had not occurred to him to look. Perhaps it hadn't. It had been a stupid thing to say anyway, given what had been between them. She wanted to take it back, to apologise, but that would have been a worse mistake than the first. She could only try to build it into a commonplace.

'Is there one more pretty than the others? Is there anyone special?'

'I'm not interested in girls,' he said, and suddenly looked directly into her eyes, for the first time as though he really saw her. 'There was only one I ever cared for.'

Anne's throat closed up. She sought for something neutral to say, but her wretched mind let her down. How would he interpret her silence? He was looking at her thoughtfully, and the corners of his mouth had softened, and she could not imagine where his thoughts might be. But when he spoke again, he said merely. 'So my sister has come out at last? Were you there? Did you see her?'

'Yes – and she was a credit to your family,' Anne said, glad to be able to offer uncontroversial praise. 'She's turned into a very attractive young woman – not beautiful, precisely, but striking, and she's very popular amongst the people of her own age.'

'She writes to me now and then – lists of gowns and dancing partners,' he said wryly. 'Those seem to be her only concern. I thank God she can still be so innocent. I thank God she was spared what happened at Chastnaya.' He lapsed into a silence she did not know how to break; it was the first time he had referred so directly to what had happened. At last he roused himself to say, 'I suppose she leads my grandmother a merry dance.'

'You haven't seen her for a long time, of course,' Anne said neutrally.

'No. I wouldn't go back to be sucked in by Gran'mère again.' He frowned, his eyes on the distance, and added softly, 'Too much has happened to me, in any case. You can't go back.'

Warmth sprang up in her for this lonely man who had shut himself away from kindness. She wanted to touch him in some way, but could think of no way of reaching him that would not be dangerous for them both. Suddenly he looked at her. 'So Basil Andreyevitch is in Moscow? I suppose you're going to join him shortly – or is he coming here?'

She was startled by the abrupt change of subject; fumbled for words. 'Sergei, Basil Andreyevitch and I, we – we don't live together any more.' He looked hard at her, forcing her to amplify. 'We had – certain differences. We felt it was better if we – had our own establishments.'

'Oh,' he said, and a variety of expressions seemed to flicker across his face as he digested the news: surprise, acceptance, gratification perhaps? And then a puzzled frown. 'But then – what are you – I mean, who is – '

She was beginning to understand a little of his state of mind, and to be alarmed by it, and to wonder how she would explain and how he would react; but he got no further with the questions he didn't know how to ask, and she had no opportunity to break it to him tactfully. At that moment there was a sound of cavalry boots on the bare polished floorboards within the house, and a male voice calling cheerfully to the butler that he had breakfasted already; and then Nikolai came out onto the terrace with a smile of eager welcome on his face for Anne. He evidently had no idea Sergei was there; when he saw his son, the smile drained away completely for an instant, and then sprang up again, new, but different. He held out his arms.

'Seryosha! My dear boy! I didn't know you were here! What brings you to Vilna? But I see you're in uniform – have you come to serve? You have a command? If not, I can get Tolly to . . . '

His voice trailed away, for Sergei had come violently to his feet, and his face was pulling this way and that with rage and pain. For an instant Anne saw the child inside the shell of the man: hurt, baffled, betrayed. He had been on the point of opening his heart to her, and this was how his trust had been repaid; now he wanted to strike out.

'Yes, I see now! I see it all! Oh this is very cosy, isn't it?' he cried bitterly. He looked from his father to Anne with identical loathing. 'No wonder your husband's left you! I should think any decent man would. Only a – a *scoundrel* like my father would dream of living with such an unprincipled – '

'Sergei!' Nikolai cried, more astonished than angry. 'What the devil are you talking about?'

'Don't speak to me! Don't dare to speak to me!' he cried out, the living pain close enough to the surface now to make his voice quiver. 'I never would have thought my father – my own *father* – would be so . . . ' He turned back to Anne, like a creature at bay. 'Don't you have *any* scruples? Is it just any man for you?'

'Seryosha, don't,' she said painfully. 'I love him.'

'It was him all the time, wasn't it, while you were pretending to be so good and pious, taking care of my sisters – my God, and with my step-mother living in the same house . . . !'

'No – not like that – !'

'I saw in Pyatigorsk – but I didn't believe it . . . I thought afterwards I'd been mistaken. I was sorry for what I'd said – I wanted to apologise. Apologise, my God!' He laughed harshly. 'And that – that *thing*,' he jerked his head in the direction of the house, 'is that his? Or can't you be sure?'

Anne could bear no more. She struck him open-handed on the cheek, putting all her weight behind it, hurting herself, she guessed, more than him. For the flicker of an instant she saw in his eyes that he almost struck her back; and then so fast it seemed like a dream, the rage and pain had gone, and the hard young face was as unmoving and unemotional as when he had first arrived, revealing nothing in any feature, showing only a faint pink mark where she had struck him.

He drew himself to attention and bowed curtly to her. 'I beg your pardon,' he said, and it was as little like an apology as if he had taken out a pistol and shot her. 'I should not be here.'

He pivoted on his heel and left them, without a glance at his father. The sound of his boots diminished through the house, and Anne, shaking with distress at the raw emotions which had been exposed, turned to Nikolai for comfort.

'He will never forgive us,' she said. 'I should have told him at once, but I didn't know how. Oh Nikolai – !'

But Nikolai was standing as he had been standing since the first outburst, staring ahead of him in the blankness of shock which precedes, and for a blessed time blots out, pain. His hands were raised a little, as though to protect himself from a blow; and he was crying.

Chapter Twenty-Seven

On the 24th of June, the Emperor gave a grand reception and ball at his newly-acquired house, Zakret. The idea once conceived grew rapidly under the encouragement of Prince Volkonsky, and word soon spread that the ball was to be a 'Vauxhall' – the currently fashionable name, as Anne had learnt with amusement, for a *fête champetre*. A parquet floor was to be built on one of the riverside lawns, and over it a flower-bedecked pavilion was to be raised; there were to be floral grottoes around the lawns, lit with candles inside coloured lamp bowls, and four bands playing at different points in the park; but the plan for the crowning glory of fireworks to end the evening was reluctantly abandoned in view of the military situation.

The preparations did not proceed without incident. On the day of the ball, at around noon, the supporting wooden pillars began to bow, and moments later the entire pavilion collapsed with a terrible rumbling crash, trapping one of the workers under the wreckage. So intense had been the interest in the project, that there were enough idlers to witness the disaster for the rumour soon to spread all through Vilna that it was not an accident at all. Napoleon had planned the whole thing as an assassination attempt on the Emperor; and the pavilion's architect, Schultz, whose name proved he was a German and therefore an ally of the French, was really his secret agent.

Demands were made for Schultz to be questioned under torture until he confessed, but they came too late; as soon as he realised what had happened, and what might have happened if the pavilion had collapsed later in the evening, the terrified architect rushed away down the lawn and flung himself into the river, and was swept away by the current and drowned.

The workmen were brought back, and by dint of frantic activity they managed to clear away the wreckage, leaving the dancing floor open to the sky. Orange trees in pots replaced the fallen pillars, and banks of potted flowering plants made up for the lack of a roof, and by a miracle all was ready by eight o'clock when the first guests arrived.

The sky had been overcast all day, though fortunately it had not rained. Now as sunset approached, the skies cleared, the clouds rolling back to the horizon to reveal a clear and tender blue. Anne stepped down from the carriage at half past eight and looked around her with a keen anticipation of pleasure. She was pleased with her gown of pale green silk, with which she wore the emeralds Basil had given her on their wedding anniversary; and in keeping with the nature of the occasion, Pauline had dressed her hair with flowers – white and apricot rosebuds, and orange blossom. She walked into the garden with her hand through Nikolai's arm, and felt that everyone ought to envy her: there was no man she would rather have as her escort, not even the Emperor himself.

Gradually the guests assembled, while at every vantage point there were crowds of onlookers who had come out from Vilna to see the Emperor arrive. The band of the Imperial Guard played softly, hidden amongst the trees surrounding the lawn; the pale, impermanent evening sky was reflected in the wide reaches of the river, while on the horizon the piled clouds rose up like fantastic mountains, rimmed with fire from the hidden sunset.

The Emperor arrived at last, dressed in the uniform of the Semionovsky Guards; tall, handsome, fair, and charming. The assembled crowds cheered lustily, and he acknowledged them with a graceful wave of the hand before he made the rounds of his assembled guests, with a pleasant word for everyone, tilting his head in that way he had which, though it was only because he was deaf in one ear, made him look so boyish and approachable.

The band struck up for a polonaise, and the Emperor offered his arm to General Bennigsen's pretty young wife, who was acting as hostess for the evening in the Empress's absence. When they had made the first circuit, other couples followed them onto the floor, and Nikolai smiled at Anne and said, 'Shall we?'

'Gladly,' Anne said, looping up her train. It was a delightful thing to be dancing with her lover under the open sky, surrounded by sweet-smelling flowers, and the beautiful colours of the gowns and jewels and uniforms. She thought of that other alfresco ball, long ago at Chastnaya; dancing with Seryosha, and Nasha sitting with the musicians and playing the hurdy-gurdy; but she couldn't be sad, not tonight.

At the end of the first dance, Prince Volkonsky claimed Anne from Nikolai, an honour she would have been happy to dispense with. The Emperor danced with Madame de Tolly, and Nikolai offered his hand to Madame Balashov, wife of the Minister of Police, a dumpy little woman who looked as though she would have felt more comfortable wearing a peasant scarf than the heavy diamond tiara which flashed in her rather coarse hair.

At the end of the second dance, Prince Volkonsky escorted Anne off the floor, bowed, and walked over to the Emperor, presumably to advise him on his choice for the third. Anne saw His Majesty's eyes come round to her; he murmured something to Volkonsky, and she saw the Prince reply with a brief shake of the head. She turned her face away, her cheeks glowing. Had she been Nikolai's wife, his status on the Emperor's staff would have required the Emperor to dance with her next; but he could not dance with an adulteress. The Prince was still talking, but the Emperor, perhaps feeling unhappy himself about the situation, silenced him with a gesture, and walked away to approach, to the surprise of everyone, the young daughter of a local landowner.

But Nikolai was beside Anne, taking her hand with a pressure of sympathy and leading her back to the floor.

'Don't mind it, my darling,' he said. 'It's not important.'

'No, of course not,' she said; but as they danced he could see the brightness of her eye and the warmth of her cheek. This was not how it should be. As a young girl, she had dreamed as all girls did of her first ball, of falling in love, of her marriage, of the subsequent glories and social triumphs which were her birthright. Her father's death had robbed her of her girlhood; and love had come too late, and in the wrong guise. What would Papa think of her now? she wondered. Would he disapprove, or understand? Suddenly she remembered his voice, speaking to her after some childhood disappointment, the nature of which she couldn't now remember: 'If we can't do better, we must make the best of it.' She had a great deal to be thankful for: let her never forget that. She smiled up at Nikolai to show she was happy, and he smiled too, relieved. He had particularly wanted her to enjoy this evening.

After the third dance the Emperor went into the house, and the senior members of the party followed him upstairs to the ballroom where there was an orchestra and more dancing, leaving the younger people to enjoy themselves more unrestrainedly in the open air. Later, supper was served outside on the lawn, and when Anne, on Kirov's arm, followed the Emperor down into the garden again, she found that the stars had come out, and a sickle moon was rising.

It was not really dark – this was after all, midsummer – except under the shadow of the trees. It was warm, and the air was quite still – not a breath to make the coloured lamps flicker, or to stir the leaves on the orange trees. Nikolai fetched Anne a glass of champagne, and they wandered down the lawn towards the river. There was a scent of stock and jasmine, and the warm smell of bruised grass; the soft voices of the guests conversing and the muted clatter of cutlery was behind them; before them the murmur of the river. Its rapid flow parted round some little islands, dead black like cut-outs against the silvered water; the moonlight rippled like shaken silk, and just before the shadow of a rustic footbridge, there was a line of phosphorescence where the water broke over half-hidden rocks.

'It's all so beautiful – so peaceful,' Anne sighed.

'Idyllic,' he suggested, and she heard the glint of laughter in his voice.

'Laugh at me if you want,' she said genially. 'There's something especially beautiful about tonight. It reminds me – '

'Yes?'

'It reminds me of one night at Schwartzenturm, when we stood on the terrace – after the picnic, the first time you took me to the waterfall. I don't suppose you remember it,' It wasn't really a question, and he didn't answer it as one. She went on, 'You'd been telling me about the magic of Russia, how it got into everyone's eyes and tangled their thoughts.' She smiled reflectively. 'I felt it, too – but I thought that you made it, especially for me.'

'Didn't I?' he said, pretending to be disappointed. 'You were impervious to me, then?'

'Ah, never that! But there is something, isn't there, about Russia, that isn't anywhere else? I wasn't wrong?'

'No, love, you weren't wrong,' he said kindly. A moth blundered past on broad, soft wings, and alighted for a moment on one of the flowers in her hair – a rose, which the heat of the house had opened from a bud to half-blown. He put out a finger to touch it lightly, and it fluttered away, swerving towards the coloured glow of the lamps amongst the trees. 'It isn't all illusion,' he said, almost to himself.

'And even if – even if Bonaparte does invade, he can't touch it, can he?'

She looked up at him anxiously, and he put out a hand to cup her cheek, loving her, wanting to preserve for her everything she found good and pleasant.

'Whatever happens,' he said, 'it will still be here. Nothing good is ever truly lost. God sees to that.'

She lifted her face a little more, and he stooped his head to kiss her, let his mouth linger on hers, feeling her lips full and soft and ready, knowing she was his and would be his. Later tonight, when they were alone, at home . . .

There was a little disturbance nearby, and they broke apart

unhurriedly and turned to look. There was a wicket gate into the garden from the road, guarded, in view of the Emperor's presence, by a private of the Imperial Guard. He had come to attention, and challenged someone who had just ridden up, and a muted conversation was going on between them, as the newcomer apparently demanded admission, which the guard denied.

A voice rose. 'Stand aside, damn you! That's an order!'

Anne looked up at Nikolai, her eyes widening in distress. It was Sergei's voice. The Count read her thoughts easily, and shook his head.

'He wouldn't come here just to upset you, Annushka. It must be something important. Wait here.'

He strode away to the wicket, calling to the guard softly as he went, 'All right, Private, I know this man.'

'I beg your pardon, sir, but my orders was to let nobody past,' the man defended himself, politely but stoutly.

Anne saw Sergei come to attention in the moonlight, which made dark holes of his eyes, and then step aside with his father out of earshot of the guard. Anne could hear nothing of what they said, but she was aware of her heart beating uncomfortably fast, as if it knew of some danger of which she was unaware. At last she heard Nikolai say formally, 'Very well, Captain. Return to your men, and say nothing to anyone.' Sergei saluted and was gone, and Nikolai was coming back to her.

She knew what it was before he spoke. He took her hands, and his were cold, despite the warmth of the night, and damp. Her blood seemed to stop and stand still; everything seemed to become very quiet.

'Sergei was out scouting with his troop near Kovno, on the Nieman. The French have built three pontoon bridges across the river, and they started crossing a few hours ago. It has begun.'

She could think of nothing to say. He turned abruptly. 'I must go to the Emperor,' he said, but before he had gone two steps, there was Balashov, apparently on his way to find out what had been happening at the wicket. In a few words Kirov told him what he had told Anne.

Balashov's grave face, the unrevealing face necessary for a minister of police, did not change. 'Very well. I'll tell His Majesty. Go and find Tolly, will you, and tell him?'

The two men went different ways, leaving Anne beached and forgotten. She stood where she was, not knowing what to do with herself, or with the picture that had been planted in her mind. She saw a broad river, silver in the moonlight; three black pontoons spanning it;

and over the pontoons, like an army of ants, the close-packed columns, more and more and more of them, more than could be counted; dark except for the white flash of their leggings, and the pin pricks of moonlight glinting from the tips of their bayonets. Thousand upon thousand, pouring into Russia with the pitilessness of insects, swarming over the bridges, marching towards Vilna . . .

With a distant part of her attention, she saw Balashov walk up to the Emperor, murmur a few words in his ear. The Emperor nodded, and then turned away and carried on chatting to the elderly lady beside him. Perhaps it had all been a dream, Anne thought. Perhaps Sergei had not really been there at all. She tried to walk forward, but her feet seemed rooted to the ground. Definitely a dream, then. She looked down at them, and they seemed a very long way away. The pale green satin of her slippers was darkened by the dew from the longer grass of the river bank; she noticed the exact shape of the mark, and it seemed somehow important to remember it.

Then Nikolai was beside her again, his hand gripping her forearm to hold her attention.

'Anna, listen! The Emperor's leaving, and I have to go with him; but he doesn't want anyone to know the news yet. He wants the ball to go on. I can't take you with me – you'll have to stay for a while. But in half an hour's time you can have a headache, excuse yourself to Madame Bennigsen, and go home. Go straight home, and tomorrow morning, begin packing. I'll come to you when I can.'

She desperately wanted some kind of reassurance, but she knew she mustn't delay him: he now had far more important things on his mind than her. She bit back the useless questions that jumped into her mouth, and said, 'Yes, I understand.'

He was already turning away, but with the last unconsumed fraction of his attention, he recognised her effort, and paused to catch her chin and deliver one hard but loving kiss. 'Good girl,' he said. And then he was gone.

The day seemed endless. During the morning the bright skies clouded over, and by noon they had drawn down in a dark blanket over the whole sky. There's going to be a storm, Anne thought, pausing in the act of folding a gown to look out of the window. The air was oppressive, like a damp hand muffling everything, making it hard to breathe; and in the back of her mind, the ant-soldiers marched, marched, their white legs swinging all together in a rippling row, left right left right, tramping down the road from Kovno. How long would it take for them to reach Vilna? How far was it? Fifty – sixty miles? The clouds were black and purple now, and the daylight was strange and muted and yellowish. It was like a dreadful omen – but for whom? For them or for the French?

A light scraping and thumping sound made her turn, and there was Rose, walking with Mlle Parmoutier supporting her from behind, her face screwed up with concentration, the tip of her tongue protruding from between her teeth. Anne held out her arms, and Rose came to her, and exchanged her governess's hands for her mother's waist. They looked out of the window together.

'Maman, why is it dark?' she asked.

'There's going to be a storm, *cherie*, that's all. Thunder and lightning. Nothing to be afraid of.'

Rose considered the answer, looking up at her mother. The crooked eye seemed a little less crooked of late, and quite a lot of the iris was showing. Anne smoothed the soft fawn hair away from the bony forehead and tried to smile.

'But *you're* afraid,' Rose observed, her one eye searching.

'A little,' Anne admitted. 'But it's silly to be afraid. Storms can't hurt you.'

'Giorgy says the French are coming,' she said bluntly. 'He's afraid of them. Will we have to go away?'

'Yes, I think so.'

'Where?'

'I don't know.'

'Will the French kill us?'

The question, so innocently spoken, exposing the root of Anne's fears, made her wince. 'No, darling. We'll be gone before they get here.'

Rose came now to the heart of her own anxiety. She tugged at Anne's waist with the urgency of it. 'Will we take Mielka?'

Anne laughed shakily, and hugged her daughter briefly. 'Oh, darling, of course we will! Mielka will go everywhere with us. We wouldn't leave him behind.'

Rose's smile became radiant, and she was content then to resume looking out of the window. There was lighting now, flickering greenish against the indigo clouds. Parmoutier came and stood beside Anne too, and they watched and waited in silence. Suddenly the air was stirred by a breath of cold wind, just as if a damp blanket had been lifted, and the governess shivered and said, 'Here it comes!'

A second later there was a flash of lightning followed instantly by a tremendous crash of thunder, so loud that it made them all jump, and Anne bit her tongue. Another cold breath, and a few heavy drops fell on the step of the verandah, leaving dark circles in the pale dust; and then the rain came down. It fell in an almost solid sheet, hissing on the dry earth and blotting out the distance. The trees shifted and whispered, and the smell of rain came in through the open windows to the waiting women, green, refreshing, delicious.

An old woman, one of the locally-hired servants, came shuffling in to push past them without ceremony and close the windows. The sound of the rain diminished; the stale warmth of the room closed round them, cutting them off from the drenched garden outside, where the lightning still flickered and flashed.

'Standing by an open window!' the old woman grumbled. 'Catch your death, Barina, and the little one too! Well, this'll teach that Napoleon to come crossing our borders. His men'll be drowning in it, and I hope he drowns too. Good riddance to him! Let me get to the other window, Barina, before that carpet gets soaked.'

Anne and Parmoutier exchanged a glance. Yes, the rain would be very bad for the marching soldiers! It would slow them down – and roads would become quagmires.

'God is on our side, madame,' Parmoutier said softly.

The old woman, overhearing, crossed herself. 'Amen to that! God is on the side of the righteous.'

Anne, her fingers moving slowly in Rose's silky hair, said, 'Yes, I hope so.'

The storm passed quickly, and a calm, bright, fresh afternoon followed. There was no word from Nikolai, and no-one came near the house. Anne's sense of unreality grew. At one moment she thought that perhaps everyone had left Vilna, and she was alone in the path of the oncoming French. At others she thought perhaps the French were not coming after all, and everyone knew it except her. As the afternoon faded into evening, and the rain-washed air grew chilly, Pauline came out to her with a shawl, and asked her diffidently if she would take dinner inside or on the terrace.

'Dinner?' she said vaguely, and became aware that she was extremely hungry.

'You have eaten nothing all day, madame,' Pauline said sternly.

Nor the evening before, Anne remembered suddenly. The news had interrupted her and Nikolai before they had had time to eat supper.

All she had had was a glass of champagne. She laughed, and Pauline looked at her quizzically.

'Yes, I'll have dinner here,' she said, and glanced towards the house. 'Is everything all right, Pauline?'

'They were all very frightened before,' Pauline answered, 'but now they see you so calm, they think everything must be well. We are all waiting for news.'

'Are you afraid?' Anne asked curiously. It must be hard for the maid, caught between her own people and her adopted people. Either side might take her for a spy.

Pauline shrugged. 'If you are not afraid, madame, why should I be? I go where you go, and as long as you are safe, so am I.'

'You want to stay with me? You don't want to go to – to the other side?'

Pauline looked contemptuous. 'They are not my people,' she said. 'That one, that Bonaparte, he holds my people in thrall as much as everyone else.'

'Ah, is that how you see it?' Anne said thoughtfully.

It was late when Kirov came home, looking bone-weary. Anne guessed he had not slept or eaten since she saw him last. She was still sitting on the verandah, beginning to feel chilly now, but unable to bring herself to go in, out of the soft summer twilight and into the stuffy darkness. Once she went in, the day would be over, and it might be her last day in Vilna, her last day of peace.

He came to her and kissed her, and sat down beside her, stretching out his legs and sighing with weariness.

'Shall I get you some supper?' she asked.

'In a minute,' he said. 'Sit with me a while first.' He reached out a hand and she gave him hers, and he carried it back to his lap and held it there, caressing it lightly, his eyes closed. Through their linked hands, communication passed. She understood that they were to be parted, and that, as she had wanted to savour the last of this day, so he wanted to savour these moments with her while he could.

At last he opened his eyes and said, 'We are to evacuate Vilna. Shishkov tried to persuade the Emperor that it was cowardly to yield the first instant the French appeared, without making any kind of a stand, and it took us all day to argue him down. Vilna would be impossible to defend, even if we had the men. We'd be trapped between the enemy and the river, with only one small wooden bridge to escape by.'

Anne nodded. 'I see.'

'So did the Emperor at last, thought not until Tolly and I rode out in person, and came back and assured him that the French really were coming.'

'You've seen them?' Anne said, startled.

His face seemed to grow older as she watched. 'Yes, I've seen them. Poor devils, they don't look as though they're marching to glory. That storm took all the air out of them – and some of the horses already look half starved. We've stripped the country they're marching over, so if they haven't brought provisions with them, they'll be hungry long before they get here. But there are thousands of them, Anna. Thousands. And how did Napoleon move so fast? It's impossible to over-estimate that man.'

'How long?'

'To reach Vilna? Another two or three days, perhaps; the cavalry might get here sooner. The Emperor's leaving tomorrow, during the night to avoid spreading panic. We're moving headquarters to Drissa. I think you ought to leave tomorrow morning. Once the word gets out that we're evacuating, there'll be some pretty scenes, I don't doubt, and the roads will be crammed with carts and coaches. You should be able to get as far as Sventsiany tomorrow – that's about seventy-five versts. Put up in the best inn, and I'll come to you as soon as I can.'

'When will that be?' she asked in a small voice.

'The day after, I expect. I'll know more by then – we'll make new plans.' He eyed her. 'Are you afraid?'

'No,' she said.

He squeezed her hand. 'That's my brave girl. Shall we go to bed?'

'You haven't eaten. I was going to get you some supper.'

'There are more important things than supper. Come, lie in my arms, *doushka*, for a few hours. God knows when we'll have the chance again! I shall have to leave you before dawn – we're taking everything with us that we can – the city archives, food, munitions – and I shall have to help supervise the packing. What we can't take, we'll burn; and then we'll destroy the bridge. He'll find the Vilia harder work to bridge than the Nieman.' He stood up, grimacing. 'It's going to be a long day.'

'Then you'd better sleep,' she said.

He grinned. 'To hell with sleep. If you argue any more, I'll think you don't want me.'

She twisted her arm round his waist. 'Always, always,' she said.

He left her arms at four the next morning; dressed himself, saying that he would shave and breakfast at headquarters; kissed her once more, thoroughly, and went away. Anne turned over into the nest of warmth he had left in the bed, and cried a little; then dried her eyes, got up, and rang briskly for Pauline.

By eight o'clock, when they were ready to leave, it was already very hot, and threatening to be hotter. She longed for Adonis's strong arms and cheerful confidence as she chivvied the servants, and supervised the loading. Rose was in a fret over Mielka, and had to be carried down the line to see him, hitched between Image and Quassy, before she was satisfied that he was not being left behind. She plainly felt her world was threatened.

'When are we going to see Papa?' she demanded.

'Soon,' Anne said distractedly.

The procession rolled away from the house, two carriages, a kibitka, and the grooms leading the riding-horses. The upper part of the town was quiet, but when they got down to the bridge over the Vilia, they had to wait their turn in a queue of carts driven by soldiers, loaded with sacks of grain and boxes of ammunition. Anne stretched her neck and stared out of the window in every direction, hoping for a glimpse of Nikolai, but there was no-one higher than a sergeant in sight.

Once out on the highway, they trotted past the slow-moving carts, and got ahead of their dust, and Anne settled back against the squabs and set her mind to entertaining Rose for the long journey to Sventsiany.

On the 27th, the baking heat of the day was suddenly masked again by lowering clouds, and torrential rain began to fall; but this time it did not blow over in an hour or two. It went on, almost unremittingly, all day, and all the next day too; the temperature dropped rapidly; the rain became sleety; there were periods of hail, and violent thunder storms, and sheets and forks of lightning.

Vilna had been abandoned, and the cobbled streets which had rung for two months with footsteps and laughter were silent. The Vilia ran fast and swollen, carrying away all trace of the bridge which the Russian sappers had destroyed after the last carts had crossed it. Only the Lithuanian residents who could not leave had remained, waiting for the French to arrive, part hopeful, part resentful. They had not loved their Russian conquerers; but would French masters be any better? Napoleon had half-promised Lithuanian independence – but he had promised many things to Poland which had never been fulfilled.

On the 28th, as the Russian army tramped briskly away on the road to Drissa, following in the wake of the Court, General Balashov and his excellency Count Kirov waited in the path of the advancing French General Murat and his cavalry, with a personal letter from the Emperor to Napoleon. They were conducted into Vilna, to the archbishop's palace, which had been Alexander's headquarters and was now Napoleon's.

The Emperor of the French received them after a long delay. Kirov thought he looked ill. He had put on a great deal of weight since he last saw him; the pale face was puffy, the eyes blue-shadowed, and the dark hair, which he had taken to wearing brushed straight forward *à la césar*, was noticeably thinning. Behind him stood Caulaincourt, who greeted both Russians courteously, but whose eyes sought Kirov's with some message of sorrow and apology. Kirov knew that he had constantly advised Napoleon against the invasion, and was probably still trying to persuade him to give it up; and that he had no hope of succeeding.

'So!' said Napoleon, with a flash of scorn, waving the letter at them, 'my brother Alexander, who was so high and mighty with the Comte de Narbonne, would now like to negotiate! He asks the reasons for this war – as if he didn't know them! – and graciously condescends to offer negotiation once my troops have withdrawn behind the Nieman!'

'Your Highness knows – ' Balashov began, but Napoleon cut him short.

'I know that my manoeuvres have already frightened you, and that within a month I shall bring you to your knees! I have not come this far to negotiate! The sword is now drawn, it cannot be sheathed. Does your Emperor take me for a fool?'

'No Sire,' Kirov answered. 'But this is a war you cannot win. His Majesty wishes to avoid pointless loss of life, which will be very heavy if your highness continues on this venture.'

Napoleon slammed his fist down into his palm. 'Very heavy? On your side perhaps! Count, my friend, count up the numbers! Your infantry numbers a hundred and twenty thousand men, and your cavalry sixty thousand – yes, you see, I know everything about you! But I have three times as many. How can I lose?'

'Numbers are not everything, Sire,' said Kirov. 'How can you feed such a great army? You will be marching through barren, wasted land, and you have no supply depots, as we have.'

'I've seen what remained of one here in Vilna! What's the point of building up supply depots, if you simply burn them and run away, instead of using them for the purpose of battle?' He whipped round on Balashov. 'Aren't you ashamed, you Russians? Since the time of Peter the Great, your country has never been invaded, yet here I am at Vilna, having captured an entire province without firing a single shot.'

Balashov's face was immobile as ever. 'I can assure your highness that Russians will fight like tigers to defend their own homeland. Patriotic fervour runs in our soldiers' veins, and they will have more urgency in the fight to protect their homes, than your men in trying to take them.'

Napoleon shrugged that away and changed the subject. 'Your Emperor is a novice in war and he conducts his campaign through a council. Now when I have an idea, at any time of the day or night, it is put into execution within half an hour. But with you, Armfelt proposes, Bennigsen examines, Tolly deliberates, Phull opposes, and nothing is done at all. You simply waste your time. That's no way to conduct a war!'

For an hour Napoleon talked to them, alternately cajoling and threatening; then he dismissed them, but ordered them to remain at headquarters. Later he invited them to take dinner with him and his chiefs of staff, and continued in the same vein to assure them that they were outnumbered, that they could not possibly win, and that they had better yield now and ask for his forgiveness.

At one point his banter descended into a kind of primitive rage, and he shouted insults at them, only stopping when he saw the look of disapproval on Caulaincourt's stern face. Napoleon's brow cleared and he put on a smile instead. 'Emperor Alexander treats his ambassadors well, charming them and treating them like his own countrymen. Here before you is one of his principal chevaliers – he has made a Russian of Caulaincourt!'

There was a heartbeat of silence, and Kirov saw with acute sympathy the pain and anger in the grave courtier's eyes. For a moment Caulaincourt could not answer; and when he spoke, his resentment was clear in his voice. 'It is doubtless because my frankness has too often proved that I am a good Frenchman, that Your Majesty now seems inclined to doubt it. The marks of kindness with which I was so often honoured by Emperor Alexander were intended for Your Majesty. As your faithful subject, Sire, I shall never forget it.'

There was an embarrassed silence, and Napoleon shrugged and changed the subject. Later, however, when the Russians' horses were called for, the Emperor showed his spite again, saying to Caulaincourt,

'You had better escort your friends to their carriage, had you not, you old St Petersburg courtier?'

Kirov felt for him acutely. To be insulted before foreigners, to have his loyalty called into question in the presence of the enemy, was too much to bear. Caulaincourt held his temper, and walked out of the room with Balashov and Kirov. On the stairs, however, he murmured to Nikolai, 'I'm not ashamed of having declared myself against this war. In doing so I prove myself more a Frenchman than those who encourage him, just to please him.'

'I know it, old friend,' Kirov replied.

'I wish he did,' Caulaincourt said with some heat. 'Since he doesn't appreciate me, I'd better ask for a transfer to some other duty. In Spain, perhaps – the further away, the better.'

Kirov touched his shoulder. 'I'm sure he does appreciate you,' he said. 'Why else would he keep you by him?'

Caulaincourt met his eyes sadly. 'Why did it have to come to this?' he said.

Balashov was waiting at the foot of the stairs, eyeing them with interest. All three shook hands courteously.

'Please convey my respectful homage to your master,' Caulaincourt said.

The Russians turned away to mount into the carriage, but Kirov turned back. They had been friends, and who knew if they would ever meet again?

'Armand – ' he said. Caulaincourt looked at him enquiringly. 'This is not between us. I wish you well, old friend, and safe.'

'And I you, Nikolai. *Adieu!*'

Anne stood at the window of the inn in Sventsiany watching the Russian cavalry divisions trotting through the town on their way to Drissa. It was the 30th of June, and still the rain poured down, smoking on the paved street like mist. The horses were rat-tailed, their coats were sleek and dark with it, and their riders huddled under their cloaks while the relentless water dripped off their cap brims and collar points and noses. The infantry were still somewhere behind them – it would be slow marching in this weather.

Many of the local gentry had fled when the first refugees from Vilna came through, packing their treasures onto carts, furniture, pictures, carpets, everything. Napoleon's soldiers had a reputation all through Europe for stripping everything in their path like locusts. But the town was calmer now, resigned, waiting for more news. Maybe

Napoleon wouldn't come at all, said those who remained; and if he did, if they welcomed him, maybe he would be a good master to them. There was a certain amount of scorn thrown on the Russian army, which had retreated the first moment without offering a fight. Anne had to listen to some pungent comments, but there was no real hostility towards her. She was generous in the matter of paying for what was provided, and inn-keepers are much the same the world over.

Inside her pleasant sitting-room, there was a large fire burning. To one side of it, Nyanya – Rose's nurse – and Pauline sat sewing; Rose herself was sitting on the floor, her legs in their hated braces stuck straight out before her, playing with a striped marmalade kitten who had appeared from nowhere as soon as the fire was lit. To the other side of the fire sat Mlle Parmoutier, reading aloud from a book of French essays.

The kitten, every inch of its small body quivering with intensity, pounced again on the straw Rose was twitching for it.

'Maman, when are we going to see Papa?' Rose asked, as she had asked already three times that day.

'Soon,' said Anne absently.

'But when? I don't like it here. I want to go home.'

Anne turned from the window. 'We can't go yet. Have you done your eye exercises this morning?'

'I don't like them,' Rose pouted. 'I want to go home. Can we keep the kitten?'

'We'll see.'

'Can we? When are we going to see Papa?'

'I don't know,' Anne said, exasperated. 'Don't keep asking the same question again and again!'

Rose burst into tears and the kitten fled under a chair. 'I want Papa! I want to go home! My legs hurt!'

This last brought Mlle Parmoutier out of her chair with a cry of concern, but Nyanya got there first, scooping Rose up with trained strength and croodling to her in Russian as she sobbed into the broad black calico shoulder.

'She's tired, Barina, that's all,' Nyanya said over Rose's head.

'She's bored,' Anne suggested wearily. 'So are we all. This endless rain!'

Mlle Parmoutier was unconvinced. 'Perhaps, madame, we should call a physician. If her legs hurt her . . . ' She had once overheard Grubernik talking about rheumatic fever, and she had never been able to shake the dread out of her heart.

'Of course her poor little legs hurt, don't they, my little soul?' Nyanya crooned, quelling the governess with a look. 'And why shouldn't they? But Nyanya knows how to make it better! A nice rub with warm oil for my little candle, and a piece of gingerbread to eat, as big as your hand, eh?'

Rose, whose sobs were already lessening, said something through her hiccoughs which the nurse evidently understood.

'Of course we can, my pigeon,' she said, and with one hand scooped up the striped kitten and stuffed it into her apron pocket, nodded to her mistress, and went out.

Parmoutier remained unconvinced and guilty. 'I'm sure she ought to see a physician, madame. And all this travelling isn't good for her. I wish we might go back to Petersburg. Do you think his lordship – '

But her mistress wasn't listening. She was craning to look down into the street, where a horseman had just arrived.

'It's him! He's here!' she cried, and was gone from the room in a whirl of muslin before the governess could do more than draw a sigh.

They had the sitting-room to themselves now. The fire was burning brightly, and a new log Anne had just put on was hissing and popping as the bark curled in the heat. Hot wine and cakes were filling the gap while a meal was prepared. Anne was anxious, though he assured her he was quite well. Much of that drawn look in his face was from shock and distress rather than physical weariness, as she understood when he explained to her what he had seen.

'Sergei's Cossacks captured a foraging party near Novi Troki, and I was called in to listen while they were questioned. The poor devils were starving. We gave them some Polish sausage and rye bread, and they ate so fast one of them threw it up almost immediately.'

'Starving already? But didn't they bring any supplies with them?' Anne asked.

He shrugged. 'They'd all been ordered to carry pack rations – rice and flour enough for three days, which was supposed to get them from Kovno to Vilna. But these men were part of the third corps, who were still fifty versts or more from the Nieman when the crossing began. They had to force-march for forty out of forty-eight hours to catch up, across land that had already been stripped by foragers. Of course they had to eat their pack rations – and once they crossed into Russia, they came across the results of our scorched-earth policy.'

He passed a hand across his face, and she looked at him with keen sympathy. 'Theirs was not an isolated case, I suppose?'

He shook his head. 'The sights we've seen – the things Sergei has told me! The horses were starving before ever they reached the Nieman, and once the rain began, they just lay down and died in their thousands! The cold and hunger, and trying to drag heavy field pieces through fathoms of mud . . . They've got no fodder for them at all. They've been trying to feed them on green rye, but it just bloats them up, and they die of colic. We skirted Vilna on our way back here, and I tell you I must have seen hundreds of dead horses just lying there, rotting.'

Anne was silent with pity. After a moment he went on.

'The footsoldiers are suffering from ague and dysentery, and when they drop out of the column for any reason, the Cossacks pick them off. There's talk of typhus, too. I know as I skirted Vilna I saw that some of the horse carcases had been toppled into the river. The men we spoke to said the terrible weather was seen as a bad omen. They're so demoralised, some of them just walk off into the woods in despair and shoot themselves.'

'Then – he'll turn back? He must turn back, surely?'

Nikolai shook his head, and told her about his and Balashov's interview with Napoleon two days before. 'He has lost a vast number of men – but the number he has at his command is still more vast. I don't believe he will turn back until he has lost every man and horse, and even at this rate, that will take a long time.'

They were silent, staring into the fire, and then he roused himself to say, 'How are things with you, *doushenka?*'

'We're all well. Rose is bored and wants to go home, and the horses are pining for lack of exercise, that's all.'

'You've had no trouble with the locals?'

'They've treated us very courteously – though I don't know what will happen when the French come nearer, and they're forced to evacuate. Stories are already coming through about the way the French army has looted every town and village it passed.'

'I don't suppose they are more than the truth. My darling, you must not stay here any longer. I must go and report to the Emperor at Drissa, but I don't suppose we'll stay there very long. It's not a good place to have to defend, and in any case, I don't believe Tolly will want to make a stand until we've weakened the French still further. Vitebsk, perhaps, or even Smolensk, will be near enough. You must go further than that, to be safe. It will not be good to be anywhere near the French army as they get hungrier, and more of the horses die.'

'I want to be near you.'

'I don't suppose I shall have the leisure to visit you, even if there were a safe place for you to stay. You say Rose wants to go home. Why don't you go back to Petersburg?'

Because it's too far from you, she thought, but she didn't say it. 'She wants to see her father,' she said instead.

'Then go to Moscow.'

She eyed him defiantly, but saw the weariness in his eyes, and understood that now she was just one more thing for him to worry about, when he already had too much.

'Very well,' she sighed.

He touched her hand gratefully. 'I'll write to you. There'll be couriers along the road all the time. I'll send you news often, and if there's an opportunity, I'll come to you. It won't be for long, *doushka*. A few months.'

'And if it is possible, if it's safe, you'll send for me? I'll come without Rose, travel fast if I have to. You'll send for me?'

'If it's possible,' he said. His voice said it would not be possible, but she had to be content with that, since she could do no better.

Chapter Twenty-Eight

Anne found Moscow in a state of advanced insouciance. The notion that Napoleon might penetrate as far as the city – a thousand versts or more! – was considered preposterous, and so the two newspapers – the *News* and the *Messenger* – proclaimed with every edition. The fiercely patriotic Governor of Moscow, Count Rostopchin, had a leading citizen arrested for repeating Napoleon's boast the he would occupy both Russian capitals within six months; and instituted a censorship on letters leaving the city, to make sure no-one passed on subversive rumours about Russian military inefficiency. Rostopchin was a favourite of the Grand Duchess Catherine, and close friend of the fire-eating Prince Bagration, which, in Anne's view, explained everything.

Basil greeted her warily, almost diffidently; but the patent delight of the reunion between him and Rose, though it hurt her a little, made her speak more gently to him than she otherwise might have. Jean-Luc, she discovered, had his own apartments in the house; but it was a large house, and he made sure he kept out of her way.

He and Basil were behaving with more discretion than she would have thought them capable of: though there was no doubt that Basil visited Jean-Luc in his own rooms, and probably sayed with him most nights, it was all done with great secrecy, rather in the manner of the Grand Monarch whose official *couchée* was followed by an unofficial exit via the secret stairway.

In public, though they continued to be seen everywhere together, they behaved less outrageously, and were less often obviously drunk. It was almost, she thought wryly, as though they had settled down after the first flush of their love affair into the comfortable behaviour of a young married couple. She hated to think about that; but for Rose's sake she had to treat them civilly when they met. It was obviously in their interest too to avoid her as much as possible and not to provoke her when contact was inevitable; and after the first few days she found she was able to dismiss them from her mind for a great deal of the time, and to occupy her days agreeably with riding Quassy, schooling Image, and playing with Rose.

Rose was glad to be home, and with the stimulus of her new pony in the old familiar surroundings, and her desire to show her father her progress, she improved in a series of bounds. Her parents developed a routine for spending time with her so that they did not confront each other. Rose spent a great deal of Anne's time prattling about what she had done with Papa and Zho-Zho, as she called Jean-Luc; and Anne could only hope that she was equally voluble with them about Maman's treats.

July was hot, and many of the leading families had gone out of the city to their *dachas*; so that when the news arrived by Imperial courier that the Emperor was to visit Moscow before returning to St Petersburg, the Governor had to send out messengers to fetch them back. There was to be a ceremonial greeting of the Monarch at the Hill of Salutation, and he was then to be escorted to the royal apartments at the Kremlin. The next day there would be a solemn service of thanksgiving for the signing of the peace treaty with the Turks, and then the Emperor was to address all the leading nobles and the leading merchants at two assemblies.

The Emperor was to arrive on the 23rd; and on the 22nd Anne was surprised and pleased to receive a visit from Lolya.

'Darling Anne Petrovna!' She came forward with a smile of welcome and outstretched hands to kiss Anne formally on both cheeks, but it soon turned into a very informal hug.

'My dear Lolya,' Anne said. 'What are you doing in Moscow? I thought you were spending the summer in Tula.'

'Aunt Shoora's brought Kira to shop for her wedding – so she says.' Lolya pulled off her gloves, and walked about examining things as she talked with the restlessness of young energy. 'Actually, I think it's to get away from the noise and dust. The whole house is being rebuilt in the grandest style – you can't imagine – all pillars and balconies! It's because of the war, of course – Uncle Vsevka's got terribly rich with his munitions factory working double-time. Isn't it nice that someone gets some benefit from horrid wars? Kira's in a dreadful panic that the building won't be done in time for the wedding, and I think Aunt Shoora wants to take her mind off it. What delicious drapes these are, Anna dearest! Are they new?'

'No, darling, I've had them for years. When is the wedding?'

'November. I'm to be a bridesmaid. She's marrying Felix Uspensky – he's a lieutenant in the Third Corps, you know, so the war had better be over by then, or he'll have to get special leave. He's rather young and shy, but he has the sweetest little moustache, and Kira thinks he's wonderful, so I suppose that's all right.'

'Where are they now? Aunt Shoora and Kira, I mean.'

'Oh, they've gone to Fontenards to look at diamonds – Uncle Vsevka wants to give Kira a necklace and tiara for her wedding gift – isn't that splendid? But I had sooner see you, so they dropped me off here, and I said you'd probably send me back to the hotel afterwards in your carriage.'

'Oh, but why didn't they call in?' Anne said. 'I should have liked to see them.'

Lolya gave her a sideways look. 'Aunt Shoora didn't like to, because of Kira's situation – 'delicate situation' she said. I must say, Anna Petrovna, you don't look a bit like a fallen woman! Or not like what I would expect, at any rate, because I don't know if I've ever actually seen one, except actresses, and I don't suppose they're all necessarily fallen, only loose, whatever that means.'

Anne coloured. 'Is that what Shoora said?' she asked quietly. 'That I was a fallen woman?'

Lolya seemed unconcerned. 'Not precisely. She didn't use those words, but that was what she meant, I think. She said she wouldn't stop me from visiting you, but I told her she couldn't anyway.'

Anne felt an enormous sadness that dear, kind Shoora should feel constrained from allowing her daughter to enter her house. She made an effort to change the subject.

'You're looking very well, Lolya – different somehow. More grown up, I think.' It was true. She seemed more self-confident, more poised, and her taste had settled down – whether of its own accord, or under guidance from her aunt Anne couldn't know; but her gown and pelisse were models of elegant restraint, while her hat was saucy but not outrageous. She seemed prettier, too, with a warm, glowing beauty quite different from her first-Season, girlish prettiness.

'I feel more grown up,' Lolya confessed. She smiled. 'I feel wonderful, actually. It's being in love – you can't imagine, Anna!'

'Can't I?'

Lolya gave her the sidelong look again. 'I suppose – ' Her cheeks pinked a little. 'Anna, about you and Papa . . . ' she said bravely. 'I – I don't mind, you know. I think it's rather splendid, in fact! It was a bit difficult to understand at first – I mean, one never thinks of one's father – well, you know – being young enough for that sort of thing – '

'*What* sort of thing?' Anne queried, amused.

Lolya grew warmer. 'You know what I mean. It's different when it's young people like Andrei and me . . . '

'Colonel Duvierge is hardly a young man,' Anne said drily.

Lolya frowned. 'Well, at any rate, what I wanted to say is that it's all right. I'm glad for you, really, as long as – as long as you really do love him?'

'Lolya, my dear,' Anne said solemnly, 'I promise you that much as you may love Colonel Duvierge, I love your father a hundred times more.'

Lolya's face cleared. 'Oh, well that's all right then,' she said with a radiant smile. 'Only you couldn't possibly, you know! Andrei is so wonderful!'

Anne felt the resurgence of her grave misgivings. The crush Lolya had on the Frenchman ought to have died down by now. Perhaps it was wrong of Nikolai to have removed her from his orbit. Absence seemed to have made the heart grow fonder – fonder, and more serious, in a disquieting way.

'Lolya, dearest,' she began, hardly knowing how to tackle the subject. 'I don't think you ought to pin too much hope on a relationship with Colonel Duvierge. It's likely, you know, that he'll be recalled to France at any moment, if he hasn't been already. I don't suppose you can even have had any news of him for many weeks now – '

'Oh, but you're wrong!' Lolya looked smug. 'Andrei was so upset when I told him I was being sent to Moscow – well, Tula, at any rate – that he made me promise to write to him, and he promises to write back.'

'Lolya! You haven't been exchanging letters with him?'

'Of course – every week! He writes such lovely letters – really long ones, and full of – '

'But darling, you mustn't! It's absolutely out of the question!' Anne was agitated. 'Not only is it very improper for an unmarried girl to carry on a correspondence with a man, but it could be construed as treasonable! Don't you understand that he's officially an enemy now? There's no doubt he reports regularly to Bonaparte, and anything you may happen to tell him will be passed on that way.'

Lolya's eyes narrowed with temper. 'Don't dare to call my darling a spy!' she said hotly.

'Lolya, that's his job! That's what he was sent to Russia for!'

'You don't know him – you don't understand! Just because he's French, you think he must be wicked – but he hates Napoleon as much as we do! All he wants is peace between our two countries so that we can be together and get married. He hates war, and – and talk of enemies – and – everything like that!'

Anne looked at her despairingly. 'Don't you understand, he's bound to say that so as to lull your suspicions, and make you talk more freely? Oh Lolya, what have you been telling him?'

Her cheeks were bright. 'Nothing!' she said angrily. 'How could you think – how could you so misjudge me, Anne Petrovna? Don't you think I know better by now than to give away secrets? Even if I knew any,' she added with a brittle laugh. 'Who would tell a chit of a girl like me anything important?'

'I don't believe you would deliberately say anything that would help the enemy – of course I don't!' Anne said placatingly. 'But consider, darling – your father is a senior diplomat, and your uncle, with whom you are staying, owns the biggest munitions factory in Russia. There's no knowing what use even an innocent-seeming piece of information might be put to.'

'Oh, you're just like all the rest,' Lolya said, turning away. 'I'm disappointed in you, Anna Petrovna. I would have thought in your position, you'd be a bit more understanding!'

The least useful thing in the present situation would be to alienate Lolya, and lose her confidence. Anne tried to soothe her. 'I do understand. I don't want to make you think badly of Colonel Duvierge – only to be careful. I don't want to see you hurt, or placed in a position . . . Lolya, he has no right to endanger you by asking for this correspondence! Don't you see? It's not the action of a man in love.'

'Of course he loves me! He can't live without me, *that's* why he wants me to write to him!' Lolya retorted.

'A responsible man – especially a man of his age – would never ask the woman he loved to do something that might compromise her. Don't you understand that?'

'It's you who doesn't understand! You don't know anything about love! I thought you were different, but you're just like the rest after all!'

'Lolya, listen to me – '

'I won't hear any more. You're just trying to poison me against him!'

'Listen to me! It's you I'm concerned with, and your safety! All the letters which leave from the post office in this city are opened and read by the Governor's official. At least while you are in Moscow, you mustn't write to Colonel Duvierge! Please, Lolya, try to understand! Even if the letter were the most innocent thing in the world, the very fact that you were writing to a senior member of the French Embassy would be considered a suspicious circumstance.' Lolya regarded her sulkily, but said nothing. 'Please, promise me you won't write to him from here.'

There was a long silence, while Lolya's pride fought with her basic common sense, and her old regard for Anne's judgement.

'Oh, very well,' she said at last, ungraciously. 'If it will stop you fussing . . . '

'Thank you,' Anne said quickly, feeling a rush of enormous relief. It was a concession; now she must turn her thoughts towards how to tackle the rest of the problem.

But the strain of the last few moments seemed to have affected her oddly: she felt her pulse beating fast all over her body, and her hands were cold and damp.

'I think it's very hard of you to lecture me,' Lolya was grumbling, 'considering I braved everyone's opinion to come here and see you . . . '

Anne couldn't listen to her. She felt rather sick, and the room seemed to be waxing and waning before her eyes. She put out a hand to Lolya, who suddenly seemed very far away, as if at the other end of a tunnel.

'I don't think – ' Anne began with difficulty; but a roaring drowned what she was going to say, and as Lolya's surprised face turned towards her, for the first time in her life, Anne fainted.

The Emperor's visit lasted six days, and during that time the patriotic fervour which was endemic to Moscow erupted into near-hysteria, which resulted in wealthy merchants accidentally pledging huge sums of roubles for the war-effort, and wealthy *dvoriane* stripping their estates of serfs, and even their houses of servants, to provide a militia for the support of the regular troops and the defence of Moscow.

The Emperor, who had entered Moscow looking distinctly worried, left it with tears of gratitude in his eyes. Deeply touched by the fervent loyalty of the Muscovites, who were traditionally rather cool and critical, his parting words to Governor Rostopchin were to give him authority to act in any way he thought fit, should Napoleon ever, inconceivably, reach the gates of Moscow. 'Who can predict events? I rely on you entirely,' he said, and drove away to visit his sister Catherine, Rostopchin's patroness, at Tver on his way to St Petersburg.

Lolya's visit to Moscow lasted three weeks, and Anne saw her often. The subject of Colonel Duvierge was hardly mentioned between them again. Lolya generously set aside their difference of opinion, and they had some very pleasant outings. Anne met Shoora several times out and about in public places, and Shoora greeted her with unreserved friendliness, though she would not visit her in her home. Anne found this hurtful, but saw in it no malice, only the results of her upbringing under Vera Borisovna and the narrowness of her education, which left her unable to be flexible over social rules.

Lolya seemed to draw no conclusions from Anne's fainting fit: certainly she never referred to it, or suggested by so much as a glance that she thought of it again. They parted on good terms, with kisses and promises of seeing each other again soon, as Lolya left with her aunt and cousin to visit friends at their *dacha* in Podolsk, about twenty-five miles from Moscow.

Basil left Moscow at the same time, to attend a house party given by the Grand Duchess Catherine, with whom he was on very good terms. He took Rose, her god-daughter, with him. Anne was invited, but declined in view of the fact that the theatre company, including Jean-Luc, had been invited to perform several plays for the guests during the stay. Anne pleaded ill health as an excuse which would not offend the Grand Duchess, and Basil, seeing that she did look rather pale and preoccupied, accepted it, and even offered some unexpectedly warm words of sympathy.

'It's probably only the heat,' Anne said. 'I shall be all right once the cooler weather begins.'

'Why don't you go down to the country?' Basil said. 'Moscow is impossible in August. Go down to the *dacha* at Fili.'

'I might,' she said. 'Don't worry about me. Take care of Rose – see she does her exercises.'

'Of course I will.'

Rose was utterly thrilled to be going on a visit to the Emperor's sister, especially with Papa and Zho-Zho. Anne went out to the carriage to say goodbye to her, and saw her sitting on the edge of the seat, with her governess beside her and the striped kitten in her lap, her face alight with pleasure and excitement. Her heart contracted with painful love, and she leaned in through the window to kiss her daughter. Rose returned the embrace with interest, and though she was plainly longing to be off, her delight at the prospect of the visit made her generous enough to say, 'I wish you were coming too, Maman!'

Left alone at Byeloskoye, Anne spent the first few days quietly, walking in the gardens, sitting under the deep shade of the old medlar, pondering her situation. It was different, of course, from last time: there was more of pleasure now, and less of apprehension – but still it was a matter for concern. There seemed, at least, no doubt about it this time. Apart from the fainting-fit, she had felt nausea several times on waking in the morning, and a second flux had not begun when it was due. She must have conceived some time during her stay in Vilna in June.

But what to do about it was beyond her to decide. She was married to Basil Andreyevitch. To leave his official protection would place her outside society, and she had already tasted, in Shoora's refusal to visit her, the sloes of being an outcast. Not only that, but it would bring opprobrium down on the heads of Rose and of the unborn child. She trusted Nikolai absolutely to take care of her in every physical and emotional way, but even his protection could not change the rules of society.

She could think of nothing to do, but to do nothing. Inside her body, the seed he had planted had begun to grow. She was with child to her love, and it was a lovely, holy thing. For the moment, she wanted nothing but to enjoy in sweet secrecy the knowledge of her fecundity. For the rest – she could only wait and see what happened. Eventually some decision must be made, some action taken; but not now, not yet.

News came regularly from Nikolai. Tolly's strategy of withdrawal was doing just what it was intended to do – slowing down Napoleon's advance, weakening his forces and lowering their morale by harrying their flanks, and increasing day by day the problem of feeding and supplying the vast overblown body of men he had brought with him into Russia.

After spending, inexplicably, more than two weeks at Vilna, Napoleon had left on the 16th of July and advanced northeast to Sventsiany, and then turned eastwards towards Vitebsk. He had marched his men fast through the terrible country: marshes into which they sank to the knees; dense forests of fir which scratched their faces and pulled at their clothes; bare roads where the dust rose so thick that the weary, hungry men could only find their way by following the sound of the drummer boys at the head of each section. By day the sun beat down mercilessly on men whose woollen uniforms had been designed for more temperate climates; by night fierce hailstorms beat down on their bivouacs, and the rapid changes of temperature brought on agues and lung sickness.

They marched so fast that their supply train was left far behind, and they had scant time to forage, even if there had been anything to find. But Tolly's army was marching before them, stripping the country as it went. All the Grande Armée found was deserted, ruined villages; and those who strayed too far from the road in a desperate search for food were picked off by the Cossacks, or slaughtered by the few native Russians who remained in the woods and more distant hamlets.

Nikolai told her in his letters of the terrible sights he had seen along the roads. Horses had continued to die by the thousand: the road was lined with their corpses, and with sick and dying soldiers, abandoned fieldpieces, carts of equipment for which there were no longer teams to draw them. The French were losing men through dysentery, typhus, festering wounds, desertion, and sheer hunger and exhaustion.

Some of the stragglers we have picked up speak of such misery and disillusionment amongst the ranks, that I imagine many are dying simply because they have no desire to live. Hardly any are Frenchmen, and most seem not to understand why they are here at all. Napoleon is promising them all they need – food, rest, clothing – when they reach Vitebsk, and that gets them along a little. But by my estimates he must have lost by now half the force with which he crossed the Nieman. Still his numbers are formidable – but they are only flesh and blood, which I think he sometimes forgets.

At Vitebsk the old argument for making a stand had been renewed amongst the Russian commanders, but Tolly's first army had not yet been able to join up with Bagration's second army, and so was still vastly outnumbered. The Russians quietly vacated the city during the night as the French approached, and withdrew towards Smolensk, leaving Napoleon to enter the next morning a city empty of inhabitants, save the very old and the very sick. Empty, also, of everything they needed – food, medical supplies, doctors, fodder for the horses.

Nevertheless, Napoleon remained there for more than two weeks, and Nikolai concluded in one of his letters that the French supremo was unsure how to proceed.

Prudence must make him realise that to advance further will only result in more loss. His advisers – Caulaincourt, at least – will try to persuade him to make Vitebsk his winter quarters, to consolidate his position and begin the campaign again next year. It remains to be seen what he will decide. We march on for Smolensk, and a rendezvous with Prince Bagration's army there.

On August the 12th, Napoleon's ambition evidently outweighed his adviser's caution, for he left Vitebsk and continued the march eastwards towards Smolensk. Here the Russians made a stand, and on the 17th of August a battle was fought, resulting in heavy losses on both sides. When firing ceased at nightfall, the French had managed to take the suburbs, but the Russians still held the old city itself.

Now Prince Bagration was amongst them, the arguments for withdrawing no further and 'finishing it' here at Smolensk were advanced with great passion. Smolensk was an extremely holy city, and to abandon it would be close to blasphemy. The whole of Russia was smarting under the humiliation of this continuous retreat, he declared. History would never forgive them for having allowed the Corsican

Bandit to penetrate so far into the heartland of Russia. Now was their chance to make amends, to prove what they were made of, to make an heroic stand, and write their names in letters of fire and blood on the pages of history!

It was splendid, stirring stuff, Nikolai wrote. *I must tell you that as he spoke, I even found my own pulse responding. After all, the French had taken a heavy loss that day, to add to their undoubted losses on the march. And I longed – and do long still – to be freed from the necessity of this war, so that I can come home to you, dearest Anna, and rest in your arms.*

But then Tolly spoke up quietly, and pointed out that the old town, which was largely made of wood and had been set on fire by French artillery shells, was burning briskly around us, and that the streets were filled with corpses. More seriously, though we might have the bridges over the Dnieper under our control, there was a ford at Prudishevo three miles downstream, and it was only a matter of time before Napoleon's scouts found it. Once they crossed the river, they would surround us, and our position would be hopeless.

So we evacuated the city during the night, burnt the bridges behind us, and withdrew down the Smolensk-Moscow High Road. We are now at Viazma, and I hear that Tolly is to be replaced as Commander in Chief by Kutuzov, who is being sent to us from St Petersburg by the Emperor himself. Poor Tolly takes it very hard; but I tell him that His Majesty is obliged to take some account of public opinion, which is as vociferous as it is uninformed. And Kutuzov is, at least, a soldier, so there may be some hope of guiding him rationally, if we can keep Bagration away from his right ear. We are to meet Kutuzov at Tsarevo on the 29th.

When Anne read that letter, she was roused out of her lethargy by a consuming loneliness and longing for him. She had been alone in the house now for ten days; parted from him for almost two months; and the crazy idea came to her that there was nothing to stop her from going to him. Tsarevo was about a hundred miles from Moscow, but the Smolensk-Moscow High Road was a good one, and she could be there, with fast travelling, in two days – and it would take the army at least two days to reach it from Viazma. She could be there at the same time as him! In two days she could see him again!

Well, why not, she argued with herself? People did travel with armies. Many wealthy, aristocratic officers travelled with an entire household, coaches and cooks and all the comforts of home. Prince Kutuzov lived like a *pasha*, with a tentful of dancing girls to soothe his brow at the day's end.

501

But *he* was not like that, her conscience told her. Like the austere Tolly, he lived hard when on campaign. Her presence would be an embarrassment. He might even think it improper of her to have come.

Then she had a better idea. Basil owned a hunting-lodge, Koloskavets, in the wooded hills above Borodino, a village on the same road about seventy miles from Moscow. There was nothing in the least improper about going there, to her own husband's property. He had told her to go out of Moscow into the country, hadn't he? And with the entire Russian army between her and the French, it must be safe. Once there she could write to him, telling him where she was, and then he could make his own time for coming to see her.

In the face of such determination, the dissenting voice retired, and she jumped up and rang the bell for Pauline with her pulse leaping at the prospect of positive action, and the thought of seeing him again.

All along the road, at every stop, Anne heard the name of Kutuzov on every lip as that of his country's saviour. The army had been retreating in the most cowardly way for months, and Napoleon had got scandalously near Moscow; but now Kutuzov had come, things would change. He would stand and fight the Monster, and beat him, and Russia would be saved! He was a true Russian – not like Tolly, who was really a German, and Bennigsen, who was a Swede. Prince Kutuzov was the real article, and a cunning old fox, and there was no need to fear that Napoleon would get any closer to Holy Moscow now than Tsarevo. Napoleon would find he had met his match at last.

Anne, who had met Kutuzov once, and knew quite a lot about him from hearsay, couldn't help wondering at the faith that was invested in the fat, elderly, one-eyed sybarite; but still she found herself affected by it. She began to think that perhaps it would really all be over in a week or two. One good battle, and the men would come home!

At Mozhaisk, the next town before Borodino, a road from the south joined the Smolensk-Moscow High Road, and here her coachman had to hold back to allow a group of horsemen – Caucasus irregulars by the look of their dress and horses, to take the road ahead of them. She wondered vaguely if they were part of Sergei's troop, and why they were scouting on this, the wrong side of the main army. They didn't seem to have an officer with them. The man at the head of the troop was a Tartar in a leather cap trimmed with black sheepskin, wearing a striped surcoat over the glint of body armour; a tall man on a magnificent bay Khabardin, with crimson tassels and gold discs on its bridle . . .

He turned his head as he reached the turning and looked straight into the carriage window, straight into her eyes; and then waving his men past him with an imperious gesture, he turned his curvetting horse three times on the spot and drove it, against its better judgement, away from its companions and up to the carriage. He stooped from the saddle to look in through the window, his teeth bared in a savage smile, and the pearls in his ears quivering.

Pauline gave a little squeak of alarm and drew back, and Anne laughed, because the situation was so strangely familiar.

'Amongst by people,' he said, 'there is a saying that where there have been two meetings, there must be a third, and that it will portend great things, for good or for ill. Twice have we met, English lady; and now I find you here, to meet a third time. May the Great One bless you.'

'And you also, Akim Shan,' Anne said. It was the most astonishing thing; and yet she didn't feel at all surprised. Russia had done that much for her. 'What are you doing here, with your men?'

'We have come to fight the battle,' he said with dignity. 'We are Tartars, and the Russians have called a Tartar to lead them at last against the foe.'

'You mean Prince Kutuzov?'

'The one-eyed, yes. So we have answered the call.'

'But this war is not your war,' Anne said, mildly puzzled. 'Why should you fight?'

He grinned. 'Because life is for battle and glory. As long as a man can sit his horse and wield his sword, he will seek honour in the field of battle, and the victor's spoil, and a noble death.'

'The tiger's death, and not the jackal's?' she said. He met her eyes keenly.

'So, you remember! It is in my heart that I should have married you, whether you would or not.'

'I should not have suited you,' Anne said gravely. 'So you have come all the way from the Caucasus?'

'To make an end, yes. Many of our people have come – but you know this,' he added, his eyes narrowing. 'The fair one, who was not your husband, he took sixty men from Pyatigorsk of the Five Hills, and another twenty have since followed.'

'Yes, I knew that.'

'So, is it that you now go to be with him on the eve of battle?' he asked with a hint of approval.

'Not the fair one, but my husband,' Anne said. Not for Akim Shan's knowing, the complication of the issue. 'I have a house in the hills near here, at Borodino, and I mean to wait for him there, and send word where I am, so that he can come to me if his duties give him the leisure.'

'Who is he, this husband of yours?' he asked suspiciously.

Concealing a smile, Anne played the game gravely. 'He is a great man, the right hand of the Emperor, and adviser to General Tolly, who was leader before Prince Kutuzov was called. His name is Count Kirov.'

Akim Shan's eyes narrow still further. 'I know this name. It is the name of the fair one who took the men from Pyatigorsk.'

'The name is the same. It is the fair one's father.'

Akim Shan considered for an instant, and then smiled with enlightenment. 'Now I understand everything! And now I see that you are a powerful woman, as I knew when I first met you, and you would not sell me the black mare! But it is not fitting that you should ride alone in this way. I, Akim Shan Kalmuck, will escort you to the place you speak of; and then I shall myself take your message to your husband. Come, tell your men to drive on! I am a prince of my people, and if you live fifty years, you will never again have such an escort!'

'I'm sure of it,' Anne laughed. It didn't seem possible now that anything would ever surprise her again.

On the night of August the 31st, Anne lay in the arms of her lover again. What did it matter if the blankets smelled rather damp, and the bed dipped spinelessly in the middle? Between her own sheets, which she had brought with her, she stretched in the luxury of being naked and feeling the touch of his warm smooth skin against her own, and of knowing that they had the whole night and most of the next day to be together.

Koloskavets was a small stone house built on one of the rolling hills above Borodino. Behind it the dense, dark pine forests protected it from the north, and presumably supplied the game for whose sake it had originally been built. Before it a small terrace ended in a wall, below which the hillside fell away, increasingly steeply, down to the village and the Kolotcha River for which the house had been named, a winding watercourse which paralleled the Highway before turning northeast and emptying itself at last into the Moskva, the river on which Moscow was built.

Inside the house was fairly primitive, having been intended only for use during the summer months as a hunting-lodge. Its furniture was sparse and old-fashioned, but solid; the air struck rather chill and damp, despite the summer heat outside, and everything was inches thick in dust. An old couple, living in quarters at the back of the house, were there as caretakers, but it was many years since any member of the Tchaikovsky family had used Koloskavets, and they had ceased to bother very much about it.

Anne soon had all the windows opened, the furniture dusted, and the fires laid and lit to air the rooms; her own sheets put upon the beds, and her own food, from an ample hamper she had brought with her, put upon the table. It was not so bad, after all; and it was only for a short time, and living rough would not hurt her.

She had entrusted Akim Shan with a letter for Kirov, and hoped for an answer within a few days. What she got was better than that, for early in the afternoon of the 31st he arrived on horseback, accompanied by Adonis.

There was little of coherence spoken between them for the first hour or two. After witnessing the first silent joy of their meeting, Adonis took the horses and ushered the servants away, leaving them in privacy. After a few minutes, they retired by common consent to Anne's bedchamber. It was what they both seemed to want most of all, and it didn't seem wrong – only necessary, and the quickest way to restore their perfect communion, after the disruption of so many weeks.

They made love with the ease of accustomed lovers, and then lay for a while in each other's arms without talking, simply savouring being together. Then they got up, and went out to sit on the terrace in the late sunshine and look at the view. Stenka and his wife Zina shuffled out with tea in a huge and ancient samovar from which the silver-gilt had rubbed brassily, accompanied incongruously by cups of the most exquisite, almost transparent chinese porcelain.

While they drank their tea, Nikolai told her that he had not come from Tsarevo, but from Ghzatsk, a village half-way between Tsarevo and Borodino.

'We arrived at Tsarevo early on the 29th, and Tolly gave orders for us to dig in. It was a good place to fortify – on rising ground, with a clear view in every direction. Everyone thought so. We'd got the men busy digging redoubts and strengthening the walls, and around noon Kutuzov arrived from Petersburg. Bennigsen was with him – they met on the road – and Kutuzov had already asked him to be his chief of staff. But as soon as he arrived he told Tolly he wanted him to remain as commander of the first army, and Minister for War.'

'Well, that's something. It must have soothed poor Tolly's pride a little.'

'A very little, I suppose. The trouble is that Kutuzov brought with him a huge headquarters staff of the sons of aristocrats, the very hot-headed young know-nothings that Tolly's been at pains to eliminate over the past months. We shall have our work cut out to counteract that influence.'

'Everyone's been talking about Kutuzov as though he's a saviour,' Anne said. 'In Mozhaisk they thought the war was as good as won.'

'He's very popular with the peasantry,' Nikolai shrugged. 'When he made the round of inspection, the men were all overjoyed, and cheered themselves hoarse over him. They think he's one of them you see, because he dresses like an Old Russian, and talks their language. He has a way of delivering short, pithy sentences in soldier's Russian that goes straight to their hearts.'

The breeze whispered through the pine trees, and the shadow of a fast-moving cloud ran across them. For a moment it was quite cool. Autumn was coming; Anne could smell it in the breeze, a smell of ending and turning towards sleep. She shivered, and turned towards her lover for comfort.

'So what did the great hero do when he arrived?'

'He didn't do very much, just listened and nodded, inspected everything, praised quite a bit. We had a meeting at headquarters, and Tolly explained the situation and the advantages of defending Tsarevo, and the old man said he agreed, and that as far as he could see everything was very well thought-out, and the work that had been started should proceed.'

'He came meaning to placate, then?'

'So it seemed. Tolly was pleased about it, as you can imagine. However, the next day various members of his suite apparently took Kutuzov's ear, and told him that it was humiliating for him to accept a battle site chosen by someone else; and that if things went well, half the credit would go to Tolly and not to him.'

'Oh, no, but surely – ' Anne protested.

Nikolai shrugged. 'They must have persuaded him. Yesterday afternoon he suddenly announced that we were to abandon Tsarevo and take up a new position on the other side of Ghzatsk. Tolly was furious – all that work wasted, and a good position abandoned! We moved out during the night, and this morning when we got to Ghzatsk, Tolly said there would be nothing important for me to do while the men were digging in again, and that I might as well make use of the lull to come and see you.'

'How kind of him! So he knew I was here?'

'He was with me when your Tartar Prince delivered your letter the day before yesterday.'

Anne told him how she had met up with Akim Shan. 'I hope General Tolly welcomed him. He's come a long way to fight.'

'Oh, Tolly knew his value all right. He's got him and his men out on the Smolensk road bringing in regular reports on the French movements. He told him when the battle began, he could join Ataman Platov's regiment of Cossacks, but your prince rather turned up his nose at that, and told Tolly very grandly that he would choose for himself where to fight.'

'Poor Tolly.'

'Yes. I don't think he quite knew how to take that. He asked me afterwards if Akim Shan could be trusted, and when I told him that he could trust him perfectly, since he hated the French far more than the Russians, he looked quite put out.'

Those were the things they spoke of in the afternoon, as the sun of the last day of August sank bloodily in the west. Supper was brought to them on the terrace, and they ate by lamplight, served by Adonis, who wouldn't let anyone else, not even Pauline, come near them. After supper there was nothing they wanted more than to go to bed. They made love again, slowly, almost pensively; and then, lying in the candlelight in each other's arms, they talked of other things.

'I couldn't believe it when I read your letter. I thought my imagination must be playing tricks on me – it happens sometimes when you're very tired. I wanted to saddle my horse right then and come to you.' He sighed, holder her close. 'It's been a long two months.'

'Yes,' she said. She had seen how long in his face. There was far more grey now in his hair, and his eyes were shadowed with more than weariness. 'I almost didn't come. I thought you might think I was a nuisance.'

'Why did you come? You couldn't have known it would be in my power to visit you.'

'I hoped, that's all.'

She was cradled safe in his arms; and his child was cradled safe in her womb. For a moment it was in her mind to tell him, but the thought of all he had before him deterred her. His being here, though for her the whole purpose of life, was for him only an interlude between worries more pressing than she could imagine, and probably more real to him at the moment than she was. No, this was not the time. A better time would come, when this could be the most important thing in the world for both of them.

'What is it?' he asked, feeling her preoccupation.

'I've missed you so much,' was all she said.

'And I you. I thought of you often, imagined you safely in Moscow, shopping in the Kuznetsky Most, seeing the play at the Grand Théâtre, riding in the park. It pleased me to know you were safe, and far from the terrible things I was witnessing . . . '

No, she thought, this was not the time.

'Will there really be a battle now?' she asked at last.

'Yes, I think so. It's time. The French are greatly weakened, and our numbers are almost even now.'

'And then will it be over?'

He didn't answer for a while. 'I don't know. If it were anyone but Napoleon . . . He is three months from the border, and winter will be here before three months are up. Caution, common sense, should have turned him back before now; but he still comes on. I don't know if it's in him to withdraw. When we fight, we will have to beat them throughly enough to convince even him. I don't know if we can. His soldiers are skilled in war, with experienced commanders. Ours are only very strong and very determined. It could go either way.'

She pressed closer. 'You will – be careful?' she said, feeling a little ashamed even as she asked it of him. Men's pride was different from women's. Women saw no point in being heroic and dead – far better to live to fight another day.

He smiled – she felt the curve of his cheek move against hers. 'Don't worry, I shall be well out of the way, at Kutuzov's elbow. Great generals and their staff command from the rear, you know! Except Napoleon – though perhaps even he may be cautious this time, having more to lose. Perhaps we can send the Cossacks after him. The French have a mortal dread of the Cossacks – even the word has taken on power, like some evil incantation!'

'The Cossacks seem to have a great respect for Kutuzov.'

'Yes, they feel he's one of them. They like Bagration, too – and I've heard one or two approving comments on young Captain Kirov.'

'Have you seen Sergei since – since Vilna?'

'Oh yes, of course. He reports to me in Tolly's absence.' He sighed. 'It's very hard to have your own son look at you as though you're a stranger. I can see, from his point of view . . . and yet, I don't know what else we could have done.'

'Nothing,' she said. And there was nothing either of them could have done to protect Sergei from his fate, from what happened in the mountains of the Caucasus. 'He'll get over it, in time,' she added, not because she believed it, but because she hoped it, and wanted to comfort him.

'I pray when all this is over he'll come to understand. I'll spend time with him, get to know him. I never really knew him you know. It seems to be the fate of males of our class. I never knew my father either – though of course he died when I was quite young. But I – I was at fault. I should have taken more trouble with Sergei, but of course my own duties . . . He was away from me too much while he was growing up. His grandmother spoiled him. And then – '

There seemed nothing more to say on that – nothing that was safe. Anne's mind wandered on over a number of thoughts, alighting here and there and moving on again restlessly. When at last she drew breath to open a new subject, she heard the small but inmistakeable sound of a snore in Nikolai's throat. His mental excitement had worn off at last, and he had fallen into the profound sleep of the exhausted.

The next morning, Sunday the 1st of September, Kirov woke early out of force of habit, and for a moment lay in a daze, not knowing where he was. The familiar feeling of dread which had attended every waking for two months past was overlaid by another sensation he could not yet identify; and then Anne moved slightly, and memory flooded back. She was there beside him, warm and smooth and sweet-smelling, everything that was soft and feminine and alive: the antipathy of war, which was cold and dirt and waste, and the stupidity of death.

The very fact of her presence seemed to throw the hatefulness of the campaign into sharp relief: six hundred miles of road lined with dead horses and dying men; with villages destroyed and burned, green fields churned into raw wounds of mud and debris; rivers polluted, crops trampled; towns that had been happy and industrious left for wrecks, filled only with beggars and with the sick and the wounded, dying of typhus and gangrene. And for what? So that one man might add another empty title to his collection.

With the restlessness of suffering, he turned on his side towards Anne. He reached out to touch her, ran his hand over her smooth flank, across her gently convex belly, up to the soft heaviness of her breasts. The two conditions, of war and peace, rested side by side in his mind, equally real – or was it equally unreal? Slaughter and mud and destruction, the campaign, the world of men; and the sleeping woman beside him, the wholeness of her unblemished skin, the scent of her clean hair.

He was aware that she was smooth and young and sweet, while he was gaunt and grey and weary. After months on campaign he didn't even smell clean any more. How could she lie with him and love him? How could he put aside what he had witnessed and love her? Could anything ever be the same again? But which was the reality – the palace from which she came, or the muddy tent where he had spent his last night? Here, this place, was a kind of half-way house, a compromise between the two worlds – and perhaps it was the only reality.

His moving hand had woken her, she was turning towards him, soft and sleep-hot and wanting him. His body responded to her automatically with a weary surge of desire, as if in the middle of death it were desperate to create life. He wished he could do that one thing – make something new and good in the middle of this desolation. If he could leave her quickened, he might leave her with less despair. He moved over her, entered her, and she moved to meet him, receiving him easily and readily, taking him into her. He held her in his arms, but he felt separated from her. His mind stood apart, knowing he loved her without being able to feel it. She smiled and curved under him, still half asleep, murmuring with pleasure; he mated her because he needed to.

And afterwards he wondered if he had succeeded, and then thought that it was a foolish thing to have done, because there would be no knowing until long after the battle whether she were pregnant or not. They slept again, both of them restless, and when they woke the second time she smiled at him and he kissed her, and Anne saw that he had already left her, that the campaign was more real to him than her, and that he had gone back to it. What was left was just the shell.

Before they had finished breakfast, Adonis came in to say that a messenger had come from General Tolly, recalling Kirov to duty at once. There had been a disagreement over the new site at Ghzatsk almost as soon as the men had begun digging in. General Bennigsen complained that it was impossible to hold, and that it had a wood in the middle of it, and Tolly, still angry over the abandoning of the position at Tsarevo, asked him tautly whether he had anything better to suggest.

Bennigsen had retorted that while travelling in his carriage between Mozhaisk and Ghzatsk he had noted several splendid places, which might have been created for the sole purpose of fighting battles. The doubtful Kutuzov had been persuaded: another move was ordered. The Russian army was once again withdrawing along the Smolensk-Moscow High Road, and Kirov's presence was urgently needed to ride out and inspect some of these 'ideal' battlegrounds and report back to the Commander in Chief on their suitability.

'I must go,' Nikolai said. 'I will send you word when I can.'

'At least you are moving nearer to me,' she said lightly.

'Anna, I may not be able to come again. You had better go back to Moscow.'

'Not yet,' she said. 'I will go when I must, but not yet. Don't worry about me, Nikolasha – I'll take care of myself, and not put myself in danger. But I'll be here, in case you are able to come again.'

He nodded, a frown of thought already between his brows, and kissed her absently, and went, almost with relief; his body following where his mind had already gone.

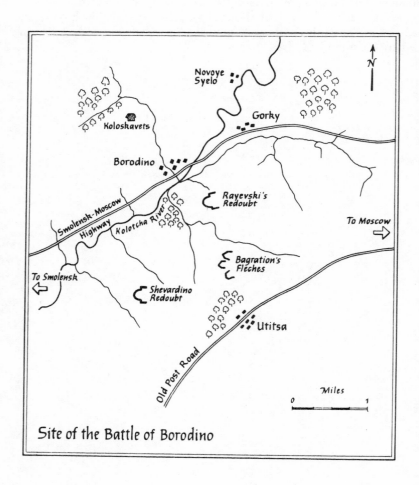

Site of the Battle of Borodino

Chapter Twenty-Nine

On the 2nd of September, the caravan of coaches and riders which was General Kutuzov's suite rolled through sleepy Borodino and on up the mile-long slope to the village of Gorky, where it stopped. This was the 'ideal battleground' settled on by General Bennigsen. It was far, Kirov thought, from ideal: hillocky, lightly wooded, dissected by the now mainly dry gullies of numerous streamlets, rising to steep hills above Gorky in the north, and descending to marshy forest around the village of Utitsa in the south.

Borodino itself, a small town – hardly more than an overgrown village, really – with its distinctive twin-towered church and white-painted houses, sat beside the single wooden bridge spanning the Kolotcha River, which ran parallel with the Smolensk-Moscow High Road until swinging northeast under this bridge and winding away to empty itself at last into the Moskva.

Utitsa lay about two and a half miles south of Borodino, on the old post road which ran parallel to the new Highway, joining up with it further towards Moscow at Mozhaisk. This old road constituted another drawback to the situation: there was a serious danger that Napoleon might use it to bypass and surround the Russians, unless it were well defended.

Whatever Prince Kutuzov thought of the site, having listened to the reports of his chiefs of staff, he announced at last that this was where they would make their stand. Perhaps, Kirov thought, he felt he could not reasonably retreat any further towards Moscow, which was now only seventy-five miles away. They had passed no place better than this for the purpose since they had left Tsarevo. Tolly, he knew, was still bitter about their having abandoned that position; to Kirov he made several stinging remarks at Bennigsen's expense about how easy this wooded and gullied area would be to defend.

As the regiments marched up, they were deployed over the ground to start preparing fortifications. The French were three or four days behind them on the road, with the Russian rearguard under General Miloradovich and the Cossack skirmishers between them and the main Russian force. Sergei's scouts brought in reports every few hours on their position and condition. Further back along the road there was persistent cold rain, which was turning the roads into quagmire. The French, with their exhausted, half-starved horses, were finding the going heavy.

As he rode about the chosen battlefield during the first day, relaying orders, reconnoitring, directing the arriving troops to their stations, Kirov glanced up from time to time at the hills above Borodino, and thought how ironic it was that this should have been the chosen place. From the terrace of Koloskavets, one would have a clear, if distant view of the whole battle. There he had known his last peace and pleasure; it was the place he had thought of as the only reality between the two opposing worlds; and at its feet, like a sacrifice, the battle would be laid.

He couldn't see the house clearly with his naked eye – just a fleck of grey against the dark green of the trees. Plainly, she must leave now, go back to Moscow. As soon as he had a moment, he would send Adonis to her with a message – no time to write a letter – telling her that he would meet her again in Moscow when it was all over.

On the 3rd of September, the first of the militiamen promised by Moscow arrived – a motley band of serfs armed only with pikes, but they were strong and docile, and were set to useful work digging trenches and raising earthworks. It was fortunate that they had several days in hand before the French would arrive, for there was a great deal to be done to prepare the defences.

A mile in front of the Russian line, and roughly in the centre, the hamlet of Shevardino sat upon a small hillock. The peasant inhabitants, already so alarmed by the arrival of the army that they had brought their goats and milch cows into their houses for safety, were moved out and sent on their way to join other refugees on the road to Moscow. The hamlet was then raised to the ground to give a clear field of fire, and the hillock fortified by earthworks into a redoubt. This would be the forward defence, intended to slow the French advance, and break the back of any initial charge.

Behind it, the main battle-front stretched roughly from Borodino to Utitsa, between the two roads. The centre of the line, where the seventh corps under General Rayevsky was stationed, was dominated by a hummock, which Tolly ordered to be fortified into another redoubt. The whole of the left wing was to be defended by the eighth corps under Prince Bagration, and Kirov noted with alarm how thinly spread the men were over this, the largest area of the battlefield. The right wing, which had the natural defences of the Kolotcha River and the hills, had by far the greater density of men; Bagration's left wing was on largely open ground.

It wasn't until the next day that Tolly had time to visit the left wing of the battlefield, and he saw at once what had alarmed Kirov. For once Bagration saw eye to eye with his old enemies Tolly and Kirov: the openness of the ground and the proximity of the old post road would make this wing very hard to hold without more reinforcements. Bennigsen, of course, was automatically against anything that Tolly was for; but after heated arguments he agreed to send over militiamen to begin the construction of three flèches on the left wing. As to reinforcements – the old post road, he said, would be perfectly adequately defended by the roving Cossack regiments. Napoleon was bound to approach by the High Road – probably he did not even know the old post road existed.

The work continued all through the day; when darkness fell, the earthworks were still not finished. Kirov was sent out by Prince Kutuzov to make a general round and report on morale, and as he rode along the line, he noted again how unevenly the forces were distributed. On the right wing, Tolly's own command, on the hill around Gorky, there was heavy artillery and solid earthworks; woods had been cut back, and the village of Novoye Syelo had been completely destroyed to leave the field of fire clear.

To the rear, in the woods, the second and third corps were stationed as reserves. Here he met young Lieutenant Felix Uspensky, Kira's affianced, to whom he spoke a few words. Uspensky had the sort of very fair skin that showed clearly every movement of his blood; and he blushed deeply at receiving the personal attention of such a great man.

'Your wedding is planned for November, I understand?' Kirov added kindly as he was about to leave.

'Yes sir – that is, if the war is over by then.'

Kirov nodded. 'If we don't finish Napoleon off, the Russian winter will,' he said lightly, and Uspensky felt emboldened to smile at what was obviously a joke.

'We will beat them, won't we, sir?' he said, and what began as a statement mutated even as he spoke into a question.

Kirov looked at him with amused sympathy.

'Are you afraid, Lieutenant?'

'No, sir,' Uspensky said promptly; and then, responding to the smile in the eyes, more hesitantly, 'Yes, sir.'

Kirov smiled. 'Good. Only a fool wouldn't be afraid, and I shouldn't like my niece to marry a fool.'

'No, sir.'

'Of course, you never show fear to your men – they expect you to be more than human. That's what you're there for. And hiding it from them helps you hide it from yourself.'

'Yes, sir,' said Uspensky, and his eyes were shining with hero worship now. 'I understand, sir.'

Kirov began to find it a little embarrassing, and with a kindly nod, mounted his horse and rode on. It did not seem so very long ago that he was Uspensky's age, he thought wryly; now he was old enough to be regarded by him as a hero.

On the slope above the main battle area he paused and looked down. The bivouac fires were burning yellow and gold all across the plain, and around them the regular troops were polishing the buttons and boots of their best uniforms in preparation for the great day. Under the admiring eyes of the militiamen, they sang satisfyingly mournful songs, and boasted of the drunken nights they would enjoy in Moscow after the victory. Kirov felt a brief spasm of pity for them. Conscription to the ranks was for life: this war had brought them far from their home villages, which, win or lose, they would never see again. The regiment was now their home, and cold comfort that must be.

He turned his gaze upwards towards the hills, where so lately he had rested in Anne's arms. She must be safely away by now, he thought, and that was *his* cold comfort: the selfish part of him wanted her near. He thought briefly about making love with her, and shivered. Those thoughts were best not indulged in now; but afterwards, he thought, afterwards he was going to retire from public service – definitely retire this time – and dedicate the rest of his life to selfish pleasure. When this was over, he never wanted to go further from home than the boundaries of his estate.

Anne had watched the regiments marching up, watching with a mixture of anxiety and ironic amusement as they deployed themselves across the plain below her. So it was to be here, then, the battle for Russia! She felt a painful kind of excitement which made her stomach flutter. Since Vilna, nearly three months ago, everyone in Russia – perhaps everyone in the world – had been waiting for the clash between these two great forces; now it was to be here, in this very place! Borodino – an utterly unimportant little country town on a sleepy and sluggish little river, where nothing had ever happened, probably, in its entire history, more serious than a petty theft or a drunken tavern brawl. Now chance had marked it out for fame. She was going to witness history in the making. The prospect was terrifying, and yet exhilarating. Not for anything would she abandon her post now.

She expected some protest or rebellion from her servants, and eyed them cautiously as they watched the troops marching up; but they seemed to feel safe, or at least detached from the scene down below. Stenka and Zina, indeed, hardly cast a glance that way when their duties brought them onto the terrace. They had lived in this house all their lives, and it would never cross their minds to leave it. If the French had marched right in here, they would have effaced themselves, endured what came, and simply waited with peasant stoicism for the invaders to leave so that they could resume their lives.

Adonis came to deliver the Count's message, which was the expected one – that she should leave at once for a place of safety. She received it with outward docility, nodded obediently as though she were already packed and poised to leave; but when she met Adonis's eye, she saw that he knew she would not go.

'What will you tell him?' she asked, half anxious, half defiant.

'Nothing, now,' he said. 'It would do no good to worry him. Let him think you are safe away. If the need arises, I will tell him you are here.'

They regarded each other steadily for a moment, and then Anne's hands unclenched. 'Thank you,' she said simply. 'You are a good friend to him – and to me.'

He shrugged. 'We both serve him in our own ways.' He looked around. 'You'll be safe enough here, unless from deserters – it's too high and too far for the battle or the wounded. Have you a gun?'

Her eyebrows rose, but she said, 'There is a gun room. This used to be a hunting lodge.'

Adonis grunted. 'Take me there. Deserters on the run are usually desperate fellows. I had better show you how to load and fire a gun, just in case.'

'Oh, but I –'

'I have to be able to face him, if he is angry with me for not making you go. *When* he is angry with me,' he amended indifferently.

'You could not make me. It is not your responsibility.'

'He will know that, afterwards. But I will show you all the same.'

When he had gone, she had called her male servants together – coachman, groom and footman – and asked if any of them knew how to handle a gun. They all said they did; and after a brief pause, the coachman asked diffidently whether the French would come here.

'No. It is too far from the road. But there may possibly be deserters on the run,' she said, eyeing them cautiously. This was the moment, she thought, when their fears would surface.

But they had nodded calmly, and the coachman had said, 'We can frighten them off all right, Barina. Don't be afraid.'

'No,' she said, enormous relief vying with gratitude for their quiet loyalty. 'No, I'm not afraid.'

Early in the morning of the 5th of September the sound of gunfire was heard from the direction of the Gzhatsk – presumably a clash between the advancing French and Miloradovich's rearguard. Shortly afterwards the Cossack detachment came cantering over the brow of the hill, and after them the rearguard, retreating at a quick march to withdraw behind the safety of the Russian lines.

Within minutes, the French advance guard – General Murat's famous cavalry – appeared over the last rise and halted at the sight of the Russians drawn up below them. There was a stirring in the Russian ranks – for some of them, it was the first sight they had had of the enemy before whom they had been withdrawing for three months. Evidently the French felt something of the same interest: faintly on the breeze they could be heard cheering, and there was a flash in the sun as Murat himself drew his sword and held it aloft in a challenging salute.

The Russians replied with a roar. Loudest of all cheered the Cossacks, who, as part of the rearguard, had had a great deal of contact with Murat, whom they always referred to by his title of King of Naples. They had an exaggerated respect for him. His daring and courage in the face of the enemy was legendary; they liked his flamboyant, colourful clothing, his horsemanship, the way he was always to the front of his men, and the last to withdraw. He was like themselves, they thought, and they had agreed privately that if he was captured by them, he was not to be killed.

All day the French troops marched up, and were disposed across the field, while the Russian commanders observed them through field glasses, noting happily the depth of mud on their trousers and the thinness of their horses, and noting unhappily the still huge number of them. The sun began to slide down the afternoon sky, dipping behind the clouds on the horizon, throwing them into dark relief, so that they stretched like tattered, smoke-blackened banners over the sunset sky, their edges rimmed in liquid fire. It was a sky of portent, Kirov thought; and then smiled at himself. Any kind of sky would have been portentous, when two armies finally took position for battle within sight of each other.

Towards sunset, while the French rearguard was still marching up, Napoleon ordered the first attack, by a division of artillery and two of infantry, on the Russian forward position, the Shevardino redoubt. A tense hush fell across the main body of the Russian army as the French artillery peeled off and formed a line behind which the two columns marched steadily forward towards the redoubt. It was a silence of nervous tension, yet there was pleasure in it too, that at last the waiting was over. Suddenly the French fieldpieces spat fire, and sprays of earth shot upwards into the golden afternoon air; the guns of the redoubt boomed in answer, the sound echoing flatly off the hills; and the hillock disappeared behind a pall of smoke.

After the long wait to get to grips with each other, both sides fought furiously. Roundshot was loaded on top of cannonball, and the advancing French infantry fell in hundreds; the French loaded their fieldpieces with grapeshot and poured death into the Russian ranks. The redoubt had been hastily and inexpertly constructed, and the cannon were so mounted that they could not swivel, limiting their field of fire. As dusk fell, the French outflanked the redoubt, firing into the Russian ranks defending from the rear; a bayonet charge followed, the Russians were driven back, and the redoubt was taken.

It was a blow to pride, to see the Russian musketmen scrambling back to the line; but the redoubt by that time was filled with dead bodies and dismounted guns, its earthworks so severely battered that its usefulness was now minimal to either side. Nevertheless, the fiery Prince Bagration, unable to bear so early a reversal, or to allow the French first blood, on his own initiative marched a division of his grenadiers up to attack, and after another bloody interlude, drove the French out of the redoubt they had just possessed.

The sun had long set. In the twilight the French threw in another division, and in increasing darkness, made still darker by the smoke, the battle was renewed. It became almost impossible to tell friend from foe in the hand-to-hand struggle in the darkness; completely impossible for anyone even a hundred yards away to tell what was going on. Both sides seemed to have been seized by fighting madness; neither would yield, and as more and more men fell, it seemed that the battle would go on all night. At last, at ten o'clock, Kutuzov sent Colonel Toll to Bagration to order him to give up what was by now in any case a useless position, and leave the redoubt in the hands of the French. Reluctantly,

Bagration obeyed; the firing thinned out and ceased, and the Russians fell back.

During the night, Kutuzov sent Tolly and Kirov round the lines, counting divisions and making an estimate of the cost of the first action. Their calculations were depressingly high. Helped by Prince Bagration's freakish humour, they had lost six thousand men dead and wounded, as well as the eight heavy guns, which could now be used against them. It seemed a high price to pay for pride. Bagration stuck out his jaw and refused to defend himself, renewing the argument instead for reinforcements on his wing, especially for the defence of the old post road.

Kutuzov yielded, and sent Colonel Kirov to General Tuchkov with orders to take his 8,000 men of the third corps down to the rear of Utitsa. Young Uspensky, Kirov thought as he rode towards the reserves' position, was going to see action sooner than he had expected.

Anne heard the firing begin, and hurried out onto the terrace to look down. She saw the columns of the French advancing, heard the stirring trumpet calls, and even, tiny and far away, the ant-soldiers' cheers. When the guns fired, the tiny figures collapsed and tumbled down the slopes of the redoubt, and more took their place. It was hard to remember that they were real men, bleeding and dying amongst the lengthening shadows.

Soon smoke from the guns obliterated the scene. As darkness fell there was nothing to be seen but the orange flashes from the gunmouths, which occasionally silhouetted some soldier in his moment of personal drama. The cannon-fire sounded heavy and flat, like doors being continuously slammed; the musket fire prickled the darkness with a pattering sound.

Pauline came out to her to try to persuade her to come in, for it was cold and beginning to drizzle, but she could not bring herself to move. Why did they go on fighting? Surely they could not fight the entire battle in darkness? She had always understood that battles ceased at sundown. Pauline came out again with a cloak, but Anne did not even notice its being draped round her shoulders. Only when the firing tailed off and finally stopped did she become aware she was cold and hungry; but still she waited, needing to know what had happened, not knowing how she could come by that knowledge.

But as the smoke slowly cleared from the valley, the bivouac fires became visible like the stars coming out, pinpricks of still light in the blackness, spreading across the valley and up the hillside. There seemed a comfortingly large number of them. Of the Shevardino redoubt she could see nothing. It lay in the blackness between the two armies, and the dead needed no cooking-fire. She wouldn't think of that: she fixed her mind instead on the Russian soldiers cooking soup and buckwheat porridge in their bivouacs, and smoking their pipes and telling stories. The fires said that everything was still all right.

The cloak round her shoulders was dewed with rain. She shivered suddenly, and went in to supper and to bed.

The next morning, Friday the 6th of September, she was up early. She thought that the battle would probably begin at dawn; she dressed herself hastily without waiting for Pauline, and hurried out into the grey morning with her hair still hanging loose down her back. But all was quiet. Down below, there were the orange points of cooking-fires, their smoke rising in faint ribbons in the damp air. There were movements in the horse lines as the troopers tended their animals; small domestic comings and goings amongst the infantry lines. As the sun came up, it caught and flashed on stacked bayonet tips, glowed on the polished bronze of mute gun barrels. The sun alone seemed to have any sense of urgency.

She turned her eyes to the French camp, and saw similar activity. But there was one person riding from place to place on a white horse, and she wondered if that were Napoleon himself, inspecting his lines – the whole world knew of his predilection for white horses. She remembered him as she had seen him in Paris, the cold piercing eyes which his smile never touched. She reached into herself for some burning hatred to throw out at him, as if she might curse him from on high like an old Roman deity; but she felt nothing for him. The scene below was like something in a theatre: a story whose ending she wanted to know. It was not real life.

There was no battle. Throughout the day the two armies sat facing each other, and went on with their preparations, as if they knew in some way that it was not to be today. Some common consent seemed to invest them – as swallows will gather through a series of autumn days, and then fly all at once on one day no different, to the observer, from its predecessors.

Saturday, the 7th of September, Anne came out onto the terrace before sunrise, and saw the whole valley filled with white fog. The air was chill, the grass silver-grey with a heavy dew. She thought of the soldiers, waking on the hard earth to find their blankets heavy with it; the patient tethered horses, their thick manes beaded as if sewn with pearls, their sweet breath smoking on the cold air. She imagined them stirring, shifting from foot to foot and shaking themselves as the camp came slowly awake. Someone would rake up the cooking-fire embers, shivering as the thought of warmth made the dawn seem chillier; a twig thrust into the red and fluttering heart would suddenly bloom a golden crocus flame. The first troopers, stretching their stiff legs, banging their cold hands together, would go towards the horses; someone would chirrup, and a ripple would pass down the line: heads turning, pricked ears and soft whickers of eagerness as they looked for their morning feed.

He would be there, too, waking chilled under a blanket on his army cot; feeling the first morning stiffness of limbs, his old campaigner's mind waking before his body. Would he think of her? Perhaps for an instant, just once, before a thousand preoccupations, discarded for the brief night's sleep, crowded in on him. Adonis would come into his tent with hot water for shaving, bringing the damp smell of fog with him. She envied Adonis briefly and passionately for being able to be with him and useful to him; she was jealous of their man's intimacy which gave Adonis a place where she could not be.

The sun began to rise, turning the white fog to gold; down below bugles began to sound reveille, like cocks crowing defiantly in the dawn, challenging and answering from one invisible camp to the other. The mist began to thin and disperse and streaks of dark green appeared through it, as it caught and tore like gauze on the branches of the trees. The sun rose, golden and lovely, lifting effortlessly into the pale morning sky. The last of the mist was sucked up, revealing the amphitheatre below; a little steam rose from the ground as the night's dew evaporated in the growing warmth. It was going to be a fine day, she thought.

Below on the plain, breakfast was over. In each of the opposing armies, the company commanders formed up their men to read to them the Orders for the Day, the last words of good cheer from their Caesars to those who were going to die.

Pauline came out and stood beside Anne, her fingers tucked under her armpits, her arms clasping her body. The sun had not yet come round: it was still cold on the terrace in the shadow of the trees. Anne wondered it the significance of the scene below would be apparent to her; but after a moment Pauline said, 'Les pauvres! Voilà la betise des hommes, madame.'

Pauline had no vested interest in the outcome of the conflict: which ever side lost, she did not win.

'*C'est plutôt leur faiblesse*,' Anne said with sympathy.

The first shots were fired at six o'clock. Two divisions of French infantry attacked Borodino itself, which was held by an elite Russian Jaeger regiment of light infantry. Taken by surprise, the Jaegers were driven back, and soon were retreating up the hill towards Gorky. The French, cheered by the easy victory, unwisely went in pursuit, streaming after them with yells of excitement. General Tolly was watching the events on horseback from the higher ground and saw the chance. He turned the Jaegers who, with the advantage of the slope now in their favour, mounted a bayonet charge whose momentum cut the French down helplessly.

But battle had now been joined in the centre, on the plain between the two roads. The most tremendous crash signalled the beginning of the battle between the opposing artillery forces. Cannon spoke, and cannon answered; roar followed flash, palls of bitter black smoke roiled upwards, as though the earth had erupted in volcanic violence. The crashes became almost continuous, so that it was impossible to distinguish one gun's boom from another; and the noise was intolerable, blotting out thought itself.

This was a new kind of warfare, never seen before: a static battle between brazen monsters, bellowing their defiance, vomiting flame and iron, dealing death on an unprecedented scale; awesome, terrible in its inhumanity. Kirov and the other staff commanders watched from the high ground in grim silence. The smoke which covered the scene seemed almost genial, in masking this ultimate madness of mankind from human eyes.

Bagration's left flank was under attack now from French infantry. Only the right flank, protected by the hills, was still standing by. A further threat was developing along the lines Bennigsen had dismissed as nonsense: Napoleon's Polish regiments were coming up the old post road, and working their way round through the woods to the south to capture Utitsa, and outflank Bagration's front.

Lieutenant Felix Uspensky had been sitting on his horse in front of his men for two hours now, trying to keep his mind off the things that might happen to him. He had never been fired at before, having only lately come from cadet school. He had joined the regiment from the reserves only at Tsarevo, and his uniform was still fresh and new and clean, unlike those of the officers who had come all the way from Vilna. When he had first tried it on, it had seemed splendid in its newness, and he had longed to show it to Kira in its pristine state. Now it seemed shameful to be so spotless; he felt his inexperience keenly. But whatever happened, he thought, he would not let his fear show to his men; he would not let his father or Colonel Kirov down.

His father had given him his horse, Svetka, for his last birthday. Uspensky reached forward and stroked the gleaming chestnut neck, and turned a lock of mane back to the right side. Svetka was a pure-bred Arabian, the most beautiful creature Felix had ever seen, and he loved her more than anyone in the world – more, he thought guiltily, even than Kira. The sun cleared the hill behind him, warming his back, and Svetka, who was being remarkably patient, shifted her weight from one foot to the other and sighed a deep groaning horse sigh that made him smile.

He suddenly thought how lucky he was to be here, with his beautiful mare, on such an important day. It would be a thing to tell his children one day, (and his transparent skin blushed involuntarily at the thought of having children with Kira), that he had fought against Napoleon at the famous battle of Borodino. Perhaps he would do something tremendously brave, and the Emperor would give him a medal. That would be a nice thing to show his son one day.

He reached up and touched his untried blonde moustache, which Lolya had admired, and of which he was proud and doubtful in almost equal proportions. He wondered if the hair tonic that his father used on his scalp would make it grow faster . . .

Suddenly the woods in front of him were seething with movement. He jerked out of his daydream. Svetka waltzed sideways and back, and then Poniatowski's famous and battle-hardened Poles on their fierce little horses came roaring out of the trees directly towards him. Everything in his body seemed to drop two feet downwards like a stone, leaving him cold and empty and weak; but it was an officer's business never to show fear before his men. He knew that. An officer's duty . . .

'Come on!' he shrieked, kicking Svetka forward. She squealed in surprise – he had kicked harder than he meant – and sprang, almost unseating him as he fumbled for his sabre. His men roared approval and surged forward in his wake. Not Frenchmen, he found himself thinking, but Poles! Still, they were the enemy too. Poles, not Frenchmen. There was horse artillery, he noticed, and he felt a thrill of fear, but distantly, almost as if it belonged to someone else.

He was still yards before the enemy line when their fieldpieces spoke; he saw their round black mouths spurt flame, and was aware of his men going down on all sides like ninepins. Then he felt Svetka slew sideways under him, her legs going out cleanly from under her as she was shot dead through the heart by enemy musket fire. He tried to kick his foot out of the stirrup, had time for one panicking thought as she fell: ' – mustn't get trapped underneath – !'

Then there was an explosion so close it seemed to be right inside his head, an explosion that was also pain.

' – loud!' he thought in hurt surprise; and died. He didn't feel the ground come up to meet him, or the rest of the charge, carried by its momentum, trample over him.

Bagration's left wing was hard pressed, and the Prince sent again and again asking for reinforcements. His fortifications, the flèches, were taken by the French, but since they were open at the rear, the captors immediately found themselves under fire from the Russian ranks who had fallen back, and it was easy then to retake them. It was a pattern repeated throughout the day, capture and recapture, again and again; the heaps of bodies mounting before and inside the flèches, the battle line swaying back and then forward like some monstrous country dance.

Rayevsky's redoubt, the main defence in the centre, was taken by the French at around half past ten, and Rayevsky was wounded. Yermolov, Tolly's chief of staff, who was passing by just then with three companies of horse artillery, intended for reinforcements further down the line, saw what was happening and rallied the retreating Russians. Amid a terrible hail of lead, he mounted a counter-attack, and retook the redoubt; the French fell back for a moment, and then counter-attacked with fresh reinforcements.

Passing through the field dressing-station late in the morning on his way back to Tolly, Kirov found Bagration, his face drawn with pain, submitting to the attentions of the surgeon, who was trying to extract a shell fragment which had pierced his shinbone.

'Kirov!' the Prince shouted through clenched teeth; his face was cheesey with sweat. 'What the devil's going on? What's Tolly doing? Tell him the fate of the army is in his hands. My men are too hard pressed. I've already lost three of my division commanders. For God's sake, get me some reinforcements!'

Kirov reported back to General Tolly, who had already had two horses shot from under him that morning. He was as calm as ever, tall and thin and erect in the saddle like a monolith, riding here and there, always on hand where he was needed. His men adored him, as much as Bennigsen and his circle hated him.

'Bagration's off the field, wounded,' Kirov reported. 'I've just seen him in the dressing-station. He's asking again for reinforcements.'

Tolly nodded grimly. 'Yes, you can see for yourself from up here that the left wing's going to collapse if nothing's done. Go to Kutuzov, with my compliments, and tell him that the left wing must be relieved at once, or the day is lost. Try to stir him up, Kirov. God knows what he's doing up there.'

It was eleven in the morning when Kirov entered headquarters, which had been moved back to safety, to a small house behind Gorky. When he was admitted to the Commander in Chief's presence, he found him engaged with a leg of cold chicken in one hand, and a large piece of bread in the other. There were dirty dishes and several empty champagne bottles on the table. He and his aides had evidently been assuaging their mid-morning appetite.

Kutuzov listened impassively as Kirov delivered the message and added a few words of his own as to what he had seen of the situation on the left wing. The meaty red face, the blind white eye, were not designed for showing emotion; the portly, elderly figure was not designed for swift action. When Kirov stopped speaking, Kutuzov said nothing, and the Count wondered desperately if he had even been listening. He glanced at Colonel Toll, who was positioned, as usual, behind the Prince's chair, and raised his eyebrows in despair.

'Something must be done, Excellency,' Colonel Toll prompted.

'Yes,' Kutuzov said thoughtfully. 'What do you suggest, Toll? Send over some reinforcements? Who have we got?'

'Why not stage a diversionary attack on our right, Excellency?' Toll said eagerly. 'We've got Ouvarov's cavalry, and Ataman Platov's Cossacks up in the hills doing nothing. If they attack the French left wing and make plenty of noise about it, Napoleon will have to move some of his troops over. He's only got the Bavarians down there, in front of Borodino.'

'Good. Good.' Kutuzov waved the chicken bone in the air with brief enthusiasm. 'Excellent idea. See to it, will you, Toll? And Kirov. Right away. Let me know how it goes.'

Outside, Toll grinned and stretched with pleasure. 'A bit of action at last!' he said. 'I'll go and find Ouvarov. You ride over to the Cossack lines, will you, and tell Platov to liaise with Ouvarov right away. I shouldn't like to be those Bavarians when that little lot bears down on 'em.'

It was typical of Toll, Kirov thought, that he should think of a diversionary action, rather than simply sending reserves over to the left wing; but if it were properly carried out, it might well tie up valuable French forces on the right, and certainly relieve the pressure elsewhere. He mounted his horse and trotted off to find the Cossacks.

Fiery little Platov, who had left the army in a fit of pique during the long march from Vilna, and had only rejoined it when Kutuzov had replaced Tolly and promised a pell-mell battle, greeted the news enthusiastically.

'Orders are to make as much noise as possible – draw the French away from the centre. It's got to look like a major manoeuvre.'

'Don't worry, my friend – we'll make all the noise you want. Ha! Action at last!' Platov rubbed his hands together, controlling his fretting horse with his knees alone. 'I've got your son with me now, you know! Joined my command with his irregulars, now that scouting duties are over. Longing for a little action himself, I understand. Quite a fire-breather, that son of yours! You must be proud of him.'

'Yes, I am,' Kirov said automatically, but wondered at this description of Sergei. A fire-breather? Stern, grim – he would have expected those epithets. But probably Platov's judgements were very subjective – he would tend to attribute his own feelings to others.

As he was leaving the lines, Kirov came face to face with Sergei, who was leading his troop down from the higher hills. Sergei halted Nabat and waved his men past him, and for a moment father and son regarded each other gravely.

'I've just brought orders for action – the Cossacks are joining the first cavalry in an attack on Borodino. You'll be going with them, I suppose?'

'Yes,' Sergei said. He frowned. 'What's the purpose? We were told this morning we weren't to try to hold Borodino.'

'It's a diversion, to draw the French and relieve our left wing. The slaughter there is terrible.'

'I see. I'd better go and get my orders.' He was about to ride on, when Kirov held out his hand.

'Sergei – Seryosha!' It was a direct appeal to their former, warm relationship. Sergei paused, but his face was unyielding. 'For God's sake, let's put the past behind us. Let's be friends, this day of all others.'

'Friends, sir?'

'You're my son, for God's sake,' the Count said painfully. 'How have I offended you?' Sergei's eyes were flinty; he didn't answer. 'If

I have offended you, forgive me,' Kirov said, opening one hand in an instinctive gesture of both offering and asking.

Something flickered in Sergei's face; for an instant, there was the shine of something warm and human and lost and afraid in his eyes; for an instant his son looked back at him, and not the stranger he had become.

But the last of his troop had passed, and Sergei visibly pulled himself back from whatever brink he had teetered on. 'There's nothing to forgive, sir. If you'll excuse me, I must be with my men.' He saluted, and Kirov responded automatically, staring dazedly ahead of him as Sergei tapped Nabat's sides and trotted past.

From their vantage point, high up the hill, Anne and her servants watched in silence the struggle going on down below. Men within a battle have no perspective on it, see only the few feet around them, the danger immediately before them. When a man lunges at you with a bayonet, you have no alternative but to try to kill him before he kills you. The internal logic of a battle ensures that, once begun, it goes on, grips the combatants in the movements of a deadly dance from which they cannot escape.

But to Anne, looking down from far above it, it suddenly seemed like insanity. She saw the coloured ant-groups surge, come together like waves of water, and mingle. For a while they seemed to struggle breast to breast, and then break apart, only to reform and clash again. She saw positions stormed and taken, restormed and retaken. Why should men die for the possession of a small hill-top, or a mud embankment? Why didn't they just lay down their muskets and walk away? There was no sense in the battle down below. It was a slow, grinding struggle over a piece of ground unimportant in every way, save to the poor people who had once lived there, and grazed their animals on the grass which was now beaten under foot and soaked in blood.

It was hard to identify one side from the other. There was smoke not only from the cannon-fire, but from the little hamlets scattered about the battlefield, which had been set on fire and burned briskly. Dust also helped to obscure the view. The noise of the battle was like the roar of a huge crowd, muted by distance: no individual, distinguishable sounds, just a mingling of shouts and screams, battle cries, the shrieking of horses, the whine of bullets and the crash of guns and the rumbling of wheels.

And above it all, the serene life of the sky went on unheeding, the clouds passing over the sun, the sun tracking slowly across the autumn sky. High up in the air, an eagle soared and drifted on fringed wings, and tilted its head in distant wonder at the clamour of death in the valley below.

'Horsemen Barina,' said one of the men suddenly. It must have been about noon. Anne was dazed with the weariness of standing so long, and the exhaustion of too much emotion; his words brought her fully alert as though she had been slapped.

He was pointing away down the hill – and yes, there were the small moving shapes of horsemen on the track which wound through the trees. Six of them, she thought, presumably deserters fleeing the battle.

'We'd better get ready. They may not come here, but if they do . . . '

There was a flurry of movement on the terrace. Within minutes the three men and Anne were all armed and ready, and standing at the parapet's edge, watching to see what the horsemen would do. The path disappeared into the trees, and Anne found her hands growing damp with apprehension. There was no reasons to suppose they would come here – but what could they be doing? They were riding purposefully, but not fast. They came out of the trees again, and she saw now that the leading pair was carrying something between them. That accounted for their lack of speed; but what could they bring away from a battlefield? Was it plunder?

Now they were coming to the place where the path branched, one track continuing round the hillside towards the village of Novoye Syelo, the other branching steeply upwards towards Koloskavets. A breathless pause. The small moving shapes of the horsemen reached the fork – and turned upwards. Someone drew in an audible breath. The path led nowhere but to the house.

But Anne was staring hard at the leading horsemen. The thing they carried, slung between them, was a litter of some sort.

'Madame,' said Pauline, sounding puzzled. 'I think that is a wounded man.'

'Yes,' Anne said. 'Why would they bring a wounded man up here, and not to one of the dressing-stations?'

But she knew. They were near enough now to pick out the colours of their clothing. They were not regular cavalry: they were irregulars, Caucasus men. She knew before she could properly distinguish his cap that the one on the left of the leading pair was Akim Shan Kalmuck; and her heart turned sick in her. She knew who it was that he was bringing to her.

He told her he would be safe, that he would not take part in the battle! She had believed him, because there was no other way she could face the long wait for news. But in the back of her mind there had always been the dread, and now it came surging like Leviathan from the black depths to torment her. He had been wounded, and Akim Shan was bringing him to her to die.

The entrance to the house was at the back, through a small courtyard which led directly off the track down the hill. Anne was waiting there when the men, at her order, swung back the gate, and Akim Shan and his men filed through on their dusty, sweating horses. Even in her state of anguish, Anne could not help a twinge of admiration. It required a considerable feat of horsemanship to keep the two lead horses the right distance apart for carrying a litter, and they were not easy horses to ride in any circumstance, still less when upset by the noise of battle and the smell of blood. Akim Shan and his companion halted their mounts and kept them surging in phase with each other. As they came to rest blood could be seen dripping slowly from the litter onto the cobbles of the yard.

Anne's eyes met those of the Prince; hers in mute supplication, his veiled and hard. She found her voice, waved a hand to the men who were standing gawping at the tribesmen.

'Lift down the litter – carefully, carefully!'

'I have brought him to you,' Akim Shan said, checking his horse with one spurred heel as it tried to back away. 'His wound is severe – it will need all your skill, I think, to save him. But I could not leave him where he was. His courage deserved better than that.'

The absurd consideration – that he deserved to be brought to her because he had been brave; when if he been less brave, he might still be unwounded – maddened her: anger, fear, anguish, outrage, closed up her throat. She tried to swallow, tried to thank the Prince for what he had done; but her mouth was dry, and she could not find any words. The servants took hold of the litter, tilting it perilously, but managed to lower it to the ground. The man-shape lay there motionless, under the covering of a black burka.

She forced herself to go forward; and then a hand slid from under the cover and slipped bonelessly to the ground. Anne's eyes widened. She knew his hands, as she knew every part of him, better than her own.

'But that's not –' she began, puzzled; and stopped abruptly. Now she understood. She crossed the few feet to the litter, was down on her knees beside it in an instant, pulling back the stiff mantle, gently turning the dust-coated face towards her. He looked, in the repose of unconsciousness, heartbreakingly young; he looked very like Sashka, asleep.

'Oh Seryosha,' she murmured. Her eyes burned with pity, and with hideous guilt that her first reaction, for just the fraction of a second, had been a surge of wicked relief.

They were carrying him inside. She issued a flurry of orders to them, and turned back for an instant to thank the Prince for what he had done.

'Won't you rest, take something to eat and drink?'

'No,' he said. 'We begin our journey at once. It is a long way to the mountains.'

'You're going home?'

'Yes. There is no honour here.' He leaned down and fixed her with a fierce gaze. 'I will tell you what happened.'

In a few, vivid words he conjured the scene for her. It had been a colourful manoeuvre: the Dragoons in dark green, the hussars in yellow, the Cossack regiments in red and blue, and the irregulars in many colours, with the red Caucasus flashes; united in being, every one of them, superbly mounted. They bore down, shrieking, on the town of Borodino, whose trim white walls were looking increasingly battered. The dust from the baked-out earth rose in spurts at every hoof fall, and drifted into a knee-high fog. A diversionary tactic is meant to divert: noise and movement, a great deal of both, are of the essence.

'When the One-eyed ordered the attack, I thought, here at last is the place in the battle for me. Our charge would draw away the enemy, and though we died, we would have saved the day. This was the death that called me so many hundreds of miles!'

The Bavarians, unnerved by the sudden and violent attack, broke and ran for cover; Napoleon's Young Guards were hastily marched up to reinforce them, and then another regiment, easing the pressure, as had been intended, on the hard-pressed Russian Eighth Corps. The manoeuvre, as far as it went, has been a success.

But Akim Shan had wanted more. The Cossacks were skirmishers by nature and experience. They were not accustomed to pitched battle. They had joined the initial charge with enthusiasm, but when they came under fire, they had obeyed their instincts and taken evasive action, cantering about in and out of the bushes, avoiding the bullets and raising a great deal of dust, but achieving nothing.

'I felt their shame on me,' Akim Shan cried, and turning sideways, spat eloquently on the cobbles. 'They had sullied the action to which

I had committed my honour. And the fair one – I could see he felt it too, for the Russians, his own people, charged only so long as the enemy ran. When the enemy turned and stood, they turned too, and fell back.'

Not a strong enough force to withstand artillery fire, Anne thought in a dazed way, seeing the scene through two pairs of eyes, in two opposing lights.

'The fair one – he longed for honour. I saw it in his eyes! The shame was on him, to see his fellow countrymen show their cowardice. So he cried out to his own men, "Come, follow me! We will conquer, or we will die!" And I thought, truly, here is a leader worth the following. So I called my own men, and we rode with him.'

He straightened in the saddle, his eyes flashing.

'We galloped straight at the enemy, straight into their fire, and they cut us down like a sickle through ripe corn! But we killed as we went. We slashed to left and right, and they fell too, and their blood mingled with ours in the dust.'

Anne felt sickened, that he saw this as something to be proud of. How different, how irreconcilable were their minds!

'How – how did you escape?' she asked through a dry mouth.

'Our charge carried us right through their lines and out at the other side. These five of my men were all that were left to me. Then I saw that the fair one had been wounded, but he stayed in the saddle, and his horse carried him clear before he fell. I thought, there is no more honour here for me. I will not fight for cowards. So I bring him here to you, and take what is left of my men home.'

His narrative was done. 'I must go to him,' Anne said. 'Will you not stay?' He shook his head.

'Then – I can only say, thank you,' Anne said again, holding up her hand to him. He reached down and took it.

'I told you,' he said, 'that our third meeting would portend great good or great evil. I hope you may save the fair one; if you do not, glory in his honourable death! We shall not meet again, I think.'

'No,' she said. 'God bless you, Akim Shan, and bring you safe home.'

He whirled around, and in a clatter of hooves they were gone. Anne pushed the gates shut, and thought of the caged tiger in Akim's mountain fastness. Had Akim Shan been killed in battle as he had hoped, the tiger would also have died. Was she glad for the tiger, that its life had been spared, or sorry, that it's unending imprisonment would now continue?

Shaking the thoughts away, she hurried indoors.

Pauline looked up in frightened relief when she came in. 'Oh Madame, I don't know what to do for him,' she cried. 'There's blood everywhere!'

The three men were standing in a helpless group, staring round-eyed. They had put the litter down on the floor in the drawing-room, and already the slowly-dripping blood had made a puddle on the polished boards.

'We must stop the bleeding first,' she said, 'and then we must get him into bed. Yurka, go to the kitchen and bring me hot water and towels. Pauline, bring bandages – anything!' she forstalled the inevitable question. 'Petticoats, tablecloths, anything you can tear. Go now, don't argue. And ardent spirits – see what Stenka has. Brandy is best – but anything will do.'

Pauline hurried out after Yurka, and Anne turned to the coachman and groom. 'Now you two, I want you to find a bed, a narrow bed so that I can get round it, and bring it in here, and then fetch sheets for it. I want it in here in less than five minutes, do you understand? Go! Hurry!'

Left alone, she bent over the wounded man, appalled at the responsibility. She hardly knew where to start. His clothes seemed all to be soaked with blood, dank and heavy with it, and his face was pale under the dust. How much blood can a man lose and still survive? she wondered. She dragged off the burka and threw it aside.

The wounds to his thighs, she thought, looked superficial: the blood on his breeches had dried already. She began unbuttoning his jacket. His waistcoat was completely sodden with blood: the wound must be somewhere to his torso. The feeling of the blood-soaked cloth was horrible, the butchery smell of it sickening. Sergei did not move at all. Was he dead? But dead men did not bleed – she had read that somewhere. Find the bleeding first, and stop it, she told herself.

Under the waistcoat, the shirt. Wet and warm and palpitating. Her throat closed up, she had to force herself to go on. The shirt seemed to be in pieces, and she peeled it away, and reeled back in horror from the wound that gaped like an evil grinning mouth from his flesh. He must have been slashed with a sabre from the side as he rode through the enemy lines. She could see the gleam of bone, the red pulse of soft tissues. Oh dear God, it was worse than anything she had imagined! She would never stop the bleeding!

'Pauline! Pauline! Bandages!' she yelled, and the sound of her own voice frightened her, unrecognisable with panic. She stood up and dragged up her skirt, and began fumbling desperately with her petticoat, trying to pull it off. Undo the laces, she told herself, while panic fluttered whimpering round her body, and that pulsing wound mocked her feeble efforts. Carefully, or it will knot! She found an end with numb fingers and pulled and oh, thank God! it came loose. Her petticoat descended to her feet and she stepped out of it. She flung herself down again beside him; but she couldn't lift him single-handed, to slide the petticoat under him. She must have help! Where in God's name was Pauline?

A footstep. Her head jerked round – it was Zina with a can of hot water, and towels over her arm. Anne's desperate eyes met hers, deep and dark in a mesh of wrinkles. What use would this old woman be? Where was Pauline?

'Poor young man,' Zina said unemphatically, 'Let me help you, Barina. This is not work for a lady.'

The old fool, Anne thought furiously. 'Go and fetch my maid! Hurry!'

But Zina lowered herself painfully to her knees on the other side of the litter, and her brown, shiny, hands, strong from a lifetime of labour, were slipping under Sergei's body.

'Now, Barina, lift with one hand, and push the petticoat through to me with the other,' she said, just as if they were doing nothing more extraordinary than making beds. Anne controlled her panicking rage, and did as she was told. Everything moved as though ordered by God; she felt the petticoat taken from her, and now Zina was drawing it round, covering that terrible, unnerving wound from sight.

'If you fold a towel, Barina, and put it over the wound before I draw the bandage tight, it will help,' Zina's quiet voice went on. Anne felt herself sinking back under control. Pressure to slow the bleeding, she thought; we need a doctor to stitch it up, but for the moment, pressure to slow the bleeding.

'Yes,' she said. 'All right.'

'Stenka's helping the men bring the bed,' Zina went on. 'Poor young man – was he in the battle, Barina? What a dreadful thing! Do you know who he is?'

The question took Anne by surprise. 'He's the son of – the son of – '

Zina nodded wisely. 'Ah. Then his father will have to be told.'

Anne hadn't thought of that. 'Yes, of course.'

'When the sun goes down, they'll stop the fighting,' Zina said comfortably. 'One of the men can go down and tell him then.'

The bed was brought, and Pauline reappeared, pale and wet-eyed, with a heap of linen which she began to rip into bandages. While the men set up the bed and put the sheets on, Zina and Anne hoisted Sergei into a sitting position against their shoulders – Zina showed her how – so as to pull off his sodden coat, waistcoat and shirt. That was when they found he had been wounded in the back, too – a bullet wound. It was bleeding very little, but at the sight of it the last of Anne's hope quietly died. There was no corresponding wound of exit. The bullet must still be inside him, which meant that he would certainly die, of fever and mortification, if he didn't bleed to death first. She did not fool herself that there was any chance of getting a surgeon up here to operate on him in time, even if such an operation had any chance of success.

She and Zina exchanged a silent look over his limp body, and took the first of Pauline's bandages and bound this second wound, too. Under Zina's direction, the men lifted Sergei onto the bed, and there the women washed him, and made him decent. He was still alive, though unconscious – Anne could feel the pulse fluttering under his jaw. All that was left, she thought, was to try to keep him alive as long as possible, and to get word to Nikolai.

The men went out onto the terrace from time to time, but Anne had no more interest in the battle. To slow the bleeding, to keep him warm – these were all she could do, but she would not leave his side. He might return to consciousness – she must be near him. As the afternoon progressed he began to show signs of life: first the flutter of eyelids, then a slight movement of the head, and his lips moved soundlessly. The movements increased. At first Anne thought he was disturbed by the distant sounds of the battle, just audible through the open windows onto the terrace; but it gradually became plain that the restlessness was caused by a fever, which was probably due to the presence of the bullet inside him. When he moved the bleeding grew worse, and she and Zina struggled to keep him still.

Suddenly, at about four o'clock, he opened his eyes, staring upwards at the ceiling. He seemed blankly bewildered; then he frowned with pain, and passed the tip of his tongue over his lips.

'Thirsty,' he whispered.

Anne had wine and water ready mixed in a cup. She slipped a hand under his head and lifted it a little, and put the cup to his lips. He closed his eyes and sipped, and again, and then sighed. She laid his head down again, and he turned and looked at her.

He didn't seem to understand at first. 'Anna?' he whispered. 'Am I ill?'

'It's all right. You're safe. You're in my house up in the hills. Someone brought you here when you were hurt.'

He frowned. 'Hills? What hills?'

'Above Borodino,' she said.

'Oh. I thought I was at Pyatigorsk.' He closed his eyes; then they flew open. 'Borodino! The battle! Is it – ?'

'It's still going on. No, don't move – you'll start the bleeding again. Lie still, Seryosha.'

'What's happening? Have they broken through?'

'No, no, the lines are holding. They won't break through.'

'Thank God,' he muttered. Then he smiled, a travesty of a smile that made her want to cry out. 'They always say it's not enough to kill a Russian – you still have to push him over!'

He was silent, gathering his thoughts; then, 'What happened to my troop?'

'I don't know,' she said. It was easier than trying to explain.

'No,' he said. 'No, I don't suppose you would.' He sighed, and closed his eyes. 'Hurts,' he said. 'Hurts to speak.'

'Rest, then,' she said. 'I won't leave you.'

He gave the glimmer of a smile. 'Anna,' he said. Then, 'Sleep now.'

Time dragged its leaden feet through the weary day. The fever mounted; the restlessness grew worse, and he didn't seem to know where he was. It was hard to keep him still. She tried to call him to consciousness, but when he opened his eyes, they only rolled sightlessly with delirium, recognising nothing. The flow of blood increased. Anne dared not remove the bandages. They added more layers, and more as they soaked through.

The evening drew towards dusk, the air cooled, and Sergei grew quiet. The firing from below was dying down. Soon Nikolai would come. Please God he would be in time.

Sergei woke, looked at her blankly. 'Where am I?'

'At my house,' she answered.

'Anna? Is that you?' he whispered.

'Yes, Seryosha, I'm here.'

'I can't see you. Don't leave me! It's dark. I'm so cold, so cold.'

It was still light in the room. She touched him with alarm, and felt the unnatural chill of his skin. She flicked a glance at Zina, who hurried off to fetch another blanket.

'I won't leave you,' she said, stroking his head. 'Don't be afraid.'

He turned his head into her caress. His face was pure white, alabaster white, like a carving in marble of a dead hero. How long could he survive such loss of blood?

He drifted, and came back to himself.

'Anna?' he said, as if he had just recognised her. 'Am I ill?'

'You're wounded,' she said with difficulty.

'Did I have a fall?' he asked. 'No – I remember. Borodino. We charged – charged the Germans.'

She saw he was rational now. His voice was hardly more than a whisper, but his eyes looked into hers with painful intelligence.

'Seryosha, why did you do it?' she asked suddenly. Akim Shan might talk of his longing for honour, but she didn't believe that was Sergei's reasoning. She had a deep inner fear that he had deliberately sought his death, and the end of his mental torment, which had begun that bloody day high in the mountains of the Caucasus. The tiger's death he had sought, swift and merciful; but fickle chance had delivered him up to the jackal.

'You were told not to try to take the town – only to cause a diversion,' she said. 'Akim Shan told me you – you went on, when everyone turned back. Why, Seryosha?' She met his eyes, and his were sad and guilty and puzzled.

'I don't know,' he said. She stroked his cold cheek again, not trusting herself to speak. He sighed. 'Perhaps I wanted to escape.' But you can't escape. What you are comes with you, always, always. He closed his eyes.

Zina came back with the blanket and they tucked it round him. Anne slipped her hand down to his side, and felt the bandages only slightly damp. The bleeding was slowing – or was it that he had too little blood left?

She thought he had drifted away again; but after a moment, without opening his eyes, he said, 'Anna? Did you ever love me?'

She couldn't answer for a moment. She looked at his pale composed face with a love and pity that tore deeply at the fibres of her heart. He might almost have been her child – within her body a child now grew who was his brother. She ached to save him hurt, to preserve him, protect him, hold him close; and there was nothing she could do.

'Yes,' she said at last. 'I loved you – I do love you.'

'I'm sorry,' he said, and she had to lean close to catch his words – his voice was only a murmur. 'I'm sorry it's like this.'

The light was fading outside, and one star was shining clear and steady in the pale green evening sky. Sergei began to yawn, as men bleeding to death often will. He had drifted away from her in his thoughts, back to the safety of his troop. After a long silence he muttered, 'Don't forget the horses. See to the horses first.'

*

It had been dark for a long time. The firing seemed to have died down, except for long rumblings, which sounded like distant thunder, from the direction of Utitsa. The main battlefield had fallen silent. It was silent inside the room, too. A lamp glowed softly in the corner, throwing its light over the bent head of Zina, who was dozing in an armchair. Anne sat beside the bed, watching Sergei. She had been still for so long, that perhaps she had dozed, too; at any rate, she had the feeling of coming suddenly to herself at the sound of voices and footsteps on the stairs.

She rose to her feet as though pulled by a string, and ran out into the hallway. Nikolai was coming up the stairs in a swirl of movement, with Stenka shuffling behind him as fast as he could, crying 'Barina! Barina! He's here!'

'Oh, thank God you've come!' Anne was across the landing and in his arms in an instant. He pressed her to him, smelling of sweat and smoke; his cloak was damp from dew; he was trembling all over, and breathing fast, as though he had been running. Their embrace lasted only an instant; she was drawing him towards the room, asking as they went. 'Is it over? Is the battle over? We could still hear cannon-fire in the distance.'

'Just a flank movement on the old road. Action's broken off everywhere else – the French have fallen back.' Nikolai's eyes went ahead of him, searching for their punishment. 'When I got back to headquarters there was a message from your prince, about Sergei. I didn't know you were still here.'

'I couldn't leave,' she said. 'Is the battle won?'

Through the door, his hold breaking away from her. 'God knows. Our losses are heavy.' His eyes found the shape in the bed. 'How is he?'

She didn't know how to tell him, but she didn't need to. When she didn't speak, he turned abruptly and read her face, and his mouth turned down bitterly. He went to the bedside and took the seat Anne had vacated, reached over for his son's hand. 'Sergei,' he said. 'It's me, it's Papa. Seryosha, look at me.'

Sergei muttered and turned his head. Please, Anne prayed inside her mind, please let him wake, let him know him . . .

'Seryosha, it's Papa. Can you hear me?'

Sergei opened his eyes, frowning. He licked his lips, and then yawned again. 'Cold,' he muttered.

Nikolai leaned closer. Tears left clean tracks down his smoke-grimed face. 'I love you,' he said; stroked the hair from the marble brow and kissed it. 'Forgive me, Seryosha. Say you understand.'

But Sergei's eyes were wandering. Anne could see he did not recognise his father.

'Don't forget the horses,' he muttered. He turned his head away, staring towards the window, held apart in the loneliness of dying. An expression of great bitterness crossed his face, as if he had suddenly seen everything with great clarity, the whole futility and waste of it, the life he had been robbed of. Anne, watching him, did not see the moment when he went. Only she became aware that the look of bitterness had faded little by little, as the light fades gradually out of the sky after the sun has gone; and suddenly from being twilight it is night, without there being one particular moment when one could say the transition occurred.

Chapter Thirty

Some time after midnight, Adonis arrived at the house, and was admitted by Stenka, who showed him silently into the drawing-room. Adonis took in the scene with one comprehensive glance; the body on the bed, covered with a burka; the old woman asleep in the chair beside it; and Anne and Nikolai on the day bed near the window, she seated, he lying down with his head in her lap.

Anne's eyes, red-rimmed but sleepless, met his blankly over the Count's head.

'He's sleeping,' she said.

Adonis looked grim. 'We're pulling out. You'll have to go too. It won't be safe here. You'll have to wake him.'

But he was stirring already. He woke from the dead sleep of utter exhaustion and looked up blankly at Anne for a moment, and she longed, helplessly, to give him a little longer in blessed oblivion.

'Adonis is here,' she said gently.

He blinked, and then groaned and pulled himself upright. That waking, he thought afterwards, was the worst of his life. He was more tired than he had thought it possible to be. Every bone in his body ached; his eyes were gritty in their sockets, his mouth was dry and foul-tasting, his head ached; but worse than all of that was the dead weight of grief that rolled onto his chest like a stone, as memory returned.

'Adonis,' he said thickly. 'What's happening?'

'New instructions, Colonel,' he said neutrally. 'The Prince-General ordered us to regroup, to renew the battle at dawn, but when they counted up our losses, he changed his mind. We're withdrawing past Mozhaisk. The artillery's on the move already – infantry to move off at two o'clock. Cossacks to provide a rearguard and cover our retreat.'

The succinct report cleared the fog from Kirov's head. 'What were our losses?'

'Forty thousand, by the first reckoning – dead and wounded.'

In the silence, Kirov heard Anne's indrawn breath of disbelief. The number was past comprehension.

'And the French?' he asked.

Adonis shrugged. 'As many, I'd say. They pulled back, out of sight of the battlefield, but by the numbers of the dead, it must be as many.' Kirov nodded, and then put his head into his hands to rub his temples. Adonis eyed him with sympathy. 'Orders, Colonel? You're wanted pretty badly at headquarters.'

Kirov looked up sharply. 'I must bury my son. Then I'll leave. I must bury him first. The General will understand that. As soon as it gets light . . . '

Adonis was not a Russian, and looked as though he would like to argue; but he held his tongue. Even on the march, with the French on their tails, the soldiers had continually stopped to bury their dead, leaving a shallow mound and a hastily knocked-together wooden cross over each. He couldn't expect his master to do less for his own son.

In the grey light of dawn, they set off down the track, turning onto the road that led past the ruins of Novoye Syelo to join the main road just beyond Gorky. Anne had left Stenka and Zina with warm thanks for their loyalty and help, and promised them a more tangible reward when the troubles were over. They accepted her thanks stolidly, and stood silently in the yard to see her off, looking as though they had grown up out of the cobbles: permanent, enduring.

Anne and Pauline climbed into the carriage; Nikolai and Adonis mounted their horses. Behind the courtyard, in the strip of rough grass between the house and the tree line, there was a newly-formed mound of brown earth. Kirov looked back at it as they rode out of the gate. They had buried Sergei in the ground, wrapped in the burka: they had no coffin for him. Stenka had promised to cover the mound with stones, to keep the winter wolves from digging it up.

As the sun began to rise, the battlefield below was revealed in all its horror, a swath of fallen men and horses, thousands dead, thousands still suffering and moaning in their mortal pain. Scattered amongst them were broken lances, shattered breastplates and helmets, shell fragments, splintered gun carriages. Around the fortifications, now battered almost level, the bodies lay in heaps like discarded rags, mute witness of the many times the defences had changed hands in the course of the battle. In the stream gullies, where the wounded had instinctively dragged themselves to be out of the firing, they were tangled and heaped, living and dead together; the wounded drowning in their own blood, crying pitifully for help, or at least for a bullet to end their misery.

The road towards Moscow was packed with the retreating army, marching wearily, but in good order. Six miles distant, the town of

Mozhaisk was already filled with wounded, who had managed to drag themselves thus far, hoping for transportation to Moscow and hospital treatment. Here a young white-faced subaltern met them with obvious relief, to say that Kirov was wanted urgently, and Colonel Toll was looking for him.

'Wait one moment,' Kirov told the boy, and dismounting, walked stiffly up to the carriage window. He reached up and clasped Anne's hand. 'Go on to Moscow as fast as you can. Don't stop for anyone, or you may find your carriage stolen from you. When you get there, you had better hide the horses. We've already asked Rostopchin several times for horses to transport the wounded, and anything that moves in Moscow will have been requisitioned or stolen by now.'

'Yes. I understand.' She felt keenly his ability in the midst of everything to feel such minute concern for her.

'I'll send word to Byeloskoye when I can. I suppose we'll make another stand further down the road, but where remains to be seen. Keep yourself safe at all costs.'

'Yes, Nikolai,' Anne said dutifully. He lifted her hand to his lips and kissed it once, and then he was turning away, duty calling him relentlessly. 'God bless you!' she called after him, but he didn't seem to have heard. She watched him take his horse's rein; but her coachman, understandably nervous, cracked his whip and drove on before she had even seen him mounted.

The last few miles of the road into Moscow were packed with refugees, deserters and wounded soldiers. Anne had been forced to travel slowly, since there was no possibility of a change of horses. She began to appreciate the value of the pair she had harnessed up, and told Tolka that if anyone tried to stop them, he was to whip the horses up and run them down if necessary. Many people looked round as they heard the horses coming, and once or twice wounded men hailed them and begged for a ride into the city, but Tolka obeyed orders, and they trotted past with the window blinds drawn. When they finally turned into the yard at Byelsokoye, Anne drew a sigh of relief. She ordered the porter to keep the gate locked at all times, and to let no-one in without permission; and told Stepan to arrange with the other grooms to keep guard over the horses twenty-four hours a day.

Mikhailo opened the door to her with a mixture of surprise and relief which would have amused Anne if she had not been so tired.

'Oh, Barina! Praise be to the saints you are safe! When we heard there had been a battle at Borodino, we were sure you had been killed.'

'Thank you, Mikhailo. I am perfectly well. Is the master here?'

'Yes, Barina – in the drawing-room. But is it true the French are coming? They say our army is in retreat. We hear such things Barina! No-one seems to know if the battle was won or lost – '

'The battle was won. Our army is withdrawing to a new strongpoint, to make another stand, that's all. There's nothing to be afraid of,' Anne said, walking towards the stairs.

'Yes, Barina,' Mikhailo said grimly.

Anne knew she had not sounded convincing. 'I'm very tired, and hungry from the journey,' she said, as if in explanation. 'Bring me up something to eat at once, will you?' And she hurried up the stairs before he could ask her anything else.

In the drawing-room, she found Basil, Jean-Luc and Rose sitting on the floor in front of the fire, playing spillikins. Basil's face was strained, and there were dark circles under his eyes, as though he had not slept much of late; he looked up as she entered, with apprehension changing to relief when he saw her. Jean-Luc looked as he always did, and his expression was inscrutable – but, he was an actor, and that was his business. She could never tell what he was thinking.

Rose looked pale and listless, but her face lit up flatteringly, and she cried out 'Maman!' and began at once to pull herself up by a chair leg. Anne was across the room in an instant, and swept her daughter up into her arms. Rose's arms went round her neck, and she planted a wet kiss on Anne's cheek, and then complained loudly, 'You missed my birthday Maman! I was three years old and you weren't here! Papa and Zho-Zho wanted to give me a party, but there's no-one here any more. Did you bring me a present?'

Anne kissed and hugged her, and then put her down. 'No, darling, I couldn't. When the war is over, I'll buy you a lovely present, but not now.'

'Are the French coming?' Rose asked with interest. 'Everybody's run away, except Papa. He's very brave.'

Anne met Basil's eye, and he gave a faint, weak smile, and shook his head.

'I'll tell you everything later,' he said with a significant look at Rose.

'I'll take Rose down to the kitchen,' Jean-Luc said, rising gracefully to his feet in one movement. 'Shall we go and make a surprise for Maman, *poupée*?'

Rose was easily beguiled out of the room, and when they were alone Anne said, 'I must admit I'm surprised to find you here, Basil

Andreyevitch. I'd have thought you'd go straight to Petersburg from Tver, in view of the situation. What brought you back?'

'Mainly the sight of so many carts laden with possessions heading out of Moscow,' he said. It might have been a joke, but it wasn't. 'Ever since the end of August, when the news arrived about Smolensk, people have been evacuating the city. So we came back to see about the valuables.'

Anne stared at him in amazement. 'You thought your possessions were in danger here – so you brought Rose back?'

He coloured. 'Don't speak to me like that. I love my daughter just as you do.'

Anne knew there was no point in quarrelling with him. She controlled her voice and said more quietly, 'Very well. But why did you come back into what you believed was danger?'

'Grand Duchess Catherine said there wasn't any danger,' he said sulkily. 'She said that once Prince Kutuzov took command, the retreating would stop, and there'd be a battle, and it would all be over. But I thought I ought to be here just in case. I thought I could still get Rose away in plenty of time if things did take a turn for the worse.'

'Everyone seems to think they have. Didn't Rose say everyone's run away? So why are you still here?'

'We did try to leave two days ago, but the damned peasants had barricaded all the city gates, and they wouldn't let anyone out – not the men, at any rate. They said it was cowardly, and that every able-bodied man had to stay and fight the French. They turned us back.'

Anne considered him gravely, but Basil's eye slid away. 'There's more, isn't there?' she said.

He nodded reluctantly. 'After we got back here, a dozen police officers came with an order from the Governor, requisitioning the horses.'

Anne remembered Kirov's words. He had had a foresight Basil apparently lacked. 'Well?' she said impatiently. 'You refused, of course?'

'How could I refuse? They were on official business. They had papers.'

Anne grew pale with anger. 'You let them take the horses? You imbecile! You idiot! You – how could you let them just take them?'

'They were in an ugly mood, and armed,' he said defensively. 'I suppose they'd had trouble with other people already.'

'Trouble? I'd have given them trouble! I'd have waded in their blood before I let them – ' She stopped abruptly, her eyes widening, and he shrank into himself, knowing what the next question would be. 'Quassy too?' she whispered.

He nodded unhappily.

Anne had no words. Quassy too, her mind repeated numbly. Quassy too.

'They'd have taken her in the end, anyway, or she'd have been stolen,' he said peevishly. 'Everyone's been trying to get out of the city. Rostopchin commandeered every horse he could find to move the city archives and public records, so even the most broken-down, spavined nag is fetching a ridiculous price, if you can find one. People have taken to stealing from anyone who has one left.'

Anne shook her head, unable for the moment to speak. Quassy, her lovely Quassy, given her by Nikolai, and Image, whom she had watched being born, and trained with her own hand.

'They didn't take Rose's pony,' Basil offered in a small voice. 'We managed to hide him. He's bedded down in one of the pantries behind the kitchen.'

She almost laughed at this pathetic attempt at placation. She drew a shaky breath and said, 'It's as well I came back when I did, or I'd have found nothing left at all.'

'But what really happened at Borodino?' he asked, relieved that the storm had apparently passed him. 'We hear such rumours, but no-one seems to know what's really happening. Rostopchin sends out proclamations all day long, and each one contradicts the last.'

Mikhailo came in with her nuncheon, and when he had gone, Anne told Basil, between mouthfuls, what she had witnessed of the battle.

'So did we win or lose?' he said at last.

'I don't know that either side could claim a victory. At the end of the day, our lines were still intact, and the French fell back. But Kutuzov ordered a withdrawal. The intention is to make a new stand somewhere further along the road, but I don't know where. At all events, the army is still between the French and us. There's nothing to be afraid of.'

'So why has Rostopchin removed all the city archives and treasures?'

'As a precaution, I suppose,' Anne said. 'I don't believe for a moment the French will be allowed to get this far, but if you're worried, you and your friend can go away, now that I'm here to take care of Rose.'

'I told you,' he said, 'they aren't letting men leave the city. In my case, do you think I'd save my skin and leave Rose here?'

'I don't know what you're likely to do,' she retorted, then she sighed and looked away. There was no point in provoking him to a quarrel. 'If you're really worried, at the first sign of danger Parmoutier can take Rose to the Danilovs. They'll take care of her. I don't like to think of her travelling without the protection of a man, but it would be all right just as far as Tula.'

'Anna – ' Basil began, and she met his eyes to read a message of even greater disaster there.

'What is it?' she asked, and felt a stirring of nameless alarm.

'Mademoiselle – she – she isn't here any more.'

'What are you talking about?'

'It was when we came back from Tver. I told you there were barricades on the city gates. They were stopping every carriage. They told us that we were welcome to come back, but that we wouldn't be allowed to leave again. Then Rose started asking questions, and Mademoiselle was answering her in French, trying to soothe her.'

He stopped, and swallowed. Anne saw his adam's apple rise and fall in his thin neck.

'Go on,' she said into that deadly silence.

'They must have heard her. Someone shouted out, she's French, isn't she? – and – and some other things, abusive things, and about Moscow being full of French spies. I said no, she was Belgian. I told them the Belgians hated the French just as much as we did. But they didn't believe me. They wouldn't even listen. They pulled her out of the carriage, said they were going to take her to the Governor for questioning. She – she didn't make a fuss – for Rose's sake, I suppose. She just – ' He stopped and swallowed again, his eyes wide and blank, as if seeing the scene again in memory. 'She went with them.'

Anne's mouth was dry. 'Where did they take her?'

'I don't know. They made us drive on, because there were other coaches waiting.'

'What have you done to try to find her?'

'I went to the Governor, had a private interview with him. He was very good about it. He sent a party of police up there to the barricade, and arrested some people, and questioned them, but he didn't find out anything. I asked for a search to be made for her, but he said he didn't have the manpower, that there were more important things to do – '

'More important?'

'He said people were disappearing every day, leaving the city – how could he hope to find one French governess?'

'Belgian!' Anne suddenly shouted. 'She was Belgian!'

Basil flinched, but went on speaking quietly. 'We just hoped she'd come back on her own somehow. We told Rose she'd gone away for a few days to help the Governor interrogate spies, and she seems to believe it. She hasn't asked anything, except when Mademoiselle is coming back.'

She was dead, Anne thought bleakly, dead for sure; dragged out of the coach by a mob . . . She didn't want to think how her death might have been achieved. Instead she took refuge in anger. 'Of course your precious Jean-Luc managed to escape! He who is really French! He kept his skin whole!'

'He kept his mouth shut. Anyway, he's an actor. It's no use blaming him, Anna,' he said quietly. 'It's my fault, for not protecting her better.'

The confession took her aback, silenced her. She suddenly felt very tired. 'Oh God,' she said, 'what's happened to the world?'

Later, when Rose had gone to bed, the three adults gathered in the drawing-room again. For once Anne did not object to Jean-Luc's presence. It seemed natural in the circumstances to draw together, like threatened animals.

Anne said again, 'I don't believe that the French will reach Moscow. The army withdrew in good order, and though the losses at Borodino were heavy, they weren't mortal. Our army is still well supplied, whereas Bonaparte's grows weaker with every mile. Kutuzov will make a stand somewhere between Mozhaisk and here, and make an end of it.'

'All the same . . . ' Basil said thoughtfully.

'Yes,' Anne concurred. 'All the same, I should prefer for Rose to leave as soon as possible, if only we could think of a way. I could take her myself – '

'It would be too dangerous,' Basil said. 'A gentlewoman travelling alone, without male escort. You'd be attacked and robbed before you'd gone ten versts. There are deserters and looters everywhere.'

'I know, but . . . ' Anne frowned in thought. The roads were dangerous, it was true – she had seen something of it at first hand. Better that Rose stay with her in Moscow than that she be the victim of desperate deserters. Probably the French wouldn't come; but if they did – she didn't want her child frightened again, as she must already have been by the mob who murdered her governess.

'Listen, I have an idea,' said Jean-Luc suddenly. He fixed Anne with a steady eye. 'I know you don't like me – ' Anne's lip curled involuntarily, and he flushed a little. 'All right, I know you hate me

– but at least you must know that I love Rose, and that she loves me.'

Anne shrugged. She had never been convinced on that point. 'Perhaps. What of it?'

'You must trust her to me. Yes! Listen! I can get her out. I am an actor, remember, and I specialise in playing women. When I am dressed as a woman, no-one can tell the difference – *no-one*! I'll get Rose past the barricades all right, disguised as a peasant woman, and take her wherever you like, and wait for you there.'

Anne was taken aback. 'But – but what's to stop you being robbed for the horses? They'll still think you're a defenceless woman.'

He grinned. 'Ah, but I won't be, will I? And I won't take the horses. I'll walk.'

'Walk?'

'We'll put Rose on her pony, dressed in peasant clothes, and with a bundle tied on behind. Make the pony look as shabby as possible – daub it with mud, chop its coat to make it look mangey. And I'll walk, leading her. There'll be nothing to tempt a gang to attack us.'

'But you can't walk all the way!'

'Once I'm clear of the city, I'll get a cart of some kind, and harness the pony. You can give me money. I'll take a pistol, hide it in my clothes. It'll be all right. Once I'm past the city limits, everyone will help me. The peasants are very good to their own kind on the tramp. We can do it. But you have to trust me.'

'I – I don't know,' Anne said doubtfully. 'Maybe I ought to take her myself.'

Jean-Luc snapped his fingers with exasperation. 'You couldn't do it! Come, Anna Petrovna, use your brains instead of your feelings! You hate me, I know – but deep inside, you know that I love that child. You, her own mother, couldn't love her more. I will take her to safety and keep her there, until you come.' His glance took in both of them. Basil was pale and silent. It was his whole life that was about to leave him – his lover and his child – but he was staring necessity in the face.

There was a scratching at the door, and Mikhailo came in, with a piece of paper on his silver tray.

'Excuse me, Barina, but one of the servants just brought this in. I thought you ought to see it.'

'What is it?' Anne asked out of the depths of her struggle.

'It's a proclamation from the Governor, Barina. They're being distributed in the streets.'

Anne took it and read it. It was a call to arms, to the defence of

Moscow. Everyone was exhorted to march out and add their weight to the army which was coming to make a stand at the very limits of the city.

' . . . Arm yourselves with whatever you can; come on horseback or on foot. Come with your crosses, take the pennants from the churches, and with these banners let us gather at the Three Hills. I shall be with you, and together we shall destroy the Villain . . . '

Anne read it, and then handed it to Basil in silence. The Governor would not have made such a direct appeal unless he thought the city was in danger. The necessity to trust Jean-Luc had just increased tenfold.

'Is it an adventure?' Rose asked. In peasant dress, she was seated on Mielka, who had bits of straw in his mane and tail and stable-stains on his quarters and belly. Jean-Luc was unrecognisable. His long hair in a plait down his back, a scarf tied round his head, a coarse wool skirt over many petticoats, a serge jacket, and a ragged shawl round his shoulders – these were the accoutrements: but the change was deeper than that. It came from within him. Anne saw that it would be impossible for anyone to guess that he was not a peasant woman, because inside him he *was*.

'Take care of her,' Anne said.

He met her eyes. 'With my life,' he said.

'If you can get as far as Tula, take her to the Danilovs. They'll take care of you both. I'll send word when it's safe to come back – or I'll come for her myself. You have the money safe?'

'Yes, of course. And the knife, and the pistol. But don't worry – we'll be perfectly all right. It's an adventure, as Rose says.'

Anne kissed her daughter, trying to appear casual, for her sake. 'Goodbye, darling. Do just what Jean – what Zho-Zho tells you. I'll see you again soon.'

Rose kissed her goodbye without concern; but when she turned to her father, and saw his expression, she was frightened, and turned back to fling her arms round her mother's neck. Anne soothed her as best she could, but when at last she released the arms from round her neck, Rose's lip was quivering. There had been too many departures lately; and Mademoiselle had never come back. Rose didn't ask about Mademoiselle . . . or Nyanya, or her cat. Glad enough that she still had Mielka and Zho-Zho, she had sooner trust to silence to restore her, some time in the future, to her normal life.

Anne turned her head away while Basil said goodbye to Jean-Luc; and then the porter opened the gates, and they slipped out into the

549

grey, twilit street. As the gate closed, there was nothing to be seen but a peasant woman leading her child on a scruffy pony.

'They'll be all right,' Anne said as they turned away.

'Yes,' said Basil.

Their voices revealed that she believed it at last, just as he ceased to.

The response to the Governor's appeal was magnificent. A huge mob of men and women tramped the three miles out of the city to the Hill of Salutation, armed with pitchforks, scythes, axes, kitchen knives, clubs, even a few rusty pikes and muskets, ready to defend with their lives the city which had nurtured them. They waited there all day; but no-one came. They saw no sign of the Russian army they had been called out to support, no sign of the French army they had been summoned to defeat. There was no sign, either, of the Governor who had promised to meet them there. At sunset they gave it up, and began to drift back to the city; and as the sky darkened, the western horizon was seen to be aglow not only with the setting sun, but with the bivouac fires of the two armies, just out of sight over the rise.

A steady stream of refugees continued to pour into the city, peasants from the land over which the French had already marched, and were expected to march, and wounded soldiers from the battle, who could find no succour anywhere along the road. The stories they told did nothing to raise the spirits of the Muscovites who had been ready to fight for their city. The army was still in retreat, they said, and showed no sign yet of stopping to make a stand of it. If there were to be a battle, it looked like being under the very walls of the city.

That night the Governor issued another proclamation, copies of which were seeded all over the city. He gave no explanation of what had happened that day; only said that early the next morning he would ride out to meet with Prince Kutuzov and discuss with him how finally to destroy the Villain. The proclamation did nothing to calm anyone's fears. There had been too many contradictory rumours. That night the taverns were full to overflowing, and the darkness was made hideous by drunken revelries, and the sounds of smashing glass and splintering wood as the revellers turned from carousing to looting.

At Byeloskoye, the day had dragged by. It was unnaturally quiet in the streets, except for the distant sounds of wheels, and the shuffling tramp of wounded soldiers making their way through the streets to the hospital. Anne could not settle to any occupation, but continually got up and walked about, thinking of Rose, wondering about the fate of poor Parmoutier, remembering Sergei, longing for news of Nikolai.

Rested now after her journey, she was feeling physically well and strong, and restless with the need for action. She remembered this stage from her previous pregnancy – a good time, when her body had adjusted to its new condition, and she was filled with energy and a sense of well-being. She ought to have told Nikolai; she wished she had told him. She supposed at some point she would have to tell Basil, but she would not do so yet. She hardly showed yet, and with a few extra petticoats . . .

She persuaded Basil to go through his precious possessions and choose the most essential which could be loaded into one carriage. When they fled, they would be able to take only the bare minimum.

'But how can I choose?' he cried. 'How can I leave anything behind? It isn't just the valuables – it's the works of art. They're irreplaceable! I've seen looters at work before. They take gold and jewels and furs, but paintings and statues they simply destroy, like wanton children. How can I leave those things to them?'

Anne shrugged. 'That's up to you.'

It was after dark when a banging at the house door startled them both. For some time they had been listening subconsciously to the distant, dangerous sounds of the city; in the streets immediately surrounding the house, there was an unnatural quiet. They strained their ears to hear as Mikhailo went slowly to answer it, spoke a few words to someone, and then came painfully slowly upstairs.

'A messenger from the Governor, Barina, with a letter for you.'

Anne opened it with suddenly nervous fingers.

My own love, I am taking the opportunity of sending this to you by military courier, so I must be brief. We have arrived at Fili; the French are not far behind us. Bennigsen wants us to make our stand here, but there are grave objections to that. If we do not stand, we must retreat through the city. I will send word tomorrow, as soon as I know what is decided, but hold yourself ready to leave at any time.

When she told him the substance of it, Basil was thrown into a panic. 'That's it! I'm leaving now! I'm not going to wait here for the French to overtake us.'

'Don't be a fool. You can't leave now. Have some sense, for God's sake! We must wait until tomorrow.'

'Tomorrow! You're mad! Don't you read what he says? The French are close behind them.'

'We must wait to hear if they are going to make a stand.'

'Make a stand!' He laughed too shrilly. 'They've been retreating for

551

months – why should they stop now? Tomorrow will be too late – the army will come through with the French right on their heels, and we'll be caught between them! I'm leaving now, while there's still time!'

He was up and heading for the door; but now she had heard from Nikolai, an extraordinary calm had come over Anne. She felt no fear, no sense of haste. He was nearby, and would take care of her.

'Listen to me, Basil,' she said. 'We won't be the only people to receive this news. Everyone's going to be out in the streets, hoping to get away with as many of their belongings as they can save. You know there's looting already in the city. If you take those horses out there now, you'll be set on and robbed, and the horses will be stolen. You'll have no chance.'

'More chance than tomorrow,' he retorted from the door.

'If there is another retreat, once the army starts to come through, people will be so frightened and desperate, they'll want nothing more than to save their own skins. They won't have time to think about anything else. They'll run like chickens to get out of the city before the French arrive. You'll be able to drive out in perfect safety. You'll have the protection of the entire army, after all.'

'You're mad,' he said. 'Quite mad. I know what it is – you want to wait for your lover. You don't want to leave before he gets here. Well, that's your business! I'm not waiting around to lose everything, including my life! I'm going now, while there's a chance. You can come with me, or you can stay, just as you please.' And he was gone down the stairs, yelling for the servants.

'Basil, for God's sake – ' she called after him, pushing herself up out of the chair. She heard his voice from the hallway.

'Get those horses put-to in the carriage we packed today. Right away! We're leaving!'

Anne ran after him, pattering down the stairs, really worried now. 'No, Basil, I forbid it! You'll ruin everything!'

He turned at the courtyard door. 'Ruin your pretty plans, maybe,' he said fiercely. 'That's none of my concern. I'm getting out.' He shouted out into the yard, 'Get on with it, man! Hurry up!'

'They're my horses!' she said desperately, catching at his sleeve. 'You shan't take them.'

'Yours! Who bought them? Who paid for them? Get away from me!' He slapped her hand away, and went out into the courtyard. Anne followed, instinctively pressing her hands to her belly.

Outside in the courtyard she saw the horses were being led out towards the waiting carriage. She caught up with Basil again.

'Take one, then! Not both of them! Leave me one, for God's sake!'

He shook her off impatiently. 'Don't be a fool – one horse can't pull that load!' Then he seemed to understand what she was saying. 'What? Do you mean you're not coming with me?'

She shook her head. 'Not now – not yet. I can't.' He stared at her in astonishment and anger. 'Leave me one horse, for God's sake!'

They were backing them up to either side of the pole, now. She saw Basil hesitate, considering; but whether he would have relented or not she would never know. There was a flare of torchlight in the street outside the gates, and someone rattled them hard with a stick, and shouted harshly, 'Police! Open the gates! Come on, now, open up! This is the Governor's business!'

Anne whirled round, white with foreknowledge. 'Take the horses back! Hide them! Quickly!'

But already it was too late. As the porter backed away shaking his head, one of the men reached through, grabbing him by the front of his tunic and jerking him violently up against the gate. He cried out as his face hit the bars, and the key on its iron ring fell nervelessly from his hand. Another hand came through and snatched it up. The porter was released and staggered back, slumping against the wall, putting his hands up to his bleeding face; the gates crashed back, and the men came surging through.

The servants shrank back behind Anne in terror, the grooms who had brought out the horses seemed frozen to the spot. She placed herself instinctively between them and the invaders, and the leader of the men halted in front of her, surveying her by the light of his torch, while his companions spread across the yard behind him, looking around them with sharp, nervous glances.

'All right, madame, there's nothing to worry about,' said the man, holding up a document, a folded piece of stiff paper with a red wax seal clearly visible on the outside. 'No harm will come to you.' He waved his men forward, and as they thrust past him he said, 'By the order of His Excellency the Governor, these horses are requisitioned on State business of the utmost urgency. That's right, Vanya, lead 'em off!'

Basil came alive. 'Don't! Don't take my horses! You can't take them, damn you!'

'Governor's business, sir. Don't get in our way, if you please, or I shall be obliged to use force. My orders – '

'You don't understand – they're the last! All the rest have been taken already! How can we get away if you take them? The French are coming! You can't take my last two horses!'

553

'Sorry sir,' the man said briefly, without interest. 'Orders are orders.' Basil grabbed at him, and the man sidestepped and pulled a pistol from his belt. 'Keep your hands to yourself, sir, or I'll have to shoot. My orders are to take the horses, at any cost.'

Anne stared. The pistol convinced her of what she already suspected. It had been rather a coincidence that they had arrived just as the horses were led out, hadn't it? Quite suddenly she knew they were not police at all. They were a band of looters, with a cunning and resourceful leader, who had seen the horses from the street and were snapping up the chance.

'Show me your orders again,' she said sharply. Behind her there were sounds of scuffling, and the rattle of nervous hooves on the cobbles.

'Barina!' One of the servants called out desperately, and swinging round, she saw him struggling with one of the men, who had pulled a soft valise from the coach and was trying to make off with it. As they dragged, each on one handle, it tore open, and a number of precious objects – gold plate and cups and so on – thudded heavily onto the ground.

'Show me those orders!' she snapped at the leader.

'Sorry, madame, no time now,' he said, his voice rising with urgency as he backed off, keeping the pistol pointing at them. Others were already trotting the horses towards the gate. Basil caught Anne's eye and she saw the truth dawn on him too.

'No!' he screamed, 'No! Robbers! Looters! No!'

The leader turned and ran. Basil stooped to grab something from the cobbles, and with insane courage, born of desperation, he flung himself after them, his arm raised above his head as if to strike down the man with whatever it was he held in his hand.

'Basil, no!' Anne cried out. In the same instant, the man in front of him turned, raising his hand, and a pistol cracked, spitting a tongue of flame in the darkness of the yard. Basil went down, skidding face downwards a few feet along the cobbles before coming to rest. The servants who had been running forward in his wake stopped dead at the sound of the shot; the horses were gone through the gates, and there was only the diminishing sound of hooves and running feet.

Anne had run to Basil, who was lying still where he had fallen. He didn't move as she touched him.

'Basil! Are you all right?'

She slipped her hand under his shoulder to try to pull him up, and found her fingers were wet. 'You're hurt,' she said in consternation. 'Oh you fool, why did you do it? You knew he had a gun!'

Light fell across her shoulder – one of the servants bringing up a torch. It wavered madly back and forth. She used both hands and managed to pull him over, and as he rolled onto his back, blood pulsed up into the air in a glittering black fountain.

Anne screamed. It was not Basil lying there, but an unspeakable horror. The shot, fired upwards, had severed his jugular vein and shattered his jaw, tearing away the side of his head. She snatched back her hands in helpless horror at the sight, even while the fountain of blood pulsed again, weakly, and then no more.

'Oh God, oh God!' she cried out, reaching her trembling fingers for the place where she should have pressed them, to keep the blood in. 'No, please! No! Basil!'

It was too late. She had had one moment, she had wasted it. Mikhailo behind her moaned 'No, Barina, he's gone.' He couldn't have lived anyway, with that horrific wound, some distant part of her brain told her; and yet she felt insanely that she had failed, she had let him go without trying, and she repented, repented, she wanted another chance.

'I didn't mean it!' she sobbed aloud. 'Basil! I didn't mean it!'

'Barina, come away, come away,' someone said. One of the men behind her was sobbing in fright like a child.

She sat back on her heels, staring in horrified despair at her bloody hands, at Basil's shattered head. Nausea rose thickly upwards in her throat, and she jerked her head away violently to look at something else, anything else! She mustn't see that – the baby – she mustn't look!

Something was shining on the cobbles in the surging torchlight. It must have been the thing in his hand which he had raised as a weapon, something which had fallen from the valise and he had picked up.

She recognised it belatedly, through her rising nausea. It was the gold tiger with the emerald eyes she had given him for his birthday, a lifetime ago, before the world went mad. One of the emerald eyes had been jerked loose when it hit the ground. She saw it glittering at a little distance, a tiny spark in the torchlight. The tiger snarled its defiance, but stared up at her sightlessly from an empty socket, even as Basil stared sightlessly at the night sky from the wreck of his face.

Anne moaned, put her fingers up to her mouth. Her stomach heaved helplessly, and she turned away and was sick on the cobbles.

Chapter Thirty-One

The original orders to withdraw from Borodino had suggested making a stand somewhere on the other side of Mozhaisk. Kirov had his doubts as to how much Kutuzov had really meant by that; although it was impossible to believe that he had intended at that point to leave Moscow undefended. But whatever his intentions, he sent Bennigsen on ahead to scout the road for possible battle sites; and Bennigsen came back at last to report that there was nowhere suitable along the way, but that the army could make its stand along the crest of the Hill of Salutation.

'He's crazy,' Adonis grumbled as he stood at Kirov's shoulder, looking over the hilltop where returning Muscovites traditionally stopped to kiss the ground in honour of the holy city. 'He's crazier than a cat in a bathtub. Who could fight a battle here?'

Kirov looked around him despairingly. The whole area was criss-crossed with deep, steep-sided gullies and ravines, virtually impossible to cross. If the army were forced to retreat – and after Borodino, who could guarantee it would not? – they would be trapped and cut down helplessly.

Colonel Toll strolled up to him. 'What do you think of it, Nikolai Sergeyevitch? I spent hours with Bennigsen yesterday, trying to get him to draw up a map of his dispositions. Even he couldn't decide where to put the defences.'

'It's impossible to defend a place like this,' Kirov replied. 'But what's the alternative?'

'Not my problem,' Toll said, jerking a thumb over his shoulder. 'That's up to His Excellency.'

Prince Kutuzov was seated on his camp stool by the roadside, with his aides around him listening to the arguments of the various generals about the positions they and their divisions had been assigned. Tolly, who had been confined to bed with a feverish cold since the battle, but had dragged himself up in view of the emergency, was attempting to talk them down and explain to Kutuzov the impossibility of the site.

At last Kutuzov beckoned Kirov and Toll over. 'What do you think of this place? Do you agree with General Tolly? Answer me frankly, now.'

They exchanged a glance, and Toll said, 'To be quite honest, Excellency, I myself would never have thought of placing the army in such a perilous position.'

Kutuzov raised an eyebrow. 'Oh, wouldn't you? And what about you, Kirov? What do you think?'

'It seems very dangerous to me, sir. I can't see how it could successfully be defended.'

'Yermolov? What's your opinion?'

Burly Yermolov, who hadn't always seen eye to eye with Tolly, was vehement now in his support. 'Impossible, Excellency! Absolutely impossible! If you tried to give battle here, you would be defeated without question, and the whole army destroyed.'

'Hmm,' Kutuzov said, his fleshy face non-committal. 'You've surveyed the ground thoroughly?'

'Yes, Excellency.'

'I think perhaps it wouldn't hurt to have another look at it. Take Crossard, here, and go over the ground again. He's had plenty of experience in several countries. Report back to me when you've made another survey.'

As it was a direct order, Yermolov had no choice but to obey, but he rolled his eyes expressively towards Toll and Kirov as he stumped past them. As he and Crossard walked away, there came, like a theatrical warning, the distant sound of firing from over the next hill: Miloradovich's men were presumably involved in another skirmish with the French advance guard.

Emboldened by the sound, Toll stepped up to the Prince, and murmured into his ear. 'Excellency, you must decide. Indecision is the worst thing of all.'

'Yes, yes, of course,' Kutuzov said. He sank his chin on his chest in thought. 'We'll have a meeting this afternoon, when Yermolov's had a chance to do his survey. Four o'clock, in my quarters. All staff and corps commanders. You can all have your say, and then I'll make my decision. Now where's my Cossack? This grass is damp, you know — distinctly damp.'

Kutuzov's temporary quarters were a wooden peasant hut in the village of Fili. The senior officers gathered in a bare room, furnished only with a long table and wooden benches, and, of course, the ikon with its red-shaded lamp in the Beautiful Corner. Colonel Toll came in with an armful of maps, which he spread across the table; Konovnitzyn was busy lighting his pipe, with which he would presently make the air foul; Tolly, his cheeks bright with fever, pointedly moved to the other end of the table, and drew out his handkerchief and trumpeted briskly into it.

At last everyone was assembled except Bennigsen, who had not come back from a further inspection of his chosen battleground. He arrived very late, to find everyone waiting for him in silence, watching the door; and finding the looks directed towards him as he entered largely unsympathetic, he took the offensive, striding to his place saying loudly, 'The question before us, gentlemen, is simply this: is it better to give battle beneath the walls of Moscow, or to abandon the city to the enemy?'

'Just a minute, Bennigsen,' Kutuzov's voice, rich with the patina of a lifetime of wine and cigars, interrupted him. 'What's at stake here is not just the city of Moscow, but the very existence of the State. We have but one army, you know! As long as it exists, we still have hope of a successful outcome to this war. Once it is destroyed, not only Moscow but all of Russia will be lost.'

Kirov met Tolly's eyes. It was what Tolly had been saying all along, ever since Vilna; it was the policy for which he had been villified, and deprived of high command.

'So the question really is,' Kutuzov went on importantly, 'should we wait for the enemy's attack in this disadvantageous position, or should we abandon Moscow to the enemy?'

Bennigsen looked taken aback, and opened and shut his mouth a few times, trying to discover the difference between his question and Kutuzov's. Tolly took advantage of his silence to say, 'The position here is so bad that any attempt to give battle would result in complete annihilation of the army. Painful though it must be to any of us to abandon Moscow, it might in the end prove to hasten the enemy's downfall. If we retain our ability to manoeuvre by removing to a place where we can keep in contact with Petersburg, and with our grainstore in Kiev and our munitions factories in Tula – '

Bennigsen jumped to his feet. 'Out of the question! The loss to the Crown of the surrender of Moscow would be inconceivable! To say nothing of the loss of morale in the army and the nation as a whole! The French have been seriously weakened by Borodino, and they're spread out at this moment over a wide front. If we move three corps over to our left wing during the course of the night, and mount a surprise attack at dawn – '

'It's too late for that kind of thing,' Tolly snapped, exasperated. 'If we tried to move a large body of men over this terrain in the dark, it would lead to nothing but hopeless confusion! Tomorrow morning would find us at the mercy of the French!'

'I must say, that does seem likely,' Kutuzov said, nodding slowly.

Several people began talking at once. The argument became general, and then heated, some advocating retreat, some stubbornly supporting Bennigsen for making a stand. Yermolov tacked off in a completely different direction by suddenly suggesting turning in their tracks and attacking the French immediately and all-out. Tolly had a fit of coughing in the middle of one tirade, and turned on Konovnitsyn, who was on his side, and offended him by abusing his execrable pipe. Toll and Rayevsky, who agreed on retreat, were engaged in a side argument about which route to take. Ostermann-Tolstoy challenged Bennigsen to guarantee that his suggested attack at dawn would be successful, and Bennigsen bristled and told him to try not to be as much of a fool as he looked.

After listening to a great deal of this, his face utterly impassive, Prince Kutuzov hoisted himself to his feet and rapped the table for silence. It fell gradually and piecemeal. The one eye roved round the table, gathering up everyone's attention.

'Gentlemen, I have listened to all your opinions. I am aware of the responsibility I am assuming, but I must sacrifice myself for the welfare of my country. I hereby order the retreat.'

His words were met with silence. Even Bennigsen had nothing to say. Kirov looked at Toll and Tolly and read in their eyes the same conviction, that Kutuzov had meant to do it all along; that he had long ago seen the sense of Tolly's policy of withdrawal before the French, but had continued to espouse the belligerent posture in order to placate public opinion.

All the same, it was one thing to talk about abandoning Moscow, and quite another to contemplate the reality of it. Moscow was the true, the beating heart of Russia, the old capital, the place where nationhood had first begun five hundred years ago in defiance of the Mongol overlords. It was the holy city. The thought of the French marching in there unopposed struck at something deep in all of them. Kirov found himself, a little unwillingly, admiring Kutuzov. There was no doubt it was an awesome responsibility, one from which he might never recover. Even if there were no other choice, the country might not forgive the man in whose name Moscow was given to the Antichrist as a present.

'Very well, gentlemen. The field commanders had better go back to their corps immediately and make the announcement; put your men on immediate alert for departure, and await further instructions. I shall need the staff colonels and the supply officer in here in ten minutes. Kirov! I want you at once.'

Everyone began filing out, and Kirov stood aside and waited until a space had cleared round the prince. Then he obeyed the beckoning finger and stepped across to him.

'I want you to go at once into Moscow, to Rostopchin, tell him that the enemy's outflanking columns are forcing me to abandon Moscow. Say 'with grief' or 'with great sorrow' – I leave the wording to you, but be tactful.'

'Yes, sir.'

'Tell him we'll be coming through tonight, under cover of darkness. Tell him I want as many police officers as he can provide to help guide us through the city and to stop deserters slipping away.'

'Yes sir. Which road will we be taking?'

'The Ryazan road.'

Kirov, startled, met the general's one eye. 'Ryazan, sir? But – '

The Kaluga road was the obvious choice, to the southwest: there were military depots and plentiful supplies; and it linked them up with Tula and the munitions factories, kept them in touch with the enemy, and gave them the opportunity to work round and sever the French supply lines. Ryazan, to the east, offered nothing.

Kutuzov gave a small, foxy smile. 'That's what I said. Listen, Kirov, you're no talking fool: I want Napoleon to think we're heading for Ryazan and Vladimir to make sure we lure him into the city. He's the raging torrent, don't you see, and Moscow is the sponge that will soak him up!'

'Yes, sir,' Kirov said doubtfully.

'Once he's got Moscow, he won't want to give it up again – then we'll have him! Bit by bit we'll surround him, isolate him, cut off his supplies, starve him and strangle him. And then winter will come.' He glanced out of the window. 'It's September now,' he said in a soft and deadly voice. 'In a month's time, six weeks at the most, the snows will begin. He has no idea, no idea at all! It's the beginning of the end for the Grande Armée.'

His face contracted with some emotion – a mixture of anger and grief, which made Kirov realise that whatever he had thought before about the old man's sybaritic indolence, he did not take this business lightly. He knew very clearly what it was he was doing. 'I'm going to see them rot!' he said fiercely. 'I'm going to see Napoleon eat horse flesh before I'm done!'

It was about half past eight in the evening of Sunday, September the 13th when Kirov came face to face with Rostopchin in the Governor's mansion on the Lubyanka, and delivered Kutuzov's message to him.

Rostopchin paled, his eyes bulged. 'But he told me only this morning, he told be there was going to be a battle! Naturally I thought we would lose it, and there'd be a retreat, but I thought we'd have several days before we had to . . . When does the retreat begin?'

'At any moment. The men are on immediate alert. There was no possibility of offering battle on that ground. The army would have been annihilated.'

'God damn and blast him! The treacherous, pusillanimous – ' Rostopchin raved. 'There are twenty-two thousand wounded in my hospitals! How in God's name am I supposed to move them at a moment's notice? How am I supposed to prevent looting? Your men will come through like locusts! I haven't got enough police officers to line the route! I need days, not hours!'

'Hours is all you have,' Kirov said, eyeing the little man with interest. He had always thought Rostopchin stupid and self-seeking, but he really did seem to care about the fate of his city. 'I'm sorry. It is necessary for the greater good of the country. The army must be preserved. Napoleon must be lured into the city.'

'Yes, yes, I see that. But it's the time I need to complete my plans . . . How can I get everything ready for the Villain before tomorrow morning?'

'Plans? What do you mean? Get what ready?'

Rostopchin looked sly. 'I have my own ideas about a reception for Napoleon. He's going to be sorry he ever came this far, I can tell you! He's going to find out – ' He stopped dead, as if he thought he had said too much, and drew himself up in gubernatorial dignity. 'I'm grateful to you, Count Kirov, for bringing me this information. And I must now beg you to excuse me: I have a great many orders to give, as you can imagine.'

'Yes, of course,' Kirov said, still thinking furiously and coming to no definite conclusions. He bowed slightly and turned away, but as he reached the door, Rostopchin called him back.

'I understand that Count and Countess Tchaikovsky are still at their house, at Byeloskoye. I do recommend that you advise them to leave as soon as possible.' He fixed him with a meaningful look. 'As soon as possible.'

Kirov didn't stop to consider how it was that Rostopchin knew he had an interest in that particular household. The warning was kindly meant.

'Thank you. I was intending to,' he said.

The streets of the city were unnaturally quiet, empty of Muscovites, and now rumbling with the vibrating thunder of heavy artillery being dragged over the wooden paving. Behind the artillery came the first of the foot soldiers. They marched in silence, looking apprehensive and unhappy. The monotonous sound of their tramping feet echoing from the shuttered houses, and the absence of cheering crowds made it seem like a funeral march; the officers rode at the heads of their columns with expressions ranging from dazed disbelief to silent rage. Some had wept when they were told that they were abandoning Moscow; others had not found the courage to tell their men, many of whom were marching in ignorance of their intent and destination.

Kirov hurried past them, heading north and west towards Byeloskoye, to warn Anne and Basil that they must leave at once. He was surprised that Basil was still in the city, having expected, if he had thought about it, that he would have left long ago at the first sign of danger. When he arrived at the house, he was even more surprised at what he found. The outer gate was open and unguarded. In the courtyard a partly-loaded carriage stood, horseless, with empty valises and boxes lying around it, as if they had been looted. He met Adonis's eyes in alarm, jumped down and flung him his reins, and strode to the door; yanked hard at the bell, rapping on the panels with the stock of his whip.

It seemed a long time before he was answered – a long time during which he imagined the worst in a number of ways. At last there was a shuffling sound within the hall, and a quavering voice called, 'Who is it? Go away! There's nothing here for you!'

'Open the door!' he shouted, racking his brain for the name of Anne's butler. 'Mikhailo, is that you? This is Count Kirov. Let me in, you fool!'

There was a brief silence, followed by the rattling of bolts and chains, and the door was swung hesitantly open. Mikhailo appeared, blinking, in the gap.

'Oh sir! It is you! Oh, thank Heaven! We've got such trouble sir!'

Kirov thrust past him. 'Where are they? Where's her ladyship?'

'Upstairs, sir, in the drawing-room. Your man had better bring the horses into the hall, sir. It isn't safe outside. We've had such trouble here. I don't know what the world's coming to . . . '

Kirov left Adonis to deal with the butler, was already running up the stairs two at a time and burst into the drawing-room with his nerves at the stretch.

'Anna! Anna! Are you all right?'

He stopped dead just inside the room. The furniture had been pushed back, and in the centre a table had been placed, and covered with what looked like a white counterpane from a servant's bed. Lying on it was the figure of a man, hands folded at the breast, the head completely wrapped in linen bandages. At the head and foot of the table stood a bronze candlestand, each bearing five candles.

Anne was sitting in a chair by the fireside, her hands folded in her lap, staring straight ahead of her. She didn't seem to hear him or notice him. Her maid, Pauline, jumped up when the Count appeared, and came towards him with her hands extended in a pleading gesture.

'Oh, sir, thank God you've come!'

'What in God's name has happened? Is that Basil Andreyevitch?' he said. 'Is your mistress ill?'

Pauline's eyes filled with tears she had been holding back for so many hours. 'It was looters, sir – they broke in and stole the horses. The master tried to stop them, and they shot him.' Her lip trembled. 'Shot him dead, sir, right in front of my mistress.'

'Did they hurt her?' he asked, his whole body trembling with outrage and fear. 'If anyone touched her – !'

'No, sir, no sir. They ran off when the poor master – ' She gulped and swallowed some tears. 'His poor head, shot all to pieces,' she whispered, her eyes looking into his pleadingly, as though he could run time backwards and make it not to be. 'Nurse bandaged him up. My lady insisted he should be laid out properly, though we hadn't got a coffin, of course, and no-one to make one, with half the servants run away. We prayed for him, my lady and I, all night, until it got light. And then she just sat down in that chair, as you see her now, and she hasn't moved or spoken all day. Oh sir, do you think her poor mind has turned? After what happened at Koloskavets . . . '

Kirov pulled himself together and laid a firm hand on her shoulder. She felt as unsubstantial as a sparrow under his touch. 'No, no, my poor girl. Your mistress is too strong for that. She's in a state of shock.'

'Yes, sir. I don't know how she bears it. What with half the servants running away, and the others in their quarters and refusing to come out, there's only nurse and me and Mikhailo to take care of her. But she won't eat, and she won't answer when I speak to her . . . '

'You've been so brave,' Kirov said encouragingly. 'now can you be brave a little longer? Can you fetch some brandy for your mistress?

And then run upstairs and pack a valise with whatever you think most necessary for a journey. We shall have to leave here very soon.'

'Are the French coming, sir?'

'Yes, child. They're coming to take over the city.' He held her eyes, willing her to be strong, and after a moment she swallowed again, and straightened a little under his hand.

'Very good, sir,' she said. 'Only look to my poor mistress! In her condition, she ought not to be subjected to such things.'

Kirov heard the words with distant shock; but he let the maid go, wanting to get to Anne without further delay. She had not moved or spoken since he came into the room, and she did not react at all when he came close to her, even when he knelt directly in front of her. Her face was pale and her eyes were wide, the pupils unnaturally enlarged. Her breathing was very light and shallow, and when he took hold of her hands, her skin felt cold to the touch. He thought he understood. She had gone away inside herself, for protection, to avoid a situation which had become intolerable. In normal circumstances, he would have left her alone to come back to herself in her own time; but these were not normal circumstances.

He began to rub her hands gently between his, calling her name quietly but persistently.

'Anna! Annushka! Look at me.'

After a few moments he saw the focus of her eyes change. She looked at him, but quite blankly, as though she did not know him.

'Anna Petrovna! Look at me. Do you know who I am? Answer me, Anna!'

She drew a small, hitching breath, and then a long, deep sigh. Her hand moved in his. A little colour returned to her cheeks. It was almost like watching someone wake from a deep sleep.

She saw him, recognised him. 'Nikolasha?'

'Yes, my darling, I'm here.'

She closed her eyes for a moment, and swayed forward, and he stood up quickly, lifted her up, and sat down again with her on his lap, holding her close against him. After a moment she put her arms round his neck and rested her face against him, and he felt her trembling.

'*Doushka, doushka*,' he said. He thought of all she had witnessed, and was filled with a directionless rage against Fate.

'Oh Nikolai,' she said faintly, 'it was so terrible!'

'Yes, darling, I know.'

'Basil – he – he tried to stop them . . . He had no chance . . . They just – just – '

'Yes, darling. Don't think about it.' Pauline came in with a bottle of brandy. She had forgotten to bring a glass. Kirov nodded his thanks and waved her away, uncorked the bottle with his teeth, and gently turned Anne's head, putting the neck of the bottle to her lips. 'Drink some of this, *doushenka*. Take a big mouthful and swallow.'

She obeyed him like a child. The brandy made her gasp and cough. She looked at him with surprised, wet eyes; shut her eyes and took another mouthful, and then pushed the bottle aside.

'I'm all right now,' she said. The last cobwebs of shock were passing from her, and the full realisation of horror and pain was beginning to dawn. He would have liked to spare her that; but she was his likeness and his equal, and he had no right to choose for her. 'Oh God!' she said, 'Oh Basil! I should have stopped him! I should have saved him!'

'You are not to blame.'

'But I am! I am!' She looked into his eyes. 'I never loved him. I shouldn't have married him. He'd be alive now if I hadn't married him – instead of . . .'

'I know. I felt that way about Irina. When she died, I felt so guilty. But there's no time for those feelings now, Anna. Later, when we have time, we'll talk about it all. I know you've suffered a terrible shock, but you must be strong now. We have to leave Moscow.'

'Leave? Have you – have the French – ?'

He took her hand and chafed it. He saw how exhausted she looked now that the numbness was gone. 'There isn't going to be another battle. We're retreating, leaving Moscow to the French. Listen to me, darling.'

'Yes. I'm listening.'

'It's the only thing left to do. We must preserve the army intact. The men are marching through the city this moment, and the French won't be far behind. They'll probably get here some time tomorrow. I've sent Pauline to pack you a valise. You won't be able to take much, I'm afraid.'

The brandy was making her sleepy now. She made a huge effort, drawing from the deepest wells of reserve. 'How will I leave? I have no horses. The looters who killed – ' She swallowed. 'They took the last of the horses.'

'Yes, I know.' He thought for a moment. 'Listen, love. I have to report back to Kutuzov. Then I'll find some horses, and come back for you. Don't be afraid. It will take all night for the army to march through, and the rearguard will hold off the French until they've all passed. Pack your valise with whatever you need. Take your jewels, if you can, and any gold you have about the house. And when you've got everything ready, try to get a little sleep. I'll be back for you early in the morning.'

He stood up, setting her on her feet. She swayed wearily, and turned towards him, clinging to him.

'Nikolasha – ' she said desperately.

He gripped her shoulders hard. 'I have to go now. But I'll be back. Do you trust me?'

She looked up at him, gathering herself together out of scattered fragments. 'Yes,' she said. 'Yes, of course.' He was all there was now; in a way, he was all there had ever been. Her focus, her anchor – nothing else mattered. She would go with him wherever he led her. 'I'm all right. You can go now.'

He smiled. 'That's my brave girl.'

He was at the door when he remembered, and turned, almost shyly, to say, 'Anna – Pauline said – is it true? Are you with child?'

A slow smile came into her eyes which strengthened him, fed him as nothing had these months past. 'Yes,' she said softly.

'When – ?'

'At Vilna.'

He smiled too, and then he was gone.

Once he had reported back, it was not easy to get away again. There was a great deal to be done, and Kutuzov seemed to find him just one more and just one more task. Shortly before dawn, he was sent off to find General Miloradovich, who was still holding the Hill of Salutation with his rearguard Hussars, and a company of Cossacks.

'What does the Prince say?' the General asked anxiously. 'Murat's cavalry are just over the ridge now. I don't want to be fighting a desperate rearguard action that's going to cost me all my men, and lose me my horse artillery into the bargain.'

'His Excellency agrees, sir, to your negotiating a cease-fire or a truce with the French, while we get through Moscow. If they hesitate, you are to tell them we'll destroy the whole city and leave them with nothing but a heap of ruins.'

'Thank God for that! I was afraid he'd say – but the sooner the better. We'll go and do it this minute. You'd better come with me, Nikolai Sergeyevitch, and then you can report back what they say to the Prince. Akinfov! Over here, man! You've got a white handkerchief about you, haven't you?'

As soon as they reached the crest of the hill, they saw a detachment of French light cavalry riding cautiously up towards them, evidently nervous about the possible presence of Cossacks. The King of Naples himself was amongst them, easily recognisable by his splendid feathered shako, and the quantity of gold embroidery on his uniform. The French party halted. Akinfov rode forward, waving his white handkerchief. They saw Murat say a few words to the cavalry commander, and then come cantering forward alone to parley.

There was no difficulty. It was plainly in the French interest to take Moscow without resistance, and to receive it intact. Murat felt confident in pledging his Emperor's word, and when Kirov rode back to report to Kutuzov, he had an unexpected bonus to offer: Murat had suggested that the Grand Armée should delay its entry into Moscow until seven the next morning, in order to allow the Russians time to get clear, and to remove some of the wounded if they wished.

'Good. Excellent. That's just what we need. He's a decent fellow, Murat. Wasted on the French. Pity he's not a Russian,' said the Prince. 'Eh? What's that? Yes, yes, take a few hours by all means! No hurry now we know we've got the whole day. You should get some sleep, Kirov – you're looking all in!'

Getting hold of horses was the hardest part. Kirov had to resort to a mixture of bullying and bribery to persuade two young, wealthy officers from the Prince's own suite to part with their spare mounts. Most of the field officers had lost theirs already, either in one of the two battles or on the long, punishing march.

When he and Adonis finally rode over the crest of the Hill of Salutation, heading for the city again, they paused in sheer surprise to look down at the extraordinary scene on the road below. The advancing French were so close to the retreating Russian rearguard, that they seemed to be all part of the same army. Now and then the French had to halt to allow stragglers and the last of the Russian baggage train to stay ahead of them, and when they did, the Cossacks rode back to stand beside their opposite numbers, chatting in a friendly way and exchanging stories. Even as they watched, they saw four Cossack riders canter up to Murat's suite and circle it for a better look at the legendary King of Naples; and Murat himself raised a friendly hand to them in greeting.

'All going according to plan, Colonel,' Adonis remarked.

Yes. I hope they don't overdo it,' Kirov said.

Kutuzov had given orders to Ataman Platov that his Cossacks were to get friendly with the French advance guard, express their admiration for Murat's leadership, and convince them that they were angry and disillusioned with the Russians, owed them no loyalty, and were on the point of changing sides. Having lulled their suspicions, the Cossacks would then let slip to the French that the army was making for Ryazan.

When they marched through Moscow and out at the other side, the Cossacks were to hold back the French and let the Russian army get ahead. Once clear of the city, the main force would turn aside off the road and begin to double back south and west. The Cossacks would continue along the road to Ryazan, and with luck, the French would follow, thinking they still had the whole Russian army in front of them. This would gain valuable time, and allow the army to establish itself in a key position to the south of Moscow before the French knew what was happening.

Avoiding the main road over the Dorogomilov bridge, which was choked with army baggage waggons, Kirov passed into the city by one of the more southerly gates, and trotted by a series of back streets towards Byeloskoye, his mind busy with plans. He didn't think he would be able to get Anne very far on horseback, or that he ought to try, in view of her condition. The town of Podolsk, twenty miles to the south on the Tula road, ought to be far enough from Moscow to be safe; and if the doubling-back plan worked, it would become the Russians army's base, which would afford her protection and allow him to be near her. Later, when she had rested and regained her strength, he would have to see about getting hold of some kind of conveyance, and sending her to Tula, to his sister.

There was a great deal of noise coming from the main route through the city which the army was taking. They no longer marched through empty streets: more and more citizens had come out to line the route, believing at first that they were witnessing the arrival of their saviours. When it became known that the army was merely passing through before abandoning them to the French, the cheers changed to shouts of anger and hostility. There was a good deal of drunkenness, too. The taverns ought to have been closed, but there seemed to be no policemen around to enforce the closure. Kirov didn't like to think how many of the soldiers were slipping away from the ranks into the crowds as the army passed through.

As they turned into the street which led to the gate of Byeloskoye, Adonis said, 'What's this then, Colonel? Looks like trouble!'

Two men were slinking along in the shelter of the wall. As soon as they saw the horsemen, they tried to make a run for it, but Kirov and

Adonis, moving as one man, blocked the way and drew their pistols.

'Stop! Stand still, both of you, or I'll shoot,' Kirov snapped. The two men stood still, watching warily, eyes everywhere, ready to take any opportunity of bolting. Adonis had dismounted, holding the horses behind him with one hand, covering them with his pistol in the other.

The two men were dressed in rough peasant clothes, and wore woollen caps pulled down close to their eyes. They had a furtive look about them, as would be expected of ne'er-do-wells; yet Kirov felt oddly that they didn't seem as worried as they ought to have been, if they had been looting.

'What are you doing here? You're looters, aren't you? Turn out your pockets!'

They didn't move, watching him warily.

'We're not looters, master,' one of them said. 'We've not touched anything.'

'Then what are you doing here?'

'We're on the Governor's business.'

'Nonsense! Governor's business – you?'

Adonis suddenly shot out a hand and snatched off the hat of the nearest man, revealing his shaven scalp.

'Well well! Escaped convicts!' he said with quiet triumph, levelling his pistol at the man's head.

'Not escaped!' the man cried hastily. 'I swear to you, master. We were let out on purpose – free pardon – to do a job!'

Kirov saw the other give him a look of warning. Making himself sound indifferent, he said, 'I don't believe you. What job?'

The second man looked at him cannily. 'Beg pardon, master, but we don't know who you are. You might be anyone. You might be a French spy.'

Adonis growled at that, but Kirov gave a grim smile and pulled open his cloak, showing his uniform. 'What job? You'd better tell me, or I'll shoot you anyway, just to be on the safe side.'

He had the feeling that the second man would have held out: there was a calm defiance in his eyes. But the first man was more nervous, and evading his companion's warning eyes, he cried hastily. 'Incendiaries, master. Mining houses. Thousands of us, let out on purpose by the Governor. The whole city's going to go up, as soon as the French are in.'

'You bloody fool!' the second man snarled.

'Good God,' Kirov said. So that was Rostopchin's 'plan'. Then,

'You've mined this house? Answer me, damn you! My wife's in there!'

'No, master, not this one. We were taking a short cut back to headquarters to get supplies. We haven't done this one yet – God's truth!'

Kirov wasn't sure whether he believed him or not, but this was not the time or place to argue. He waved his pistol peremptorily. 'Very well. Go on, get off with you. Adonis – the gate!'

The two men scuttled past and disappeared round the corner. Kirov's mind was seething: incendiaries? The whole city? It would finish Napoleon, finish him completely. But it would also finish Moscow. Moscow, the holy city, would burn! He ought to report back – but the most important thing now was to get Anne out to safety. The men might have mined the house after all – he couldn't trust their word. Sly Rostopchin! Determined, too. Who would have thought it?

While Anne made her final preparations, Adonis instituted a search of the cellars and outhouses to make sure no incendiary devices had been planted. It seemed the men had told the truth; and the servants who were staying on were now alerted to the danger, and could be trusted to look after their own interests. Some of them, resentful at the turn things had taken, remained in their quarters, and would not emerge even to see the mistress leave. For the others, there was a tearful farewell in the courtyard.

'The French won't harm you,' Anne assured them. 'You should have enough to eat, with all the stores in the cellars. Keep yourselves safe at all costs. We'll meet again, when all this is over.'

Mikhailo, his eyes red, spoke for all of them. 'Yes, Barina. The good times will come again.'

The servants who had been with her in Koloskavets shook her offered hand shyly. Old Nyanya sobbed and begged her to take care of the little Countess, and make sure she had her hot oil treatment every day. Despite the few hours of sleep she had had last night, Anne was numb with weariness, and that was good, for it prevented her from feeling too much sorrow. She mounted the horse Nikolai had brought her and looked briefly at the Greek facade of Byeloskoye, and was sure she would never see it again; yet she felt no emotion with the thought. It was already a part of the past, to be left behind and forgotten. What the future might hold, she could not imagine; but she had everything that mattered – with the new life inside her, and Nikolai beside her, they were going to join Rose.

Pauline, very doubtful about riding cross-saddle, had been helped to mount; the valises were firmly strapped on behind the saddles and covered with blankets; the gate was swung open, and they were off, clattering out into the road under the hazy morning sun. It was September the fourteenth, and there had been a slight fog that morning. Autumn had definitely come.

When they reached the stone bridge over the Yaouza river on the east side of the city, they found General Tolly sitting on horseback watching the soldiers marching over, and pulled out of the columns to join him at his vantage point. For the last part of the route, the road had been lined with cavalrymen, evidently posted to stop the soldiers from deserting. Tolly, however, greeted Kirov with a shake of the head and the words, 'God knows how many we've lost. I even sent my own aides back to the main intersections, but you can't keep your eye on everyone. I could have used you earlier. Rostopchin didn't provide a single policeman, as far as I could see.'

Kirov now had a fair idea what those policemen had been doing, but he said nothing. The fewer people who knew about the plan the better: word had a way of getting around.

'We saw plenty of signs of looting back there,' he said. 'I suppose it's inevitable.'

Tolly shrugged. 'Not our problem now. Here, Khastov! Turn those carts aside! Civilians must wait for the infantry to pass over first!'

'Has the Commander in Chief come through yet, sir?' Kirov asked.

'Not yet. He's only going as far as Panki today – that's where the new headquarters will be.' He glanced with mild curiosity at Anne and her maid, and said, 'You can go on, if you like. It might be better for you to get your party settled before the staff arrive – make sure of a decent lodging. There's going to be quite a crowd later on.'

'Thank you sir. I'm sure you're right.'

'All right. Khastov – let the Colonel's party through.'

They were about to ride forward to join the column at the bridgehead, when there was a distant loud explosion behind them, from somewhere near the centre of the town. The horses snorted and laid back their ears, and the soldiers faltered and looked back over their shoulders.

'Keep 'em moving, sergeant!' Tolly called out. A column of black smoke climbed up vertically into the sky, growing thicker even as they watched. Tolly snapped his fingers for a telescope; and after a moment he said, 'It looks like a fire in the Kitai-Gorod section. I suppose some looter or deserter's been careless. Nothing to do with us, anyway.'

Kitai-Gorod was the merchant's section of the city. Kirov thought they could hardly have chosen a better site for the first incendiary: it was a tightly-packed area of wooden buildings, shops and warehouses full of oil and wool and rope and candles and paint and spirits – everything that would burn most readily. He said nothing, and escorted Anne forward to cross the bridge. At the highest point of the span, he turned in the saddle to look back at Moscow and salute it inwardly, for what he knew, now, was the last time.

Once they were over the bridge and outside the city walls, they were able to slip out of the column and overtake the slow-moving infantry and waggons. Further towards Panki, they caught up with a convoy of oddly-shaped covered carts, and it was only as they were passing them that Kirov recognised them belatedly as the municipal fire-fighting pumps. Rostopchin must have ordered them to be taken out of the city that morning. He had certainly, Kirov thought, done his job thoroughly.

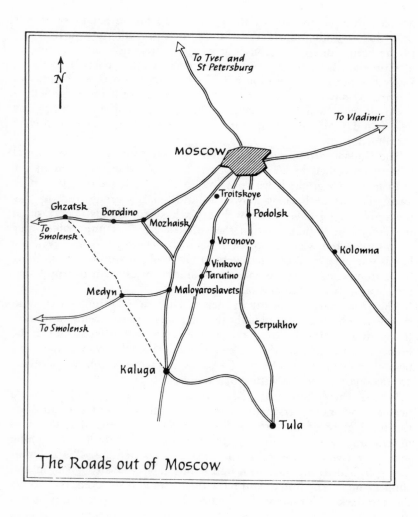

The Roads out of Moscow

Chapter Thirty-Two

Moscow burned for almost three days. The fire in Kitai-Gorod was only the beginning, for even while French grenadiers were hurrying to the scene, dragging goods out of the warehouses and fighting to contain the blaze, fuses were smouldering in other parts of the city. Every few hours an explosion would signal an outbreak in yet another district. By dawn on the 16th, the fires were out of control, fanned by a strong wind which, by changing direction several times during the next two days, ensured that more and more buildings caught and were consumed.

The Russian army, moving crablike, slowly south and west around the city, travelled by the light of the blaze. During the night of the 16th it was so bright it was possible to read by it six or seven miles away. The whole horizon glowed a lurid, ghastly orange-red; by day the smoke hung over Moscow like black storm clouds. The task of the French fire-fighters within the stricken city was impossible: they soon discovered what the Muscovites of course knew – that even the handsome palaces of the rich were in fact built of wood, with nothing but a thin facade of stone, marble, or stucco, insufficient to stop them, too, from catching fire and burning fiercely.

The army marched mostly in silence. There was nothing cheering in that distant glow, or the thought that the holy city was being devoured. It was thin comfort to know that it would not now offer shelter to the French; a little more comfort to know that the French advance guard had been thoroughly fooled by the Cossacks and were even now following an imaginary army down the road towards Ryazan.

In the early hours of the 18th, rain began to fall, growing heavier and more persistent as the day went on, and extinguishing the lurid glare of the fire on the horizon. Travelling that day was miserable: low clouds closed in the horizon, and shrouded everything in a grey twilight; the rain was cold and unrelenting. The columns first splashed, then squelched, and finally laboured through deep and slippery mud. The horses laid back their ears and shivered, their coats flat and dark with rain, as they hauled the heavy caissons and waggons along the rutted road. Ditches became fast-running streams, sometimes overflowing across the road in a tea-coloured flood. By the time they arrived at last at Podolsk on the Tula Road, everyone was thoroughly soaked, chilled, and liberally splashed with sticky mud.

Kirov sent Adonis on ahead to secure some kind of lodgings for them, for he was worried about Anne, who had been increasingly silent as the day went on. She was suffering, he thought, from a reaction – and it was not to be wondered at. The things she had witnessed in the last month would have been enough to destroy a weaker woman. She drooped in the saddle, rain streaming from her collar and the brim of her hat, tendrils of soaked hair dripping on her cheeks. Her condition was only less pitiable than Pauline's, who was suffering, in addition to everything else, with severe saddle soreness from the unaccustomed cross-saddle position.

Adonis met them on the outskirts of the town, and directed them by a side road away from the centre to a little inn on the back road to Kolomna. Here, thanks to Adonis's threatening appearance and his liberal handling of his master's purse, they were received kindly, and given a decent room, with a small private sitting-room attached, in which a birch-log fire was burning, still a little fitfully, under the chimney.

'They've promised a truckle bed in here for the maid,' Adonis announced, going in ahead of them to stir up the fire.

'And what about you?' Kirov enquired ironically. 'Or didn't you think to ask?'

Adonis gave one of his equivocal grimaces. 'I'll sleep with the horses. I don't trust anyone, not this close to Moscow. But don't worry – I know how to make myself comfortable.'

Pauline, her fingers stiff from cold, but simply grateful not to be sitting down, was helping Anne to take off her sodden cloak and hat. The room was musty-smelling and a little chilly, for the fire wouldn't draw properly: even as Adonis poked at it, a spat of rain came down the chimney and sizzled on the logs, sending a cloud of pale smoke out into the room.

'The wood's damp,' Adonis announced. 'Have you got your flask there, Colonel?'

A capful of vodka thrown into the flames caused a minor explosion but made them burn up bright and blue for an instant; and soon there was a cheerful sound of crackling from the logs. Kirov looked at his drooping love and her numb-fingered maid, and took pity.

'Pauline, go next door and get out of your wet clothes. I'll take care of your mistress. Go on, now, don't argue with me.

Adonis, do you think you can get them to send up some hot wine?'

When they were alone again, Kirov sat Anne down by the fire, and knelt before her to pull off her wet boots and stockings, and to chafe her feet with a rough towel. She blinked with pleasure at the returning warmth, and then bent her head while Nikolai dried her hair.

'I never thought,' she said, 'that I would ever have you at my feet like this.'

He smiled in approval, and started on the buttons of her jacket. 'That's better! Your spirits aren't completely quenched, then?'

She looked round the dim little room with something like pleasure. 'No, not quenched. Everything that's happened seems to have had the effect of narrowing my vision. Just now, I find it is all I can manage to be glad of being with you, and out of the rain. I can't seem to care about anything else very much.'

He kissed the end of her cold nose. 'Good. That's as it should be. As soon as I've got you dry. I'm going to put you to bed and give you a little hot supper, and then I expect you to sleep the clock round.'

'You're so kind to me.' Her eyes smiled sleepily at him. 'I don't think I'll find that at all difficult.'

The next morning, Anne was still asleep when Kirov set out from the inn to ride to headquarters and report. Scouts had already been up to the Sparrow Hill that morning to look down on the ruins of Moscow. The rain had extinguished most of the fire, leaving a blackened, smouldering mess of beams and rubble. About two thirds of the old city had been destroyed. It was a sobering thought.

'It looks as though the Kremlin is more or less untouched, though,' Toll told him, with a mixture of relief and regret. 'So Napoleon will still have a palace to live in.'

'What are the plans for us now? Do we stay here?'

'Not if our Tolly can help it. We need to be still further west, so that we can cover the two Kaluga roads. Napoleon still thinks we're heading for Ryazan, but once that ruse falls through, he's bound to think of Kaluga. We're going to press the Old Man to push on across country to Troitskoye. It's between the Old and the New Kaluga Roads, so we can cover them both from there, at a pinch.'

'It'll be hard travelling in this weather.'

'Fathoms of mud,' Toll agreed with a grin. 'His Excellency's favourite going! We'll try to get him to order the move for tomorrow morning. I don't suppose there's any chance of winkling him out today.'

As Kirov was leaving, one of the Prince's aides, Colonel Kaissarov, came through the room and nodded a distant greeting, and then paused at the door to say casually. 'Oh, Kirov, by the way – did that messenger find you?' Kirov looked puzzled. 'There was a messenger looking for you – civilian – some kind of artisan, from Serpukhov I think.'

Serpukhov was on the Tula road. 'No, no I didn't get the message,' Kirov said.

Kaissarov turned away, saying indifferently, 'I expect one of the company clerks has it.' The Prince's inner circle tended to have a short way with outsiders.

Kirov was back at the inn in the early afternoon, and hurried up to their rooms, sure of bringing Anne news that would cheer her. He found her in the sitting-room, crouched over the fire, which was burning better today, now that the chimney had warmed up.

'I've got a letter for you,' he greeted her cheerfully, bending over to kiss her cheek. It felt burning hot under his lips, and he straightened to look down at her with consternation. Her eyes were bright, her cheeks painted with fever. 'You're ill! What is it, love?' he said, alarmed.

'I seem to have caught a cold, I'm afraid,' she said. 'Nothing to worry about, Nikolasha. What is this letter? From whom?'

'It was addressed to me and sent to headquarters,' he said, unconvinced, but allowing himself to be sidetracked. 'But when I broke the wafer, I found it was really meant for you. Someone's been using his wits about the surest way to find you.'

Her face lit. 'From Jean-Luc? News of Rose?'

He gave it to her, and she turned to the firelight to read it.

First of all, it said, *I must tell you that we got safely away. No one troubled us in the least. We reached Podolsk by evening; now I have moved on to Serpukhov.*

A family has taken us in – very kind – the Belinskis. He owns a furniture factory; she thinks I am clever and amusing. They have a daughter, fifteen, who longs to go on the stage, and a son, eighteen, who longs to join the army: they beg me to tell my adventures over and over. I am very popular as you can imagine!

We are comfortable here, and they love Rose, so I don't see any point in going on further. I shall wait here for news.

We heard that the French took Moscow; and today we heard that it was burning. I pray you both got safely away. I tell Rose you certainly did, but pray send word soon to reassure her. She is well and happy. They have given her a white kitten, and Belinski fils is teaching her the piano.

I send this care of Count Kirov as being the surest way. Everyone always knows where the army is; and he will surely know where you are.

Adieu! – De Berthier.

Anne read and re-read this unsatisfactory epistle. There were a hundred things she wanted to know; but at least Rose was safe, and being cared for. The letter was typical of him, she thought, trying to read what was unwritten, between the lines. What had he told these Belinskis? How had he explained his relationship with Rose? Had he hidden the fact that he was French? It maddened her to have to leave her precious child in that man's protection, and under his influence.

'Did you read it?' she asked Nikolai. He nodded. 'It's good to know they are safe, at least; but I wish he had gone on to Tula.'

'Does it occur to you, love, that if he did that, he might find himself separated from Rose? I'm not sure that he would be entirely welcome at the Davidovs'. I don't suppose Shoora would understand about him and Basil, but Vsevka might thank him and firmly show him the door, especially since he has two unmarried young females in the house.'

'Yes, Lolya and Kira. He would not care to have them associate with such a man.'

'By remaining where he is, he can stay with Rose, and tell them what he likes.'

Anne sighed. 'I'm sure you're right. We must go and fetch her as soon as possible. Now that her father's dead – and there's another thing: how can I tell him about Basil? How can I tell Rose?'

'I don't know,' he said gravely. 'I think, for the moment, it is better to leave things alone. Send them some non-committal word which will satisfy them for the moment, until we can – Anna? Are you all right?'

She shivered, feeling herself first hot, then cold. 'I think I have a little of a fever,' she said.

He touched her brow. 'I think you have a lot of fever,' he said, alarmed. 'I think you had better go straight back to bed.'

Her limbs ached, and the thought of lying down was very tempting. 'Yes,' she said, 'perhaps I will.' But she found she couldn't get up; Nikolai had to carry her into the bedroom.

The following morning, the army moved out from Podolsk to march the twelve miles or so to Troitskoye. Count Kirov was not with them. Anne's temperature had climbed all through the day, and by the evening she was plainly very unwell. Adonis, despatched to headquarters in search of a doctor, came back with General Tolly's personal physician, sent by that kindly soldier with a note expressing his concern.

The physician diagnosed an influenza, and Kirov, whose mind had been running on typhus, smallpox and other such horrors, drew a sigh of relief. 'Thank heaven!' he said, and almost smiled.

'An influenza is not to be taken lightly,' the doctor reproved him sternly.

'No, no of course not,' Kirov murmured, quickly straightening his face.

'A young and healthy person, with good nursing, should recover from it without permanent disability. But you must take no chances. These are bad times – a lot of infection about, and winter coming on! And there is always pneumonia to think of, my dear sir!'

'Yes, indeed. I shall be very careful.'

'Yes – well,' the doctor looked a little mollified. 'Make sure she's kept warm at all times, and quiet. Saline draughts until the fever breaks, and then a light diet for the first week. After that, as much nourishing food as she can take. You'll find she's rather pulled by it – convalescence can be slow. But in a month or six weeks – I think in two months' time you may find she is quite herself again.'

'I understand.'

The doctor looked at him curiously. 'You know the army is leaving tomorrow? She mustn't be moved, of course.'

'No, of course not. I shall speak to the Commander-in-Chief.' He frowned a moment in thought. 'If he won't allow me leave, I shall resign my commission,' he said finally. 'I can't leave her now.'

When the physician had gone, he discovered a sense of relief inside him at the thought of resignation. He was very tired, more tired than he had realised, and the thought of letting go was very pleasant. Everything told him it was time to step out of the current of events, and rest a while.

Anne was very ill – so ill that many times Kirov thought the doctor must have been mistaken in his diagnosis. Her temperature climbed, sinking back a little during the middle of the day, and then rising again towards evening, when she would sometimes become delirious. She complained at first of aching limbs and a severe headache; then she developed an exhausting cough, and her throat became too sore to speak.

It was Adonis, oddly enough, who took charge of the nursing. The inn-keeper's wife inclined to the burning-noxious-vapours and swallowing-live-insects school of medicine, which had flourished in the previous century: and Pauline, though willing enough, knew nothing of the business, beyond what her grandmother had once told her, that sick people should lie with their feet higher than their heads so that the infection could drain out of their ears.

This didn't strike Kirov as very helpful, and he was relieved when Adonis sent her away kindly but firmly, saying that she was not robust, and should not be exposed to the sickness, or he would have two of them on his hands. Pauline was at first scandalised that he, a male, should propose taking care of her lady; but once she learnt that the innkeeper's wife was to perform the more intimate tasks for her, she relented; and seeing how skilled Adonis was at nursing, she soon ceased to regard him as a male creature at all.

It was Adonis who prepared saline draughts and herbal infusions, and who persuaded the delirious patient to drink them; it was he who propped her up on pillows when she found it hard to breathe, bathed her hands and face with rose-water, and mixed a soothing syrup for her throat. Most of all, it was he who calmed Kirov's fears by telling him again and again that she was doing very well, and that it really was just an influenza; and dealt, successively, with his master's fears of smallpox, scarlet fever, diphtheria, and, when the cough began, consumption.

At the end of a week, the fever broke at last, leaving the patient with all the symptoms of a heavy cold, cough, and sore throat, which even her distracted lover could believe she might ultimately recover from. It was as well that she did show this improvement, for on the 26th of September the cavalry of the French advance guard, who had several days before realised they were following a party of Cossacks on a wild goose chase, discovered at last where the main Russian army had got to. They began advancing southwards, and Prince Kutuzov, not seeing any need to gratify them by giving battle, gave the order for another withdrawal, towards Kaluga.

This left Podolsk in a rather exposed position, and after a brief consultation between them, Kirov and Adonis agreed that it would be more dangerous to remain where they were than to remove Anne to a safer place.

'Now the fever's broken – as long as she's well wrapped up, and put in a coach of some sort – ' Adonis said.

'Yes, I agree. But where can we go? We don't want to travel too far, but we need to be safe.'

'Somewhere out of the way – off the main roads. I'll make enquiries, Colonel.'

His enquiries produced a small house on the side road from Voronovo to Kolomna belonging to a local *dvorian*, whose finances had become so perilous in the hard years leading up to the invasion that he was willing not merely to rent it but even to sell it, and to remove himself at a moment's notice to the home of a married sister in Tarutino. The deal was rapidly concluded, and Anne was wrapped in a large quantity of warm clothing, and placed in a *telega* hired for the purpose, and they removed to Litetsk on the same day that the first French company came clattering into Podolsk.

Although only ten miles further on, Litetsk was much more isolated, standing on an unfrequented road, and sheltered from casual view from the road by an exceedingly overgrown park and almost impassable drive. It was very unlikely that any French patrol would even use this road, and still less so that they would think of leaving it to penetrate the tangle of the driveway for any reason.

The four of them settled in, to light the fires, screen the draughts, and make themselves comfortable. The move had exhausted Anne, who was suffering from the normal severe debilitation of influenza. She slept a great deal, and when awake, had no energy for anything but to lie looking at the fire. For the others, the sense of security of Litetsk was enhanced by the knowledge that there was nothing they must or even could do until Anne was well again; after strenuous effort and worry, the reaction caused a depth of relaxation in all of them amounting almost to lethargy.

Nikolai spent his days sitting in a chair by the fire. When Anne slept, he dozed and daydreamed, going over the events of the past, taking stock, repairing the thousand tiny lesions in heart and mind that a full life and an active career had left. He was very, very tired, and for the first ten days at Litetsk he rarely stirred from his chair; eating and drinking with infantile docility whatever Adonis put before him; caring nothing about the progress of the war; retiring early to bed, to a deep and dreamless sleep.

As Anne grew stronger, and was able to sit up and take notice, so Nikolai recovered too. She was still very weak and pulled, and a little of any activity sufficed her. He sat with her and read to her, played cards with her, but mostly just held her hand and talked to her. At first they talked randomly, of neutral subjects; but they both had a great deal of mourning to do, and there were shocks they had sustained whose effect had been, through necessity, deeply hidden. The time came when it was right for those events to be relived, and for the pain to surface and be suffered and dealt with.

They talked of the flight from Moscow, and of Basil's death, and then of Borodino, and of Sergei. Their grief over Sergei's death was compounded by the knowledge of his deep and ineradicable unhappiness; and for Kirov, by the knowledge that his son had died without forgiving him, without reconciliation. Speaking of it now, for the first time, with Anne, he knew that he had not yet come entirely to feel it, that there were layers and layers of suffering still to be realised. Anne might grieve for Sergei, mourn the waste of so promising a life; but Kirov's anguish was of a different order. This was only the beginning for him of knowing that his son was dead.

Moving backwards through pain, they talked of Vilna, of Anne's marriage, of Pyatigorsk, of Natasha, of Irina. There was a day when Anne was able at last to weep, and once begun, she could not seem to stop. Nikolai took her in his arms, and she cried on his shoulder until his jacket was soaked through, cried until her head ached, cried herself into a fever again. The next day she was prostrated, and Adonis was for the first time really worried, thinking she was suffering a relapse. But on the day after that, she was herself again, and plainly on the mend. As the physical fever had burnt out the infection, so the fever of weeping had burnt out the grief.

They could talk then of good things: of being together, of the child that was to come. Anne was now approaching the end of the fourth month, and was beginning to show. She would lie with her hands curved over her belly, and smile at Nikolai that transfiguring smile that belongs only to pregnant women.

'We must be married before he's born,' Nikolai said one day. 'I don't wish him to be disadvantaged.'

Anne smiled, but felt a fluttering inside, as if she were a green girl in her first Season. 'You have never asked me to marry you,' she said teasingly, to hide her foolishness. 'Perhaps I may not accept.'

He looked at her carefully, to see how serious she was. 'Shall I do it properly? Shall I kneel?'

'You needn't kneel – but, yes, seriously, I should like you to ask me,' she said.

He took her hand and kissed it, and then covered it with both of his. 'Anna Petrovna, since I first met you on the Isle de la Cité, in Paris, nine years ago, my love for you has never faltered – only grown. You are everything in the world that I want in a woman. You are to me entirely lovely.'

Her throat closed up at the strength of the words, at the depth of emotion she saw in those shining, green-gold eyes. It seemed almost frightening to be so much to someone: and yet she loved him as strongly, loved him wordlessly and absolutely, as she loved daylight and the air she breathed. Why should she be surprised?

'I love you, too,' she said. 'I have no words to tell you how much.'

'Will you marry me, then, *doushenka*? Will you marry me, little soul?'

Absurd that it should be so important; but she had heard at last the words from him that for so many years she had never dreamed she would hear. She felt happy, peaceful, triumphant.

'Yes,' she said. 'Yes please.'

At the end of October, a letter arrived for Kirov from General Tolly – a private letter of farewell, informing him that he had resigned from his position, pleading ill health.

My health has certainly been impaired, and I have not been fully well since Borodino, the letter said, *but I have no hesitation in telling you what I have already said to the Prince, that my resignation is hastened by deep dissatisfaction with the way things have been handled. The army has become a monster with two heads: administration and command, both, have become a chaos of incoherence and ineffectuality.*

I am retiring to Kolomna for a few months, and will write a full and detailed report to His Majesty, concealing nothing that has gone on. I regret nothing in leaving, but that I have not had an opportunity to say goodbye to you, Nikolai Sergeyevitch. I have a great admiration for your abilities: I hope if you return to your duties, that you will be better appreciated than I was.

When the letter came, Kirov was still sunk in his indolent period, and he was roused by it no further than to feel deeply sorry for the general who had been consistently undervalued and villified, and yet who had done more than anyone else to keep the army together and capable of operating. The two heads of the monster – Bennigsen and Kutuzov – must have come close many times to driving Tolly mad, he thought. He hoped sincerely that the Emperor, who had always admired Tolly, would find some way to reward him, and to do him public justice.

It was not until the middle of October that Adonis began to bring his master back snippets of news from the outside world, when he ventured out for supplies. Napoleon was still sitting in Moscow, he told him, and suffering apparently from the same curious indecision which had marked the whole campaign. It was known that he had sent three times to Emperor Alexander offering terms for peace; it was thought that the Emperor had simply ignored them, had not troubled to answer. Yet Napoleon did not seem to have come to any conclusions as to what to do next, and neither moved on, nor retreated, but merely sat still in the ruined city.

The Russian army had retreated as far south as Tarutino on the Old Kaluga Road, where it was in touch with Kiev and Tula. Kutuzov was waiting for reinforcements who were at that moment marching up from the south. He made no attempt to engage the French in battle, and Kirov felt he was doing absolutely the right thing. The longer Napoleon remained in Moscow doing nothing, the more completely he was trapped; a hostile move on the Russian side might prompt him to action. Besides, the Russian army grew stronger day by day as the French grew weaker, and the threat of the army was as effective in confining the enemy as a battle would be – and much less costly.

The French advance guard under Murat had followed as far as Vinkovo on the same road, and stopped there. The two forces remained ten miles apart, facing each other in uneasy equilibrium. It was a curious period of inaction. The only hostilities were the Cossack raids on the supply lines along the Smolensk-Moscow High Road, and the relentless picking off of foraging parties whenever it could be done without risk.

The weather had remained unusually warm for the time of year – a factor, Kirov thought, in Napoleon's continued delay. He had evidently been lulled into a false sense of security by the Indian summer – but the snow might begin in a fortnight, or a month, or tomorrow, and then the city would be cut off, and he would starve. Already the nights were increasingly cold, and there was sometimes a sharp frost for the oblique sunshine to warm away in the morning.

The mild weather which was perhaps deceiving Napoleon, also extended the idyll of Nikolai and Anne in their rural retreat. They were perfectly happy together, doing nothing but enjoying each other's company, and the bliss of unimpeded love. In the middle of the day it was often warm enough to sit out of doors, and Anne, who was now out of bed and growing stronger day by day, was amusing herself by pottering in the overgrown garden, and bringing in bunches of late, overblown roses and Michaelmas daisies to decorate the dinner table. They dined simply, and the plain food was delicious and satisfying as no banquet had ever been. In the evenings they sat by the fire and talked, or played cards, or read aloud to each other. They went to bed early, and made love, and then slept in each other's arms, peacefully, like children.

It was a rude shattering of this idyll when Adonis came in one rainy day when they were confined indoors. He sought them out in the drawing-room without even taking off his wet *tulup*, and stood before them, dripping on the hearth rug, his one eye regarding them sternly.

'That's it, Colonel,' he announced grimly. The return to the military title – of late he had been calling Kirov "master" or the neutral "sir" – shook the Count out of his reverie. 'They've upped and gone!'

'What? Who's gone?' He read the answer in Adonis's face. 'The French?'

Anne drew in a breath of surprise and alarm. 'The French have left Moscow?'

'Four days since,' said Adonis. 'Started off on the Old Kaluga Road, just as if they were going to challenge us to a battle; then turned off and went across country to the New Road. A sort of feint, it looks like – but the Cossack scouts were following 'em all the way, and soon saw what was going on.'

'Across country? But that's all marsh land that way. Those roads won't take the weight of a whole army.'

'So they've found out, Colonel,' he said with relish. 'That's why it's taken 'em so long – and from what I heard, you never saw such a circus as Napoleon's got along with him! Not just the footsoldiers and the cavalry and the artillery, but carts and carts of plunder, a host of boulevard carriages they've picked up in Moscow, and such a crowd of hangers-on as you never did see, including, they say, the whole of the Théâtre Francais – afraid of being lynched if they stay in Moscow after the Grande Armée's gone! Christ, I'd like to see Napoleon shift that lot along! This rain's all but finished 'em off.'

Kirov was on his feet, walking up and down as his mind began to work again for the first time in weeks. 'Moving south, is he? But if he has all that train along, he can't be meaning to mount a military campaign. He must be retreating – heading back for the border.'

'Then why is he going towards Kaluga?' Anne asked.

'In the hope of capturing our supply depots, and taking a more southerly route to Smolensk, I suppose. He wouldn't want to march back the way he came, along the High Road – it's picked clean. There's nothing there but trampled fields and burnt villages.'

'Yes, of course. I hadn't thought of that.'

'There's more danger than that on the High Road, Colonel,' Adonis commented neutrally. 'A lot of the peasant who cleared out when the French came through have drifted back now. Their field crops have been trampled and their villages destroyed, and they're out for vengeance. There are bands of armed peasants in the outlying villages, and living rough in the woods, just waiting for a chance to show the French what they think of them.'

'But why did Napoleon make that elaborate feint along the Old Road? I suppose he must be hoping to slip past our army on the New Road without a battle. What are our generals doing, Adonis?'

'Wasting time, as usual, Colonel,' he said with a grimace. 'The Prince-General got the news yesterday, but he said he couldn't move off until the horses that were out on foraging parties had come back into camp. They're going to march off tomorrow, to try to catch the French at the road junction at Maloyaroslavets.' He grunted. 'Thank God for this rain, and Napoleon's cleverness! If he'd gone directly by the High Road, he'd have passed our army before the Prince-General woke up, and be in Kaluga by now!'

The mention of rain made Anne aware of the state of the hearth rug. 'You'd better go and get dried off,' she advised, 'before you come down with an influenza too.'

Adonis looked offended. 'I've never been ill in my life,' he said. 'That's for women and weaklings.'

Anne laughed as he stalked off, but when he was gone, she turned to Nikolai, her smile fading like June snow. 'What happens now?' she said quietly. 'It is the end of this place for us, isn't it?'

He nodded slowly. 'Yes, I think so. It's time to move on.'

'Are you going back to them?'

'I don't know. It depends a great deal on what happens next, how Kutuzov means to handle it. In his position I think I would simply let the French go, confine them if possible to the worst road, harry them and delay them where possible, and let the winter take care of them. But there's bound to be pressure on him to attack and finish them off.'

'They shouldn't be allowed to escape,' Anne said. 'Especially Bonaparte. If he gets away, the war will go on, maybe for another twenty years.'

'No, my love. This campaign will finish him. He will have lost his reputation as well as his army. Didn't I tell you he had overreached himself when he invaded Russia? His star is waning – all things have their season.'

Anne was almost in tears. 'No, you don't understand! He's a monster! He's a black magician! If he gets away he will somehow – somehow – make it all right with his people. He'll find another army, and it will all begin again. He must be destroyed.'

'He will be. Don't be afraid, Anna! It's all over for Napoleon, I promise you!'

She looked unconvinced, but said, 'What about us? What shall we do now?'

He thought for a moment, and then said, 'I think we had better collect Rose and take her to Tula – that's the first thing. I should like to see Lolya again, too. Then we can decide what to do.'

She searched his face for information. Would he be able to leave the campaign alone, having come with it so far? Wouldn't he want to be in at the kill, if kill there was to be? He said "we can decide" – but he meant "I shall decide".

'We'll be farther from the army at Tula,' she said quietly.

'There are regular military couriers coming to Tula every day. We'll get the news there as quickly – and more accurately – then we get it here,' he said.

She had her answer.

They arrived in Serpukhov early in the afternoon of the next day, to learn that a piecemeal battle was being fought at Maloyaroslavets. Kirov was evidently disturbed by the news, and even more so by his inability to find out any reliable details of the action. It seemed that a French advance guard had reached the town the night before, and the Russian advance guard, arriving this morning, had driven them out, but failed to finish them off. Since then other divisions had been arriving singly through the day, and each side had pitched some, but not all, of them into the battle.

Prompted by Anne, he managed to return his mind to the task in hand, and asked a passer-by for the direction of the Belinski house. They found it without difficulty – a small but modern and well-built house on the outskirts of the town, with a very young pleasure-garden to one side of it, and the factory to the other.

Adonis was prepared to jump down and knock on the door, but Anne forstalled him, thinking the sight of him might well frighten any provincial servant into fits. She went herself, and was glad that she had, for a round-eyed maid of no more than fourteen opened the door to her, and stared up in awe and consternation at Anne's hat.

'Good afternoon,' she said kindly. 'I am Madame Tchaikovskova, and I believe you have my daughter staying here with you.' The maid's mouth hung a little open, but she didn't seem to be able to think of an answer. 'Is your mistress at home?' Anne pursued.

'Tanya? Who is it?' a voice emerged from the depths of the house,

587

closely followed by the very ornately dressed figure of a middle-aged woman, with high-piled curls of a shade of gold nature surely had never intended. 'Ask the name, you stupid girl! How many times have I told you – ' She stopped dead at the sight of Anne. 'And who might you be?' she asked, with a suspicion Anne could not wholly blame, in view of the presence only forty miles away of the Emperor Napoleon's Grande Armée.

'Madame Belinski? I am the Countess Tchaikovskova, Rose's mother. I believe she is staying here with you?'

A remarkable series of expressions passed across the marshmallow-pink face, which seemed to leave its owner as incapable of speech as the maid. Kirov had now descended from the carriage and came up behind Anne, and she heard his voice from behind her, gently prompting.

'I'm afraid we're letting the cold air into your house, madame. May we come in?'

'Oh – oh, why, yes – do! My manners! I'm so sorry. You must excuse – we weren't expecting you, you see, and dear Zho-Zho didn't say – ' Her hands fluttered about her like panicking birds, alighting now on her hair, now her bosom, now brushing down her skirts. 'I'm not dressed for receiving visitors, as you see. You really must excuse me, dear Madame – and Monsieur Tchaikovsky – oh, do come through into the drawing-room!'

'Please, you mustn't disturb yourself,' Anne said, following the retreating figure. 'I am sorry to have come upon you unannounced like this, but as things are at the moment – '

'Oh, time of war – of course, of course! And the things you must have witnessed, madame, are not to be told! Moscow burning! Such a terrible thing! Those French are monsters, monsters, and so I've always said! And Belinski was beside himself when he heard – well, I shouldn't have liked to be a Frenchman coming into the room just then! To set fire to our holy city, and after all we've done for them! Well, I said to Belinski, I said it would serve them right if we all stopped speaking French after this, just to show them! Only of course one can't speak Russian in the drawing-room, it sounds so odd, and I never learned English . . . '

Anne passed behind her into the drawing-room, a heavily furnished, crowded, but comfortable room, and saw Rose sitting at a table near the window cutting out paper dolls. Jean-Luc was sitting beside her, watching her, his chin resting in his hand. His hair, she saw at once, was much shorter. The luxuriant cascade, which had reached to his waist, had been cropped just below the shoulders, and he was wearing it neatly tied in a queue. He was dressed very plainly in trousers and tunic, and if he was wearing make-up, it was certainly a great deal more subtle than Madame Belinski's.

He looked up as she came in, and a strange expression crossed his face for a moment; then the veil descended, and he assumed his usual inscrutability. Anne couldn't quite decide what the expression had been. He looked taken-aback, as though he had not expected ever to see her again – as well he might, since he had not heard from her for so long. But it was not the look of someone glad to see her: he looked, she thought, stricken, as though her appearance foretold some doom.

But all this passed through Anne's mind in a second. Her eyes had gone immediately to her daughter, who looked up, regarded her for a moment in surprise and wonder, and then wreathed her face in joyful smiles.

'Maman! Maman!' she cried out, and struggled down from her seat to limp across the room as fast as her legs would carry her. Anne met her half way, and in an instant she was in her arms, and they were embracing with all their strength. Behind her Anne heard Madame Belinski sigh sentimentally.

'Isn't that a pretty thing to see? There's no mistaking our little Rose's mama, is there? I always say, don't you, Count Tchaikovsky, that there's nothing stronger than the bond between mother and child! So natural, so pretty!'

Anne, her face buried deep in Rose's neck and thin silky hair, turned to face them as Nikolai, gravely concurring with this deep philosophical truth, went on to explain that he was not Count Tchaikovsky, but Count Kirov, a friend of the family.

'Oh, not our little Rose's father, then?' Madame Belinski said brightly, but with a glint of suspicion in her eye as she looked from Nikolai to Anne.

Anne, however, had no attention for her. Jean-Luc was on his feet, and at the mention of Rose's father, he had sought Nikolai's eye with a questioning look. Nikolai returned the gaze steadily for a moment, and then gave an almost infinitesimal shake of the head. Jean-Luc read it, understood; his face aged, almost visibly. Anne was shocked to see the change in him. She had never liked to think about the relationship between him and Basil; it hurt her dreadfully to have to acknowledge that the Frenchman had loved her husband, but there was no doubt about it now. He had truly loved Basil, as she had not.

Anne found her legs trembling, and was forced to sit down, taking Rose, who was clinging to her like a marmoset, onto her lap.

'I am so grateful to you, Madame Belinski,' she heard herself say in a light, shaky voice which was hardly her own, 'for taking care of my daughter. I don't know how I shall ever be able to thank you.'

'We have enjoyed having her, Madame – and her brother,' Madame Belinksi said. 'Or – I suppose I should say, her *half*-brother?' A hint of a question mark crept into her voice as the puzzlement surfaced on her painted face. 'For I see now – excuse my impertinence, madame, but you are much too young to be dear Zho-Zho's mother! Not, of course,' she went on, with curiosity strong in her voice, 'that there's a great resemblance between him and Rose – but that would be accounted for, perhaps . . . '

Anne dragged her wits together. So that's what he had told them! Clever – or was it more devious? 'Yes, of course – a previous marriage,' she said vaguely. 'I dare say he resembles his mother more strongly.'

Nikolai spoke from behind her. 'I wonder if I might have a word with you – er – Zho-Zho – in private, if Madame Belinski would graciously excuse us?'

'Of course, of course – please do,' Madame Belinski smiled and blushed, and Anne guessed that Nikolai was being charming over her shoulder.

'And then, I'm afraid, we shall have to be taking our leave. I hate to descend on you and leave again so suddenly – '

Madame Belinski looked taken aback. 'But no, surely not – you will stay to dinner at least? My husband will want to meet you – and the children are out visiting – they will be heartbroken. Oh, surely, after Rose has been with us so long, you will not just take her away helter-skelter like that!'

Nikolai was grave. 'Madame, I regret the necessity deeply – and the appearance of haste and ingratitude it must present to you. I assure you nothing but the most urgent considerations of national importance would persuade me to leave so precipitately, but where His Majesty's business is at stake, all else must come second.'

Madame Belinski was flattened by the speech, which contained at least three words she didn't understand. 'Oh, of course, of course,' she whispered meekly. 'I quite understand.'

'And I assure you, dear madame, that as soon as the present emergency is over, we will return in order to thank you properly for all the kindness you have shown, and to allow little Rose to visit you again. Indeed, I hope she will often be visiting you. I'm sure she regards you now as her second family.'

These sentiments set Madame Belinski chattering about kindness and obligation, which she directed at Anne as Nikolai took Jean-Luc out of the room – she supposed to tell him about Basil. Anne listened patiently, aware of the great and real debt she owed this kind woman; and feeling guiltily glad that Nikolai had made it possible for them to get away.

It took over an hour to do so, despite the fact that there was very little to pack, for it was very hard to stop madame talking. The Belinskis had given Rose a number of toys and new clothes, and there was the white kitten, too; and then Rose had to say goodbye to all the servants individually. Anne was afraid the rest of the family would come back before they had left, and it would all begin again; but at last they were all squeezed in the carriage, with Rose on Anne's lap and the kitten on Jean-Luc's, and they were off.

Jean-Luc had hardly spoken a word since they arrived at the house, and Anne was not very surprised, considering the nature of the news Nikolai had given him. She was surprised when they travelled only another ten miles towards Tula, and stopped at a posting-inn in a village, where Nikolai announced they were to spend the night.

They bespoke rooms, and an early supper; Anne acquired some bread and milk from the kitchen for Rose, and had the pleasure of sitting with her while she ate, and then of bathing her and putting her to bed herself. When she tucked her in, however, she asked for Jean-Luc to come and kiss her goodnight. Anne shrugged inwardly, kissed her daughter, and went downstairs to find him.

She couldn't help wondering what was going to happen at Tula, if, as Nikolai said, the Davidovs would not admit him to the house. His position was now equivocal, to say the least; and when they settled again in their own home, what then? Without Basil, he had no place in her household, except as Rose's "friend". How much he really cared for her daughter she was unsure: not enough, she hoped, to make him want to stay near her.

She found Jean-Luc with Nikolai in the coffee room, and delivered Rose's message.

'Very well, I'll go up at once,' he said. He hesitated a moment as though he would say more, and then shrugged, and with a strange grimace, left them.

Alone together at last, Anne and Nikolai turned to each other. 'He told the Belinskis he was Rose's brother,' she said.

Nikolai looked grim. 'It was his solution to a deadly problem,' he told her. 'I've been talking to him – had it all out of him. He stumbled, you see, though he didn't know it at first, into a household of the most rabid patriots and Francophobes in the province. If Belinski *père* had discovered the truth about him, he would have handed him over to the town committee, who would probably have hanged him without further ado. Fortunately for him, his acting skills enabled him to hide any trace of his nationality. His great fear was that Rose would betray him accidentally – but I don't think they were terribly discerning people.'

'No,' Anne said thoughtfully. 'Poor Jean-Luc. It must have been very bad for him.'

He raised an eyebrow. 'You feel sorry for him? I thought you hated him unrelentingly.'

She gave a painful smile. 'I do – I did. But I wonder sometimes . . . I can see just a little what he must feel. Did you tell him about Basil?'

'Yes. Also about the Théâtre Francais leaving with Napoleon's train: that his old company, to a man, are heading out of Russia as fast as they can go.'

Anne looked puzzled. 'Why did you tell him that?'

'Because he needs somewhere to go.'

Anne studied his face carefully. 'He's leaving? He's going with them? He does not mind, then, leaving Rose?'

'Do you want him to stay?'

'No – of course not – but – '

'Then be grateful.' He stood up abruptly and walked to the fireplace, resting one elbow on the chimney-piece, and said, 'Now that Basil is dead, there is nothing for him here. He will be an embarrassment to you and to himself, besides being a danger to Rose – moral and physical. For her to be in company with a Frenchman now – and later, for her to be under the influence of a known sodomite – ' The brutality of the word made Anne wince and he met her eyes briefly and then turned away to look into the fire. 'Yes, I put it to him that way, in those words. So he's decided to go back to Paris, to his own people.'

'You put it to him?' she said slowly. 'What else? Nikolasha – what else?'

He didn't turn his head but spoke still staring into the fire, his forehead resting against his arm. 'I threatened him a little, too. Told him that once I married you, I wouldn't let him see her. I said that if he didn't go, I would see to it that everyone hereabouts found out he was French.' A pause. 'That would be like sentencing him to death.'

There was a long silence. She looked at his back, and didn't know what to say, or even to think. All he had said of Jean-Luc was true; yet

592

Jean-Luc had brought Rose safe out of Moscow, and Rose loved him. There was no place for him here now; he must be sent away. Nikolai had done what he did for the best, she thought, but it was not the sort of thing she would have expected of him.

He stirred, as if he had heard her thought. 'I don't like myself very much at the moment,' he said.

Jean-Luc left early the next morning, not wishing still to be there when Rose woke. Kirov did his best for him, gave him money and a fur coat and a good horse; and wrote him a letter which would get him safely through any Russian military hands into which he might fall. 'When you get near the French, make sure you destroy it, or they'll think you're a spy. You had better buy provisions as you pass through Serpukhov and carry them with you. Travel as fast as you can – stay at the head of the French column. With a good horse, you should get through – but take care of it. If it dies, you die.'

Jean-Luc received everything – money, horse and advice – in hostile silence. Kirov eyed him thoughtfully. 'It's for the best,' he said. 'When the Grande Armée has gone, it won't be a good thing to be French.'

'No. But that isn't why you want me gone. You don't give a damn about the safety of my skin.'

'No – but Anna does. And I care about her – and Rose.'

At the thought of the child, his face crumpled for an instant, before he regained control of it. 'Take care of her,' he said. 'If you let any harm come to her – I may not be able to hurt you in this life, but I'll pursue you beyond the grave, I swear it.'

'I'll take care of her,' Kirov said gravely. 'I – I wish you well.'

The mask was in place, and Jean-Luc gave him a smooth and seamless look. 'God damn you, Count Kirov,' he said calmly. 'And God damn Napoleon Bonaparte – if he hadn't invaded Russia, none of this would have happened.'

'I think God has damned him already,' Kirov said. 'Take care you don't get caught in the blast.'

It was hard to explain to Rose that Jean-Luc had gone. She accepted it at first, but Anne realised later that it was only because she hadn't understood properly, and thought he had only gone for a few hours. When they prepared to leave the inn, she dug in her heels and refused to move. They must wait for Jean-Luc, she declared. They couldn't go without him.

Anne tried to explain the situation, and Rose's lip began to tremble.

'I want Zho-Zho!' she cried ominously.

'Darling, he's gone away, back to his friends. He can't stay with us any more.'

'When's he coming back?'

'He isn't coming back, poppet. He's going to live with his own people from now on, in France.'

Rose's eyes filled with tears, and the tears overflowed. She had lost Mademoiselle and Nyanya and Papa and the ginger kitten, and had clung through all of it to Zho-Zho, who had taken her to a safe place where they gave her a new kitten and nice things to eat and a dozen people cuddled her all day long. But if Zho-Zho went, there was no firm foundation to her life: chaos loomed, and the only way she knew to respond to that was to cry, loud and long.

She was still crying when they carried her to the carriage; she cried on and off for the next three hours, and only stopped crying in the end through sheer exhaustion. As they drove at last into Tula, she was asleep on Pauline's lap, her thumb in her mouth, and the kitten dozing in her arms, her tear-swollen face drawn in lines of weariness and sorrow. Her eyelids flickered now and then as they drove through the streets, and when they pulled up in the sweep in front of the Davidov house she took one quick look, and then turned her face into Pauline's bosom and closed her eyes determindly. Unconsciously imitating her mother in her own childhood, she retreated from intolerable reality into sleep.

The butler opened the door as the carriage pulled up, and a footman came out to help put down the step. Nikolai stepped down, and turned back to offer Anne his hand; but before she was out of the carriage, there was the sound of light feet on the gravel, and Shoora came running down the steps and towards them.

Kirov turned to catch her by the forearms as she flung herself at him; at the door of the house, Vsevka had appeared, looking grave, and behind him Kira, wearing black bands for her fiancé who had fallen at Borodino.

'Nicky! Thank God you've come!' Shoora was crying. Her face was pale and her mouth bowed with tragedy. 'You got our message then? Oh, what's to be done? We've been worried out of our minds!'

'Shoora, dearest girl, calm down! What message? I haven't had any message from you,' Kirov said.

Shoora's eyes grew rounder, her mouth made a soundless "o" of shock. 'Then – then you haven't come to – you don't know about – '

'What's happened?' he asked, gripping her hands firmly; but his heart was cold with apprehension.

'We sent a letter to you straight away by the military courier, to headquarters. We thought you'd be there, or that they'd know where you were. We didn't know what to do for the best – but it wasn't my fault, Nicky, you must believe me! I had no idea what she was going to do!'

'For God's sake, Shoora, *tell me what's happened*!'

'It's Lolya – she's gone. She's run away.'

Chapter Thirty-Three

The all was soon told, and it was very little. Lolya had gone out riding, accompanied by her maid; when she did not return for dinner, Shoora had been alarmed, thinking she must have met with an accident, and Vsevka had sent out servants to search the estate.

'You didn't miss her until dinner time?' Nikolai said incredulously.

'It was nothing unusual. You know how she loves to ride. She was often out all day without noticing the time,' Shoora protested. 'She used to wear out that maid of hers, but of course I wouldn't let her ride completely alone, in case of accidents.'

'You should have sent a groom with her,' he said hotly. 'A girl of her age, to be allowed to jaunt all over the country with nothing but a silly chit of a maid – '

'That's not fair, Nicky. Lolya's not a child – she's eighteen, and quite capable of knowing what she must and mustn't do. Of course if she had gone outside of our own estate, I should have insisted she had a groom with her, but in our grounds I didn't think there was any need.'

He bit back his next angry words. 'I'm sorry. You're right, of course. Go on.'

'Well, we searched and searched, thinking she must have had a fall. It never occurred to us that she'd run away – well, who would think of such a thing?'

I would, Anne thought, but she said nothing yet. A suspicion was forming in her mind which she didn't want to admit.

'And then we found the letter she left,' Shoora went on. 'One of the maids went up to turn the beds down, and there was the envelope addressed to Vsevka and me, pinned to the pillow.'

'Have you got it there? Let me see.'

Shoora took it from her pocket and handed it over. 'And then we found that she had taken a cloak-bag with various things – her toothbrush and hair brushes and nightgown and so on, and her jewellery, and the miniature of her mother, and the cachoux-box you brought her from Paris . . . '

Nikolai read the letter, and handed it to Anne. 'What the devil does this mean? Have you any idea, Anna?'

Anne scanned the scrawled lines.

Dear Aunt and Uncle, I'm sorry to leave like this without saying goodbye, but you'd be sure to try to stop me, and I can't allow that. Please don't worry about me, for I shall be quite safe. I shan't be coming back, ever, but I will write to you when I am settled and tell you all about it. Thank you for all your kindness to me. Please tell Papa I shall write to him, too, and that he mustn't be angry with me, for I can't be happy here any more. My best love to you all – your Lolya.

Oh Lolya, Anne thought, you silly, romantic child! She turned to Shoora. 'Tell me,' she said, 'has Lolya had any letters while she's been here?'

'Yes, several, from her friend Varsha in Kaluga – you know, she used to be Varvara Salkina until she married the eldest Surin boy in the summer. She wrote to Lolya every week. Why do you ask?'

'Did she receive a letter on the day she disappeared?'

'I don't remember. Wait – yes, the evening before, I think.'

'And her decision to go riding was quite sudden?'

'She announced it as she was going up to bed,' Vsevka put in drily. 'She said she was tired and went early, but at the door she said she'd like to go out riding the next day. I thought at the time it was an odd thing to think of, if she was tired, but you know what girls are like.'

Nikolai caught Anne's arm and turned her towards him, his fingers biting into her flesh. 'What do you know, Anna? Do you know where she is?'

'I don't know, but I can guess. She's in love with Colonel Duvierge of the French Embassy – or thinks she is. He will have been with Bonaparte in Moscow these last few weeks. My guess is that he's been writing to her, and that the last letter she got was to tell her the French were leaving, and going back to France.' She took a breath. 'I think she's gone to join him.'

'But the letters came from Kaluga,' Shoora said.

'Obviously she told him to write care of her friend, so that your suspicions wouldn't be aroused.'

'What reason have you for thinking this?' Nikolai asked sharply.

'She's been writing to him ever since she left Petersburg. She believes he's really on our side, and hates Napoleon – she thinks he only wants peace for the world. Now I suppose she thinks he's going away and she'll never see him again, so she's gone off to join him.'

'That would be just the sort of hare-brained thing she'd think of,' Vsevka said. 'But Duvierge? – I find it hard to believe she'd fall in love with a Frenchman.'

Nikolai was unconvinced. 'I don't believe it. You've no evidence for all this whatsoever.'

'Where else could she have gone?' Anne said. 'She says she's never coming back.' His fingers were hurting her arm, and she sighed and touched them. 'But she couldn't have done it without help,' she said.

'That maid of hers was completely under her thumb,' Shoora said.

Vsevka shook his head grimly. 'I think there's someone else who might know something about it. Shall we ask Kira?'

Kira had been hovering in the background all this time. She had edged towards the door at the beginning of the conversation, but couldn't quite bring herself to miss what was being said. Now they all turned towards her, and she was trapped. She shrank back a little, and then lifted her pale face defiantly.

Nikolai released Anne's arm and bore down on her. 'Kira, what do you know about this? Is it as Anna says?' Kira didn't answer immediately, and he took her shoulders and shook her violently, startling her. 'Tell me what you know! This is serious, you silly chit!'

'Yes! Yes, she's run away to join André!' she cried out, and then burst into tears.

Nikolai removed his hands and turned away, looking so white that Anne thought he was going to be sick. She moved closer to him. Vsevka looked at his daughter incredulously.

'If you knew about it, why didn't you tell us? For God's sake, Kira, why did you let her do such a crazy thing?'

'It isn't crazy,' she sobbed. 'Lolya loves him, and he loves her.'

'Nonsense! He doesn't care a jot for her. He was just trying to get information out of her,' Anne said.

Kira turned a tearful, stricken face from one to the other. 'You see, you don't understand! She knew you wouldn't – that's why she made me promise not to tell. And I helped her, and I was glad to! You don't understand, any of you, what it's like to be in love! My Felix is *dead*! Lolya wanted to have her chance of happiness, but you'd have tried to stop her.'

Her sobs overcame her, and Shoora went automatically to put her arms round her and comfort her. Vsevka looked at his brother-in-law.

'What will you do?' he asked quietly.

Nikolai's shoulders were bent, as though under a terrible burden, and Anne, who could see his face, saw the loss in his eyes, and wished she could have protected him from this. But an instant later he straightened, and his face became hard, his eyes determined.

'I must go after her. I wish to God I knew which way she

had gone, though. It will be like looking for a needle in a haystack.'

Anne turned to Kira, and said gently, 'Did she tell you, Kira? Did she say which way she was going? You must tell us if she did – her life may be in danger.'

It took a while for Kira's sobs to subside enough for her words to be understood; then she told them that Lolya was riding to Kaluga, to Varvara Surina's house, where Colonel Duvierge would meet her as the French army passed through on its way to Smolensk.

Nikolai whipped round. 'What? Then – good God! – she's probably still there! Why didn't you say so at once, you stupid girl?' He turned to Vsevka. 'We guessed that the French were hoping to get to Kaluga, but our scouts spotted them on the way, and they were intercepted at Maloyaroslavets. They never reached Kaluga, so Lolya will still be waiting at the Surins' house.'

'Oh, thank God!' Shoora cried. 'Kira, why didn't you tell us?'

But there was no time for recriminations. 'I must go at once,' Nikolai said. 'Vsevka, can you give me a horse?'

'Of course. Do you want me to come with you?'

'I'm going with you,' Anne said firmly.

He stared, seeing at once her determination, trying to gauge her reasons. 'Nonsense. You can't, in your condition.'

'Don't be silly. My condition is nothing. I'm coming with you, so don't waste time arguing.'

'I have to ride fast.'

'I promise you, if I can't keep up, I'll give you leave to abandon me,' Anne said drily. 'If Lolya's there, you'll need me to chaperone her, don't you see? What will be the point of rescuing her, if the scandal ruins her? My coming with you will make all look right.'

And if she's not there, she thought, I shall be more likely to be able to get information out of Varvara Surina than you, in your rage. She didn't voice it, but she thought the second possibility was the more likely. Lolya was far more determined than Nikolai had any idea of.

Nikolai, Anne and Adonis reached Kaluga at dusk on the next day and rode straight to the Surin house. The butler was unwilling at first to let them in, evidently doubting the claim to gentility made by a couple who travelled on horseback rather than by coach, and accompanied only by a villainous-looking foreigner. However, when he learned that Nikolai was Lolya's father, he looked relieved, concerned and guilty in quick succession, and stepped back to admit them, saying that he would see if his master were at leisure.

He had no need to bother; as the party stepped into the hall, Vanya Surin came out of his study to see what the noise was about.

'Count Kirova, sir,' the butler announced, with an air of passing over the problem lock, stock and barrel to his master.

'Oh lord!' Surin said, with an expression of dismay that would have been comical if the matter were not so serious. 'You'd better come upstairs, sir, and talk to Varvara. I know she and Lolya have been plotting something, but what it is I've no idea. She's the maddest creature!'

'Is she here? Is Lolya here?'

He looked surprised. 'No, sir. Were you expecting her to be?'

Nikolai's heart sank, and for a moment he couldn't speak. Anne took over. 'Has she been here?'

'Oh dear, I don't know.' He looked from one to another. 'I've been away for several days on business. I only came home last night. You'd better come up and ask Varsha.' The implications began to dawn on him, and his handsome young face puckered with concern. 'You don't mean – you don't know where she is? Oh lord! Come up, sir, at once. Will you have some wine? Boris, bring wine, and lay extra covers for dinner. No, no, I insist. You can't go anywhere tonight, whatever happens. It's almost dark.'

Varvara was sitting on a sofa in the drawing-room, a picture of feminine contentment, with a lap-dog curled up beside her, a piece of embroidery in her lap, and a box of candied plums on the little table before her. She had a pretty, foolish face, and a great deal of lace about her gown, and when Anne and Nikolai stepped into the room, she dropped her work and put her hands over her mouth with a little, startled gasp.

Her husband looked as stern as it was possible with a physiognomy like his. 'Varsha, what's been going on while I've been away? And where's Lolya Kirova? You see her father's come to find her. What have you been up to, you mad creature?'

'Oh dear, oh Vanya, don't be cross with me! It wasn't my fault, really! I told her not to go, but I couldn't stop her. I mean, when Lolya wants to do something, she does it. I *told* her it wasn't proper, but she said they were going to be married as soon as she got there, and so it would be all right. So, you know, what could I do?'

Anne gripped Nikolai's forearm warningly. Losing his temper with this goose-witted woman would only delay matters.

'Where has Lolya gone, Madame Surina? Did she tell you?'

'Why, to join Colonel Duvierge, of course. They've been betrothed all summer, and now he's going back to France, so she has to go with him. He's got a house in Paris, near the Opera – imagine! I'd love to go to Paris! – and a palace in the Bois de Boulogne. Lolya says we can visit her there when the war's over, Vanya – won't that be nice?'

The war to Varvara Surina was evidently of little more import than a cold in the head.

'There was another letter, I suppose, from the Colonel?' Anne asked casually, holding the men silent with a commanding glance.

Varvara grew more confident in the uncontentious atmosphere. 'Oh, yes, it came on the day after she got here. He was supposed to be meeting her here, you know, and when he didn't come she was very upset. But it seems they couldn't come after all, and had to go another way, so he sent her a letter to say he would meet her somewhere – I can't remember where,' she added vaguely.

'Try to remember,' Anne said gently. 'It's important.'

'Well, I didn't see the letter, you know,' she said, looking round-eyed from Anne to Nikolai, who was holding silent only by the greatest effort. 'Lolya didn't show it to me. She just said she would have to go and meet him – somewhere – and I said it wasn't right, because you know if he had come here, I could have chaperoned her until they were married, but as it was, she only had Sophie with her, which doesn't really count. But then she said they would be married as soon as she got there, by the army chaplain, and she wouldn't listen to what I said . . . '

'Where?' Nikolai demanded, losing control at last. '*Where did she go*? God damn it, how could you let her just . . . ! You silly, hen-witted creature! Think, damn you! *Where*?'

'I say, sir, there's no need to shout at my wife – '

'There's every need! Don't you realise my daughter has ridden off completely unprotected to try to reach the remains of the fleeing French army? They fought a battle – for all we know they could be fighting again! She's going to ride through a battlefield full of deserters and wounded men and starving refugees, in order to run away with a Frenchman, and your wife helped her do it!'

'Oh no!' Varvara said brightly. 'She wasn't going to where the fighting was. She was going to take the short-cut across country and meet him at Medyn.'

Nikolai looked at Anne. 'There's a road from there directly to Ghzatsk. If the Grande Armée is retreating down the Smolensk High Road after all, they could meet up with it there.'

Vanya Surin was watching them thoughtfully. 'You'll be going after them, I suppose?'

'At first light,' Kirov said. 'I wish to God we could leave now, but . . .'

'I'll provide you with anything you need,' he said. He bit his lip. 'I'm sorry, sir, that my wife should have helped Lolya to do something so – so foolish. But you must understand –'

'Lolya's very determined,' Anne said. 'It would be hard for anyone to stop her once she'd made up her mind.'

Surin looked grateful. 'Yes,' he said eagerly, 'and Varsha's never really had any influence over her.'

'You'll see that Madame Tchaikovsky gets safely back to Tula,' Nikolai began, but before Surin could answer, Anne said firmly, 'No. I'm coming with you.'

Surin looked from one to the other, and then said to his wife, 'Varsha, come with me into the morning room for a moment. I want to talk to you. Excuse us, won't you, please?'

Alone with Anne, Kirov said, 'Anna, this is different. It may be some time before I catch up with her. The hard weather might start at any moment, and I shall be travelling through rough country. The going will be hard, and it may be dangerous; and there will certainly be some dreadful sights on the way. If I can't catch them before Ghzatsk, I shall be travelling over the road the French took on their way to Moscow. You can imagine what that will be like.'

Anne let him finish, and then said, 'I'm coming with you. More than ever you need me – if you find her you will need me to take care of her on the journey back; and if you don't find her . . .' She did not need to finish that sentence. 'The hard going is nothing – I am very strong and healthy, and I ride as well as any man. As for the danger –' She shrugged.

'The danger is real enough,' he reproved her. 'Do you think I would let you risk yourself – and the child? You must go back to Tula and take care of Rose and our unborn baby.'

She stepped up close to him. 'Listen to me, Nikolasha! If there is danger, I want to share it with you. Not being with you hasn't spared me, has it? I left you at Borodino to be "safe" in Moscow! No, let me finish! I don't know what will happen, I don't know how long we will have together, and I won't waste another minute of it. If you go away without me, I may never see you again. I would sooner die with you, than live without you.'

'Anna, it isn't a matter of –'

'It's no good! If you don't take me with you, I shall follow Lolya's example, and come after you. Better to have me under your eye, isn't it?' He opened his mouth to protest at the joke, but she shook her head and made a denying movement of the hand. 'She's my responsibility, don't you see? Yes, there are Rose and the new baby too, but Lolya came first, before them; and now she's in danger. Rose is safe with Shoora and Vsevka; the new baby can take care of itself; but Lolya is out there in danger she doesn't even perceive, and it's partly my fault. I knew about her and Duvierge, and I did nothing to prevent it. If I had warned you, warned her aunt and uncle – spoken more forcefully to Lolya herself – '

He saw the truth of her arguments, but could not bring himself to accept them. He put his head in his hands, and she touched his shoulder comfortingly. 'Let us be together, my heart. It's all I care about now. We'll find Lolya and bring her back together.'

They started for Medyn the next day. It was mid-morning before they set off, for whatever his desire for haste, Kirov knew that this journey was not one to undertake lightly. In a few days it would be November. Already the nights were bitter with frost, and the snow could start at any moment, and they must be prepared for it. Moreover the horses Vsevka had lent were not suitable for the hard journeying they might have to face: Adonis was sent out to buy four Cossack ponies, and one of Surin's footmen was despatched down to the mill to buy a sack of oats for their feed.

Varvara, still not fully understanding the seriousness of the situation, was nevertheless good-naturedly willing to lend Anne whatever clothing and furs she might need. She was shocked and thrilled to learn that Anne meant to ride cross-saddle, and therefore required not a smart riding-habit with Hussar frogging on the jacket and a full skirt of *bleu royale* velvet, but a pair of baggy Cossack trousers and a thick, loose woollen tunic, under which she could wear several layers of underclothing.

'What an adventure! I almost wish I were coming with you!' she said, rummaging in a drawer for warm stockings. 'But how will you manage without your maid? Who will dress your hair for you?'

Anne assured her solemnly that she had learned to plait it for herself while staying in the Caucasus, and that she wouldn't mind not having her front hair curled, as it was an emergency. A young footman who was about the same height as Anne provided, with many blushes, the peasant tunic and trousers required; Varvara provided the furs, hat and gloves and boots.

The fourth pony was loaded with food, arms and blankets, and extra clothing in case Lolya hadn't thought about the oncoming winter. The Surins saw them off, waving from the doorway, Varvara all smiles, as though they were going on a picnic, Vanya looking grave.

'Good luck,' he called. 'I hope you find her soon.' The tone of his voice revealed all too clearly his doubts on the subject.

The road to Medyn was little more than a series of farm tracks. The deep ruts of September had been frozen by the frosts of October into a series of icy ridges, like miniature mountain chains. Now and then the tracks petered out altogether, and they had to ride across fields, guessing the direction from the sun, or asking the way from the peasants who were still working in the fields, pulling the last cabbages and potatoes. The ponies were sure-footed and intelligent, however, and picked their own way nimbly over the rough ground.

They reached Medyn with about an hour of daylight left. Kirov was for pushing on, but Adonis argued against it. It was dark of the moon, and they had no idea what accommodation, if any, there would be along the road to Ghzatsk. They did not want to have to sleep out unless they had to. Better to stay here, get a good night, and start off at first light the next day.

Anne sympathised with his impatience. They had come across no trace of Lolya so far, though she had hardly expected it: the peasants had too much to do at this time of year to be noticing passing horsemen – or even horsewomen. But she agreed with Adonis. To sleep in Medyn, at an inn, would allow them to preserve their supplies for later, when, possibly travelling over barren land picked clean by the army, they would need them.

Kirov yielded to common sense, but the evening passed very slowly. He had no desire to talk, and yet there was nothing else to do. After a period of watching him pace about the room and answer her comments with a snap, she suggested he went down to the coffee-room and talked to the local people, and found out what they knew of the military situation.

He returned late, smelling of pipe smoke, and told her that after the battle at Maloyaroslavets, which had resulted, like Borodino, in heavy casualties and no clear victory for either side, the two armies had marched off in opposite directions, the Russians southwards down the road towards Kaluga, and the French northwest towards the junction at Mozhaisk with the Smolensk-Moscow High Road.

'Why on earth didn't our army pursue them?' Anne asked.

Kirov shrugged. 'I suppose Kutuzov thought they were going to press on towards Kaluga, and he was retreating to make sure the route was covered. Why Napoleon turned northwards, instead of taking the south road to Smolensk I've no idea. But at any rate, Kutuzov must have realised later what happened, because he retraced his steps, and *he's* taken the south road. So now he's marching parallel with the French: I suppose hoping to intercept them at Viasma.'

He was calmer now that he had had something to think about, and a little while later they went to bed, in order to be able to leave at first light the next day, at about half past six. In bed, he kissed her and turned on his side away from her without speaking, and she lay for a long time staring upwards into the dark, thinking about Lolya. The thing that exercised her most was wondering whether Duvierge had actually invited Lolya to come with him, or whether it had been Lolya's idea from first to last. If the former, it suggested that he cared more for her than Anne had believed. She hoped it was so – in that case he would take care of her, and they need not worry about Lolya's safety, only her virtue.

She thought Nikolai was long asleep; but suddenly he said out of the darkness, 'I'm glad you came with me Anna. I don't think I could bear my thoughts if I were alone.'

She reached out and touched him, and he caught her hand and pulled it round him; she turned over and tucked herself against his back, spoonwise, and they slept.

It was fifty miles from Medyn to Ghzatsk, and the road was narrow and unfrequented. For part of the way it paralleled the river Lutza, and in several places the river had overflowed its banks, and the road disappeared. They had to take to the fields then, and pick their way through near-marsh. Once they passed beyond the head of the river onto higher ground, the road ran through pine forest, dense and gloomy, and unnaturally quiet; but the surface underfoot was hard and dry, and they were able to pick up speed.

It was beginning to grow dark, and they were all wondering silently where they would be able to spend the night, and whether they would have to sleep out, when suddenly a party of Cossacks sprang out from the trees and blocked the road in front of them. The ponies started and jostled about; Kirov reached automatically for his pistol, and then realised that several guns were already pointed at him, and lowered his hand reluctantly.

'And who might you be, and where are you going?' the leader asked with an insolent grin. 'Mighty well covered-up, aren't you? What's on the baggage horse? Loot stolen from Moscow?'

'Steady your men,' Kirov said sternly. 'We're not French refugees. I'm a Russian officer.' Moving his hand slowly and keeping it well in sight, he unbuttoned the collar of his fur-lined cloak and pulled it open to show his uniform. The guns were lowered, and the Cossacks pressed their horses forward curiously, wanting to know what they were doing and why they had a woman along with them.

'One of the French officers has stolen my daughter,' the Count said succinctly. 'My wife and my servant and I are going after them, to bring her back.'

There was an approving clamour.

'Why, good for you, Colonel! And Madame Colonel!'

'Dirty French scum! You ought cut his balls off when you catch him!'

'You've missed 'em by two days, Colonel, but you'll catch up with 'em!'

'We've seen off fifty or more in the last few days. We pick 'em off as soon as they drop out of line.'

'When we catch 'em, we give 'em to the peasants,' the leader explained with relish. 'They make it last a good, long time!'

Anne shuddered to think what would have happened to them if the Cossacks hadn't believed Nikolai.

'The French have passed this way, then?' he was asking now.

The leader nodded, and waved a hand backwards over his shoulder. 'They came along the highway, and passed through Ghzatsk two days since. They thought they'd find supplies there – a supply train all the way from France – but we got to it first. We killed the drivers and drove it off before they'd got a sniff of it! We took all the food and fodder – all they found was some fancy French wine, and much good may that do 'em!'

'So Ghzatsk is empty now? How far are we from it?'

'Five or six versts.' The leader shook his head. 'But you wouldn't want to stay there, Colonel. Full of corpses and sick men. Stragglers still coming in, too. Besides, the French pretty well destroyed it the first time through, on the way to Moscow. There's nothing much there now but ruins and canals choked with dead horses.'

'We have our own provisions,' Kirov said. 'All we need is shelter for the night. We'll ride on in the morning.'

The Cossack leader nodded. 'Don't you worry, sir. Come along with us, and we'll find a peasant house where you can stay. You don't mind roughing it, I suppose?'

606

'Not at all. A barn will do, provided it's sheltered.'

'We'll find you somewhere better than that. And we'll pass the word down the line, that you're to be looked after. There are plenty of *izby* off the road that haven't been destroyed, if you know where to look for them. The peasants are out for French blood, and they like chopping up the prisoners we bring them, and the foragers who stray too far from the road. But they'll take care of you all right, and your good lady, don't worry.'

Kirov exchanged a look with Adonis, who shrugged slightly, and then nodded. It was not, he thought, as though they had any choice about accepting the Cossacks' help. But it would make their journey easier, and it would be as well for them to be granted safe passage, in case the angry peasants mistook them for French refugees.

The Cossack party crowded round them, and they left the path under their escort and rode through the trees, the pace picking up, despite having to wind in and out of the trunks, to a fast trot. Anne had to keep her wits about her so as not to part company with her mount when he dodged one way round a tree, and she the other. It was almost completely dark when they trotted into a clearing and confronted a log-built, two-storey peasant house, from whose chimney a cheering plume of smoke was rising ghostly grey in the gloom.

The leader gave a high chirruping call, like the *kee-wick* of a hunting owl. It was evidently a signal, for at once the door of the *izba* opened and a trapezium of yellow light fell out across the invisible grass. A stocky peasant stood there, with a precautionary short-handled axe in one hand, and what looked like a piece of bread in the other.

The leader jumped down from his pony and held a short, sotto-voce conversation with him, after which he turned to Kirov and said cheerfully, 'All right, Colonel. Lev here will give you all a bed for the night, and put you on your way tomorrow, first light. We'll pass the word about you. You'll be all right.'

'Thank you,' Kirov said. 'We're very grateful.'

'Nothing to it, Colonel!' He mounted and wheeled round after his men. 'Don't forget,' he called cheerfully as they trotted away into the darkness, 'when you catch him, cut the bastard's balls off!'

Inside the hut was just like any other – the stove, the long wooden table, the benches, the shelves high up with their few belongings. Anne made automatic obeisance to the Beautiful Corner, remembering the first time she had made the gesture, long ago in the company of Irina, and how strange it had seemed. It came naturally to her now. She wondered what her father or Miss Oliver would think to see her cross herself before an icon of St Sergei. How shocked they would be! England was far away now, like the most distant of dreams. She did not believe that she would ever see it again: Russia had taken hostage of her now.

The peasants were kindly, shy and monosyllabic. They offered them a seat near the stove, and one of the women began preparing tea, while two of the young men went out with Adonis to settle the horses.

'We won't take your food,' Anne said at once, thinking they probably had very little to begin with, and would be worried about their stores being depleted by the unexpected burden of two *dvoriane* and a large mercenary. 'We have brought food of our own with us.'

But one of the women, middle-aged and broad-bodied, but hard, like a rosehip, rather than fat, drew herself up with unexpected dignity and said, 'No, Barina, you are our guests. You keep your food for later. You may need it.'

'You are very kind,' Anne said. 'But we do not wish to leave you short.'

'While we have food, we will share it. So God orders us to be hospitable, lest we entertain an angel unawares. You are welcome to all we have, Barina.'

So they shared the evening meal, a simple affair of cabbage soup, black bread, and salted cucumbers. Afterwards the man of the house brought out a flask of kvass, and a pipe was lit and passed amongst the men. Kirov bravely shared it, and they all talked about the war and what would happen next. Meanwhile one of the women had guessed Anne's condition, and on the women's side of the stove there followed a deep and detailed discussion of all the pregnancies and labours they had known. Anne fount it interesting that none of them suggested that she was doing anything out of the ordinary by riding with Kirov in her condition. They were perfectly accustomed to working until the last moment of their own gestations; the idea of taking to the sofa for nine months was alien to them.

When the time came to retire, they gave Anne and Nikolai the best places on top of the stove, where they slept warm – almost too warm. The night seemed to pass very quickly. The old woman was up before first light, stirring up the stove and lighting the samovar for tea; and by the time the sun rose mistily on the first day of November, they were mounting their ponies in the clearing, their breath smoking on the cold, uncharitable air.

They came up to the road a few miles west of Ghzatsk. The first thing they saw was a five-foot long, elaborately-wrought gold torchère, lying at a drunken angle half in and half out of a deep rut at the side of the road: a piece of plunder from Moscow, presumably, that had fallen from a cart. A little further along, however, they came upon a trail of scattered goods – a dozen beautifully-bound books, a pair of candelabra, a rolled-up tapestry tied with string, a canteen of silvery cutlery, a framed portrait of a woman in the dress of the previous century. It looked like a deliberate attempt to lighten the load of a carriage in trouble.

They rounded a bend in the road, and there before them was the carriage itself, at the bottom of a slope which led into a ford and up again. The carriage stood – or rather leaned on a broken axle – across the ford, its doors hanging open, more plunder scattered around it, as the occupants had presumably searched amongst their loot for the most portable objects. As they drew closer, they saw something else lying on the ground beyond the carriage.

Half a dozen carrion crows flapped and hopped away from it as they approached, and Anne turned her face away, feeling a little nauseous. It was a dead horse – so thin its ribs and hips seemed almost ready to break through its dull hide. Its tongue hung out of its mouth, and there was a white tide mark along its neck where its labours had raised a foam. What was peculiarly horrible was that chunks had been roughly hacked out of it – and not by the beaks of carrion crows, either.

Kirov remembered Kutuzov's words: *I'll see him eat horseflesh!* It was plain that the retreating French army was desperately short of food; as desperately as it was short of fodder for the horses. This one looked as though it had died in the effort of dragging the carriage out of the shallow ford into which its momentum had carried it; and to judge by its condition, it had been lucky to get this far.

Adonis jumped down from his horse and passed the reins to Kirov, walked over to the dead horse, and bent to examine its hooves. He straightened up and called out, 'Come and look at this, Colonel.'

Kirov urged the horses nearer, until they caught the scent of their dead brother, and snorted and goggled and would not go any further. Adonis lifted a hoof and angled it towards him.

'No spikes. These aren't winter shoes,' he said. 'See – smooth as glass, and a ball of frozen mud on its sole. No wonder the poor beast fell and couldn't get up.'

'Not winter shoes?' Kirov said dazedly. 'But – Napoleon sat in

Moscow for a month doing nothing! Surely to God he must have had all his horses reshod? If he did nothing else, he must have done that!'

Adonis shrugged, and dropped the hoof, and came back to reclaim his mount. Anne watched in silence. Even she knew that every horse in Russia was reshod at the end of autumn with spiked shoes, so that they could get a grip on icy ground and packed snow. Without winter shoes, they would slip about hopelessly and fall every few steps.

Adonis was mounted. He took the rein of the packhorse, and they trotted on.

That was the first they saw of the debris left by the retreating Grande Armée, but it was not the last. Discarded plunder littered the road: statues and paintings and candelabra, gold plates and silver goblets, icons and altar furniture, tapestries and carpets, silk gowns and gauze scarves, ormolu clocks and porcelain figures, silver-inlaid tables and delicate Louis Quinze chairs. The Grande Armée had stripped Moscow of everything it could carry away; but the desperate state of the horses had forced them to jettison their booty in the attempt to save their lives.

They soon stopped counting the dead horses. Every hundred yards or so they found another, and almost all had been rudely hacked by the starving soldiers, desperate for something – anything – to put in their stomachs. There were abandoned carts, and boulevard carriages whose light frames had not survived the roughness of the road. Some of them had evidently been partly destroyed to provide firewood to cook the lumps of horsemeat, for they found the remains of many fires, and occasionally charred bones, and the sticks they had speared the meat on.

They found any number of discarded arms, brestplates, helmets; cannon, too, usually dismounted or spiked to prevent their being used by the enemy, presumably abandoned when there were no more draught horses to haul them. What was fleeing before them was evidently no longer an army, but a rabble of desperate men hoping to save their lives.

They found dead men, too. It was a grim sight. Some had evidently died of exhaustion and starvation; others told another, harsher tale. Bandaged or treated wounds suggested that they had been brought along in hospital carts, and had either fallen out, or been dumped like the excess baggage. More than once they found clear evidence that the unfortunate, in falling or being thrown from the cart, had been run over by the vehicle following.

The path of the Grande Armée cut a great swath across the land, spreading out far to either side of the road. Beyond it, in the fringes of the woods and what remained of the fields, they found evidence of the work of Cossacks, picking off men who strayed out of line, possibly foraging or perhaps wandering in delirium. Adonis, scouting further into the woods, found in a clearing evidence of a grimmer sort. The trunk of a fallen tree lay across the clearing, and lying in a line along it were the bodies of seven French soldiers. They had evidently been captured and handed over to the peasants, who had obliged them to place their heads on the tree trunk, and had then, with great thoroughness, smashed their skulls to pulp with clubs.

He returned to the road and rejoined Kirov and Anne, and said nothing about what he had seen. He had been ready to propose leaving the road, so that Anne might not have to witness any more unpleasant sights; but he had an idea that what had happened in the clearing to the seven Frenchmen was amongst the more merciful ends that the peasants were likely to mete out; and he did not think his master would want her to be exposed to that kind of reality.

They reached Viasma, and skirted the town, which, despite the biting cold which had set in over the last couple of days, they could smell a good way off. Outside the town, they came across the remains of a bivouac camp: more abandoned carts, rudely hacked to provide firewood; a score or more dead horses, which presumably had succumbed to the bitter cold of the night; and at least a dozen human corpses, some of which seemed to have been stripped of their clothing, presumably by colleagues desperate for warmth. Two of them were bare-footed, but those who still had shoes revealed that suitable footwear had not been provided for them any more than for the horses.

They hurried past this grim sight, and beyond the town they were intercepted by a group of four Cossacks, who plainly knew of their approach.

'Best stay off the road now, Colonel,' they told him. 'It's not a nice sight up ahead. And you're not far behind the stragglers now.'

'We've caught up with them?'

'Only the back end. The French army's spread over such a distance now, it takes 'em three days to pass through a place. Most of 'em wouldn't notice if you rode right past 'em, but one or two are still armed, and all of 'em are desperate enough for a horse and a warm coat to kill you with their bare hands.'

'How far ahead is Napoleon himself?'

'He and his party are at the head of the column. They're travelling fast. You won't catch 'em up on this road. You'll need to take some short-cuts.'

'Can you direct us?'

'Better than that, Colonel – we'll take you. We'll head straight for Smolensk – you'll catch him there all right.'

There had been light flurries of snow on and off for several days now, but not enough to settle, though the ground was hard with cold, and the air was bitter. Then for two days it grew milder, and the grey clouds threatened, but did not release their load. Nikolai, Anne, and Adonis were passed along the line, from one set of guides to another, sleeping at nights in peasant *izby*, either inhabited or deserted, and one night in a half-ruined barn.

Then on the 5th of November the wind changed and blew from the north. The temperature plummeted, and the first serious snow fell. By the afternoon of the 6th it was snowing in earnest, and out of the shelter of the trees it was hard to see more than a yard in front through the dazzling whiteness of the air. Remembering what they had seen of the soldiers' clothing and shoes, they had no difficulty in imagining what state they were in now. The Cossacks brought them reports of what they had seen and found: soldiers whose light clothing soaked through and then was frozen stiff on their bodies like a carapace; their beards and moustaches hung with the icicles of their breath. They stumbled along in their thin, worn-out shoes, and when they slipped or fell over a hidden stone or branch, they had no strength to rise again. The snow quickly covered them; the road, the Cossacks said, was a series of such mounds, small ones for the men, large ones for the horses. The snow undulated with them like a quilt.

The Cossacks rejoiced in these stories, but Nikolai and Anne received them silently. It was impossible to feel much rancour for these ordinary soldiers, who had been brought to Russia against their will, and had probably never understood what they were doing here. Nikolai was also forced to wonder about Lolya, and how she had fared. From what he knew of Duvierge, he was sure that he would contrive to make himself comfortable, and Lolya would therefore be comfortable too. He pinned his hopes on the news that came down the line that Napoleon and his immediate circle were at the head of the column and still provided with horses and carriages. Duvierge would be one of that circle. They were closing the gap.

The weather brightened a little on the 7th, but on the next day the temperature dropped again, and went on dropping, freezing the surface of the snow so that even the well-shod Cossack ponies had some difficulty in getting along. They were not far, now, from Smolensk, approaching it across country from the southeast, where they had cut off a long bend of the road, but as the temperature dropped ever lower, Kirov decided they must take shelter well before the sun went down: once it grew dark, they might easily freeze to death.

They spent that night in an abandoned hut in the woods. They brought the ponies in and tethered them at one end, and dragged in the entire stock of firewood from under the eaves, and built the fire up as high as it would go. Even so, and huddled together, it was miserably cold, and Anne, who had held up so far better than any of them, longed for home and warmth and comfort, and came close to wishing she had never left Tula. What were they doing here? she wondered, close to tears, feeling her bones ache as the cold ground sucked the vitality out of her. They didn't even know that Lolya was with Duvierge. She might be anywhere. She might be already dead. It was hopeless. They would all die of the cold, and what use would that be to anyone?

It was hard to get up the next morning – easier to remain lying huddled together in the warmth of each others' bodies. Adonis dragged himself up first and loaded more logs onto the fire. Once it burned up, everything seemed better – but then it was hard to bring oneself to leave the fire and go out into the bitter morning. The thermometer outside the window registered minus fifteen.

When they got outside, they found that the wind had dropped, and the air was sparkling clear. Anne's spirits rose again. Today they would reach Smolensk for sure, and since Napoleon was bound to rest for several days in the city, they would be sure to find him there. They would find Duvierge; they would find Lolya.

'Best have your pistol at the ready, Colonel,' Adonis said as they led the ponies out. 'And you, mistress – you'd better have mine. I'll keep my musket to hand. There'll be some starving soldiers between us and the city, I dare say. Stick close and don't stop for anyone, nor matter what he says. Got your white handkerchief ready, sir?'

They had to get onto the road in order to get over the bridge, for Smolensk sat on the river Dnieper. Soon they saw the golden domes and spires gleaming in the sunlight against the pale sky; then the stout fortifications reared above the horizon; then they saw the road.

It looked like a battlefield. That last bitter night had killed thousands, and thousands more had survived by some miracle, only to collapse in the last desperate effort to reach the shelter of the town. The road was littered with dead men, over many of whom the still-living crouched, stripping off their clothing to add to their own inadequate coverings. Dead horses lay along both sides of the road; and the men who still moved looked like tattered ghosts, their haggard faces and ice-hung beards unnaturally white above the motely rags they were wrapped in, as they stumbled in terrible silence towards the city.

The Kirov party did not need their white flag or their arms. The men they passed were too weak to threaten them, too desperate to reach safety themselves to care who it was that was passing them. One or two threw them frightened looks when they heard the sound of horses, evidently fearing that they were Cossacks, and them stumbled on gratefully when they found they were left alone.

By mid-morning they were clattering over the bridge to the town gate, and there they met the first real soldiers they had seen – a detachment of the Old Guard, haggard and weary, but still in uniform and under discipline, holding the gate and watching the relics of the army straggle in.

'Hold up!' a sergeant commanded sharply. 'Who are you? What do you want?'

They halted.

'I am Count Kirov, formerly of the Russian Embassy in Paris. I am known personally to your Emperor, and to General de Caulaincourt.'

'The devil you are! And what do you want, sir?' the sergeant said, his eyes going over Anne and Adonis with equal astonishment and suspicion.

Kirov realised that to try to explain now would delay matters considerably, and this was not a good place to delay.

'I wish to speak to General de Caulaincourt personally, on a matter of great urgency. Would you have the goodness to conduct me to him? I promise you he will see me – we are old friends. You need only mention my name.'

The sergeant considered the proposition, but only briefly. 'You'll have to leave your weapons aside, sir,' he said almost apologetically. Having divested them of their arms, he beckoned to a corporal of the guard, and told him to take two men with him and escort the visitors to the Grand Equerry's quarters.

'And I hope you are a friend of his,' he muttered to himself, turning away as the corporal led them away, 'otherwise the old man will have my guts for fiddle strings.'

Chapter Thirty-Four

Much of Smolensk had been burned down during the previous occupation, when the French were travelling towards Moscow; but at the top of the hill there were several stone-built houses which had survived intact, and here Napoleon had settled himself and his immediate staff. Leaving them to wait in the street, under the curious eyes of the two privates of the guard, the corporal went in to report.

After a wait of about ten minutes, they were conducted inside to a sparsely-furnished room, where Kirov at once recognised Caulaincourt's travelling-desk, which went everywhere on campaign with him. It was covered with papers and maps, and behind it stood Caulaincourt himself, haggard, grim-faced, looking ten years older than when Kirov had last seen him, at Vilna.

The two men, old friends, exchanged a long look in which the same awarenesses were shared. Everything Caulaincourt had warned of from the very beginning, even back in Paris, had come to pass: Russia itself, rather than the Russians, had defeated Napoleon's grand design and destroyed his Grande Armée, the pathetic relics of which were hobbling even now on blackened, toeless feet into a city which could not feed them or clothe them. The invasion had been an abject failure; but Kirov could not rejoice. It was he who spoke first.

'Armand,' he said hesitantly. The big things were too big to be addressed. He said instead, 'I heard about your brother. I'm sorry.'

Caulaincourt's younger brother Auguste, a gallant and popular cavalry officer to whom he had been deeply attached, had been killed at Borodino. Caulaincourt's face registered the pain anew. He said, 'Your son, too.'

Kirov nodded; and then he lifted his hands. 'Old friend, we never wanted this – either of us. This isn't even war – it's madness.'

Caulaincourt looked down at his hands. 'You don't know – you haven't seen the half of it!'

'But Armand,' Kirov said abruptly, 'the horses – no winter shoes! You're the Grand Equerry! Surely – ?'

Caulaincourt turned his head away, staring towards the window. 'I gave the orders for every horse under my command to be reshod, and for every man to have proper boots and winter clothing. But I'm only responsible for the Household. When I begged His Majesty to give orders for the rest of the army, he only laughed.' He put a hand to his head. 'I tried again and again to warn him, but he wouldn't listen. "Tales to frighten children!" he said. "Caulaincourt's losing his nerve!" he said. And the autumn was so mild, as if God Himself were on your side, lulling him, making him delay and delay . . . ' His eyes were bleak. 'The horses were starving to death even in Moscow; but all he would say was "Send out for more fodder".'

He stopped abruptly, aware that what he was saying was close to disloyalty. He met Kirov's eyes again, knowing that he, at least, would understand. It was above all the strain of his love and loyalty towards his Emperor, when his Emperor consistently ignored his advice and plunged them all into disaster, which had aged him; that, and the terrible things he had witnessed.

'It isn't war,' he repeated Kirov's words; then he pulled himself together. 'What are you doing here, Nikolai? You have not come from your Emperor?' His eye betrayed a glimmer of hope.

Kirov shook his head. 'No, I am here on a personal matter. You know nothing of it, then? My daughter — I am looking for my daughter.'

'Your daughter?'

'There is a certain Colonel Duvierge, who has been maintaining a correspondence with her,' Kirov said grimly. 'I have reason to believe he has abducted her.'

Caulaincourt's eyes opened very wide. He thought a moment. 'I cannot say that I know anything of that. Many of the senior officers have women with them, as well as servants and plunder — that's their privilege; and there are a great many civilians following the army — too many! I begged His Majesty to limit the following.' He grimaced. 'When we left Moscow, it looked more like an Eastern caravan than an army . . . '

'Duvierge is here, in Smolensk?' Kirov interrupted urgently.

'Yes, he and de Lauriston have travelled with the Household all the way. I know little of Duvierge, but I always thought he was a gentleman. De Lauriston seems to think highly of him — but then he's a soldier.' There was a hint of the old rivalry, the old jealousy, in his words.

'I must see him. Can you arrange it for me, old friend? If my daughter is with him — '

'Of course. At once. If you will wait here, I will send a message to bring him here to you. It will be best, I think,' Caulaincourt said thoughtfully, 'if I summon him to see me, without mentioning your name. If he has abducted your daughter, it will be better not to give him time to think of excuses.' He gestured towards the fire. 'Make yourselves as comfortable as possible. I will have some coffee sent in to you. Oh yes,' with a wry expression, 'I still have a little left. I made good provision for myself and the Household. Would to God I could have done it for the whole army.'

Left alone, Kirov walked over to the fireplace, and Anne went to stand near him for comfort. They did not speak. There was nothing in their minds but the hope that Lolya was with Duvierge, and safe and well – for bad though that would be, any other possibility was infinitely worse. The wait seemed very long. The room was quiet except for the crackling of the fire, but from outside in the street came noises which by their irregularity told the grim tale of an army in disarray.

At last the door opened, and Caulaincourt came in, met Kirov's eye warningly, and stepped aside to usher in Colonel Duvierge. He looked, Anne saw with mingled relief and anger, as immaculate as ever, smoothly handsome, unmarked by the terrible flight or the hideous scenes he must have witnessed. He stepped through the door with an expression of polite enquiry on his face, and then stopped short when he saw Kirov. A flicker of something passed through his eyes; and then he allowed his gaze to rove insolently over the three travellers, and he raised an eyebrow in ironic enquiry, as though he had come across someone improperly dressed at a drawing-room reception.

'So! Monsieur de Kirov, what an unexpected pleasure,' he drawled. 'And Madame Tchaikovskova too, I see. Your servant, madame. Your presence suggests that this is a social, rather than a diplomatic visit – you should have warned me, Excellency,' he added, with a glance at Caulaincourt which revealed a glint of anger.

'You know why I'm here,' Kirov snapped, his anger fanned by Duvierge's shameless composure. 'Where is my daughter?' Duvierge's eyebrow climbed again, but before he could answer, Kirov went on hotly, 'Don't trouble yourself to lie about it! We know that she has been writing to you, that you enticed her away from her home and family. Where is she? If you have harmed so much as one hair of her head . . . '

'Calm yourself, monsieur,' Duvierge interrupted. 'And please, let us remember our manners. I have no intention of lying, and I find it offensive that you should suggest I would do so.'

Caulaincourt made a movement to intervene, but Kirov's temper snapped before he could speak. 'How dare you make a joke of it? How dare you speak to me like that? Good God, man, have you no shame? Have you no morals at all? You seduce an innocent young girl, abduct her from her home, subject her to the horrors of this retreat, and then have the impertinence to bandy words with me, as if we were at a tea party!'

'Nikolai,' Caulaincourt began, seeing Duvierge's face begin to redden. 'Be calm.'

Kirov swung round on him. 'Be calm? No, by God, I won't be calm! He insults me, he insults my daughter, by his lightness! I tell you, Duvierge, you will speak to me with respect, or I shall knock you down like the puppy you are!'

'And I tell you, Count Kirov, that I did not abduct your daughter – no, nor seduce her! It is impossible to seduce a virtuous girl!'

Anne drew a breath of shock and fear, and Kirov, with a growl like a goaded bear, stepped towards Duvierge with a raised fist. Caulaincourt placed himself swiftly between them, catching Kirov's wrist with slender, steely fingers. There was a moment of frozen silence. The difference between the two men was so marked: Kirov, bundled in his travelling clothes, dishevelled and mud splashed, blazing with a searing rage; and Duvierge, immaculately uniformed, his handsome face a little pale, but his expression still cool and haughty, refusing to flinch before Kirov's anger.

It was not, she saw in that instant, shame or guilt that made Duvierge behave so insultingly: it was hatred, plain and simple, for Russia and the Russians. Lolya to him was not the issue. He was a Frenchman, brought up since the Revolution, come to manhood in the blaze of light that flooded the world from the new sun which was Napoleon. He was one of the new breed of men, belonging to the new world: he despised Russia as old, corrupt, decaying, impotent; and yet the greatest soldier in the new world had not managed to conquer it.

And Lolya, poor simpleton, had fallen in love with his careless good looks, and had persuaded herself that he loved her. But André Duvierge loved only two things, as Anne saw very clearly just then: he loved power, and he loved André Duvierge, and the two things were inextricably linked.

All this passed through her mind in the instant of time it took Caulaincourt to catch Nikolai's raised hand; even as she gasped, he was saying, 'No, Nikolai, not that way! Duvierge, guard your tongue! I will not hear any woman insulted, least of all the daughter of my old friend.'

Duvierge gave Caulaincourt one glance, in which Anne read the contempt he felt for a Frenchman who could call a Russian a friend; and then his face was smoothly expressionless again, and he said in his light, polite voice, 'I beg your pardon, Excellency. I was in error. Madame, my apologies.'

He bowed to Anne, who felt her body rigidly refuse to acknowledge the gesture. Her face was stiff with resentment as she said, 'Will you please tell us, Colonel Duvierge, if Lolya is with you. We have travelled far in great anxiety: do not prolong our sufferings.'

Was he ashamed? Anne hoped, but did not think so. He answered easily, just meeting her eyes. 'Yes, she is in my lodgings.'

Nikolai, whose body was braced against Caulaincourt's restraint, made a small movement of relief so intense it could not be articulated. Anne saw some of the tension go out of him. Caulaincourt released his wrist, and he lowered his hand slowly to his side. Anne waited for him to speak, and when he did not, she went on, 'Is she well? Has she been taken care of?'

Duvierge raised a brow again. 'She has travelled in one of my coaches, attended by her maid, and has eaten as well as I have. Do you not think I take care of my – guests?'

Anne had an uncanny certainty that he had been about to say "possessions".

Nikolai was able to speak at last. 'Take me to her,' he said harshly. 'I have come to take her home.'

Duvierge gave a slight bow in his direction. 'I will take you to her with pleasure. But I should perhaps warn you, monsieur – explain to you, rather – that you are wrong in your assumptions. I have not abducted your daughter, nor do I keep her here against her will. She wished to come with me.'

'Take me to her,' Kirov growled. 'And keep your mouth shut, or I'll shut it for you.'

'Take them to your lodgings, Duvierge,' Caulaincourt said, making it clear that it was an order and not a request. 'Take the guard with you from the ante-room – to ensure your safety, madame,' he added apologetically to Anne. 'They will escort you back to me when you have – completed your business.'

Anne nodded, grateful for his kindness. She remembered her own earlier misgivings, that the flight to Duvierge had been Lolya's idea. It seemed that they were about to be confirmed.

Duvierge had set himself up in a house off the main street, and Anne saw at once that he was not a man to travel in discomfort. She suspected that having lived a little while in Petersburg, he had absorbed enough information about the Russian winter to respect Caulaincourt's advice more than Napoleon was inclined to. In the courtyard of the house were two strongly-built carriages, mounted on runners instead of wheels, and two peasant *kibitkas*, loaded to the canvas with supplies. The door to the house was opened to them by a suitably-dressed servant; there was a heap of furs on the hall table, and a smell of coffee on the air.

Duvierge met her eyes as she sniffed, and gave a shrug. 'When we first reached Moscow, there was plenty of everything, but the fools who plundered the houses first loaded themselves with furniture and gold candlesticks. I had more foresight: I made sure of the commisariat first.'

'Yes,' Anne said neutrally. It was good for Lolya that he had, but it did not make him easier to like.

'Never mind that. Where is my daughter?' Kirov said impatiently.

'Come this way, please.' Duvierge led the way into a drawing-room. Again it was sparsely furnished – stripped during the first occupation, Anne guessed – but the few pieces that had been placed around the fire were good, expensive, and harmonious, and she thought he had probably brought them with him from Moscow to make his journey more tolerable. It took only the fraction of a second to notice that; then she was looking at Lolya, who had jumped up from her seat by the fire as the door opened. Her expression of delighted welcome changed to one of dismay as her father entered behind Duvierge, and the book she had been reading fell from her hand and hit the polished boards with a solid thump.

'Papa,' she said in a small, frightened voice, and she looked from him to Anne and back with the expression of a child caught in some naughtiness – an expression comical in its inadequacy to the situation. Then she laughed nervously. 'André, you should have told me we were expecting guests,' she said, trying to sound like a sophisticated hostess.

She was looking well, Anne noticed with relief. She looked rosy and healthy, warmly dressed in a long-sleeved gown of fine grey-blue wool, with an expensive cashmere shawl draped gracefully round her shoulders, and her hair had been dressed by her maid's skilled hand into a cascade of Roman curls. She seemed to feel the incongruity of it when she looked at Anne, dressed in Cossack trousers and sheepskin jacket, and with her hair in a plait, for she touched her head with nervous fingers, and tweaked a curl out of place.

Kirov felt all his rage seep out of him at the sight of her. 'Lolya, child,' he said, his voice shaky with relief. 'You're safe! Thank God!'

Duvierge walked away to stand at a little distance, his arms folded across his chest, as though he had no part in the scene, was merely watching it as one watched a play at the theatre.

'Of course I'm safe,' Lolya said, sounding genuinely surprised. 'Didn't you read my note? I told you I'd be all right. André takes care of me, just as I knew he would.'

Nikolai went on as if she hadn't spoken. 'How could you do such a thing? To betray your aunt's trust – to give us all so much worry – so much trouble. We've been breaking our hearts over you! Thank God we've found you! But what on earth possessed you to go with him – a Frenchman, the enemy of your country?'

Lolya's surprise gave way to disapproval, and the last few words hardened her expression. 'Now, Papa, I can't have you speaking badly of André. And as to trouble, you needn't have come all this way, just to see if I'm all right. I told you in my note I would write when we got to Paris.'

'We've come to take you home, child,' Kirov said, understanding her words with difficulty. 'Pack whatever you need as quickly as you can. Your maid is still with you, is she? Anna Petrovna has come to chaperone you. We may yet be able to hush this up. No-one knows but your aunt and uncle, and your silly friend in Kaluga.'

Lolya interrupted. 'Stop it, Papa! I'm not going with you. I'm staying with André. We're going to Paris. I've *told* you! Why don't you listen to me?'

Her eyes were defiant, but Anne saw in them a shadow of fear. Was she afraid that he would persuade her to leave – or that he would not? Anne said, 'Lolya, you remember what I told you before, in Moscow?'

'You told me a lot of things,' she snapped, turning on her swiftly. 'You told me he didn't love me, that he was only using me. Well, you were wrong. Now you see it, don't you?'

'I told you that no man who loved you would do anything to risk your safety. By asking you to come with him on this – this hellish journey, he has proved he doesn't love you. Can't you see that?'

'He didn't ask me,' Lolya said with a defiance that covered a world of hurt. 'I suggested it. It was my plan – he only agreed to it. So you can't blame André for anything. Blame me if you want – not that it matters now.'

'Matters? Of course it matters! What are you talking about?' Kirov cried, frustrated by the irrelevance of the talk.

Anne intervened again. 'Colonel Duvierge,' she said, turning to him, 'won't you please speak to Lolya? You are a gentleman. I don't believe you are without principle. Lolya must come back with us – you must see that.'

But he only shrugged. 'I see nothing of the sort. Hélène may do as she pleases. She came of her own free will: I do not keep her here by force. If she wishes, she may go with you. Ask her, not me.'

'I don't wish!' Lolya cried passionately. 'I want to stay with you, André!'

He gave her a small smile, devoid of any affection. 'Then stay,' he said indifferently.

Anne stared hard at him. 'Why did you let her come with you?' she asked abruptly. 'You don't love her.'

'Oh, love! You women talk endlessly above love! Hélène wished to come with me to Paris: why should I prevent her? It is – a *pleasant* thing to have a companion on a journey such as this.' The irony of his tone in choosing that word Anne could see was not lost even on Lolya. She pressed her advantage quickly.

'You see, Lolya, he doesn't love you. He only finds you convenient – *pleasant*. Something to make the journey comfortable – like this furniture.'

'Not true! Not true! How dare you say it! I hate you, Anna! André loves me, he does!'

'Come back with us, chérie, while there's still time. Even if you get as far as Paris, do you think he will go on finding you *pleasant* for ever?'

'Stop it! I won't listen!' Lolya pressed her fingers to her ears.

'He denies none of this, you see,' Anne went on remorselessly, her heart aching for the young woman she must hurt to save. 'If he loved you, he would deny it.'

Lolya turned a frightened, harried look at her lover, who met her gaze with a small, cool smile, and a lift of an eyebrow, which seemed to say *choose between us – safety or excitement; respectability or romance.* He said nothing, promised nothing; and suddenly a change came over her. She put her hands down to her side, straightened, lifted her chin, looked at her lover with a frightening pride. In a calm voice she said, 'I wouldn't ask him to deny it. What he says is true – I am here of my own free will. The choice is mine.'

A flicker of something like respect was in Duvierge's eyes as they met hers, and it hardened her resolve. She turned to her father.

'I'm not coming with you, Papa. I'm sorry if – if it hurts you. But I love André.'

'I've heard enough of this nonsense,' Nikolai said. 'I'm not asking you, Lolya – I'm telling you. You're coming home with us, now.'

'No,' Lolya said calmly. 'I won't come, Papa, and you can't make me.'

His fists clenched in frustration. 'Lolya, for God's sake, what is all this? Can't you see that this man is a scoundrel? He'll use you and then discard you! I know his sort. How can you think you love him? Haven't you any self-respect?'

Lolya blazed suddenly with anger, and she looked in that instant uncannily like her father. 'Oh! I'm tired of you talking to me like a child! I'm not a child any more, but you still think you can stop me having what I want! You've got what you wanted, haven't you? You've got Anna – and you're not even married to her! So don't talk to me about respectability and morals and – and – ' Her rage went as quickly as it had arisen: it is hard for a child to quarrel with a parent whose authority she has always respected. She looked down and bit her lip. 'I'm sorry, Anna,' she said briefly. 'I didn't mean to hurt you.'

Anne tried once more, dragging the words up from a heavy heart. 'Oh Lolya, please don't do this. Come back with us. It's for the best – I swear to you.'

For a moment Lolya looked at her, and Anne saw with a terrible pity that she knew Anne was right; that she knew he didn't love her, and that she had deceived herself wilfully. But she lifted her head proudly and stepped over to stand beside Duvierge, and said quietly, 'I'm sorry, Anna. It's too late, you see – I belong to him. We were married in Mozhaisk.' She sought something in Anne's eyes. 'But even if we weren't, it would be too late. *You* must understand that.'

Anne looked at her with enormous sadness. 'Yes,' she said, so quietly that it was almost a sigh.

Kirov looked at his daughter in bewildered pain. 'You choose him? You won't come with me? Lolya – my child – '

'I think you had better go now,' Duvierge said. 'You see that she makes her choice freely. I do not keep her against her will.'

Kirov turned on him. 'By God, I should like to kill you!'

'Yes, no doubt. But it would not help, would it?' Duvierge said indifferently.

There was nothing more to be done; and yet he could not bring himself to leave. He stood with his hands hanging uselessly, looking from his daughter to the Frenchman. Suddenly Lolya ran to him, put her arms round his neck, and pressed her cheek briefly against his. 'I love you, Papa,' she whispered; and before he could touch her, she disengaged herself and stepped back, and said with dignity, 'Please go now. I want you to go.'

Duvierge followed them out, returning them to the care of the guard. At the last moment Kirov turned on him again, and anticipating him, Duvierge lifted his hands, and looked at him cannily, and said, 'Yes, yes I know! I will take care of her – you have my word. I am a Frenchman, not the Devil.'

He would take care of her, Anne saw that – not because he loved her, but because she was his possession. Lolya would have to settle for that – and who knew but that in the lottery of marriage she might have done worse?'

Caulaincourt received them gravely, listened to Kirov's few broken words about the interview with Lolya.

'What power I have, I will use to see that she is taken care of,' he said at last. 'When all this is over, if she wishes to return, I will send her back to you. There are bound to be cartels of exchange. God knows how many Frenchmen have been taken prisoner.'

'Thank you,' Kirov said bleakly.

'And now, though I would like to offer you hospitality, I think it would be better if you were to leave Smolensk immediately.' He tapped a document lying on the corner of the desk and said tonelessly, 'We have just had a report, you see, that your army under General Kutuzov has captured Vitebsk, and seized our garrison stores there.'

Kirov stared, his mind dragged away from his own problems for a moment. Vitebsk was the major town linking the route from Smolensk to Vilna – Napoleon's escape route.

'Your stores?'

'We have been relying on those stores to get us to the border. Now we have nothing – and even the direct road is blocked to us.'

'What will you do?' Kirov asked at last.

'We shall have to go another way,' Caulaincourt said, and then his control wavered and broke. 'We have only fifty thousand men left – fifty thousand, out of such a multitude!' he cried. 'They're starving to death! If you'd seen, as I saw, the whole road littered with bodies – men dead of hunger, cold and misery! Even on a battlefield I never saw so much horror!'

'Yes,' said Kirov. To say "I'm sorry" would be inadequate, and yet he was, desperately so. He held out his hand, and Caulaincourt stared at it for an instant as if he didn't know what it was. Then he took it and grasped it.

'You had better go now,' Caulaincourt said. 'I will have you escorted out of the town – when this news about Vitebsk spreads, it will be dangerous to be Russian. You have what you need for your journey home?'

It was a curious courtesy from a general of a starving army, but neither of them seemed to see it so.

'Yes, we have what we need. Armand – when it is all over – if we should meet again – '

Caulaincourt nodded. 'It was not our fault, none of it,' he said. 'But I wish to God I had died at Borodino with Auguste. A man who has seen what I have seen has lived too long . . . Adieu, Nikolai. God send you a safe journey.'

'God bless you, old friend,' Nikolai said painfully.

Caulaincourt shook his head. 'I think He has forgotten us,' he said.

Caulaincourt's escort took them out of the city by one of the northern gates, since the remains of the Grande Armée was still straggling in by the eastern gate. They rode north at first, and then struck eastwards, travelling across country, taking a direct line towards Moscow. A week later they came back to the Smolensk-Moscow High Road at Ghzatsk, far enough behind the army to have avoided the rearguard under the fierce old warrior, Marechal Ney, and even the stragglers.

The temperature had gone on falling, fourteen, fifteen, sixteen below. The days were breathtakingly cold, and dazzlingly beautiful, with skies of a vivid purity arching dark blue to the zenith above them; sunrise and sunset turning the snow to rose and carmine. The intense cold froze the crust of the snow and the surface of the rivers, making the travelling easier, and the hardy, sure-footed ponies could cover five or six miles an hour during the short days.

But when they had passed Ghzatsk, the clouds gathered, and the snow began again, lightly at first, but gradually thickening until it was impossible to see more than a few yards ahead. Adonis looked towards his master for instructions, and then, seeing that he was sunk deep in thought, shouted out to him, 'We must take shelter, sir. Shall we turn back to Ghzatsk?'

Kirov looked at him, bemused, and shook his head as though to shake his thoughts into order. 'What? Shelter – yes, we must have shelter,' he mumbled.

Anne almost laughed. 'Koloskavets is up ahead, you fools! Zina and Stenka will make us comfortable! There'll be food and firewood and fodder for the ponies, too.'

'Provided the French army hasn't been there first,' Adonis said, annoyed that he hadn't thought of it himself.

It was snowing so hard by now that it was difficult to find the path up the hillside. The snow had covered everything, every landmark, in a featureless white blanket, and for a time they were completely lost, casting about, unable even to be sure that they were on the road. Surprisingly, Anne discovered that is was not even possible to tell whether one was going uphill or downhill, and that was most frightening of all.

The ponies trudged on uncomplainingly, their faces and manes crusted thick, even their eyelashes loaded with soft white flakes like overhanging eaves. As time went on, and they still could not find their way, Anne knew the first pang of fear; and, warmly wrapped, fed, and mounted on a sturdy pony, she had suddenly a clear and piercing sense of the plight of the French soldiers she had seen. For the first time she had some idea of the almost unimaginable agonies they must be suffering, clad only in thin woollen uniforms, without boots, without food, without shelter. The pain they would suffer from the agonising cold would be relieved only by the numbness that proceeds death – a numbness they must surely come to welcome. Only fifty thousand of them left, she remembered – and how many more were yet to die?

'Over there – look!' Adonis suddenly shouted, his voice muffled by the snow and his upturned collar. 'That must be Borodino – we've wandered off the road. Come on, this way! Stay close!'

To their left, a vague shape rearing up was the remains of the twin towers of Borodino's church. They had strayed, Anne realised, onto what had been the battlefield, though the snow of the past weeks, thank God, had spread a uniform blanket of white over the horrors beneath, freezing the undulating crust hard. Dead men and horses, discarded arms, dismounted cannon, all were buried deep under the innocence of whiteness, like laundered sheets, which took the ugliness from everything.

In the spring, when the thaw came, Anne could imagine what would be revealed. It would not be a good place to be in the spring. The new snowfall lay like feathers over the old crust, and Anne had a sudden terror that the weight of her and her pony would break through it. Vividly she imagined them plunging through some weakened place into a gully full of corpses, which the carrion had not had time to pick clean before the snow came. She shook the hideous image away, and concentrated instead on the thought of Koloskavets and a blazing fire.

Taking their bearings from Borodino, they found the path at last by the pine trees growing along its margins, and Adonis sent his pony up the hillside in a series of plunging leaps, with Anne close behind him, and Nikolai leading the spare horse bringing up the rear. Now they were so close, every moment of delay before reaching shelter seemed intolerable. Surely it had never been so far up the hill as this? Surely they must have missed their way again, and be riding away from the house instead of towards it? Anne was desperate now to be out of the saddle, to rub her numb hands and feet, to rest, to eat hot food. She felt that another five minutes out here in the blizzard would break her heart; and yet five minutes were followed by five minutes more.

And then, quite suddenly, they were there: the grey walls had been invisible in the background of whirling snow until they came in sight of the black iron gates. They rode into the yard and out of the wind, and suddenly the snow was falling gently like a tame thing, like a holiday thing, for making snowballs and toboggan slopes with. And there was Stenka in *tulup* and fur hat and huge boots, grinning toothlessly as he stumped forward to take the horses' heads; and there was Zina in the doorway to the kitchen, smiling serenely, as if their arrival were nothing untoward, as if they had only been away on a day's hunting.

'Come in, Barina, and get yourself warm. If you wouldn't mind stepping into the kitchen, Barina – the fire in the drawing-room's laid but not lit. I'll go up and do that as soon as I've helped you off with your things.'

'Thank you, Zina. I shall be glad to get out of this saddle.'

Zina nodded calmly, watching them with her unfathomable eyes, accepting, unjudging. 'The samovar's almost on the boil. I can have tea for you in a few moments.'

Anne dismounted stiffly and handed the reins to Stenka, and trudged towards the open doorway and the light and warmth. War and invasion had convulsed the land, death and disease and starvation and horrors of every kind had been unleashed; men were this minute lying down in the snow and dying from cold and hunger; but it was impossible to think of any of that now. Zina had said the magic word *tea*, and somewhere in there ahead of her there was a fire.

The blizzard lasted for three days; but even had it stopped during the first night, they would not have gone on. They had reached a haven, and for the moment they did not want to leave it. Nikolai remembered how before the battle he had found Koloskavets a single reality set between two opposing and equally unreal worlds. Now, with nothing to see beyond the windows but endless, featureless whiteness, it seemed the only reality, a small place hanging in oblivion, which had somehow survived the wiping-out of the rest of creation.

They had everything they needed. Zina told them they had not been troubled by looters or stragglers: too far off the road, and the French terrified equally of Cossacks and what they called Partisans – the returning peasants bent on revenge. There was firewood enough for the whole winter, if they needed it; there were roots and sacks of grain and smoked, dried meat in the cellar; and when the snow stopped, if they remained, Adonis and Stenka could go out into the forest and shoot game for fresh meat. Eventually, of course, they would have to leave. Anne supposed vaguely that they would go back to Tula in the first instance, for Shoora and Vsevka would need to know what had happened to them and to Lolya; but for the time being, they had reached a resting-place, and they were staying put.

The relief of being safe and out of the saddle was so great that they all experienced a kind of euphoria for the first few days. They discarded their travelling clothes, they bathed luxuriously – Nikolai shaved in hot water and emerged looking ten years younger, only very gaunt and hollow-cheeked. Anne washed her hair, and curled it, and when Nikolai saw her with it dressed for the first time in weeks other than in a plait, he smiled a long, slow smile and told her he'd forgotten how beautiful she was.

During those days of the blizzard when they were confined to the house, with nothing to do but sit by the fire looking into the flames, they talked. Not of the war, which was too horrible, and too unreal, nor of the past, which contained too much sorrow, but of their future together. They talked of Schwartzenturm, and what Nikolai meant to do to improve the land, the new succession-houses he meant to build, the modern crops he meant to try out.

'Unless, of course,' he said suddenly during one conversation, 'you don't want to live there? It occurs to me that perhaps you'd sooner we sold it and bought a new *pomestia* somewhere else.'

Anne laughed. 'A fine time to have scruples, after you've planted acres of turnips and built a pinery! No, love, I'm happy to live there. I like Schwartzenturm.'

He smiled gratefully. 'I don't think Irina ever did,' he offered, and she understood him.

'I'm not jealous of her,' she said. 'I have you now – that's all that matters.'

He put his arm round her and drew her against his shoulder, and she sighed comfortably. 'We'll be married as soon as possible,' he said. 'In Petersburg, I think. I don't think Moscow will be a good place for either of us now.'

'No,' she said. 'I don't want to go back to Moscow. We'll collect Rose, and go back to Petersburg. I wonder how she and Sashka will like each other?' She smiled. 'I shall have Sashka again! I can't tell you how happy that makes me!'

'I'm glad you feel like that. The poor child has lacked a mother so long. Even when Irina was alive, she never had any love for him.'

Anne grunted in acknowledgement, her eyes on the leaping flames. Outside the wind soughed around the house, but inside there was no sound but the conversational crackle of the fire, and the ticking of the clock on the chimney-piece.

After a while he said, 'Where are you?'

'I was thinking of Schwartzenturm,' she said. 'I was looking at the view from the top of the Black Tower; and taking Rose to see old Marya Petrovna and the tame pig; and going to mass in the little white church; and having guests to dinner, and sitting on the terrace in the White Nights.'

'The White Nights!' he said in a tone that told her how fantastic that seemed to him in the present circumstances. 'Very proper, domestic dreams they are, too,' he added. 'Have you no higher ambition, Countess Kirova? Don't you want to travel and see the world?'

'I've done that already,' she said. 'Now I want to stay home.' But the words had broken the mood. She thought of the rest of Europe, of England, of the seemingly endless war. 'This will be the end of it for Bonaparte, won't it?' she asked him in a subdued voice.

He was a long time answering. 'Yes,' he said at last. 'I think so. Even if he escapes with his life, I don't see how he could survive politically, having failed, and having lost his whole army. It must be the end of him.'

'And the end of the war?'

He didn't answer that, deep in his own thoughts. 'I told you once, didn't I, that when a war is over, no-one can really remember what it was all about. No-one ever wins a war. We just survive it – or fail to.'

His son Sergei had died in this very room, turning his face away from his father, unyielding, unforgiving. The firstborn, dearest to the heart as the firstborn must always be: special, never-to-be-replaced. Without really being aware of it, he freed himself from Anne's embrace and stood up, walked away towards the window, the pain of his thoughts needing movement. All his children lost: Sergei and Natasha – even Sashka, for he hardly knew him, the war having kept him so long away from home.

And Lolya, more lost than all, because she lived, and he would never see her again. Duvierge would survive, he was sure of that; he had the knack of it; and Lolya would survive with him. They would escape out of Russia, and she would be his, his possession, loved or unloved, trammelled by him, used by him; her youth and vitality passing untasted in the service of a man who could never deserve her.

He stared bleakly out of the window. Gone, all gone! Natasha and Yelena and Sergei; and how many others? So many thousands dead; and crops trampled, villages burned, lives torn apart, never to be put together again. No winners; only losers.

Anne got up and came to stand beside him, and seeing the blackness of his expression was afraid to touch him, though she needed him, needed his reassurance. The white wilderness of snow beyond the glass was an emptiness, a desert, as featureless as darkness.

'We've lost everything,' he said.

'No,' she said. If he thought that, it was the worst thing of all. 'No! We still have so much.' He didn't respond to her, and she grew afraid, and tugged at his arm to bring him back to her. 'We survived.'

'Did we?'

His eyes came back to her reluctantly, and for a moment he looked so old and so tired that she felt a kind of terror, that she would lose him, because he no longer had the strength to love her. 'Nikolasha,' she said, and reaching out wildly she took both his hands and placed them over her belly. 'This is what we have! Our love for the rest of our lives; being together! And the child!'

He felt the tautness of her belly under his hands, the heat of her blood through the firm flesh and thin skin. He was tired, so tired – she seemed infinitely far away, and young, and he was old. Too old to begin again. Too old to try any longer. He could not bear to feel anything ever again.

But she called him, relentlessly, with the insistence of the life that was so strong within her. Life cannot be ignored, he thought; it must be lived, it must be answered to. It was the condition on which they held the earth, the price of their tenure of the beautiful world God made: the beautiful world which would shake off the blight and horror of war which men had laid on it, and in a few years be green and blessed again, as though none of it had ever happened.

The glow of the firelight behind her lit the curve of her cheek and gilded her eyelashes; there were gold lights in her brown hair; she was beautiful to him. And like a miracle, he felt the stirring of life again within his weary body, and feeling her flesh under his hands, he wanted her. She was ripe with life, her belly was full of his child, and he wanted her, he wanted to hold her and fill her again and again, until black memory retreated; as every new day was filled with the light of the sun, driving back the darkness.

'I love you, Anna Petrovna,' he said abruptly, and she looked at him for a moment doubtfully, quizzically. And then she laughed: not because it was funny, but simply because she felt good. He put his arms round her and pulled her roughly against him, and she tilted her head up, looking up at him and laughing; and against his belly, through the muffling layers of his clothing and hers, he felt the child within her kick him lustily.

Epilogue

Nobody knows exactly how many men crossed the River Nieman into Russia in June 1812; probably the total of the Allied French forces taking part in the campaign was between five and six hundred thousand. Those who straggled back over the frozen river in December numbered between thirty and forty thousand.

In the six months in between, half a million men had been lost: some in battle, killed or taken prisoner; others from starvation, exhaustion, typhus, pneumonia, dysentery, gangrene; and on the long march back from Moscow, others still perished from the effects of the pitiless Russian winter. Unprepared for the terrifying cold, without food, fuel, or adequate clothing, they died by the thousand. Frozen to death, they fell like winter sparrows, unheeded beside the road, and no-one ever recorded their names.

The name of Napoleon Bonaparte is known throughout the world: the greatest soldier who ever lived, and the man who, more than any other, shaped modern Europe.